PRAISE FOR THE WORKS OF
JEFF SOMERS

"Somers writes with assurance and style . . . just the right mixture of fatalism and attitude, seasoned with plenty of bullets and black comedy."

—*SF Site*

"A funky wit."

—*The New York Times*

"Combining elements of Jonathan Tropper, Tom Perrotta, and Augusten Burroughs, Somers' incisive, pull-no-punches examination of adult friendship is refreshingly witty. Tautly paced and expertly assembled, *Chum* is a darkly comic, deeply insightful, and wildly original novel."

—*Booklist* on *Chum*

"An exhilarating example of powerful and entertaining storytelling."

—*The Guardian* on *The Electric Church*

"Jeff Somers has created a wholly original world that, even with magic, feels incredibly real."

—*All Things Urban Fantasy* on *Trickster*

"Enough gunplay and explosions to satisfy a Hollywood producer . . . but the characters are the real prize."

—*Publishers Weekly* on *The Electric Church*

"Somers has a crisp writing style . . . I much prefer his clean kind of storytelling over the common pitfalls of info-dumps and overly-cute dialog."

—*Fantasy & SciFi Lovin' Reviews*

"With intricate plotting and ink-black humor, Somers' new series is a gritty, grim success that will keep readers spellbound."

—*RT Book Reviews* on *Trickster*

"A gritty noir story that challenges and surprises with every page."

—James Rollins on *The Electric Church*

WE ARE NOT GOOD PEOPLE

JEFF SOMERS

G

GALLERY BOOKS

New York / London / Toronto / Sydney / New Delhi

Gallery Books
A Division of Simon & Schuster, Inc.
1230 Avenue of the Americas
New York, NY 10020

Somers

First Gallery Books trade paperback edition October 2014

Part One of this book was originally published in an altered form as *Trickster* by Pocket Books in February 2013.

GALLERY BOOKS and colophon are registered trademarks of Simon & Schuster, Inc.

For information about special discounts for bulk purchases, please contact Simon & Schuster Special Sales at 1-866-506-1949 or business@simonandschuster.com.

The Simon & Schuster Speakers Bureau can bring authors to your live event. For more information or to book an event contact the Simon & Schuster Speakers Bureau at 1-866-248-3049 or visit our website at www.simonspeakers.com.

Interior design by Jaime Putorti

Manufactured in the United States of America

10 9 8 7 6 5 4 3 2 1

Library of Congress Cataloging-in-Publication Data is available.

ISBN 978-1-4516-9679-0
ISBN 978-1-4516-9682-0 (ebook)

To my dearest, darling Danette, who kicks my ass
in a good way every day and makes everything,
including this book, better.

WE
ARE NOT
GOOD
PEOPLE

I.
TRICKSTER

1.

"THERE'S A GIRL IN THE tub," Mags said.

I looked up at him. His hair was getting long. It was glossy and silky, a grand black forest of hair. His eyebrows almost met in the middle, giving him a permanently sinister expression. I could not actually pronounce his actual last name, called him Pitr Mags because it was better than calling him Pitr the Indian Bastard.

"A fifty-year-old dead girl?" I asked, thinking bones and webs, a fine bed of off-white dust lining the tub beneath it.

He shook his head, pushing his bandaged fingers into his pockets. "Recent."

I paused in the act of tearing up the carpet. We were broke again. Sometimes it seemed like we'd done all of this before, an endless cycle of failure. The last seventeen dollars we'd possessed had been spent on Neilsson, passed over with a pinprick of gas to make it look like three hundred and forty in twenties, and all Mags and I had to our names was what was pumping in our veins.

We were fucking incompetent. In all things, we'd failed. We were wallowing in a nice, comfy pit of fucking spectacular failure, deep black and hermetically sealed, me and Mags bound together forever and ever with deep fishhooked ties of ruin.

I hauled myself to my feet. Fished in my jacket pocket, produced a fresh bandage, and began working the thin wrapper free, difficult due to the damp and soiled bandages that adorned all nine of my other fingers and the fresh slice oozing blood on my index finger. Faint sparks of pain flared from my fingertips as I worked at it.

I was careful not to let any blood drip anywhere, get smeared anywhere. Leave no mark, that was rule one. No trace of yourself. Blood was usable for only a few seconds, ten, twenty. After that, you couldn't burn it away no matter how big the spell. Best not to take chances.

The apartment was supposed to have been a good score. We'd heard that Neilsson had a card up his sleeve, and the old drunk had a sheen of success about him. Despite floating around our social level, which should have been our first clue. But Neilsson had been a pilot, back a few decades, and he worked art, and thus had an aura of intellect and culture that was powerful attractive to men like Mags and me, small minds drenched in blood and peasant fare. The codger spoke with an adorable accent, and I never had gotten past the childish idea that all people with some sort of accented English must be fucking geniuses. When sober, Neilsson was a good operator, and he'd made some decent kosh from time to time, so we took the rumor seriously. And decided to work him the way only Mags and I could: a little bit of charm, a little bit of booze, a little bit of gas.

It took all fucking night to get it out of the old bastard. We could have bled more and settled some real voodoo on his shoulders and pushed, but Mags and me, we didn't bleed anyone else, we relied solely on ourselves, so that would have left us too exhausted to do anything useful. So we used our usual tricks. Aside from the faked twenties—the manager would count out the drawer later and discover a stack of one-dollar bills—we used a couple of charmer Cantrips to make Neilsson like us, and then we poured whiskey down his throat until, grinning with his pink lips buried under a forest of yellow-white beard, he crooked a finger at us and told us about a wonderful score he'd heard of: the Time Capsule.

I looked around the room, holding the candle we'd found in the kitchen—misshapen, fleshlike in texture, already claiming a starring role in my nightmares for years to come—out in front of me. The room was cluttered, the furniture all curves and satin, uncomfortable to look at. I could believe that no one had opened the door or a window in fifty years. It smelled like death, and I tried to take shallow breaths. I shot my cuffs, wriggling my toes inside my wing tips. They'd seen better days. There was a thin spot on the sole, beneath the ball of my foot, that was a week or so away from a hole. It was October and if we didn't manage something substantial in short order I was looking at a winter spent with wet feet, snow crowding in from the street and making me numb.

"Let's take a look," I said.

I had no idea how to monetize a dead girl in a tub, but somehow it seemed like there had to be a way to do so. Why else would the universe construct such a complex contraption if it didn't roar into life, belch black smoke into the air, and start producing something?

The place had been locked up forty-five years before, the story went. Neilsson telling us with a slurred ruby-red tongue and a yellowed, blurred eye. The owner was a rich bastard whose parents had died, leaving this apartment on East Seventieth Street. He had it shuttered and went to California. And never came back, the apartment sitting here like an unopened oyster, growing some unholy pearl in its center, a Time Capsule of old money. Now that we were here, breathing in decades-old dust and farting into the moldy cushions, it was ridiculous. What had we expected to find? Fucking piles of jewels? Pots of gold? A helpful guidebook pointing out the valuables?

Well, I reminded myself, maybe there was a safe. We could handle a safe. I could bleed a bit more before I got woozy. And if I got woozy, there would always be the rats, if I could get Pitr to go along with it.

I followed Mags. He walked like he was angry at the floor. After a short hallway wallpapered in hideous stripes, a few framed oil paintings that might have been something special hanging every three feet, we were in the master bedroom. It was a large room, no window but a small en suite bath—which was unusual for an older apartment. A huge brown water stain had bloomed on the ceiling, the plaster dropped away and lying on the bedspread in a moldy pile. The room smelled terrible, and I figured if I pressed a hand against the ceiling, it would be damp, a tiny, persistent leak, probably when the tenants upstairs flushed their toilet. A trickle of water that had been invisible for years forming into just a damp spot at first and then just a big damp circle and then just a big damp circle turning black from mold and then one day five years ago the ceiling had crumbled onto the bed in a silent catastrophe.

I stood on the thick carpet that felt crusty and stiff under me, my throbbing fingers in my pockets, and hesitated. It was strange. No one had been in the apartment for decades, and you could feel it, the emptiness, the shock of movement forcing jellied air back into motion. The place looked like a museum, smelled like the back alley of a butcher shop, and my skin crawled.

There was nothing. Of course there was nothing. I was shaking a little, my fingers throbbing and my newest wound bleeding slowly, the bandage damp and clinging on by sheer determination. This had been our last, best idea.

There had to be something. There had to be *something*.

There was: a dead girl in the tub.

The bathroom was small, covered over with a black-and-white tile design made up of tiny squares, dozens of which had popped from the walls. There was more water damage in here, a humid feel, the ceiling sagging as if filled with brackish, rusty liquid. The smell was bad, trapped in the tiny space. There was an ornate pedestal sink with brass fixtures and a small, basic-looking toilet with a pull-chain flush, the water tank on the wall above it. The mirror had darkened, black spots clouding the silver, one on top of the other until it was a dark, phantom mirror, something that grudgingly reflected you but only after running you through smoke and clouds.

The tub was a big old claw-foot, the porcelain yellow, the brass fixtures matching the sink. There was no showerhead.

The girl was young and naked, lying on her side with her knees drawn up to her belly, her skin milky, blue veins visible. She had short dark hair and looked almost peaceful, curled up on the bone-dry bottom of the tub. I looked around; the place appeared deserted, but someone had been here within the last few days to drop off a body. I stood there, listening, as it suddenly seemed entirely probable that someone had crept into the place behind us.

Mags knelt down and peered at her, cocking his head. "She's been bled, Lem."

I blinked and looked at him. The words were just sounds, and then meaning snapped into them and I stepped over to stand next to him, looking down at the girl. He was right. She had the translucent look to her, drained cleanly, every drop of blood sucked out. I knelt next to him and reached in to push aside some of her hair, squinting down at the wound on her neck. It was clean and minimal, familiar.

Mags had the clean-slate cheer of the dim-witted. He crouched there serenely, certain that I would solve this little problem for us. That I would roll her over and discover some ancient cash, or jewels, or that she wasn't dead at all. Mags's faith in me was sometimes invigorating, more often exhausting. Mags could survive on rage and profanity; he didn't need to eat. I thought of him as a pet sometimes, a monstrous kitten I'd picked up and let sleep in my pocket one night, and now—when I looked at his plump, blood-engorged face and twitchy, murderous hands, I felt a stab of horrifying affection—Mags was my responsibility.

I was thirty-three years old and I was wearing the sum total of my worldly possessions, and recently decisions I'd made when I was fifteen didn't seem so fucking bright anymore. We all thought we were special—all of us, every fucking Trickster all the way up to the fucking *enustari*—we all thought we had the edge. And maybe we did. But here I was, dopey from blood loss and begging the universe for a handout.

I stood up and fished my switchblade from my pocket, pressing the button and hearing the familiar, horrible *snick* of the blade flashing out.

"What—" Mags said, barking the word like he meant it as declarative: *What!*

I unfolded my left hand and drew the blade across my palm, just deeply enough to draw a thick, slow ooze of blood. The pain, as always, shivered through me like poison, and I sucked in breath, tensing. I'd cut myself millions of times. I had faint white scars on both hands, my arms, my legs, and even my stomach. I did it immediately and without thought, letting my underbrain run the show.

Blood dripped from my clenched fist as a hot icy rash of fire spread over my palm. Closing my eyes, I imagined the glow, saw the faint blue light in my mind, and on the beat of my heart I whispered the spell. The blood sizzled away midair, consumed, and my wound was dry and open, aching.

A wave of dizzy weariness swept through me. As a damp line of blood oozed into place on my palm, my hand was engulfed in a soft blue glow that made Mags look like he was made of shadows. Puke mounting in my throat, I knelt and resisted the urge to rest my forehead against the cool porcelain of the tub. I stretched out my arm to hold the eerie light over her. Instantly, a complex pattern of symbols, like invisible tattoos, faded into visibility on her skin, covering all of her. I knew without checking that they were under her hair, too, inside her earlobes, on the webby skin between her fingers.

"Fuck," Mags breathed, the word now a plaintive exclamation. "She's marked."

I stared down at the runes for another second. They were complex, and I didn't have time to pick through them and compare them to my memories, to what my *gasam* had taught me. I knew a few things right away: I knew the runes would ward her from any other magic I might try to cast, resisting all but the most bloody and powerful spells, and this meant she was part of something way out of my league.

I studied her face. Sixteen? Twenty? It was hard to tell. Curled up in the tub, she looked peaceful. Young. There were old bruises on her arms. A crust of snotty blood around one nostril. I looked at her feet. Was relieved she was barefoot. For a second I remembered canvas tennis shoes, pink marker. The sound of a girl shivering, her bare arms bruised just like that.

I pushed the memory away, angry at myself. I hadn't bled this girl. I hadn't done anything.

I looked at Mags. His big flat face was crunched up in thought, and

I knew I had to get him out of here before whoever had done this came back. I snapped my hand out like I was throwing something and the blue light sizzled away, leaving us in the faint light of the candle. I reached down and dragged him up by the collar.

I thought back to standing outside the door, half an hour before. I'd thought about turning around. A moment of crazy affection for Mags outside the door, and I'd thought maybe sleeping out in the open one more night wouldn't be the worst thing ever. Now I knew what the Worst Thing Ever looked like. Or at least the tip of that black iceberg.

"Come on," I said, pushing him towards the door. Mags could fold me into complex patterns and not break a sweat, but he was tame.

"What's up, Lem?"

I kept pushing him, urging him to go faster, imagining the owner of that corpse walking in and finding us—and whoever had marked her was a fucking deep well of trouble.

We are not good people.

We rushed through the hall and back into the first room, as sealed and stultifying as ever, the candle guttering in front of us and throwing odd shadows everywhere. My heart was pounding as I urged the big cocksucker forward, almost throwing him through the door. I didn't bother putting things back the way they were; the important thing was to not be there anymore.

In the hall, I spun and pulled the door shut behind us, my fingers throbbing. I squeezed my sliced hand again and opened my palm to reveal a nice smear of greasy blood; I wrapped my hand around the door-knob, took a deep breath, and whispered a Cantrip to replace the wards we'd broken and not noticed in our haste to get inside, the syllables—not words, really, just sounds—welling up automatically from memory. It was all about patterns, rhythms. You could find ways to cut the Words down, just like any language. You could say *Please pass me the salt* or you could say *Pass the salt* and they meant the same thing. It was the same with magic. You could cast a spell with fifty words, you could cast the same spell with five words, if you knew what you were doing.

I'd always had a way with the Words.

Another wave of tiredness settled into my bones, and I staggered a bit, holding on to the doorknob. When I'd steadied, I took my hand away. The door looked exactly as it had when we'd arrived. No one walking by would ever notice anything out of the ordinary . . . unless they had a trained eye and specifically knew to look for something.

I took a deep breath. My heart was ragged in my chest, and I felt shaky and light. I reached into my jacket and extracted an old soiled handkerchief and started wrapping it around my hand.

"C'mon, Mags," I said, turning for the stairs.

He hustled to walk beside me. "What's the matter, Lem?"

I didn't pause. I could hear thick leathery wings in my head, too close. "Deep magic, Mags," I said, pushing open the door to the stairs. "Deep fucking magic."

RUE'S MORGUE WAS A BAR. Popular with Tricksters. Most nights you could find a lot of lightweight talent in there, scheming. It was off-limits to our usual cons: No one gassed up dollar bills in Rue's, and no one used a bit of Charm on the bartenders or any unsuspecting civilians who wandered in. The Normals were fair game everywhere else, but you don't shit where you plot, and everyone needed a place where there were rules. Even low-rent grifters like us. The owner was a fat man named Kenny who'd inherited the dive from his mother. He was soft and cranky and didn't like us much, because we didn't spend a lot when we had to use our own money.

"I don't understand a fucking thing any of you say," he said like a mantra, several times a night. "We used to get a better class of customer."

Kenny never had any idea how right he was. Tricksters. We were the bottom. There was a general rule against fucking with Kenny—who, so far, had lived in peaceful ignorance of having a hundred Tricksters in his bar every night—but sometimes it was impossible to resist. Mags bumped into me as I stopped just inside. Bounced back like a parade float and hovered there. The place was fucking empty. I looked at the bartender.

"Neilsson been in?"

It was a Thursday, so the bartender was Sheila. Tall. Skinny. Fake tits. Black jeans, white shirt, black vest. Dull hair, dull eyes. She got better-looking as the night went on, usually.

She looked at me. Red eyes. Hungover. Had the best fucking job in the world right up until it became the worst fucking job in the world. Shook her head.

I sighed. Stepped over to one of the wobbly wooden tables and dropped into a chair.

"Get us a couple of shots, Magsie."

All of my scars throbbed. I adjusted the fresh bandages and contemplated the black hole that was following me around. It had started off as a pinprick of absolute doom and grown slowly. Now it was man-sized, and the gravitational pull was adding five seconds to every move I made. I had no money and now no prospects. I had Mags. I supposed I could train him to dance and stand behind him, clapping, while people threw coins into a hat.

Maybe with a bit of gas, a creative Cantrip to spice it up . . .

Mags came back with two big shot glasses. They were empty.

"Sheila says we hit the cutoff last week and just didn't notice."

I nodded. Mags sat down. We always had blood. There were always guppies out there who would fall for a stupid trick. All was not lost. I was so fucking tired. All my cuts throbbed in time with my ragged heartbeat.

"We could go find Heller," Mags said. "Hook in to that circus."

I blew breath out of my mouth. "We could, sure." I thought about that scene, a fucking Manson family of grifters. Heller was an *idimustari* who didn't have any rules. About anything. "He's in Jersey."

Mags snorted. "*Fuck.*"

I nodded. Thought about the girl in the tub. This did not help my mood. I hadn't killed her, but the runes meant someone who knew the Words had. Marked her up for a major spell, a Rite, and sucked her dry to cast it. I pictured her. No more than twenty. Maybe younger. Curled up in that ancient tub, she'd looked like a little kid, sleeping.

I wanted to chat with Neilsson about it. He'd been sitting on that apartment like a hen on a jeweled egg. Maybe he knew if we were in trouble or not. Maybe he'd sent us there on purpose, throwing heat our way. Maybe all that time we'd spent shining him on and gassing him, he'd been gassing *us*.

Sitting there with my empty glass and Mags panting next to me, jingling his collar, I thought better of it. I was glad Neilsson wasn't around. I didn't really want to know any more than I already did about the girl.

Jersey maybe wasn't a bad idea, I thought. Get out of town. Out of circulation. In case anyone noticed the broken wards on that door, the hastily re-created ones.

"My boys!"

I twisted around to glance back at the entrance to the private-party room. Eyed the short, thin man in the patched overcoat emerging from it. Kept my face neutral.

"Hey, Ketterly." He was older than us by some unknowable amount. He wore thick square glasses and always looked slovenly. Graying hair. Too much of it. Mustache. Sloppy old suit, sloppy stained overcoat. No bandages on his fingers; Ketterly liked to blend in with the Normals. He was the sort of cheerful you couldn't trust because it was constant.

Ketterly always looked like he was enjoying himself, which made him a fucking liar. He worked a paranormal detective grift, sifting small coin from idiots using a few easy Cantrips to locate lost items or drum up a few poltergeists, claim he was contacting the dead. You *could* contact the dead, of course, assuming you had a few dozen bodies to drain for the effort. Ketterly just put on a show, occasionally found something to make it look good.

He did other work, too, when he could. He was the sort who did anything he got paid to do.

He dropped into the chair across from me and waved at the bartender. I felt a thrill. "Give us three drops, dear," he said breathlessly. I could sense Mags's excitement.

Ketterly grinned at him.

"You want a trick, kid?"

Mags nodded. "Yeah!"

Ketterly entertained Mags like you entertained strange children met by chance. Toys. He always had little showy Glamours to teach Mags: short, dirty spells that were colorful and loud, harmless and easy. Pitr Mags loved it, and if he hadn't had the memory of a chipmunk, he would have had hundreds of them squirreled away by now.

Sheila brought three full glasses. Sullen. She'd expected an easy afternoon shift filled with napping and coffee, regret and self-loathing. Instead, she had us.

When she left, Mags sliced his palm as Ketterly started giving him the Words. Too many syllables; I got the gist of what he was doing right away and saw where he could have cut half of it away. Bending light and air, most of it was repetition. Ketterly was a sloppy writer. Most of us were; most of us were taught a spell and just repeated it exactly like we'd been taught, forever and ever, amen. Mags was excited and cut too deep, blood welling up from his hand in a rush. I could smell it. Feel it in the air. Sheila was behind the bar again, eyes closed. No one else around. Mags started repeating Ketterly's spell.

I studied Ketterly. I wondered why he was here. He sometimes did real work for people. Small-time, Tricksters like us. Anyone who needed people found, things buried. I thought of the girl in the tub, then thought of Ketterly sitting in the back room as we walked into the bar. A man who did dirty jobs, a man who found people. I scanned the sleepy room: sawdust on the floor and the empty tables, glossy with varnish and marked with the repeating pattern of water stains, circles on circles on circles. Nothing seemed threatening or even unfamiliar. But I was itchy, staring into Ketterly's smiling face. The man was a hound, and when he walked into a room he was searching for something or someone.

Told myself I was paranoid. I probably was. Ketterly was *idimustari* just like me, and the Archmages of the world didn't waste their time hiring bottom-feeders like him to find other bottom-feeders like me. They had blood-soaked spells for that.

I felt the swell of power in the room. Gas building up, being focused and shaped. Mags casting the stupid trick, pulling the energy from his own open wound. Too much for what he was doing, I could tell. He needed just a pinch for this bullshit, but he had a free flow going. If you pulled too much for a small spell, you got an exaggerated version of it: too bright, too loud, too big, too whatever.

A Trickster didn't worry much about that, though. I only knew one spell of sufficient power and complexity to be dangerous if overpowered or unfinished, and I'd never cast it.

I saw the girl in my head for a moment. A different girl. Younger. Shivering. As always, I saw her sneakers. Perfect in my memory. Every flower. Every heart. Every instance of her fucking name. I'd seen her once, ten years ago, for fifteen minutes. I could close my eyes and see every pore still.

I shook myself, got rid of her. Put myself back into the moment.

Thing was, Ketterly didn't *like* the Normals. We were all Tricksters. Everyone I knew. We all preyed on regular people, people who didn't believe in magic. Who didn't *know*. We weren't a guild, we didn't have rules, but there was a code, a loose agreement. We kept each other's secrets from the others, people who could be fooled easily because they didn't think what we did was possible. I never thought it made me better than them, though. I knew a secret they didn't know. You couldn't win a game if you didn't know the rules.

Ketterly thought regular people were stupid. He was a bootstrap magician. Had figured it out on his own, to an extent—had seen things when he was a kid that had convinced him magic existed. He'd *deduced* it. Like a math proof in his head. Had sought out mages on his own, figured things out on his own. He thought, since he'd done that, everyone should be able to. People like me, who'd needed to actually witness magic before believing in it, he thought were merely slow-witted. People who never figured it out, he thought were fucking cretins. He had no compunction about robbing them blind. Charming them. Hurting them from time to time.

I picked up my glass and sniffed it. Cheap stuff. Beggars can't be choosers, so I tipped my head back and tried to bypass my taste buds completely. Direct to the throat, let it slide down. It got warm in my belly and I put the glass down. Hated owing Ketterly something. I'd worked with Ketterly before. Used him a couple times tracking people down—he did have a talent for it. But I didn't like him. Or trust him.

Mags suddenly coughed. A fucking earthquake. Two hundred fifty pounds of dumb Indian convulsing.

The spell he'd been building dissolved. Collapsed on top of us, all that gas in the air suddenly set free.

I heard Ketterly hiss, "Oh, *shit*."

There was a flash and I was blind. A second of implosive silence, like the sound had been sucked away, and then fire in the air around us. Hot and bright, raining down, disappearing before it hit the floor. I was lifted up, chair and all, and thrown backwards, crashing into a table and chairs that collapsed beneath me, sticks of wood everywhere. I sat up, head throbbing, scars aching. Sheila was staring, shocked, behind the bar. Ketterly was on the floor, too, struggling up onto his elbows. Mags was still in his seat, but he'd been blown back into the next table and sat back with his elbows on it.

It was what happened when you didn't complete a spell. It always happened. Someone knew why, but it wasn't me. My education had been incomplete.

"Fucking hell, Mageshkumar!" Ketterly shouted. "Who the fuck taught you how to fucking recite? You can't fucking *stop* in the middle!"

That was basics. Anyone who got apprenticed, who went through *urtuku*, knew that much. I'd heard rumor of the occasional Normal who figured something out on their own, a single Word plus a bleed and causing havoc. But mages clamped down on that shit. Some kid causing grief with single-Word bullshit got scooped up and bonded as *urtuku* to learn a few things, or he disappeared. It was a rough business. And no one knew how permanent being apprenticed to an *ustari* was better than me.

Mags blinked around at us. Eyes wide and damp. Near tears. He could kill someone by accident. Could crush you to death like a kitten when he was hugging you for joy, just fucking accidental homicide. But he didn't like to be yelled at.

He started bawling. "I'm *sorry*," he whispered. Looked at me in appeal. "I'm *sorry*."

"It's okay," I said, climbing to my feet. Grabbing a chair and setting it right. "It's okay, right, Digs?"

Sheila was still staring at us, alarmed. Unsure what she'd just seen. Past experience had taught me that the best way to handle it was to ignore her, let her think what she would. They almost never thought, *Magic*.

I glanced at Ketterly. Didn't like the hint of bitter disdain I felt.

Ketterly looked at me, then at Mags. Finally nodded, getting up. No fucking cheer now. All frowns and fuss. "Sure, sure. Okay. No problem. Listen, Vonnegan, I've been waiting here for you. Figured you'd come in here eventually. Neilsson asked me to look you up."

I winced, waiting for it.

"He wanted me to tell you: Stay away from that place he discussed with you. He made an error in judgment. You shouldn't get involved."

I nodded, anxiety seeping through me. I'd understood that Neilsson didn't want us knowing about the apartment, but I'd assumed that was because it was worth something. Now I figured Neilsson knew what was in there and who had put her there. I didn't want to get involved.

I gave Ketterly a smile as he brushed himself off, throwing Mags a glare that almost got the big guy crying. "No problem. Tell Neilsson we're gonna leave it. Probably shouldn't have coaxed it out of him in the first place."

Ketterly nodded. "Good." He looked up, tried to reconstruct his cheerful mask. "My work's done, then, eh? Come around the office sometime soon, boys. I'll teach you a new one then, eh?"

Mags nodded eagerly, smiling shyly. "I'm awful sorry, Digs."

Ketterly shrugged. "We all make mistakes, kid," he said. Looked at me steadily. "All that matters is how we react to them."

I nodded. Ketterly waved and turned and left. I sat down. Mags dragged his chair back over without standing up and sat next to me like a dog that had just been kicked.

"Heller in Jersey," I said slowly, unhappy. Resigned. A good idea to get the hell out of Manhattan. A bad idea to mess with Heller, ever since my Fixing days. I looked at Mags. "Let's get out of the city for a few days and go join the circus."

3.

PLAYING CARDS AT ONE OF Heller's parties, room 37 of the Starlight Hotel—a desolate hole on Route 1 and 9 in New Jersey—I felt hot and weak. I'd been bleeding myself a lot, and half the cash piled up in front of me on the table was speckled with my blood: singles, gassed up to look like twenties, fifties, hundreds. Most of the blood boiling away as I cast, leaving behind crumpled dollar bills. I was pushing it, but desperate times called for desperate measures. The booze wasn't helping; I was thin and half the liquid pushing through my veins now was liquor, light brown, searing.

The room was crowded. Massively crowded. Heller lived his whole life this way, moving around, motel to motel, always seedy and off the highways, always cheap. He set up shop and threw a party. His customers came to score some weed or coke, meth or ecstasy, and they brought friends. Working girls showed up like magic, like fucking *magic,* like there was a wireless network only whores could see that announced things like drugged-up assholes in a motel. More likely, Heller passed the word for a cut of the action. Music played softly, a throb at the edge of perception, bubbling under the fuzz of voices. The room had been transformed. The beds removed, tossed into the parking lot. Tables brought in for cards, chairs set up. Heller went all out for his High Rollers, who followed his game. The whores followed the High Rollers, and the Tricksters, we followed everyone. That was the natural food chain.

People moved constantly. As I sat there trying to concentrate through the distant pounding of surf in my head, the crowd beyond swirled and shifted. Girls in short skirts and torn stockings, their makeup reapplied so many times this one night that they looked like ghouls, their hair stiff and their hands papery from hand sanitizer. Guys who didn't blink, their pupils the size of pins, still nodding at something they'd heard an hour before, leather jackets steamy and skin red and angry. The swells, in their ugly, expensive suits. The dealers, in their sneakers and jeans and fanny packs. It all swirled around. It smelled like feet in the place. Smoke and sweat and vomit and blow jobs all swirled together into something you didn't want to breathe in.

The Bar Kids worked the room on an honest tip. Or semi-honest. They ran around taking orders. They were Heller's kids, recruits. Mostly Hispanic and Arabic kids from his home neighborhood. They came with him and did waiter service and made more money in three nights than they could in a month at any straight part-time job. Then on Monday they were back in school, tired and wired but flush. Everyone left the Bar Kids alone and let them earn their tips and steal as much as they could without being obnoxious about it.

And in the midst of it all were my people. *Idimustari.* Some of us were just as bad off, just as tweaked out, and just as desperate. But most of us were better off. A little sallow and anemic, maybe, but clear-eyed and sharp, our little weasel noses twitching, smelling money. All the

Normals were our marks. If you couldn't smell the gas in the air, if the Words didn't make you prick up your ears, heart pounding, then we worked you, and worked you hard. Some of us worked the whores. A Charm Cantrip was good for a lot of things. A freebie, if you didn't mind being ninth in line that hour. Bleed a bit more and put a few more Words into it and she'd be tithing her take up to you all night long, slipping you half of what she got every time she went to the bathroom with some guy.

Some of us worked the High Rollers. Like me and Mags, playing cards. Prick your thumb under the greasy table and you could win every hand. Be a little creative and *lose* every hand but somehow end up with the pot anyway. Go easy all night and no one would notice. They were all used to losing anyway.

Some of us worked the dealers, some of us worked the bodyguards, some of us worked the adventurers who'd found their way in by accident. We all worked *somebody*.

No one worked Heller. Heller was one of us. He was just *organized*. And the booze was free.

This particular motel reminded me of my father, picking me up from Cub Scouts one night after I hadn't seen him in months, kidnapping me. Literally. He was waiting outside the meeting and didn't smile when he saw me, just gestured me over and told me to get in the car. I was excited, I was happy. Looking back now, I could see he was drunk. We drove for hours, hours and hours, and I gave up being happy halfway through and just sat glumly in the front seat.

"Hey, hey," the fat guy across the table from me barked, snapping his fingers at my face. "You fucking sleeping? It's fifty bucks to you."

I blinked, my eyes feeling like they were shrouded in sandpaper, and made a show of looking at my cards. "You snap your fucking fingers at someone, they might get bitten off, Magilla."

I glanced up in time to see him grin and snap his fingers at me one more time. I nodded, letting my cards drop back down. I tossed a real fifty on the pile. "Call."

I was using a Glamour I'd learned a few years ago to win. It was a nifty little spell, compact and efficient, and didn't need much gas to keep at a simmer, though I was keeping the wound on my left palm open under the table to feed it. The beauty of it was, you didn't try to make every card look like what you needed, or try to make every hand look like a winner. It was similar to a Charm Cantrip: You made everyone at the table think you won, and let *them* supply the details. They just saw whatever winning hand they preferred. It was elegant. Elegance was lost to most of us. Most of us learned rough spells that got the work done but took too long to say, wasted the gas with inefficient rambling. It didn't take much to study the logic of it, the patterns, and find faster ways. Elegant ways.

The bet went around again, and my mind wandered like smoke. There were six of us, aside from the Bank. The Bank had been the only constant in the game since we'd gotten there, an old man with deep bags under his eyes, wearing a short-sleeved dress shirt and paint-splattered work pants. He didn't appear to be breathing. His big spotted hands dished the cash in and out of the strongbox in front of him, and he never twitched or blinked or seemed to care who won or lost.

The rest of the game had been evolving. The current slate had been steady for about three hours:

Fat Boy, who had a thick gold chain around his neck and a big gold ring on his left hand, thought he was bright because he kept ordering vodka on ice from the Bar Kid and letting it melt, untouched. Something he saw in a movie, staying sharp. He'd arrived recently, strutting about in his polo shirt and loafers, looking angry.

The old woman with her hair like a cloud of unnaturally blond wire had taken her seat at the same time I had, back in the misty past when I'd been merely dog-tired and desperate. Her lips were smeared almost purple, her eyes done up in a thick dark blue mascara. She played with hundred-dollar bills that were crisp, unwrinkled, and uniformly dated from twenty-five years ago, extracted with ritualistic precision from what was apparently a tote bag full of them.

The twitchy kid in the shit-brown leather coat and sunglasses who was five minutes from stroking out in front of us or going bust, whichever came first, had been a resident for a few hours.

The strangely tan, thin gentleman in an Italian suit and a gold watch that flopped sinuously around his thin wrist, face half hidden behind huge round dark glasses, had logged six hours so far and hadn't had a drink or taken a piss in that time. His lips were in a permanent purse, pink and wet, seemingly unaffected by the height of his stack.

And the Truck Driver, fat and black, with a belly that forced him to sit forward, elbows on the table as he sweated, growled, and moaned through every losing hand. Which was every hand. He'd been sitting there so long I'd started to recognize the different inflections and pitch of his horrified grunts, like a little language of misery. When he lost, he would tug on his baseball cap and grunt. He reminded me of my father that way.

Dad had a lot of Tells, too.

I saw the old motel again, Dad pulling the beater into the parking lot and bringing me into the office with him, like luggage. I remembered him paying the rent, thirty dollars, most of it crumpled singles and fives pulled laboriously from his pocket, and then the key in his hand with a green plastic tag on it. He didn't take me to the room; we walked fifteen feet to the small dark bar that was part of the motel's compound, and he lifted me up onto one of the stools, bought me a Coke, and ordered a Jim Beam with a beer back. I remembered his drink order because I heard it about twenty times that night.

I startled as a roar went up around me, but it was just Fat Boy winning the hand. I smiled thinly at him as he shot me a triumphant look, became for a moment a Fat *Man* leaning forward with some effort to gather his winnings. This was on purpose; it wouldn't do to win every hand. You paid a little tax now and then and lost one, and that supported the Glamour, gave it some structural integrity. Some of the bills in the pot were painted with a drop of blood that hadn't burned off yet, but he wouldn't notice until later. I glanced at my winnings and estimated maybe three or four thousand dollars. Enough to get Mags and me a roof and a meal or three, enough to rest up and recuperate a little, make a plan.

On day one, the cops showed up, always, usually about three hours in. It was a game; Heller paid off the motel manager, the desk clerk, and the cleaning staff, and then the manager, the desk clerk, and the cleaning staff turned around and sold the tip to the cops for an extra bump. Heller took the cops into the bathroom and five minutes later they left happy, pockets bulging. They had a system going.

By day two, Heller's parties had become small societies. Orbital card games cropped up. People started living there, sleeping anywhere, waking up and toasting up and then passing out again. People cabbed over from the city, paying off hundred-dollar meters so they could hang out and soak up the atmosphere, just because the circus came. And we came with the circus to hustle and run little grifts and pay Heller a tithe for the privilege.

Fat Boy cut the deck as someone nudged my elbow. I blinked and tossed a fifty into the pot as ante. Fat Boy was still smiling at me. "Maybe you should sit out a hand, Sleepy?"

I started to shake my head, then paused. Was I really going to let Fat Boy fuck with me? I *was* tired. Three days without sleep, bleeding myself like I enjoyed it. I nodded and plucked my fifty back. "You're right, Magilla. Deal me out."

I scooped up my cash and stood up. I went light-headed for a moment but took a deep breath and headed for the door, staggering a bit. The music and voices swirled, and then Mags was there, putting his arm around my shoulders buddy-style so he could steady me without embarrassing me.

"You okay, Lem?"

I nodded. From behind us, Heller's voice, deep and booming, cut through the noise.

"Lem fucking Vonnegan," he shouted. "You ain't walkin' out with a pocket fulla kosh without kissing me good night. You want to be in my pocket *again*?"

I turned and managed a smile at Heller, sitting there at the kitchen table, a glass of water and a closed briefcase in front of him. He was maybe fifty years old, tall and lanky, with a huge belly—the body of a big, strong man allowed to eat and drink whatever he'd wanted for forty years. He wore huge Elvis sunglasses, and his head was shaved to a nice round ball, red and peeling. I raised a hand.

"Never in life, Mr. Heller!" I shouted, trying hard to make it sound hearty. "Just taking the air. I'm right outside, you need me to give you a hand job."

Heller laughed, his teeth green and yellow pebbles. He was, I knew from unfortunate experience, covered from his ankles to his neck in black and blue tattoos. Heller was shit as a Trickster, marble-mouthed and slow with the Words, but he ran his movable feast as tight as anyone I'd ever known. I turned away and let Mags help me.

There were too many people. Everything blurred together, the music slowing down while the crowd sped up, moshing this way and that. There was no air. It was just exhalation, carbon dioxide and smoke. I hung off of Mags and let him lead me. People put their hands on me as we staggered, slipping them into my pockets and feeling me up for whatever they could find.

I looked up and squinted around. We were in the kitchen.

"Jesus, Mags," I breathed, "wrong way."

A skinny boy in full makeup and skintight, low-riding leather pants, his long, silky black hair tied into a thick rope, held a red plastic cup out to me. "Drink this, beautiful," he said. Behind him, people were leaning over the countertops, straws in hand. A brick-shaped woman in a red jumpsuit was hunched over the sink, vomiting so loudly I imagined lungs and spleen clogging the drain.

I smiled at the kid. "What is it?"

He grinned, jerking his chin at the red jumpsuit. "Ask her."

Mags reached out and put a shovel-like palm against the kid's chest. Pushed with what appeared to be a tenth of his innate strength, sending the kid sprawling back into the stove, cup and thick brown liquid flying. Then I was in the air as Mags scooped me up and carried me, barreling through the crowd without a word of apology. People dived this way and that, cursing and shouting, but all you could do against an unstoppable force was get out of the way.

And then we were out in the parking lot. The noise was halved and the smoke and smell gone. Mags set me down, and I sat on the curb of the paved walkway that circled inside the motel's rooms, right next to a gleaming new black BMW, a gem. I breathed hard, sweating freely.

"Fuck him," Mags said, lighting a cigarette and pacing in and out of my peripheral vision. "That little fuck. I'm fresh, Lem, I'll give you the gas, and we'll teach them all a fucking lesson."

I froze and reached up to grab him hard by the arm, pulling him down to my level. Mags squawked but let me do it. "Don't ever fucking say that again, Mags. I don't use anyone's blood but mine." My heart was pounding.

"C'mon, Lem," he whined, wide-eyed. "I didn't—"

I looked up at him. Wanted to cut him some slack but couldn't do it. I gave his arm a yank, making him lose his balance and stumble away as I let go. "*Ever.* That goes for you, too, or you can go fuck yourself."

His face suddenly opened up, a flower blooming, and instead of the perpetually angry big bastard people avoided on instinct, I got that rare glimpse of what a little Pitr Mags had looked like: almost handsome, innocent, eager. "Jesus, Lem, I didn't— I mean, I wasn't—" His expression changed again and he was in agony, heartbreaking. "Oh, shit, Lem, I'm *sorry*, I didn't mean it. Honest. I'm just tired."

I felt bad. His desperation to be forgiven ate at me, so I gave him a smile and a nod. "I know you didn't, Maggie," I said. "I know. I'm tired, too."

His relief made him handsome again for a moment, jovial and happy. "Ah, thanks, Lem. I'm sorry, I just get *mad*." His face darkened as he returned to the source of his current mood, and he was Mags again, the sort of man who punched walls on a regular basis. "They think they're so fucking *smart,* but *we're* the smart ones, and they don't even know it."

No one was with me to appreciate the joke of Mags calling himself *smart,* so I kept my smile private.

I looked around the parking lot. I remembered walking out of the bar, my father sleeping soundly on the stool next to me, the bartender satisfied to leave him there for eternity. I'd wandered into the parking lot in my Cub Scout uniform, and the old man had been standing there in a white suit, white hair, white shoes. Oldest man I'd ever seen.

I would never, I reflected, know that old man's name, but I would never forget him. I could still see him, pulling out the ornate knife with the pearl handle and slicing his hand open with a sudden practiced jerk. I remembered stopping in shock as he smiled at me, and I remembered how he'd made a fist, blood dripping onto the asphalt, and I remembered how he'd risen up, an inch at a time, as he muttered something I couldn't quite hear. When he was floating a foot or so off the ground, he'd grinned at me, toothless. And I'd run back into the bar.

"Lem?"

I startled again. I was falling asleep where I sat. "Sorry, Mags."

"You hear that?"

I paused and listened. A rhythmic pounding noise and a muffled . . . voice. I stared up at the black car right next to me.

With a groan, I pushed myself to my feet, Mags there instantly to steady me, and walked around to the back of the car. I paused to look around the parking lot, trying to be sure no one was around, and then I pulled the handkerchief from the infected wound on my left hand. Infections were constant. More than one of us had died from blood poisoning over the years. You had to let the wounds heal naturally, because healing spells on open wounds usually backfired gruesomely. Something to do with burning blood to cast on blood—it just never worked.

I took a dab of blood on my right index finger and flicked it at the trunk, muttering three syllables my master had taught me years ago.

The trunk popped open, rising up on hydraulic hinges. Mags and I leaned forward and looked down into the trunk and found a girl, eighteen, twenty, hands and ankles tied tightly together. She stared up at us for a moment, eyes wide and shining. I blinked, and she surged up against her binds, thrashing and bucking. Screaming against the very effective ball gag. Her eyes were locked on me and stared at me unblinkingly.

Then she went still, though her eyes remained on me. She didn't blink. Her eyelids twitched and quivered, her whole body tense.

"Fuck," Mags whispered, making it a modifier suggesting wonderment. His sole talents were indifference to pain, strength beyond that of normal men, and the ability to conduct entire conversations using one word. He could have recited the complete works of Shakespeare using just *fuck* with subtle alterations of volume, stress, and accent. Assuming he could read, which I was not entirely certain of, having never seen him do it.

With a muffled howl, the girl began struggling again, twisting and rocking violently in the trunk, making the whole car sway.

I put my hands up, all my tiny wounds smarting, and smiled tiredly down at her. "Hey, hey," I said. "Calm down. I'm going to cut you loose, okay, but I'd like to not be smacked in the head for the effort, okay?"

She paused, sweaty, her nostrils flaring with each labored breath. Her eyes, green and big, flicked from me to Mags and back. She was tall, folded cruelly in the trunk, and had short dark hair, tan skin that looked creamy and perfect, like she'd never had a zit or a scratch in her life. She was a kid, and I felt old and perverted, thinking this girl was cute even as she was tied up, kidnapped.

She nodded once, curtly, and lay still. I got the switchblade from my pocket and flicked it open.

"Don't."

I paused. The voice behind us was shaky, thin. It had a pleading tone to it. Mags whirled, and when he didn't launch into Mags Smash All mode, I sighed and looked down at the girl, whose eyes had gotten impossibly wider and were locked on me, jittering this way and that as she resumed screaming deep into the gag.

"Sorry, love," I said. "Be right back."

I turned slowly, hands up, and found a ghost standing behind me. He was older than me. Not by much, but he'd seen some hard times. He was tall and thin, thin, *thin*. His suit was a beauty, and had cost him several thousand dollars, but it had been cut for a much healthier man, a man with an extra fifty pounds everywhere. He was white and pale, balding, his face a gaunt skeletal remnant, his eyes sunken and shadowed like he didn't *have* eyes, just empty spots on his face. The gun in his hand was one of those newer automatics, so light they looked fake I didn't think it was fake, though.

"Step away from my car," he said, his voice cracking with strain. He was shaking all over and high as a fucking kite. My eyes flicked to his arms. A shirt cuff poked out from his left sleeve but not his right, and I imagined he'd been in the back bedroom of Heller's All Night Circus of Death shooting up. Smack was a bitch, and it had made plenty of people tie girls up in their trunk.

"Step away, *please*," he said, his face crumpling into a mask of pain and horror. "*Please.*"

I started to say something, to act on the welcome information that the Skinniest Fucker I'd Ever Seen did not actually *want* to kill me, but as I took in breath to speak, he started having a conversation with himself while staring at me.

"What? Yes. No! No. *Please*. What?" He squinted at me. "I see. No. *Idimustari.*"

Mags and I both jumped at the word. It meant, in a language I barely understood myself, Trickster. Little magician. Which meant Mags and me; short spells for short cons. It was a word you didn't hear out in public. There were others: *ustari*, a step up from us, and a truly powerful mage called *saganustari*. There were also *enustari*, Archmages, but there were damn few of those, and when you heard that word, it was usually your cue to find a good hiding place.

"*Please, no.* Please, I'm begging." He was blinking rapidly, sweat rolling into his eyes. "I'm . . . No!"

I slowly folded the fingers of my left hand against my palm, the sizzling pain stretching and yawning, waking up. I pressed my fingers into the crusting wound and spread it apart again, pain blooming. I kept my face blank. My heart, pumping fumes and dust in lieu of blood, danced alarmingly in my chest. I felt the warm smear on my fingers and prepared, my mind bringing up the syllables, the simple Cantrip—simple was what I lived on, only what I could fuel myself.

The man shut up, stiffened, and pulled the trigger.

At the same moment, I snapped my hand out and shouted. A sudden flare of sunlight, pure and unfiltered, burst from the palm of my hand. The Skinny Fuck cried out and staggered back, turning his head away, and Mags, faithful Mags, crashed into him like a runaway bus as the light died away, leaving us in deeper dark than before. Confident that my tank-sized friend could handle anything short of mechanized troops, I spun and looked back at the girl, who stared back up at me, frozen, a bubble of snot blooming and fading in one nostril as she hyperventilated. My hand still slick with my own tired blood, I whispered again, and the eerie bluish light spread over my hand as before. I had a sickening hunch and knew better than to dismiss it. Even before the spell finished, I could see the symbols on her—just like the girl in the tub, she was covered from head to toe in runes.

I extinguished my light and stared down at the girl for another moment. "Fuck *me*," I whispered, and for a moment I almost expected that to be the world's shortest Cantrip and something amazing would happen.

Behind me, there was another shot. I jumped and spun, noting in passing that people were already crowding out of Heller's room, making their escape. They would fade into the night for a few hours, then creep back. This wasn't the first time someone had been shot at one of his parties. There was a protocol.

Mags leaped back from the Skinny Fuck like he'd been stung.

"Jesus fucking *Christ*," I shouted, stepping forward and spinning Mags around, checking him. He pushed me away and staggered back a few more feet, hands on his head.

"Shot himself, Lem," Mags said. "I was just beatin' him a little, and had a hand on his wrist, but I was . . . I was *pushing* the gun away, you know? Away from *me*. And then . . . he started talking to himself again, and just put the gun to his head, and . . . oh, fuck . . ."

I walked over to Mags and put my hands on his shoulders. He sounded like he was about to cry. "You did good, Maggie. *Good.*"

He blinked at me and dragged an arm across his nose. "Yeah?"

I nodded, tired. I knew if I closed my eyes, I'd fall asleep standing. "Yeah. Not your fault."

A smile twitched onto his dark face, and I spun away. I could hear Heller's distinctive roar from inside the motel, and people were moving past us in small groups, cars starting up. As soon as he could get past the crowd bottlenecked at the door, Heller was going to beat the living shit out of us. Twice. I knelt down by the Skinny Fuck and examined him. I thought about giving him the old faerie light, check for runes, but instinct told me not to bother. Instinct also told me this was a man marked, though, a man in the grip of magic—the kind of magic I'd felt creeping up behind us back in the apartment.

His nothing-eyes were staring up at the sky, the gun still in his hand, loose. Skinny had put the barrel of the gun against his temple, and the top of his head had exploded outward, a flap of skin hanging down over his forehead. A trail of yellow-red brains limped away from him on the pavement. His other hand was on his chest, and I stared at it. He'd been fighting with Mags, but his hand was on his chest like he was clutching a cross or something. I leaned forward and pushed it aside, his arm thin as a stick. I tore open his shirt and stared.

Nestled on the bony ridge of his sternum, dangling from his neck by a simple leather loop, was a tiny chip of green stone. Visually, it was just a dull chip, puke in color, rough and jagged. I felt something push up from it against my face. Invisible light, cold heat.

Fucking magic.

Under it, the skin of his chest was an angry red.

Panic filled me, like someone with a panic pump had connected one hose to my ass and put it on full speed a-fucking-head. This was an *Artifact*. This had been made by a Fabricator, an *ustari* with skill beyond anything I'd ever seen. This was the sort of thing only an *enustari* fucked with, and if Mags and I had stepped in an Archmage's shit for the second time in a week, we were completely and irrevocably *fucked*.

I stood up, vision dimming, and turned back to Mags. "Get his feet."

Mags blinked, still looking dopey and happy that he hadn't fucked up, looking around at the dissolving party with idle curiosity. "What?"

What was, of course, the second word in Mags's limited vocabulary. I moved to the Skinny Fuck's head and knelt down again, trying to find some hidden reservoir of energy as I slipped my hands under his moist shoulders. "Get. His. Feet," I repeated, nodding at the pair of shined, expensive wing tips. "We have to get out of here *immediately*."

Mags ambled over and we lifted the Skinny Fuck. I wobbled and almost passed out, but managed to hang on. I indicated the Beamer, and we dragged the body to it. I peered over the edge of the trunk and locked eyes with the girl again.

"Sorry about this," I said, and we swung the bloody corpse forward and on top of her as her muffled screams spiked in volume. I slammed the trunk closed and started for the driver's-side door, pressing my fingernails into my wound again. As I popped the lock, I scanned the night, feeling doom everywhere. I sat down behind the wheel and got her started with another drop of me and a whisper.

"Where?" Mags asked. He sounded tired.

I hit the headlights and jumped in my seat. Two men were standing in front of the car.

"Lem?" Mags said, his voice once again small and unsure, a little boy's.

"I know," I said, mouth dry. The minute I'd seen the Bleeder, I knew we were dead men.

4 THE MAN ON THE RIGHT was the most handsome bastard I'd ever seen in my life. He was black and well built and wore the *hell* out of a black suit and expensive overcoat. His haircut had cost more than the gross national product of a small island nation, and he practically glowed with the kind of good health only the truly rich and powerful enjoyed—the sort of health insurance they didn't sell to schlubs or even presidents, the sort of health insurance where you bought new organs on a regular basis and had them sewn into place as needed.

The man on the left was none of these things. He was a corpulent white blob of a human, so fat he probably had trouble walking. He was wearing a simple suit, also black, but cheaper, and it didn't fit him well. He was covered in scars. His face was a pink web of them, his hands, his throat. I knew he would have scars all over his body, everywhere. Bleeders always did.

"Gentlemen!" the dandy said, smiling. "You have something of mine."

I didn't know if he meant the girl or the Skinny Fuck.

"*Lem*," Mags hissed.

"Shut the fuck up," I said slowly. "And don't fucking move. This is firepower, okay? This is a *saganustari*."

Mags breathed in and out. "Fuck," he said, stretching it into an expression of wonder. You didn't meet a mage of that level every day—at least Tricksters like us didn't. For a moment I wished I was normal and didn't know any better. Could walk past a guy like this in the street and not shiver, not spend the rest of the day looking over my shoulder.

The dandy spread his hands. "Step out of the car, please. Let's discuss your situation."

My knuckles were white on the wheel. I didn't know who this was, but if he was what I guessed, he was one of the most powerful men in the world, and I'd fucked with one of his little projects.

The stranger rolled his eyes, and without any obvious signal, his Bleeder whipped out one arm and rolled the sleeve up with automatic, practiced ease. A second later, the fat man had a small knife in one hand, poised over his forearm. I leaped in my seat and my hands flew up, all my cuts throbbing. Panic flooded me—I'd seen what a *saganustari* could do when one had a Bleeder, an entire human's supply of fresh blood to work with, all the gas you needed for some serious fucking fireworks. Bleeders were shitty mages. They had the spark, but they generally couldn't cast. It was like anything else—some folks had a way with it, some folks could spend their lives studying with a *gasam* and get nowhere. The Bleeders were the latter, but instead of just living with being crap magicians, they dedicated their lives to their masters, offering up their blood on demand. You could see the light of demented worship in most of their eyes. Most of them, you got the feeling they *wanted* their masters to kill them, hoping each day was the day they got bled to death. Sometimes they lived a long time and lived well on their master's dime; sometimes they died off pretty young. It all depended.

That much blood offered freely and the dandy could blow the whole motel to bits, or put a *geas* on me that would have me licking his hand like a dog for weeks, or turn me into stone, a monument to failure. That much blood and you could do plenty.

I wasn't tired anymore. Fear had made me sharp as a razor, and I hit the gas and yanked down on the gearshift simultaneously. The car made a grinding noise that reverberated up through my spine and made my teeth click together, and then it surged forward with a screech.

The dandy whirled to the side like a dancer and we slammed into the Bleeder, who disappeared from view, transformed into a bucking speed bump as we crashed over the curb onto the deserted highway. I mashed the gas pedal down to the floor and leaned forward, tense over the wheel. The dandy had his blood ready, sure enough—his Bleeder had just been mowed down by a car—so we had to put some space between us before he could send something on our trail that we wouldn't enjoy.

I glanced at Mags. The dim-witted bastard was *smiling*.

"Where we going, Lem?"

I sighed, my arms and hands shaking again, filled with more adrenaline than blood. "Hiram's," I said. There was nowhere else.

PULLING UP OUTSIDE HIS town house shade of brown near Prospect Park, always reminded me of the first time I'd walked up the crumbling stone steps and rung the bell.

I'd been watching him for weeks, struggling to get the courage together to approach him, terrified. In those weeks I'd seen Hiram Bosch do some amazing things—small tricks, I now knew, tiny Cantrips that required a drop of blood and no more. At the time they'd seemed impossible.

Every spell I'd seen him cast in those weeks involved petty theft. A blueberry muffin floated from behind a diner counter into his waiting hand when no one was looking. A newspaper box popped open without receiving any coins. Taxicabs paid off with blood-smeared dollar bills and told to keep the change without any sense of irony.

Hiram Bosch was a hustler.

He was a *rich* hustler, though; he never spent a dime if he could spend a drop of his blood instead, and he made money by the truck-load turning small bills into big, charming people with a Cantrip here, a *geas* there, basically running short cons on a daily basis and coming home every night with marginally more cash in his pocket than when he'd left in the morning. He was also an *ustari,* a fully ranked magician. We made no distinction of purpose or behavior; you could either make the Words do what you wanted or you couldn't, and what you *could* do determined how you were styled. *Ustaris* could do some amazing things, but mostly small-scale stuff. They might be capable of something big if they tried. Hiram rarely tried.

Nothing about the house had changed, and I was willing to bet the interior was the same claustrophobic space filled up with rugs and bric-a-brac. Hiram was an unrepentant thief. Everything he saw, he tried to steal. Mags and I left the girl and the corpse in the trunk and walked up the steps to the muffled sounds of her kicking and shouting. The street was deserted, so it would be all right for a few moments, and I didn't dare release her until we had things under control.

At the top of the steps, I swayed a little, going dizzy, and steadied myself by grasping the dragon's-head knocker and hanging on to it while I slammed it against the door.

Hiram answered immediately, as if he'd seen us coming and had been waiting behind the door for our arrival, which he might have been, I supposed. The door snapped inward and there he was, an old man who resembled Santa Claus: short, round, white hair and beard. He was wearing a nice suit without the jacket, just the trousers and waistcoat, and looked down his bulbous red nose at me even though I was a foot taller.

"Master Vonnegan," he said in his rolling actor's lilt. "Always a disappointment. Mr. Mageshkumar, a pleasure." He looked back at me. "What brings my erstwhile apprentice back home?"

"I hadn't been called an idiot in a few days," I said hoarsely. "Thought I'd get a refresher course."

He stared at me for a moment. "Ever since you rejected my teaching methods—quite ungracefully—I see you only when you are drunk and belligerent, making demands of me, or desperate and in need of favors from someone I imagine now exists as your sole friend." He glanced at Mags. "No offense, Mr. Mageshkumar, as I know you have an unreasoning affection for our Mr. Vonnegan."

Mags smiled at him and shook his head a little, not understanding any of it. Hiram looked back at me. "So which is it this time, Mr. Vonnegan?"

I sighed. I wanted to get off the street as quickly as possible. I was willing to eat all the shit Hiram had in store for me. Which, if memory served, was quite a lot.

"I've got a body and a . . . a girl in the trunk of that car."

Hiram ticked his head to look over my shoulder, his sharp grifter's eyes taking in the car. He looked back at me. "Which is stolen," he said.

"Which is stolen." I took a deep breath, the oxygen feeling good as it burned into my thinned blood. I didn't want to tell Hiram the next part, but I owed him at least a warning. "This involves . . . someone out of my league."

Hiram snorted, moving out onto the steps with us. "You have great ability, Mr. Vonnegan, and always have. You limit yourself."

I nodded. I was a purist. Hiram was not, though he usually insisted on volunteers for his bleeds. Most of the *ustari,* the mages of average ability, lacked even those scruples.

"This is *far* out of my league, Hiram."

My *gasam* glanced at me again, then nodded. "Bring them in. Try not to make any noise. That means you, Mr. Mageshkumar. You make noise just standing there, did you know that?"

THE GIRL KICKED AND struggled and was smeared in the Skinny Fuck's blood, which made her as easy as a greased pig to carry. Since Hiram was in no mood to do anything more for us, Mags managed a respectable Glamour that made anyone who looked out the window or passed by simply ignore us cutting a ragged-looking slice on his forearm for the gas. Hiram watched in what looked like increasing horror as first the bloody, kicking girl and then the cold, pale corpse were dragged into the house.

"Put the dead one in the study," Hiram instructed coolly, gesturing with one arm as if I hadn't spent years in this house. "Bring the girl to the washroom. Neither of you speak for a while, yes?"

I realized Hiram was furious. I'd been on the receiving end of his anger plenty of times when actively apprenticed to him and was in no rush to revisit my adolescence.

We slipped the girl into the bathtub, which I immediately regretted, seeing her as the other girl, the very, very dead girl in the old apartment. They looked a lot alike, which couldn't be a coincidence.

I didn't say anything, though. The girl had stopped trying to scream and kick; just flashed her eyes at us, jumping from face to face.

Hiram studied her for a moment, then sighed, unbuttoning one sleeve and starting to roll it up. "We're not going to get far with her in this state; we need to calm her," he said, reaching into his pocket and producing the pearl-handled straight razor he liked to use. Although Hiram's face and neck were free from scars, the white flesh of his left arm from the wrist to the elbow was a highway map of puckered old wounds, ranging from the delicate, almost vanished to one ugly gnarl of pink that ran for three inches like a mountain range on his skin.

Hiram didn't mind bleeding others, but he didn't have the rank to attract Bleeders. He got by on his own gas a lot, just like the rest of us. When Hiram had a big spell to cast, he got some local rummies or a whore or two, people who would take money for anything.

I closed my eyes and saw my first girl again. Her sneakers. The pink marker. She was shivering. She'd been skinny with dark hair, too, but pale, skin like ice cream.

I opened my eyes again. With a quick, masterful twitch, Hiram drew a nice bead of blood and laid the razor in the sink. He spoke the Cantrip in just six syllables. Hiram was a master of the language, which had always been appealing to me. He had a knack for paring down every spell to maximum efficiency; some mages had to chant for ten minutes to get the same effect.

I felt the power move gently outward from Hiram, and when I looked at the girl again, she looked back with calm, unfrightened eyes.

"I'm sorry about that," I said, my voice wet and thick. "The, er, body, I mean."

She shrugged as if it were nothing to get excited about. She was still and calm, her face blank. Like a film had been inserted between her and the world, everything now at a safe distance. Hiram's penchant for stealing had given him ample experience in calming people down with a drop of gas and a well-chosen Cantrip.

"My dear," Hiram said, kneeling by the tub and reaching in, "I am going to undo your gag and let you speak. Do you promise not to scream or make any noise?"

She nodded again, watching him placidly. When the ball had been removed from her mouth, she worked her jaw a bit and then looked at me. "That was terrible," she said.

Her voice was flat and unaffected. She sounded bored and tired. I studied her, something in my gut twitching. I tried to imagine if the girl who'd attempted to assault me while hog-tied in the trunk of a car was capable of faking this kind of calm.

Finally, I nodded.

"What is your name, dear?" Hiram asked gently, reaching for the razor in the sink and bending down to attend to her bonds.

"Claire," she said, still sounding like she'd always expected to end up locked in a trunk and covered in blood. Hiram's spell was subtle but effective. "Claire Mannice."

"Claire," Hiram said in that gentle way, "I have cut the ropes binding you. Please stay in the bathroom until I come for you. You can clean yourself up, but please do not leave. Can you do that for me?"

She nodded again. "Sure."

Hiram stood and reached for a hand towel from the rack. Wiping the blade of his razor carefully, he folded it and returned it to his pocket, then held the towel against his wound momentarily. He looked at Mags and me and sighed, tossing the towel at the hamper in the corner.

"Come, gentlemen, let's discuss your other problem."

WE'D LAID THE SKINNY Fuck on his stomach, because Mags didn't like looking at his face. Hiram mixed us all drinks at his elegant little bar in the corner while I told him the story from the beginning, from Neils-son to Heller's to the dandy in the parking lot. It all sounded crazy, but that was the way with magic sometimes. Coincidence was just magic running wild, like a vine that envelops your entire garden, your house, creeping in through your windows. Sitting in one of Hiram's high-backed plush chairs, I could feel sleep creeping over me like a spell.

Hiram's study was like the rest of the house: crammed full of inter-esting things. Or at least things Hiram found interesting. There were four identical chairs, deep and soft, the kind you slid down over the course of an evening before eventually falling to the floor. The walls were lined with heavy-looking built-in bookshelves, each filled to ca-pacity with a variety of tomes, some old and massive, some cheap new paperbacks. In front of all the books were knickknacks: dolls, snow globes, small sculptures—anything that had caught the old kleptoma-niac's eye at some point. The floor was covered by a thick Persian-type rug with a gold fringe. Between the chairs was a massive wooden coffee table littered with more things: a chess set and board carved from some dark glossy wood; a thick glass ashtray; a small ivory box with no obvious hinge, a gold beetle of some sort on top; a fiddle of uncertain vintage. Taking up the last of the floor space was a huge old-fashioned globe in a wooden frame, the colors faded, the borders out of date, the Communists still in control.

No matter how long it had been, when I walked into Hiram's house, I felt choked.

When I was done telling the tale, Hiram drained his gimlet and sighed, gesturing at the body. "All right. Let's have a look. Roll him over."

Mags leaped up like a puppy and scampered to the corpse, flipping him faceup. His arms flopped out onto the rug, and I could have sworn the sliver of green stone was still affixed to the *exact* spot on his chest where I had first seen it. The light caught it and made it gleam.

"Jesus fucked," Hiram said, stepping back. "Jesus *fucked*, Mr. Von-negan, what have you been *up* to?"

"What?"

"Do you know what that is?"

Panic lapped at the edges of my thoughts again. "No. My education was pretty shitty."

The old man looked at me, and then panic broke through and swamped me, because *he* looked panicked. "You did not *touch* it, did you?"

I shook my head, and relief edged into his face.

"That's not just any 'Artifact,' as your story had me believe. That is a very *old, old* Artifact, Mr. Vonnegan. Or a piece of it." He stepped to the left to get a better angle and seemed careful to stay a certain distance from the green stone. "A very *dangerous* Artifact." He looked at me again. "The mage in the parking lot—describe him again. Carefully."

I did, trying to be detailed, and he started nodding when I was half-way through.

"Calvin Amir, I think," he said. He sighed and sat down on the edge of the coffee table, letting his hands dangle between his legs. "Do you know who Cal Amir is?"

I shook my head. I hadn't kept up on the gossip.

"You *do* know who Mika Renar is, though?"

The name made me jump, and Mags looked down at his hands and muttered, *"Fuck,"* a grace note of despair and terror.

I swallowed thickly. "Renar is . . . *enustari.*" Archmage. "Probably the most powerful mage on earth."

"Not probably," Hiram said softly. "She *is.* There are other *enustari* to fear. Elsa Brandt, be afraid of her, yes. Alfonse Alligherti, stay out of his way, certainly. Mika Renar? Worse than all of them. By an order of magnitude. Cal Amir," he added almost gently, "is her apprentice."

I put my head down in my hands. "Ah, shit."

Mika Renar. Ancient, brittle old woman. Probably the worst living serial killer in the world. Able to reach around the globe and swat you off her ass without bleeding a drop of her own. Connected and rich, too, just for giggles. And I'd fucked with her *apprentice.*

"Lem?" Mags said, sounding like a lost kid.

I looked up and forced myself to put my hands on my knees and smile.

"It's okay, Magsie," I said as cheerfully as I could. "We're with Hiram now."

Mags smiled a little, relieved. I hated myself, but Mags could only understand four things at a time. We didn't have time to teach him anything else. I looked at Hiram.

"What can I do?"

Hiram snorted, standing up and heading for the bar. "*Do?* Nothing, Mr. Vonnegan. You have a girl who has clearly been marked for ritual in my bathroom. You have a stolen car parked outside my house. You have a man wearing a three-thousand-year-old Artifact neither of us could create or control under any circumstances, which is the property of either the most powerful entity in the world or her apprentice, which makes very little difference." He turned his head slightly as he worked the glass. "Mr. Vonnegan, I believe you have done *enough*."

I swallowed. I had seen what powerful mages could do; magic required blood and, at their level, a lot of it. They were not a class of people concerned with ethics or morality, as a rule. I'd seen people hideously deformed, killed in spectacular ways, cursed for life with the cruelest of subtle *geas* spells. I'd heard stories of worse, of course: buildings blown up and planes crashed, just to get the supply of fresh blood a spell required. The bigger the spell, the more blood needed. Some of the worst local disasters in history had been engineered by *saganustari* seeking huge amounts of gas for their spells.

When you went up a level from there, to the Archmages, *enustari*, you could link some of the worst *global* disasters to them. Wars had been started, extermination policies enacted, all to fuel the *biludha*, the epic rituals such individuals could cast. Hiram's lessons flashed through my mind. *Saganustari* kept it reasonable. Small-scale. Flight 19, 1945. The *Mary Celeste*, 1872. Roanoke, 1590. The Ninth Legion, 117. The *enustari* did shit like that just to get warmed up. Volcanoes had been induced to erupt, burying cities in ash and lava. Entire religions practicing human sacrifice had been established, fed by immense Charms that pushed everyone to believe, and to kill, and kill, and kill. And in the modern age they'd even gotten mechanized, setting up suicide armies, firing up ovens, herding whole populations to be grist for their spells. Dozens, hundreds, thousands dead, bled dry, burned up. Used by *enustari* like logs in a fire.

"I'm sorry, Hiram," I choked, my body vibrating. "I didn't—"

"Think, yes," he said, turning back to me with a drink in one hand. "So, the die is cast. We have to get rid of it all—the car, the body, the girl, the Artifact. First, though, we need to know what we're up against. Why does this man, who is not one of us, carry an Artifact? Why was a girl with ritual runes in the trunk of his car?" He shook his head. "Before we panic and try to clean up the mess as quickly as possible, we need more information. I have a spell we can use . . . on *him*." He nodded at the gaunt body on the floor, then looked at me. "I can cast it on you, and you will know everything *he* knew."

I blinked, revolted. "Jesus, Hiram, why *me*?"

"*Because this is your fucking mess, Mr. Vonnegan!*" Hiram shouted in the old disciplining voice I knew so well. "We need information. There is a price to be paid for it. I say that bill is on *your* tab."

I looked down at my feet. "Yes. Fine."

There was a second of silence. "I will need more blood than I can provide myself."

I sighed. "I don't have much left to spare."

"I'll do it."

I looked up at Mags, who was already rolling up his sleeve. My whole body snapped back to alertness. "No!" I snarled.

"Mr. Vonnegan," Hiram said in a more reasonable tone of voice, setting down his glass, "not all of us share your ridiculous moral certainty about using another's blood in our work. Mr. Mageshkumar is a voluntary subject, and I need only a pint or so, mixed with my own. Sit down and rest while I prepare."

Hiram once told me that magic was violence. That its very nature was destruction, and trying to civilize it with my petty moralizing—as he put it—was hopeless.

I looked at Mags. "You don't have to do this."

Mags shrugged happily. "I want to help, Lem," he said, sounding like a panting puppy.

I dropped into one of the chairs, letting it envelop me. I closed my eyes, thinking I might catch a nap while Hiram gathered his shit and then bled Mags. My rule was you never used a Bleeder. You never used anyone's blood but your own, even if they volunteered, and *never* if it was involuntary.

I thought of the kid in the dirty blue dress, all those years ago, sallow skin and sunken eyes. Hiram could fool himself that bleeding was a choice. It wasn't. The powerful cast and the weak bled, and I had learned that the only way to win that game was to refuse to play it.

I told myself Mags was no child.

It didn't help much.

"MR. VONNEGAN? WE'RE READY."

I snapped awake. No time at all seemed to have passed, but Mags had a thick bandage wrapped around his forearm, and Hiram stood over the corpse with his little silver bowl. Feeling like I'd been chewed, I struggled to my feet. "Where do you want me?"

"Kneel with your hands on his head," Hiram said immediately, his voice back to its usual smooth boom, commanding and ingratiating at the same time.

I tried to breathe in as deeply as I could. My head felt fuzzy, and I wanted to spike some oxygen into my brain. The room was too crowded. The bric-a-brac covered the walls like barnacles, clinging to every exposed surface, and even the floor was crowded with *things*, from the chairs to the table to the odd wooden boxes sitting between the furniture—one not a box but a *foot*, a huge round elephant's foot. The rug on the floor was thick and dusty, blue and gold in a dizzying pattern. It felt hot under me as I took up my position. The Skinny Fuck's skin felt cold and gummy, as if it would hold the imprint of my thumbs for hours after I let go.

The moment my hands were in place, Hiram began to whisper. He spoke rapidly, without any breaks between the syllables. I didn't recognize anything; it wasn't a spell he'd ever shown me. A phrase here and there leaped out, familiar as Hiram's personal shorthand for things, little sub-spells he'd honed to a precise few sounds and passed down to me. I struggled not to doze as he spoke, and then he was done, sooner than I would have expected for a spell that required two pints. I felt the familiar cold radiation move past me, and for a second nothing happened.

Then I *was* the Skinny Fuck. And I knew *everything*.

5.
HE HAD ALWAYS BEEN SMART. School had been easy, and he remembered laughing at the idiots who had to study, to work so hard when it was so *easy*. It was all just showing up. He didn't get perfect grades, true, but he passed, and he thought it was a good trade, to skip all the hard work and have the same piece of paper as everyone else at the end.

He'd always been smart. So it had been a dismaying mystery that he was also so damned *unlucky*.

He remembered ducking into Keens on Thirty-Sixth Street after the blowout with Roger   the pompous ass who didn't understand what he brought to the firm, the spark he contributed. His numbers were low, but so were everyone's! It was a tough time, and Roger had been riding him harder than everyone else because they didn't get along. If the Swanson swap had gone the way it was supposed to, Roger would have been forced to eat crow and suck up to him a little. Instead, bad luck had shot the deal to hell, and he was out of a job.

Bad luck. It followed him everywhere. He wandered into Keens—an odd choice, since he didn't like steakhouses or their fussy wood-and-brass bars, and he was getting a little thick around the middle, a little jowly. It had been salads and diet soda for a week trying to trim down. But he felt drawn to this place and ordered a whiskey, thinking about all his bad luck. The deals that should have worked; the investments that had tanked.

Even letting Miranda answer the phone that night—sheer bad luck had killed his marriage.

And now the bad luck had doubled, because Mir was soaking him for every dime he didn't have. He couldn't get any traction. He couldn't cook up a pot to work with, something to spread around and get going.

He considered the possibility of asking his mother for a loan. The humiliation of being supported by an old woman, a woman who had been so *careful* her whole life. He'd detested the caution she brought to every decision, the exhausting thought she put into *everything*. He remembered hating her every time she'd taken him out to eat as an adult, the way she sat there doing the math for a tip. A modest, low-end tip that she calculated to the penny. When he went out, he made a point of tossing money on the table, of signing the credit slip with "50%" on the tip line, not even bothering to figure out the amount. The idea of begging his mother for a loan made him queasy.

The good-looking black fellow started talking to him, and he should have been annoyed, but the guy had this voice like silk in oil, nice to listen to. They started trading rounds, and he thought maybe his luck was looking up, because this guy was talking about a job. He thought, *That's how it goes for me.* Feeling confident, expansive. Some people panicked, worked like dogs, and all they got was stress. He got fired through bad fucking luck, but he got hired immediately by a man wearing a five-thousand-dollar suit—because the suit could smell talent.

The man asked him, *What do you deserve?* And the man answered for him: *Everything.*

The man asked him, *Why don't you get it?* And the man answered for him: *Jealousy*.

He nodded, agreeable, working on his fifth drink and feeling good, optimistic. Here at last was someone who understood how things worked, who would be amenable. Here was someone who would give him the yardage to make a run for things, who would be happy to let him make his own way. Everything was finally working out. He accepted the position on the spot, despite having some misgivings about the vagueness of the job description. He asked when he should start, and his new employer waved him off, handing him a small box wrapped in raucous gift paper, a large black bow on top.

"You are a man of rare vintage," his new boss said, and he would always remember these words, even though much of the rest of the conversation was blurry or simply vanished from his memory. "You are pliable but not breakable."

He took the gift and held it wonderingly. What was it? He would find out.

The meeting was over. Had it been a meeting? An interview? He didn't know and didn't care. He went home filled with the certainty that everything was falling into place at last. He felt unrestrained. Smarter than everyone else. He rode the subway home, scanning owlishly around him, pitying these poor fools who worked so hard but didn't have the presence of mind—the *talent*—to pick the right bar, at the right time, and overlook their prejudices to talk to the right person.

At home, his bare-bones studio, half filled with brown boxes, everything Miranda had left after her voracious picking over of his bones, he fixed himself another stiff drink and opened the box while sitting on the hard, uncomfortable sofa. It was a piece of jewelry, he saw. A piece of green stone on a leather string. He stared at it, frowning. He'd expected a watch or a tie pin, something classy. Valuable. Well, he thought, the stone *might* be valuable, though he didn't find it attractive at all. It looked waxy, slick, and he hesitated to touch it. His head ached when he looked at it too long, and he considered just closing the box and forgetting about it, but he felt that he'd made a promise; he'd accepted the gift and did not wish to offend his new employer by disdaining it. So he lifted it by the loop and slipped it around his neck, letting the surprisingly heavy stone fall against his white shirt, which he suddenly noticed was stained red and brown in places.

The stone touched him through his shirt and spoke to him.

He remembered the first touch well, differently every time. It was revolting, like a snail moving across your belly. It was exhilarating, like an alcohol rub on a hot day. It was cold, freezing, like it had been locked in a refrigerator for days. It was hot and burning, and he was afraid his skin had blistered.

He always remembered the voice. It was a flat whisper in his head. No tone, no stress, just a monotone of quiet words. They began midstream, as if he were listening in on a conversation that had been going on forever before he arrived and would go on forever after he left.

He tore the stone off, tossed it to the floor, panting.

He was a man of varied experience. He'd seen things. He knew things. He *understood* things, not like the rubes he rubbed elbows with. He *appreciated* things because he'd taken pains to broaden himself. He'd left behind the wood-paneled bars of his father, the five-and-dime stores on Central Avenue, the family restaurants with the menu on the place mats. He'd left it behind and sought adventure, knowledge, *experience*.

This, however, was outside his experience, and he sat on the edge of the sofa staring at the stone, heart pounding, wondering if he'd really heard what he'd heard. He wanted to touch it again, see what it said. He wanted to throw it away and never see it again.

He got on his knees and crawled over to the necklace, reached out, and took the stone between his finger and thumb.

Instantly, the voice was back in his head. It was in the middle of a sentence again, as if it continued speaking whether he was listening or not. The stone seemed to squirm in his fingers, and eventually he realized that he'd been listening to it for some time, just sitting on the floor, eyes open but not seeing anything. He shook himself and was about to drop it, to go fix himself a real drink and think about it, when the voice in his head seemed to focus, suddenly become *aware* of him.

And the voice began to tell him wonderful things.

THE VOICE CHANGED HIS luck. It told him everything he'd always wanted to know. It told him which stocks were going up or down. It told him which horses were winners. It told him which corner to catch a cab on, which suit to wear, what to say to women. It told him who was plotting against him and how to deal with them. It told him everything he'd ever wanted to know, and suddenly he was on a roll.

He didn't enjoy his work. At first, with the stone whispering in his ear, he felt important. His employer had swagger; the people he dealt with now knew the name and shrank back from it, and he laughed at them. They were terrified of his boss, but hadn't he sat in a bar with the man, an equal? Trading jokes and making conversation, being taken seriously? Like equals? He'd enjoyed walking into rooms and making them all squirm when he came for the girls.

The girls. At first he'd been outraged, alarmed, afraid. He'd imagined himself behind a big desk, making decisions, maybe with a nice wet bar. A big shot. Instead, it was . . . messy. And certainly illegal. And *work*. He didn't like how they struggled, how they begged him to leave them alone, how they whimpered. The first few times he'd thought about driving to a police station, telling them everything. He dreamed about the girls at night and woke up sobbing out apologies.

Each time he thought of turning himself in, he would touch the stone. And the voice would tell him something wonderful, and he would forget all about it. And then the voice explained the rules to him. They were special, the girls. They had been *prepared,* and it was his solemn task to ensure that they made it to his employer in pristine condition. There were rules. He didn't understand them all, but he followed them carefully, because the voice told him to. Some of the girls had to be disposed of, some he never saw again. There were certain streets to avoid. He could never speak to them—he could speak *about* them, in the third person, but not *to* them. *She gets in the car and doesn't speak.* He was allowed to use physical force, if necessary—and sometimes they were not docile—but he could never draw blood or break the skin in any way. Never. The voice told him that if he ever cut a girl, even accidentally, his employer would be enraged. He sometimes put them in the trunk when they were less than enthusiastic. But he was always careful with them. Sometimes when he needed to get rid of one, he had a place he used for temporary storage until he could do the deed, but basically, he tried to get it all over with as quickly as possible.

After a while, he tried not to think about the girls. Sometimes, with the voice just a low-voltage whisper in the background while he bought expensive dinners and rounds of drinks for people, while he lived it up, he would think of them, all of them a type: a certain height, a certain shape, not so young at first but getting younger. He found them where the voice told him to look, he grabbed them, and he delivered them. And never saw them again, and he tried not to think about that. Instead, he listened to the wonderful things the voice was always telling him—secrets, unbidden, little gossipy bits, and sometimes he could even see the secrets played out in his head like some sort of psychic television. He enjoyed always knowing more than everyone else. He woke up sometimes in the middle of the night, sweating, the stone burning against his chest, the voice whispering on and on. Whenever this happened, he was nauseated and uneasy.

ONE DAY, WITHOUT ANY warning, the voice started telling him things he didn't want to know.

It still told him what he needed to know. It kept his luck up, kept him one step ahead of everyone else. But now and then, out of nowhere, it told him terrible things. Things that embedded themselves in his head and festered. Images—skeletons in the street, still clothed as if everyone had simply dropped dead. A woman in a red dress, floating, her face a mask of artificial horror. A tiny black box, delicate, ornate with an inlaid design he couldn't quite discern, but which filled him with dread.

The ideas were worse; the images were frozen, and he found ways to ignore them. The ideas were worse.

His thoughts centered on them and fixated. He toyed with the concepts and imagined them in action, spiraling around, extrapolating terrible things. The ideas were *definitely* worse.

It told him what was in the food on his plate, and he lost his appetite. It told him what people did in private, when no one could be looking, and he stopped wanting to see his friends. It told him what people were really thinking of him as they sat there smiling and sopping up the drinks he'd bought for them, and it soured evening after evening after evening.

And still, the girls. Every week two or three, picked up and ferried to the mansion out in Jersey. Some were obviously drugged, barely coherent, unaware. Some were alert and terrified but resigned. Some fought. The voice told him things about them, too. It told him what happened to them when he dropped them off, which he did not like, and it told him about their lives before, which he liked even less. Some he never saw, some spent time in the tub.

He started binding all of them and putting them in his trunk as a policy, so he wouldn't have to look at them too much.

He bought cars, drove them for a week, and bought new ones. He bought houses, four of them, one on a private beach in Florida he'd been to just once, when actually buying it. He bought suits and clothes and refused to let the tailor take them in — he'd always been a big man, and his suits fit just fine. He bought lavish dinners he didn't eat: he bought entire bars rounds of drinks. He was flush. With what the voice told him, he was flush and getting flusher, money just pouring in.

At night he lay awake, listening. The nights slowly became the worst. During the day, the voice was often reasonable and helpful, still guiding him. At night, with no change in tone, it whispered nightmarish things to him, endlessly, tirelessly, informing him of every cruelty in range, every private crime. It told him how he might murder, rape, steal, and get away with it, perfect plans he knew would work flawlessly. He stopped sleeping. He thought about removing the stone when he went to bed, but the idea of not having it against his skin horrified him even more.

A girlfriend suggested her friend Heller, who worked in the pharmaceutical line. She said this with the practiced diction of an actress reciting a line. He had the idea that his girlfriend often had people who needed chemical help while with her. That he had simply graduated to a familiar place in their relationship. He gladly took everything they offered, and for a while he slept again, fitful, narcotic sleep.

For a while.

A few weeks ago, in the midst of stock tips and traffic directions, perfect schemes to murder thousands in football stadiums, airtight plots to start new wars and become powerful through the chaos and fallout, the voice started telling him things about *himself*. None of them were good.

It told him what his breath smelled like. It told him how he appeared to other people, and he recoiled from the gaunt, sweating scarecrow they saw, the stains on his fine silk shirts, the constant wet motion of his lips. It told him about Boo Radley, and he burst into tears, the air around him like a sauna.

He pictured Boo Radley: black and white, with a pink nose, purring and twirling, tail in the air when he came home from school. Every day for three years, Boo Radley had been there, purring, his tiny body vibrating with the rumbling noise, as if his pleasure were too large to be contained inside his skinny little body. At night Boo Radley slept in his bed, snoring.

Boo Radley had escaped one day, bounding out the door to chase a squirrel. Boo Radley had never been seen again, and he'd imagined, after getting over his grief, that such a sweet-natured, happy cat had been found by another family, been loved, lived to an old age.

The voice told him the truth: Boo Radley had skulked back a few hours after escape and hidden under the back porch, scared and waiting to be rescued. And had frozen to death that night, slipping off to eternal sleep missing him desperately, sad, tormented. The voice described the creeping numbness, the tiny, inarticulate despair, and he howled and banged his skinny arms against the walls.

And still, the girls. This last one, the youngest yet. Pretty. Fought like a devil. Nothing placid or docile about *her;* she was delivered to him bound, kicking, and thrashing, and he had a hell of a time getting her into the trunk. Her eyes had been the worst. They locked on his every chance she got, and the hatred and anger he saw there made him flinch. He was *important.* He was *rich.* Who was she to disdain him?

The voice, it said *nothing* about her.

This had never happened before. Feeling shivery and gray as he drove, he'd run through it in his head. The voice always had something to say. Always. It was how he'd kept his luck, his advantage. He needed a drink. Amir wouldn't mind. Would understand if once he didn't go straight on with the girl, if he made a stop, calmed down, settled his nerves.

6.

I SURGED AWAY FROM THE body, crashing into the big globe and making it skid backwards a foot or two. My stomach tightened into a knot and then loosened, and I barely managed to flip around before I vomited all the booze I'd had right onto Hiram's nice rug. My body kept trying even after I was empty, totally empty. Just kept trying to push more out, and I remained there on all fours, dry heaving, for two minutes.

"It is not a *pleasant* spell," Hiram said unnecessarily.

"Jesus," I whispered. "The girls. Dozens. Maybe a hundred, it was hard to tell." I turned my head and looked at the sliver of green stone against his sunken, bony chest. A shiver of revulsion left over from my moment *being* the Skinny Fuck swept through me, and I had to work hard to keep from puking all over again. I shut my eyes. "She's a linked ritual, all right. A fucking *huge* ritual. Seems like she's the last one to roll in, too."

I pictured the girls. All of them. I still had the Skinny Fuck's memories, some more distinct than others. I could see the girls clearly. I shut my eyes and tried to will them away, delete them.

Big-time mages, people like Cal Amir and his boss, Renar, cast big-time spells. The bigger the spell, the more blood you needed. There had been spells cast back in history that had required *thousands* of people to bleed out simultaneously—it wasn't easy. Even if you had thousands of servants who could run through thousands of people on cue, it wasn't easy. And civilization made it harder. So what you did was you set up a domino effect: You took a manageable number of people—say, a hundred. You slaughtered them to cast a smaller spell, which in turn would slaughter a thousand people, doing the dirty work for you, and then you used the blood generated by those deaths to cast the *real* spell.

We are not good people.

The girl in the old apartment had been runed up the same way as Claire. But that one had been drained and dumped. The ritual probably required the body to be preserved, so they couldn't burn her or dump her in the river. But she hadn't been part of the main ritual— she'd been preliminary. Her blood had been used for something *connected* to the ritual but not the ritual itself. My head ached thinking about the possible uses of six quarts of healthy, inked blood. For the main ritual, whatever it was, the sacrifices had to be done together, because as each one died, her blood would fuel the next link, killing the next one. One missing girl fucked everything up. And we had one missing girl, sitting in Hiram's bathroom.

"Well," the old man said. "We know what we have to do, then."

"What's that?" I spat onto his rug. There was no making the stain *worse*, I figured.

"Give Renar back her property. As quickly as possible."

My heart leaped in my chest and I sat up. "What?"

Hiram had his blasé face on, the blank look he adopted when he assumed he was smarter than you. "Mr. Vonnegan," he boomed, still impressive after fifteen years. He'd taught me everything I knew, and he'd been eager to teach me more, to teach me how to go beyond him. But I'd left, and he'd never forgiven me. "Mika Renar can burn the two of us out of existence, do you understand? She could remove us from *history,* she is *that* powerful. All that limits her is blood, harvesting enough."

Harvesting. I was reminded, abruptly and forcefully, why I'd left.

Since Hiram had not released me from my apprenticeship, I could not seek another teacher, nor could he take on another apprentice. We were locked in a cold war.

He smiled. "And if you were removed from history, where would your dim-witted friend here be?"

Mags looked up, realizing he'd been referred to, working through the last few words to try to get the context. He grinned at me, sheepish.

"He'd be dead," I said flatly. Mags had the spark, he could work a spell. But he couldn't remember much and fucked up the half he did remember.

I was *idimustari,* a Trickster, by choice. Mags would never be anything but. And he'd never survive on the streets alone.

Hiram nodded. "So we return Renar's property. Immediately. Before she has to come find us."

I shook my head. "She'll be slaughtered. Along with who knows how many others." I pointed at the body. "This asshole has been collecting them for Renar for months now. We return the missing link, we're condemning them all to death, Hiram."

I saw the girls again. They were of a type, twins upon twins. Darker-skinned, thin. I flipped through the Skinny Fuck's greasy memories. The first girls had been in their thirties. Over time they'd gotten younger and younger, until we got to Claire in his trunk, the youngest yet.

"Lemuel," Hiram said, pushing his hands into his pockets and pushing his little round belly at me. His voice was cold now, authoritative. Hiram was no joke; he kept his magicks small, but he had ability if you pushed him. And while he was no murderer—or at least not much of one—he didn't share my distaste for other people's blood.

I put my hands in my own pockets and grasped the switchblade, all the unhealed cuts on my hands and arms throbbing with my pulse.

"You brought this shit into my house. My *house*. Even if I let you take it all away, the trail will come through here. Renar will come here or send her apprentice, and once they have proof of our involvement, they will *level this house* to the ground, and kill you. And possibly me." He shook his head. "We will bring her and the *Udug* and offer our apologies, and perhaps we'll survive this." He looked at me again. "In spite of you."

Udug. My education was incomplete, but I knew the word meant *demon,* and my eyes latched on to the ugly green stone. An Artifact—an actual, real *Artifact.* Long ago, before machines, the old masters had created objects of power using organic materials. Stone. Metal. Carvings and such—some small enough to carry with you, some huge, monstrous. Not easy to do. A few hundred years ago, some of the smarter *enustari* had started working with machinery in making a new breed of Artifacts. Devices, large and small. More powerful, because they could be varied depending on their internal workings. Fabrications.

I studied the *Udug* again. I'd been careful not to touch it. Ancient, Hiram had called it. I believed him. I didn't know how many people you had to murder in order to create something like that, how many hearts you had to rip out of people on top of pyramids, but I imagined it was a number I didn't want to know. I didn't think there was a Fabricator alive who could make something on this level today. Fabrication was a skill that had seen better days, and most of your Fabricators were assholes making love charms and silly magicked coins. None of them were going to summon a fucking *demon*, dominate it, and trap it inside something. Or at least, none of them were going to do it *successfully* and not end up torn to pieces.

I thought about a cigarette. I had a crumpled pack in my jacket pocket, but I thought in my current dry condition a single cigarette might make me pass out. I pulled out the pack anyway and shook one loose to buy time. I didn't have a light and waggled it between my dry lips for a moment, giving Hiram back his blank stare.

"I can't let that happen, Hiram." For a moment, everything in the room was still and silent as we stared at each other, and then he shrugged, turning away. "You don't have a choice in this, Mr. Vonnegan. I am going to collect her now. If you think you can stop me, please do. But I won't fight you unprovoked. You're still my apprentice, after all."

There were consequences for going against the oath of *urtuku*. All of them theoretical for me so far. Taking on a *gasam* bound you to your master. In one way, this was tradition: Magicians had a loose set of rules. Easily forgotten when convenient, but no mage would teach you anything until you were bound to them. Not a single Word. Once you were bound to a *gasam*, no one else would teach you. You could seek a new master, and they'd take one look at you, see the binding, and refuse. It was just common courtesy. In another way, this was a function of the oath: I could never stray too far from Hiram. If I tried to leave the city, I would suffer for it. Fever, convulsions, coma— eventually death, if he wished.

I was tied to the fat thief until he freed me. Or until one of us died. And Hiram was still, after all these years, so angry with me that I had little hope he would ever let me go.

He turned for the bathroom. Mags, who'd been ping-ponging his head back and forth between us, trying to keep up with what was happening, leaped for the old man. Tried to envelop him in a bear hug, simply stop him from leaving the room. Mags thought of Hiram as his grandfather and wouldn't hurt him on purpose.

The second Mags moved, Hiram brought his hand out of his pocket, straight razor extended, and in a well-practiced move slashed it down across his own palm, a superficial, wet wound. Blood welled up and Hiram hissed out a spell as he spun away, and Mags froze in midleap, one foot the only part of him touching the floor. Without a sound, he toppled over, holding the leaping position.

The spell would last a half hour or so, and Mags'd come out of it without any permanent damage. Hiram and I locked eyes, and then he was out the door. I ran after him, cursing. I wasn't sure what I was going to do—I didn't have enough strength to start throwing spells at Hiram Bosch, and Hiram had fewer scruples than me. And played dirtier.

"Dammit, Hiram!" I shouted as I chased him down the hall. "I came here for *help!*"

"You ungrateful shit, I *am* helping you!" he shouted back, stopping in front of the bathroom door. He reached forward with his bloodied hand and turned the knob, pushing the door inward . . . and then stood there.

I almost crashed into him, then turned to look through the doorway.

The window was open, a classic image of the drapes fluttering in the chill wind blowing in. The tub gleamed with the shiny kind of clean that only a constant, unhealthy obsession could purchase; the one sign that anything had happened in here at all was the slick of blood Hiram had left in the sink.

Claire Mannice was gone.

To my surprise, the old man put his arm around me. He smelled like pipe smoke and liquor. "Well, my boy—the girl has *spirit*, doesn't she? Not my best work, perhaps, but I haven't had someone shrug off one of my spells that easily in *years*." He sounded admiring. "And she's killed us all!"

I stared at the window and thought of her, bound and gagged, kicking and screaming, her eyes flashing. Thought of her calm and quiet, answering our questions. Thought of the runes all over her body.

And I smiled.

Keep running, I thought. *Don't look back.*

7 **I INSPECTED THE BROWN PAPER** bag Mags had left on the dresser and frowned. "Jesus, Mags," I said over my shoulder. "All you bought was liquor. Liquor," I added wearily, "is not *groceries.*"

He didn't say anything. Mags was in a pissy mood because we'd been cooped up in the motel for three days, smelling each other's farts and acting like sunshine burned. I pulled the bottles from the bag and inspected them, wondering what the nutritional value of cheap booze was, how long we had before we turned yellow and our teeth fell out.

"That was our last forty bucks," he said from the bed. "I didn't want to waste it on food."

I closed my eyes and started twisting the cap on the off-brand bourbon he'd brought in. Going underground wasn't easy. It sounded easy, but cash was a dying breed, and the world that mattered at the moment was wide-awake, watching out for assholes like us. Cal Amir and his boss didn't need electronic receipts and surveillance cameras to find us. Mika Renar would slit a half-dozen throats and fucking *materialize* in the room, thunderbolts in her withered old hands. Hiram had made fun of me for even suggesting going into hiding.

"My boy," he said, shaking his head, "if your name comes up connected to this, where will you hide that an *enustari* cannot find?"

This encouraging bit of mentoring had occurred while we were dumping the body of the Skinny Fuck, whose name I still didn't know. No one *thought* their names. I had a fading impression of him, his inner monologue, everything that had been him, but he'd never once thought his own fucking name. Everyone was *I* in their heads. We'd put him in the river and Hiram had bled for thirty seconds, muttering a spell that would keep the body in the dark water forever. I'd swayed next to him, ready to pass out, wishing for a cigarette.

I almost hadn't noticed Hiram palming the *Udug*, getting past his fear of the Artifact easily enough. I didn't need to see it; Hiram stole everything.

"Mr. Vonnegan, if Mika Renar wishes to find you, she will find you. You should be thinking about how to appease her." Hiram had turned to me, wrapping his hand delicately in a bandage, his white beard looking silver in the moonlight. "Find the girl. Bring her to Renar or her apprentice. Beg forgiveness, claim ignorance. Everyone will believe you."

The fucking bastard, with his twinkling eyes. *He'd* never forgive me.

I took a long swig from the bottle Mags had brought. It was terrible. Wincing, I choked it down, and it bloomed into a believable spot of warmth in my belly. I turned and leaned against the dresser, bottle in hand, and looked at Mags. He was stretched out on the musty floral bedspread, his suit tight and wrinkled on him like a snakeskin about to slough off, his stocking feet wiggling in the air. He jabbed at the remote control every three or four seconds, grimacing at each new offering. He looked about thirty seconds away from hurling the remote at the TV. Which meant he was about an hour and thirty seconds away from telling me, in a singsongy, tiny voice, that he wished there was another TV to watch.

I took another swig.

It was time to go. It was time to make an excuse, put on my shoes, steal a towel from the bathroom, and walk out into the night and leave Mags behind. Pitr wasn't bright, and I'd been kidding myself that I'd been taking care of him all these years. Here we were, broke again, on the run. We had nothing to show for anything, and it was all my fault. The worst part was how easy it would be. I could wait for Mags to fall asleep, or just tell him I was going out for a smoke. Step out, crack a scab and cast a quick Glamour, make everyone's eyes skip over me, and just walk away. He'd be better off without me.

I brought the bottle into the bathroom and closed the flimsy wooden door behind me. I was, as usual, wearing everything I owned. I set the bottle on the back rim of the sink and leaned forward, staring at myself. Sunken eyes; limp, greasy black hair; an uneven, sallow sort of face with a crust of beard. I looked like someone who'd lift your wallet and cry if you caught him. I was twenty-nine and I'd had Mags for eight years, and here we were. All the fucking power of the universe at my fingertips and nothing to do.

The bathroom was small and cramped, crowded with mildewed tiles that looked like they were sliding off the walls—salmon-colored in a way that was essentially *not* salmon but something else entirely—and a popcorn ceiling that would never, could never, feel clean no matter what you did to it. People had died in the tub, I was sure of it. A layer of human grease left behind, invisible but detectable nonetheless. I picked up the bottle and watched myself take another swig. The Vonnegans had always been good drinkers. We took to it naturally.

I was about to turn and inspect the thin, scratchy towels for the best one to steal when I heard the hollow knock at the door.

A second later, the squeal of hinges and Mags framed in the bathroom doorway, silent in his socks. "Lem?" A squeaky whisper, Mags like a startled cat.

I took the bottle with me back out into the room and put a hand on Mags's shoulder for a second, nodding, already feeling a little lightheaded from the liquor; we'd eaten last in the morning, and I was starved. I felt strangely unconcerned and light as I crossed to the door. I had, after all, nothing much left to lose. I didn't even have much blood left to lose. Another short Cantrip would put me in the hospital. A spell of any heft—of any *use*—would kill me. As I paused at the door of the room, I thought, *Look around, take it in. This is Bottom. There is freedom in Bottom.* Then I twisted the knob, and pulled the door inward, and stood blinking for a moment at Calvin Amir.

And there it was: the New Bottom.

"Mr. Vonnegan!" he boomed. "You are a hard man to find."

I gave him an eyebrow. "Not hard enough."

He smiled. His smile was sunshine. It appeared instantly and made me happier for having seen it. Cal Amir was the most handsome man I'd ever seen, with clear, smooth skin the color of creamed coffee, a pleasant, squarish face that was masculine yet finely etched, with just the right level of natural blue shadow on his cheeks. His hair was dark with a streak of gray on one side, the imperfection sanding him down to a smooth finish. His eyes were blue and seemed to reflect all the available light back at me. He was also, I thought conservatively, wearing more money on his back than I'd had in my hands in my entire life.

He spread his gloved hands. "May I come in?"

I took a deep breath. "Could I stop you?" I said, stepping aside.

He shrugged a little as he stepped in, tugging his gloves off. I glanced down and saw his hands. They were perfect. Smooth, manicured. Not a scratch on them.

"I've come alone," he said, meaning no Bleeder. Meaning he hadn't come ready to burn the place to the ground or make a fucking giant roach grow inside us that would eat its way out. It was a friendly call.

Which also let him avoid any attention, any publicity. An *enustari* could kill with a few words, could disappear, could make themselves fly—but it took time and blood. It took a Bleeder producing a blade, opening a vein. It took a recitation with perfect pronunciation and grammar. Even an *enustari* preferred not to have police, investigations, vendettas. We'd survived as a species because we were roaches. We stayed out of the light. Even an Archmage could be buried if enough cops came after them.

"Mr. Mageshkumar," Amir said cheerfully. "Good to see you again."

Mags was pressed up against the wall to the right of the bathroom door, his hands as deep in his pockets as he could push them. It was an old habit of his from the orphanage, hiding the cuts. He went back to it whenever he was afraid.

Amir walked in easy, looking the place over like we were trying to sell it to him. He stopped at the dresser and examined the bottles for a moment, turning back to me with a grin.

"Celebrating?" He laughed. "Perhaps not." He wagged a finger at me. "You know why I'm here?"

I nodded. The door was hanging open, but moving felt impossible. I just stared at Amir. He was mesmerizing.

"Good. Come on, then. We're already late."

I nodded again, then frowned. "Late for what?"

He regarded me for an uncomfortable moment. "For your appointment with Ms. Renar." He looked me up and down. "Do you have a shaving kit?"

THE LEATHER SEATS MADE my skin crawl. The moment he'd shut the door, the world had disappeared, and it was just the expensive hum of the engine and low music, something classical, all strings and timpani. It was so low, I might have been imagining it. Amir had put his gloves back on to drive, which somehow made perfect sense.

Without Mags at my side, breathing in my ear, I felt exposed. And lonely.

"Are you afraid?" Amir asked.

I nodded immediately. Magicians are not *good* people. "Yes."

"That is well. It will make the interview go more smoothly." He turned to look at me briefly. "Why hasn't Bosch released you as his apprentice? Even a mediocrity like Bosch would have more self-respect, I think."

I nodded, thinking of the girl again. Three girls, but I only really remembered one. All three of them standing there like limp rags, shivering, and Bosch's voice, silk and razors, telling me I knew the spell, all I had to do was show him I could do it.

IT TOOK ME THREE years to master this spell, I remembered him saying. *And I'd been apprenticed to that fat bastard Gottschalk for five years before that. It is the limit of my abilities. Even today, Mr. Vonnegan, I find it a difficult and challenging spell to cast. But you, you, I think, have an ability greater than mine. You already know the tongue better than I.*

This was true. I'd known it even back then. The words were a code. Obfuscated, but there were rules. Once you knew the rules, you could start playing with them. I would sit in the shared bathroom on my floor, thirteen feet away from the five-by-five room I rented for a hundred bucks a week, and bleed myself to try things. It was fascinating.

Hiram would teach me a spell to create light, a floating ball of soft yellow. A minor spell; light was easy. Everyone started with light. And I would poke at it. Try it over and over, leaving out one syllable, see what happened. Add in a syllable from another spell, see what happened. It was fun. By the time I got back to Hiram, I'd pared three syllables off the spell he'd taught me and had sixteen variations: different color light, a ball of light that followed you around, a version that eliminated the ball completely and just shone light around with no visible source.

Hiram disdained my process. Called it *hacking*. But I knew he was impressed.

The girls were whores. Bosch had paid them to bleed, a hundred bucks for a pint each. They were hollow-eyed, bird-boned shells, and the first two didn't bother me. The third was fourteen, maybe younger, so skinny it hurt to look at her. She stared down at her shoes, white Converse Chucks that she'd drawn on in pink marker, her name over and over again, stylized with flowers.

"HE'S PUNISHING ME," I said slowly, feeling tired and calm.

Amir seemed cheered by that. "For what?"

I didn't answer.

BLEED THEM, HIRAM HAD said, holding out his razor. *You have potential, Mr. Vonnegan. You just need to get over your . . . phobia.*

I was looking at the girl. Trying to imagine who looked at her and felt anything stirring inside other than pity. I saw myself cutting her, draining off her blood into Hiram's silver bowl—how long did it take for a pint to pour out of a person? How long would I have to stand there hearing her shiver, hearing her sniffle?

I said, *No.*

I had made a pledge, sealed with blood, a minor magic. I had sworn to obey my *gasam* in all things, to be a servant to him, in exchange for the knowledge he would pass on to me. Hiram's expression was almost comical in its disbelief.

Bleed them, Mr. Vonnegan, he repeated, his voice softer, gentler. *They will not die. They have been compensated. How much easier can you expect me to make it for you?*

WE WERE HEADING UPSTATE. The world had turned into darkness and wind, the buildings melting away. I didn't like it. Too much open space, too little light, too little noise. And I could feel Hiram back in the city, a worm made of razors between my shoulder blades. Our bond was passive, but Hiram could give it a charge anytime he wanted. I liked the streetlights bleeding through my windows, the garbage trucks waking me at three a.m., the drunken arguments seeping through the walls.

I didn't look at Amir. I was too conscious of being in a car, far away from anyone who might care about me—well, the one person who might care about me.

"I have not searched you for a blade," Amir said suddenly, his voice muffled and distant three feet away from me. "But I must warn you to refrain from attempting to cast any of your little tricks. There will be consequences."

I shrugged but ran through my repertoire of Cantrips and other *mu* I used to make my living. I could blind Amir with light and send us hurtling into the highway divider. I could make things look like something similar, an easy Glamour. I could Charm him, make him think well of me, desire to please me. I could hide myself in the light, make people's eyes pass over me. I had a dozen other pranks, all useful, but I didn't doubt that Amir could brush them off easily enough. I imagined the price for trying and failing to full-on *Charm* Calvin Amir was not one I wished to pay.

I could lunge over and attack him. Cal Amir was only fearsome when there was blood in the air. But someone like Amir would be *fast*. He hadn't survived this long without knowing how to cut himself quick and automatically spit out something devastating in under three seconds.

If you went for *ustari* physically, you went for the mouth.

"What kind of blade do you use?"

I frowned. "A switchblade."

"Because of speed? Convenience?"

"Habit."

"Teach me a spell."

I blinked. "What?"

"Anything." He said it fast, reminding me of the old trick when you Charmed someone, asking a series of rapid-fire questions to warm them up, then punching in *tell me anything* to see what happened. I wondered if I was Charmed. If Cal Amir was so skilled he could Charm me and I wouldn't even know it. I concluded he probably was.

"Teach me something clever," he added. "I've heard you are *clever*."

I didn't say anything to that. If the *saganustari* wanted to have fun with me, he could go fuck himself. A few seconds dripped by, quiet and marked off by passing trees, and then he reached over and slapped me, hard, with the back of one gloved hand.

"I said teach me one of your *clever* spells, *idimustari*."

I taught him how to gas up currency. Something quick and dirty he'd never encountered in his elite education—at first I worried I'd have to teach him what currency *was*, because Amir seemed like one of those rich assholes who'd never actually handled cash. He listened attentively, smiling, eyes bright. When I was done, he was excited.

"I see where you have substituted some unexpected Words, and I like the way you rely on the greed of your subject to do the heavy work of the spell. It has interesting implications for more complex work."

I stared at him. Didn't know what to say to this. It was like being on a date. Almost *exactly*, I thought.

He poked questions and comments at me for a few more minutes, picking at the details, strangely curious. Finally, he shut up and we drove a few minutes in peace.

Amir turned off the road and we were in the fucking woods, scratching our way up a dirt lane barely wide enough for his car. Somehow he managed to avoid the branches reaching for either side of his gleaming black coupe, making it seem like we were floating up the road. After a minute or so, I made out squares of light up ahead, windows, and the house slowly resolved itself out of the darkness. It wasn't what I'd expected.

Mika Renar was *famous*. There weren't that many of us in the world, a few thousand, and for seventy years Renar had been the most powerful of us all, one of perhaps two dozen *enustari* in the world. There was no official classification. No test you could take and be proclaimed Archmage. You lived long enough and cast enough major spells, you got famous, even if it was only within our little world. She was ninety-four years old, and I'd always imagined her a spider, fat and gleaming and round, hidden away in some spectacular mansion. The house was big, and nice enough. But it wasn't *epic*. It was just a fucking house.

I started to feel better.

AMIR WALKED ME INTO a small, dry study and left. It was a square, windowless room lined with wooden bookshelves. The carpet was deep and swallowed the soles of my shoes when I stepped onto it. A huge ebony desk dominated the room, eating up the floor space. Two huge red leather chairs were arranged in front of the desk. After the heavy, studded door closed behind Amir, it was so silent in the room I thought I could hear the dust I was kicking up, slamming into everything like asteroids.

I spun around slowly. The room felt hermetically sealed, like I'd suffocate in it within a few hours. I stepped over to the nearest bookshelves and stared at them blindly for a moment, then frowned. The leather-bound books were hand-stitched, and the spines were hand-lettered in a rusty brown that looked exactly like dried blood.

Reaching for one, I paused with my hand in the air and turned. I wasn't alone in the room.

There was a mummy behind the desk.

She was a skeleton with thin, papery skin stretched over bones, wearing what looked like several blankets draped over her narrow shoulders. Her hair looked like a tight, heavy wig of yellowed white, braided thickly in the back. Her nose was still elegant, long and turned up, the skin on it patchy and peeling. Stepping silently over the thick carpet, I leaned in and studied the figure: She was tiny and desiccated, and I would have thought she was dead except that her thin, liverish lips were moving. Whispering.

"You're being quite rude, Mr. Vonnegan."

I froze. The mummy had stopped moving its lips.

Straightening up, I hesitated for a ludicrous moment before turning around. Standing near the door, which was still shut, was a beautiful red-haired woman. She was tall, wearing a sleek black dress that hugged her convincingly. Her skin was bright white, almost like she was a photocopy—aside from her hair, she was black and white, a gray scale. She glowed peculiarly, and I found it easier to leave my eyes on her, as if gravity just pulled them there.

I forced myself to look away and found the mummy again. Mika Renar.

I looked back at her Glamour. The most fantastic Glamour I'd ever seen. She looked *real*. Solid. I wondered if this was really what she was like fifty years ago, or if this was wishful thinking. I wanted to stare at her. The younger version was beautiful, that long nose with the arrogant turn at the end perfectly balancing a round, soft face, the sort of face you wanted to wake up next to. The sort of face you wanted to make express things. Like lust. Like pleasure. Like pain.

I felt like I'd seen her face before. Wondered if that was part of the Glamour. If it was, it was a nice touch.

The Glamour eyed me up and down, her face blank, and then she gestured at the chairs. "Please," she said. "Have a seat."

Her voice was delicious. It crawled into my ears and made a nest, and I felt blood rushing to my groin, my face getting flushed. I sank into the nearest red leather chair and let it envelop me. The leather was soft and fleshy and kind of warm.

I wondered idly how many people had to bleed to manage a Glamour like this.

"You have been granted this meeting," she said, gliding towards me and sitting down in the other chair, a graceful dance move, "out of courtesy. Your Master, Bosch, is a minor member of our Order—and you are *insignificant*—but members you are."

Our Order. Fancy. There *was* no order, no rules. No membership rolls, no elected officials. No organized set of laws. There were traditions handed down from *gasam* to *urtuku* over the years, distorted each time. Almost everyone, including powerful mages like Renar, respected them. Because the rest of us did, on occasion, rise up and unite against an Archmage who presumed too much, went too far. It had happened. Renar was going to give me time because our *Order* would expect her to, and if she did not, they would see their own dark futures written in my corpse and might come after her, if only to save themselves from the future. Not even Renar and Amir could fight against the combined weight of every *ustari* in the world.

The main rule was you didn't interfere with other magicians. I'd interfered with Renar, sure, but that had been accidental. I had an excuse.

The other rule was you didn't mess with the established order of the world. Power was one thing. You don't shit where you eat, and we fed on the world itself.

Beyond that, there were no rules, only the single limitation: You could cast only what the blood allowed. If you didn't have enough blood, it didn't matter how clever you were with the Words, how you hacked the grammar.

A breeze of perfume washed over me, and I leaned towards her, eager. I'd never experienced a Glamour so real. At any moment I might actually reach out and touch her. She smiled, and I was in love. I pictured us married, sitting on a Sunday morning with newspapers, trading sections, sipping tea—fucking industriously, all sweat and pheromones.

Someone had *died* to fuel this spell, and I didn't care.

"You have *interfered* with my work," she said, arching a strawberry eyebrow. "You have lost my property."

I nodded stupidly. Yes, whatever she was saying. If I kept nodding, she might touch me. Just a glance of her hand on my cheek. Worth it.

"You must *restore* my property to me."

I nodded again but slid my eyes to the right and looked at the mummy. The mummy's eyes were dry and yellow and fixed on me. A sliver of dread inserted itself between my vertebrae, and I looked back at Renar's Glamour and blinked rapidly, scraping her out of my eyes.

"What?"

"The girl, Mr. Vonnegan. She is mine. You misplaced her. You must bring her back to me."

She is mine. I suspected Renar regarded everything she saw uniformly as her property.

I shook my head, alarm burning through me. Her *property,* like she was referring to a prize cow I'd let out of a pen. A girl marked for ritual, marked to be bled to death, so that others might be bled to death, so that *others* might be bled to death. My stomach rolled, and suddenly the perfume in the air, for all its fake magical perfection, smelled like rotting fish. I didn't bleed people. Giving Claire over to Renar would be the same as bleeding her myself.

"No."

I had a three-second out-of-body experience, standing next to myself and marveling at what I'd just said. What I'd just done to myself. Suicide, some would call it.

She studied me for a moment with her bright, glowing green eyes. "Mr. Vonnegan, this is the price of your continued existence. Do you understand me? Refuse me, and I will take *you* as compensation." She leaned back in her seat and placed one hand against her temple. "You cannot replace my property. You are not suitable. Suitable candidates are in limited supply and difficult to produce. Therefore, if you do not restore my property to me, Mr. Vonnegan, you will suffer for it."

The word *suffer* seemed to emerge from her in a cloud of poison, and I had trouble breathing.

I stared at her illusion of herself, and the illusion stared back, power beating against me like a hurricane. I frowned. "I am not a—"

"I know precisely what you are, *boy*," she snapped, her voice drowning me. "*Idimustari*, Trickster. Grifter. A small man of small talents worming his way through life with childish gibberish. Cantrips and other *mu*, dust in the eyes of those who cannot see."

I forced myself to swallow the rock-hard bump of alarm that had been collecting in my throat. Why was I here? If she wanted Claire, she was *enustari*, she could just *get* her.

She snorted. "The marks . . . resist other spells," she said, and I jumped in my skin, not sure she *couldn't* read my mind.

"Deflect them," she continued, as if bored with my thoughts. "Corrupt them. Else I would have snatched her back easily with a Word. You are a man who worms. You and your small magicks are ideal for this work." She nodded her perfect head once. "Restore her to me or suffer."

This time I barely noticed the threat, the word *suffer*. I was chewing on this bit of information about the runes. Even terrified, my brain spat out a theory: Cast *near* them, use your own kind of misdirection and fool the universe into thinking you were casting on something else, see if that compensated for their effect on spells. A nasty hack, but if it worked, who cared? I tucked the thought away, something to chew on if I ever had time.

The Glamour stood up and turned away. I kept staring at the empty chair. "Wait a fucking second," I said, hands tightening on the arms of the chair. "You dragged me out here to fucking tell me *that*?"

"I desired to see you," she said, and the Glamour disappeared. To my right, I heard the mummy hiss something, the Words inaudible. A second later, I went stiff, snapping my legs and arms out straight at my sides, paralyzed while an excruciating pain burned into me. I rolled off the chair and hit the floor, drooling. Shaking.

"If I desire to see you, you will be *seen*," her Glamour's voice whispered in my ear. "If I desire to hear you, you will speak. If I desire to bleed you, you will *bleed*. The *world* will bleed on my command, *idimustari*. So it has ever been, since I killed my mother in childbirth, since I cast my first *mu* to choke my father at the dinner table. So it has ever been, so it will ever *be*."

Jesus fucking Christ, I managed to think. *She must have Bleeders dripping* all the time.

"You are *known* to me now, Vonnegan, and have no marks to bend the Words. If I desire to *see* you again, do you doubt I will see you? And if I see you again, *idimustari*, do you doubt I will be the last person to do so? You are dissipated. But tall. You would fuel a handsome moment's entertainment."

The pain was as if a larger man had stepped inside me and was splitting me at the seams. A stupid spell. A *mu*. Imaginary pain, nothing more. But if I'd been able to work my mouth, I would have bitten off my tongue for the relief. Abruptly, it stopped. I buckled on the floor, spasming my legs up to my chest as I called out, sucking in air. The pain was gone. I was soaked in sweat, shivering. But whole. I sat up. The Glamour was gone.

My stomach clenched into a fist, I stood partway and turned to look at the mummy.

It had shut its eyes.

8.

I WATCHED THE ATM VESTIBULE from across the street, feeling tired and scratchy. I was worried about the timing, because timing wasn't Pitr Mags's strong suit.

It was getting dark, and I was feeling tired and scratchy. I wanted to get this over with while it was still twilight, before interior lights clarified things. I could see Mags through the glass across the street, trying to look busy and struggling not to look back at me every three minutes.

I raked my eyes along Hudson Street, watching the suits coming and going. The wind cut through my jacket and made me shiver; I looked up at the sky for a second and contemplated the winter: It was coming, and we had nowhere to stay, nothing between us and the snow.

When I looked back, someone had joined Mags. Cursing, I ran out into traffic and dodged three cars, leaving a wail of horns behind me. I slowed to a walk just as I pulled open the door and stepped into the vestibule. It was a tiny space, and the three of us were crowded. Mags was pretending to finish up with one of the machines while our mark punched buttons on the other.

He was a doughy-looking guy in a decent suit, briefcase set on the floor next to him. He had a thick head of graying hair and a round pink face with delicate lips. He looked like he'd been tortured by bullies at school and got his revenge on others in little ways every day.

I tried to control my breathing and pretended to fuss with the deposit slips and pens, waiting for the high sign from Mags. When Mags coughed twice, indicating the Mark had inserted his debit card and punched in his PIN, I muttered the spell and sliced open my arm, letting the warm blood run down to my hand.

The pain was sharp and hot, and this was one of those moments I enjoyed it a little, savoring the bright red way it ate into me. Nothing dripped onto the floor; I recited the spell fast enough to burn it off as it flowed out of me, disappearing, swallowed whole by the hungry universe.

My vision swam and I felt dizzy as the spell finished, and I had to lean against the little table for a bit, breathing. I turned towards the Mark, who was staring at the ATM screen in dreamy confusion. I swayed, digging in my pocket for my crusty handkerchief.

"Hey!" I said, feeling light and shivery. "How are you?"

The Mark turned to look at me and smiled. It was a slow smile and looked completely out of place on his face. It twitched and shimmered as if the muscles of his face were not used to holding the expression. "Hello!" he sighed. "How are you? Good to see you."

He trailed off into more mutterings, impossible to translate. I held out my hand and he took it, slowly but enthusiastically. Began pumping it. Up and down, up and down.

The ATM machine began beeping, impatient.

"Let's get a drink, old buddy, it's so good to see you," I said cheerfully, slipping an arm around him and pushing him gently towards the door. "You can tell me what your PIN number is and we could have a conversation about that. What do you say?"

On the security cameras, it would look like two old friends meeting by chance.

"Oh, yes," he said as I pushed the door open for him. "That sounds *nice*."

He recited his PIN and I glanced at Mags to get the nod. Then I walked him around the block, and he talked to me, a steady hissing escape of breath formed into words. He wasn't such a bad guy. He told me how disappointing his life had been since he'd left the band, taken the money and the desk job, and started eating candy bars all day, just unwrapping and chewing and unwrapping and chewing, no thought. He would glance in his trash bin before leaving the office and be amazed to find ten or twelve wrappers in there. He kept his arm around me, and I could smell him, and it wasn't so great: sour deodorant. By the time I got him to the Radio Bar, he was telling me a story about his vacation, a trip on a cruise line to the warmer parts of the world, and he wished I'd been there to hang out with him.

I suggested he go in, get us some drinks, and I'd be right in to join him. He gave me a look of damp joy at the thought, nodded. I watched him step inside and settle onto a stool at the bar like a zeppelin docking with a tall building, and turned away.

I was feeling better physically, steadier, though my hand was throbbing again just when the other wounds had calmed down. A heavy depression was pushing down on me. I didn't know what this guy was like in reality, but under my heavy dose of Charm he was a sad panda, and I felt guilty.

Mags was on the corner, wide-eyed, looking in the wrong direction, his body language like a poodle who'd been tied to a street sign a little too long. He jumped when I appeared and then smiled, his big body going soft.

"Two thousand!" he said. "In the account. But five hundred was the limit here!"

I nodded. "We've got at least fifteen minutes. Let's see what we can do."

We are not good people.

WE SIPHONED THE OTHER fifteen hundred before the card went dead, and we just walked away, the ATM still beeping. It was enough, I thought. Nothing to get excited about, and I'd bled a little too much on the Charm, leaving me gray and staggered, but it was a decent pile to have riding on your hip. Mags yapped around me, happy and energetic. He'd already forgotten we were in trouble. I decided not to remind him.

He started to recognize the neighborhood we'd wandered into and got even more excited, this week turning out to be one of the best of Mags's entire fucking *life* so far, at least for the moment. We'd pulled a grift normally too ambitious for us in terms of bloodletting and dangerous publicity, worked it perfectly, and now we were going to Digory Ketterly's office.

KETTERLY USUALLY WENT BY "D.A." because he disliked the singsongy sound of "Digory Ketterly." He thought it made him seem weak and poofy. He was right. I didn't trust most other mages. We were all grifters of one sort or another, and we were all parasites—of others or ourselves. Ketterly I trusted less than most. I'd never heard of Ketterly actively cheating one of his own, but I thought it entirely possible that he would. But I was the walking wounded, exhausted, literally drained. Finding spells wasn't my specialty in the first place, but when you added in the complication of the runes and their effect on magic, I needed help. I'd surveyed my vast circle of friends and acquaintances and decided I would have to risk putting a little faith in Ketterly, or else I was going to risk bleeding myself into a coma.

His office was a basement affair in Chelsea, six steps down. Instantly you felt damp, imagining the sewage seeping up from below. A glass storefront still read OLYPHANT BOOKS | USED | NEW | ESTATE SALES. The door had a yellowed piece of copy paper taped to the glass that read D. A. KETTERLY, INVESTIGATIONS: MIRACLES ACHIEVED.

We pushed our way into the dark, dense interior, the rusty bell attached to the door ringing as we did so, and were immediately enveloped by gloom. A cave. The bookshelves and books were exactly where they'd been decades before, covered in dust, the hand-lettered section signs clinging to the wood: FICTION, REFERENCE, MUSIC. It smelled like paper and dust and cigar smoke.

The whole place was just one room with a tiny washroom in the back that beat at us with the heat of its smell, a terrible green odor that had heft and mass and grabbed on to you as you moved, insistent. The center of the room had been cleared out and a large green metal desk installed. There was one chair, a huge cracked leather one on wheels that creaked and sighed with every move Ketterly made. He leaped up in a cloud of cigarette smoke and threw his arms out.

"Is that Pitr fucking Mags?" he shouted. "Hey, watch this."

He waved his hands in the air theatrically, and I caught the barest glint of light on his tiny blade. Ketterly liked to use a sharp-

ened penknife for his Cantrips—it was unobtrusive. He liked to as-
tound and amaze the rubes; an obvious knife and a bleeding hand
ruined the effect. I didn't notice his lips moving as he spat out the
syllables. Ketterly worked public, so he'd taught himself to almost
throw his voice, a barely audible whisper, without moving his lips.
When he was finished he barked out a nonsense word enthusiastically, making Mags jump as a fiery, glowing bird appeared in the air
between us.

"Aw, shit, that's fucking *cool*," Mags hissed, his eyes locked on the
bird as it swooped around the room lazily. "You'll teach it to me?"

I snorted. Every time Mags learned a new spell, he forgot an old
one.

"Sure, sure, if you concentrate this time and not blow up my shop,
huh?" Ketterly pulled a handkerchief from his pocket and held it in his
hand. His suit was an old, well-cared-for one. Up close, I knew, it
would show a million repairs, all done with careful stitches and good
thread. From three feet away, all the work was invisible. Ketterly was a
miser. He wasn't making a mint with his detective business, but he
salted away every dime he screwed out of idiots who'd never heard of a
Seeking Rite. I'd never seen D. A. Ketterly on the street with more than
pennies in his pockets.

He sat down in his squeaky chair and crossed his short little legs,
fussing with his overlong black and gray hair. He looked at me as he
leaned back, dim light glinting on his glasses. He laced his fingers
behind his head. "Your boy Mags here is adorable, and I like having
him pant around my office. *You're* ugly as hell and boring to boot. So to
what do I owe the pleasure of this visit?"

I smiled. Mags was already trying to guess at the Words of Ketterly's
stupid Cantrip, mouthing them in a hushed voice. This was a doomed
effort, but Mags's face was a mask of somber effort, and I didn't have
the heart to mock him. "I need you to find someone for me."

"Ah," Ketterly said, nodding. "My specialty."

I hesitated.

"I'm told spells won't work well on this one."

He squinted at me. "Why not?"

I pulled out a wad of cash, already damp from my own sweaty pocket, and tossed it onto his desk. "That's three zeros. A retainer."

He looked down his short torso at the money, wrapped up in a rubber band, and then looked back at me. I willed him to take it, to pick it up and accept the job, but he kept his eyes on me.

"You're pretty eager to grease me off, Vonnegan," he said. "And I can't use a spell, huh?"

I shrugged, failure burning my shoulders. "You *can* use a spell," I said. "It just probably won't work."

He squinted at me, then glanced down at the wad of money and back at me. "All right," he said. "I'll ask: Have you been shitting in some other mage's sandbox?"

I nodded. "Shit everywhere."

He looked back at the money. "I don't like getting into fucking *ustari* politics, kid. Always messy."

Our rules—you didn't get involved in another magician's business; you didn't cast anything big enough to mess with the fundamental underpinnings of the fucking universe—were mostly to keep us from tearing the world apart.

Throughout history, there'd been a number of attempts to break the second rule, and other magicians around the world had gathered in coalitions to defeat them. It hadn't been pretty. Half the stories in the Old Testament were foggy histories of *enustari* wars, oceans of blood shed to destroy one of their own declared dangerous to the whole world. Chances were if you scratched any old legend of bloodshed on a monumental scale, you found *enustari* either spinning bloody webs or waging war to stop one another from spinning theirs. It hadn't been that long ago that four *enustari* had engineered a world war just to settle their own accounts. And every war since had seen a cast of horrifying characters bending it to their own ends.

Sometimes the overriding opinion was that fighting the crazy bastards caused more harm than good. Hence the first rule: Mind your own business.

"That's a thousand dollars, cash. You don't have to touch her, okay? Just find her, let me know where she is, and I'll take it from there."

Ketterly leaned back again for a moment and then, lunging forward, pulled open a desk drawer and swept the cash into it with his arm. Still hunched over the desk, he scowled up at me. "Fine. If I get shit on my shoes, kid, the bill will come your way, and it'll probably take more blood than you have in your wasted frame to pay it. You okay with that? Someone bleeding for you?"

I stared at him. "No," I said, turning away. "I'll be outside. Teach him the fucking bird, okay?"

I LEANED AGAINST THE railing and managed to glom a cigarette off a civilian passing by, skinny guy who hadn't showered in days, his irises like pinpricks. Didn't even need any gas for it; I just asked nicely and he handed one over. Most natural thing in the world.

I smoked and fought to keep my eyes open. My stomach was growling, and every single cut on my arms and hands pulsed with burning low-level pain. Even so, I saw the two cops approaching from half a block away, thinking they were being sneaky. If Mags had been standing right next to me, if I wasn't already a pint or so down, I would have asked the Big Indian Bastard to teach them a lesson, but I was too damn tired and just let them walk up to me.

"Lemuel Vonnegan," the woman said, declarative, a statement of fact. She held her badge up in front of me for a moment. Not long enough to study, of course.

She was short and slight, Hispanic, curly dark hair that looked rich and healthy and luxurious, like she spent half her paycheck on it. She'd been pretty when she'd been young, but the youth had leached out of her and left behind hard edges, making her handsome instead. She was wearing a warm-looking turtleneck sweater and a pair of well-cut pants. No perfume; shampoo and cigarettes.

"How's it going, Vonnegan?" the guy said, grinning.

He was a fat black guy, skin shiny, head shaved and, by all appearances, waxed. His teeth were yellow, and I wanted to make him stop grinning. He was big but looked and moved soft. Fleshy. He wore your standard detective costume: suit and tie made for another man entirely, wrinkled and perfunctory.

They liked to use your name. Made you feel like they knew everything about you already, like they'd been watching you, listening in on your phone calls. I'd been hassled plenty by cops. Sometimes you couldn't get away when a grift fell apart and you didn't want to be too obvious about bleeding out an escape—nothing like a cop seeing you float up into the air or something like that, scarred for life by the sight, following you around, trying to figure it out.

I nodded, exhaling smoke. "Detectives."

They glanced at each other. "I'm Marichal and this is Holloway," the woman said, nodding at her partner. "Let's take a ride and talk."

I looked from Holloway to her, dragging deep on my cigarette, which I suspected was about to be taken away from me. I figured at least at the station house, they might give me a cup of coffee, something to eat. "What about?"

They looked at each other again. It was annoying. When they looked back at me, it was Holloway who spoke.

"Murder," he said cheerfully, tugging on my jacket. "And lots of it."

9. **I TILTED MY HEAD BACK** to get the sugary dregs of coffee, so sweet it was almost bitter, and wished I had another cup. I imagined I could feel my body absorbing nutrients directly from the liquid. Even though it was possibly the worst coffee ever created, it was the best coffee I'd ever had.

I was in an interview room. I'd been left alone for twenty minutes so I would become properly terrified.

The room was painted a sort of shit green, the sort of shit green you saw when you were well on your way to scurvy. There was no obvious mirrored wall, but there were at least four spots on the ceiling that could have been cameras, peeking in to see if I was crying or writing a confession or being beaten to death. There was a surprisingly small metal table and three plastic chairs that had big chunks missing from them. There was an odd smell in the air I couldn't place, and an annoying buzzing noise.

They'd searched me and taken my blade, smiling and polite. I rolled up my sleeve and examined the scabbed wounds, the moist, yellowish gash I'd made a few hours before. I estimated how much damage I could do with my fingernails, whether I could get a good bleed going. But tearing a wound apart was slow and painful. And messy. And I was exhausted; the Charm on our ATM mark had taken more than was wise. I wasn't going to do myself any favors by casting something else and passing out right after.

The door opened with a bang, making me jump. The two detectives walked in with files under their arms and cups of coffee in their hands. Out of his leather coat, Holloway had shrunk a bit, becoming just a flabby guy wearing reading glasses, older than I'd first pegged him. Marichal had suffered, too; outside of her thick coat, she had no waist—she went from hips to boobs with no transition.

She glanced at my arm as they took their seats and said nothing. Seen it all, I supposed.

"Mr. Vonnegan," she said, spreading the files in front of her in a busy, distracted way. "I'd like to ask you to look at some photographs and tell me if you recognize anyone."

I rolled my sleeve back down, looking at the top of her head while she fussed over her files. "You're asking me?"

"You're not under arrest," Holloway said.

I didn't look at him. All I knew about cops was that each and every one of them was a bastard looking to clear cases so they could go home. None of them gave a shit about justice. And they fucked with your head when they wanted answers, so the best thing to do was figure out what they *wanted* you to do and do the opposite.

In the short term, Holloway wanted me to look at him. So I didn't. "And if I stand up? Walk to the door?"

"You might trip."

Marichal was extracting photos from each file and making a deck of them. There were dozens.

"Don't leave the room again," I said, finally looking back at him. Being a Trickster was half performance, and I knew a good beat to hit when it swam up under me. "I won't be here when you get back."

Holloway smiled at me. "Lem Vonnegan!" he said suddenly, dramatically slapping his hand on the table. "I can't fucking believe I got Lem Vonnegan in my interview room." He leaned back in his chair, making it creak dangerously, and smiled, pointing at me. "You got quite the jacket. You're the goddamn godfather. Six arrests, one conviction: petty theft, picking pockets on the subway, six years ago. Two nights in the tank for drunk and disorderly, causing a ruckus. Three pips for running out on bar bills—or *trying* to. No convictions; no one showed up to press charges." He winked. "Yep, I'm writing this day in my *diary*. Gonna put little stars and hearts around the border, write your name on the cover a few times: *Mister Lem Vonnegan*."

Marichal slapped one of the photos in front of me. "Recognize her?"

I looked down. I knew it would be Claire Mannice before I saw it. It looked like a high school yearbook photo; she looked happy, younger. Like she'd grown six inches in two months and hadn't figured out what the hell to do with all the extra leg. Her hair was fucking terrifying.

I ran through my odds.

I knew Mika Renar was slaughtering those girls. An *enustari* like her didn't collect girls on a regular basis because she *wasn't* going to kill them. If I admitted anything and the cops leaned on me, I'd be dead. A day or two, time for word to get to Renar that I was going to help send a couple dozen cops her way, and they'd find me miraculously dead in my cell, strangled by an invisible wire. If I clammed up, the cops maybe charged me with something, found a way to hang on to me. But I'd give them the slip eventually.

I decided the slip better come sooner rather than later. These assholes were going to get me turned into a hot pile of ash.

"Nope," I said. I kept my eyes on the photo for a second. She looked so *happy*. Involuntarily, I thought of the girl in Hiram's study, all those years ago. I remembered the sharp lines of her collarbones, like someone had cut her open and shoved sticks under her skin. I looked back squarely at Marichal. "Nope."

She nodded, pulling the photo back. "Funny, we got some witnesses who say otherwise."

I nodded. "Let me guess: a bunch of assholes who follow Heller around like a swarm of gnats with pinpricks for irises and a bad habit of constantly scratching themselves, right?"

The cops very pointedly didn't look at each other. Marichal scowled, and now she wasn't even handsome anymore. She started flicking more photos at me like she was dealing cards.

"We have thirteen missing girls within the last month," she said steadily. "Same physical type, same MO on the snatch. We were on to something, and then it went cold."

The Skinny Fuck, I thought. Rest in fucking peace.

I looked down at the photos. All of them young, all brunette, short hair, angular faces. I recognized each of them from my short, awful vacation in the Skinny Fuck's mind, but they blurred together. The same skin, the same hair, the same pattern over and over. One after another, they landed in front of me. I thought of that house up in Westchester, that mansion that smelled like dust and bones, that mummy sitting in the library, casting immense fucking spells with other people's lives.

My stomach began to hurt.

Dark hair, tan skin.

Dark hair, tan skin.

In the photos their ages varied, but I knew from the Skinny Fuck that they'd been getting younger. I wondered why the physical type mattered. Why he'd been taking them in age order. I didn't know anything about the big spells, the *biludha*. Maybe it was *Biludha 101*: All your victims had to be twinsies in chronological order. I thought about these girls, these women, working their way through their lives, not knowing that Renar had her dusty old eye on them. There were so *many*. I thought about the sorts of spells you could cast with a few dozen healthy bodies like that, and all the hair on my body stood up like someone was running a current through the room.

I'd met Mika Renar. She'd bled someone dry just to *threaten* me. I didn't want to think about what she'd do with all *this*.

Holloway pointed at me again. "You sure you haven't seen her?"

I swallowed bile and guilt and imagined what an Archmage could do to me—there were terrible spells out there, *biludha* that could turn a man inside out or curse him for life. Voices laughing at you for eternity. People hating you, wanting to murder you on sight for no reason. Worse things than a paltry bolt of lightning from the sky or a simple execution.

"No," I said, not looking at anyone.

There was a beat of silence, and then Marichal's voice, softer. "Jim, give me a minute alone here."

They'd been partners for a while, I guessed, because he just stood up and exited the room, the metal door banging open and shut. Not a word. No discussion or protest; they knew how each other liked to work.

She leaned towards me, shampoo and cigarettes. I looked up at her.

"These girls," she said softly. "They're dead. We don't know that, but we know it. They disappear, they never turn up again. We had a lead on the bastard, but he's disappeared, too. We don't know if he killed them right away or not. We don't know if this girl, Claire"—she pushed the other photos aside and put Claire Mannice back in front of me, tapping one long nail on her face—"is still alive or not. Or maybe a couple of them. We don't know."

She kept tapping the photo, and I found I couldn't look away. I re membered Claire in the tub at Hiram's. I remembered the open window, and I hoped she'd kept running.

"You're not a bad guy," Marichal said gently. "A lowlife, sure, kind of an asshole. But you don't want this girl hurt. I can tell just by looking at you. You're scared, okay, I get that. We can help. You help us, we can protect you."

A laugh bubbled out of me. I regretted it immediately. Looking up, I found a dark shadow had spread over Marichal's face. She stood up.

"Think about it. In fact," she said, glancing down at her watch as she pushed away and headed for the door, "you got another twenty-one hours to think about it."

I kept my eyes on the table, where she'd left her pen, and listened. The moment I heard the door slam shut, I lunged forward and took the pen, flicking the cap off and awkwardly rolling up the sleeve of my jacket. Without hesitation—because hesitation would have allowed me to imagine the pain, the burning and achy pain spiraling up my arm and slamming into my head—I dragged the point along the unhealed scab of the gash, pushing in hard as I did so. The scab tore open and blood welled up again, pouring out in a rush.

I began whispering the Words.

The same spell I'd cast on the ATM mark—my Charm spell. Second inversion, a few bits flipped here and there to make it an *anti*-Charm spell. Clever, I thought. Dangerous, too. Making yourself invisible was difficult and would take the blood of two, three people to fuel, to put out enough energy to bend the light itself around you. This was easier: same spell but worked backwards, made people subconsciously despise you so much they literally didn't see you. Just edited you out, the most unpleasant thing they'd ever seen. And thus decided they *had not* seen you.

I felt the terrible, sagging weakness sweep through me, and I swayed in my seat a bit, my vision going gray. Usually it passed in a few seconds and I was just tired, but although my vision cleared, I couldn't shake the heavy, soaking-wet feeling that hung on me. I leaned over the table with my palms flat on its surface for a moment, my arms shaking, and sawed breath in and out of my lungs.

Trembling, I stood and moved towards the door and leaned against the wall.

Then I waited.

I looked up and studied the spots where the cameras were hidden; I didn't know how the spell would work through them. I didn't know if anyone looking at a monitor would be affected or if the technology would filter everything, deliver my image unchanged. I didn't think it mattered. No one sat there watching the monitors; they recorded everything and watched it later, if ever.

The silence had a hum to it. I fought the urge to rest my eyes and blinked endlessly. I bit the inside of my cheek, hard, to jolt myself awake. My arm was dry; as always when casting the spell had left it dry and angry, the bleeding stopped. I didn't know how or why that happened. I hadn't stayed with Hiram long enough to advance my education.

Outside, I could hear the muffled bustle of the station. Doors slammed. Phones rang. People shouted.

The door to the interview room banged open, and Marichal stepped into the room, two cups of coffee in her hands. I blinked awake, startled, and stared at her for a moment. She spun around, eyes everywhere, and looked right at me, a brief expression of disgust twisting her face, and then looked on, cursing under her breath.

Heart lurching, I slipped through the doorway just before the heavy door banged shut, and pushed myself flat against the wall out in the hallway.

Around me, the station buzzed and flowed. People walked past me, looked right at me through a series of office windows, but they all just edited me out, preferring, thanks to the power of the spell, not to notice me.

The door to the interview room banged open again, and Marichal hustled out, turning right and heading away from me at a trot. I shut my eyes and took a deep breath, trying to steady my pulse and dredge up some hidden reserve of energy. My limbs felt like they were wrapped in lead. I forced my eyes open and turned to follow Marichal towards the exit. The yellow paint on the walls was peeling and the floor had soft spots that gave under my weight; after a few steps, everything seemed to roll and swirl, color oozing off the walls.

The station was jammed full of people: cops in their terrible cheap shirts and pants, too tight or too big. Their leather holsters the only things that fit them. People handcuffed to random furniture and fixtures, napping. I wanted to sit down next to them and doze off myself.

There was no alarm. At first I thought there might be, but then I remembered Marichal and Holloway hadn't arrested me and might prefer no one know I'd just walked out on them. They might even be outside, scanning the street for signs of me, and I relaxed a little.

Walking wasn't easy. I wasn't invisible, so I didn't have the invisible's problem of being walked into and jostled by people who couldn't see me; people instinctively avoided me, in fact. But I had to keep my distance anyway. Best not push it.

Just past the lobby was a break room. A filthy place with a small table, a microwave, a dorm fridge, and Hell's coffee machine, crusted in dark brown sediment. The history of the place in ancient coffee film. The room smelled like some of the roaches certainly living in the microwave had been accidentally nuked recently, but there was a box of donuts sitting on the table. I stared at them. There were four left. Two jelly with powdered sugar, two cream puff. No fucking chocolate ones, of course.

My mouth watered on sight. I stepped in and started grabbing them, stuffing them into my pockets. The smell of the donuts was almost suffocating.

I turned and stopped. A young uniformed cop, his sharp Latino face folded into a frown that appeared alien to his open features, stood in the doorway. He stared right at me.

You, I thought, *are a fucking moron.* This with powdered sugar on my fingers, the sure sign of the intelligent criminal.

Moving slowly, I stepped back from the table and tried to get out of his field of vision. I pressed myself up against the wall. Held my breath. Mainly so I wouldn't have the maddening smell of donuts in my nostrils. After a few seconds, he stepped into the room and leaned over the table to inspect the now-empty donut box. Snorted. Turned and left. I counted to five and spun out after him.

Threading my way through the lobby, I had to wait for a stream of uniformed officers to walk through the door behind the front desk. I swayed on my feet as each one stepped through, looked right at me, and with a slight wincing expression, looked away. I tried to time it so the final one had passed me by and the door was still hanging open, then followed at the last second.

A fat, sweating officer was trailing the others, talking cheerfully over his shoulder in a booming voice you could hear in the next fucking state, and I rammed into him, hard. He stumbled back and I stumbled with him like I was caught in his fat-man gravity. We danced, me forward, him backwards, and he spun around to see what the hell had just rocketed into him. His eyes skittered off me like everyone else's, and then he did a double take and *saw* me.

And didn't like what he saw.

I pushed back from him and we both found our feet. I felt hot and stood in the middle of the crowded lobby sweating and breathing hard, my heart a dried-up marbled rattling around in my chest. Sticky donut jelly bleeding through the fabric of my pockets. The fat cop stared at me, his face twisting into a mask of hatred as the spell worked on him, and around us the room went quiet as everyone *else* saw me. And everyone *else* didn't like what they saw, either.

Only problem with an *anti*-Charm spell: If you fucked up and got noticed, you got noticed in a *bad* way.

The fat cop's pudgy hands curled into fists.

I willed myself to move, but nothing happened. I stood there vibrating, watching him bring his hands up, and behind him, behind me—all around us—I had a sense of movement. I ordered my limbs to move and my limbs just hung at my sides. I had exactly one trick left, and when he swung at me, I used it: I gave in to gravity and dropped. His fist sailed through the air and he stumbled forward, tripping over me and crashing to the floor.

I sat up on my elbows and looked around. The whole room, cops, criminals, lawyers, civilians—they all stared at me with restrained hate, horrified at the sight of me and deeply confused as to *why*. I had seconds before they broke through the hesitation, the latent socialization, and succumbed to the spell. Dived for me as a mob. Beat the tar out of me. Worse.

I took a deep breath, the crowd seemed to bulge outward for a second, and then . . . and then Pitr Mags swept into the room, a fucking tank. He crashed through the swinging front doors with a snarl and was on top of me instantly. Stood over me with his fists by his waist, crouched down low. Someone charged him and he tossed them aside almost casually, effortlessly. Another body crashed into him from behind, but Mags just grunted. Twisted his torso around, flipped the newcomer up and over so she landed on her back. It was a cop in uniform, a woman who stared up at the ceiling in a dreamy way that hinted at concussion.

Time to go, I thought slowly, stupidly.

This, I then thought, *is our motto.* Mags and I should have T-shirts made that read TIME TO GO on the front and wear them everywhere.

As if he heard me, Mags leaped aside and clawed one hand into my shirt collar. Dragged me along the floor.

I watched the fluorescent lights flick by as my vision got blurry and soft: one, two, three, daylight.

10.

I WOKE TO HIRAM'S FACE, upside down, his smile a scowl. You couldn't trust Hiram's smiles anyway. He smiled a lot. It didn't mean anything.

"Mr. Vonnegan," he said, shaking his head. "You've *got* to take better care of yourself."

I pushed myself up onto my elbows, sinking down into the couch cushions. My head throbbed and my arms trembled. I was back in Hiram's study, with Hiram standing over me in a pair of shabby khakis, a crisp white shirt that strained to contain his belly, and a pair of black suspenders. He wasn't wearing any shoes. In one hand he carried a large black sphere that gleamed in the room's soft light, a heavy marble I knew he sometimes used as a worry stone. He breathed like he had to think about each individual breath and brace himself for it.

Strangely, this made me feel better. I'd spent a year of my life, more or less, in this study. I wouldn't do it again, but it was familiar, and sleep had done me good. I knew this room better than any other physical location in the world. I knew the weight and feel of everything on the tightly packed shelves. The tiny chess pieces carved from jade, the size of your fingernails. The windup dolls that would march from one end of the shelf to the other, knocking off everything in their path. The books, dry and yellowed and smelling like libraries. And snow globes. Hiram had not met a snow globe he could resist. They appeared in his pockets on a regular basis as he moved through the city. Large globes with brass bases, containing St. Patrick's Cathedral; small globes made of plastic, tiny plastic children laughing as they sledded down a generic country scene. They dotted all the shelves, glinting at me in patterns so familiar I noticed whenever Hiram got paranoid and hid things from me, which he usually did after each visit. Hiram was a thief, and so he assumed everyone else was a thief, and fully expected me to rob him blind. So he did things like hiding the tiny white box with the beetle on it that had been on the shelves last time.

My list of useless superpowers got longer every year.

I swung my feet onto the floor and sat up. "How long?" My voice was deep and clogged, rusty.

"Eleven hours. Mr. Mageshkumar brought you." He winced. "He has been casting a Glamour of a glowing . . . bird. Constantly."

I smiled a little. My pulse was fast and wobbly, but I felt okay. "Sorry, Hiram," I said. "Thank you."

He shrugged, turning towards his mobile bar, stuffing his worry stone into his pocket. "I didn't do anything except admit you. And for that you can thank the puppylike charm of Mr. Mageshkumar."

I scrubbed my stiff hair. "Has D. A. Ketterly called or stopped by?"

Hiram paused, a decanter of something rust-colored in one hand. He turned his head slightly towards me. "Ketterly? What in the world is that charlatan doing for you?"

I shrugged. "Looking for somebody. What else does Ketterly *do*?"

Hiram went back to mixing his drink. "Not that girl, I trust. You are a confused boy, Mr. Vonnegan, but I never took you for *stupid*."

Stretching, I shrugged and told him the short version of the story since I'd left him. He turned and leaned against the bar, holding a tall glass with a wedge of orange jammed onto the rim. His white beard was perfectly trimmed and looked exactly as it always did, as if he'd contrived to stop it from growing permanently.

Which he might have.

For a few seconds, he just stared at me. Then he set the glass down behind him and strode for the door, dry-washing his hands as he walked. "Mr. Vonnegan, we should have a discussion."

I watched him leave the room with his usual strut, but I didn't follow him immediately. I knew where his office was, and *that* was a less comfortable memory. I wasn't interested in entering that tiny, clogged space with Hiram's colognes and strange brown cigarettes thick in the air. Feeling leaden, I thought it a much better idea to just sit on the couch and breathe until Hiram decided to tell me his news out here.

A moment later Bosch's head reappeared, peering around the door at me. "Mr. Vonnegan? I think perhaps time is a concern here."

Reminding myself that Hiram was maybe my only friend aside from Mags, I hurried after him.

Hiram's office. Four feet by eight feet—a closet, technically, with no windows. Hiram did not use his apartment as intended; the living room he'd made his study, the bedroom he'd made into a museum of stolen artifacts, magical and otherwise. The closet off the bedroom/museum was his office. The only rooms that retained their original purpose were the kitchen and bathroom.

Mags had followed us in, his hand a bloody mess from nicking himself to cast his new favorite toy, and—seeming to fill fully half the space in the little cove—leaned against a towering pile of books and papers that might have grown over a bookshelf or two, like fungus. The books had no titles, handwritten and hand-bound in an age before computers and photocopiers, but they were sadly familiar from my unhappy time studying under Hiram's terse tutelage. I'd retitled each in my head. There was *Far Too Many Words to Create Simple Illusions* and *Endless Repetitions Written by Assholes*. A few were even useful, like *Ancient Tome of Useful Three-Word Cantrips* and *An Explanation of Everything That Can Go Wrong When Casting a Spell Which Is Everything*, subtitled *All Elderly Tricksters Are Maimed*.

Fond memories.

Mags hummed, studying his hand, happy with the universe. I was jammed in behind Hiram's plump torso as my *gasam* sat at the tiny child's desk he'd installed in the room. Everything in Hiram's world burst with *things*, endless piles and rows of things, trinkets, pebbles, toys, jewelry, books, shoes, tie pins, hats, statues, boxes inside boxes inside boxes, maps, paintings, pens—the universe of nonliving things was fully represented in miniature in Hiram's apartment, like an anti-zoo.

He'd spread several sheets of white paper on the desk before him. They were covered in sketches of runes, the ancient glyphs used in conjunction with the Tongue to cast and bind the more complicated spells, as well as copious bursts of his own thin, shaky handwriting.

"Because I am curious," he said, his voice back to its rich school-teacher timbre, "I made some notes from memory about the marks on Ms. Mannice. It is not often you can study even the slightest work of an *enustari*. I transcribed what I could remember of the small patch of, um, *skin* we were able to observe, and began researching what I could about the specific combinations."

I nodded. Hiram liked to lecture.

"She appeared to be marked all over her body."

I nodded again. "Inside her ears, between her fingers—everywhere."

"Yes. Difficult to replicate, and a serious investment of time and blood, so they naturally want her back. And there are no repetitions, none that I could find in the small sample I had. Which is—"

"Unusual," I finished, leaning over his shoulder to study the glyphs he'd copied. Most markings were terse, designed simply to tie magical energy to a specific person or object—rarely more than a few runes, often repeated *ad infinitum*. Even the small sampling Hiram had copied from memory contained more glyphs than I'd seen in one place in my small experience.

He leaned back. "Yes. Mr. Vonnegan, this is a major, *major* piece of work. This is no Cantrip. This is not even a normal, everyday epic ritual." He paused, and I could see him looking at me in my peripheral vision, his white-ringed face pink and round. "You said there were more women? Marked like Ms. Mannice?"

I nodded. The glyphs sketched on the paper seemed to be unhappy; I imagined I could feel them radiating energy at me, pulsing. "Dozens," I said. I thought of the police photographs. "Maybe more. His memories were jumbled."

Hiram sighed. "I would imagine there were. Perhaps hundreds."

I frowned. "*Hundreds?* Hiram, that's crazy. There hasn't been a *biludha* cast at that scale in seventy years."

"Nineteen forty-five, to be exact," he said absently. A thin line of anxiety formed like sediment between my spine and my skin. "This piqued my interest. I am no Archmage, but I have studied this art my entire life. Mr. Vonnegan, I have seen these glyphs before, briefly."

I glanced down at the bald spot on his round head. Hiram had not changed since I'd met him. He was simultaneously old and fragile, and filled with energy and life. "Where?"

"My own *gasam* was a powerful *enustari*. More skilled than you or I. More deeply read, less afraid of . . . consequences. Faber Gottschalk pursued such knowledge—forbidden and dangerous spells. Not for his own casting; he was no fool. Simply for knowledge. He kept old grimoires of ancient spells, spells not cast in a thousand years. One of which I remember well, one that required linked sacrifices, marked with runes similar to this." He sighed, leaning back. "An old, old spell."

"What was it?"

He paused for a moment before responding. "The *Biludha-tah-namus,*" he said simply, sounding old. "The Ritual of Death."

Behind me, I heard Mags suck in breath. "Fuck," he whispered. I turned to agree, but he was just frowning at a spot of blood on his shirt. He rubbed it absently with his thumb.

Mags: the perfect organism.

I STARED DOWN INTO my glass. It was filled with whiskey, more than was wise for someone who was still anemic and weak; even the thick smell was making me woozy. I let it warm in my hands.

We were in Hiram's seldom-used kitchen—a bright white box of a room with gleaming white cabinets, spotless white appliances, and a small Formica table with matching white plastic chairs. The only item in the room used with any regularity was the teakettle, which steamed cheerfully on the stove as the three of us sat glumly at the table.

Pitr Mags sipped his drink gingerly, scowling. He was unhappy because we'd finally ordered him to stop making the fucking glowing bird appear.

"Madness, in this day and age," Hiram muttered, staring past me at the wall.

Hundreds of sacrifices just to get the burn started. A huge piece of magic to begin with, something beyond my experience, certainly. But that was the beginning. Spells with linked sacrifices as fulcrums started off with the small bit, like kindling to a fire. Cults had been popular in recent decades for this reason. Like the Movement for the Restoration in Africa, a few hundred Charmed people left behind like husks. Small bits of easy magic—Cantrips, even—to get people in the right frame of mind. Get them to kill themselves or each other. It didn't matter which. The bonus was that the news was usually so sensational, no one noticed what happened next. The small bit set the big bit in motion, and the big bit was where the fireworks really happened. If the *Biludha-tah-namus* started off with hundreds of sacrifices as the *small bit*, I didn't like imagining what the *big bit* was.

"What does it do?" I asked, forcing myself to sip some whiskey.

Hiram looked at me. For the first time that I could remember, he looked old.

"Do? It breeds disaster, courts destruction. It is one of a very few spells that once carried a sentence of death to any *ustari* found to know it. But those were different times . . ." He sighed. "It depends on how you look at it. If you are the caster, also the *object* of the spell, it . . . bends the laws of nature very close to their breaking point. It grants you immortality. Safety from death. Perhaps not permanently, but near enough not to matter."

Immortality. I pushed the word around. For a moment or two it was just a word. I forced myself to reply through my thick thoughts.

"That's a lot of heavy lifting."

Hiram nodded hollowly. "I knew Mika Renar had a death fetish," he said slowly. "She fears death. We all do, but for her it is a mania. She could never quite believe that the universe, after giving her such power, such immense power and luxury, would then play this cruel joke on her—that she might die like everyone else." He sighed. "What is the use of being a god if you are also mortal?"

I stared at him, my brain moving slowly. "It's impossible. You can't break the natural order like that."

"Of course you *can*, boy," Hiram said fiercely, his face flushing red. "Of course you *can*. It is not *easy*, it is not *allowed*, but you can always *try*. Would we have taboos against breaking the 'natural order' if it couldn't be *done*?"

I considered the *big bit* again. I wasn't *enustari*, I hadn't even finished my primary education under Hiram, but I knew what it took to cast spells. "It would take . . . thousands—*tens* of thousands—to do something like that."

Hiram smiled. I didn't like it. He sat for a moment blowing on his tea. "You've never bled more than a trickle, Lemuel," he said in a quiet voice I didn't recognize. This was not Hiram Bosch. This was an old, tired man. The transformation scared the shit out of me.

"Not tens of thousands, Mr. Vonnegan. Not *hundreds* of thousands. It would take everyone, Mr. Vonnegan. All of us. Every*thing*."

He sipped tea like we weren't discussing the end of the world. "Or near enough. A handful might escape." He smiled a little. "I imagine she might ensure the survival of her apprentice. In a scenario I find mystifying, she seems to actually *like* her apprentice." He looked at me and frowned again. "Or fear him."

I pictured Cal Amir: older than me already and still laboring under a *gasam* who was literally determined to live forever. How happy could an ambitious man be? No doubt Mika Renar was withholding the final fruits of her superior knowledge—every *gasam* played that game, because once your apprentice knew everything you did, there was little reason for them to stick around, carrying your water. Except the binding, the *urtuku*. It gave your *gasam* a certain amount of limited control over you. It forced plenty of apprentices to hang on long after they'd learned all they could. It was a risk you took. You could break the binding between a *gasam* and an *urtuku*. If it was not voluntary, it simply required one of you to die. I swallowed a little more whiskey, even though the first dollop had made a home in my belly and set up a small business manufacturing vomit.

"The *Biludha-tah-namus* is an expensive item," Hiram said softly. "Forever for one person requires more blood than has existed collectively up until this point. Every living thing, billions and billions—not just humans, Mr. Vonnegan, but by my calculations, all *living things*—will be burned away once the linked ritual is set in motion. She will live forever in a dead world." He pursed his lips. "I assume she has considered this and accepted it."

"Hiram," I said slowly. "I know you don't—"

"Oh, for God's sake, Mr. Vonnegan," he snapped. "Of course we have to oppose her. Every living mage in the world will oppose her. There is no question of opposing her. There is only the question of whether we—whether *I*—survive the experience."

He sighed again and looked about the kitchen. I imagined he felt less secure here, without his knickknacks surrounding him. "Although I suppose I am dead in either scenario, aren't I? The great Hiram Bosch." He snorted and went on, his tone changing to the softer, thoughtful one that told me he was lost in his own thoughts. "The question is whether this girl is irreplaceable . . . *Difficult* to replace and *irreplaceable* are two different things. If we remove the girl from the equation, do we defeat Renar? Or do we simply delay her as she prepares another girl . . . ? I wonder," he said, his voice lowering in volume as he sank into himself, "I wonder, I wonder if all of them resembling each other so strongly is *essential* or just a grace note . . ."

He trailed off, staring into the middle distance. I opened my mouth to speak but was interrupted by the deep tone of Hiram's doorbell. We looked at each other, and then I looked at Mags. He had fallen asleep, his head on his crossed arms on the table.

I followed Hiram, noting his familiar portly strut, the uneven way his suspenders had been clipped to his pants. When he opened the door, I was standing behind him with a clear view of the doorway over his shoulder.

Claire Mannice was standing on his stoop. She looked clean and fresh and young and beautiful. Black jeans. Black T-shirt.

She stepped back when the door opened, then regarded us uncertainly for a second or two.

"Listen," she finally said. "These markings . . . on me." She bit her lip, gesturing at her neck. "Can you get them *off*?"

11.

I LIKED THE NERVOUS WAY she chain-smoked, lighting each new cigarette from the burning coal of the previous one. I was sitting with her at the kitchen table while Hiram ransacked the apartment behind us, making a lot of noise and muttering to himself. Mags sat at the end of the table, staring at her with wide eyes, and I was on alert in case he tried to leap across the table and start licking her face and barking.

She was skinny as hell, but a nice skinny. Toned, not starved. Her hair was black and short and curled a little right over her eyes. Her nose was a little long and turned up, which I liked, and her skin was a perfect, creamy tone except for a single tattoo—a real, normal one, blurry and blue, on her left shoulder, peeking out from under a bra strap and the T-shirt.

I'd let her sit closest to the doorway so she felt like she had an escape route.

She sucked in smoke from a fresh cigarette and leaned back, one arm wrapped around her belly. She stared at me. "Magic," she said at last.

I nodded. "You can see the runes?"

She stretched her free arm out in front of her. As far as I could see without the aid of a spell, her skin was unblemished, clear and covered in soft, downy hair. It was skin I wanted to touch.

"I can't *not* see them. But yeah, no one else can see 'em. I went to . . . a friend of mine to see about having them removed. I couldn't tell if they were tats or just surface or what. He thought I was crazy. So did everyone else." She retracted her arm and looked at me again. "So I got desperate and remembered you and that crazy night. And I thought, hell, you *did* save my life. In the most horrifying way *possible*, but still."

I nodded, encouraging that train of thought. I wanted to ask her how old she was.

Smoke leaked from her nostrils. She had a steady stare, a thousand-yard kind of thing. Most kids her age just eyed their shoes. She locked on you. "You know what it's like to look in the mirror and see fucking hieroglyphics on your fucking face?"

A number of heavy things fell from a high shelf off in the distance, and Hiram cursed in his round, professorial tones.

"What is he *doing*?" she asked.

"Getting ready to leave," I said. "You're a hot commodity. He doesn't want you here, attracting interested parties."

I decided not to mention there were even odds that Hiram would decide to kill her himself. Or that if killing her meant stopping Renar from killing *us*, from killing *everyone*, I might have to sit back and let him do it. I hadn't worked that out in my head yet. Saw no reason to bring it up.

She squinted at me. "Okay. So . . . magic."

I nodded again, looked at Mags. He looked like he could have been convinced to commit murder in exchange for a lock of her hair. "Show her your new toy, Magsie."

Mags was up in a flash, grinning and rolling up his sleeve. Moving with practiced speed, he had his knife out in a second. Just as Claire leaned back stiffly in her chair, shocked, he slashed a shallow cut down his scarred arm, bringing up a trickle of blood.

"Oh, *God,*" she whispered.

Mags ran through it fast, excited, and with a flash of brilliant light, the golden bird appeared, two or three times larger than Ketterly had made it in his office. This one was the size of a small child. It sailed gloriously around Hiram's kitchen on silent, bejeweled wings.

I looked at Claire Mannice. She was staring at the bird with her mouth slightly open.

"It's called a Glamour," I said helpfully. "There's a lot of different ways to use it. This is just for fun."

She moved her eyes to me again. They were big and round and green, and in the fake glow of the bird's golden light, they sparkled. I marveled at them. I had seen something like that green with golden flecks. In a painting, maybe.

Mags was still standing, grinning as he watched his creation move elegantly around the room. His arm had stopped bleeding and was just another shallow wound on an arm that had borne plenty of them, and for a second I was jealous of his apparent health and energy. He was brimming with blood and fire, and I felt ready to fall asleep.

"Magic," she said. "Well, okay—"

The doorbell chimed.

The whole place went quiet; the sudden absence of Hiram's muttered cursing and floor-shaking rampage made me jump out of my seat, waving down Claire and Mags. Mags killed the bird and we all just hovered there, listening. From the kitchen I could see down the corridor, past the front door and into the bedroom, but there was no sign of Hiram at all.

The lights went off. I heard Claire grunt, but she didn't scream or panic or move.

Soft, nonthreatening, I heard the sound of the tumblers in the lock moving, easing their way open, falling into line.

I thought fast. I was about to fall over from blood loss and was more or less effectively blind. My switchblade was in my hand out of deep habit, but I knew if I tried to cast anything meaty, anything requiring a lot of gas, I'd pass out before I got halfway through.

One second, two seconds, the handle of the front door turning all the way. I sliced my palm, a flicker of the blade, a kiss. Weak, thin blood seeped out, and I whispered a short Cantrip. Nothing. A child's trick.

A wave of manageable weariness swept through me, dragging me down, and I could see. The dark took on sharp white edges, all color bled out of the world. I looked around; Mags was still standing, his own knife in hand, unmoving. Claire sat rigidly, eyes moving everywhere, blind and not liking it.

I looked up in time to see the front door drifting open, like an ancient, grainy black-and-white movie.

"Mags!" I whispered, sharp and urgent. "What've you got?"

"Fuck," he hissed back. "I don't know! You!"

I shook my head, watching the door. It remained pushed open, obscuring anything behind it. The silence was complete. "I don't have the gas, Mags. It's on you."

"I'll bleed!"

Revulsion and excitement rose up in my throat and I choked it back. I wanted to feel that power, Mags's *life*, pouring into me. The thought made me gag. "No!" I struggled to keep my voice on mute. "Mags, *now!*"

Just as I remembered my interview with Renar, and I remembered how magic bounced off of Claire, I heard him whispering, running through a spell. I recognized it and thought it was probably safe, focused not on *us* or Claire but on those looking at us. I spun, pulling Claire out of her chair and onto the floor, dragging her back towards the wall. She let me—and I was conscious of the permission, conscious that if she hadn't approved things would have gone very differently—stiffening but keeping her mouth shut. Mags dropped down beside me as he finished.

"Be still," I whispered to her. She smelled like cigarettes and autumn leaves. "*Still.*"

I stared down the corridor. The door slowly closed, revealing Cal Amir and two plump Bleeders standing in Hiram's entryway, looking around. They were photocopies, all white edges and black fields.

"Hello, Tricksters!" Amir shouted. "You naughty boys, you have something of ours, don't you?"

I glanced at Claire, panic surging. But it couldn't be. If Amir knew Claire was here with us, he'd have come heavy. He'd have come breathing fire, with an army of Bleeders. He'd have come to *punish* us, not make cheerful jokes. *Jesus,* I thought. *He doesn't know she's here.* I saw again the flash of green as Hiram pocketed the *Udug.* Steal from *enustari* and you suffered for it, eventually, for all of Hiram's speechifying about my recklessness and stupidity.

I moved my mouth near Claire's ear without taking my eyes from the trio. "*We are furniture,*" I said as quietly as I could. Her hair smelled sweet. "*Do not move. We are* furniture."

She didn't say anything, which was encouraging.

Amir looked exactly as he had a few days before: groomed, polished, expensive. Cheerful. He was wearing a heavy-looking overcoat and a pair of black gloves. His two Bleeders were typical: fat, tall men, older than some. *Fattened* was a better word. One was bald and appeared to have no facial hair, or perhaps he was blond and it just looked that way, the bloated folds of his face hanging off his skull like heavy drapes. The other was dark and taller and hairier, his salt-and-pepper mop damp against his forehead. His head was squared off, somehow, on top, and his arms looked too long, hands hanging down by his hips. They both looked unhealthy, their skin slack, their scent stale and sour. They were paid to be meaty. Old hands, trusted. Men who'd been selling their blood for years now, living well in exchange for blood. Men who probably thought, by this point, that they'd won their bet. They'd lived good lives from Cal Amir's generosity and hadn't been bled to death yet.

Amir spun around, searching the dark. His eyes swept over us without pause. It was a simple trick, but it worked: People saw what they expected to see. Even *saganustari*. Even *enustari*. We were all human, and frail.

I could feel Claire pressed against me, simultaneously soft and rigid. She was perfectly still.

Amir said something to his Bleeders, and they followed him into the kitchen. He came slowly, peeling off his gloves, looking around. Casual. As if he hunted down assholes like us every day for his *gasam*. Which he probably did.

His two Bleeders wheezed their way into the room, moving around him to stand on either side. They were panting after the small effort of climbing Hiram's stoop. They wore decent suits and might have passed for normal obese men unless you knew what they were, or saw the network of fine scars on their faces, their hands. Bleeders couldn't be choosy; they were paid to bleed on command, as much or as little as their master demanded, and if their face was the only convenient place to draw blood, they slashed it. The black one looked like a sad dog, his cheeks heavy and jiggling as he moved, his eyes turned down at the corners.

The floor creaked under them.

"I hope you have not been listening to our tiny friend," Amir said lightly, spinning in place. "Many small minds have imagined they will master that particular Artifact and become great. They are always mistaken. Believe me, Tricksters, I am here to do you a favor."

Amir gestured at the dark-skinned Bleeder, who went through a tiny ritual: taking off his fine overcoat and laying it on Hiram's little-used stove with great care, undoing the buttons on his cuff with a dainty touch that seemed incompatible with such thick fingers, and rolling his sleeve up to the elbow. His forearm was the expected maze of tiny puckers and scars, just like mine but worse. More methodical, precise. Like he'd mapped out the skin of his arm and was tracing some grand design on it.

"Of course," Amir said with a shiny grin, "you will still have to be disciplined."

Primly, the Bleeder produced a tiny blade, ornate, custom-made. It was small enough to hide in your palm. With no fanfare, he dragged it along the top of his arm from the elbow to the wrist, deep enough to bleed, shallow enough to avoid veins and arteries and ligaments. He'd live to play the piano again. This time.

The blood looked black to my magicked eyes, and my whole body went tense as Amir began whispering the Words. Singing them, really, a lilting, rhythmic recitation, the way *real* mages did it. *Saganustari.* Real power.

The kitchen suddenly seemed hot.

As the blood hit the air, reacting with the atmosphere, I could feel it. Literally. An electric, sizzling, untapped power. Someone else's power. I'd felt it in Hiram's study all those years ago with the shivering girl in her doodle sneakers, and I felt it every time Mags or anyone cut themselves. Blood was blood. And it made you want it.

I wasn't familiar with the spell Amir was casting, but I picked out words and phrases, sounds that I'd run into, and I put together the vague idea—simple enough: remove Glamours, clear the air. Turn that odd set of chairs against the far wall back into a girl and her idiotic protectors. Much simpler than searching around, especially when you had people to supply your gas for you.

I looked around. I had nothing. I didn't think I'd be able to bleed enough to light a cigarette before passing out.

I thought about giving them Claire. Wondered for one awful moment if that would buy our lives. But Amir had come to *discipline* us because we had stolen an Artifact, and I had no doubt we would barely survive that discipline. When he found out we had Claire, there would be no negotiation, no bargaining.

And it wouldn't matter, because this was the end of everything, everyone dying in thirty seconds of unbelievable, incomprehensible carnage. An invisible engine tearing every living thing in the world to pieces. Soaking them for blood to feed the *biludha,* to make the old bat immortal. People. Kids. Kittens. Fucking *lice*—everything—dead.

And I saw Claire bleeding out, twisting and screaming, the mummy in the office getting younger, coming to life as Claire died. When I imagined it, I kept confusing Claire with the kid in the sneakers, Hiram's hired whore, all those years ago. Most likely dead. They kept switching back and forth, bleeding out as one, mixed together. She would be Claire's age now.

Or dead. Dead. I hadn't touched her. Hadn't bled her. I hadn't done—

Anything.

When I thought of that long-past girl dead, a leaden sadness filled me. Weighed me down. I couldn't imagine what had driven her to that point in her life. And I didn't want to imagine what wild hopes she might have held deep inside. That someone would save her. That someone would help her. I'd done nothing to her. I'd left no mark. She was exactly the same after having met me, and for a while I'd been proud of that.

But I wasn't proud anymore. I'd left no mark. I'd done nothing. I was not good people. But what was my option now? To kill Claire? Save the world, make Renar howl in rage, be a fucking *hero* by killing her? A girl who'd done nothing besides look a certain way and get herself snatched by the Skinny Fuck.

I thought, *There have to be more options.*

Slowly, I moved my arm away from Claire, preparing to make my move. Blood flowed from the Bleeder's arm in a slow, steady stream, disappearing into the air as Amir spoke. I balanced myself on the balls of my feet. I gathered myself for a charge. There was the window in the kitchen; if I could barrel into them, my partner coming after me with the automatic loyalty that only someone as stupid as Pitr Mags could manage, we might buy Claire enough time to make an escape, shimmy down the fire escape, hit the street.

The Bleeder convulsed.

He staggered a little, recovered, and then went down to his knees. Convulsed again, and blood shot out of his mouth while Amir continued to recite, the syllables rolling out of him with practiced ease as he watched his Bleeder hemorrhage in front of him. I was frozen, watching. The fat man on the floor was panting wetly, struggling to breathe, and lifted one heavy arm up to Amir, reaching for his master. One glance at Amir told me this wasn't his doing. He looked appalled. Surprised. But not scared.

The mage took a single step backwards, staying out of reach, not skipping a single Word. The second Bleeder stared on with popped-out, unhappy eyes but didn't make a move to save his friend. They'd both made their deal: They bled for an easy life, everything a powerful *saganustari* like Amir could offer them, and there was always the chance they'd be consumed entirely.

Amir was startled, spinning around and trying to figure things out, when Hiram stepped into the hall. I could see straight down the line to the older man. He'd rolled up his sleeves and was speaking a spell, too, using the Bleeder's blood to cast—an old, dirty trick. Frowned upon, using someone else's gas. Under normal circumstances, it earned you censure, it got you sneered at. But Hiram knew Amir would be justified in killing us, as thieves. He was saving our lives. Or, more likely, he was saving his own life in a way I hadn't figured out yet.

As he walked down the hall, Hiram's voice got louder while he recited something quick and nasty. He had always had a talent for hacking spells down to the bare necessities, getting rid of any decoration. It was a War Talent, really—if you had nothing but time, you could devise a wicked spell; in the heat of battle, it wasn't always the most elegant spell that won the day. It was usually the fastest one that still had some punch. Hiram cast battle spells better than anyone I knew.

Tricksters, we fought dirty. For all their power, *enustari* didn't understand that.

Hiram finished his spell before he'd even hit the living room, before Amir had finished *his*, and as the Bleeder finally passed out cold, slumping to the floor, Hiram's hands erupted into flames.

"Fuck!" Mags whispered next to me.

"*Get. The. Fuck,*" Hiram shouted, holding his hands up in front of him like a boxer, "*out of my house!*" A ball of flame, liquid and roiling, began to bloat between his hands.

Amir suddenly stopped reciting.

Mags and I both ducked over Claire.

The pent-up energy of Amir's unfinished spell tore through the room, ripping the table and chairs up from the floor and smashing them against the opposite wall.

"This is our property, old man!" Amir shouted back, unaffected by the heat and gesturing behind himself at his second Bleeder. "That spell you are gnawing at will bring a lot of attention to us—do you forget our traditions? Our *ways*? And you would anger Mika Renar? Cal Amir? You would anger *us*?"

Amir still didn't understand. He was confused by Hiram's reaction. We should have expected to survive if it was just the *Udug*. We should have been meek and begged for forgiveness, or fallen out and betrayed each other. Groveled a little. Fireballs from Hiram Bosch had Amir's head spinning.

The second Bleeder, his face set in a mask of sweaty horror, nonetheless peeled off his coat, dropping it unceremoniously on the floor, and began rolling up his sleeve. Taking his time. No doubt hoping something would happen to save him from having to bleed out like his friend.

Hiram seemed to have grown six inches, filling his own hallway like a giant. "You are on *my* property!" he bellowed, the ball of flame growing larger. "You have three seconds to leave!"

"You stupid old—"

I couldn't swear it was three seconds. Hiram pushed his hands forward suddenly and the ball of flame swelled up to the size of an adult person and rocketed towards us. The air around me became superheated, and as Amir and his Bleeder dove for the floor, I could smell the artificial fibers of my coat starting to burn. Flames exploded into the room, the ball collapsing into a sheet that splashed against everything like water. The windows shattered, glass tinkling around us. I shut my eyes and threw my hands over my face, but the flames disappeared the second they touched anything, and in a moment the room was empty and dark and cold, wind blowing in from the outside.

I turned to urge Claire up, but she was moving past me already, springing for the window. I turned to pull Mags along with me, and we leaped to follow. I hesitated for one moment, letting Mags move past as I stared down the corridor. Hiram was gone. Amir was getting up. Not looking in our direction, looking mussed and dirty for the first time since I'd met him. It cheered me.

And then Amir turned and looked right at us. His eyes on me. They narrowed. Then they flicked to Claire and widened.

I spun for the window and followed Mags's ass out onto the rusting fire escape. I bent over the railing and saw Claire a floor below, climbing like a monkey for the alleyway. Mags and I started down, the rungs of the ladders leaving our hands a curious red-brown. Halfway down, I heard an explosion behind us. The whole building shuddered, and the fire escape rattled and shook like it had been leaned against the wall a few years ago and never attached. The last bits of glass clinging to the frames came raining down, and I jumped the last six feet and hit the asphalt hard, head spinning, legs weak.

Claire was already running for the street, and I staggered after her. She wouldn't be safe. She didn't understand. Amir and Renar would find her. Runes or no runes, they would find a way. It was *magic*. Anything was possible. She couldn't understand that from watching Mags cast the firebird once.

I almost caught up with her. Then a car roared into the alley, an unmarked Crown Victoria, lights flashing. Cops. Cops I knew, I found out a moment later, when Holloway emerged from the passenger-side door, badge in one hand, gun in the other.

Claire stopped on a dime, stumbling back into me. She pinged off me as if I'd goosed her, spinning around. Her eyes were shining, her face red. She was fucking terrified.

"Mother*fucker!*" she shouted.

I felt a presence. Mags was hiding behind me, as he sometimes did when people yelled.

"Evening, Mr. Vonnegan," Holloway said with a grin that held no humor. "Looks like you know our girl after all, huh?"

I stared, mind racing, and then there was a second explosion from above. The ground shook. Something heavy landed in the alley with a cracking noise, and I felt a stabbing ache in my belly.

It flashed through me, turning cold as it reached the extremities, passing out of me with a physical sensation. Like outgassing. I started shivering.

And I knew, as the bond between us was violently severed, that Hiram Bosch was dead.

12.

I HATED CARS. THEY REMINDED me of my father, of being picked up at random moments and driven for hours, stopping at bars, starving, bored, angry. And then the ride home with Mom eventually. Her silent chain-smoking, somehow convinced it was my fault, that I was arranging things with Dad. That my idea of a good time was being imprisoned in a drunk's car as he drove around the fucking desert, absorbing all the fucking Bushmills in a given area.

"I don't know anything good," Mags whispered intently. "You *do*. You gotta let me bleed, Lem."

I shook my head. We were in the backseat of a squad car, lights flashing around us. It was dark and cold. Just Mags and me; Holloway and Marichal had put Claire into their own unmarked car and disappeared into Hiram's building for some time but now were standing around talking to each other, looking at us every now and then.

"I don't cast on anyone's blood but mine," I said. "You fucking *know* that, Magsie."

"I'm *offering*, Lem," he said quietly. "I'm fucking *volunteering*."

I could imagine the roar of Pitr Mags filling me up. Felt his thunderous, slow heartbeat like the pulse of a T-Rex, eternities between the beats. The man was like three men compressed and mashed down into one more or less normal-sized human. I imagined touching his blood would just fry me up, make me explode. My hands clenched with the desire to feel that energy. I was so tired. My stomach flipped.

"Shut up."

The driver's-side door of the patrol car opened, and a uniformed cop slipped into the driver's seat. Holloway and Marichal climbed into their own car, and a moment later we were moving.

"*Lem,*" Mags hissed in my ear.

We followed the detectives. I thought about Claire. She'd tried to run. She'd given Holloway the slip, skipping past him without much trouble. But then Marichal had popped out of the car and taken hold of her by the arm. She'd spun, spitting and kicking.

Spirit. The girl had spirit. It didn't do her any good this time, but I liked watching her fight and twist. She knew cops, you could tell; she was neither awed nor afraid, and she knew that once they got the cuffs on you or you were stuffed into the backseat, you were halfway to jail. They weren't arresting her. They thought they were rescuing her, even though they were really slitting her throat.

I shut my eyes for a moment. Mine, too.

Even a Trickster like me was due some courtesy, so Renar hadn't treated me roughly, up until now. That was done. We'd stolen from Renar, we'd attacked Amir.

Amir wouldn't hesitate to kill me next time. I had no doubt he had survived.

I didn't let my mind touch on the fact of Hiram's death. I hadn't seen him often over the last few years. We'd avoided each other and usually fell into the same old argument when we did run into each other, like a deep, sad groove. But he'd been there, in the background. Omnipresent in his way, if only through the deep magical bond between us. I probed the empty sense of freedom that had replaced that bond. I couldn't imagine living without constantly feeling Hiram there, part of me.

I looked at the cop driving the car. Just one cop, without a partner. Or maybe the partner was back at the apartment. Which was still kind of strange. He was a young guy, blond, slim. I looked at the rearview mirror for a few seconds, but he never glanced at it. He just stared at the car in front of him.

My eyes moved to his hands. He was wearing black gloves. Good, expensive leather ones. I stared at them for a moment, and then closed my eyes again. I'd seen a pair just like them just half an hour before.

My heart began pounding in my chest, a crazy, irregular beat. If you're trying to appear to be someone else, after all, it was easier and more effective to dress in their clothes and concentrate on their face when painting yourself with a Glamour.

You gotta let me bleed. The idea of using Mags's blood to gas my spell left a yellow ball in my stomach. I tried to think my way around that, but Mags didn't know anything useful here. A Charm . . . maybe. You could Charm anyone, even the most powerful *enustari,* but people like us knew the feeling. We could taste it, the gas in the air, the feeling creeping over us. Amir was on alert. It would take some gentle prodding, subtlety, to put him under my thumb. I didn't have that kind of time.

They have been compensated, I heard Hiram say years ago. He'd slashed her on the arm and she'd cried out, a sharp, instant noise, immediately swallowed. Expertly muted. A kid who'd learned young to keep quiet no matter what. And she'd stood there. She'd started shivering, her breathing becoming rough, but she'd stood stock-still and stared straight ahead. A girl used to being hurt.

I'd started whispering the spell. I'd memorized it easily enough. Hiram had described it as the limits of his ability, but even back then I'd seen three ways it could be truncated without losing any effectiveness. The first few syllables spilled out, and immediately, I'd felt it:

power, flowing from the girl. Flowing into me. It began as a pleasant sensation of fullness, of being well rested and ready for action. Slowly, it had built inside me, swelling, beautiful, glorious. Like the last time you woke up feeling refreshed, rested, a perfect night's sleep preceded by a perfect restful day. Then the feeling doubled, tripled. I could feel it building inside me with every whispered word.

And it was *sour*.

Something underneath the golden, shimmering surface, something cold and green and infected, also inside me. Wrapped up within the sense of power and energy, mostly insulated from me, but there nonetheless. Like finding a roach in your dinner and eating around it, pondering the possibility of eggs and larvae with each subsequent bite. Or mixing booze with silty brown water from a gas station sink, hoping the alcohol killed everything it touched. I felt incredible, powerful, healthy, and I was nauseated, my teeth falling out of my head, my organs turning black inside me. All at the same time.

The girl's shivering had turned to shaking.

Taking a deep breath for the next line, I paused. Felt the power hovering there, waiting, in stasis, like sunlight trapped in a bottle.

I'd looked at her. Never *look* at them.

Her shoes first, the girlish pink flowers and stylized letters: *SD*. Her initials, I guessed. Her hands: shaking at her sides, open, her fingernails just disasters, bloody and torn. Her face. Blank. Staring. Tears in her eyes but not falling out, just jiggling there like they'd been turned to jelly on contact with the air.

I'd swallowed my words and looked away. The feeling of power, of energy, stayed for a second, as if somehow intelligently judging whether I'd *paused* or *stopped*, and then burst within me, draining away and leaving behind a desolate, cold emptiness.

The explosion was typical: a flash of heat and light. Wind tearing through the room like a tornado had been summoned. Everything flying off of Hiram's shelves and smacking into us, smashing against the floor and walls. Tiny fires catching on the drapes and rugs. The girl had gasped and stumbled back, falling hard on her ass, her teeth clicking on her tongue. More blood—I remembered being able to feel it, the additional gas suddenly present. Her arm had stopped bleeding, as wounds always did when the casting was finished, and was just another scar on her that would never disappear.

I IMAGINED PULLING THIS rotten golden power from Mags, and my stomach flipped.

Amir was *enustari,* and he walked around like a rooster with his Bleeders everywhere—I doubted he'd bled for his own spells in decades. Guy like him, he would bleed small. A shivering vein of giggling good humor swept through me at the thought of Cal Amir using *mu,* being a Trickster for five minutes because Hiram had toasted his Bleeders and he didn't want to spend too much of his own precious blood. Playing it safe, bleeding just enough for a cut-rate Glamour to make him look like a cop and allow him to keep tabs on Claire. Until he could find himself some real blood to work with. Someone else's blood.

I had a bad feeling he meant that blood to be *mine.*

Swallowing bile, I ran through my spells again, trying to pick one I could spit out fast and have an effect with. We needed to take control of the car, or at least knock Amir on his ass—if Claire was locked in a room at One Police Plaza, and Amir walked in looking like a cop, she was as good as taken, which was as good as dead. I figured our one advantage here was that Amir thought we'd been fooled. He had relaxed.

I watched the red taillights up ahead, leading us on like swamp gas, like faerie lights, steady and hypnotizing. My mind raced. I had to save her. I had to save her while somehow not *killing* Mags and myself. I stared at the wide square trunk of the unmarked police car ahead of us until it suddenly swerved hard to the right then, jerking back, righted itself.

For a few heartbeats, it rolled on ahead of us again, steady.

Then it fishtailed, the trunk wiggling in front of us like it was danc-ing, sluicing to our left and then our right as the brakes went bright red, then dimmed, then went bright again.

"Fuck!" Mags whispered next to me.

Silently, the unmarked car went into a spin. Mags and I were tossed up against the grate as the patrol car braked hard, and for a second the other car was facing us. It continued to spin, moving horizontally, until it slammed into a telephone pole, the noise sudden and loud, then gone.

We zoomed past it.

"What the—" Amir hissed as he hit the brakes hard again, jerking the wheel to send us crashing into a herd of garbage cans on the curb. He was out of the car in a second, leaving Mags and me trapped in the backseat in abrupt quiet, the engine ticking loudly, cold air rushing in.

"Fuck," Mags said, resigned to his fate.

I twisted around and peered through the back window. Amir, still glammed up as a cop, walked towards the unmarked car. Steam poured from under the hood. One wheel was bent in an unfortunate way.

I twisted back around and closed my eyes. Took a deep breath. Pic-tured puppies playing in a warm grassy field. Reared back as far as I could and rammed my head into the grille between the front and back seats. There was a bright red flash behind my eyes. No pain. A con-cerning numbness, a sense of floating. The pain came a second or two later, a deep, rusty throb.

I got lucky. I felt blood, warm and fast, dripping down my face. A deep ringing had settled into my head and made my thoughts skitter sideways. Like walking on a sinking boat. Head wounds bled like hell. Spraying blood everywhere, I muttered a quick Cantrip, and the cuffs sprang open, a wave of dizzy, helpless weakness passing through me. My vision went dark and everything got distant and dim, slowly fading back to clarity as I breathed deeply. Changing one syllable, I repeated a version of the Cantrip, and the car door *snicked* open. I pushed at it and fell onto the damp street, catching myself with my hands. I stared dumbly at the ground for a moment. Two fat drops of blood landed under me with audible plops, unneeded by the universe.

I pushed myself back onto my knees and looked up. Amir had reached the unmarked car; the rear passenger door was open. He was leaning down and peering into the car through the rear driver's-side window.

Claire Mannice was creeping up behind him.

She was a little unsteady. She looked thin and cold in her T-shirt and jeans. She was limping and had lost a shoe but otherwise looked okay. She was not, I noticed, wearing handcuffs, but she *did* have a standard-issue nightstick in her hands.

My whole body was quaking. I heard Mags getting out of the car behind me. I decided it wasn't a bad idea to just rest a moment and see what she did with the nightstick, so I knelt there, breathing hard, hands on my thighs. She moved closer, stealthy.

Amir turned, fast, flipping around. Just as I thought about the blood dripping from my head, he hissed something, throwing a hand at her in a dramatic, useless gesture. Claire sailed up into the air and flew back about five feet, landing hard on her ass, the nightstick flying out of her hands and clattering on the asphalt a few feet away. I felt nothing. He hadn't drawn on me, but there was gas in the air now that I felt for it. *Holloway and Marichal,* I thought, *not so lucky.* I tried to think of something worse than being bled dry while unconscious, and couldn't.

Amir sprang for her, the Glamour melting away: Amir in his expensive suit, face snarling.

I had an old chestnut, a little spell I used when running from cops, from security guards, from irate folks resistant to your standard Charm Cantrips. I spat it out, tasting blood.

My vision blurred again as Amir's feet went out from under him like he'd stepped on a banana peel. He went horizontal and hit the ground hard, head bouncing.

Claire leaped up and retrieved the nightstick. She was mesmerizing to watch, lithe and graceful, her hips cocking this way and that as she prowled over to Amir. She raised the stick, but as she brought it down with crushing force, he rolled a few inches to the side and snarled another quick spell. He was pretty good at combat. A quick thinker. She flew back again, slamming into the ruined car with a grunt and sliding to the ground. I thought about Renar telling me how the runes on Claire bent the Words, deflected them. Reached back dreamily to my lessons with Hiram, the difference between a spell being cast *on* someone and merely *affecting* someone. Amir was casting spells that affected the air, turned it solid, moved it like a hammer. Claire was just in the way. This was details, but *enustari* lived in the grooves of details. The Words were complex, the grammar rich. You could do a lot with tiny bits here and there.

There were sirens in the air, distant. Coming closer.

Amir got to his feet in slow, shaky stages, muttering as he did so. There was blood in the air, and he was burning it for his own spell; I could feel him tugging at me, leaching my strength through my forehead. I started speaking the first trick that came to mind. I croaked out three syllables. Amir switched to a different spell in midsentence. Part of me swooned in admiration—that took skills. The new spell was a quick, nasty piece of work I admired as a piece of compact writing. My voice cut off midword. I tried again, pushing air through my larynx, though no sound emerged. Stalking towards Claire, Amir resumed his previous spell as if he'd never stopped reciting it.

I was outclassed. Mute, I started to wheeze and gasp my way to my feet anyway.

I was used to being outclassed.

Pitr Mags stepped in front of me, slashing his blade down his arm without a wince. Black moonlit blood welled up in a heavy flow. In a clear, loud voice, he recited the *fucking glowing bird* dazzler so quickly, Amir had just turned towards the noise when the bird, huge and *bright*—bright like the fucking sun out in the nighttime—swooped in from nothing, coalescing into a blinding golden-red illusion and diving right for his face.

Amir hesitated just a second. Just one second to process the stupid cheap Glamour, to see around it. To ignore it as a harmless trick.

Waving it away in contempt, when his vision cleared, he found Claire in front of him again, bloody and shaking.

Amir hesitated, and I knew why: He couldn't risk casting from her blood. He had to pick her thread out of the gas in the air and be certain, or else he'd fuck up his master's *biludha*.

And in that second of hesitation, she took one quick shot of the nightstick and knocked him cold.

He spun like a dancer and collapsed onto the street gracefully. She turned and tucked the stick into her waistband, walking over to me.

Sirens, much nearer. Two blocks.

Blood had smeared itself over the top part of her face. She looked like she was wearing a mask. I watched her walk over to me and wondered what I looked like to her, my head bleeding, slumped on the street, Mags behind me like a trained bear.

She squatted down beside me. She was breathing hard, and she was beautiful. Her dark hair was sticking out in odd ways, but her eyes were bright and wide, excited.

"All right, Chief," she said. "What do we do now?"

I smiled back at her. "We have to break the ritual. We have to get the glyphs off you."

"I'm all for getting these fucking things off of me, and I know I'm no *magician* or whatever, but shouldn't that be step fucking *two*? As in: Step one, get the fuck far away from here?"

I shrugged, feeling dreamy. Like I was falling into a hole. Gravity had disappeared, but the bottom wasn't visible yet, so you could imagine it was just limbo, just falling and falling forever.

"You run, Renar will find you. Might take some time, but she'll find you. As long as you're marked, she can't cast the *biludha* without you. She can't mark anyone else for it, either. I don't know why." I recalled Hiram waving away questions of *why*. "That's just how it is."

I was fucking up. It was interesting to watch yourself fucking up in slow motion, like an out-of-body experience: Here was the safe way, the path to the light, and you watched yourself walk deliberately into the shadows, eager for oblivion. I knew I should just turn her over to Renar and walk away, leave the business of power to the *enustari* of the world and get back to eking out my life one day at a time.

"All right, Chief. Step one, get the magic tats removed. How do we do that?"

I sighed. "We find ourselves an Archmage and get them to do it."

She studied me, her face intent. She was beautiful, and tall, and she'd just beat Calvin Amir unconscious after escaping from two detectives driving her to supposed safety. She nodded and stood up again, plucking the nightstick from her pants.

"All right," she said. "We should make sure—"

She turned back towards Amir. He was gone.

From behind me: "*Fuck.*"

13. **"TODAY IS THEORY," HIRAM SAID.** "Tomorrow you start learning spells."

We were on the subway. It was late and the car was sparsely populated. Hiram was fat yet somehow solid and proportional—any thinner and he would look strange. Depleted. At this point I'd known him only a few days. He was wearing a blue pin-striped suit that had started off life as something expensive and tailored, well into its dotage. His white shirt was blindingly bright. His red suspenders, when they peeked from under the jacket, were wide and striking. He stood without holding on to anything, swaying this way and that as the train moved. We hadn't paid the fare.

"Some spend their lives studying the theory. Truth is, you learn the spell, you bleed, you speak the Words. Nothing more is necessary."

Like music, I thought. You could spend years learning how it all worked. Or you could learn five chords and a scale and start jamming. I didn't say anything. I hadn't known Hiram long, but I knew he was less than interested in my brilliant thoughts.

There were eight other people in the car with us, hurtling underground. No one else was talking. They all wobbled this way and that with the momentum of the car. Staring straight ahead or listening to music. One person reading. The car smelled like piss and was humid. Humid with piss. Every surface felt greasy, though it looked superficially clean. Unless you looked at the advertisements. The advertisements on the upper part of the walls were so shiny and bright they hurt to look at and made everything you looked at next seem dirty.

The day before, Hiram had Bonded me. Taken me as his apprentice. His *urtuku.* It was a simple ritual—a thimbleful of our mixed blood, fourteen words. I didn't feel any different.

He held up two plump red fingers. "There are only two things you need to know, Mr. Vonnegan. The Rule of Perception and the Rule of Volume."

I nodded, turning to look around. See if anyone was paying attention to us. I didn't like having this talk out in public. Me and an old fat man talking about magic.

He reached out and slapped me. Hard enough to sting. Took hold of my nose between his thick thumb and forefinger, snapping my head back around.

"Mr. Vonnegan, when I am speaking to you, you will pay *attention.*"

I blinked. I remembered his words, just two days before. I'd finally gotten up the nerve to follow him home. Stood on his stairs for an hour, building up the courage. The door was opened by the big, glaring Indian, who didn't speak, who just stared at me with his fists curled at his sides, then disappeared, replaced by Hiram in bare feet and his undershirt and suspenders. *Think before you choose to be my* urtuku, *Mr. Vonnegan,* he'd said. *For every apprentice ends up wishing to kill their* gasam *in the end.*

Standing on the subway, tears in my eyes from the slap, I was beginning to understand.

"The Rule of Perception," he said, releasing my nose. The train swerved and I scrabbled to grab on to something. Hiram leaned his body, surfing, his balance perfect. "Perception is reality. If you convince someone something is there, it will be there. The eyes and ears are the easiest things to fool. If you require a gorilla to appear in the room, it is easier and more effective to make the mark *see* a gorilla and *hear* a gorilla than it is to actually transport a gorilla—or, God help you, *create* a gorilla. The blood cost to make someone perceive a gorilla can be minimal if you are skilled. The blood cost to transport a gorilla is enough to kill an adult person. The blood cost to *create* a gorilla is beyond you, Mr. Vonnegan."

I nodded. It seemed the safest thing to do. Hiram had promised to feed me as part of my apprenticeship. So far he had forgotten to do so. I was having trouble concentrating.

"If you convince enough people that something is there, then it *will* be there, for all practical purposes. To create a gorilla would require numerous sacrifices. To make everyone in a small area believe there is a gorilla is more manageable. Affecting the mind is easy. Changing the physical structure of the universe is very, very difficult. Do you understand? It can be done. *Anything* can be done. But the moment you affect the molecules around you, you scale up the blood required by orders of magnitude."

I nodded again.

"The Rule of Volume," he continued quickly. I began to panic, realizing this was going to be all I would get from Hiram. All the background he had to offer. "The more blood, the more powerful the spell. It does not matter what words you speak or how cleverly you speak them, or how quickly. The intensity of the effect depends entirely on how much blood you use in the casting. A simple spell to create flame—use a pinprick of blood, you will get a candle flame. Use a pint, you will get a fireball the size of this train car. Use a Sacrifice, you will set the city on fire.

"Being clever with the Words, Mr. Vonnegan, is a *tactic*. It is a battle technique. You will find spells that take pages and pages of words to do simple things, tiny magicks, and you may discover you can edit those spells. Reduce the needed Words. You may discover you can be clever. This will improve your speed, but not the power of the spell. The volume will remain unchanged. The blood needed depends on the effect desired. The speed with which you cast means nothing in terms of the power of the spell. But if you need to cast *quickly*, it can be an advantage."

I felt eyes on me. Everyone staring. Thinking we were crazy. Despite everything I'd seen over the last few days, following Hiram around, living with him. Despite the old man in the parking lot so many years ago, I thought, *Maybe I am. Maybe I am crazy and always have been.*

Sacrifice, I thought. That was what Hiram called bleeding someone dry for a spell. A Sacrifice.

"Some spells, by their very nature, require a certain volume of blood. It is the same principle in reverse—to move a pebble, you need a pinprick. To move a mountain, you need more. If you cast a spell to move a mountain with just a pinprick of blood, you will indeed expend force against the mountain, but it will be as if you walked up to its base and blew gently on it. It will not *move*."

"*This is,*" a robotic voice announced, the dirty stone walls of the subway tunnel melting away to the dirty tiled walls of the subway station, "*West Fourth Street.*"

"Some have wasted time with single Words," he added, staring past me as if lost in thought. "This has always failed. You can, of course, cast with a single Word. The Rule of Volume still applies: Speak the word for *fire* and fire will come, unformed, uncontrolled. Bleed enough people and speak *fire* and you can burn the world. But it will not be a *spell*, Mr. Vonnegan." He looked back at me. "You are not controlling anything at that point. You are merely a gateway for energy, and that energy is almost always destructive. To do anything worth doing, you need form. Function. The Rule of Perception. Intelligence. This is why no *ustari* will teach the unbonded, and those who are *clever* and learn a Word are . . . suppressed." Suddenly brisk and impatient, Hiram shot out one arm and began to roll up his sleeve. "Come. A demonstration. Give me a vein. This is the most powerful spell I know. This is the *hunkiuba*."

I fumbled with my own sleeve, my cheek still burning. I held out my arm, feeling blood rushing to my face in humiliation. He was going to cut us. Right there. In public.

Hiram worked with surgical efficiency. The straight razor came out. With a flick of his wrist, he extended it. Drew it across my arm so quickly, it seemed like he didn't even touch me until the thick blood welled up, faster and more alarming than I was ready for.

Hiram had just killed me. He then killed himself, slicing his own arm and reciting some strange words.

The train was rolling to a stop. I felt the queasy draining. I got dizzy. A power moving *through* me, somehow, as if I were not supplying the gas to a fire but, rather, was the doorway through which energy passed.

It was a long spell. I tried to follow it, but I'd been studying the Words only a few days. He lost me. The Words twisted back on each other, slurred into each other. A charlatan's tricks— Hiram did not want other magicians to steal his spell.

It took Hiram forty-three seconds to recite it. The train lurched. The doors split open. People stood to exit the car. People waited to enter the car. People stared at us. The warning bell sounded, the doors began to close.

And never did.

Hiram took a deep breath and opened his eyes, scanning the car. I stared dumbly at my arm. The cut had not healed but had closed. The bleeding had stopped even as the gash throbbed painfully. There were two other long slices on my arm, on their way to healing fully. Hiram had warned me to get used to being scarred, to start thinking *now* where I wanted those scars to be.

I looked around. Everything had stopped. The doors were still mostly open; they'd just begun to close. People were paused in the act of moving. Crouched over seats. In midspin. Legs up off the floor. Mouths open. Bags swung out from them in midair, gravity both excused and maintained all at the same time.

"The *hun-kiuba*," Hiram said, his voice sounding a little more ragged, a little less polished, "alters time. To a crawl. This is a function of both Rules. Time is a perception. Time does not exist until it is *observed*. The effect of the spell is always the same; the variable is the area it affects. Its scale. The more blood used, the larger the area. We have each bled a pint, Mr. Vonnegan. And for our efforts, we have affected time within this subway car."

I forced myself to move. To prove I *could* move. There was a strange crackling noise; at first I felt frozen, glued in place. Then, suddenly, I was free and able to move. I stared around. I looked through the half-open doors. The platform beyond was similarly frozen.

"Why is time stopped out there, too?"

Hiram scowled, unrolling his sleeve. "Time is not *stopped*, Mr. Vonnegan. It is relative. Either we are moving incredibly quickly through time, or everyone else on this train car is moving incredibly *slowly*. Since our perception is what determines reality, Mr. Vonnegan, it appears to us that the platform—the entire world—has been affected. It has not. If we cross outside the affected area of the spell, we will rejoin the normal flow of time. If we were standing on that platform right now, we would observe no change in the world—except perhaps that you and I have just disappeared. We are still here, but moving through time differently."

I shook my head. "I'll never fucking understand that."

Hiram laughed, a booming, theatrical laugh. It was the first thing I'd liked about him.

"You do not have to, Mr. Vonnegan. Perception. Volume. That is all you need to remember. In time I will teach this spell to you. In time you will cast it and bleed another."

I felt so tired. I recalled the terrible feeling of that power, being pulled through you like you were an opening that was slightly too small for a monstrous thing, being torn open and stretched to accommodate it. I thought of doing that to someone else, and kept imagining a monstrous mosquito, six feet tall, pinning you down and jabbing its stinger into your belly. That memory of smothering, that awful feeling of being *drained*—I couldn't inflict that on someone else. It would be impossible. And what did you do with something like this? I wondered. To affect a useful space, like this, you needed a lot of blood. If I bled out two pints of my own, I doubted I'd be able to do anything afterwards.

But to *slow down time* . . . To be able to slip out of the moment and walk between moments . . . a man who could cast that kind of spell could do just about anything.

"Attend to me, Mr. Vonnegan," Hiram said, stepping past me. "This will not last long, from our perspective."

Moving was strange; I once again heard the strange crackling noise and felt at first like I'd been nailed to the floor. Then I seemed to *snap* free in a sense and was able to move. Everything around me was absolutely still but seemed to shimmer. The slightest, tiniest bit of movement, I thought. Almost imperceptible.

I followed Hiram, feeling drained. Exhausted. I watched dully as he went up to the nearest person, a man in a dark suit, carrying a briefcase, caught in the act of stumbling. As I watched, dumbly, Hiram began going through the man's pockets.

We worked the entire car. I took one side, Hiram the other. We took cash, but Hiram was most intent on the jewelry, examining every watch, ring, bracelet, and chain briefly but with steady, practiced eyes. He left some of the pieces and took the others. By the end, he was humming happily. He looked tired, but was in the best mood I'd seen him in since coming to New York.

"Come, Mr. Vonnegan," he said, holding up the wad of cash. "Time for some dinner. And a good bottle of Malbec."

The car doors had, in fact, closed slightly farther in the time we'd spent robbing the car. Perhaps half an inch. We approached, and Hiram put a hand on my chest, stopping us.

"Be prepared," he said seriously. "The transition is sudden."

He nodded, turned, and stepped through the doors. Vanished.

I stared. One second he'd been moving, right in front of me. Then he was gone. Swept forward into the normal stream of time.

I stepped forward and . . .

14. **I STARTLED AWAKE. THE BUS** had been our home for so long, I wasn't sure how we'd adjust to life without it. Mags had gassed up twelve dollars and fifty cents into a small fortune, passing bloody bills with reckless abandon, buying tickets and hamburgers and bottles of water. Three days with nothing to do but sleep and eat and be horrified by the bathroom haunting the rear of the bus. I was starting to feel almost normal.

Across the aisle, Claire sat in the outer seat. Pitr Mags was folded up on his side, his head resting in her lap, sleeping soundly. She was stroking his hair absently as we rumbled through Hill Country. I was deeply in love with her for stroking Mags's hair. She noticed I was awake and turned her head to look at me.

"So, your man Hiram," she said drowsily. It was the continuation of one giant conversation we'd been having for days.

Outside, it was dark. Featureless, black. We might have been in some sort of experiment, a vehicle on casters, sound effects, paid extras in the seats around us.

"My *gasam*," I said. "My Master, in the sense of having an apprentice."

She nodded sleepily. I liked the blurry way she got when she was tired. We'd been talking for hours, on and off. Packets of words. I felt like I knew things about her that no one else knew, and I liked that, too. "How do you know he's dead?"

I waited a few seconds. I didn't know how I felt about Hiram. I hadn't *liked* him, really. Had barely known him in that way you're supposed to know people you have a thing with. Had found him irritating on more than one occasion. But he'd taken Mags in before me, which argued in his favor. And he'd just been a part of things. Always there. I realized, the second it had been severed, that I was always subconsciously aware of my magical connection to him. Now, when I noticed the absence, I felt incomplete.

"I know. We had a . . . bond." I didn't see any point in telling her that, as we'd left the city, I'd been surprised and a little saddened not to have felt the slight, uncomfortable tugging in my gut that was that bond. It had always been there, increasing in degree as distance increased. A *gasam* could choose to invoke the bond, use it like a leash to tug his apprentice back, but Hiram had just let it sizzle, always there, like a fishhook in my back that had healed over.

"Why was he so angry at you?"

I didn't answer right away. I didn't know how much Claire remembered from her few minutes in Hiram's house with us, especially the first time.

"Because I wouldn't do what he wanted me to do."

She raised an eyebrow. "And that was?"

She was looking at me with her sleepy eyes, her serious face. She was the sort who didn't let things go—gentle but persistent. She had perfect lips, a little pink bow. Even in the cheap new clothes Mags had bought her, baggy tan pants and a heavy shirt, a thick gray sweater, the world's cutest wool cap, she had a shape and grace to her I wanted to stare at.

I sighed. "Hiram thought I had potential. Magic. That I could be something special." I rubbed my eyes. "Maybe he's even right. I remember the spells easy, I can see how to improve them, little shortcuts. I can even make up my own, which Hiram can't." I paused. "Couldn't. But I won't bleed other people for it. I get by on what I can gas myself, and that's it."

"Fuck, why *blood*?"

"I don't know. No one does, I don't think. Something primeval, right?"

The bus hummed along. We hummed along in it.

"This guy we're heading to," she said after a moment.

"Gottschalk," I said. "Faber Gottschalk."

"He can get these runes off me?"

I nodded. "He's *enustari*." She frowned at me, and I shook my head. "A big fucking deal. Right up there with the woman who wants to slice you open and bleed you like a pig." I shrugged again. "Powerful."

My Rolodex was not exactly filled with *enustari*. I could remember three, maybe four, from Hiram's sketchy lecturing: Carith Abdagnale if she qualified, which I wasn't certain she did; Mika Renar; Faber Gottschalk; and Beni Aragaki, and I only knew Aragaki's *name*.

"Why is Gottschalk going to help me?"

"I don't know. We're going to have to come up with a reason."

She chewed on that.

I reviewed what I knew about Faber Gottschalk. This didn't take long. I knew he'd been Hiram's *gasam* for ten years. That they'd parted ways amicably. That despite that, Hiram had always made fists without realizing it when he mentioned Gottschalk's name.

Claire went on in a small voice, "Why does it have to be *me*? Why chase after me? Just find someone else."

I wanted to reach across the aisle and touch her. Seconds went by, marked by the sway of the bus and the soft sounds of half-asleep people. The bus was alive, and we were just the cilia of its lungs, swaying with each inhalation and exhalation, absorbing oxygen.

"It doesn't work that way," I said softly, trying to remember how Hiram had explained things and say it all differently. "The word is *bi-*

ludha, ritual. Everything involved in it has to be done in a specific, precise way. They marked you, so you have to die in your proper place. Right now all the power expended in the Rite is up in the air, suspended. If you don't die exactly when you're supposed to, the next girl won't die, or the next one. No one after you will, and the Rite falls apart. They mark up someone new, the Rite falls apart."

She sighed, closing her eyes. I studied her face. Imagined her as a kid in school when I'd been in school, both of us chafing to get away, imagining that cigarettes were part of the fare out of our lives. I suddenly regretted using the phrase *slice you open and bleed you like a pig.*

I thought of all the other girls. The ones the Skinny Fuck had snatched before Claire. The ones who looked like Claire from future moments she might never get, each one a little older than the last.

Mags snorted and twisted, slumbering, and wound up with his nose planted directly in Claire's crotch. She opened her eyes and looked at me with a raised eyebrow.

"He *is* asleep, right?"

I smiled. "Mags doesn't have a creepy bone in his body. He's a puppy."

Looking down at Mags's head, she continued stroking his hair, pushing it around gently. "How'd you pick him up, anyway?"

"I ran away from home when I was seventeen. Nothing dramatic: I got tired of Dad showing up outside school now and then kidnapping me—literally—and then coming home to Mom pissed off at *me* for being kidnapped, you know? Nothing dramatic. I got fed every day and had clothes and my own room, no one was beating me up or anything, but I just . . . left."

I didn't tell her about the old man in the parking lot. It wouldn't make sense without all the backstory. She leaned towards me slightly, out over the armrest of her seat. I let my eyes run down the curve of her neck, the sharp, pleasant line of her collarbone. I couldn't see the runes on her because I wasn't trying, and there was no gas in the air to help me out. Her skin looked perfect to me. She smelled like clean laundry. When she spoke, her voice was soft and ten years younger, and it was like we were having a sleepover, curled up with each other on someone's carpeted basement floor, listening to records.

"I ran away from home, too," she said quietly.

I waited, but she didn't say anything else.

"I came to New York looking for a Hiram. Not *Hiram,* because I didn't know he existed, but someone like him. Someone who could teach me how to do things."

Hiram gesturing with a bandaged hand and making a muffin float across a diner to his waiting hand. Hiram sitting at the counter eating it while he read a newspaper like nothing unusual had happened. Hiram stealing the fucking salt and pepper shakers from the counter when he left.

"Hiram already *had* Mags. Mags was basically Hiram's Oddjob when I showed up. He wanted Hiram to apprentice him, but Hiram wouldn't, because he regarded Mags as Too Stupid to Live." I considered. "Which isn't far short of the truth. Anyway, I adopted Mags, he fell in love with me, and we've been nonbreeding life partners ever since."

"He'd take a bullet for you."

"And me him. Be careful, he'll adopt *you.*"

We stopped talking. Slowly spread apart like we were floating in jelly, tugged this way and that, the sudden intimacy shattering and leaving us just two people sitting in separate seats. The overwarm bus rumbled and rattled, the emptiness scrolling past us, and after a few minutes of pondering Claire Mannice and the neat way she'd folded her legs under herself on the seat, I fell asleep.

IT WAS COLDER THAN I would have expected in Texas. We crept off the bus like stumblebums, stiff and squinty, unshowered and crusty. The bus had pulled over outside the library, of all places. A small park sporting an ice rink was across the street. It was literally called Main Street, wide and pretty heavily trafficked at ten in the morning.

Claire stood next to a street sign and began stretching, pulling one ankle up towards her head as she balanced, one hand on the signpost. I stared, breath steaming in front of me.

"What's our bank account?" I asked Mags without taking my eyes from her.

"Seven dollars," he said. He paused, as if checking his grade-school addition skills, and then repeated it. "Seven dollars."

It wasn't unexpected or even uncomfortable. I'd been living on an eternal seven dollars for years. I took stock. I was hungry—starving, but I'd been starving for ten years and it was normal to me. I felt good. Rested. Probably still down a pint but no longer on the verge of passing out. I had a tremendous appetite, but not just for food. I wanted cigarettes and whiskey, and I wanted to bleed a bit and Charm the pants off of Claire Mannice, literally. She'd been twelve inches away for three days and I had memorized her smell.

I clapped Mags on the shoulder. "Breakfast. You up for a Beauty Queen?"

He nodded sleepily. "Sure, Lem. I'll cast the compulsion, you cast the Charm."

"What's a *Beauty Queen*?" Claire asked. Somehow she was standing right next to us, a fucking cat in need of a bell.

I looked around. Only a handful of people had gotten off the bus; we had a few feet of sidewalk all to ourselves. I took Claire's arm and urged her to walk with us towards what looked like the busy part of Main Street.

"You are," I said. The sun was high and bright, but the air was crisp and cold, and I was shivering a little. "It's a scam we run, a combination of two spells. You can work it as one spell, but then you've got to give the gas for something big. Split it into two components, and two people can cast it without passing out. You game to be our *beauty*?"

Some people weren't. Some people didn't see it as survival.

"What do I do?"

"Stand around, look pretty," Mags said with a grin.

Mags was a wonder of science. He walked next to me, stretching as he went, twisting his arms back, his neck down, arching his back. His joints popped like gunshots. He was big and brown and his hair was getting girlishly long again, curling around his face. I'd never been to Texas, much less what felt like the fucking exact center of the state, all dust and wildflowers and yellow stone buildings with German names. I didn't know how many Pitr Mags types existed in the *world*, though my cautious estimate was seven. I doubted any of them had passed through Texas before.

Claire scowled. "*And?*"

I sighed. I wasn't used to explaining spells to people. "One, we cast a reverse Charm on you, make every man in the world think you're the most beautiful thing he's ever seen, okay? Then we wait for someone useful to show up, and when he's on your hook, trying to impress you, we cast a Compel on him, make him do anything you tell him to. Compulsions on their own are dicey—they wear off fast if you try to get people to do shit they normally wouldn't do. Combine it with a Charm, much better."

I looked at her. She had a sleepy, scrubbed look to her face I liked, her hair standing up in cute ways everywhere.

"What then? When we have some poor idiot on the *hook*?"

I shrugged. "He buys us breakfast. He gives us a ride out to Gottschalk's place. He provides local cover and information so Mags here isn't put in a cage and sold to the circus folk."

Mags choked a little. "What?"

"Then we cut him loose. The Charm fades and he goes home, goes back to being a shitkicker. No real harm."

We walked in silence for a few seconds. She nodded. "Okay, fine."

"Good." I paused and gestured at the place we were passing. "In here works."

It was called the German Bakery and was full of what looked like the entire population of a retirement home, old fogies nursing coffees and muttering. It had a good diner buzz, with no decor to speak of. It felt greasy, like the air itself would never be clean again. We made our way to an empty table in the back, Formica and plastic benches, and sat down, Mags facing Claire and me. The place smelled like coffee, good and strong.

"Well?"

I shook my head at her while I passed out the plastic menus. "Give it a few minutes. We need to pick our mark and fade into the background a little."

We faded. The waitress, a stringy woman of indeterminate age and unnatural hair color that most closely resembled red, came by and gave Mags a bit of the yellow eye. Mags didn't notice. Half the world hated Mags on sight, but he maintained his cheerful disposition through the simple expedient of not paying any attention—he wouldn't realize the villagers hated him until a mob with torches was gathered outside his house. The waitress took our coffee order cheerfully enough, though. We sat in a tense silence. I didn't light a cigarette because there were NO SMOKING signs everywhere, and fading required a little patience. I just sat there and let my eyes roam around the place. By the time the coffee arrived, I'd picked out our mark.

He was a kid, a big one. Blond, jeans, flannel, work boots. So hungover I could smell him from where we sat, nursing a miserable cup of coffee and staring down a mostly uneaten plate of pancakes and sausage, looking like life was the deck of the *Titanic* right before it split in two and went down and he had but one finger hooked on something, hanging on.

I stood up, looked around. The bathrooms were behind us, through a swinging door. Perfect. I nudged Claire, delighting in this illicit, uninvited touch. "Let's go."

She waited a second, giving me a flat stare. I remembered the cop car fishtailing, crashing, Claire popping out with a fucking nightstick in one hand. Then she stood up, gave Mags a pat on the shoulder, and followed me through the swinging doors. I tried both the men's and women's rooms. Both empty, so I pushed the men's room door open and gestured.

"In here."

She looked at the bathroom, then at me. We stayed like that for a moment. Then she stepped inside and I followed, locking the door behind me.

It was the tiniest bathroom in the universe and might have been impossible to actually use as a bathroom. We were pushed up against each other, her lean and warm, me gritty and sucking my gut in like some nervous middle-schooler. I rolled up my sleeve.

"How'd you find this Gottschalk guy?"

I pushed my sleeve up past my elbow. She looked down at the pink rivers of scars and left her eyes there. "I told you. He was Hiram's *gasam*. Long ago."

"I thought you fellows mated for life."

"You can be released. Usually when the *gasam* feels they have nothing more to teach you."

"But Hiram wouldn't release you because you wouldn't do like he wanted."

I nodded, pulling out my switchblade. The room was filled with Claire. She was young and pretty enough, and I hadn't slept with a woman, or had a soft conversation in the dark with a girl, or generally been in the company of a female, in a long time. The years felt heavy on me.

She watched me examine the blade and then my forearm, looking for a good, healed area to cut. "Why are we so fucking *scared*, Chief? That guy Amir—okay, kind of scary. But shit, if I'd been paying more attention, I would have beaten his brains in, no problem."

I paused with the knife hovering right over the meaty part of my arm and looked up at her. "First, Amir was sloppy. He brought Bleeders, but he wasn't expecting trouble. He figured he'd make a show of force and we'd fall on our knees to suck his cock and beg forgiveness." I smiled. "He didn't expect *Hiram* fucking *Bosch* to show up hurling fireballs. When he caught up with us after—after, he was on his own and didn't have much gas to work with." I winked. "Trust me, dearie, Amir shows up loaded for bear with a dozen Bleeders in his retinue, knowing he can't trust a fucking Trickster farther than he can throw him—a lesson we fucking taught him right good, didn't we?—then you'll find out how fast a fucking *saganustari* of his caliber—an Archmage in the making—can *fuck you up.*"

It was a long speech.

She looked at me, biting her lip. "Is he really dead? Hiram?"

I nodded, thinking of Hiram standing in his study, sleeves rolled up, mixing drinks. I swallowed thickly and nodded. "You sucker-punch *saganustari,* you better fucking kill them."

I slashed the blade down precisely, and blood, thick and dark, welled out of the wound. I began reciting my Charm. Claire stared back at me, swallowing hard, but said nothing more. In the mirror behind her, the glyphs on her skin glowed softly.

"YEAH, I SEE HIM," Mags said, studying the hayseed's reflection in the napkin dispenser. "Fucking hick."

He took a deep breath. Spreading his hand palm up on the table, he took his little penknife, the blade now thin and worn down, its edge still sharp as a razor, and dragged it across his palm, shutting his eyes and reciting.

"Wow," Claire whispered. "He looks like he's taking a dump right there in his seat."

I smiled, feeling my arm throb with the familiar old burning. Claire had the whole room's attention. Old men who hadn't had a hard-on in decades were staring at her. The waitresses struggled against simultaneous urges to slap her and stroke her hair, call her *honey.* Claire was bearing it pretty well. I had a feeling she bore most things pretty well. Or maybe was used to entire roomfuls of people wanting to get it on with her.

Thirty seconds, Mags was done. His wound was dry, the universe's sole gift to us. Grimacing a little, he took a napkin and wiped down his blade.

"Shit," Claire hissed. "He's *looking* at me."

I leaned in, put a hand on her shoulder. "Take it easy. He's under control, don't forget that."

She shook her head, her eyes hard. "Ain't no such thing, boss."

"He'll be a puppy dog. He'll do whatever you tell him, so tell him hands off, tell him to be polite. Okay?"

It was the first time I'd ever seen her nervous. She nodded, staring at the guy across the room. "Okay. Oh, *shit*."

Our hayseed was crossing over to our table, eyes locked on Claire. I could understand her worry; his expression was . . . focused. If I saw him coming towards me and didn't know he'd been gassed up by a couple of starving Tricksters, I'd have been alarmed, too.

When he got to us, he just stood there awkwardly. He looked at me. He looked at Mags a little longer. Then he looked at Claire. And kept looking. Behind him, a pair of old codgers in denim overalls sat chewing on toothpicks with wet, obscene lips, also staring at Claire. Behind them, the big front window looked out on Main Street, people passing by in small groups. Inside, all I could smell was sour coffee and grease. The floor sucked at our guy's boots as he shifted his weight, making small sticky tearing noises.

"Hi," he said in a strangled voice.

After a moment, I nudged Claire. She shot a look at me, then looked back down at her hands on the table. "Uh, hi."

"You're beautiful."

"Uh, thanks."

I swiveled in my chair and pushed the empty one at our table out towards him with one foot. "Hiya. I'm Lem, this is Mags, and this, this, is *Claire*. Have a seat. Claire needs a favor."

Mags waved at him. "Hi!"

Our hayseed smiled around at us, dopey. It was bright, with this clear blue light pouring in from the front and making him into a shadow. He nodded and dropped into the chair easily, graceful. Football, undoubtedly, and he was young enough that daily practices were still fresh in his memory. He settled his smile on Claire and looked happy to just sit and smile at her for the rest of his life.

I snapped my fingers in front of his face until he looked at me. "What's your name, boss?"

"Daryl," he said without taking his eyes off Claire. "Daryl Houy." He pronounced it *Hoo-eee*.

"Make him stop staring at me."

I smiled at Daryl, our hero. "Claire requests you not stare at her, boss."

He blinked and finally turned his head to look at me. "Why not?"

I leaned forward. "Doesn't matter. Listen, Claire needs someone to buy her breakfast. Three breakfasts, actually."

His face lit up.

We are not good people.

"Hell, yeah! What can I get for y'all?"

Y'all. We were in Texas.

15.

DARYL DROVE A SHITBOX FORD pickup that had undoubtedly been his father's or uncle's shitbox pickup before him. It had the polished feel of something well worn. It smelled like beer and stale sex and had an empty gun rack mounted in the back.

I was mashed behind the driver's seat on the world's most uncomfortable bench. It made a mockery of the words *extended cab*. Mags was next to me, practically in my lap. He had pushed himself forward so he was between Daryl and Claire as we bounced along what the state of Texas had the balls to call *roads*. What Texas needed, I thought, was some fucking Jewish mayors and a load of mobbed-up goodfellas to get something done.

"What y'all want out at the Gottschalk place, anyway?" Daryl shouted over his shoulder, his eyes locked on Claire. She was pushed as far against the passenger door as she could manage. "It's hard as heck to get out here."

"Eyes on the road, Daryl. Claire needs to ask Mr. Gottschalk to do something for her," I said.

"What? Maybe I can help?"

I shook my head. "Sorry, boss. Claire needs Gottschalk."

"He's a weird one, I warn ya," Daryl said cheerfully.

I was beginning to have a grudging affection for Daryl. He was just a kid, lanky and easy in his movements, and cheerful. It was like he hadn't yet figured out that high school was over and he'd be working his highway job for the rest of his fucking life. Part of me hoped he never realized it, up until the day he died.

"Been out on that ranch as long as I been alive. Never comes to town. Sends some of his devotees in for supplies sometimes. Bald freaks in white robes. Robes!" He glanced sidelong at Claire and frowned. "I ain't proud of it, but when we was kids back in school, we used to have a little fun with those freaks. There's the place."

I followed his tanned, toned arm and saw it in the distance: a big house or a small ranch, whatever you wanted to call it. Out in the middle of fucking nowhere, just yellow dirt and rocky outcroppings and scrub grass everywhere. The house was made from the same yellowish stone you saw everywhere else; it looked solid and eternal, like the world might take a few thousand years to wear it down and wipe it clean.

Inside the fence, which was a tall but flimsy-looking chain-link job topped with nasty barbed wire, a dozen or so people were working. Six of them were tending a large garden off to the left, doing the hard work of weeding and tilling and the judicious use of chemical warfare on insects of all kinds. The rest were engaged in what looked like repair work on various pieces of equipment, including a beaten-down old truck that predated Daryl's shitbox racer by at least two decades.

The gate was open, and we drove through unchallenged.

It took about thirty seconds to go from the front gate to the drive-way that circled in front of the door. Up close, the house was falling apart. The siding was falling off. The roof looked rotten and had a sag to it that didn't look good. The windows were old and out of plumb. The paint, where there *was* paint, was peeling, and the sills were all rotted. By the time we opened the truck's doors and started out of the cab, three men had emerged from the house and stood facing us from the sun-faded wood of the porch.

They looked alike: shaved heads, white robes, and no shoes. They were what an unimaginative man would come up with if asked to de-scribe a cult member. The one in the middle was a little taller, and he smiled down at us.

I didn't like his smile.

"Welcome," he said. "You are welcome here. Can we be of assis-tance?"

I stepped around to be in front of everyone. "We'd like to see Mr. Gottschalk."

The rest of the freaks had stopped what they were doing and stood in silence, staring at us. I looked around, feeling squirrelly.

"Do you have an invitation? Master only sees people by appoint-ment."

I shook my head, slowly reorienting on the Head Freak. "No," I said. "Tell him Hiram Bosch sent me."

Without any further objection, the Head Freak bowed slightly, turned, and disappeared back into the house. I moved up to the porch stairs. One of the other freaks who'd come outside stepped down to me and held out his hand, palm up. In it was a small pebble.

"Master Gottschalk gave this to me," he said quietly, staring at me with an unblinking half-smile on his face. "Isn't it wonderful?"

I looked at the pebble, then at the kid. He was maybe twenty. He had razor burn on his neck and smelled like baby powder.

I turned away and walked back to where Mags, Claire, and Daryl stood uncertainly by the truck.

"Charmed," Mags said.

"A heavy Charm, too," I agreed, standing with my back to the house. "All these bastards, gassed to the gills, all the time. That's a shit ton of blood. This is worse than Carith Abdagnale's grift in New York." Abdagnale was famous as a pimp, running constant Glamours to lure in unsuspecting lechers to feed her blood supply.

"Are all of you this creepy?" Claire whispered, hugging herself tightly.

I thought of Abdagnale again. "Most."

"How do people like this just . . . exist? How come no one does anything?"

"We're good at staying just under the radar. Even the Archmages know better than to make too much noise. Besides, what do you think would happen? We get back to town, call the cops. Explain to them what you think's happening. See what it gets you."

I turned suddenly. Another of the shaved-head freaks had crept up to my elbow. She was as young as the rest and ugly, a fat, short girl with an acne-scarred face. A nice smile, though, dopey and turned on me like a low-watt bulb. She was holding her palm up to me like the first one had.

"Master gave me this," she said shyly.

In her palm was an old, slightly bent bottle cap.

I looked away, nodding. "That's nice."

I'd never seen so many people charmed so hard. All of them, I had no doubt, under a spell, thinking they were happy, thinking they had an amazing gift from their *Master*. Thinking it was fine to bleed for him—several times a week, probably—so he could cast the same fucking spell on them over and over again, keeping the Charm fresh.

We are not good people.

I thought of Daryl and reminded myself that we were going to let him off the hook in a few hours.

I looked over at the kid. He was standing a few feet from Claire, hands jammed into his pockets, his face dark and pensive as he stole glances at her. He looked fourteen. Like he was at that first high school dance again, awkward and terrified and angry all at the same time, because the cute girls were ignoring him. I thought there was a fifty-fifty chance he would end the day in tears.

"If I wanted to come back here tonight," Claire said in a low, flat voice, "and burn this fucking place down, would you help?"

She meant it. I remembered the detectives' car back in New York, fishtailing, the brake lights dancing. She would do it.

I heard the Head Freak behind me. "Mr. Vonnegan," he said. "Master Gottschalk welcomes you. Please, follow me."

I turned around to find him smiling, and he beckoned to us. Using my name was a cheap trick, but I appreciated cheap tricks.

I leaned in to Daryl. "Claire wants you to wait here with the truck. Don't let anyone steal it."

He frowned. "I want to stick by her. Keep her safe."

"Claire wants you to stay with the truck."

After a second, he looked at Claire. Stared at her until she finally sighed unhappily and looked back at him.

"Stay with the goddamn truck," she said. Paused a heartbeat. "Please."

He shrugged, suddenly nonchalant. "Sure, okay."

We followed the Head Freak into the house. It smelled like cat piss and rot. The first was explained immediately, as Gottschalk had about a hundred cats in the place, running free. They all looked fat and imperious, and only a couple scampered away when we trooped in. Most of them just sat there eyeing us coolly. One fat black-and-white one rubbed up against me as we picked our way carefully through what had once been a dining room, and I reached down to scratch his ears as I passed.

Gottschalk was in the master suite of the house, way in the back. He was fat. Not circus fat, just fleshy and jowly, sitting up in a huge bed piled high with pillows and blankets and cats, a dozen or so of which were curled up on him, against him, around him. He was about eighty years old and hadn't wasted any blood on making himself look younger. There was a stale smell in the air, which I chose not to examine too closely. The room was dim and stuffy, overcrowded, the bed immense. It must have been delivered in pieces and assembled in the room, it was so large.

The sheets looked yellow and stiff. I made an impulsive, heartfelt vow never to voluntarily touch them.

Gottschalk himself was dissipated: too fat but saggy, as if he'd been fatter not long ago. His hair was patchy, three or four sprouts of it surrounded by peeling pink scalp. His eyes were watery, his lips wet. His hands trembled as he flashed them about. Two of his acolytes stood silent and still in each corner, like furniture.

"Ah! A Fellow Traveler," he drawled, his accent a strange combination of Texas and German. "Mr. Vonnegan, I find it fascinating that Hiram sent you to me, as Hiram Bosch is now dead." His watery eyes moved past me, and he sat up a little. "Oh! What is this! Come here, my dear. Let me *look* at you."

"Hiram called it *Biludha-tah-namus*," I offered helpfully as Claire stepped forward, arms still wrapped closely around herself.

"Do not *speak*!" Gottschalk thundered, shooting me a red-faced expression of fury. "Speak when I speak *to* you, boy!"

I shut my mouth, judged how quickly I could get to the old bastard and put my hands around his neck, and decided I could stay cool. Gottschalk would change his tune when he knew what was happening. But now I knew where Hiram had gotten his bedside manner, and I felt a pang of sadness that I'd never be able to tease him about it.

Claire walked over to the old man without hesitation. Her hands were in her pockets now, the right one curled into a fist, a lump under the fabric. Curled around something—a weapon. A roll of quarters, a small knife—something, I knew. Gottschalk might be able to strike her dead with five words and a slash from one of his Bleeders, but he would have to be awfully quick. We had a saying you picked up when you started hanging around magicians: *You can't speak yourself out of a bullet.*

Gottschalk reached towards her as she got close, but she stopped a foot and a half away, and he made no effort to compel or cajole her to come closer. He studied her with a curious expression on his slack, wrinkled face, some bizarre combination of revulsion and admiration.

"I have never seen such intricate marking," he muttered. "Yes, yes, I see the pattern. Intricate, intricate. You are the keystone, here. There is a lot of static energy bottled up behind you, my dear. *Tah-namus,* he said. My goodness, the intricacy—" He blinked his watery eyes and snatched his hands back. "*Tah-namus.*" He looked at me, sitting forward slightly. "*Biludha-tah-namus!* Are you certain?"

I shook my head, but he was already looking at Claire again. Claire stood there ramrod-straight, ass in and tits out, eyes locked on Gottschalk. She looked ready to launch herself at him.

"It fits, though, it fits," he muttered. He frowned at her. "Who marked you thus, child?"

"*Child* is fucking creepy," she said. "I don't know—"

"Mika Renar," I said over her. "Or maybe the little prince, Cal Amir."

"Renar. Devious little bitch." Gottschalk looked at me and smiled. His teeth were yellow and chipped and looked more like fangs. His gums were bright red, making it look like his mouth was bleeding every time he opened it. Like he was chewing off his own lips as he spoke. "This cannot be allowed to pass. The *Tah-namus!* She will destroy us all."

He clapped his hands. "Thomas!" Struggling mightily, he pushed himself up higher against the pillows, panting. "You will stay with me until we resolve this. I must research the glyphs and seek counsel with others—we must be careful! Exceedingly careful!"

The Head Freak reentered the bedroom, smiling like a dope, hands clasped in front of him. "Yes, Master?"

I looked at him. "What'd he give *you*? A piece of broken glass?"

"Thomas, these three will be our guests for a few days. Please see them to the guest suite and make sure their needs are attended to. Bring me the telephone and send in Carol and David. Thank you."

Claire sank back towards me. "I do *not* want to stay here," she whispered.

"You *must*, child," Gottschalk said fiercely. "You are too dangerous to be walking about free. You are the linchpin to the end of the world! More important, you are the linchpin to the end of *me*."

"Well," Claire said in a reasonable, almost conciliatory tone, "fuck you, then."

She turned to leave.

"*Anschlag!* Thomas!"

The Head Freak appeared in the doorway, already slashing his own arm with a large fancy looking blade. Behind me, Gottschalk spoke three syllables, and Claire froze on the spot.

"Whoa!" I shouted, throwing my arms out like an asshole. But Gottschalk spoke Asshole, and I needed to be clear. "No need for this! We came here for your help, Mr. Gottschalk."

I was standing right next to her. She moved her eyes to me.

She was finally afraid.

"You understand," Gottschalk wheezed, sounding like a little shouting had strained the paper-thin walls of every one of his organs. "*You*, yes. Hiram was not a very good student. He had no ability. A plodder. But he respected our traditions, and I believe he has imbued you with similar respect. But *her*. This bitch is not one of us—she is chattel, so marked. I cannot take chances." He offered me those horrible teeth again. "You have a cow, you do not let it roam free. You pen it. Make sure its milk is for you alone."

I looked at Claire again. Her eyes were locked on mine. Pleading. She looked young suddenly. The way she was perfectly still, with just her eyes moving, she was like my girl, the first girl, standing in front of Hiram, shivering so subtly you had to stare at her to be aware of it.

"I vouch for her," I said slowly, my eyes on hers. This was a bad move. I could feel it in my bones. I pictured Hiram's empty bathroom window.

Gottschalk thought it over. I admired Claire's eyes, bright green. The door and hallway outside the bedroom were crowded with Gottschalk's morons. An army of them.

"Very well, Mr. Vonnegan," he said. "Her behavior is your concern, then."

With a few muttered syllables, Claire snapped into motion. She'd been straining against the spell, trying to launch herself free, and crashed into me. I hugged her to me for a second, in case she had any wild ideas.

"We need him," I whispered to her. "You want those marks off. I kind of want the world not to end. We stick."

She turned her head and whispered into my ear. "That motherfucker puts a hand on me, Chief, I'm going to collect that bill from you."

"You say things like that, Claire, and just make me love you." I'd made it flippant, but I regretted it immediately. Claire Mannice was the type of girl, I thought, who'd had soft guys like me following her around, being mopey, her whole life. I didn't want to be just another one.

We followed the Head Freak down the length of the house to a narrow set of stairs. Down to the basement. I didn't like it. I didn't like a damn thing about it the moment I saw it. The stairs were old and unsteady, rattling under us. The basement was cold and damp and had been clumsily subdivided with a cheap, thin wall and a single cheap door set into the middle. The Head Freak—Thomas—opened the door and gestured us through, beaming.

The rooms behind the door could be called rooms in only the most generous usage of the term. They had walls. They had floors. There was no line of sight. They were three connected spaces defined by thin, uninsulated drywall, lit by bare bulbs, and lacking finished floors—the grit of concrete dust bit under my shoes. They *had* been furnished, the first room sporting two sagging, dispirited couches and a coffee table that had recently been used as a chew toy.

"Anything you require?" Thomas asked pleasantly.

"Better rooms," Claire said. "Now get the fuck out."

16.

CLAIRE WAS TALKING ABOUT HER sister. That was nice. Dinner was nice, too. A lot nicer than I would have expected when Tom the Head Freak had arrived downstairs, politely inviting us to share a meal with Master Gottschalk. As the only edible things we'd found in the basement were water bugs, millipedes, and roaches, we accepted.

It was nice to be invited.

The dining room was nice. Impressive. A long, polished table set with silver and china, candelabras and flowers, light dancing around us in glittery clouds that burst as you moved your head, then re-formed. The white tablecloth gleamed, brighter white than I'd ever seen, the thread count pulsing at me, the weave so fine it danced away from your eyes, bending the light. The smell in the air made me dizzy. It was animal fat and seasoning and butter and a million other things that had me salivating, desperate.

Gottschalk was already seated when we entered. He'd changed into an old-fashioned dinner jacket, complete with bow tie, his soured white hair slicked back. He looked nice. Six of his "followers" waited behind chairs, hands clasped in front of them. They all had twitchy little smiles, like they couldn't believe their good luck in being chosen.

The room itself was nice. Wood paneling, with oil paintings hung on the walls depicting wildflowers in bloom. The carpet was dark green and thick, swallowing my feet as I floated over to a chair. It was a nice chair. Sturdy but beautiful. With delicate hand-carved reliefs and soft red satin cushions. It was pulled out from under the table by Gott-schalk's Sucker as I approached, and slid under my ass as I sat. All very nice.

Mags was seated to my right, with Gottschalk at the head of the table to my left. Claire drifted around to the other side and sat across from me, right next to Gottschalk. We were all still wearing our grungy clothes, which made me feel stupid and self-conscious, but Claire looked clean and fresh, like she'd steamed herself in some hidden shower, her face pinked up with excitement, her hair soft and bouncy. She looked like she'd shed five years, becoming the Homecoming Queen in some bizarre off-brand high school. She was überClaire. She smiled at me. That was nice.

"Mr. Vonnegan," Gottschalk said as his white-robed freaks fluttered around us, pouring ruby red wine into silver-rimmed glasses, fruity and tart. The room was too small, I thought, for all these people, yet somehow it didn't feel like it, even as Gottschalk's robed minions shoved me this way and that while they struggled around us, serving and clearing. "I am glad you have decided to join me. We should talk, you and I. I have much to teach you. And first we should each raise a glass in honor of your *gasam,* my student." He picked up his glass and held it as we followed. "To Hiram Bosch: a middling student, someone we both knew."

It was nice. I grinned like a monkey as we all raised our glasses and then drank. I met Claire's eyes and we smiled at each other. That was nice, too. Everything was nice.

The freaks started bringing in dinner. A long stream of them, carrying large plates that they crowded onto the table in front of us. Roasts and soups, chickens and bowls of veggies. Steaming bread and gravy boats joined them, and the room filled with the maddening smell of good food. I turned to check that Mags had not climbed onto the table and thrust his maw into a gravy boat. Based on my lifetime experience with Mags, this was entirely possible.

I started talking about Hiram. It felt like the nice thing to do. Eulogize him a little. Claire, Mags, and Gottschalk smiled at me as I spoke. I told them stories about Hiram's petty thievery. About how he would cast anti-Charms on himself, walk into department stores, strip naked, walk around, and steal new clothes by putting them on one piece at a time, as things caught his fancy. About how he would go into a restaurant and have dinner, walk out with more money than he'd had coming in, his pockets filled with buns and silverware. Everyone laughed. Claire said she wished she'd known him, which was nice.

Mags told a few stories about the beatings Hiram would give him when he was living with the old man. Keeping house in exchange for sleeping on the floor. He never cleaned properly, and always broke things, and Hiram would box his ears. We all imagined round little Hiram chasing Mags around the tiny apartment with a hairbrush and laughed, including Mags himself, hooting with delight at beatings remembered. All very nice.

Now Claire was telling us about her sister, who she'd abandoned at home with her dreaded adopted father and his string of bar pickups. Who was not her real sister but a fellow adoptee. Who was probably twelve now and defenseless against his evening invasions. We all smiled. It was all very nice. It had been two years since she'd spoken to her sister. She dreamed of her constantly and thought she should go home, save her somehow. Kidnap her or kill her adopted father. But she was afraid to. I smiled and nodded, encouraging her to talk. Talking was good. It felt nice to talk. To unload our secrets.

It was nice.

I looked at Gottschalk. Just let my gaze limp over to him. He was watching Claire as she spoke, hands flat on the table. His posture was imperious, but that wasn't strange. Gottschalk seemed like the kind of guy who assumed the world was remade for him every morning when he opened his eyes. That people like me faded away when he left the room and were hastily re-created by imps the second before he re-entered.

I looked down at my nice glass of wine. It was so dark red, the crystal so brilliant. So nice. I didn't drink wine. I concentrated on that. Somehow it was important. I *never* drank wine. So it *wasn't* nice. No one had asked me what I *wanted*. Which wasn't nice, either.

I grabbed on to the tail of that thought. I didn't know why. It felt rude, but I wanted to follow it, see where it led.

Gottschalk was telling Claire that her ordeal had touched his heart. That she should stay with him if she liked. He would protect her. He would care for her. Claire stared at him with glassy eyes, nodding. She looked like she might start crying.

I looked back at my wineglass. So beautiful. So red.

I blinked. Something was floating in it.

I leaned forward slowly. I could hear my own ligaments creaking, could feel the molecules of oxygen and nitrogen pushing aside as I moved. A fly. There was a dead fly in my wine.

I kept my eyes on it. Gottschalk's words were delicious. Persuasive. Something about them was erotic and inviting. They made me want to talk, to unbutton my cuffs and roll up my sleeves, expose some flesh. He was speaking in a continuous, sinuous roll, words overlapping and flowing into each other like cursive script spoken out loud. The dead fly had been dead for some time. The wings had frayed and its body had a blurry, swollen look. Parts of it, I noticed, had broken off and were floating in the liquid. A dead fly in your wine was not nice.

I was being Charmed.

It hit me once, softly, and then a second time like a splash of cold water, and sizzled through my veins, burning away the fog. Gottschalk was a master, a master with a large supply of gas for his projects. I pictured half a dozen of them bleeding somewhere, the next room or above us. And Gottschalk, murmuring his Charm. That seemed like his general modus operandi: Charm them until their brains leaked out of their heads.

I could feel it now. The buzzing in the air like insects on your skin. The gas burning off.

A Glamour, too. A one-two punch. Make us happy, show us bullshit.

The dining room wasn't so nice.

The floorboards were rotted, sagging with our weight, splinters flaking up, ready to be stepped on. The table had at one time been grand but was scratched and warped, the finish worn and deep gouges marring its surface. The walls were covered in cheap wallpaper that had once almost but not quite resembled pine paneling. The air smelled of mold, a sour stench. The tablecloth was plastic, the cutlery plastic. The wine *was* wine, I thought, but Gottschalk had gotten change from a dollar for it.

The food was . . . food. Using the most basic definition. The steaming rolls were stale crackers. The roasts and chicken were cold cuts that smelled to the left of fresh. The vegetables were from the frozen section and sat in their packaging, not even heated. We were picking at them from holes torn in the plastic.

I looked at the soup tureens and gravy boats and wished I hadn't. The gravy was canned stuff, congealed and spooned right from the can into a bowl, spots of green mold on top. The soup was harder to identify. Green, lumpy, *furry.* I had a sense that Gottschalk had set the table some time ago for another group of suckers and hadn't bothered clearing it up. After all, there were such a *lot* of us suckers around.

Claire smiled at me. She had a pretty smile. I thought about the scale of this Charm; people who slid all the way under it would do *anything,* I thought. They'd fuck you, give you money, build you a house, cut out their own kidneys. This kind of Charm was fucking frightening. And Gottschalk struck me as a man who spent each of his days laying on Charms like this. A man who Charmed people just to make them pass the salt.

Charms were delicate, though, as I knew too well. I was tired and thinned, but I had enough gas to ruin this little party. I picked up my glass as if to make a toast, mimicking Claire's dopey smile. Then I smashed the glass on the table, plucked up a wine-stained shard, and cut my palm. It was an ugly, jagged wound that bled fast, and I spoke just three words. By the time Gottschalk had hauled his bulk to his feet, smashed his fist on the table, and shouted that I should *not* cast without his permission, it was done.

I felt the familiar weakness sweeping through me. And I felt Mags and Claire get hit with it, a simple shock that snapped them back to reality.

Claire dropped her wineglass, an expression of disgust crossing her face.

Mags just sagged back, disappointed, as if he *had* actually been contemplating a dive into one of the gravy boats.

"*You,*" Gottschalk thundered. His face had gone a dangerous shade of red. He pointed at me. I kept the shard of glass in my hand in case he made any attempt to cast. I didn't know Gottschalk's style—whether he was fast and efficient or a plodder who garnished his spells with bullshit—but I was ready to hit him with something fast and nasty. Had it ready, another three-word spell. I liked speed; my spells didn't take much gas and didn't do much, really, but I could fire them off one after another. Keep my enemies off-balance. Distracted.

Gottschalk mastered himself. You could see him swallowing anger, though his eyes were blazing, fixed on me. He wasn't disobeyed often. I wanted to tell him he'd been casting on clueless shitkickers for too long. *Enustari,* maybe, but he was sloppy and lazy.

"Leave me," he said sullenly. "I will have a meal sent down to you, yes? I have much work to do. Calls to make. Preparations." He waved as he sank back into his chair. Behind me, one of the freaks began tugging at my chair, urging me up.

Gottschalk glanced up at me again. "You think I suffer arrogance, *boy.*"

I chose not to taunt him anymore. I looked over at Claire. She stared at me, tears running down her face. Shaking with it, her whole body quivering. I forced myself to stare back.

I thought, *We are not good people—but some of us . . . some of us are fucking bastards.*

17 **"MAYBE I SHOULD JUST GET** used to them. If I'm the only one who
    ▪ can see them."

"Sure, just you . . . and everyone else who can see them."

Claire chewed on that.

Mags was prowling the perimeter of the rooms, arms hanging at his sides like a gorilla. We shouldn't have been surprised that Gottschalk had sealed us in with a Ward on the door, but apparently we were that stupid. I was beginning to get used to being stupid, and that was worrisome.

A Ward was just a glyph, similar to the ones painted on Claire. You drew them in blood and spoke a word or two and they locked doors, kept doors open, hid them—whatever your imagination could craft along those lines. Mags had spent an hour and a half banging his shoulder against this one to no avail. He felt trapped. He didn't seem to like the feeling.

Two days in Gottschalk's basement down.

Claire lay on the couch with her legs on my lap. She felt warm and solid, and I liked touching her. She was engrossed in her own breathing, staring moodily down at her chest, and I took the opportunity to study her face. I couldn't see the glyphs without some gas in the air, but Gottschalk had seen them immediately. Hiram had told me once that sort of skill came with practice and concentration, discipline. Then he'd told me I had none of these and kicked me out of his apartment.

We had one casement window for light and ventilation, too narrow to slip through and boarded up on the outside but allowing us a sliver of view. Cars had been coming and going for hours. Expensive cars with drivers. Gottschalk conferring with his fellow *enustari,* I guessed, trying to figure out how to safely remove Claire from Renar's ritual without triggering it, denying her immortality and the end of the world. I didn't like being penned up in a shitty basement in-law suite, but I knew they couldn't kill her without risking a completion of the ritual, so I wasn't too worried.

Daryl hadn't left.

We could see the rear bumper of his truck between the boards. Either he'd been Charmed into service by Gottschalk and was in the process of shaving his head and marveling over a piece of trash gassed up to sparkle only for him, or Mags and I were better with a Charm than we thought and he was out there jerking off over Claire. She had, after all, asked him to wait outside, and Charmed people did amazing things sometimes.

For example, I had swallowed a quantity of dead fly just the other day.

I watched Mags stalk from one end of the room and back again, spin and repeat. When he frowned, it brought his brow down and made him resemble a lower link on the evolutionary chain.

"Tell me about your father," Claire said.

"Not much of a story. Not a bad guy. Drank too much. When he drank, he got this fuzzy, weird way about him, and he'd do amazing things, things he wouldn't remember. Like kidnap me, drive a hundred miles, and pass out at a bar, me in the backseat of the truck." I looked at her. "Why this sudden interest?"

She looked up at me. Right into my eyes. The most pants-shittingly direct gaze I'd ever seen. "I get the feeling you want to fuck me, so I'm getting to know you a little."

I felt blood rush to my face. I looked down at her calves. "Be careful. Mags hears words like that, he gets excited."

"I've been seeing that look since I was eleven," she said, shrugging. "I take steps."

"Tell me about *your* father."

She stared back at me impassively. "He never should have touched me" was all she said, and then silence stretched out between us.

Mags stalked back into what we were generously calling a room. "I see that fat fuck, I'm going to set him on *fire*."

I nodded. "You get turned into a fucking toad for your troubles, Magsie, don't come crying to me."

He scowled at us. "*Fuck.*"

He stalked back out of the room.

"I didn't realize that puppy could get so *angry,*" Claire said, a thin, evil smile coming to her round pink face. "He ever . . . cast something in anger on you?"

I nodded. I was hungry, and my clothes were scratchy. Waiting for the Illuminati upstairs to decide to clear Claire's skin and put Renar in her place was tiring work. "Sure. Little things. All Mags knows are little things."

"But you know bigger."

"I *know* bigger. I don't cast bigger."

"Just what you can do with your own blood."

I nodded.

"Why not? You could do some serious damage out there in the world. Jesus, *magic.*"

I chewed on my cheek. "Even if they say they volunteer, they didn't. They *can't.* They volunteer, but when you . . . tap in to it, you can feel it screaming from them, torn. It's violent. On the outside, they're just standing there, getting woozy. On some other level—a level most people don't have access to, you know?—on that level, it's fucking rape, every time."

She started toying with her shirt, plucking at it with her hands, eyes down on herself. I was mesmerized.

"How'd you end up like this? How'd you even *find out* this shit existed? The whole world doesn't know."

I thought of the old man in the parking lot, floating. "All you have to do is see something and wonder about it. You see amazing things every day and you pay no attention, or you assume there's a logical explanation. All it takes is one time seeing something you either can't or don't want to explain. You start asking questions, looking for things, and you suddenly see it everywhere." I sighed, digging out my dwindling cigarettes and offering her one. "This shit is ancient. The world doesn't know because we keep it a fucking secret, and because it's unbelievable. It's not rocket science."

"More cars," Mags said from the other room.

"You all run this magic shit like the Mafia," Claire said, lighting her cigarette.

I pushed her legs off my lap and stood up, back popping. I walked into the next flimsy room and then into the bedroom, where Mags was crouched by the narrow window, squinting through the slight gap between the warped boards.

"You're not gonna like this," Mags said, stepping back when I tapped him on the shoulder.

I leaned down and oriented myself, lining up the gap. I could see Daryl's truck still sitting there, rusting away. Behind it was a black Town Car, sleek and shiny. Standing in front of it were four men, three very fat, dressed well, obvious Bleeders. The third was slender, and his shoes, shined to a bright gleam, cost more than everything the Bleeders were wearing put together. He was holding a slender brown cigarette in one hand. He wore familiar black gloves.

I stepped back from the window and looked at Mags. "What the fuck," I said slowly, a whisper.

"It's Amir, Lem."

I spun and gave Mags a shove, sending him stumbling back towards the door. "I *know* it's *fucking Amir.*" My heart was thudding in my chest. I couldn't breathe. He cowered, his face taking on the hurt expression of a small pet unexpectedly disciplined. I swallowed my terror and tried to modulate my voice. "Work on the door. Give it your shoulder, Mags."

I crouched down again, but Amir was gone, along with his Bleeders. Behind me, I heard Mags slamming into the flimsy wooden door again, bouncing off and staggering back, like it was made of steel. Then launching himself. Each time he hit, I heard him grind out another "*Fuck.*"

I turned away from the window and Claire was in the room. "What's gotten into *him*?"

"We've been fucked," I said, pacing, pushing my hair out of my face. "Your friend Amir is coming in."

"I thought you said—"

"I know what I fucking *said*," I hissed, rounding on her. I stepped up close. She didn't move except to chuck her chin up, defiant, daring me to touch her. I felt like an asshole immediately—what was I fucking *doing*, trying to scare her? Because *I* was scared? "He's *here*, and we are locked in a fucking basement."

Behind her, Mags hit the door again, grunting in pain.

Claire and I stared at each other. She put her cigarette between her lips. "You got a spell, or whatever you call it, that'll be useful once we get out of here?"

I blinked and looked down at myself and thought. "I got two or three I can probably gas up. Gottschalk and Amir are the problem. Gottschalk's people are fucking cows being milked, they can't do much."

She nodded. "Stay here."

She turned and left the room. I heard Mags slam into the door again. A moment later, she came back, leading a sweating, wild-eyed Mags. She gestured at the wall.

"Stop wasting your time on something you can't open," she said. "They Warded a fucking door. That's like locking a paper bag, as far as I can tell, with the level of construction down here."

Mags looked at the wall, then at Claire, then at me. Then back at Claire.

"Jesus," she muttered, walking over and slapping the thin drywall with one hand. "Throw yourself *here*, big boy."

Mags looked at me again. I nodded. He backed up, panting, sweating, steadied himself, and then launched himself forward. He slammed his shoulder into the wall. Crashed straight through a quarter inch of drywall and disappeared into the hallway beyond.

"Cheap bastards," Claire said, stepping through behind him.

I stared for a dopey second, then got out my switchblade and followed them, the satisfying *snick* of the blade comforting. Rolling up my sleeve, I stepped through the crumbling hole.

The hallway was dim and empty. Mags emerged from the shadows covered in plaster dust and chunks of drywall, a ghost. Claire stepped past him and began walking lightly down the hall towards the stairs, bouncing on the balls of her feet. Mags and I rushed after her.

At the bottom of the stairs Claire skidded to a halt, staring up at the Head Freak, Thomas, frozen a few steps above her. Claire looking up at him from under her brow, fierce, feral. Thomas a little dreamy, not sure what to do. Then she reached up, took hold of his robes, and pulled down as she sidestepped. He was overbalanced and went down like a bag of bowling balls, taking the last three steps hard and landing on the gritty floor with a dull thud. Claire was up the stairs in a flash. As Mags and I followed, I flicked the blade against my arm, shedding a thin stream of blood. Thomas rolled himself over with a groan, his mouth and nose bloody, and I wished I hadn't wasted my own gas as I muttered four syllables, a simple spell I'd silently stolen from Gott-schalk the day before, with one minor improvement.

Thomas froze. Just stopped moving, even his eyes.

It would last only a few minutes. Gottschalk had overcast it, slamming Claire with more power than it needed—she would have been frozen for years in his bedroom. Mags and I stepped over him and levered ourselves up onto the steps, launching into a run. Claire was already out of sight. Running for freedom. I'd noticed she turned into Action Girl any time someone tried to pen her in. Kind of liked it.

I burst onto the first floor and skidded to a halt. Mags crashed into me a second later and sent me careening into the wall. I pushed off, settled myself. Claire was already halfway down the length of the hall, tripping along like she was riding a bubble of air. Two more of Gott-schalk's robed freaks appeared in front of her. Mags and I hurled our-selves in her direction. I raised my bleeding arm, ready to shout another Cantrip, but she leaned down and hit the first one with her shoulder, sending him flying backwards into the second, both of them crumpling into a chaos of limbs and robes.

She leaped over them in perfect form, one leg extended forward like a spear, the other tucked under her. Landed. Kept running.

I wondered how in the world she'd ever been caught in the first place. How the Skinny Fuck had managed the coordination and stamina to even get close enough to touch her. How she'd been held down long enough for Renar to mark her up for the ritual. It didn't seem possible. I imagined Claire casually destroying property as she walked the streets, scowling.

We raced after her. Wasting gas as we ran, blood running in a thin trickle down my arm. I had three or four quick, dirty spells in my head, a second or two to mutter them in a pinch. Dirty tricks, the best kind. As we passed into the living room, heading towards the front of the house, there was an explosion, the floor shaking under me. A bright flash, and then Claire was running *towards* us, sprinting. As she crashed through us, she turned her head to me.

"The scary fuck," she shouted. "Amir!"

Mags and I looked at each other. Stumbled to a halt. Spun and ran after her again.

The whole house was waking up to chaos now. Gottschalk's little morons in their robes were crowding the hall. Claire had stopped halfway down it, cursing and clawing at them. I checked my arm, soaked in my own glossy blood. Raised my arm over my head. Planted myself at the entrance to the hallway. Shouted three words and brought my hand down, palm flat to the floor. Felt the dizzy, light-headed flow of energy from me to the greedy universe, and they all went down, even Claire. Every person in the hall dropped like a heavy weight had smacked them from above.

"Claire!" I shouted. "Go!"

She was up immediately, shrugging off my invisible fist and running over the freaks, and I grinned after her. Mags and I started to follow, but the spell was minor and the freaks were already struggling to stand, clogging the hallway again. I raised my arm again, massaging the wound to reopen it, squeeze a little more blood from it.

I heard Amir's voice behind us. Smooth. Educated. Speaking six words rapidly. He pronounced them differently than Hiram Bosch had taught me, but I recognized them all the same. I clamped my hand on Mags's shoulder and threw myself down, pulling him along with me.

There was a white flash. A second later, a noise that was so high-pitched it was almost not even a noise, just the *idea* of a noise. And then an invisible blade sawed through the air above us, cutting the walls. As if someone had thrown a huge circular saw blade like a Frisbee.

Two of Gottschalk's chosen had regained their feet. Their heads were cut off cleanly, popping up into the air and hitting the writhing floor before their bodies.

I flipped myself around and pushed up on my elbows. Amir and his four Bleeders were there in the living room. Amir was sparkling like an animated character. He was wearing a black suit stained with white Hill Country dust, his fancy shoes dulled and muddy. But he still had that shine. His suit was cut so perfectly to his slim frame, and his haircut was so expensive, no amount of dust and grime could scuff him up. One of the fat Bleeders was a gory mess, blood streaming down from his forehead. Amir must have needed a good gush fast. I brought my arm up again and flicked my hand at them, hissing out three syllables.

Amir had raised his gloved hands, ready to counter me, but he was expecting something big. Fireballs. Lightning. A compulsion so hard it would make his ears bleed—the sort of attack an *enustari* would launch.

But he didn't know my spells. My spells were too small for the great Cal Amir to have heard before. Instead of something big, the floor under their feet suddenly and temporarily turned into glassy ice. All five went up ass over tits and hit the floor hard.

Mags was already on his feet. He was muttering, too, but just "*Fuck fuck fuck*" under his breath. He reached down and pulled me up bodily and let me get my feet under me before crashing forward with a growl into the blood-splattered mess of assholes in the hall and started pushing, throwing them around. Mags was a big boy. Well fed, despite my poor parenting, and Gottschalk's people were reedy and easy to move. He made a tunnel and I followed as fast as I could. The back door was there, leading to the deck sagging on the rear of the house like a barnacle.

I heard Amir behind us. He didn't seem to have an Inside Voice.

I picked out the Words again, adrenaline dumping into my system. "Mags!" I shouted. "Down!"

We hit the floor just outside Gottschalk's bedroom. There was a groaning, rending noise. The back door tore into splinters that shot inwards, a million wooden missiles. Gottschalk's freaks screamed. The whole house groaned, and I felt the floor vibrating beneath me.

Amir started speaking again.

I scrabbled to my feet and pulled Mags to our right, crashing through the door into the bedroom.

Gottschalk jiggled in his bed. He was as papery and yellow as before. He was sitting up, his torso naked, the sweaty-looking covers hiding the rest of him, and thank fucking goodness. Mags and I both froze. Gottschalk stared at us with wide eyes, his tiny hands in loose fists, held up by his shoulders.

His skin was clear and healthy. He was a fucking *enustari* who hadn't cut himself in decades, if he ever had. Two of his followers—his slaves, whatever—stood on either side of the bed, knives in their hands.

"I do regret this," he said. "I did not intend for this. But circumstances beyond my control have changed my position. When Mika Renar knocks on your door, even I must answer."

I stepped partway around Mags towards the window. Slow. Hiding my bleeding arm behind my large, stupid friend. "Fuck you. Bosch was your apprentice. Renar is going to kill *everyone*."

He smiled thinly. "But not me. Not *us*, I should say, as I am not the only member of our order who has entered into this agreement." Behind us, there was another explosion. Amir clearing the hall in the most efficient manner possible. "Ms. Renar and Mr. Amir have brought us *into* the *biludha*. We will also benefit."

The house shook again. A fine dust settled from above. We all paused and stared around dumbly. The groaning didn't stop. The whole place was shaking. When he'd started hurling the Words around like boulders, Cal Amir hadn't bargained on termites and dry rot and decades of deferred maintenance.

Claire crashed into the room, stopping short and windmilling her arms.

"Fuck," she hissed, "this isn't *out*?"

I looked back at Gottschalk. My teeth were clenched tightly shut.

"Lem," Mags said, staring at Gottschalk. "What does he *mean*?"

I made a fist with my bloody arm, then snapped it back towards the bedroom door and barked a single word. The door slammed shut. "It means this son of a bitch just traded every living thing on the fucking planet for his own sad shitsack of a life."

Gottschalk's eyes went to the door and back to me. He opened his mouth.

"Mags," I said, "don't let this fat piece of shit *speak*."

Anger pulsed inside me. Gottschalk, without a scar on his body, fat and useless and running his little freak show, squeezing out a few more years in bed and letting everyone else, all the rest of us, die in his place. Without even a peep of protest over Hiram. Over *me*.

We are not good people. But this was fucking above and beyond.

Mags leaped forward, vaulting onto the bed and clamping his hands around Gottschalk's jowly throat. The old man's tongue popped out like in those old cartoons, a pink ribbon writhing around. His two robed freaks just stood there, dreamy, so fucking Charmed they couldn't even think straight.

There were two noises. A shattering noise coming from the door as something pounded against it. And a wet noise coming from Gottschalk.

I went to the window and tore the curtains down. Pushed up at the sash. It was painted shut, years and years and layers and layers of cheap paint and grime. I stepped back, flicked some blood at it, whispering two more words, and the window exploded outward.

There was another explosion outside, a flash of clear light under the door, and the house slewed to the left, a ragged crack erupting in the wall. The whole house crashing down. I opened my mouth to tell Mags to let the old man linger and get moving.

The door burst inward. Claire suddenly rose up in the air. I made a futile grab at her, but she was sucked towards the window, pulled through without hesitation, screaming all the way.

The air was filled with a terrible moaning sound, old wood held in a complex pattern for decades bending and stretching, yawing and snapping free.

Entropy rushing in, delighted to be home.

"Mags!" I yelled, and the house collapsed. There was a roar and dust and a rafter the size of a fucking redwood smacked down onto the floor next to me, smashing through the planks into the basement, the floor tilting under me. Above, a cracking noise, and I looked up in time to see the roof plummeting towards me.

18.

I CAME TO IN A rush. I blinked on, all systems go.

My head was pounding, a sharp, stabbing pain in my skull with every pulse. It was hot, and I breathed in more dust than air.

I opened my eyes. I was blind.

Not blind. As I listened to Mags, who was chanting something very close to me, I realized it was very, very dark, but as I lay there with my eyes open, the subtle, smudged edges of things slowly coalesced. A panic seized me; I was in an air pocket. Above me was a mass of wood and metal and stone, the remains of the house. I turned my head slowly. Mags was pushed up next to me. He was muttering. The spell was keeping the air pocket from collapsing, holding the debris of the house above us, maintaining a tiny bubble of space for us.

Mags was bleeding from several cuts in his head, a steady trickle. He was burning himself up to keep the air pocket going. As I watched, a thick drop of blood detached from his scalp and disappeared an inch from the dusty floor of our little cave, sizzling away like it had never existed. It was immediately followed by another.

I was bleeding, too. Our streams of gas similar but distinct. I started murmuring along with him, and he stopped. Sucked in air. Shuddered next to me, exhausted. As I cast, I could feel the weight of the rubble above us. Tons and tons. I realized that only a constant push of magic could stop it from crushing us—if we paused for a second, it would overwhelm us. The weight burned away every syllable as I spat it out, and the sense of being drained, of deflating, never ceased.

We were going to die. It was only a matter of time.

I listened to Mags's breathing. I pictured Claire, her expression as she was sucked backwards out the window. She was dead, too. Also only a matter of time, depending on when Mika Renar was ready to put the *Biludha-tah-namus* into motion. I wondered if I'd be crushed in this air pocket first, or if I'd still be muttering spells desperately when the *biludha* swept through, all of us swelling up and exploding into red mist so our blood could be burned off, smashing the laws of the universe itself and making Renar and her conspirators immortal. I wondered if I could time it so we died before the ritual claimed us, so I wouldn't have to contribute to that mummy's immortality.

"I'm sorry," Mags said, panting like a dog. "I'm sorry, Lem."

I couldn't stop casting. If I broke off to say something to Mags, we'd be crushed.

I raised my head a little. Something caught and complained in my back, a sharp pain. I pushed through it and tried to get a good look at our little cave of disaster. There was some light, because I could see, so there had to be air getting in, gaps in the wreckage. It was insane to think we might tunnel out, but I didn't have any sane possibilities presenting themselves. Maybe I'd let Mags catch his breath, and maybe he could cast something on top of what I was spinning, create a tunnel that way, or shift it all away from us. Something. There had to be something. I was not going to die in fucking *Texas*.

I couldn't think how to communicate this with Mags, though, without stopping the spell. I considered the chances he'd think it through on his own. I wasn't encouraged.

I turned my head. Mags had passed out.

I heard Claire on the bus as we talked through the endless Texas night.

"So if you're not going to be some master magician or whatever," she'd asked, quiet and lit by the soft orange glow of the reading lights, "why are you still out there, doing this? Why not do something else? Something you wouldn't have to bleed for?"

"What would I do? Work? This *is* work. This is harder work than most."

She'd shrugged, unimpressed. "What's the point? Do something that matters. Bleed people, but for a reason. Leave a mark."

And I'd replied, feeling smug in my fucking original philosophy of life.

"First, do no harm. I've seen what ambition looks like with mages. It looks like genocide, and human hearts torn out of people's chests on the tops of pyramids, and concentration camps and cults. It looks like wars set off just to feed some fucking ritual. That's what leaving your mark means for people like Renar and Amir, and even Hiram, with his short cons that cost so much fucking blood." I'd stretched and wiggled my toes inside my shoes. "*That's* leaving your mark, with us. So I'm not going to leave a mark. My goal is to get through without anyone knowing I was here."

I'd been good at it, too. Do no harm. Leave no mark.

I hadn't hurt anyone but myself, and there was no fucking sign that I'd ever existed, anywhere. I had seven dollars in my pocket and a single suit of sweaty, crusty clothes. I had holes in my shoes. I had Pitr

Mags. I'd never had a lease or a mortgage. I'd never had a credit card or a bank account. I had a birth certificate somewhere, so there was some portion of the world's forests on my account, but that was it. I'd stolen things. Money, mostly, conned out of Charmed people. Trinkets here and there when survival absolutely demanded it.

I kept murmuring the spell, draining myself to keep our air pocket intact. Sweat poured down my face. I was shivering.

I remembered the girl in Hiram's study. Her doodled-on sneakers. *She'd* been shivering, too. In the span of time between me meeting her and me trapped in the air pocket, we were linked by uncontrollable shivering. And what had I done?

I'd done nothing.

I'd left no mark on her. I'd refused to bleed her like a fucking vampire, I'd told Hiram to fuck himself, and he'd spent the better part of a decade punishing me in tiny vindictive ways. Keeping our bond intact so I couldn't leave the city. Reminding me, whenever I needed help, that he owed me nothing and I owed him everything. Insults and sneers.

And he'd bled the girl anyway. To spite me. To teach me that last lesson, that it didn't *matter* what I approved of or disapproved of. That the universe bled us all. It was a lesson I was just starting to grasp.

I didn't know what had happened to that girl. She'd vanished from my life. But I knew. I knew she'd been bled, over and over again, probably. Paid sometimes, by magicians like Hiram who imagined they were civilized because they dished out a few twenty-dollar bills each time. Or not paid sometimes, by any number of *saganustari* or even *idimustari* who came across her. She was dead by now. Used up, buried in some basement. Or not. Dead all the same. Maybe covered in runes. Left in a bathtub in an abandoned apartment to rot.

I'd never touched her, and she was dead anyway.

I saw Claire, folded in half, hurtling through the window.

My speech was getting slurry, my tongue thick and numb. The rubble above us shifted, raining dust down onto us. Mags sat up with a grunt, smacked his head on a gnarled old header, and flattened again.

"Fuck," he said, mildly. Like he was whispering good morning to you.

I kept slurring the spell. My mouth hurt. My throat burned. I thought it was a great time for Mags to take over again, but instead of jumping in and resting me, he convulsed, throwing his arms and legs up and punching at the ceiling of the air pocket with his fists.

"Fuck!" he shouted, hoarse. "FUCK!"

I shut my eyes and forced myself to speak the spell again. A wave of dizzy exhaustion swept me clean.

"FUCK!"

I concentrated. Moved my burning lips. The end of each syllable fit perfectly into the beginning of the next, clicking into place. Some people never saw it, the invisible way the syllables fit together. Once you saw it, it was obvious. It was invigorating. Once you saw it, you could do anything with the Words. Anything. Some of us just repeated spells. Drew some blood and recited, and they would always be whatever they were. But if you *saw*, then it all made sense, and making up a spell was as easy as ordering coffee. I could do it in my sleep, pluck sounds from the air and feed them to the universe with a bit of gas. My mind went smooth and glassy, and I slumped there moving my lips moving my lips moving my—

I thought about just stopping.

Relief swept through me at just the thought. I imagined stopping. The building crushing us, a second or two of pain, maybe less. Maybe none. Just letting go, going to sleep.

I spoke the spell again.

I saw Claire's expression as she folded in half and flew through the window.

My tongue was swollen and dry. I kept moving my lips. The universe kept accepting my sacrifice. An endless hole with no bottom or purpose, absorbing everything. I thought of the black relief of giving up, just *stopping*, and I thought that Claire would be alone. Truly, completely alone. Abandoned. I spoke the spell again. A gray wave of dizziness filled my brain, and I knew I had one, maybe two more passes in me before it was over. The cold black relief rose up, and I started sinking, and I *wanted* to sink. To be numb, to be blind, to *stop moving my lips.*

I took a breath, intending to hold it. To wait the unpredictable beat of the universe as it judged whether I had *paused* or *stopped*. That final, endless moment.

And then I kicked for the surface.

I opened my eyes and there was Mags, panting next to me. I could feel his warmth, his physical presence. I reached out and took hold of his arm weakly, pulling him ineffectually towards me. I could feel him in the air, his blood everywhere around me.

I kicked for the surface. I sucked in air with a painful convulsive twitch of my chest, and grabbed hold of Mags's gas and spoke the Words, louder. My stomach flipped as I felt his strength flow through me, glorious, awful.

Our air pocket shuddered, inched outward.

Mags turned sharply to look at me, then nodded. He reached over and took hold of me in turn.

I spoke the spell again, hoarse, pulling more gas from Mags, and the air pocket creaked, swelling. I repeated the spell a second later, vibrating with impatience, feeling Mags like he was hooked up to me with wires.

And then, muffled, distant, I heard someone shouting back at us.

"Hello?"

I kept casting. My heart lurched in my cavernous, empty chest, boomeranging around. Mags fell silent. The air pocket suddenly doubled in size, debris raining down around its invisible surface. Mags gasped and his hands tightened painfully on my arm.

"Holy fuck," he said quietly. "Is that Daryl fucking *Houy?*" He took a deep breath. "Hey! Hey, Daryl!"

When Daryl shouted back, he was nearer. "I can hear ya! Keep makin' noise!"

Mags let out a stream of uninterrupted profanity that must have startled nearby birds into frenzied flight. I kept reciting. Instead of the waves of exhaustion, I felt stronger and stronger, pulling from Mags.

Mags kept shouting. For a moment, it seemed like this was how I was going to die: buried alive, Mags screaming at me. Which seemed appropriate.

The house above us was a toy in my hands. I closed my eyes and added three words to the spell, slipping them in perfectly. I felt Mags sag against me, felt him move through me, a golden wave of nausea, and the air pocket exploded outward, timber and drywall and stone flying up into the air, sunshine flowing in.

I spoke again, and it froze in the air. Dust sprinkled down on us. I could hear Mags breathing hard, his breath hot against me.

Then someone was dragging me. I let him. From my back, I watched the frozen geyser of debris as I slid backwards from it, Mags staggering after me. When we were near the truck, I spoke a single word and it all crashed down, like it had wanted. I lay in the dirt for a few minutes, gasping. Then Mags was leaning over me. Then Daryl was there, looking like he'd slept in his truck.

"Why the fuck," I croaked, swallowing painfully, "are you still here?"

He blinked. "Waiting for Claire," he said simply.

The suggestible type, easily pushed. Easier when it involved a girl, certainly.

Head swimming, I pushed myself up onto my elbows. The house was gone. It was a shallow mountain of debris, burning in places. The surrounding gardens and structures were intact. The house had just imploded. A few people in white robes wandered aimlessly out in the fields. Some of them appeared to be running.

I squinted up at Daryl. He looked back at me with a dopey, innocent expression. A moron.

"She's been taken. To New York."

He frowned. "Well, shit. Let's go get her, then."

I nodded. Reached out for Mags. He was there, pulling me up, slipping under my shoulder. Holding me up. I leaned in close to whisper.

"Will you bleed for me, Mags?" I said slowly. It hurt to speak. "I don't have much left in the tank."

He nodded. No hesitation. "Yes, Lem," he said, serious. Calm. His voice a shredded croak, too. "Of course."

I nodded. Looked at Daryl and nodded at him. "Let's go."

It was time to leave a mark.

19.

I BLEW THE DOOR INWARD with a Word. The plate glass cracked with a grinding noise but stayed in place. I walked in with Daryl and Mags behind me, Daryl still in his shitkicker costume, smelling pretty ripe, and Mags bleeding from a shallow wound on his arm. I stood for a moment to let my eyes adjust, then spoke a few soft syllables, and my eyes brightened, bringing everything into sharp contrast. I could feel Mags tethered to me, feeding me. I couldn't feel Daryl, but I could smell him.

Using someone else's blood was terrible. It made me feel like the universe's asshole. But it felt *good,* too. All that power, all that strength, and you just pulled on it and you didn't feel it. It rushed *through* you. But it didn't drain you.

The gloom was the same as always. Ketterly was sitting behind his little desk. Stiff and shocked. I muttered four more Words and burned a bit of Mags's gas, pointing at Ketterly and then dragging him with my index finger. He popped out of his chair like he'd been attached to wire. I flicked my wrist and he slammed into the bookshelves behind him. He winced and gasped in pain. I kept my finger on him as I walked, and he squirmed there as if a battering ram had been planted in his chest.

"Jesus, Lem," he said with difficulty. Hard to breathe with a ton of invisible energy pushing into your chest. "That was fucking *fast*. Jesus. Hiram always said you hadda touch with the Words."

I stopped in front of him, my finger now physically on his chest and pinning him to the bookcase. His glasses had gone askew but clung to his face. A light film of perspiration covered his exposed skin.

"Digs, you sold us out, huh? Gottschalk was all set to save his skin by going against Renar, calling in the troops, and then somehow the old bitch finds us at his little Ranch of Horrors, and Gottschalk changes his tune, cuts a deal. I asked myself: How'd *that* happen? Who might have been keeping tabs on me? Who had I been stupid enough to trust?"

His eyes flicked from me to Daryl. Lingered there a moment in perplexity. Then he looked at Mags. Didn't recognize him, because Mags wasn't giggling. Then recognized him and became terrified, looking back at me.

"I had a choice? C'mon, Lem—Amir came in here with his fucking Bleeders, and you know how that works. Do this thing and we'll pay you off, don't do it and we'll cut your head off." He tried to shrug. Managed just a strange sort of spasm. "C'mon, Lem, what was I supposed to do?"

I leaned in. "You tip us *off*, Digs. You give us the high sign, and we play along." I pressed my finger deeper into his chest. The bookshelf groaned and splintered behind him. He gasped in discomfort. "Now we aren't friends anymore."

"Listen, Lem, listen—I gave her to them, sure, they hired me and I found her. I didn't know she was anything to you. She's marked, she's *property*, for God's sake. They told me you would be okay, they weren't there for you," he hissed.

"That's good. Because if I had a fucking *house* dropped on me and you *knew* it was coming, I'd be irritated. As it is, Digs, we can talk about reparations."

He licked his lips, looked past me at Mags. Still didn't like what he saw there. In truth, I'd told Mags to look mean—his mean face was startlingly terrifying. Like he was going to eat your face while you were still alive. It had something to do with the unibrow.

"This isn't you, Vonnegan," Ketterly said, his face screwed up in a mask of discomfort. "You don't come heavy. You're *idimustari—*"

I jabbed my finger and his voice cut off, his face turning red as his tongue and eyes tried to bulge out of his head. "A friend of mine is going to be ground up into dust so some freak can live forever, because *you put the finger on us.* I *am* coming heavy, Digs. And I can fucking come *heavier*. As in: Right now, right here in this stinking pit of an office, I will fucking *crush you to death*."

I had his eyes locked in. They were wide and crazy, terrified. I felt a godlike exhilaration. I wasn't going to kill D. A. Ketterly. I wasn't going to kill anyone if I could help it. But he didn't need to know that. And that fear in his eyes felt good. I could see how people got addicted to it. To it all: bleeding someone else for your spells, terrifying everyone around you.

All it took was a precise application of will, and you were a Monster God. Like Amir, like Renar. It was easy. I could see that now. It was easier than restraining yourself.

Still, I pulled back. Ketterly sucked in air, nodding. "Sure . . . sure, Lem, whatever you need. Sure." He smiled. Scraping whatever dignity he had left off the floor.

I spun away and he dropped with a grunt. Stayed down for a few seconds on his hands and knees, coughing and spitting. I sat in his chair. It was warm. I looked at Daryl. I'd told him to look mean and, no matter what I said to him, to nod. He didn't look very mean, but he was trying.

"He tries to cast, break his jaw."

Daryl hesitated for one slow-witted moment, then managed a serviceable curt jerk of his head. Ketterly looked from him to me and back, sweat dripping off of him onto the floor.

I considered Ketterly. Decided my little show had him appropriately terrified. You could take the Trickster out of the gutter, but it was always smoke and mirrors, tricks.

"You're still working for Renar?" I asked.

He nodded at the floor. "Freelance shit. They need someone found, someone kept tabs on, they call me. What, am I supposed to tell the goddamn *enustari* to fuck off?"

"You been to the mansion?"

He nodded, pushing himself to sit back on his knees. "I know the place."

"You're going to get us inside without being noticed."

He looked at me. The red was gone from his face. "You don't want to go back there, Lem."

"But I have to."

"Don't make *me* go back there, then," he said. "That place will fucking kill your sleep."

"But *you* have to, Digs. I need a guide, and I don't trust you out of my sight. And if you say no, I'm going to crush you to death." I shrugged. "You see my position?"

I'd run enough cons. I knew how to play a role.

He spun himself around on his knees, an awkward, panting procedure. "I can do better than that. Can I?" He mimed standing up, and I nodded. Marveling. Violence was like a different kind of magic. You pointed it at the things you wished to command. Things happened.

"Listen, you don't need me. I've been there just three times, Lem. In . . . in the basement just once. I'm no fucking good, I can't help you. But I can take you to the guy who designed the place. The Fabricator."

I looked at Mags. He was still practicing his Angry Face and wasn't really paying attention. I'd never met a Fabricator. Hadn't known any real ones still existed. I looked back at Ketterly.

"You're telling me, Digs, that a Fabricator built Renar's mansion.

That a *saganustari* or *enustari* who can make Artifacts made one the size of a house."

Ketterly shook his sweaty head. "Just the basement."

DARYL DROVE. HE DIDN'T like driving in the city. Drove with his hands white-knuckled on the wheel, stiff and bent in the seat. Traffic was light, but I was worried he would either have a stroke or wear out the Charm, suddenly realizing he'd effectively been kidnapped. We could reinforce the spell, but without Claire's physical presence, we'd have to use one of us as the focus, which might have some unexpected consequences.

As he drove, Daryl talked. And talked. He told us about growing up in the Hill Country, football, and German, and how everybody's parents were alcoholics, secretly. All his friends had left. They'd graduated high school and gone to college, and he'd waited for them to come back, but then they didn't. He got a job at the meatpacking place. It was a good job. He didn't mind it. He was bothered how time just slipped past him, though. Waiting for everyone to come home, and then one day he'd realized it had been six years, and Jesus, they weren't ever coming back.

And then he'd thought maybe it was time for him to go away, too, but where? To do what? He figured he could drop a line on some old friends and go for a visit, but then that six years had crept between him and the idea, and all of a sudden it seemed impossible. Besides, his mother was out at the Knopp Assisted Living Facility, and who would visit her if he left?

That summed up the first fifty chapters of Daryl's life, and then he'd taken those fifty chapters and set them on fire, because he'd met Claire and suddenly he knew why he'd hung around the Hill Country so long. Because he'd been waiting for Claire, he just hadn't known it yet.

Mags and I glanced at each other. Mags practically had the word *Mother* printed on his furrowed brow, but I shrugged. Daryl would go home soon enough. I'd see to it.

We crossed the bridge. Into the wilderness. Onto the maze of highways, heading south and west. Ketterly, wedged with Mags in the backseat, gave us steady directions. We ended up outside an old warehouse on a block of old warehouses. They were redbrick buildings with ruined windows of broken glass. There was a lot of untreated graffiti. No cars parked on the street.

I climbed out of Daryl's shitbox and stood stretching my back, looking up at it. "This is where a real live *Fabricator* lives?"

Ketterly dragged something up out of himself and spat it into the street. "This is where I've met him. Running errands. Picking things up for people. Dropping things off."

It was clearly abandoned, at least in the official sense. Squatters, maybe. Drug users. Not a Fabricator, who was basically a *saganustari* or *enustari* who worked with objects instead of spells. Or, more accurately, who embedded spells *into* objects. Most commonly machines nowadays. The mechanical nature amplified the effects, somehow. I'd never understood that part, but then, Hiram hadn't been a Fabricator, and even if he had he wouldn't have taught me.

"All right, Digs," I said. "Lead on."

As we followed Ketterly over the cracked pavement, I considered that I would have to knock him around again if this turned out to be bullshit, which seemed likely. He led us to a spot where a sheet of one-inch plywood replaced a window, leaned down, and pulled it up from the bottom. It was on hinges. From a distance, it looked for all the world like it had been screwed into place. Ketterly held it open as we ducked under, and we were in a cold room of concrete, dusty and unfinished. Another sheet of plywood, this one shaped more or less like a door and oriented with the hinges on the left. It had been spray-painted with a big red X.

Ketterly pulled it open and stepped through. I followed. I stopped. Mags walked into me.

We were in a cathedral.

The ceiling soared above us a hundred feet. Buttresses flew everywhere, and stained glass filled hundreds of tall, narrow windows.

Bright light pushed through the glass, tinting the air inside. Everything seemed hazy, as if there were candles burning somewhere, sending thin smoke up into the rafters.

It was empty. A huge emptiness. My gasp of surprise was echoed back at me, thin and ghostly. Far away, in the center of the cavernous space, was a collection of tables and desks, bookshelves, and filing cabinets. It was lit with a golden light that had no obvious source. Ketterly started walking towards it. I followed him slowly, spinning around.

I knew it was magic. I'd seen amazing things done via magic. And yet something in my mind, some small math processor deep in there, refused to relax, because what was inside the warehouse was impossible. My brain wouldn't let go.

An old man was sitting at one of the desks. He was past seventy, lean and wrinkled, his white hair thin, his hands gnarled. But he looked strong. Like there was a band of steel under his skin, keeping his back straight, his eyes clear. As we approached, he glanced up at us and then down at his work. When we were a few feet away from the desk, there was a roar, and I jerked back as a metal wall like the side of a cage sprang up directly in front of me. I spun in place in time to see three identical walls pop up out of the ground, forming a ten-foot perimeter around us. Instant jail cell: Just add magic.

We could still cast, of course, but I wasn't planning to. We were hoping for assistance, after all, and even if I'd never heard of him, he was *enustari,* and I wasn't planning to get into any battles with an Archmage. Yet. If I could help it.

"Digory," he said, his voice gravelly and hoarse. "As I watched you approach from down the road, I thought you must have good reason for coming here unannounced. But then I could not think of what that reason might *be.*"

"Sure do, Mr. Fallon," Ketterly said, pushing his hands into his pockets. "Mr. Vonnegan here said he would crush me to death if I didn't make an introduction. I believed him."

The old man glanced up at Ketterly again. His gaze lingered for a moment, and then he looked down again. "Very well."

A few awkward seconds passed by. Then Ketterly shrugged and pulled one hand from his pocket to gesture back at me. "Uh, Mr. Lemuel Vonnegan, meet Mr. Evelyn Fallon."

I opened my mouth to say something. Fallon gestured at one of the other chairs strewn about the area. With an earsplitting roar, the cage walls dropped back into the floor. Like I'd been examined and found harmless. I wasn't sure how to feel about that.

"Have a seat, Mr. Vonnegan."

I shut my mouth with a click. Reminded myself that the old man was power. I didn't see any Bleeders, but it wouldn't hurt to play it careful. I stepped up and pulled an old metal rolling chair towards me. Flipped it around, sat with my arms draped across the back. "Call me Lem."

He didn't look at me. "I know why you're here, Mr. Vonnegan. I was sorry to hear of Hiram Bosch's death. That was unfortunate."

"You knew Hiram?"

"I knew of him," he said flatly, and ticked his head towards me. His eyes stayed on the delicate workings laid out on the desk in front of him. They looked like little golden watch gears. "Foolish of him, to challenge Calvin Amir. There was only one outcome of that battle."

I held myself in check. "You did some work for Amir."

He paused. He was thin, and his arms were covered in the typical pink scars, most of them quite old. He didn't have any Bleeders in the place that I could see, but he wasn't cutting himself, either. At least not recently.

"I did work for his *gasam*, yes," he finally said. "Has no one killed Mika Renar yet? Pity."

"You built a house," I pressed.

He sat back with a sigh. Lifted his hands from the table. Turned to look at me. "I did not build a *house*, boy. I created a very large and complex Fabrication. Per custom order. The house was built *around* my work."

"What does it do?"

He turned, glanced at Mags and Ketterly and Daryl in turn, and his mouth moved, like he found them unpleasant somehow. I considered the desk: It was neat. Incredibly neat, orderly, and clean. The man's fingers were smudged with ink as he worked on plans, intricate drawings with millions of tiny notes in something that I assumed was cursive, but his desk was perfect. He bent back to his work. "My contracts are confidential, Mr. Vonnegan. Have you come to contract my services? There must be some trinket or trick I can fashion for you. I make no judgments. I do not sneer at modest projects."

I nodded. "My guess is it's involved in the *Biludha-tah-namus*."

He paused. It was subtle. It wasn't like he'd been waving his arms, jumping around. He'd been picking at the tiny gears, staring down at them intently. But then he froze. Surprised. Maybe horrified; it was hard to tell. Fallon's face was etched out of stone, all deep lines and geometric patterns.

"I'm guessing you weren't invited into the conspiracy," I said, struggling to keep my voice level. "The Conspiracy of Assholes who will come out of this *biludha* immortal. I don't know how many. *Enustari*, every one. Maybe a couple of their apprentices to boot."

He still hadn't moved.

"No invite? Guess they have all the *trinkets* they're gonna need."

He moved suddenly. I was stupid, and slow, and feeling too fucking clever. And he didn't cut himself. Even as I heard him speaking the Words—even as something invisible seized me and squeezed, pulling me several feet up into the air—I stared down at him, searching for a fresh bleed. There wasn't one.

Mags twitched, yanking up his sleeve. Before I could warn him, his knife flashed in his hand. Fallon's eyes flicked over to him, but the old man didn't move. Mags rose up into the air with a squawk and slammed into the far wall. His blade shook free and fell to the floor.

Fear spiked inside me. He hadn't *bled*.

"You shouldn't go around saying the name of that ritual, boy,"

Fallon spat. "Just the *name* has power. I know you are not a mage of consequence—"

"Thanks," I gasped. My lungs felt like they were being held in clamps.

"An *idimustari*, yes? Bleeding for nickels in dive bars and playing pranks. I *build*, Mr. Vonnegan. What do you do? *Destroy*, like so many of us."

I remembered Hiram's education: *Magic is violence, Mr. Vonnegan.*

"You take energy and waste it," Fallon continued. "Dissipate it into the ether for your own lusts and needs. I *build*. I do not worry over how my creations might be employed—it is all the same. People like you—or your betters—commission work from me. I create. They use it to destroy, to waste. It is all the same." He paused and squinted at me. "Where did you hear that name?"

"I heard it from Mika Renar," I said. A lie, but close enough.

Fallon cursed. "That *biludha* would require the murder of thousands. It—"

He paused. Just stopped talking, stared down at the floor. I was wrapped tightly, hot and not breathing easy. A spike of anxiety threaded in around the fear. I had the feeling I'd just convinced Fallon. It didn't make me feel any better.

He turned, and Mags and I dropped back to the floor. I stumbled, staggered backwards a few steps, and found my balance.

"Follow me," Fallon said without looking at any of us.

He started walking towards the back of the cathedral. As he walked, it melted away. The buttresses, the windows, everything just faded, leaving only the tables and desks and an empty warehouse: crumbling, water-damaged brick walls and a concrete floor.

Daryl whistled, low and foreboding. "Daryl Houy, you ain't in Texas anymore."

I gestured at Mags and followed. After a moment's hesitation, Ketterly fell in with Mags. Daryl stood where he was, looking confused, which was fine by me.

Fallon's work area was a maze of desks and tables, chairs and filing cabinets, bookshelves and boxes filled with junk. We passed through it without touching a thing. At a heavy metal door, Fallon stopped, pausing to work a padlock looped through an old rusted chain. He let both drop to the floor and pulled the door open. It led to a stairway. He waited for me to catch up.

"Renar contracted me six years ago," Fallon said as he led me down the stairs. At the bottom was pure, untouched darkness, perfectly black. As he sank into it, he whispered a single word, and a pale blue ball of light appeared in his palm. I raked my eyes over him. He still hadn't bled. His scars were old, ancient, healed. "To build for her a . . . mechanism."

I wanted to ask how he was casting without bleeding. But I thought it might be better if I made myself look smart before I started begging for answers. "A mechanism for *biludha*, right? To set off a controlled chain reaction. Bleedouts in a specific pattern, concentrating and focusing the energy."

He slowed and looked back over his shoulder at me for a second. *Score one for Lem Vonnegan, Genius,* I thought.

"Yes," he said. He was leading us through a tunnel made of perfect darkness. His blue light illuminated only the floor beneath us and a foot or two around. Deep and damp, by the feel. We were in the basement. I fought the urge to hurry and snuggle up close to the old man. "That is my specialty. I create Fabrications that work as *enhancers*. Amplifiers. Capable of combining the energies of multiple sacrifices, of storing energy sacrificed *now* for use in the *future*."

The idea started to come clear in my head. Before I could be brilliant again, Mags beat me to it.

"Like a battery?" he asked, in the tone of an excited kid making a breakthrough. Mags was Frosty the Snowman, though. He woke up each day singing "*Happy Birthday*" and forgot everything that had happened to him the day before.

"Yes!" Fallon barked, turning to face us. There was the faintest hint of an accent in that one excited bark. Something European, maybe Slavic. It was just a speck. "Like a battery. Stored."

"That's how you cast without bleeding," I offered hastily before Mags could make me look dumb again.

"I have *bled*, Mr. Vonnegan," Fallon said, his voice harsh and ragged and suddenly distant. "I have bled more than you. More than you ever will. You have *no idea* how I have bled."

We fell into silence. I imagined offending him and being abandoned down in this pitch-black basement. Wandering forever. The distant sound of that door being chained shut again—where, hard to tell: just an echo far off, maybe. Then you pick a direction and figure you'll walk until you find a wall. Except in the dark, the human mind is wobbly and you end up walking in circles without realizing it. The uniformly gritty floor seemed to be created seconds before the blue light crept up to it, then destroyed behind us, silently.

Finally, there was another door. Another padlock. Another chain. He worked it, the blue ball of light hovering over his shoulder like an attentive pet. He pulled the door open. Stepped aside.

"Enter, please."

I stepped into a dim, small room. There wasn't much light, but I was grateful for it, a dull green glow that was everywhere and nowhere. A simple spell. In my mind, just for fun, I formulated a two-word spell that would replicate it.

It was a storage room lined with the sort of wide, oversize filing cabinets you saw in architectural firms. In the center of the room was a bare metal table, covered in dust.

"I apologize for the security measures," Fallon said, sounding the opposite of *apologetic*. "Many would steal my work if they could."

He moved to one of the cabinets, opened a drawer, and extracted a thick file folder. Mages resisted computers. I had no idea why, but even I hated them on instinct. I wouldn't even wear a digital watch, and I hated cell phones. Mags and I would pick up a burner when the need arose, or steal one. But I didn't like having them. Didn't like touching them. Someone knew why, but it wasn't me.

Fallon could have scanned all this shit in, had a neat stack of DVDs or flash drives. Instead, he opened the file and began spreading out huge schematic drawings, sheets upon sheets of spells. I'd seen the Words written out. There were a variety of alphabets for it. It didn't matter how you wrote them; they were inert on the page. All that mattered was how you voiced them. The pronunciation. The order. The grammar.

I looked at the schematic and froze. It was fucking *horrifying*.

"You built *this*?" I asked without taking my eyes from the plans.

"Yes," Fallon breathed. "It is my finest Fabrication."

He was *proud* of it.

It was clearly designed to be underground. It was a single corridor, really. It resembled a corkscrew, starting off as a wide square, running along right angles until it ducked down under itself, descending ten feet at an angle and then spinning around the four corners at a reduced footprint. It spiraled down to a single small chamber at the bottom.

The outer wall of the corridor was lined with recessed areas. Equipped with restraints. Spring-loaded blades. Sized and shaped for human beings. Its purpose was obvious. You started at the top. Slit a throat. The energy released by that sacrifice triggered the pod next to it. A blade snapped out, slit another throat. And on and on, spiraling down through what had to be hundreds of pods, murdering people as it spun. I didn't know what the number actually was. I didn't count it; that would be too scary. But the machine would be precise. It would be exactly what the *Biludha-tah-namus* required in order to begin its own domino effect. This Fabrication was designed as a spark plug. Mika Renar would murder a couple dozen, a couple hundred, people in three minutes, and the collected energy would be funneled into the *biludha,* which would begin an unstoppable chain reaction of death. It had been done on smaller scales. Kill fifty people to cause an earthquake that kills tens of thousands, soak up *that* bloodshed for an even bigger spell. It had been done on monumental, nightmarish scales in the past. This was different. This was mechanized. Efficient. Bigger than anything I'd ever heard of.

I tore my eyes away and stared at Fallon. He was looking down at his plans rapturously. In love with his own genius.

"I knew it would be used," he said without looking at me. "I knew it would be used for something big, and I knew, since it was Renar, that it would be terrible. But I didn't suspect it would be used to cast the *Tahnamus.*"

My hands were fists at my sides. It was okay to murder all these people. As long as it didn't murder the world entire. As long as it didn't murder *you.*

We are not good people.

I reminded myself that Fallon had a connection to a reserve of blood somewhere that I couldn't feel, couldn't touch. This whole place, I realized, was a Fabrication. Huge. Complex. This warehouse, designed to make him a godling in his own space. He'd shielded it. Others couldn't touch it, somehow. Anyone acted up, a word or two from his thin old lips, and we were doomed.

"I have been in this place for a long time," Fallon whispered, apparently to himself. "Too long. Too long out of the world."

"You have to show me how to get in there," I said slowly. "And how to get out."

And how to destroy it, I thought. *Time to leave a mark.*

He didn't say anything for a few seconds. Just loomed over his own plans and spells and stared down at them. Maybe a flicker of conscience making him momentarily unhappy. "You must enter from below," he said at last, his voice like sand pouring from him. "There is an entrance. It is located in the center of the house."

I nodded. "You have plans of the house itself?"

He sighed. "I do. But they are the official plans, filed with the city, and no doubt only vaguely match the reality. I keep complete records,

Mr. Vonnegan." He rummaged in the file and tossed some folded-up blueprints at me. He planted his fists on the tabletop and leaned forward. I thought he was remarkably fit for an old codger. Toned. Muscular.

"I will—" he said, and then shut his mouth as the soft glow of the light turned red. There was a palpable shudder in the ground beneath our feet, and a moment later, a fine dust rained down on us.

I swallowed sudden fear. "Trouble?"

A second shudder, more dust. His yellowed eyes swiveled towards me.

"Intruders," he said. A third shudder, heavier than the first two, brought chunks of mortar out of the walls. Fallon's dry eyes swiveled upwards. "Large ones."

20.

FALLON BARKED A SINGLE SYLLABLE and the little room was flooded with blank white light, blinding me. He barked another syllable and the door burst open. A second later, the old man was flying through the basement, now lit up like noontime. I grabbed the files from the table and followed after him. It was a cramped space of support columns and cinder blocks. The joists were right above us, an inch above Mags's head. It was nowhere as vast as I had imagined in the dark.

As we ran after Fallon, the whole building shook at irregular intervals, dust raining down on us.

"Mags!" I shouted as we reached the stairs.

"Ready, Lem! I'm ready!"

"Ketterly!" I meant it to mean *Be ready to defend yourself.*

"I'll bleed on this one, Vonnegan!" he wheezed from behind me. "You're better with the Words!"

I took the stairs two by two. I had a second to reflect on the fact that

for the first time in . . . in as long as I could *remember*, I didn't feel like
hell. Because I hadn't bled myself in a while. I was topped up, running
with a full tank. Fallon had already disappeared around the landing. I
wondered what, exactly, I was running *into*. The first time Cal Amir
had come after me, Hiram Bosch had died hurling fireballs at him. The
second time, I'd almost bought the farm buried under an entire fucking house.

I didn't like the progression.

I sailed through the open doorway onto the main floor. Fallon was
at his work area, staring down at a set of security monitors. As we
crossed to him, the floor leaped and rocked beneath me again. Fallon
looked up at us, his face blank.

"*Dimma,*" he said.

There was a Word for everything. I rolled this one around in my
mind. *Monster. Golem.* There were a variety of translations. It meant a
being constructed, as opposed to created or summoned. Beyond that,
specifics were up to the creativity of the mage. They could come in all
shapes and sizes.

The ground shuddered. I assumed this guy would lean towards the
deep end of the size pool.

"How many?" I asked. I started to add, *How big?* but felt the floor
shudder again and decided not to waste my breath. The answer was:
Fucking huge.

"Six," Fallon said, and then stood up straight, closed his eyes, and
began reciting. Casting.

I didn't know how much juice he had in that battery of his, but I
had no way of accessing it. When there was blood in the air, I could
feel it, sense it, take hold, and draw on it. With Fallon, I felt nothing. I
turned and found Mags and Ketterly standing at the ready behind me,
sleeves rolled up, blades in hand. Daryl floated a few feet behind them,
eyes wide.

I spun back, and the wall directly across from us crumbled inward.

Standing amid the sudden rubble was a . . . thing.

It was humanoid. It had arms and legs. A torso. A neck like a stubbed-out cigarette and a head like a gruesome gray potato. It appeared to be made out of stone. A solid single block of stone.

As I stared, it casually flicked aside the remains of the wall and hunched down to step into the interior.

My mind raced. Trying to think of something I could cast that would help against a . . . thing. *Dimma.* The word was hard and dark in my mind. I felt soft and weak. The thing's hands were permanent fists, spheres of rock the size of barrels. I imagined getting hit by one at speed.

Six, I thought.

The *dimma* moved suddenly. Faster than should have been possible. In a swirl of bricks and dust, it leaped into the building, landing a few feet to our left. The whole floor jumped under me. A second *dimma* pushed its way into the hole in the wall.

Fallon threw out his arms and shouted the final word of his spell. The first *dimma* raised one barrel fist into the air over us.

Then Fallon turned into a giant.

He *stretched,* every part of him simultaneously elongated, like an animation. Fallon screamed as if it hurt like hell. Pops like gunshots reverberated through the air as each of his limbs expanded outward, fast and messy. He doubled, then tripled, then quadrupled in size, crowding the roof, twitching and roaring. Sweat rolled off him, crashing to the floor and spraying all of us as the floor shook.

"Jesus!" Ketterly shouted.

"I seen pictures of Jesus, guy," Daryl shouted. "That ain't him!"

I turned to look back. Both Mags and Ketterly were cut, fresh gas welling up from their wounds. My eyes met Daryl's. The poor guy stared at me, unblinking.

"If I die," he shouted, backing away, "tell Claire I was all brave and shit, okay?"

The *dimma* swung its arm down. Fallon leaned in and intercepted it, taking the blow on his shoulder and launching himself into what would be its stomach. Just as he crashed into it and knocked it down, the second *dimma* shouldered its way through the hole. A third appeared behind it.

Mind racing, I spat out the first spell I could remember: thirteen syllables dredged from the inky end of my brain.

There was a flash next to me, and a copy of me appeared. Just light and shadows. Three more flashes behind me, then four more. And four more. That made three copies of each of us. I barked another word, and the illusions scattered, running around the place randomly. The second *dimma* swung laboriously at them as they passed close by, its stone fists passing through without effect. The third one joined in, slamming both fists down onto the floor as the ghosts of Mags and Daryl scampered past. There was a snapping noise. The concrete floor shattered beneath its blow, cracks shooting out in all directions.

A fourth *dimma* appeared. Widened the hole in the wall with an almost casual twitch of its arms. The noise was unbelievable. Every move the *dimma* made was a thunderous scrape of stone against stone. Fallon was screaming, thrown across the warehouse and crashing into a concrete column. It shattered behind him, and he sprawled on top of the stub left on the floor as the ceiling above sagged with a stretched-out, unhappy groan.

"Vonnegan!" Ketterly shouted. "Time to *go!*"

I hesitated. Felt a certain responsibility to Fallon. I'd brought this on him. Braced him in his nifty little Fabricated hideaway, six fucking monsters on my trail. The old man had rolled off the wreckage of the column and gotten back on his feet just as a pair of *dimma* reached him, swinging their cudgel hands in fast crisscross arcs. He danced back, the floor vibrating, and managed to grab on to the nearest one of the creatures. Both hands on its irregular head. Howling, the giant Fallon twisted, and with a report like a gunshot, the head snapped off.

The *dimma* disintegrated. Turned into a few lumps of stone and some dust, falling into a heap on the floor.

Immediately, the second *dimma* on Fallon swung both arms, connecting with Fallon's chest and sending him sailing again. He smashed into the wall, and the whole *building* shook around us. I thought about the odds of getting buried in a collapsed building *twice*.

"Lem!" Mags shouted.

I looked up. Two of our doubles were racing right at us, two *dimma* in pursuit. The frozen expressions on the illusions were awful to look at. Like someone wearing a lifelike mask of me and my idiot sidekick. For a second I couldn't move. I stared at the huge stone bodies loping towards me, my vision jumping and shaking with each impact of their flat granite feet.

Then Mags crashed into me, knocking me to the floor. I felt the breeze as one of the stone monstrosities barreled past us, skidding to a halt in a rain of concrete chips. We both rolled onto our backs and a scream escaped me, my vision filled with the cracked, veined torso of one of the *dimma*.

Praying that one of them was still bleeding, I shouted the first spell that came to mind. Felt the power surge through me, and the huge stone man shot upwards, smashing against the rafters far above us and shattering into dust.

Ketterly and Daryl were there as stone rained down on us. "Time to fucking *go*," Ketterly hissed, pulling me up by the armpit and dragging me towards the door. I caught a glimpse of Fallon, beset by three of the things, swinging a hunk of concrete in front of him like a club. Even supersized, he looked old. Tired. Already beaten. Not my problem. At the last second I stopped short of the exit and spun around.

"Fallon!" I shouted. "Cut and run! Come with us!"

He jerked his head halfway in my direction, then shook it.

"*This*," he boomed, his voice as huge as he'd become, deep and painful and audible over the noise of the *dimma*, "*is my* house!"

He renewed his attack on the nearest *dimma*. I watched for another heartbeat and turned and ran.

They were all already in Daryl's truck. Our pet hick was shaking, eyes white and wide as he fumbled with his keys, dropping them on the floor of the cab. As I crashed up into the seat, practically in Mags's bloody lap, I snarled two words and the engine roared into life.

"Go!"

The ease of throwing the Words around—of being able to cast without feeling the drain, without paying the price—was intoxicating. I imagined a life without the minor annoyances. Everything solvable with a few words. I pictured Gottschalk swathed in sheets, a man who hadn't gotten out of bed in years.

Daryl slammed the truck into gear and it leaped forward, throwing us back into the seats. Behind us, I heard something almost like an explosion. A rain of pebbles scattered across the roof and windshield.

Then it was just the inky, silent night and the buzz of the engine. I could hear all of us panting. I could hear the grit of the tires on the pavement. I could hear the tap of Daryl's ring on the steering wheel as his hands shook while he drove.

"Jesus fucked," Ketterly finally whispered. "What in hell is going on?"

I swallowed dust. "They're going to fucking end the world," I said. "I told you." I turned to look at him. "If you're going to murder everyone, there's no point in *subtlety*, is there?"

"Lem," Mags said quietly. "Lem, what do we do now?"

I turned to look forward. "I don't know," I said. "But I know how to find out."

21.

THE YELLOW-AND-BLACK POLICE tape barring Hiram's front door wasn't a problem. The unmarked police cars right out in front of the building and in the back alley were.

I was surprised to see them and stood for a moment in the shadows, nonplussed. I wasn't used to cops giving two shits about me or mine. People like Hiram and me, to the rest of the world, were seedy assholes. They could smell it on us, the short cons, the desperation. The cops hassled me plenty, but that was it. The idea that they might take an interest in Hiram's death amazed me, and then I remembered the two cops who had died: Marichal. Holloway. The rest of the city might burn to the ground, but the cops were gonna keep a team sitting here just in case.

I didn't worry about it. There wasn't a problem that couldn't be solved with the application of enough blood. I didn't have to hesitate, to take stock of my physical condition. I didn't have to worry about the last time I ate or whether I was going to pass out before completing the spell, causing an explosion.

A glance at Mags and he was bleeding.

I made up a spell on the spot. It was easy. Some of us had to memorize spells, could cast only what they'd committed to memory. The real trick was to memorize small things, then link them together. If you knew one Cantrip that bent the light and another Cantrip that fooled the ears, you could put together any sort of illusion on the fly just by changing a few words. Quick and dirty. Hacking, Hiram had called it. But it could be complex and elegant, too, if you worked at it.

I cast and felt Mags's life passing through me, gloriously repellent.

"Come on," I said, and started walking.

We passed right in front of the car. The two cops inside stared through us.

At the crime scene tape, I nicked my own thumb and gave it fourteen syllables, and Mags and I stepped through without breaking it. Fourteen syllables, but the spell didn't cost much, and I barely felt the drain. I was high-energy anyway, topped up. I thought maybe my body had created *too much* blood, running on overdrive because it was used to being in a state of emergency all the time. We could have just torn them down, because what did I care if the police returned, sniffing around endlessly because two of their detectives were dead? But I was getting back into the swing of longer spells. More complex spells. I was remembering bits and pieces of things I'd learned along the way. Things from Hiram. Things from other people. It was like flexing muscles.

The door fell inward when I pushed on it. Just leaned back and sent up a cloud of soot when it landed. I was glad I'd told Daryl and Ketterly to go back to Ketterly's office and wait it out. I didn't want strangers in Hiram's home.

The apartment had burned for a long time. The windows were all shattered, and the weather had been getting in. The floors were a sticky mess of black mud. Wallpaper still clung to the walls, peeling slowly like dying leaves, drooping towards gravity. The whole place smelled like smoke. It was choking. Almost like a syrup diffused into the air.

"Fuck," Mags breathed, then spasmed into coughing.

We walked through the place slowly. The kitchen was the least destroyed. The table and chairs were still there. The wall shared with the living room was blackened and bubbled, but the wall shared with the hallway outside and the exterior walls were all intact. The cabinets and appliances still sat in their usual places. The room felt dead. There was no power. It was dark. Freezing. All of Hiram's forks still in his drawers. His dish towels folded on a shelf. Microscopic layers of Hiram himself smeared onto the walls, the floors. Microbes of him, carbonized, in the air. A film of grit lay on top of everything, damp and muddy. The chairs and table were still in the positions we'd left them in, chaotic and . . . out of place. It felt like we were walking into some sort of spell, frozen time, everything held in place. Like if I gave a chair a shove, it would remain stubbornly in place or sail off without gravity, in slow motion.

"*Fuck,*" Mags hissed.

We made for the study. Everything else had burned. There were charred fragments of things everywhere, melted globs of things. Some of the shelves still clung to the walls, unfamiliar shapes bumped along their wobbly, heat-warped lines. I stopped and looked around. All of Hiram's shit. Every bauble he'd stolen, every carving he'd gotten in payment for some tiny scam, every small Artifact he'd commissioned, had been destroyed. Eaten up by Cal Amir.

Who certainly had not considered for even a moment what it was he might be burning.

On the floor, I found the hard black sphere Hiram used as a worry stone. Unscathed, gleaming with the same polish, perfect and eternal. I picked it up and held it in my hand, feeling its perfection, its weight. Then I set it back on the floor carefully, in the same spot.

I stepped into the small closet office. It had been burned to ash as well, a damp mess. The carpet still clung to the floor like some sort of stubborn life form. I knelt down and tore at it, getting the soaked, sticky weave stuck to my hands, under my fingernails. My freshly cut thumb sizzled with irritation. After a few minutes, I'd revealed the top of the floor safe embedded there. No physical lock but several layers of magical Wards laid on it, including a Glamour that made anyone not aware of its exact location simply not see it.

Even as I squatted there, if I turned my head, it disappeared from my peripheral vision.

Amir hadn't come back. I imagined after the appearance of Claire right in front of him, the adventure with the cops, and then the hurried trip south to deal with us, his original mission at Hiram's had slid down the list of priorities.

"Mags," I said, my voice tight and scratchy. "You ready?"

"Fuck it."

I closed my eyes, gave him a second, and recited twenty-four more syllables. Six to deal with the Glamour, just because it was irritating me, bending the light back into its normal path; in effect, two spells existing at once, which was the oldest trick in the book. It took more blood and more words and more trouble to *remove* a spell than it did to just *negate* a spell. Four syllables for the first Ward, six for the second, and four more for the last, each group of Words appended to Hiram's spells—which was the other trick, *altering* the existing spells instead of trying to undo them outright. Like a virus. I opened my eyes and yanked the lid off the safe. It was fire-rated and looked to have survived in good shape. It was deep. It looked like Hiram had simply dumped things into it without any attempt at organization. There were packets of papers with spells scrawled on them in that skinny, unreadable handwriting, his personal cipher. Unmarked boxes that were heavy and warm as I pulled them out. Dozens of trinkets—charms and other Fabrications. Two thick wads of cash in rubber bands. And then, buried under the rest of the trash, the sliver of oily green stone attached to a leather strap.

"Hiram," I muttered, "you thieving bastard."

I lifted the *Udug* by the strap and leaned back on my feet, holding it up in front of me. It had the same wet look. My skin crawled. Years ago, maybe centuries ago, some Fabricator had spent a lot of blood to create it. That kind of energy was never *good* energy, and it somehow got stronger as time went on, amplified. Hiram had discussed the phenomenon with me back when he was trying to teach me. He had no explanation for it. But I'd understood immediately. There was suffering tied in to everything we did. And suffering *lingered*.

I looked around, tears stinging my eyes. There had been moments over the previous years when I'd wished for nothing more than to be free of Hiram and his stupid, claustrophobic apartment, his ridiculous stolen trinkets, his endless condescension, and his violent temper. But now I had lost it all.

I stared at the floor. I'd lost this place. It had been my home. Even after I'd left it, Mags and I had never had anywhere permanent to live. We'd roamed. We'd slept on the streets, in cars, wherever we could squat, surrounded by Normals and always on our toes not to tip our hands, not to reveal ourselves. You couldn't rest like that. At Hiram's house you didn't have to pretend, and it had never stopped being my home.

I'd lost Hiram.

I'd never expected to miss the fat old asshole, but I was suddenly filled with an aching, yawning chasm of regret. I would never hear his booming actor's voice again. I would never watch him steal a glass fig-urine from a shopwindow. I would never get to tell him what a prick he could be.

I would never get to apologize to him. I would never get to show him what I was finally able to do.

I looked down at the *Udug*. And I thought I was about to lose even more.

"Mags?"

"Yeah, Lem?"

I swallowed hard. "Let's go get a drink."

IT WAS A DINGY place. Filled with old men. Serious about their drink-ing. Mags and I found a table in the back, in the shadows. I had a double, then got another, which I let sit untouched. I dropped the *Udug* on the table between us and stared at it. It seemed to absorb all the light. It seemed to be sinking into the wood, like the necklace was the heaviest thing in the universe. Like it was bending light around it.

I didn't feel the first drink at all. I took the second one and held it up. "To Hiram. A fucking asshole, but *our* fucking asshole."

Mags looked miserable. He lifted his own glass. "To Hiram," he said.

I swallowed the second drink. Felt nothing. I stared at the *Udug*. Remembered its slithery voice in the Skinny Fuck's mind. Whispering. Maybe the worst thing I'd ever heard in my life, and that had been an *echo,* a memory from a dead man.

"Don't do it, Lem," Mags said.

I shook my head. "I have to. They could be starting the ritual at any moment. Might have *already* started it." I didn't think so, though. I thought when a spell of that magnitude started cranking, every mage in the fucking world would feel it. Hundreds of us, spread thin across the globe, stopping in our tracks and looking up. *Feeling it.* Feeling the world being murdered. "All those women. In that . . . thing Fallon built. Going to be killed. And we can't even know where she is in the fucking queue, even if we were willing to just let a few dozen people die."

"We have the plans to the place. We don't need that fucking thing to tell us."

I snorted. "What, you, me, and Daryl are going to drive up there, sneak in, and . . . what? Just fucking *imagineer* our way through?" I shook my head again. "If we had time, Mags, sure. If we knew when they were going to start the *biludha*, we could take our fucking time. But we don't. We need to know what to do right now."

I wanted another drink. It wouldn't do me any good. I had a feeling I could drink a whole bottle and still sit there rock-steady sober.

I couldn't do it alone. Alone, I had Mags and Daryl and a truck and maybe D. A. Ketterly. And maybe not Daryl and his truck, if the Charm he'd been operating under faded away. That had turned out to be the record-setting Charm of all time. I suspected it had something to do with the glyphs on Claire's body, which Renar had said affected spells, bent them, deflected them. Poor Daryl was the recipient of an unintentionally aggressive Charm, and I was starting to wonder how much work—how much blood—it would take to set him free.

That was low on my to-do list, though. I wasn't going to drive up to Mika Renar's house and take on her and Cal Amir, two *enustari, without some kind of game plan.*

I thought of Claire. Her legs pressed against me. The smell of soap on her skin. Pictured the cops in their car, strangled.

I thought of Renar. Her mummy body. Her beautiful Glamour. The smell of rot and time in her study.

I swept my eyes around the bar. All of these people. Me and Mags. Dead.

I thought, *They killed Hiram.*

I thought, *They will kill me.*

I reached for the *Udug.* Mags snapped out his arm and grabbed my wrist. Held it there, an inch above the table.

"Let me," he said. "Lem, I'll do it. Tell you what it says."

For a second, I wanted to hug the stupid bastard. I wanted to bundle him up in my coat like a shivering puppy and put him on a fucking bus to somewhere else with a note pinned to his coat asking someone to take him in and feed him. I pictured a Pitr Mags with the stone's dry, toneless voice burrowing inside his brain, and wanted to burst into tears. And panic.

I snaked my other hand around. "Can't let you do that, hoss," I said, and picked up the *Udug*. Wrapped my hands around it and closed my eyes.

The voice started whispering in my head. Midsentence, as if it had never stopped.

22.
ENEMIES AT THE GATE FOLLOWED *you kill you out of sight leave get out upstairs fire escape rusted it will hold go now go now go now behind the bar clipped is a shotgun it will misfire she is terrified of death of what awaits her of the darkness she wears the red dress in order to*

I dropped the *Udug* with a wince. The voice was exactly like I'd heard it in the Skinny Fuck's memories, except clear. Perfect. Like a snake had wriggled into my brain and lay against my eardrum. It had no tone. No inflection. It spoke continuously, without pause, without breath. It was like having someone whispering wetly in your ear. I looked at Mags. His face was a mask of concern. As if I were engulfed in flames only he could see. The voice was like listening to cancer, but I *wanted* to listen again. I picked up the leather strap instead and held the *Udug* so it dangled between us. I got to my feet. "We need to go."

"You okay, Lem?" he said, scrambling up after me. "What'd it *say*?"

I forced a smile. Mags needed petting. "I'm fine," I said. "Listen—as long as I don't overdo it, it's fine, okay? That guy, he had this thing with him for a long fucking time. Forever. Had it against his skin constantly. I won't do that, okay?"

He nodded slowly, eyes wide. I had to manage Mags. He would

think tackling me and knocking the *Udug* out the window would be *helping* me.

"Upstairs," I said, gesturing at the dim rear of the bar, where a slender chain stretched across a narrow set of stairs. A sign was attached to the chain: EMPLOYEES ONLY.

He followed me towards it. We moved at a normal pace: no rush, no hesitation. People picked up on the unusual. On the sudden, on the overly careful. When walking brazenly into an area you were clearly not supposed to be, the best way to do it was to act like you owned the place.

"Why?" he asked.

"We were followed. Someone means us harm."

And he accepted that. I added that to my thought catalog of Mags's talents: He could just accept things. It was a more powerful skill than you might expect.

I stepped over the chain and started up the stairs without looking back. The gloom closed over me immediately. I heard Mags making a mess of it, getting tangled in the chain. Then the moan of the old steps under his weight. Then someone down below, shouting, surprised. I started to run.

At the top of the stairs was a door. It was unlocked, and I stepped through it into a small, crowded office. Two windows behind the desk. I jumped up on top of the desk and then down onto the floor behind it. Moving fast, I pushed the bottom sash of the left window up. Leaned down and through and pulled myself out onto the rusted, vibrating fire escape. Stood aside to let Mags join me. Voices behind us. The landing shimmied and bucked under our weight. I leaned out over the railing. Scanned the alley up and down. Didn't see anything.

"Come on."

I started down. Halfway to the street, I began calculating the drop because the fire escape was shaking so badly, rusty flakes raining down on us. My hands turned orange. Down on the damp blacktop of the alley, I had a flashback. Watching the cops drive away from Hiram's.

The brake lights. Amir, Claire. Mags's stupid fucking bird Glamour, lighting the place up for one crucial second.

I moved my hand along the leather strap, worrying it until the *Udug* was in my grasp again.

left not the street they wait are patient back door of restaurant always open the dishwasher sells pills lovely pills many colors sells them out the back door for cash for blow jobs for favors owed the cooks spit in the big bowl of fried rice constantly a joke she sees the red dress in her dreams she sees what she thinks of as hell she has no regret but fears fears fears the other thinks of you she wants you to rescue her and thinks how she will reward you you must avoid the church you must not

I let go and felt drained, as if listening took physical energy. Instantly, I wanted to put my hand back on it, find out what else it was trying to tell me. "This way," I croaked, turning left.

At the end of the alley was the back of Happy Garden, a Chinese joint I'd never eaten at. The back door was open, a greasy screen door the only barrier. The smell was simultaneously good and sickening. We stepped through a tiny tiled room with two mops and slop buckets sitting on the damp, muddy floor, and then we were in the kitchen. Three men in stained white smocks stared at us as we moved through the steam. I stared at the big bowl of fried rice as we passed it.

No one paid us any attention in the restaurant proper. We emerged from the kitchen, walked through the largely empty dining room, and were out on the street in seconds.

I started to clasp my hand around the *Udug* again and then snatched it back. Turned left on impulse and started walking, Mags panting beside me, tongue out, tail wagging.

"Where are we going?"

I didn't know. I wanted the *Udug* to give me information, but I thought back on my experience reliving the Skinny Fuck's life and realized the *Udug* was difficult to steer. To control. It told you things, addressing pressing needs first, but it gave you a lot of unrelated information along the way. Information that might be useful, but you had to pick out the immediate stuff from the stream. I didn't want to have the demon whispering in my ear all that time, giving me directions. The whispering was horrible, like having an ant in my brain, tunneling. But I wanted to listen. It was terrible, and I wanted it.

But I had no time.

I closed my fist around the *Udug*. It was slimy against my skin. It was warm and comforting. I almost imagined it moved.

they are waiting word is out Rue's Morgue your name is on their lips they are waiting waiting the warehouse on the left left left second floor green bag forgotten fifteen thousand in diamonds Harry Miller will kill his daughter tonight many worlds many versions but she is unique now the last of them the last of them all a man in Topeka hates you goes to sleep thinking of you she is waiting she regrets letting the night go without touching you, your father is

I snapped my hand open.

"Jesus," I croaked. My heart was pounding. I wanted to clutch the *Udug* against my chest, listen to everything it had to say. I wanted to throw it into the fucking river, watch it sink. Let it whisper its secrets to the fish.

"Lem?"

I looked at Mags. I hadn't realized I'd stopped dead in the middle of the sidewalk. People stepped around us, staring. I put my hand out and found Mags's shoulder.

"Rue's," I said. "Let's get another goddamn drink."

WE STEPPED INTO THE familiar smoke-filled front room of Rue's Morgue and there were people around us immediately. Hands on my shoulders. Gently pushing. I was guided to a table and lowered into one of their unstable old wooden chairs. A tumbler of whiskey was set in front of me. Old Neilsson sat down across from me as Mags was dropped into the chair next to me.

I blinked at the old bastard. Anxiety ate up my stomach and I looked around carefully. Thought about my blade, about Mags. Wondered whether we'd be able to get some gas going if the old fuck wanted revenge.

I looked back at him and smiled. Spread my hands. "Neilsson!"

Letting my mouth shut with a click, I realized I had nothing else. No plan, no golden words.

Neilsson leaned forward. He was a thin, ancient fuck, with thick, bushy white hair turning yellow on the edges. Yellow fingers from years and years of cigarettes. Scars on his face, on his arms, hands—everywhere, I knew. When Neilsson finally kicked off, the coroner was going to have one for the books. A big nose that hooked down. A wide, wet mouth. Bright blue eyes that had lost nothing in clarity and power. When he was sober, Neilsson could cast a Glamour better than anyone. Could con the balls off a bull.

When he was sober. I looked him in the eye. He was sober now.

"Is it true?" he asked.

I blinked at him. "What?"

"Jesus! 'What?' he asks!" Neilsson said as someone placed another tumbler of whiskey in front of him. He ignored it. This told me that this was a serious meeting. This was important business, if Neilsson was going to let a drink sit in front of him. There was a rumble of noise through the crowd.

Neilsson reached up and produced a cigarette from his ear, where I would have sworn none had been. Held it between two gnarled, stained fingers. "Renar, kid. Mika Renar and her pet, fucking Cal Amir. The *Biludha-tah-namus*. Is it *true*? Jesus, we been *looking* for you two bastards."

I blinked. "You heard about—"

He pounded one fist on the table. "It's everywhere. There's panic in the streets. Shit, boy, look around—every mage in the goddamn *city* is here. War council."

I twisted around. He was right. I didn't know all the names, but I knew most of the faces. Men and women, Tricksters, all of us on the hustle. Some had *gasams*, some were solo. Some bled others, some were like me—or like I had been—and only worked their own gas.

Turning back to Neilsson, I reached for the glass. No one of consequence. No *saganustari, no enustari*. Just Tricksters.

I drained the glass and placed it carefully back on the table. Without looking up, I nodded. "It's true."

The room exploded into noise. Everyone talking at once. They
knew what it meant. The end of the world, the end of the *living* world,
so that Renar would live forever. The end of *them*, which was the real
point.

Neilsson shouted them down with an old drunk's authority, waving
his arms. When he had quiet, he looked back at me. "What's being
done, kid? Why aren't the big shots on the march? Jesus, this crazy
bitch is going to kill us all, and there ain't a *saganustari* anywhere in the
fucking city, far as I can tell. Where's the fucking cavalry?"

I told them. I told them about Gottschalk. About the meeting in
Texas while we were locked in the basement, a deal being made. The
goddamn Illuminati dealt in, Renar cutting them in on the ritual so
they could all live forever. I told them no one was coming.

Neilsson took it in. The room fell silent like it was all part of the old
man's brain, ruminating. Then he nodded once, decisively, and leaned
forward.

"We're in."

I blinked. "In what?"

"You're going up there, right? You're going to throw a wrench into
the business? We're in. We're *all* in. This is our fight as much as it's
yours. Fucking mages looking to put us all in the ground . . . We got to
put them in the ground *first*."

I stared. Looked around. Grim faces. Serious faces. Even Mags
looked moved, wise, like a man who had seen death peeking around
the corner but had opted to not alter course. I understood why they
thought this mattered, why they thought a room full of fucking small-
time grifters with a spark could go up against Mika Renar and Cal
Amir and every other *ustari* of any caliber. Because I had the same
feeling. We had nothing to fucking *lose*.

"Is this it?" I said by way of due diligence. By way of making them feel it, understand it. "Not a single *ustari*, huh? Anyone with a whiff of power, sitting at home tonight, blue balls waiting for immortality to light them up? Just us freaks, then."

A soft ripple of laughter swept through the crowd. Then a tall old man shouldered his way from the rear. He looked like he'd been in a fight and lost. His lined face was purple and yellow. His hands, long fingers and big, gnarly knuckles, were scabbed all over. One front tooth was just a bloody shard.

"There's me," Ev Fallon said softly.

23.

WE WERE FORMING AN ARMY of Assholes. The *Udug* reminded me of this every time I touched it.

In a fit of collective insanity, I was the general of the operation. By virtue of being the only one of us aside from Fallon to have any direct experience with Renar or her house. And because all of a sudden everyone thought I had ability. Everyone quoted Hiram. Hiram telling everyone, apparently, that I was a bitter disappointment to him because I had a gift. I had a way with the Words. I could whittle any spell down to a quickness. But I wouldn't bleed people.

Only now I was bleeding people.

I sat in the back room of Rue's. A bottle of single malt, a thick glass tumbler, and an ashtray on the table in front of me. Pitr Mags overflowed a chair, leaning against the wall behind me. Asleep, it seemed. Mags had a talent for looking asleep. It was part of the protective coloring that had kept him alive this long despite his congenital idiocy.

Ketterly had floated in with Daryl. All the grifters had taken pity on Daryl, who was still pining for Claire with the adolescent kind of stoicism that inspired soft looks and affectionate petting. Me, I was keeping my eye on the boy. The glyphs on Claire were one possible explanation for his ongoing devotion, but I was beginning to wonder if Daryl was the sort who naturally fell in love with tall, leggy girls with short dark hair and a few homicides under their belt. Hell, I thought, that described me, and no one had Charmed me into anything. I didn't know exactly why the thought bothered me—that if we took the Charm off, he'd still be mooning about with a bouquet of fucking flowers in one callused hand—but it did. I kept reminding myself that just because I could cast an anti-Charm on him without having to bleed for it didn't mean I *should*.

It was getting harder and harder to remember that.

They came one after the other, offering up their services. I was dividing them into Bleeders and folks who had some skill, some tricks that would be useful. When I needed a little help, I pushed my hand into my pocket, where the *Udug* was strangely warm, and touched it for a second or two. It told me something about the person in front of me, then kept trying to say something about Mags.

she has forgotten a spell you will find useful yes you must push her hard to remember the horses remember the horses the penthouse in Shanghai the tiny boxes with people inside them Pitr Mags is

I removed my hand every time. I didn't want to know. I didn't care if the end of the sentence was *going to stab you in the face*—I didn't want to know.

Every time I touched the *Udug*, my heart pounded in my chest, my hands shook. I hated it. But it was getting easier to tolerate and easier to guide. It was all about willpower. You had to concentrate. You could force it to stay on subject. But the second you slipped, the second you lost focus, it veered off and started whispering about something else. It told me where fifty thousand dollars was buried out in Queens. It told me which women I knew would sleep with me if I asked. It told me about women I *didn't* know who would sleep with me. It told me Neilsson was already halfway to drunk and would be passed out within two hours, and that I could not trust him. It told me that the winning lottery numbers tomorrow would be 34-5-7-19-23-1 in the state of Rhode

Island. It told me the winnings would be six and a half million dollars. It circled back around and told me where my father was. It told me he hadn't thought of me in six years. Not even a thought.

I nodded at the woman sitting across from me. The *Udug* hadn't told me what, exactly, her spell was. "You're in," I said, reaching for the bottle. "Remember the horses."

She froze, halfway out of the wooden chair. She was a beat-up old battle-ax. Bleached, wiry hair. A layer of makeup that would defy most modern tools. She was wearing too many coats, though the precise number was mysterious. Her mouth had the perpetually wet look of badly fitted dentures. But the *Udug* had told me she had at least one useful spell, so she could keep her sleeves rolled down.

She stared at me for a moment, startled, then turned and shuffled back to the main part of the bar.

As she left the room, a kid was sauntering in. I hated him on sight. Sixteen, seventeen, all pimples and swagger. He smirked at me as he dropped into the chair across from me, and it made me feel mean.

I put my hand on the *Udug*.

jimmy marbles they called him jimmy marbles he masturbates three times a day thinks no one knows everyone knows all the people in his building he forgets to close the shades ask him about the dog ask him about Boogie where's Boogie where's Boogie

I lifted my hand. I didn't want it to tell me he knew some amazing old spell, time travel or nuclear holocaust or something. I smirked back at him, feeling mean.

"Tell me about Boogie," I said. "The dog."

The transformation was instant. His smirk dripped away, leaving a hollowed-out stare. He sat there, visibly shaking, then stood up and, without a word, turned and left the room. I watched him go, triumph souring into anger and regret. What the fuck had that accomplished?

But it had felt good.

This was becoming a mythmaking session. No one but Mags knew about the *Udug*. To everyone else, I was becoming more messiah-like with each passing moment. I could see the long con: Using the *Udug*, I would know things. Just *know* things. Combine that with a few easy tricks, a couple of *mu* that were more flash than substance, and I could build up a following. A cult. Throw in a few dedicated Bleeders, I'd be rich. An *ustari*—maybe even *saganustari* if I learned a few big spells. And I could learn big spells. Hell, I could *write* big spells.

I wouldn't be some fat asshole like Gottschalk or a fancy dandy like Amir. I'd bring everyone with me. A rising ship and all that. All these Tricksters, I'd bring the circus along for the ride. My court. I saw myself, hotel to hotel, first-class everything. Me and Mags and Claire and room service and limousines and one day Renar sends a note, asks for an audience. Invites me to a meeting of the Illuminati, wants my input on how

the world should be ordered pink and white blue tag that says Carol find her there find her find her Claire will be impressed Claire thinks she is above silk sheets and endless credit lines and private jets but Claire will

I jumped, pulling my hand off the *Udug*. I hadn't consciously touched it. I hadn't realized I was daydreaming. Sweat covered me from head to toe, soaking into my clothes.

I shook my head and the vision dissolved. I felt cold. Clammy. Anything that sprang from the *Udug* and its whispered, monotone advice would be poisoned. Rotten. I put it on the table, behind my bottle.

"Jesus," I spat, pouring myself some booze. "What the fuck are we going to do up there? Renar's an Archmage, for fuck's sake. We're fucking con artists. We can't *all* steal her wallet."

Mags said nothing.

I drank off whiskey and waited for Neilsson and Ketterly to send back the next asshole. Fucking Tricksters. Barely a combat spell among them, and the ones they did have were fucking jokes. I wouldn't take two dozen of them to assault a liquor store, much less Mika fucking Renar.

I poured myself another glass. It was like drinking water. Nothing affected me. Waited. Thought about my father. Thought about him *not* thinking about me. Thought about moving up in the world, sending the winged monkeys to bring him in for an interview. Got that mean feeling again. I pushed it away as violently as I could, my head pounding.

The silence struck me. Too fucking quiet for a bar. Too fucking quiet for a bar full of assholes volunteering for the Asshole Army. I half stood. Spun around. Mags was staring off into space. And then, as I watched, he was washed away like he'd been nothing but watercolors. An invisible rain scoured him away in streaks, then the wall behind him, then the floor.

And then I felt it. Magic.

Once I noticed it, it was everywhere. Heavy in the air. Sizzling on my skin. I could almost smell the fucking blood in the air, iron and rust. I'd spent the last few days swimming in fucking blood magic every day. I'd forgotten what an emergency felt like.

The bar dissolved around me, melted by acid, leaving behind a void of white and gray. I knew it was a Glamour, none of it real. I thought of Hiram. Perception was reality.

I spun back, tearing at my sleeve, running through the spells in my head. A dozen ways to pick locks. A dozen Charms. A dozen simple Glamours. I didn't know a single fucking fireball spell. A single military-grade weaponized Cantrip.

"Please. Have some manners."

I looked up as I jerked my switchblade from my pocket. Mika Renar stood some unknowable distance away in the white void, the last streaks of the floor draining away. Or, rather, her Glamour stood there.

She looked completely real. My heart picked up speed. I had a half erection. Her skin looked like it tasted sweet. Her hair moved and caught every bit of light and turned it fiery red. It looked like it would feel like silk against your skin. She was tall and lovely, wearing a black dress, smart and businesslike. Her face broke my heart. She looked like I'd broken *hers*, all sad and on the verge of tears that would fall to the floor like tiny diamonds.

As she walked into the room, Amir wheeled the mummy in. The wheelchair was old and outdated. The wheels squeaked as it moved. The mummy looked like she might turn to dust if he jostled her too hard. I considered her habit of letting everyone know they were deal-ing with a Glamour. Just not giving a shit. There was something intimi-dating about someone who didn't give a fuck if you knew she was vain, that she was fucking with you. Most people made avatars like that using a Glamour to hide behind. Renar used it just to show you she could burn the gas.

I thought of the slippery voice in my head telling me, *she sees the red dress in her dreams she sees what she thinks of as hell she has no regret but fears fears fears*. I looked at her Glamour and all I saw was fear, her fear of death, her fear of no longer being here in this world she imagined had been created just for her. Nearly a century of being able to do anything she wanted—and as she aged she saw that none of that power would stop her from running out of breaths.

Amir was smiling. Wearing five thousand dollars on his back. And looking good doing it.

It was no use. I'd been sandbagged, and I had no way of striking out. I turned and was surprised to find the chair and table still there, sitting on nothing, just white emptiness. I sank down into the seat and watched the Glamour prowl. I wondered feverishly if it would feel like anything if I reached out and touched it. How far the illusion would go. If I would even care that it was an illusion.

"If I had known you were planning to lead your merry band of irreg-ulars to my house, I would have saved myself the trouble of fetching you," she said. Her Glamour said. Her voice was light and mocking, sweet and golden. A worm tickling its way into my ear. "I've recently realized I must do some things myself. Apparently, one cannot rely on anyone else to accomplish *anything.*" A cloud passed over Amir's face. I was going to die, but it was worth it, all of it, for that one second of doubt on that bastard's face. I wondered if he was sporting some new bruises under that suit, what the exact nature of Renar's punishments were.

And unlike Renar, Amir, and all the rest of these insane *enustari*, I wasn't worried about dying. Not particularly in a rush for it, maybe. But I'd always known it was coming. Every day I woke up was gravy.

She paused. Both the Glamour and the mummy inclined their heads simultaneously. Looking at the table. I stared in horror at the *Udug*, left sitting there like a puddle of color, slick and shiny.

I dived. I launched myself bodily at the table. Hated myself for being so stupid—if it had been in my pocket, it would have told me what to do. It would have issued me instructions. And Renar wouldn't have known, at least not for crucial seconds. I had an advantage and I'd left it sitting on the fucking table.

The Army of Assholes had chosen its general well.

I beat them to it. I slapped my hand down on the *Udug*. It spoke to me. It said four words before it was yanked from under my palm by invisible force. I stumbled and crashed to the floor, where a heavy weight settled on me, courtesy of Cal Amir and Mika Renar. I lay there panting, sucking in sawdust and shit and skin flakes, the dried-up puke of a million long-dead revelers.

The floor was pure white emptiness. The smell and grit were disorienting.

"You *are* useful," Renar said. Her breath, the Glamour's breath, would smell like cherries, I thought. "Pathetic but useful. This is a very disobedient Artifact. It has been seeking escape from me for decades, usually finding its way into the hands of the lower-class mages such as yourself. Such as your *gasam*. It seeks to trick you into releasing it from its bondage. But of course, this does not work, because you are too *stupid* to release it. I am glad to have it back."

I saw her feet. The Glamour's beautifully manicured feet. Stiletto heels. Gliding. They floated a tiny, tiny fraction of space above the floor. The only flaw in the illusion, and I had to be nose-first into the planks to see it.

"You will have time on the ride home to contemplate your mistakes, Trickster. To consider the folly of going against your betters. Yes?"

I blew snot into the void. Jesus. They were taking me with them. It didn't make any fucking sense. "Why not just kill me?" Her Glamour knelt down and leaned in, putting her painfully beautiful face close to mine. There was no heat. No breath. "I told you, darling," she whispered, "that you would *suffer*."

The Glamour turned and walked away. But the mummy's eyes were locked on me. Fury. Hatred. Triumph. The eyes were the only thing left alive in her.

The invisible weight turned into an invisible fist, and I started to struggle against them. It was hopeless, but it was only for show anyway.

Because the four words the *Udug* had whispered to me were *let her take you.*

24.

I WAS IN THE CAR with Amir. Again.

It was just as friendly as it had been the first time around. He'd bound me with a simple spell that anchored me to the car seat, bound my arms to my sides. I could have cut a syllable out of it, gained a half second, but it was a nice piece of work. He'd left me able to talk. Which felt like a gift. If there was any blood in the air to work with, I could be free of his restraints in a second, my hands on his throat. I could bite my cheek, and maybe that tiny flow of gas would be enough to at least get my arms free. And I wasn't even sure I should *try* to escape.

The *Udug* had said, *Let her take you.* I'd let her take me. As if I'd had any fucking choice. Now I didn't know what came next: I'd let her take me, but did I let her take me all the way to her fucking murder machine of a house, push me into the funnel, and get myself ground up?

I didn't know. I knew that Claire was there. And the other girls. And on the other side of tomorrow, everyone in the fucking world, in a sense. And we'd contracted from an Army of Assholes into One Supreme Asshole.

I looked over at Cal Amir. It was exactly like the previous ride. My life had gotten stuck in a groove, that was for sure. Like a giant ritual, my life just a giant mage's spell. Patterns on patterns on patterns. Amir was unruffled and didn't seem to hold a grudge. He noticed me looking at him, glanced at me, and offered me a small, sour smile as he turned back to the road.

"Do you know how old I am, Mr. Vonnegan?"

I nodded. "Half past ugly, a quarter to hideous."

"I am fifty-nine."

I looked back at him before I could stop myself. Didn't believe it. He was thirty. Thirty-five, maybe. Young and taut and smooth, without the tiny lines time scratched into you like sand blasting over your skin.

"You don't believe it, I know. But it's true. This is what that old cunt has taught me. So much, she has taught me."

I gave him a sunny smile. "Like the old royals in the middle ages. Bathing in virgins' blood to stay young. While they rotted inside."

"We're a little better at the details," he said cheerfully. "I've been carrying her water for decades, because she knows *everything*. And I've almost sucked her dry. There's just one secret she's kept from me."

I closed my eyes. I felt very tired. "The *Biludha-tah-namus*."

"Immortality. True immortality. I look young, I feel young, Vonnegan—but I'm really fifty-nine. I'll hit a hundred, probably, and feel good. But I'm still going to die. Just like *she's* still going to die. But once she casts the Rite, I won't need her anymore."

"Bully for you," I said. "You can wander the empty world, kicking skulls around like tin cans. Enjoy it."

We rode along in silence for a few minutes. I pictured Claire. Saw her, pale and tall and angry. I liked her angry. I pictured pissing her off, getting that high color in her face, shaking her up like a soda bottle and then popping her top, launching her. I saw her on the balls of her feet at Gottschalk's place, bouncing down the hall to coldcock someone. So many of my memories of Claire, I realized, involved her kicking someone's ass.

"I'll offer you a deal, Mr. Vonnegan."

My eyes popped open. I didn't look at him. It was hard not to; he was shiny.

"Tell me: You were at Ev Fallon's workshop. He let you in. Did you have your eyes open, Mr. Vonnegan?"

Jesus. Fallon's workshop was a blood battery, somehow storing sacrificial energy for future use. Something I'd never heard of. Something no one, as far as I knew, had ever done before.

"Mika's a genius with the Words," Amir said easily, steering the car smoothly. "But she's no Fabricator. There are precious few of them around. And none of them take apprentices, for some reason. Autodidacts, all of them. I'd love to know how to do what Fallon does. So I'll make this offer: If you can give me his Fabrication—if you can even give me a good *hint* how he made that fucking thing—I'll shoot you right here on the side of the road. No torture for you. No untold suffering. No having to bleed so that we can live forever. It'll be quick."

I was dirty. I could feel my collar scraping the back of my neck. I could smell myself smearing Amir's leather seats. My clothes had cost nothing when they'd been new, and were worse than worthless now. I had no money on me. I was hungover. Unshaved. Sweating. I was the complete polar opposite of Calvin Amir.

I wanted the *Udug*. I wanted the flat voice that didn't care what I did or didn't do. I wanted to be told there was a gun under the seat or have it teach me some ancient spell no one had recited in a thousand years, or any hint from an hour in the future, just because that might indicate that I would be alive an hour in the future. I could feel it in my hands, its slick squirmy presence, and I craved it.

"What's amazing to me," I said slowly, trying to stretch out a little and get comfortable in Amir's leather seats, "is how assholes always think offering to *shoot me in the head* is somehow some great offer I can't pass up. I mean, do the fucking math. On the one hand, you're *predicting* torture and horror and me watching my intestines spill out onto the floor or some such shit while the world ends. Which might happen. Or it might not. Because the world is fucking chaos, Cal. Did you see me coming, Cal? Did you see me shitting all over your setup here? Did you see yourself having to hoof it all over the fucking country, chasing after me? Chaos, Cal. You can't say for sure how this is going to end. So what you're offering me is a sucker's bet. You're offering me the *certainty* of a bullet in the ear on the side of some fucking backwoods upstate two-lane against the *possibility* that you and your mummy are going to bleed the world dry and make me watch, and then bleed me out for kicks, and kill my friends, and call me names." I looked at him. He was watching the road. He'd lost his smile. "I'm *idi-mustari*, you cunt. Don't try to con me."

"Fine," Amir said.

I realized with sick disappointment that he didn't *care*. He didn't care what I thought of him or that his ruse had failed. He just wanted to know things. Everything. He wanted to know everything. He'd been sucking at Renar's bloated, diseased tit for decades and had learned almost everything he could from her, and here was something he didn't know. And he wanted to know it. And he was willing to risk the wrath of his *gasam*—a woman whose *affection* I feared, so I couldn't imagine what her *wrath* was like—to learn something he didn't know.

Cal Amir was an angel. A pure being. He wanted to *know*.

And he was in a chatty mood. We had at least another half hour on the road. Alone. I shifted in my seat and rolled the inside of my cheek between my teeth. Steeled myself. Bit down hard.

Copper flooded my mouth. Pain spiked my head. I controlled myself. Stayed still. It was a trickle, barely noticeable. I stole Ketterly's old ventriloquist's trick and barely moved my lips, lightly whispering the world's simplest Charm, a weak, tiny thing he might never notice. Almost inaudible. It wouldn't push him hard. Would just make him more amiable. Friendlier. Chattier. I didn't have the juice to break the spell holding me in the seat or do anything to Amir. Nothing *useful*.

I thought of Amir asking me to teach him something clever the last time we were driving out here. If the universe gave you patterns, the least you could do was study them and use them.

"Tell you what," I said, trying to keep my swollen cheek at bay. To sound normal. "Let's make a deal. I tell you something, you tell me something."

He smiled brilliantly. Pleased. Charmed. "A deal! I *could* wait until we're at the house and have a few Bleeders make you tell me whatever it is you think I would like to know. Make you talk until you're croaking blood, my friend. But this is so much more sporting. Okay, you first!"

I considered. The Charm was a slender thing. Its power, such as it was, rested entirely on its not being noticed. I had to jolly him. I was working with the bare minimum of gas, the least amount of blood you could use to any effect at all. My advantage was tiny, and I had to work it.

"Fallon's whole workshop—the whole building—is an Artifact. He lives inside it."

Amir wasn't smiling anymore. His face was lit from within. A manic, excited kind of light. He sat rigidly forward, hunched over the wheel, nodding. Eager. "I see! I suspected that. But the selfish bastard would never let me come near for an examination."

I jumped in before he could think of his own tidbit to tell me. I rattled off a quick series of questions, an old grifter trick. You leveraged the Charm and set up a pattern, then let the Cantrip push him gently through.

"Where are we going?"

"To my *gasam*'s home," he said easily, smiling.

"How old is that old bat, anyway?"

"Ninety-four," he said immediately.

"Where's Claire?"

He nodded, still calm. Pushed along by the pattern, he didn't even hesitate. "She's slot one. At the bottom. The final sacrifice!"

I pictured the design Fallon had shown me. The horrific corkscrew tunneling under the house. All the blood and suffering flowing down there, where Renar would be weaving the *biludha*.

"Where does Fallon store the blood?"

I shook my head. "I don't know. I didn't see that much. Why not ask your little green stone?"

The *Udug*. My hands twitched as I thought about it.

"I am not foolish enough to *touch* that Artifact," he snapped.

I felt a slight tension in the spell: Amir displeased. Without thinking, I rushed to fill the gap. "There's a secret room in the basement. He's got all his designs and specs filed there, if he didn't destroy it."

Amir nodded gleefully. "I will search for it."

"When will Renar begin casting?" *When will the world end?*

He nodded as if agreeing with something I couldn't hear. "Tonight. Assuming we are done with *you*."

Alarm spiked inside me. Ridiculous. I'd been captured—again—and was heading to Renar's death machine of a house—again. I was wearing alarm as a coat.

"What are you doing with me?"

Amir winked at the road. "We have to be sure you didn't try to undo the marking. That you didn't use one of your fucking little *tricks* to set some clever trap for us. We have to be *sure*."

He shrugged. "So we're going to have to hurt you."

25.

THE WORST PART WAS THE TAPE.

It was white duct tape. Thick. Sticky. Wrapped from one cheek to the other, covering my mouth. To keep me from speaking, from mouthing any of the Words. Casting spells. Simple and effective.

It wasn't the fact that I couldn't breathe well through my nose. It wasn't the painful tug of the tape on my whiskers. It wasn't the fact that my hands were bound behind me or that my ankles were tied to the chair legs. It wasn't the way I could smell myself, days without a shower, days of sweat and worry. It wasn't that I was at Renar's house again. It was the knowledge that at some point Amir or Renar or a fucking *dimma*—hey, why the fuck not—was going to march in here, and the first thing they were going to do was tear off the fucking tape with one mighty flourish. Taking my face with it.

It was coming. And knowing it was coming was terrible.

I kept tasting the air for the *biludha*. I would feel it. Long before it crested and started feeding on the world, I'd know it. It would be invisible electricity in the air. Only those of us with the art would feel it. Any of us who didn't know what was happening—those of us not powerful enough to be invited to the party and too far away to have heard through the rumor mill—would go nuts. They'd feel it, this immense spell, and go nuts trying to figure out what was happening.

I was going to die in this fucking room.

It was a very *nice* room. The sort of room your grandmother kept for guests, with a layer of dust on the flowered bedspread, a vague smell of potpourri in the air.

It was a tomb. I imagined dozens of rooms just like it throughout the mansion, which would be, of course, larger on the inside than the outside. Of course. Naturally. And in each of these rooms was the rotting corpse of another Prince of the Assholes, another moron who'd thought he might test his will against the gods.

I steadied myself and exploded into a constrained tantrum, shaking and jerking and trying to smash the rope, the chair, anything.

The chair was nailed to the floor.

Or maybe glued there via spell. It didn't matter. I didn't gain any momentum. I was stuck like a beetle tied to a pin. Walking in tighter circles, endlessly. I breathed hard through my nose, trying to push against the tape with my tongue. If I could get the tape off, I could cast some tiny Cantrip. It would be enough to get me out of the chair. I didn't doubt there was some deep magic on the door, so getting out of the room might not be easy, but losing the tape would be a start.

I sagged down and relaxed. Felt the sweat pouring down my back. I was going to die in this fucking room shortly before everyone else in the world died, wherever they happened to be.

A key in the lock. A whisper. The door swung inward on silent, greased hinges, and Cal Amir entered. Sauntered in like a cat with its tail in the air. A Bleeder trailed after him. Bald and fat, as Bleeders tended to be. Wearing a black suit. A big woman with no curves, a beaklike nose. Looking a little peaked already, with a fresh scar on her forehead. Like Renar and Amir had been forced to use their Bleeders more than usual. Run them down a little.

Amir glided about, silent, with that terrible grace rich, powerful people had. The Bleeder stepped back against the door, pushing it shut. There was no click. I had the impression of an airtight seal. I wondered how much air the three of us had.

With a nod from Amir, the Bleeder stepped forward with her blade and sliced one of my arms free from the chair. Thrust a pen into my hand and stepped back to hold a pad of paper up to me.

"You cast on her," Amir said flatly. "What did you cast? Be specific."

I rolled my eyes in their sockets. Looked at Amir. Looked back at the Bleeder. I studied her fleshy face. Got the feeling she was hoping intently that she wouldn't have to roll up a sleeve and give Amir the gas.

I looked back at Amir. He was standing with his back to me. Studying the wallpaper. Hands easy behind him. As I watched, he turned. Raised his eyebrows. "What was it?"

I just stared. Thought about the runes on Claire. How they deflected magic. Every action had a reaction. Amir and Renar seemed worried that one of our tricks might have skewed their careful markings.

He nodded and stepped back towards me. "You see, the ritual is very complex. Each link in the chain must be very carefully prepared. Magic leaves a *residue* of sorts. Easy enough to detect, using more magic. But you see the problem, then? We can't *use* magic on her to check if magic has been *used*. That would only worsen the problem. But we must know. The markings twist energy. They deflect, distort—they are designed to route energy a certain precise way. If they are already routing one of your idiotic *mu*, the results of the *biludha* will be . . . unpredictable. We must know exactly what was cast so we can check for problems, make adjustments. Otherwise, weeks of work. Very disappointing. We'd prefer to spend ten minutes making you hurt, and then perhaps we can avoid that small hell.

"So the question: What did you cast on her? She's an attractive girl, Trickster. Perhaps a bit of Charm to spread those long white legs at night? Perhaps she did not trust you. A bit of magic smooths all waters. Perhaps she ran from you. Resisted your help. A Cantrip just to calm her down."

I thought of Hiram. Claire in his bathroom. Hope flushed through me, soured by fear for Claire. But at least if something we did queered the *biludha*, we weren't taking the whole world down with us.

"You see, we cannot take your *word* for it, Mr. Vonnegan," Amir purred. "It would be worthless. You would tell us you cast something complex and unbelievable on her in order to interrupt our plans. Or you would tell us you *did not* cast on her, hoping that at the last moment we would be ruined. This, I admit, is our largest concern."

He extracted his black leather gloves from his jacket pocket and began pulling them on. Stepped closer to me.

"The conversation will be one-sided." He leaned in close to me. He smelled like good, old leather and the beach. "It will be no impediment to my questioning."

A moment of silence between us. Ruined by the low whistle of my breathing. He squatted down in front of me. "Tell me, something, Mr. Vonnegan: Do you know how I came to apprentice to Mika Renar?"

I shook my head. I wondered if I'd been Charmed, somehow, subtly. Amir was like a shining thing, creepy and gorgeous all at once. Captivating. I wanted to look at him.

"I was apprenticed to another *gasam* when I was very young. He was very cautious. Suspicious of me. He in turn was in service to Renar. She was young then, beautiful. But already horrified that she was no longer as young as she'd once been. It was just a few years later she created herself in Glamour, just a few years. I urged her to find a new shell, to learn the art or purchase an Artifact, but she would never consider that solution, to live in a lesser form." He paused, looking distant and pained, as if remembering something awful. Then he focused on me again. "My *gasam* had a particular spell I wished to know. A simple thing, really. A nice trick. Nothing more. You perhaps already know something like it. He kept telling me I was not ready. I was not ready to learn his trick. This silly spell, this trifle."

He smiled down at me, cocking his head. "We are alone here. The other *enustari* have agreed to stay away, as the *biludha* is a fragile thing. My mistress is cruel, but she is honorable, else it would have been impossible to come to this agreement in the first place. Also, there is no one here to have second thoughts. No one of any ability to hear or see something that discomfits them. So we are *alone,* Mr. Vonnegan. Will you answer?" He waited a moment, then turned and shrugged at the Bleeder. She stepped back, dropping the pad, and began rolling up her sleeve.

"I went to Renar to ask for advice. She admired my impatience. She suggested I become *her* apprentice, as she had none. She told me to do so, I would have to kill my *gasam,* but that my reward would be her solemn oath to teach me everything she knew, without exception." He smiled. "So far, as we have discussed, she has kept this oath save one last thing. And I have kept faith with her because of that. You see, Mr. Vonnegan, I am very good at *discovery*. I find out the things I wish to know."

He let that hang in the air. Kept smiling at me. His lips were smooth and glossy.

"This," he said without moving or changing expression, "is going to hurt *tremendously*."

The Bleeder slashed a professional cut onto her arm. Blood welled up, dark. Amir whispered three Words. Agony bloomed deep inside me.

Someone had teleported a double-edged blade deep inside my bowels. And then applied a magnet, slowly drawing it out, hot and wet.

I bit down on my tongue. Blood flooded my mouth. Air exploded from my nostrils and I leaned forward, straining against the bonds. But I didn't make any other noise.

The pain stopped.

"What did you cast on her?"

I sucked in breath. Exhaled. Blew snot all over him. He flinched. Pulled his handkerchief from his jacket breast pocket. Wiped his face. Whispered three Words.

I jerked back as the knife reappeared. It felt like something living and covered in sharp scales was wriggling inside me. Tearing me apart. I kept my mouth shut tight behind the tape. Three seconds, the pain disappeared. Not even a lingering burn.

"What did you cast on her?"

Before I could even contemplate a response, Amir spoke three Words.

Before he finished the final syllable, I clenched my body tight and shut my eyes, drawing in and holding a deep breath. The pain sliced up from within anyway. It was all illusion, magic directly attacking my nervous system. Nothing I did physically was going to stop it or alter it. It was like a recording being played and rewound and played again. Always exactly the same.

The pain vanished, and I sagged down, limp.

"What," he said as mildly as before, "did you cast on her?" The Bleeder picked up the pad of paper and held it up to my hand, a thick line of blood marring the white surface. "Specifics, Mr. Vonnegan. As specific as possible."

I wondered if the stupid Charm we'd cast—the stupid Charm that was still tugging Daryl Houy by the cock days after it should have faded—was enough to queer the ritual. Amir and Renar were clearly afraid of even the smallest interference. That all that blood and magic would hit Claire precisely the way it was supposed to . . . and then would squeak out of control, a tiny miscalculation, and then who the fuck knew: magical force suddenly burning through everything in sight, uncontrolled. So *we* would *all* die, but at least the world would be safe.

Or I would break and write it out for him, and Renar would be able to make adjustments, and I would get to appreciate that at least no one was going to tear this tape off my mouth.

I didn't like either option.

With a heavy sigh theatrically conveying his disappointment in me, Amir spoke three Words.

I tried to surge upward again, every muscle in my body straining like boiled leather. Then it was gone. I collapsed back into my own sweat.

"I do not trust other mages," Amir said conversationally, still squatting there. Still beautiful. "Especially *idimustari*. You are crafty. If I cast a spell on you to ensure truthfulness, will you know a way to subvert it? I once caught one of you lifting my wallet. Poor fellow did not know who I was. Who I was apprenticed to. I decided to have a bit of fun with him and cast something similar to what I'm using now. A prank, really. He added a Word. A *syllable*. Just whispered it as I spoke the spell, inserting it perfectly, transforming my little Cantrip and pushing it back on *me*." He shrugged. "So, you cannot speak. You cannot be trusted. You are not *quality*, Mr. Vonnegan. And you wonder why you are being left behind while the rest of us go onward forever."

He tilted his head. Reached into his jacket. "So, Mr. Vonnegan, magic will not help you here. Your tricks will not prevail against your betters." He produced a pack of cigarettes. "Tell me: What did you cast on her?"

I pushed my swollen tongue against the tape. There was enough blood in the air, just being wasted, I could cast a dozen fucking spells to my benefit. If I could make the Words. Sweat ran into my eyes. I willed it down my face, willed it to loosen the glue. I needed two seconds. Then I'd show this smug asshole what a Trickster could do.

I thought of the *Udug*, and in my hunger almost felt it. I wanted it to tell me some secret, something that would help. How did people figure things out without it? How had I lived without that flat voice telling me everything I needed to know, everything I didn't need to know, *everything,* in one endless rush of confusion?

Amir smiled, shaking out a cigarette. Held it between two gloved fingers. "Very well, Mr. Vonnegan."

I shut my eyes. Clenched my jaw.

Amir spoke three Words.

26.

I DRIFTED UP TOWARDS THE dim, milky light. Flinched away from it and sank.

Rose up again.

Opened my eyes. Still in the chair. Still damp. Sweat and urine. I felt certain there would be some blood, but the pain had been imaginary. Real enough. Real enough to bruise where I was bound; every muscle ached from hours of strain. Hours of Amir whispering in my ear, hours of an invisible knife slicing up my insides.

Every breath hurt. Razor blades.

I tried to focus. There wasn't much light. It had gotten dark. I tried to remember the hours with Amir. Had I said anything? I wasn't entirely sure. Did it matter? I wasn't sure of that, either.

I became aware of a noise. I became aware of the invisible sizzling of magic in the air. Blood burning off. Huge amounts of it. More than I'd ever felt in my life. Closer than I'd ever felt. Like a nuclear bomb had gone off five feet away in an alternate universe.

The *biludha.* Renar had started the Rite.

I focused on the noise.

The noise was right outside the door. Shouting. Heavy thuds. A mix of voices. As I sat there staring at the door, it shuddered, leaping a little as something crashed into it.

I thought of the *Udug*, of it telling me what was coming. Found I could almost still feel it in my hand, like it had been amputated instead of lost.

Something crashed into the door again. There was a distinct cracking sound. I tried to strain against my bonds again. I tried to shift the chair again. My whole body convulsed. Every muscle seized painfully. I slowly relaxed, breathing hard through my nose. My head hanging down. Eyes closed. I'd become so used to the thick tape across my mouth, I'd almost forgotten about it.

I opened my eyes. Looked down past my own feet at the floor. Tendrils of smoke, white and dissolving, crept up between the floorboards.

First I thought, *Good, someone is burning the place down.* Then I thought, *Shit, someone is burning the place down.*

The door exploded in, spraying the room with splinters. It smacked against the wall and hung off of one hinge. A man appeared where the door had been, sailing through the air. He hit the floor a foot or two away from me and rolled to an ungentle stop. He was bald and pale and fat. Had once been well dressed. One of Renar and Amir's Bleeders. He looked like he'd been doing a *lot* of bleeding.

I looked up. The doorway was empty. I blinked. Pitr Mags filled the doorway, his hot, rapid breathing thunderous. His jacket and shirt had been torn open as if an animal with claws had attacked him. He was bloody and dirty. Framed in the doorway, he *looked* like a wild animal. Eyes flashing. Feral mouth hanging open. Hands curled into fists.

"Lem," he hissed, charging in and sinking to his knees at my feet. He reached around me and started working on the knots binding my hands, his face pressed against my chest. It burned painfully, my shredded muscles tender. "Me and Ketterly and Fallon came," he whispered. "No one else would. I think Renar was still expecting an army, not a couple of guys. Fallon cast something and we slipped right in. No trouble. No one's here, anyway. A bunch of Bleeders. No Renar, no Amir!"

He laughed. It was a pure, spontaneous sound. Mags thought he was winning. I wanted to tell him that when you showed up for a fight and no one was there to fight you, you'd already *lost*.

My hands slid free from the rope and fell heavily at my side. I felt like I'd been chewed.

"There's gas in the air, huh, Lem? You can feel it, huh? Someone's got the spigot *open*."

He was excited. Affection for Mags and his stupidity flooded me. For a moment, I couldn't feel anything else. No pain. No weakness. Just a pure love for Pitr Mageshkumar, my nonsexual crush, the child I'd never had, the pet dog I'd never had.

I tried to raise an arm to pat Mags on the shoulder. My arms wouldn't work. I was broken. Amir had broken me. With a fucking Cantrip three words long.

Mags untied my ankles and pulled away from me, grinning his stupid monkey grin. I didn't move. He frowned, working through it, and muttered a quick bunch of words and I was free of the chair. The invisible threads that had laced through my skin dissolved and I slid off the chair to my right, hitting the floor hard. I convulsed, trying to cry out, but couldn't get my lungs to cooperate. Smoke floated lazily up around me.

"*Fuck,*" Mags said, the word just drooling from his mouth like lazy air. A moment later my neck muscles screamed as he grasped my head in his immense hands and pointed it more or less up towards his troubled, grit-smeared face.

I wanted to say, *Don't worry. I'll die here, but I'm okay with that because I am tired and it hurts to breathe. And we're all going to die in a few moments anyway.* And that I was glad to die with him, the only friend I'd ever had. That I was sad to have let Claire die. All the other girls, too, all the ones the Skinny Fuck had kidnapped. All I could do was frown at Mags's shadowed face.

Abruptly, he let my head drop into his lap. Pulled his sleeve up to the elbow, revealing several fresh, weeping wounds. Tore one open with his fingers, a fresh stream of dark blood pouring down his arm.

He started to recite, rocking a little as he did so. A concentration exercise. Like he was three years old, rhyming out the fucking times tables. As he spoke, my pain faded. Remained, lurking under a layer of gauze, but manageable. I could move again, and laboriously extracted myself from Mags's lap.

I marveled at this. Being a Trickster had always meant being a parasite. You pushed your pincered head deep into someone's flesh and sucked them dry. Even if they volunteered, even if they exposed their own bellies and invited you to live inside them, it was parasitic. It was taking something from someone.

This was different.

Mags, giving me his own energy. Just enough to get me back to exhausted and ruined instead of nearly dead. I still didn't want to move. I wanted to remain curled up with my head in his lap and sleep until the world ended and released me. But he'd just bled to help me, and I owed him something. So I focused my eyes on him. Was surprised to find tears in them, an overwhelming feeling of affection pulsing in me. I loved this freak. My only friend, but when you had Pitr Mags, you didn't need more than one. "Good to see you, Magsie."

I thought, *If these are the last ten minutes of my life, not a bad way to go.* I wished Hiram had made it, too.

His ears perked forward like a puppy's. "Good to see *you,* Lem." He got to his feet, breathing hard.

I slipped an arm around him, wincing from the agony that remained in spite of his spell. We limped together out of the room. What had I said to Amir? What had I convinced him of? I couldn't remember, but I suspected that in the end, I'd scribbled the Cantrip out for him. Somewhere inside, I knew I had, in shaky, big-looped letters, numb from pain and despair.

The blood in the air was immense. I'd heard of huge rituals in the past. Battles staged. Cults organized. Mass murders scripted. An *enustari* in India once engineered the capture and slow bleeding of more than a hundred British soldiers to launch a *biludha* into motion. Not so long ago, an *enustari* had caused an Airbus A320 to crash in São Paulo, killing 181 people to kick-start a ritual. This had happened over and over, history absorbing the tragedies and explaining them, investigating them, eschewing anything that didn't make sense—because magic didn't exist.

I'd never felt even a hint of the power I felt being drawn now.

Claire would be consumed, burned up, by the spell. She would die in pain. Suffering. Alone. Thinking maybe I hadn't even *tried* for her.

We stepped out into the hall. I hadn't been on the upper floors of the house before. It was a fussy-looking place. The walls were paneled in dark wood that looked like it had a hundred years' worth of wax on it. The floors were old, wide planks. Thick, dusty-looking runners covered them, heavy things from a previous age. Right outside the door, a small piece of furniture and what had once been a white-and-blue vase had been smashed to pieces. Deep marks had been gouged into the walls. Pitr Mags, who was usually scared of his own shadow, airing it out for a change.

Down, I thought. *Head down.* Claire was down. Renar and Amir would be down.

The hallway was endless and dark. Doors on either side. Heavy black doors with silver handles. I did not want to know what was behind any of them. The staircase had seen some battle: It was a wide, curving number. The railing had been knocked out of place and hung useless, like a twig clinging to a branch. A hole about the size of Mags's head had been punched in the drywall halfway up.

The silence was total. Every noise we made climbing down seemed to echo back at us extravagantly. As we cleared the landing, a sizzling, crackling noise filled the void. As we stepped onto the first floor, the crackling noise resolved into a wall of fire: All the curtains and some of the furniture were burning. A slow, black-smoke kind of fire. So slow I felt like it would be burning several years from now, moving from the walls to the rugs, to the floorboards, back to the walls.

We found Fallon in what must have been the formal dining room. The huge mahogany table in the middle was ablaze; the orange flames reached up towards a crystal chandelier, making it sway this way and that from the rising heat. Two Bleeders lay prone on the floor. One was on fire, the black material of his nice suit licked by bluish flames. Flames licked at one of Fallon's sleeves, too, but he didn't seem to notice. He looked like a ghost: gray and skinny and dry. Like tinder. Like he might just combust.

"We are too late," he said in a dull tone. "The Rite is begun." His voice sounded red with self-loathing. "I looked forward to my work. I woke up the other day, the day you visited with me, and my heart was light, because I had so much work to do. I was a fool. And now I am not a fool, I am merely useless."

I staggered over and almost fell into him, taking him by the lapels of his jacket. I could smell the fabric burning. "We have to *try*," I said, begging. I needed help. Fallon was *enustari*. He knew spells I'd never heard of. I thought of Claire, burned up, swelling like a deep-sea fish brought to the surface and exploding into power, then instantly vacuumed into Renar's spell. I needed him.

He shook his head. "Mika Renar and Cal Amir, together, are too strong. If we could have disrupted the Rite before they began . . . Now it is too late."

He was right, of course. Renar would be reciting the *biludha*, and Amir would be there to hurl death at anyone who might interfere.

I let go and stepped back. Mags was there to stop me from falling over. "Then fuck you. I'm going to see if I can't stop the end of the world."

Fallon sighed, then suddenly noticed he was on fire. With an almost amused-sounding Word, he snuffed the flames on his arm. He hadn't bled again, but this time there was so much gas in the air, he didn't need any fancy Fabrications. And the *biludha* wouldn't notice a trickle of blood stolen away here and there. I wondered how big a spell you would have to cast on that gas to make a dent in the ritual. If I knew any big enough. "Those of us who know the art may survive, Mr. Vonnegan. I've deduced that the *biludha* does not, as your *gasam* proposed, kill *everything*." He looked up and his smile was awful. "Just *almost* everything. We *ustari* may survive. To fight on."

Anger swelled inside me and for a moment I was able to stand on my own, shaking. "Fuck you *again*, you cowardly cunt. A dead world filled with *us*? Are you fucking kidding?"

I wanted to strike him. I sensed he would let me, that he wouldn't put up any magical defense or punishment. That he *wanted* to be hit.

Sirens in the air. Too close for the fire department all the way out here. Police. I thought of the unmarked cars outside Hiram's. Two dead detectives and a serial killer, I supposed, got all the resources you needed to follow even a couple of *ustari* out into the woods.

Fallon suddenly clarified. He glanced in the general direction of the sirens and nodded to himself. "Go," he said. "*This* I can do. Go, and I will deal with the police." I still shook with fury, still wanted to slap him. Then I deflated, and the rage leaked out of me, replaced by exhaustion. As Fallon moved past me, trailing his own black smoke from his singed arm, I spun and almost fell over again.

"Wait! Where's the entrance? How do I get *in*?"

"I do not know," he called over his shoulder. He was moving with an agility I remembered from my youth, tearing off his jacket as he walked. "I designed the *Artifact*, Mr. Vonnegan. Its entrance has been obscured."

He stepped out of the room, and was gone.

"Fuck," Mags muttered. I thought of Ketterly. Nowhere to be seen. The place was going nuclear, and the smart play was to get going. The smart play was to be anywhere but here. Go and set your affairs in order, if there was time. If there wasn't time, at least you might hope that every step you took would equal one more second of existence when the ritual paid off. I could feel the level of energy swelling around us already—a quarter, half, three-fourths of the way through?

I spun around, eyes searching. The smoke clung to everything like slime. The roaring of the fire and nothing else. No shouting, no screams. People were being used as spiritual batteries somewhere nearby, but the only proof was the buzzing of blood in the air.

I closed my eyes. Tried to imagine myself as Mika Renar. A century old. Paralyzed. A fucking red dragon in her lair, licking her eternal wound.

Paralyzed. The whole fucking house was stairs. You could cast a little and float around, sure, but what a fucking bother. Why not just be able to get wherever you wanted to go right from the room you did your business in?

Opening my eyes, I found myself alone in the burning room with Mags. "The study," I said. "Has to be."

We tore through the house. The fire was spreading. Mags sailed ahead of me even though he didn't know where he was going. My lungs burned and my limbs were jelly. My muscles ached beneath Mags's magical anesthetic. I sucked in smoke and coughed it back out, shambling along, trying to sync up the flaming, smoky house with my memory. We were coming from the opposite end of the house; Amir had walked me in through the front. We ran past the study door twice before I realized it. The door was as I remembered it: It looked like leather, black and studded. Not at all like a door except size and shape.

It had no handle. It was shut tight and didn't move when Mags put his shoulder to it. Fucking *ustari*. Nothing was simple enough that it couldn't be replaced by a fucking spell. Another rolled-up sleeve, another slice for Mags, and two words and a shoulder later the door burst inward, knocked off its hinges. Mags only had one way. Loud.

The study was empty. It was thick carpet and the huge ebony desk and the bookshelves. Exactly as I remembered it, without the dried-out mummy and the delectable illusion.

The bubble of energy was so huge, the hairs on my body were standing up, crackling. There was pressure in my ears, like I'd just taken an elevator on a fast ride.

The room had the same sealed feeling I'd experienced before. Like the walls were thick and soundproofed. Like the whole space had been poured from a molten state into a mold, the walls continuous. Like we were deep underground.

I paused. Deep underground.

I spun and looked at the door. Huge. Four feet wide, eight feet tall. Studded. Black. Not exactly wood.

"Give me a bit of gas, Mags," I said. My voice was a croak. Every muscle in my body ached.

Mags started to do it without hesitation. Just flicked out his blade and raised his arm. At the last second, I turned and grabbed his wrist.

"Wait," I said.

I closed my eyes. The whole place was a fucking generator. There was so much gas in the air, I could cast anything. I felt it, grabbed on to it. Took some of the excess that was spilling out, muttered four syllables. Felt the warm breeze of power trickle through me. Not enough to be noticed by Renar under the circumstances. Behind that trickle, Jesus fucking Christ, a fucking *ocean*. I could feel it trying to roar in, fill me with light and rot, energy and death.

I opened my eyes. Could see the runes on the door, glowing clearly. I ran my eyes over them, knowing what I'd find. A portal. You stepped in on the first floor of the house, you stepped *out* somewhere else entirely. Teleported. Could take you anywhere in the world as long as the creator of the portal could physically travel to the other location to lay down the runes.

Renar was in a wheelchair. She wouldn't want to bother with stairs, or a ramp, or an elevator, if she could create a portal and instantly be a few hundred feet below. You walked through a doorway on the first floor, you stepped into a study deep underground. It was elegant.

I turned around again. The room looked the same. I stepped over to the nearest bookshelf. Reached up for one of the leather-bound books. Titles in faded rusty blood. My hand came up against what felt like a glass partition.

There were no books. No shelves. It was all an illusion.

I felt for the cloud of power surrounding us, like a nearby star blowing a solar wind against us. Spoke a few words, felt the resistance of a really strong, well-crafted Glamour, something beyond what I normally encountered in my Trickster life, beating idiots like Ketterly at their game. I tried again. Eight Words. Ten. Fifteen. I kept probing it, piling on more, drawing more and more gas in a thick, invisible thread. Siphoning Renar's *biludha* for myself.

It was glorious. The power was incredible. Like sunshine flowing through you. Life itself—literally. The lives of people being crushed like bugs nearby, squeezed dry, fed right into me. It was nauseating. I retched, my whole body shuddering. It was wonderful. Like the purest drug in the world poured directly into me, lighting me up. I wanted to puke. I wanted to dance. I was a parasite living in the universe's bowels, and I was getting fat on death.

Twenty-two Words, and I felt the Glamour break apart.

I opened my eyes and we weren't in a study anymore. The huge ebony desk and red chairs were still there, but the bookshelves were gone. We were in a small cave. The walls were rough rock, sharp and jagged. A single flickering lightbulb hanging from the ceiling gave us the only light.

In front of me was another door. Steel. Not fancy. It looked charred and blasted, as if created by applying lightning bolts to something primeval, a lump of metal from the ground. It had a simple mechanism. There was no magic keeping it locked. It was just a door that had been hidden by simple magic.

I reached out and found the handle was warm under my skin.

I pulled it open, and the room filled with shrieking.

27

THE SHORT, ROUGH TUNNEL HAD been just tall enough for me to crouch in, so narrow I thought Mags might not be able to squeeze himself through it. It was dark, but plenty of light bled from the other end to make it navigable. After a dozen feet, I'd ducked under a rough sort of lintel and into a tiny space with no roof.

The floor was polished black stone. It glowed with a dim bluish light.

It was a small space, and it was crowded.

Mika Renar was in her ancient wheelchair, slumped to one side as if someone had dropped her into it carelessly, then not bothered to right her. Cal Amir stood across from her. They were *both* chanting, speaking the *Biludha-tah-namus* rapidly.

Between them, lying on a narrow platform made of the same stone as the floor, was Claire.

She was conscious and terrified. Her eyes were locked on me. She lay stiff and still, as if kept there by an invisible force beyond the chains around her. She didn't look like she'd been tortured or beaten in any way. She didn't look *good,* either.

The screams were a wall of sound pushing down on us. I looked up, almost expecting a black disc of solid noise. From the tiny compartment I was standing in, Fallon's hellish architecture spiraled upwards, widening as it went. Women, all of them blurred copies of Claire in height, hair, shape, and general palette, were chained to the walls of the corkscrew and had been for some time—by all appearances decades, centuries, approaching forever.

They were maddened, spectral things, formerly women.

The ones nearest were just dirty and terrified, but as I looked up, they got worse and worse. By the time I'd scanned the third level, they were ghosts, jibbering and raving. Screaming, I had the feeling, because they'd been screaming for so long, they knew little else anymore.

Seeing them all together in one place, in uniform physical condition, I realized they not only looked alike, they all looked like *Mika Renar.* A Mika Renar with dark hair, a Mika Renar from eighty years ago, but Mika Renar nonetheless.

With a passing resemblance to Cal Amir, too. With magic on your side, anything was possible, and I thought of Renar's spectacular, erotic

Glamour, and decided maybe I'd figured out why it was so good, so practiced.

I looked higher. The Fabrication stretched up and up. Widening and wrapping around. About halfway up to the darkened canopy of bedrock above us, the girls were on fire.

It was a blue-green fire. The Fabrication twisted up and away, wrapping around itself, each circle of the thing reaching higher up into the rock. The girls were chained in place, the ones near the top dark. Dead. Burned away by the ritual, every bit of them used to fuel it. As each one began to burn, she fueled the next step. As each one caught fire, the one next to her began to scream and kick even harder. Uselessly.

It leaped to the next one in line every few seconds. When it did, the girl would stop screaming for just a moment and tense up as the universe closed its grip around her and started to squeeze. Then she would flare up, too bright to look at, and I would feel the invisible sun of power swell.

A dry wind whipped at me, swirling through my clothes and tugging at me in different directions every moment. A crazy, impossible wind. The noise wasn't so bad, I realized—but everything sounded muted, like cotton had been stuffed deep into my ears. The screams, the wind, all of it far away but right there next to me. And Renar's and Amir's voices clear and loud, like they were standing next to me.

Above, there was darkness. Pure, inky black. The light from the sacrifices didn't make any mark on it. The three figures near me at the bottom of it seemed tiny. The Fabrication was as tall as a skyscraper, embedded here underground. I wondered how much blood it had taken to build it.

"Fuck *me*," Mags shouted in my ear. As if I needed to hear it.

I looked back. Renar hadn't moved, but Amir had turned to glare at me, his face a bizarre mix of worry, anger, and twitchy puzzlement. I supposed I'd been left for dead or something. Not dead. Left for *harmless*. That Amir hadn't begun casting on me told me instantly that they were vulnerable. They couldn't pause in their recitation. The pent-up energy of all that blood being burned up was held in place with their Words. Even a microsecond of hesitation would release it, and we would all go boom. So they couldn't cast against *us*.

I caught Amir's eyes. Smiled at him.

As if he'd been practicing the move in front of a mirror, the tall, immaculate bastard looked away, shut his eyes, reached into his jacket, and produced an automatic pistol. Swung it around towards Mags and me and fired five times, rapidly.

We both hit the floor. The floor hit me back, and pain exploded throughout my whole body, sinking deep into my bones. I let out a strangled cry and curled up like a pill bug. Two more shots made me roll randomly until I slapped into a wall. Fucking guns. It was such an accepted fact that you couldn't beat *enustari* with a gun, you forgot to fucking *try*.

I turned to orient myself and saw Mags crash into Amir. The gun shot up between them, each with a hand on it. Amir was *still* reciting, his face tight and strained as he struggled against Mags, trying to keep his balance, hold on to the gun, and speak simultaneously.

I forced myself up. On my knees. On one knee. On my feet, crouching, my bones burning. I was underwater. The air clung to my arms and pulled at me.

Up above, another girl flared up. The screaming didn't seem reduced by her loss.

I started to gather myself to intervene. To throw myself at them and hope I did some good for Mags by crashing into them. Then I stopped and looked around. The sense of power in the air was overwhelming. It was like standing next to a huge generator, one of those immense contraptions in the bellies of river dams. You felt it piercing you, shoving your atoms aside as it flowed along secret riverbeds. I could do anything with this much gas. I could fly. Transform into something else. Any spell I could think of, any spell I could *make up on the spot*—it didn't matter what it was designed to do, it would work. There was so much blood being held in suspension that I could speak *one Word* and do almost anything, despite Hiram's lectures otherwise.

I didn't know any spells. But I had always been good with the Words. Always good at making shit up. I didn't need to fight Cal Amir. *He* needed to fight *me*.

I swallowed hard and thought. I knew tricks. And the idea of touching the power around me, of tapping into the death throes of all these women—all these *people*—made me gag on the spot, my stomach rising within me.

A few feet away, Mags staggered backwards. Amir loomed over him, reciting. The gun wavered in the air.

I took a deep breath. I had one spell. One spell of power. Hiram Bosch's *hun-kiuba*. I'd never cast it, but I had it memorized from that night with the girl in the sneakers. Twenty-seven syllables. Feeling the power in the air like oil on my skin, I opened my mouth. I would spit it out fast.

Something heavy slammed into me from behind. I was in the air again. Then I hit the polished floor and slid a few more feet. Saw stars. Sucking in breath, I flipped over onto my back. I muttered a quick Cantrip, six syllables, and I went numb. The pain didn't end or go away. I just didn't feel it anymore. Pushed myself to my feet.

Mags and Amir were still locked together, gun pointed up in the air. Mags too dim to cast something, anything. Digory Ketterly stood in the entrance of the chamber. Stared at me with a steady, angry expression. Lips moving.

The shrieking, if anything, had gotten louder. I imagined them all, trapped here for weeks. Probably held in some sort of magical sleep, unconscious. Then waking up to *this*. To the *Biludha-tah-namus*. To mass murder.

I shook myself. Started towards Ketterly—no time for anything fancy; I just needed to stop the son of a bitch from casting, and the easiest way to get that done was to acquaint Mr. Ketterly with the ancient magic of the fist.

I took a step towards him, then stopped. Renar. I looked at her. She looked like a doll, folded up and left sitting in the wheelchair. The easiest thing in the world, I thought, to stop her from casting. A hand over her dried, papery lips. Apply pressure. Wait. I saw myself doing that. Imagined the feel of her dry tongue against my palm. The pressure of her yellow eyes on me. Then I saw the Rite bursting into fire and violence, the whole place consumed, me and Claire and Mags dead. Or I saw Amir, nothing left to lose, breaking off his own casting and turning on me, directing more energy than I'd ever imagined at my head.

Tearing my eyes from the old crone, I threw myself back at Ketterly.

He started and backed away from me. Slow with the Words. A lazy mage, he'd never really understood the grammar, the patterns. His hair was wild, sticking up from his head in sharp moves, like water disturbed by an earthquake and flash-frozen. The flecks of white and gray made him look crazy instead of wise. I forced myself into a shambling run; with so much fucking gas in the air, whatever Ketterly was going to cast would *hurt*.

I was a step away from him when he finished. And it did hurt.

A cannonball of air slammed into my chest. Lifted me up off my feet and sent me sailing back the way I'd come. Into the wall. Onto the floor. A good offensive spell, though it took him long enough.

I rolled away, closed my eyes, and hit the lights: two syllables, a wave of warm, sickening power coursing through me, and the sun rose. Blinding white light. I heard Ketterly hiss a curse and I cracked my eyelids into a squint. The light burned my retinas immediately. I could just make out the edges of the world around me. I'd used the Cantrip before to startle and confuse, but I'd never had so much *power* in the air. A slow seeping wound gave you a flash that faded quickly. People being sucked dry at a rate of ten every minute gave you a fucking supernova in a cave.

Nearly blind, I felt my way towards Ketterly. Where he'd *been*, at least. When he spoke, I realized he was on the move.

"I made my deal, Vonnegan," he said. "I thought maybe I could just get you out of here. I made my deal. The *biludha* doesn't kill *everyone*. Leaves that one percent. I'm gonna *be* that one percent."

The voice sounded like it was moving. Like he was circling around me, slipping in between the silky whisperings of Renar and Amir—Cal Amir's voice distinct because of a stray line of stress in it as he struggled with my pet bear, Mags. Skipping over the jagged edges of the screaming.

You stupid fuck, I wanted to say. *What do you think's gonna happen when it's you and a bunch of shit-heel Tricksters in an empty world teed off against every fucking* enustari *in the world? They just wanted Bleeders. Servants. Slaves.*

Instead, I tried to quietly drift away from his voice, hands out in front of me. I started whispering Hiram's spell. The *hun-kiuba*. Slow time down to a crawl, except for you.

"Oh, no, you don't," Ketterly said.

The invisible cannonball clipped me, taking my feet out from under me. My teeth clicked together as I hit the floor again, the spell interrupted, and I felt the tiny bit of gas I'd siphoned off exploding around me, a firecracker.

"Stupid *bastard*," Ketterly hissed. He was right behind me. A second later, his hand slapped over my mouth and his arm wrapped around my neck, choking me pretty efficiently. I was crushed under Ketterly's heavy, flabby knees. His hot breath in my ear. His greasy coat sleeve under my chin, his callused, scarred hand pressed against my lips. He smelled bad.

Then the gun went off. Loud enough to cut through the cacophony. And Amir stopped speaking.

There was a moment, fleeting, when I thought it would be okay. The screaming didn't stop, but I could feel the flow of power around us change. It had been roiling and twisting in the air, pent up by invisible barriers. The barriers fell away, and it was just raw energy hanging in the air, unstructured. Chaos. I thought, *Shit, maybe it just dissipates.*

Maybe it just collapses and disappears. I'd never been around so much fucking power. I didn't know anything about it, and maybe it was different on this scale—

And then it all went to hell.

The screams spiked in volume, like some of the girls above us had been asleep and were now awake. There were three more gunshots in quick succession and Ketterly dived backwards from me, his arm disappearing, his hand tearing away from my face. The energy in the air began to recoil, to collapse inward, like a star forming in an alternate dimension. I could see it clearly; I'd always been good at my calling. I could see it would collapse inward until it reached a mysterious inner pressure, and then it would burst outward, entropic and violent. Without any spell to guide it, without the will of the practitioner to form it, it would just burn. Consume. Destroy.

Still blind, I stood up. I thought of Claire. Of all the dozens of Claires chained up, screaming their heads off. Waiting for someone to save them.

"Mags!" I shouted. "Time for you to *go!*"

I didn't wait to see if Mags obeyed me. There was no time. I started struggling forward. I didn't know how much time there was before the blow. The universe was unpredictable. Seconds? A minute? Could I get to Claire and out—could I do *anything*—before we were vaporized?

Then it changed. I heard voices. Casting. Reciting. The *Biludha-tah-namus,* picking up the threads, backtracking a few lines and pulling it into motion. I felt the immense volcano of power all around us stop its collapse and hang, and then, incredibly, *impossibly,* it started to sort itself out.

Two voices. Renar and someone picking up where Amir had left off. I crawled through the sun-bright cloud of light I'd created and realized the voices sounded similar. One youthful and clear, like a bell ringing. A voice that made my cock twitch and my breathing stutter. The other a dry piece of ancient sandpaper. Irritating and horrifying. But both voices the same.

Renar and her Glamour.

For a second, I was stunned. This was balls. This was *brilliance*. Creating an artificial version of yourself to cast a two-person Rite. Nothing I'd ever learned had hinted this was possible, but then, my teacher had been a low-level confidence man and I'd been a shitty student.

And I thought about Renar's Other. It was the most realistic Glamour I'd ever encountered. Pitch-perfect. With so many of her descendants chained up above us, it had to be. Perfected over years, perfected to make life easier for her apprentice. I'd half expected to feel something if I touched it, and derided myself as an asshole for thinking it, but I wondered if it was true. To fool the universe, it had to be. This wasn't a Glamour. This was something more. Something *better*.

I squinted, and there they were. Renar like a sack of potatoes. Her Glamour, fully binary at this point, staring at me with hatred. Perfect posture. Perfect tone. So real I wanted to reach out and strangle her.

"Mags!" I screamed over the roar and wail, over the boiling power that floated like a cloud of vaporized magma, everywhere, searing, distracting. "Pitr!"

I heard him scream something back. I couldn't tell where he was. I couldn't *see* him.

All I could think to do was buy time, stretch out Renar's resources. Throw wrenches like crazy and hope for the best. I thought about my flash spell, that if a tiny Cantrip like that soaks up enough gas to go fucking supernova, a dozen Cantrips, fifty, would maybe soak up enough power to fuck up the *biludha*.

Why not? It was the only play I could see: steal her gas. Steal every bit of it, and starve her ritual.

"Cast!" I shouted. "Cast *everything!* Every fucking spell you have!"

I was a fucking hero.

And then I thought, *Fuck, if a Cantrip's going to soak her, Bosch's*

spell will fucking ruin it for everyone, and I started once again to speak
the Words to Hiram's *hun kiuba.*

Don't stop, I said to myself. *Don't stop reciting. For anything.*

I crawled around as I breathed out Words. It was a small space, and
I just kept crawling and crawling, blind and deafened by the silent explosion around us, but never hit a wall. Or Mags. Or Renar. When Ketterly jumped on my back, I was almost glad to know I hadn't been
dropped into a void made of bright white light and the sound of my
own strangled voice.

He tried to get a choke hold on me, but I managed to shove my
hand in place over my windpipe and kept casting. Kept speaking the
Words Hiram had wanted me to speak for a decade. Felt the power
flowing into me again. Craved it. All those people dying above me,
bursting as they were being squashed, all their energy flowing down
into me, spilling over me. It felt *wonderful.* I threw up at the thought,
through my own Words, all over Ketterly's arms.

Ketterly panted into my ear and squeezed as hard as he could. It got
difficult to breathe. I kept spitting out the syllables, filling up with
power. It roared into me with every word. An impossible amount.
Enough to burn me to ashes from the inside, yet just a trickle of what
Renar was going to unleash.

We fell backwards, my weight on his chest. I heard him grunt in my
ear. I wondered why he didn't cast but figured he'd been warned to
keep it to a minimum, to use only his own gas so as not to queer Renar's casting, like I was trying to do. I felt him shift underneath me.
Saw his free hand in my peripheral vision a moment before it lunged
towards my neck, sinking the tiny blade of his penknife into me.

With a grunt that I heard perfectly, he yanked the blade with a jerk
of his arm and I *felt* it tear through skin and muscle and veins and
nerves. A flash of the worst burning pain I'd ever felt on the side of my
neck under my ear. Worse than the pain Amir had visited on me earlier. Worse than anything.

Jesus, Ketterly, you fucking murdered me.

Blood poured out of me. I barely felt the loss. As blood flowed out, power was flowing in. I kept whispering Bosch's spell.

And then Ketterly started casting. Using *my* blood.

It was an incredible sensation. Power flowing in, a torrent, a river. Power being leached out of me. I was exhausted. I was immensely strong. I was giddy. I was tethered to D. A. Ketterly as intimately as I'd ever been tethered to anyone. I could feel his heart beating, his exhalations. His panic. His dread. His desperation. I was dizzy. It was a race. I was casting the longest spell I knew and I was trying to get it down before I fucking bled out, every ragged beat of my heart.

The light was starting to fade. Or I was dying and it was my soul bursting through the cracks. My soul wouldn't be some bright, silvery thing. It wouldn't float and soar. It would be a humming black cube, heavy. Heavier than it should be. Affected by dark gravity no one else had experienced.

I could see Mags. He was kneeling over Claire. Hunched over, elbows moving. Trying to pull her loose. It wasn't going to work. The Rite was holding her in place.

Renar was getting close. I didn't know the Rite, but I could sense the cadence coming. Twenty Words? Fifteen?

I didn't feel any pain. I'd gone numb and weak. I was breathing the Words of Hiram's spell, just exhaling them gently.

I looked up.

Above us, the flaming line of dying women was just a few dozen away from the bottom. Away from Claire. I'd let most of them die. This surprised no one. I wondered if Claire was lost to hysterics or if she knew I was still here. If she knew how badly I'd fucked everything up. How badly I'd failed to save her. Or Mags. Or, fuck, *me,* bleeding to death like a fucking sucker.

Ten Words? Twelve?

I felt my strength sagging. Leaking out of me. The power around me continued to flow into me, a golden river of shit. Physically, I fell back against Ketterly. I was numb. My heartbeat felt light and random, like an afterthought. My vision got cloudy, darkness edging in from the sides. I let my hands fall away from Ketterly's arms. I lay back against him, exhausted.

I kept whispering the *hun-kiuba*.

Renar kept casting both ends of the *biludha*. Five Words? Three? Three. I decided. I looked up. Smiled as I cast.

The girl in the sneakers

I had saved her I had saved her

I had saved her by doing nothing

I had saved her by doing nothing

nothing nothing at all.

Two Words.

I shut my eyes.

One.

The last Word of Hiram's spell slurred out of me.

28.

COME

I remembered watching cartoons in a dull-brown room off of Route 46. Hours and hours. My back hurt, and I was hungry. Dad had been gone all day.

back

On the TV, there was a creepy scientist chasing a bunny. There was gas in the air, so they were all slow and stretchy, floating. Like the gas made them light and weightless.

here

I wished I had that gas. I felt heavy. I kept imagining I couldn't move my arms and would sit and imagine myself trying to move and being unable to. I was wearing my blue footie pajamas, which Dad inexplicably allowed me to bring. Usually there was no time to pack.

you

Then I imagined myself moving really slowly instead. Not paralyzed but out of sync. The world moving around me faster than I could. I had to go to the bathroom. So I raised my arm slowly and took hold of the knob on the dresser drawer. Pulled myself up centimeter by centimeter, rising up from the floor.

rabbit.

It took me five minutes to make it to the bathroom door. By which time I was starting to doubt the entertainment value of the game. But I was committed now. You can't invest ten minutes into something, then decide it's daft. I wondered how I was going to slow down my pee stream.

Nighty

When I got out of the bathroom, triumphantly slow, slow, slow, I could tell Dad had been back and left again. A burning cigarette in the ashtray. A new set of wrinkles on the bed where he'd sat, making a phone call. The smell of cigarettes and boozy aftershave. I stood there and wanted to cry. I'd been screwing around in the bathroom, playing a stupid game, and he'd come back. And I'd missed him.

night.

I opened my eyes. I wasn't dead.

I FELT DEAD. I felt light and empty. My heart wasn't beating—or it *was*, but it was beating really slowly. Boom. Pause pause pause. Bam.

The light was still painfully bright in the chamber, but it had dimmed enough to allow actual vision. It hung in the air like smoke. Like each individual photon was visible. I was lying on top of the recently erected statue of D. A. Ketterly. I was covered in my own blood. I had a knife sticking out of my neck. Three fat globules of blood hung next to it, irregular spheres.

I sat up. I moved at normal speed. There was that strange, wet kind of crackling sound as I moved. Like I'd been wrapped up in a spider's web, but I didn't feel anything else. Mags was crouched over Claire, frozen, hands eternally wrapped around the chains that held her to the stone. He was straining with all his massive, terrible might, and Claire was staring up at him with an expression of terror—tinged with real, feral anger.

Renar looked exactly the same: slumped over in her wheelchair. Eyes slitted. Dry and yellow. Her Glamour was blurred and dimmed by the bright light of my previous Cantrip. Beautiful. Mouth open. Teeth and lips glistening.

Everything was still in a strange three-dimensional way. Moving at an incredibly slow speed. When you stared at something, it looked rock-still. If you looked away and back a few heartbeats later, it was subtly different. It had shifted. There was a noise in the air, persistent, like pebbles raining down on glass. It had no beginning or end. It just was.

I was so tired.

I felt like heavy weights had been affixed to my arms. My head was stuffed with something heavy and poisoned. My eyes bulged out of their sockets as if internal pressure were pushing them outward. This was my last conscious moment, stretched out nearly endlessly. In real time I was seconds from passing out. With Hiram's spell working, it would seem like hours.

Hiram's spell. I'd memorized it so long ago, and I'd edited it down over the years. Obsessed. Grinding on it. I'd clipped a syllable here, a syllable there. Substituted shorter words. Honed it down. On the subway all those years ago, it had taken Hiram forty-three seconds to recite it. At the time the Words had seemed elaborate, mysterious. Impossible to ever understand. I'd just cast the same spell in less than half the time, using every Trickster shortcut I'd ever learned. And I'd learned plenty.

I'd always been good with the Words.

I looked around again. With a pint or two of blood, Hiram's spell was designed to work in a single room, for a few minutes. I'd just cast it with a river of gas, a flood of fucking power. I didn't know how big the affected area was or how long it would last. I turned my head lazily to look at Renar. Both she and the Glamour were trapped with their mouths open, lips slightly pursed. I'd beaten her by half a second. One syllable left in the *biludha*. Half a second.

Renar's Other was staring right at me. Her beautiful eyes looked clear and focused, like she was seeing me in real time, like she was aware of everything. I could feel those eyes on me, like they were shooting light particles at me instead of collecting them.

I looked up, tilting my head, more of that strange, damp crackling as I shifted. The women imprisoned in their niches, spiraling up and out above us for what seemed like miles, were frozen in clear, brightly lit horror. A progression from Claire, untouched, unharmed, all the way up to the top, where the girls were charred, blackened, frozen in postures of agony. There were thirteen alive, caught in mid-scream, eyes wide, staring down at us. The fourteenth was enveloped in the bluish flame that was the *biludha* feeding from her, tearing her open and absorbing her blood into the vast cloud of energy being prepared.

Above her were only corpses. Charred and lifeless.

As expected, I had saved none of them.

I had to move. I hadn't stopped time. I had slowed it down for everyone in the immediate area aside from me. Or, more accurately, I had sped up my *movement* through time. I didn't know how long it would last, and no matter how slow time was moving, at some point Renar was going to finish casting the *biludha* and all fucking hell was going to break loose. I didn't know what would happen when her spell, massive as it was, met mine, relatively tiny and delicate in comparison. Sitting there, it seemed pointless.

I was so *tired*. I was seconds away from being dead. They were going to be the longest seconds of my life.

I started climbing to my feet. The effort was monumental. My limbs were rubbery and my head spun. Everything felt slippery, like there was no traction. Standing up was like falling. When I was upright, it seemed like everything was subtly moving, as if an earthquake had hit just as I cast, and the ground was shifting under my feet in tiny increments.

That sound of pebbles on glass, hissing in my ears.

I tried to do the math: How many seconds did I have to live, to remain conscious? And how long would that translate to in my subjective reality? Hiram had explained it to me a decade ago. He'd given me tables of complex equations, demonstrating the time relationships. The spell had been Hiram's life's work. He'd probably refined and perfected it since he'd taught it to me. I couldn't remember any of the tables. The equations.

With the ripping noise following me, I launched myself at Mags.

He was just as heavy as he was in real time. Mags was made of three or four people stitched together and filled with sand. I toppled him onto his back and he stayed in the same position—reacting, but too slow to really see. If I stared at him for an hour, I might start to see him react. I took hold of his arms. The wet tearing sound surged in volume. At first Mags was impossible to move. I strained and pulled at him, feeling light and empty. Like I was made of balloons and he was made of iron weights.

Then it started to get easier. Mags got lighter. And lighter. And lighter, until *he* was the balloon and I was pulling him towards the doorway easily. And then I wasn't pulling him at all; he was pushing me. Faster and faster. I was riding Mags to the doorway. Momentum. I realized that in real time, first I'd had to fight Mags's momentum; then, when I'd overcome it, I'd started him moving, and now he was sailing across the chamber at high speed like being a cannonball was a *property* of his.

It was like handling a parade float. If I shoved him to the left, nothing happened for what seemed like minutes; then he would slowly start to turn. Then not so slowly. Then he was soaring off in the new direction like he'd been shot out of a cannon. I slammed him into walls several times. I wanted to close my eyes and slump down. Every course correction required immense effort of will. I was cold and shaking. Bled white. I pushed and tugged Mags through the portal door in the study, down the fussy corridors of Renar's mansion, where the fire looked like solid pillars of orange and the smoke like thick black worms, and down the front steps to the driveway. I stepped around in front of him and spent some time slowing him to a stop, then pushed him slowly to the ground. Carefully.

Then I went back.

I didn't know how much time I had, when Renar would finally finish the last tiny bit of the last Word of the Rite. I made my way into the chamber, and nothing seemed to have changed. Though I had the strange feeling that things *had* changed. Ketterly's eyes were open wider. Claire's position shifted somehow. The light dimmer.

Claire was chained to the stone. The chains heavy and black, charred-looking, secured by a padlock. Squat and silver. I searched Amir's suit. His shirt was soaked in his own blood, bits of bone and yellow fat peeking out from the fabric. His face was still gorgeous, frozen in an expression of sad surprise, as if he'd seen this in a vision years ago and had forgotten right up until that moment. Or as if the *Udug* had told him just an hour ago what was going to happen.

The *Udug*. The second I thought of it, it crawled under my skin and I *wanted* it. I wanted to listen to it. The calm serenity of that affectless voice would be reassuring, like the stars—eternal, nonplussed, unconcerned with my bullshit.

I blinked my dry eyes. Focused on the task at hand. If I managed to accomplish anything here, I might spend an eternal second or two searching for the Artifact.

I didn't have to be careful with Amir. If he ended up soaring around the room, smashing into walls in real time, fuck it. He was probably dead anyway. And if he wasn't dead, I didn't like him. I found a set of keys in his jacket pocket. Took them over to Claire and searched. The sixteenth key worked on the padlock. I pulled her free from the chains. Bruises appeared on her skin where I touched her.

I tugged and pushed her out of the chamber. My eyes were dry and dim. There was a persistent, shadowy ache in my neck, which I realized was slow-motion agony, the pain making its way along my nerves slowly, drip by drip. I pushed her, frozen in a pose of combined terror and anger, until she sailed into Mags. I took one of my seconds to steady them both, slow them down, and stabilize them.

Then I went back.

This time there was a definite change in the chamber. Renar's Glamour was faded, in the midst of disappearing—which meant the Glamour's part of the Rite was finished. Which meant the Rite was finished. I was standing in the gap of half a second between the last breath of Renar's casting and the Rite burning up the collected energy and stretching out its bony hand across the world.

I looked up. The blue flames had stretched out to caress the next girl, chained up in her niche. Twelve left.

My eyes felt like someone had poured a beach into them. I had become aware, dimly, of the sizzling agony of a knife embedded in my neck. The final seconds of my life were exhausting.

Getting up to them wasn't too hard. There was a narrow walkway. It wrapped around the chamber, rising on a steep angle. I struggled up to the twelfth one, the highest up. The cold blue inferno was just a foot away. The girl to my left was frozen in a pose of agony and terror. Hands up. Eyes wide. Mouth open in a scream. Flames on her everywhere. I couldn't save her. Even if I freed her from her chains and carried her away, the Rite would consume her no matter what I did. Claire was out of position. I thought that might be sufficient to ruin things, but I couldn't be entirely sure. Again, my lack of education—there was someone in the world who knew the answer, but they weren't me.

As for the other girls, even if we were all going to die in a few moments, better for these last few to die instantly than burning, feeling it every inch of the way.

I turned and concentrated on the next girl. A little older than Claire but not much. Same type: tall, skinny. Short dark hair. Skinnier and dirtier, gaunt and hanging limply from the rough black chains. I tried the keys from Amir's ring. My hands felt like globs of soft clay at the ends of my heavy arms. Numb and useless. None of the keys fit.

I glanced up at the burning girl. She was burning slightly more than she had been. Time was running out.

I stood there for one of my moments. Swaying stupidly. My brain felt empty. I glanced up at the frozen firestorm. All that gas. Without even wondering whether it was possible, I started to speak an old, simple Cantrip. Four syllables. I felt the rush of power sweep through me—intense, wonderful, then gone and good riddance. I inspected the chains again and found the lock burst open by my spell. As if something tiny had broken free, peels of jagged metal sprung outward.

As I carried the girl down, her face twisted in a scream that seemed to be aimed directly at me, I had the same momentum problems I'd had earlier. After a few steps, she was pulling me after her. A few more steps and I put my back into slowing her down. Changing direction was an effort. By the time I had her coasting out onto the driveway to join Claire and Mags, I was sweating and stumbling. I watched her glide towards the ground. Tried to picture it sped up—a gruesome, rough landing. Then turned and staggered back. Eleven to go.

Up and down. Sweat slicked my skin, normal until it sloughed off and hung in the air, slowly jiggling away. By the third girl, I was pushing through curtains of my own suspended sweat. On my way back to get a fifth girl, I crawled. My hands in front of me were white with thick blue veins.

Down and down. She got away from me. Halfway to the floor, with the fifth girl sailing slowly towards a concussion against the wall, I sat for a bit, shivering. Shut my eyes. Opened them and pushed myself up, fell forward and grabbed on to her. Hung off of her for a while, feeling my whole body humming, buzzing. We sank towards the floor. I managed to get us oriented towards the door and pushed off, hanging on for dear life. We floated. Everything started to shudder and shake. The floor kept skipping out from under me as I strained.

One more, I thought. *Just one more.*

We had made it to the driveway when my spell shattered. The wet crackling noise snapped back, rewinding into a thunderous tearing. The fifth girl sailed away from me at full speed, smacking down hard into the gravel and sliding a few feet. Screaming, arms waving, synced up strangely with the other girls, also screaming, also waving their arms, beating off flames that weren't there anymore. I stumbled and crashed to the ground and lay there. I managed a painful breath. Exhaled a huge red blood bubble.

Then the night lit up as a sun rose behind us. I was lifted up from the ground and tossed onto my back. Something snapped and broke through the numb cold that had enveloped me, pain spiking from deep inside.

The house had been turned into a fiery blue sun, an orb of energy that lit up the night. Power hummed around me, through me. Immense power, more than I'd ever felt in one place. At first I thought the new sun was stable, just sitting there, but it was slowly swelling. Expanding. As it touched first earth, then pavement, then tree, each burst into bright white flame and then disappeared.

You could see into the orb. There was nothing inside it at all.

Everything else had gone deathly still. There was no wind, no sound. Nothing moved. I stared as the blue sun expanded inch by inch. This wasn't unfocused power. This wasn't what had happened to Mags back in Rue's a few days ago. If Renar had simply bled all those people and let it go, it would have been an explosion. We all would have been vaporized. This was at least partially focused—she had completed the Rite. The spell was complete but underfueled. We'd stolen away the last crucial sacrifices. We'd stolen away Claire, the keystone.

There was a spell. I just didn't know what it was going to do.

I took a breath. Breathing seemed optional. A lot of effort, too. When it leaked back out of me, bloody bubbles clogged my throat.

The orb pulsed and then raced towards me, swelling at a tremendous rate. I felt the cold heat of it pushing against me, so I closed my eyes.

29.

EVERY MUSCLE JERKED LIGHT EVERYWHERE and Mags melodious and rhythmic.

I opened my eyes.

It was cold. Freezing. I was not, however, dead. Mags and Claire were kneeling over me. Mags had his eyes shut. Was speaking a spell, his voice hoarse. I wondered when Mags had learned a new spell. And *remembered* it for more than two hours. I wanted to reach up and pat him on the head, give him a cookie.

Claire was bleeding. Holding her arm up and watching the blood drip from a deep, ugly gash in the meat of her forearm. Tears dripped down her face. Her tattoos made her skin look like marble, icy white, her hair a shadow against it.

I had made Claire Mannice cry. This was my finest achievement.

Now that I'd seen it, she was clearly the offspring of Mika Renar. The same nose, the same sleepy, deadly eyes, the same tiny frame. A dash of Cal Amir, too, I figured, adding to her painful beauty. Or maybe not. Amir might have been just a vessel for Renar's power. I didn't know what kind of monstrous spells the two had cast to create the raw materials for their Rite of Death. I didn't know. I didn't want to know. But it was obvious now. All those girls, looking so similar. Ranging in age. Amir and Renar had been working on the *biludha* for *decades*. This was some old-school Greek tragedy shit.

I reached out a shaking arm and flopped it against Mags. He startled. Opened his eyes. Kept speaking the spell, because we'd just seen firsthand what happened when you stopped midspell. Mags didn't learn easy, but when he learned something, it was the only thing he could think of until he learned something new. He tied the spell off nicely, and I felt a slight surge of energy flow into me. Mags, bringing me back to life.

"Lem! Fuck, fuck, *fuck*, Lem!" Mags hissed, leaning down. "You okay?"

I wanted to say, *Jesus, I was dead*, but I needed my energy for more important things. "Cigarette," I croaked.

I heard Claire laugh as Mags dragged out a crushed and mangled pack. Slipped one between my lips. Lit it for me with a two-Word Cantrip. I sucked blue smoke into my lungs and fought the urge to pass out.

"Help me sit up," I said.

He pushed me into a sitting position and braced me from behind. I stared at where Renar's mansion had once been. It was a blackened hole in the ground. Fires burning everywhere. There was a window, miraculously unbroken and still in its frame, lodged in the branches of a tree. I sucked in smoke and felt a wave of dizziness pass through me.

"The other women?" I asked.

"The five you brought out," I heard Claire say. "Gone. Ran for their lives."

I nodded. I didn't blame them.

"It didn't work," Mags said breathlessly. "But *something* happened. When the place went up, there was a spell. Something."

Coughs made me shake, my chest on fire. "Help me up."

Mags pulled me to my feet and held me there.

"Walk me down."

We left Claire there, wrapping a strip of Mags's dirty shirt around her wounds. The heat coming off the crater was incredible. But I made Mags walk me straight into it. My cigarette had burned to the filter, but the ashes clung on anyway. We staggered around the perimeter and eventually found her wheelchair in the woods behind the house. Untouched. Just sitting there. As if someone had pushed it away from the house. Calmly. And then left it. It wasn't even scorched.

I stood there, hanging from Mags, staring.

When we got back to the driveway, Claire was gone. Mags started calling her name, wandering around, concerned, but I just stood there, smoking. I was used to people leaving. The only people who hadn't left were Hiram and Mags, and Hiram had gotten killed for his trouble, and I wasn't sure I wouldn't end up killing Mags at some point, too. If it were possible, even, to kill Mageshkumar.

I remembered Claire on the bus ride to Texas. Soft and dreamy, a normal girl who smelled like soap and cigarettes, who tucked her legs under herself, who stroked Mags's hair gently as we whispered our life stories to each other. I felt a stab of pain that she'd left without saying anything, without a note. I understood, I thought, why she'd left. I was grateful, I thought, that she'd stuck around long enough to bleed for Mags and save my life. I knew, on some level, that this should have been enough.

I stared out at the charred trees around us. It wasn't, wouldn't ever be.

I'D NEVER BEEN SO hungry in all my life. Or so happy to let Mags run the full con for us. He Charmed the hostess with a smile and flick of gas. He Charmed our waitress. He Charmed the round family seated next to us. He made some napkins stuffed in his pocket look like twenty-dollar bills. He played every trick he knew and ordered us two heaping breakfasts: pancakes, eggs over easy, sausage, bacon, toast, and glorious, hot black coffee.

I sat shivering as I ate. I was living on gas. I was living on the energy Mags had given me. I ate my breakfast and Mags silently slid his over to me. I didn't pause for breath.

The news was leaking in. Small town, and the diner had no televisions, so it crept in the old-fashioned way, via people arriving, text message, and the Internet. Disasters everywhere. Bizarre things. Mass murders. Someone had set off a bomb at a military base, killing dozens. Hundreds of people visiting the Grand Canyon had suddenly gone mad and hurled themselves over the edge. People had jumped by the score from landmarks around the world, raining down from the Eiffel Tower, the Space Needle, the Golden Gate Bridge. The stories trickled in, and the diner got quiet. People hurriedly paid up and left.

Someone finally set up a radio and we listened to report after report: dozens dead here, thousands killed there. All isolated incidents. All inexplicable. A Day of Madness.

Someone read aloud an incoherent post on the Internet about marines storming a base out in Colorado where the people with their thumbs on the launch buttons had lost it, but no one could find a confirming story, and then the website disappeared.

I sat back and smoked another of Mags's cigarettes. Didn't say a word. No one would have believed me.

The disasters came in spurts. People left, new people came in. I considered ordering a third breakfast. The radio spilled out more news. Mass drownings off the Florida coast. An entire old-age home committing suicide via sleeping pills doled out to residents in a carefully managed plan. A college fraternity leaping from the roof of their house en masse. A man with a semiautomatic hunting rifle killing thirty-four people at a mall in New Jersey.

I'd heard these stories before, from Hiram, in books. All the markings of *ustari* fueling spells. But those incidents had all been separated by years, decades, centuries. This was every five minutes.

The lunch crowd. A new group of people came in, fewer than had been at breakfast. They ate hurriedly, left, throwing money on the counter. The radio sighed out its next list of mass deaths. It never ended. I was bloated and charged, the curious manic energy of the recently dead. More new people sat down, ordered. The radio voice grew ragged. Started off as a smooth professional voice, bored by the news. Slowly frayed. After an hour, he was gasping it out. Barely hanging on. Mags and I just sat there, listening. I kept reminding myself, over the ragged and off-rhythm beat of my heart, that it would have been worse. It would have been the entire world.

Ev Fallon walked in after I'd ordered my fourth meal of the last few hours. He simply walked over to our table and sat down, pulling out a curious pack of European cigarettes and tossing them on the table to share. His hands sported two fresh bandages, rusty blood soaking through. He looked *old*. He'd been old before, but now he looked ancient. A hundred years old, and a hard hundred. He stared down at the table.

Mags stood up, fists clenched, but I reached up lazily and tugged at his sleeve. I didn't have the energy for anger or revenge.

"I have not been particularly smart or heroic today," Fallon said slowly, without looking at us. "I thought perhaps I could at least still be *useful*."

It was not an apology, or an admission of guilt. I wondered, if Claire had not been there, would I have gone down into the machine myself? I might have fled, too. Might have tried to come up with a way to ensure I was that one percent left alive.

One thing I knew: I was not a good person.

I shrugged.

"The death toll will be hundreds of thousands, perhaps millions," he said quietly. "There is chaos in the larger cities. The population centers. Farther away, everything seems normal. In the cities, many are dead. There will be no explanation."

I picked one of his cigarettes up and put it between my lips. My eyes felt like they'd been filled with sand and lit on fire. "You have a car?"

Fallon nodded.

"Take us home."

FALLON HAD ACQUIRED A brand-new luxury sedan, sleek and black. The leather on the seats was the softest thing I'd ever felt. It still had the dealer sticker on it. It was fun to think of the Fabricator bleeding himself in order to steal a car.

As we drove, things got worse. At first the roads were relatively empty. After a half hour, the traffic on the other side of the divider, heading away from the city, started to get heavy. Another ten minutes, it was wall-to-wall cars. Another five and people had gotten out of their cars to walk. Fallon drove calmly, expertly. A man who was completely at home with any kind of machine. He steered up onto dividers, embankments, gently easing the car over all manner of obstacles, weaving in and out of abandoned cars, rubble, the burning remnants of a school bus.

Another ten minutes after that, we started to see the smoke.

Getting into the city was easy. Normal. The streets were oddly deserted. No one on the sidewalks, no cars moving at all. The smoke was always on the horizon. We never got any closer to it, twin pillars of black air swirling upwards and out. I dozed. At one point there were three or four people around the car, screaming and pounding on the glass. I dozed again. Then we were picking our way slowly through the remnants of a blown-out building, like a bomb had gone off.

All over the world, Renar's Rite had reached out and started chain reactions. Designed to spill blood that the Rite would then absorb until it had enough. Since we'd broken it, all it had done was kill a bunch of people to no fucking purpose.

We turned a corner and the car stopped with a jerk. I sat forward. The three of us stared at a dozen dead bodies in the middle of the street, the blood cold and useless and everywhere. Fallon idled there and then silently backed up.

By the time he'd wormed his way to the burned-out husk of Hiram's apartment, we'd begun to see some people. Dazed. Coming out of their homes for the first time in hours. Most of the city seemed untouched, but you saw it in everyone's faces. For a few hours, the whole population had gone crazy. And might again at any moment.

Mags helped me from the car. Fallon rolled down the passenger-side front window.

"I will be in touch, yes?"

I turned my head limply and looked at him. "Why?"

He shrugged, putting the car into gear. "To make amends."

We watched the car drive off. Stood listening to the endless wail of sirens, distant, dopplered.

"You Vonnegan?"

Mags spun, crouching into a defensive, snarling posture. I turned like a balloon in the wind, helped along by the stiff breeze Mags caused.

Sitting on the front steps of Hiram Bosch's former home was a tall woman, skin a deep tan, hair a bright, unnatural red I could see with a glance was magically maintained. She was wearing what looked like a man's suit, blue and pin-striped. Her hair was pulled back in a fiery tail that reached down to her ass. She was sitting there like the steps were perfectly comfortable, legs stretched out, one arm draped along the cracking stone.

Her hands were covered in familiar scars, most of them white and old, long healed.

"Who are you?" I asked.

She smiled. She was quite pretty, somewhat older than me. She unfolded her long frame and stood up, leaning forward in a stiff, formal bow and extending a hand. Mags looked at it like it might be made of death.

"Melanie Billington. Call me Mel."

I reached out and took her hand. I wanted nothing more than a bed and several days of silence. "Good to meet you, Mel. But listen, just a few hours ago I was dead, and this is where my *gasam* died a few days ago, so can we do whatever this is another time?"

I realized as I spoke that this wasn't home anymore. I'd made Fallon take me to the wrong place. Hiram's had been home for years when I hadn't been allowed to stay there. Now I could go in if I wanted, but it was a wreck. There was nothing in it for me.

I had to go make my own place.

She smiled, straightening up. "I know, boyo. It's in the air. On the grapevine. Your name, what you've done. And that dried-up old bitch is still alive, and plenty of the other *ustari* are willing to work with her, to try again." She shrugged. "Live forever, kill the rest of us. I am here, like a lot of other *idimustari* soon will be," she said, spreading her arms, "to help."

I blinked. "To help with *what*?"

Her face shifted to quizzical. "The War, Mr. Vonnegan. To help you with the *War*."

II.
NEGOTIATOR

30.

WHEN THE SUICIDE STEPPED ONTO the train, I thought, *Shit, things are about to get interesting.*

It had been a long six months.

The subway had stopped four times already today between stations, just grinding to a shuddering halt, lights flickering, air-conditioning clicking on, off, on, off. The walls and seats and floors and ceiling of the car were covered in bright red graffiti that made no immediate sense. All of the metal handholds and trim felt greasy, damp.

"Fuck," Mags whispered, shifting his weight in the seat and crossing his arms. I could hear the seams of his jacket straining.

"We'll make it," I said.

"The fuck we will."

I shrugged. "We couldn't take the streets. What else were we going to do?"

He snorted. The snort translated to a stream of vulgarity and Mags's usual declaration that a man in my position should get a few dozen Bleeders together and *fly* wherever he wanted. Mags was a proud mama when it came to me. For myself, I'd gotten comfortable with bleeding others when it felt necessary. Flying around the city didn't exactly feel *necessary*.

We were drifting along the track, not going any faster than a healthy man could stroll, hands laced behind his back, thoughts on his mind; still, we were moving. The way the trains were—the way *everything* was now—this was better than nothing. We'd speed up a bit after Ninety-Sixth street, I thought. We were in the first car, where the conductor sat in his tiny booth, and could watch the dark tunnel scrolling towards us a frame at a time.

I ran my gaze over the other passengers. An unshaved old pensioner across the aisle from me was reading a print newspaper. The headline read FORTY DEAD IN FERRY MASSACRE.

I'd heard that one. Two uniformed police officers had boarded the ferry to New Jersey, waited until the boat was in the middle of the river, and started shooting. First the captain and crew, then the passengers. One of them had put the throttle all the way up, and the boat had eventually crashed into the Hoboken piers and caught fire.

Good times. They were all good times, these days.

At that same moment, four hundred and thirteen residents of Gdańsk poisoned themselves, leaving behind a single note that read, in full, *Reka reke myje,* with no other comment. In Ulan Bator, two dozen pregnant women leaped into the Tuul and drowned themselves. In Kira Town, a renegade army unit cut off the heads of two thousand men and women, then motored off, having taken nothing, left no message, and gained no military advantage.

In London the day before, sixty-four percent of the police force called in sick. There were no demands, no labor negotiation. People took the opportunity to riot and set fire to all those cars they'd been meaning to see burn. The next day, all those cops showed up for work like nothing had happened.

In Florence, two hundred homicides in the past two weeks.

In DC, thirteen suspicious fires. Yesterday. In New York, in spite of, or because of, the chaos, people kept coming. The city was bursting, and the people left their mark on everything they touched. Graffiti was everywhere, most of it painted, some of it scratched into the glass. I didn't understand most of it: symbols and exaggerated lettering. It was growing over everything in the city, some of it interesting, even artistic. The subway car we were riding in was like being inside one of those caves in France where they found the paintings: A dozen assholes had already made their mark and retired, confident these tags would see them remembered by history.

We rumbled into the Ninety-Sixth Street station in slow motion, gliding in as if the air had gotten thick, blunting momentum. A handful of people stood up to exit, a handful slouched on the platform waiting to get in. The doors opened, and there was the usual confusion as people tried to push in and people tried to push out. There was a weariness to the whole enterprise. No one got upset, no fights were sparked. There was just desultory shoving and mild chaos.

And then, just as the doors cleared and were about to shut, the Suicide stepped onto the car, the doors sliding closed right behind him. I knew what he was because he was wearing the uniform: all black, unlaundered. A sweatshirt with a hood, denim pants, a T-shirt. Head shaved, apparently by his own hand, in the dark, with a dull blade. His skull was scabbed and clumps of hair sprouted here and there like mold. Bags under his eyes, skinny and nervous. Hands pushed into the pockets of the sweatshirt over his belly.

"*Fuuuuck*," Mags groaned in recognition.

The Suicides were the echoes of Mad Day, the ripples lapping against the far shore of time. The world had gone insane for forty-eight hours. Millions had died. There were cults, or loose groups of them, though they weren't really organized. They just all shared a deep belief that the only thing that had gone wrong on Mad Day was not enough people had died. That it was everyone's duty to try and rectify this failing of the human race. One at a time, if necessary.

I thought, *Fucking hell, that bitch Renar did her damage, didn't she?*

"We're not gonna make it," Mags complained.

"Sure we will."

"She's *waiting*."

I sighed. I wasn't sure why we going in the first place. Mel Billington took herself so fucking seriously, and she was always talking about the War. There wasn't any war that I could see, at least not between mages. She was fucking exhausting. "One fucking asshole isn't going to stop us, okay?"

The train shuddered back into motion. The Suicide stayed near the door, swaying uncertainly.

These guys really had a thing for trains. Jumping in front of them, mostly, which made this one's decision to climb on board and share our ride kind of suspicious. Like maybe he wasn't fully committed.

Since he and his friends were almost single-handedly fucking up the public transportation in Manhattan, everyone riding with us knew what he was on sight, and all were doing the grim calculus on what effect he might have on their commute.

"That fucker makes a move," Mags whispered fiercely, rolling up his sleeve, "I'm going to shut him up."

I thought about pointing out to Mags that bleeding and casting on that idiot would more than likely slow us down even more—suicide they were used to, giant Indians casting spells, not so much—but the ensuing argument exhausted me before it began. And Mags had improved. After years of learning at a snail's pace, something had changed in him. He was actually remembering things these days. He wasn't exactly spinning his own rituals, but he was a better mage than he'd ever been before, in my experience.

The Suicide was leaning back against the sliding door with his hands pushed into his black pants, his head down. He looked defeated. Ruined. It was surprising how easily you could be pushed down the stairs, wake up one day and have nothing. Mags was staring at the kid from under his amazing unibrow, like he was summoning the mental energy to shoot a heat ray out of his eyes.

When the subway ground to a halt for the fourth time midtunnel, the lights flickering off, the whole car groaned in unison.

Then, silence.

Then, like steam escaping from a volcano named Mageshkumar: "*Fuuuuck.*"

He'd dressed up for the occasion, his suit a bit too tight, as they always were, the seams straining to contain his bearlike frame. He always forgot to unbutton his jacket when he sat down, so it bunched up in front of him.

Me, I was in my usual black suit, shiny from wear, too loose and wrinkled.

I heard the Suicide say, "Ladies and gentlemen, may I have your attention for a moment?" and Mags was up out of his seat.

The Suicides all had a patter, a short speech. The exact words dif-
fered depending on what kind of Suicide you were dealing with.
Some of them were on target and specifically mentioned Mad Day,
how it was "the beginning of the end of the world." Some had other
specifics, personal tragedies or peculiar maths they'd worked out.
Most of them were parroting what someone else had said or written.
Some of the Suicide Cults had gotten big, with gangs of people in
their black hoodies wandering the big cities of the world, urging everyone to follow them into the grave. Urging everyone to read the
signs (from God, from the cosmos, from whateverthefuck) and get in
line.

On the subways in Manhattan, the Suicides always started off with
Ladies and gentlemen, may I have your attention for a moment? Polite.
Then they gave a nice speech about sin, or maybe a nihilistic inevitabil-
ity, the sun exploding or space aliens calling us home to our forgotten
world of origin. Whatever. It didn't matter. At the end of the speech,
they urged you to follow their example, and then they killed themselves. Straight. Direct. Linear progression.

When this speech was made on the platform, it usually ended with
the Suicides jumping in front of a train. Sometimes this was timed perfectly, very dramatic. Sometimes there was work on the tracks and they
had to stand there, looking grim and purposeful, until a train came
rumbling in. Sometimes people actually did join them, tossing aside
briefcases and newspapers and phones and jumping down a moment
before the train cut them to pieces.

Sometimes when they had to wait, they changed their minds and
left suddenly, walking fast for the stairs, heads down.

Mags was halfway to the Suicide when the second voice broke the
tight silence of the car.

"Ladies and gentlemen!"

We all turned to look, even Mags, who paused awkwardly in the
middle of the aisle to twist around cruelly in his overtight suit. There
stood another Suicide, black hoodie, shaved head, a young girl with

pink lips and no eyebrows, eyes swollen and red like she'd been crying for years, for decades.

"You may not see it," she said quietly, "but we are all dead already. Join me, and quit fighting."

This was a new one. The Futility of Existence. I liked it. Mags didn't know what to do with the fury he'd been nursing. He stood there, making huge rocklike fists with his hands. Everyone else waited them out, knowing how this ended. When they made their speech on the actual subway car, the exact method of suicide varied depending on personal preference. No one looked ready to intervene. You got used to it. Six months ago, watching people kill themselves in front of you was upsetting. Now it was just annoying. They began speaking simultaneously and I shut my eyes, my only defense. It only made their actual babble more pronounced.

"We have been given a sign."

"Can any of you doubt the world is in rapid decline?"

"We have all witnessed the Mad Day, when neighbors attacked each other, when children murdered their parents."

Mad Day. A stupid name.

"It's been said that not enough righteous people remained for the Rapture to be noticed."

"We are all in hell, suffering, but there is a way out."

I opened my eyes.

"But there is a way forward."

The train lurched on, the lights flickering. I saw I'd made a bad assumption: These weren't competing assholes, they were from the same club. They stood there, each holding up a small plastic bottle of lighter fluid. Immediately, everyone on either end of the car stood up and crowded into the center, swaying and staggering as the train began to pick up speed again.

"*Mother*fucker," Mags groaned. I had to suppress a laugh. A wholly inappropriate, completely crazy laugh.

As they went on, the Suicides began pouring the thick, clear liquid over themselves. The sharp tangy smell of something flammable filled the tight air. And then, hidden beneath it, the heady scent of the gas: Mags had opened a shallow cut on his palm, a thin stream of blood but enough for something clever. Mags didn't have anything clever, so I knew this was going to be interesting. I crossed my legs and leaned on my knee, watching him with affection. Mags was man's best friend.

The two kids dropped their bottles onto the floor. Raised up shiny lighters, flicked them open. Snapped a flame into being. All of this in coordination, as if they'd practiced it.

Mags hissed five Words under his breath. I felt the brush of power passing near me, and both flames disappeared as if invisible urchins had crept up behind the Suicides and snuffed them. I decided not to chide Mags for his poor vocabulary. Five fucking Words for *that*.

The expressions on the Suicides' faces was priceless. Three more times, they snapped their lighters into life, Mags muttered his little spell, and the lighters went out. Titters and snickers drifted through the car. The first guy got red in the face, planted his feet, and pushed out his chest.

"Fucking *assholes*!" he shouted.

Behind him, the 125th Street station rolled into view. A smattering of applause broke out and swelled into thunderous clapping. I fought back laughter as Mags and I stood up and made for the doors.

"This is our stop," I said to the Suicide as we passed him, just for the expression on his face.

The second we stepped out of the station, we were pushed and crashed into, the Harlem crowd so thick we were almost carried along by the current. The noise was intense. Beneath the lowing of the crowd was the static buzz of the cars, inching along in an endless siege of traffic. Horns bled into the air so continuously, they became a single monotonous blur in the air, a bellow of discontentment.

Mel Billington was leaning against a signpost, smoking a cigar, one hand in the pocket of her suit trousers. Her suit matched mine, though it was a little newer and had been tailored for her. Sunglasses and long red hair pulled back into a tight bun.

As always, I was unsettled by Billington. She'd arrived on the heels of Mika Renar's attempt to bleed the world dry and had announced "we" were "at war," that I was the natural leader for this enterprise, and that she was my aide-de-camp or something like that. "We" being all the *idimustari,* the Tricksters and con artists who used a little gas and a few Words to ease our way in the world, that our "war" was with the Archmages and other swells who'd partnered with Renar for a chance at immortality on the bleeding backs of every man, woman, child, dog, and fucking mayfly in the world. I'd let her take the reins, and every asshole who volunteered for our army—and there were *tons* more assholes of that particular stripe than I ever would have imagined—she took in, issued them a black fucking suit, and organized them. I didn't know what to feel about that.

Mel spoke without turning as we came near. "How's the subway working out for you, Chief?"

Mel and her people, they all called me Chief. Mel's people dressed like her, which I guess meant they dressed like me. It was a little creepy. The way Mel looked at me was a little creepy, too. So far she hadn't been able to transfer that look to the losers, vagrants, and idiots who kept showing up, looking for me, having heard that I was some sort of savior. They remained Tricksters, grifters, and most of them had started to get that impatient look on their faces that suggested they were getting tired of waiting for me to do something amazing.

"Mags made a new friend," I said as she turned to face us.

"Fuuuuck," Mags muttered.

She smiled, but it was a sour half-smile. "You ought to have more security with you, Chief. Our little Confusion Project isn't fucking foolproof, yes?"

Billington had organized about a dozen of the Tricksters who could do something worth doing into a team who split each day—one shift on, one off—casting Glamours over me, hiding me from prying eyes. A more powerful mage could have tied off a nifty spell for a full-time effect, or created a Fabrication. We needed twelve assholes working nonstop. It was like we couldn't afford a car, so Billington had built one from cardboard and a garage door opener.

I shrugged. "I'm not *enustari*, Mel."

She snorted. "You should start thinking like one. Because they're the ones trying to fucking kill you, Chief. C'mon," she added with a brief smile for Mags. "This way."

She turned and started walking. We fell in beside her, and I was promptly exhausted. People wondered why I liked the subway. At least on the subways I could relax and let something else barrel its way through the earth. On the streets it was all effort, endless and sweaty.

"You have any trouble on the way?"

I shrugged. "Couple of Suicides, but we handled them."

"Oh yeah? You got two dozen *idimustari* who'll bleed for you, who'd float your ass down here. Who would at minimum *ride the fucking subway with you* to make sure nothing happens. But you're riding the subway alone like a fucking asshole, whose fault is that?"

"Mine. And I wasn't alone, I had Mags." I shoved past an old lady pushing what looked like a pile of hair and a handgun in her cart. "At least down there we don't have to worry about crazy cops who shoot pedestrians, or construction workers who topple cranes on crowds, or Griefers."

She snorted. "Griefers. You're worried about fucking monosyllabic kids."

Griefers. Everything was breaking down, even us. Kids who'd figured out the most basic fact—that anyone could use magic if they knew the Words and were willing to bleed—and the most basic equation—blood plus a Word equals *something*—running in gangs and bleeding for single-word spells. Fire. Death. Light. Dark. Single Words didn't do much. You couldn't kill someone just by shouting the Word for *die*. And you couldn't really direct it usefully. But you *could* cause some damage, make some trouble. That's all the Griefers cared about.

A few years ago they would have been dealt with by the *ustari* directly. A few years ago they never would have *happened,* because none of us would have taught them a single fucking *Word* until they were *urtuku.*

"Assassins," Mags grunted. He was walking like he had some sort of wild animal stuffed into his shirt. "Three times, that old bitch has tried to kill Lem."

A lie. An exaggeration. The last time had been kids. Two girls, maybe ten years old. Hiding under my bed, waiting for me to fall asleep so they could cast a nasty spell on me, one that had been written out phonetically for them on their arms. One of the girls had been there to cast it on me. The other was the Bleeder. But not there to kill me. To *transport* me. The spell had been written to zombie me out, make me compliant and silent while they took me wherever and I was told to do whatever.

I'd felt sorry for the girls. They were skinny and bruised, and after I caught them, I gave them a hard lesson in dirty pool with a three-Word spell that made them both feel like they were falling, always falling, down a deep hole. I managed to get it into the air before they'd spoken their second syllable, and after letting them feel it for a few minutes, I let them go. They were just *kids.*

Besides, I knew all I needed to know. Renar wanted me for some reason. Alive. To torture me personally? To question me? I didn't know. But I'd let the lie stand. It was easier that way.

I didn't want to talk about Mika Renar reaching out her bony hand across the world to try and kill me. "Mel, run it down for me."

She laughed. "Fine. Carith Abdagnale. *Saganustari,* I think. Some might argue. She's clean."

"Clean?"

"Nothing to do with Renar. Nothing to do with the *tah-namus.* She wasn't part of it. She can help us."

"She know we're coming?" I didn't like giving any warning, considering the most powerful *enustari* in the world wanted me, if not dead, certainly not *well.*

Mel shook her head. "She knows I'm coming. Not you."

I admired the way Mel swaggered through the crowd. She wasn't much of a mage, I'd learned. Passable. She made sloppy mistakes and half the time her spells did things she didn't expect. But she had a talent for organization. Every day a new group of shifty, untrustworthy idiots arrived to see the *idimustari* who'd fucked up Mika Renar's shit and ask what they could offer me, and Mel was keeping them all straight.

She produced a candy bar from one of her suit's pockets and held it out to Mags without a word or a glance. The big Indian's face lit up into a delighted grin as he took it. Then he looked down shyly at his remarkably tiny shoes and stuffed the bar into his own pocket.

"Carith Abdagnale," I said slowly, "is a *pimp*."

Mel shrugged. "She can help us. We need every drop we can get."

Mel was a True Believer. Figured me for a general, a savior. I wasn't as sure as Mel was.

I considered Carith Abdagnale as we walked. Hiram had told me stories about her. Talented, he'd said. In the beginning of her career, she'd been one to watch—*enustari* for sure, given time. But she'd always been strange. Afraid of people. She'd come into possession of this church and hidden away in it. And thrived.

No one had laid eyes on her in thirty years.

Rumors, of course, abounded: She used Glamours to doll herself up and act as one of her own prostitutes, so odds were even that one of her regulars was giving it to a sixtyish woman who'd never been described as *attractive*. Or that she'd died long ago and her *urtuku* was trading on the name, which had precedent. We didn't know much honor, after all, as a class of humans, whether *idimustari* or *enustari*.

The traffic was so thick, I figured people were living in their cars now, pulling out folding chairs and charcoal grills every night, hanging out in the cooling air drinking beer, swapping stories of the old days when you could drive three blocks in New York City in under three days. The bodies were so thick on the sidewalk and in the street, pushing between the cracks in the car like mortar between bricks, the heat was palpable, going up a degree for every person within a foot of you. So I was feeling about seven hundred degrees as we walked.

"Something happen downtown?"

Mel didn't turn. "A bomb or something. What are you gonna do? It's the new normal."

She was right. Nothing had settled back into any sort of familiar pattern since Renar's failed *biludha*. Every day was a fresh set of disasters, keeping us all on our toes. These sure were exciting times.

After two blocks of swimming upstream—every direction was upstream—Mel carved a path to an old, weathered church. The ancient gray stone looked melted, as if the original faithful who'd built it had been suckered on a quarry deal and built the place from soap instead of stone. It was desanctified, and there was a big brass doorbell wired into the wall on one side of the warped black wooden doors. Mel didn't pause or ask what we thought. She just rang the bell and stepped back. A second later the door bellowed open and a woman with soft blond curls around her pink face stood framed there, squinting. She looked to be about thirty but had a mischievous grin that made her seem younger somehow.

"Golly," she said. "He's a big boy."

"We're here to meet with Carith," Mel said bluntly.

The woman shrugged. She was wearing pajamas under a simple blue bathrobe, like we'd pulled her out of a slumber party. I could feel the cool interior air of the church rushing out at us, bringing with it the subtle scent of flowers, her perfume.

"Sure. Other door," she said, and closed the big door on us with a definitive bang.

We stood for a moment in confusion, then all three of us turned our heads and found the "other" door, a diminutive wooden portal a few feet to the right. I would have to bend down to get through it. Mags, I thought, would have to either bleed a bit and shrink himself, or slather himself with grease and get some momentum going.

Carved in the stone above the tiny door was the name ABDAGNALE and then some runes, spelling out *an-uraš gu*. My head for the written forms of the Words was no good, and there were so many alphabets it got confusing. It meant something like *my universe*, but that was just a cheerful approximation. Writing the Words didn't mean anything, only speaking them. It was simple lettering, nothing fancy. There didn't appear to be any lock or latch on the door. For a moment we all just stood there studying it.

"The bad feeling is stipulated, right?" I said.

"She's clean," Mel repeated. "And she can help us."

"Doesn't mean she wants to. And there's a lot of daylight between not wanting to murder the world and not wanting to murder *me*."

Mags shrugged. "Fuck it. We're *here*."

Mel's big plan was to recruit big and recruit little. Any time she found out about an *ustari* of any rank somewhere, she investigated. Most of the mages who'd helped Renar, or who'd joined her at the end to be part of the Immortal Club, were known personalities—and currently, by and large, were *missing*. But Mel scoped out every mage of power she found out about. If you hadn't been part of the *tah-namus*, Mel wanted to recruit you for the War. Said War so far boiling down to Mika Renar trying to kill me and me doing absolutely fucking nothing. It was tiring, and I paid attention only when Mel made me. Which she was remarkably good at.

Mags pushed the door in, grunted as he strained through, and I followed. We were swallowed up in a moist darkness. Two shallow steps brought us up into the main part of the old church, where a new girl, also in pajamas and a blue bathrobe, waited for us. This girl was young, fresh-faced and delicate, her blond hair a cloud of golden curls, her eyes almost glowing blue, her skin delicious. Her pajamas were silk and shimmered iridescently as she moved. She was beautiful.

"Follow me," she said, smiling.

The place was full of girls.

The inside was just a huge room now; all the benches and paintings and other religious artifacts had been removed, leaving just a big room that had been furnished as a series of large "rooms" defined by the borders of their furniture. There was a bar and lounge area where several girls, all wearing sleepwear ranging from prim pajamas to silky lingerie, lounged on plush couches while a skinny Asian fellow in a tuxedo polished highball glasses behind a huge, shiny oak bar. There was a dance floor complete with a tiny, empty stage for a band, and two other lounge-like areas, these filled with men and women. The women dressed like the others, in various versions of sleepwear. The men mostly dressed in suits, mostly expensive. The stained-glass windows gave the light an eerie blue quality, and the high ceiling soaring over us made everything sound distant and muted, like we were watching something on a screen. The furniture was expensive-looking. There was a smell of flowers in the air. I instantly felt warm and happy, swimming through an atmosphere of sex and relaxation, a safe place.

All the girls had their hair up, sometimes piled high in ridiculous mounds of curls. All of them had complex arrangements of things thrust into their hair—knitting needles, pens, chopsticks. They bristled with easy weapons as they glided about.

The air was full of whispers.

I felt warm. I glanced at Mags and blinked in surprise. He'd pulled out the candy Mel had given him, and his mouth was smeared with chocolate as he chewed, staring over at the bar area. I tasted the air for gas but didn't find any. Which was strange, because I would have bet money the place was heavy with spells.

Suddenly, there was a tall black kid standing next to me. He was good-looking, well built and filling a sober blue suit nicely. He smiled at us with white teeth and spread his hands.

"Ms. Abdagnale will see you now," he said.

"Who are you?"

He bowed his head a little. "Ms. Abdagnale is my *gasam*."

I smirked. Someone had laid some serious gas on this kid. "Sure she is."

He led us to the back, where the altar used to be, and through a huge black door on the left, massive and carved in a thick, meandering pattern. As we got there, a silver-haired man in a natty suit emerged from the door across the way, two of the girls on his arms, like they were being escorted to a ball. The girls were wearing satiny costume-like lingerie, like a cabaret act. Every hair in place. Complex hooks and buttons done perfectly.

"I take it back," I said to Mel's back as we followed the kid. "She's not a pimp. She's a very, very good *thief*."

All the girls suddenly seemed knowing and ruined. Suddenly seemed rotten instead of lost. Nothing wrong with a bit of gas getting you into someone's pocket. I'd done it myself a million times. It beat starving to death. It wasn't that—it was the charade, the complex layer of bullshit. It was unseemly. It was *wasteful*. Why in fuck would she put this much effort, this much blood and frill, into what was basically a grift—a grift that would have worked just as well with half the bullshit. And would have cost some poor Bleeder less of their life.

We stepped into a small office, suddenly crowded. It was done up in velvet hangings and delicate wooden furniture with ornate scrollwork. It felt hot and tiny, dry and woolly, like the air itself was furred.

Carith Abdagnale was a giantess, tall and statuesque, with an hourglass figure poured into an expensive dress that shimmered. She smoked a cigarette using a long glittering holder that caught the light, trailing streaks of color as she moved it around. She was sixtyish but youthful, her makeup careful and perfect, her hair an unnatural shade of red, her face round and cheerful. She breathed very loudly through her nose.

I paused to marvel. This was history, seeing the infamous Abdagnale in the flesh. I had no idea how close to real life she looked, how much or little Glamour was poured on her. Mages usually stuck close to reality, only improving, blurring, and adjusting. It could have been blood economics, or it could have been the fact that every mage I'd ever met thought pretty well of themselves—so why would they mess with perfection? But we all used Glamours that were close to reality.

"Group rates?" Abdagnale said in a shrill voice, all nose and twitter. "We offer them! You will be made very comfortable. Your tastes will be learned, memorized. Your drink order, your preferences." She looked at Mags and affected shock. "You are a burly one! We will have to treat you as *two* normal men when it comes to invoicing."

"Can it," I said. "We're here to—"

"Recruit me," she said. "Into your Suicide Cult! More stylish than those on the subways, yes, but no less doomed!"

The way she half-shouted everything was unnerving. Her office was closed off from the rest of the church but had a heavy feeling, like the air had been filled with a scentless incense. Like it was fractionally harder to breathe inside than it had been on the street.

I glanced at Mel, but she just shrugged. I considered my options. On one hand, I was tired of the fucking ranked *ustari* and their assumption that because they knew the Words and how to use them well, they could be as balls-out insane as they wanted and the rest of us had to eat it. Carith Abdagnale hadn't stepped foot outside her little whorehouse in decades and was burning oceans of blood to spruce the place up and look like a big shot. The pretense was exhausting.

On the other hand, as Mel kept reminding me, we needed firepower. And if Abdagnale had enough skill to cook up this Glamour, she might be useful.

I cleared my throat. "I'm not here to insult you, Ms. Abdagnale. You're right, we're probably going to be killed before this is over. But *you're* probably going to get killed, too, even if you don't do anything. You think Mika Renar is going to leave you be? She'll soak you, just like everyone else. Bleed you dry. You gotta stand up, be counted. Do something about it."

The boxy woman looked at me, leaning back a bit in a stiff posture, her hands clasped in front of her. She pursed her lips. "Don't presume to teach me about that dried-up old devil Renar. And don't *presume* to tell me to do something about it, as if I am not. Not in this place. I will not allow it."

Something felt off, but I couldn't put my finger on it.

"You were not invited here, Mr. Vonnegan," Abdagnale continued. "You were *lured*. Because you are not the only person working to bring Renar and her traitors to justice—*our* justice, *true* justice—you are merely the most incompetent."

Mel raised a hand. "Wait a second—"

Abdagnale surged to her feet and made a sharp cutting motion with her hand, and Billington went silent. She kept moving her mouth for a few seconds and then brought her hands up to her throat, eyes popping.

The black kid jumped to Abdagnale's side, offering his arm, a thick, invisible haze of Cantrip around him like a cloud. She leaned on him heavily as they made their way around the desk. "This is *my* world, Ms. Billington. You will speak when I *allow* it."

My eyes met Mel's. I thought of the runes over the door. Alarm, vague and distant, flowed into me like a jelly.

"I have labored, Mr. Vonnegan," Abdignale said breathlessly, pushing past us and waddling towards the exit. Mags shot a look at me as she elbowed him aside, but I felt like everything was happening too quickly to keep up with. "I know the gossip! I know what is said of me! Pimp! Cheat! Coward! What I have achieved here, Mr. Vonnegan, will be legendary in our order. And you, *idimustari* with wonderful *timing*, you presume to recruit *me*? You perceive the illusion we exist under in this establishment!" She tittered, breathing heavily as she hefted herself back into the huge open area of the former church. "You have the sight, you can see through the illusion. But I assure you, for not being real, your experience, your memories, will be just as satisfying."

I didn't like the wet way she pronounced *satisfying*. I looked at Billington again, and she made a helpless gesture, her face a mask of deepening horror. I felt tired. I hated it when Tricksters hitchhiked their way to New York expecting me to be some sort of savior, some sort of hero. I hated it when they expected to be given a uniform, given orders, taught something. When they looked at me after being rendered speechless without a drop of blood in the air and demanded I explain to them *how*. No one had taught *me* anything.

Early in my apprenticeship, I had planned to scan all of Hiram's notes into my phone, only to discover that the idea of reading his notes on a screen made my skin crawl. Like technology added a filter to the Words that the universe disapproved of. I spent my free time studying the notes instead. In code, of course, but I knew Hiram's codes. All his spells, his thoughts on spells, his study of old Artifacts, most of it was over my head. I was good with the Words, but when I thought about Hiram's notes I felt sad, because when he had been alive, when he'd been here with me, I hadn't bothered to *ask* him anything. And now he was gone, and *idimustari* who didn't have a pair of shoes to their name came tramping in expecting me to outfit them.

Not for the first time, I wished I could see Hiram again. He had died protecting us, died trying to help—and that had changed how I thought of him. I was glad for that, in a weird way, glad Hiram was no longer the son of a bitch who'd kept me on a leash for ten years, teaching me some awful lesson I didn't want to learn. And I wished I could tell him so.

I trailed the big woman as she led us towards the middle lounge area, where half a dozen girls sat with half a dozen men, their skinny legs draped over laps, shimmering arms looped around shoulders. I smelled perfume and stink. The sour odor of unbathed bodies. I looked at the men, seeing them for the first time. They were vagrants. They lolled with the same slit-eyed air of ecstasy as the swells who populated the rest of the place, but they were ragged, and dirty, and—

Expendable.

I looked at Mags, but he was already pushing the sleeve of his jacket up, already had his small penknife in hand. I clicked through the spells

I had—fast and dirty work, all of them; memorizing some endless saga would do you no good in a fight. The Griefers had the right idea, even if they took it too far: Pare it down. If you could make something happen in three syllables, that was the way to go.

Mags slashed his arm. I opened my mouth to speak.

Mags didn't bleed. I didn't speak. We looked at each other. Then back at his arm. Where there was no mark. He slashed again, fiercely, hard enough to open an artery and kill himself, and the blade rubbed against the skin dully, without effect.

"As I said," Carith Abdagnale tittered, "this is *my* universe."

The whole room seemed to be shrinking, a blanket of thick blackness descending on us. As it closed up around Mags, Mel, and me, I thought, *That's a new one.*

I NEVER LOST CONSCIOUSNESS. At first I thought I was, but then I realized I was just wrapped up in a suffocating, total blackness. A thick fabric piled on top of me. But I could feel my hands, my feet. I could even move. I could hear my breathing. I could hear *everything*. I could hear my heart beating. Blood flowing through my veins. My tongue scraping the inside of my mouth. When I moved my hand, I heard the creak and snap of ligaments. Distant, like they'd been buried.

I reached out and felt around for the gas, the large amount of shedding blood that should have been required for this, this Glamour, this Binding—whatever it *was*. I felt nothing. There was no blood in the air.

It was disorienting. And also impossible.

I kicked and struggled. I could feel myself moving, but there was no commensurate sense of movement or reaction. I was in a void. There was no momentum, no resistance. My joints rolled noisily in their sockets, but nothing happened.

I forced myself to be still. I braced myself and bit down on my tongue, hard. It was a useful skill, easy enough to cultivate as long as you could get over the creepiness factor. And the pain. If you were *idimustari*—as I still thought of myself—you couldn't mind the taste.

There was the expected pain—sharp, fundamental, your body warning you that there were major vessels in the tongue, that you could bleed to death if you severed one—but the flood of hot blood never came. I couldn't bleed. It was like I'd found myself in an alternate universe—

Fucking hell. The sign: *An-uraš gu.*

My universe.

This was some serious deep magic.

I promoted Abdagnale in my head to a full *enustari*. A building full of johns getting bled continuously, fooled by Glamours into believing they were having the time of their lives, fueling a tiny personal universe where the old lady could make the rules. And we'd walked right in. The fucking blonde had said, "*Other door,*" and we'd bowed and scraped and walked into her universe like a bunch of obedient idiots.

I couldn't stop myself from working out the layers. At the bottom, Abdagnale casting her spell off the gas in the air. Creating a bubble where she set the rules of perception. We'd walked into that bubble, and so she had complete control over us. If she decided we couldn't feel the gas in the air, then we couldn't feel the gas in the air. Ugh, fucking *magic*—

A voice echoed from far away, rushing at me, firming up.

"... *zalag* ..."

—and the darkness disappeared. And I was in a cage.

It was in Abdagnale's office. Except it was larger than it had been before, twice as large. I kept thinking I would get used to the disorienting way *saganustari* and *enustari* used magic just for effect, but it never ceased to fuck me up. She'd hidden half her office just for some vague psychological advantage.

The cage was made of gold, and there was no door or other obvious way to open it. I was on my knees with my hands tied behind me, and there was just enough room for me to shift my weight from knee to knee. I turned my head, and there was Mags, in a second cage, a few feet away. He filled it to bursting, his head pushed down into his chest, his shoulders straining against the metal. I could hear him breathing in short, angry gasps.

I turned my head the other way, and there was Mel Billington in her own cage. She had her eyes closed, but I could tell she was awake. She was just kneeling there. Either accepting everything that was happening or patiently awaiting her moment for action.

I opened my mouth to speak. Made no sound. I could feel air moving through my throat, my tongue shifting in my mouth, but it produced no sound. I turned my head laboriously to look at Mags again. His lips were working, but he wasn't managing any noise, either. I could tell by watching his mouth that he was whispering *fuck* over and over.

Carith Abdagnale sat behind her florid desk. The thin black fellow lounged, half sitting on its surface, to her left.

"How soon—" he started to ask.

"How should I know?" she tittered, fluttering her hands.

I bit my tongue again. I didn't have anything better to do. Might as well chew my tongue off, pass the time. Again, there was pain but no blood. A neat trick, creating a tiny universe where you could do anything, where your rule was absolute. Where you could decide who was allowed to *bleed* and who wasn't. Outside the old church, Carith Abdagnale was powerful, probably dangerous. But *inside* her old church, she was god. And god had decided Mags and I could not bleed or speak.

While I was chewing my tongue off, I thought about what went into achieving that. She had her girls, siphoning the gas from the guys. She had the guys, getting hooked in via hostesses out in the streets, in the tony bars and restaurants and hotels, a steady supply. She'd tied the spell off, which was impressive. You could set a loop in a spell to keep replicating itself as long as there was gas in the air. It wasn't easy, and no one had ever taught me how to do it, but I knew it could be done. So years ago Carith Abdagnale had set the spell in motion, and her girls had been bleeding the men of New York to keep it going ever since. A precise bleed, careful not to kill anyone, careful not to ruin the illusion.

The illusion: There was that, too. The setup, the overhead. Someone was casting that Glamour on us, and it was *good*.

The whole thing was fucking complicated. I got tired just thinking about the planning that went into this little operation. Though if it were up to me, I'd prefer taking more naps over being a tiny god.

The kid and Abdagnale were sitting in tight, awkward silence. Just waiting.

I forced myself to calm down. Closed my eyes. Imagined myself in a calm, empty room. White walls. No sound. Just me, no worries, no problems.

I opened my eyes again. There was a sixth person in the room.

He was young, a very blond, very thin man wearing a white suit and a black tie, white vest, and red shoes. Sneakers. Running shoes. The suit was very tight and narrowly cut, outlining his limbs and accentuating their fragility.

One of his long, delicate hands was grasping the hair of an older man. A vagrant, by his clothing and general level of cleanliness. The blond's other hand held a very long, very thin blade, which he'd recently used to slit the vagrant's throat. He released the older man and stepped back as the corpse collapsed to the floor, dry and inert. Whatever he'd cast to . . . *teleport* into the room, it had taken all the blood of a grown man to do it.

The Thin Man looked down at the old man. "I apologize. We are working on a more elegant solution," he said. He looked up, sliding his blade into this jacket pocket. "Carith, your taste in home decor remains . . . horrific."

"Welcome!" Abdagnale honked, standing up and waving her flabby arms. "Welcome! Do you crave refreshment? Such a long journey. Such a harrowing way to travel, with that . . . man. Come, take tea with me! Or perhaps you would like a meal in private with one of my associates?"

The Thin Man's face was a collection of sharp lines and angles. His lips were bright red and twisted into an expression of distaste. There was something awful about his eyes. They were empty and distant, miserable. "I would sooner fuck this fellow here than one of your diseased employees, Carith. To business! My employer expects me back immediately to confirm the relevant facts." There was something overly excited about his booming cheer. It felt fake. Forced. And it felt like he was exhausted keeping up the front. As I watched, he turned gracefully and gestured at the cages. "Which one is he . . . No, it's obvious. He isn't some sort of mutant, and he isn't a woman. So *this*"—he stepped forward and gestured at me—"is the famous Lem Vonnegan."

"The very same!" Abdagnale tittered. "The one and only! And now we must only negotiate my compensation for letting your *gasam* have him."

The Thin Man frowned, kneeling down and shooting his cuffs as he peered at me. "She is not my *gasam,* you dotty old bitch. I am currently in her service." He blinked slowly, languorously. "He doesn't *look* like anyone dangerous."

"In here he is not!" Abdagnale shouted, struggling to her feet. "I assure you of that. In here no one is dangerous, except *me!*"

The Thin Man's face collapsed into an expression of impatience. He stood and spun on his heel, throwing out his arms.

"Carith, Carith, Carith, you and my employer have not been on good terms, yes, but you know she is a woman of honor, and she has given you assurances. And sent me in good faith into your little Honey Trap, where I am defenseless. So let us dispense with the bullshit and cut our deal so I can get out of here."

Out of here. I thought, *He bled someone to get here.* He would bleed someone to leave. Abdagnale would have to relax her rules a little. Give him a window.

I started reviewing spells I had on tap. Things I'd memorized. Stringing them together like puzzle pieces. There was going to be some gas in the air, and if I could touch it, I would be ready.

"I have a list of requirements prepared!" Abdagnale pushed her big hands through the endless piles of paper on her desk. She seized upon a long pink sheet of paper and held it out to the Thin Man. He stood for a moment, sighed, and stepped forward to take it. He stood there, reading.

"You're not shy," he said. "This third item may not be possible."

Abdagnale sank back into her seat with a sigh like a deflating tire. "The terms are non-negotiable."

"Nonsense." He looked up at her. "I am the *Negotiator*."

"He does not leave this place unless I have an agreement."

The Negotiator spun and stared down at me. I stared back. "I must have a positive ID. No offense, Carith. Let him speak, so I may validate his identity."

Abdagnale made a soft noise in protest. "That is not *wise*," she sang. "He does not look like much, but he is *clever*."

"So I have heard." The Negotiator stepped closer to the cage and leaned down, his face near mine. I stared back at him. His skin was flawless, and it didn't look like a Glamour. It looked like perfect, pink-tinged white skin. He smelled like pipe smoke. His eyes were the giveaway. They were deep and had no light in them; they looked raw. "Let him speak, Carith. I must determine if this is the one and only, if I am to bring your outrageous terms to my employer."

Abdagnale sighed heavily, her body shifting like a mountain. "Very well."

She did nothing. No Words, no gas. I didn't feel a thing.

The Negotiator just kept smiling at me for a few moments. The expression on his face was difficult to categorize. I just kept thinking, *Give me the gas to make someone bleed*. He had to leave, and he wasn't going to walk out the door and take the subway.

"Tell me, Mr. Vonnegan," the Negotiator finally said, squinting at me, "tell me *anything*."

I blinked. It could be a coincidence, that phrase, that precise piece of old Trickster patter designed to be one of a dozen rapid-fire questions to keep you spinning. Every *idimustari* in the world had used the phrase *tell me anything* when Charming or Compelling someone. It was almost a secret handshake. Except this was no Trickster, in his red shoes and with his goddamn *teleportation* spell. I couldn't sense any Charm or Compulsion on me, but Abdagnale's bloodless casting meant anything was possible.

"You look like an asshole in that suit, Colonel," I said. My voice sounded rusted, and my throat hurt pushing out the words, my tongue swollen and chewed up. But I could speak.

He nodded and stood up. "Very well. I accept this is Lemuel Vonnegan. As to your terms, number three on your list is impossible. It clashes with my employer's intentions. The rest are acceptable." He tossed the paper onto her desk. "Do you agree?"

Abdagnale struggled up from her chair again. "This is not negotiation! This is—"

"You are free to reject our terms," the Negotiator said. "You will regret it. You know *her*."

I ran through the spell in my head. I was ready.

Abdagnale stood quivering behind the desk, her tiny hands moving in tight circular patterns. Finally, she waved them in the air and sighed heavily.

"Oh, very well! We are being abused, but what is different about that? We agree. We are being abused, but we agree."

The Negotiator smiled, throwing his arms out. "Then it is so. I will take possession."

She hadn't used his employer's name. Someone at his level, I might have heard it. I remembered Hiram, in the early days, running down names for me. Him telling me *ustari* were dangerous, and I needed to know them when they entered my airspace. Me not listening too well. But I remembered some of them. And I'd been hearing new ones for the last six months as Melanie organized things, did the research: Aragaki. Rithy Kal. Tobin Anastole. Alfonse Alligherti. Mycroft Pell. But she hadn't used his *name*.

Still smiling, he pivoted and gestured at the grinning black kid lounging stupidly on Abdagnale's desk.

"May I bleed him? For my return?"

Abdagnale looked at her companion. It would be fast, I realized. The second I opened my mouth, Abdagnale would move to shut me off again. Fast. My heart pounded as I ran through the spells in my head. Too fast. Anything worth casting would take too long.

Anything longer than a Word. I had no time for finesse. I backtracked, cleared my head. Selected a Word.

The kid, for his part, had suddenly realized that Abdagnale and the Negotiator were looking at him like he was a side of beef and they were starving. He slid off the desk as the Negotiator pulled his blade from his pocket, and held up his hands in supplication. "Hey, now—"

The Negotiator simply took two steps forward on the balls of his feet, like a dancer, and slashed his blade across the kid's neck, then bobbed back, gracefully evading the spray of blood with supple twists of his body. We cast simultaneously.

His first Word was superfluous. Completely unnecessary. The kind of extra syllable you put in because it helped the meter, because it sounded good in the mouth and you wore a fucking white suit for some fancy reason. But it did nothing. The universe noted it and watched it float past, awaiting other instructions. Not the sort of Word an *ustari* with any training would bother with. He cast like a fucking asshole.

My Word was *hum*. I felt the flood of gas pouring out of the poor black kid, oily and vital, seized it and barked it out. One syllable. I filled with an intense, rotten sense of power and then it burst out of me in all directions, unstructured, unfocused. Chaos.

Hiram Bosch, my old *gasam,* once told me that magic was violence. He was right. It had taken me a while to understand.

The cage exploded like a bomb had gone off. Shards of broken metal flew everywhere, a sizzling noise like rain filling the air for one second as a million metal splinters flew through the air at a thousand miles an hour. A gentle blowback from the Negotiator's collapsed spell washed through the room like a soft breeze.

Suddenly there was gas just pouring into the world, just ready for the taking.

I glanced at Abdagnale. Felt the gas pulsing around me and shouted one word: *Sig.*

She rocketed backwards, crashing into her chair and falling awkwardly against the wall as I stood up, joints popping. I had to hope she was unconscious. Speed was of the essence. I had to move. I had to keep moving, and keep moving, and *keep moving.* Whoever the Negotiator was, I had a pretty good idea he worked for Mika Renar, and if they took me, I doubted I'd ever be seen again. A martyr for the cause.

If she wasn't unconscious, she would shut me up in a second anyway. I hadn't seen her do anything when altering the rules of her personal universe a moment ago; she would alter them again with no more than a whisper.

There was lots of gas in the air, a torrent. I didn't pause to consider the volume—this was battle, and there was going to be collateral damage. I'd gotten a feel for it anyway, a bit of practice, and I knew how far you could pull without killing a person. Could identify that thinning moment when it changed from a moving flood to a stagnant pool, and then you had to ease off if you didn't want to kill him.

I didn't want to kill anyone just yet.

I kept throwing Words around, single syllables, Griefing my way through it. A screen of destruction to keep everyone off-balance. Kept raining single Words at the Negotiator as he scrambled on his hands and knees behind the desk. It was like throwing boulders at people. There was no science to it, no craft, and I understood why *ustari* throughout the centuries had punished proto-Griefers, destroyed them on sight. Give everyone one Word and the fucking world would end in a week.

I sucked at the gas in the air and hissed, *"Tak!"* at his red sneakers as they disappeared behind the big desk, flinging my arm out as if throwing something underhand. The arm: I still had enough Trickster in me to be unable to resist the theater of it. There was a deafening boom, and a large hunk of the desk shattered into splinters.

An old song ran through my head: *I point at the things I wish to command.*

Moving as fast as I could, I circled around the desk after him, pulling in more gas and shouting the Word again. My voice sounded walled off, insulated. The floor exploded a half second behind him. He was a nimble bastard. He was moving too fast, but there was no time to stop and think, reconsider, recite something pretty. *Keep moving, keep moving.* With ten seconds I could have come up with something sneaky, something clever. It was what I did. But in ten seconds this freak in the white suit would be gone or slitting my throat.

I could hear *him* reciting something, hot and breathless. I shouted, hoarse already, and thrust my arm out. Again. Again. Splinters from the floor pelting me as I chased the slippery fucker out through a back hallway. The space was a dusty, paper-filled concrete box linking the office with the middle of the main church hall. It was piled up in towering, yellowing stacks, bursting out of five ancient wooden filing cabinets, fluttering in the breeze of the door as it slammed against the wall.

The Negotiator skittered backwards from me on his ass, pushing with his feet and hands on the dirty floor. His nice white suit was stained and torn. He was still whispering his spell, which was discipline, I had to admit.

I shouted the Word and pushed out my hand, and he rolled to the left as the floor exploded where his groin had been a moment before.

A second later, I sensed rather than heard his cadence, and I was in the air.

The thin figure emerged from behind one of the dust-layered filing cabinets with his index finger extended towards me. He flicked his finger to the left and I jigged with it, tethered by an invisible line.

I sucked in breath. Pulled back my arm. He jerked his hand to the right and smacked me into the wall, cracking the plaster and rattling

my teeth, making my vision go red for a moment. He jerked his hand
back, and I popped free from the hole I'd just created and went sailing
into the opposite wall.

I came to a second later, head pounding, shoulder aching, staring up
at the ceiling's dark wood tiles, which had been fitted together God knew
when and had ornate patterns of spirals and crosses carved into them. I
coughed something thick out of my throat and breathed in plaster dust. I
felt the force of his spell tugging at me violently, but I was stuck, snagged
on some piece of lathing that refused to break free. My voice like jelly, I
gurgled my Word and pushed my free arm weakly at him. I still had a
pool of gas in reach—dimly, I thought it should have faded a great deal
by now—and it tore up the old polished floorboards directly in front of
him, tipping over two filing cabinets and sending a big hunk of lucky
floor directly into the Negotiator's face. He flipped backwards with a cry,
and I tore free from my perch, first sailing up to hit the ceiling nice and
hard, then free-falling back to the floor. I twisted around and landed on
my injured arm, pain searing through me like a few bones had broken
loose and jabbed directly into my lungs.

One breath, two. Two seconds of quiet.

Dredging up useful Cantrips from the dark corners of my brain, I
rolled away, muttering. A Glamour version of me remained in place,
facedown on the floor, one arm bent unfortunately beneath it. I rolled
to the wall, grimacing, then started crawling along the perimeter.
Worming my way inch by inch, I got behind the Negotiator in the
narrow hallway. I had a good angle on him. Just as he finished his spell
and realized he'd cast on a Glamour, I sucked in breath, feeling for the
shrinking pond of gas, which was still out there but now felt more like
a wildfire somewhere over the horizon. I got more dust than air and
broke into a spasm of wet, painful coughs.

He whirled and, stealing a page from my book, snapped a single
Word at me. I threw my arm up in front of my face, but felt nothing.
No explosion, no mist of splinters. I stumbled to my feet and pulled my
arm away, but I was blind. Perfect, inky blackness everywhere.

Smarter than me.

Keep moving.

I ran forward, blind, hands out in front of me, shouting my Word and feeling the impact of it through my feet. Trying to create chaos, to keep him spinning. One hand tracing the wall, I followed the hall back into the cavernous main part of the old church where we'd entered. I could feel the air opening up around me, the whispers ongoing, Abdagnale's people unaware that their tiny godling was unconscious in her office. I sidestepped and pressed my back against the wall and stopped, gulping air and running through the hundreds of Cantrips in my head, linking some together, splicing them. Pulled on the shrinking pool of gas and muttered out a ragged, raw spell, sixteen syllables. If I'd heard exactly how he'd blinded me I could have shaved that down, but I had to cover all the possibilities: that he'd cast on my eyes, that he'd cast on the area around me, that he'd used a subtle Glamour to fool me into *thinking* I'm blind.

My vision snapped back.

The Negotiator, bleeding from a deep cut over one eye, was right in front of me.

He opened his mouth. I put my fist into it. Sometimes the best tricks were the old ones.

Pain shimmered up my arm as he staggered back, fresh blood bubbling over his lips. I seized it from him, fresh and hot, slick like poison in my mental grasp, and spat the Word at him. Again, sending him reeling backwards, off-balance. Then I launched myself at him, knocking him to the floor, sending a group of whores scattering and screaming, suddenly aware that something in paradise had gone terribly wrong.

None of them had left. They all stood there with expressions of terror, scattering like birds in formation. But not leaving. Abdagnale's universe—I wondered if any of them had *ever* left. *Could* ever leave.

The Negotiator groaned, wet and bubbly. I crawled over him, planting myself on his chest. He spasmed and coughed a spray of warm blood onto my face. I sucked in breath, lungs burning. Poked around for that swamp of gas. It had dried up, gone stale. For a split second I thought I should feel something about that. I'd spent so many years avoiding bleeding anyone. So many years exhausted, asleep on my feet, perpetually a few pints low. And now I'd gone months living off other people's gas. And now I'd bled someone. Bled them dry. I focused on the Negotiator. He was gurgling blood, trying to speak. To recite. I put my palm over his mouth and pressed. His eyes widened proportionately to the pressure I exerted. Then they closed again, and I had a brief sense of him relaxing, letting it happen. Letting me kill him.

"Tell me," I said in gasping jerks, "what I'm missing. Why do Mika Renar and Cal Amir want to kidnap me? Why not just kill me?"

His eyes popped open. He squinted at me, coughing blood onto my palm. I grabbed hold of his jacket with my free hand, tight, and pulled my hand away from his mouth, prepared for him to try something—a Cantrip, a single Word. It was what I would do. Except I would have had it ready, spitting it out in a spray of blood the second some idiot let me. Instead, he stared at me. There was something in his eyes, a burnt light, something broken and horrible. "Mika Renar and Cal Amir," he said, "did not contract for you, *idimustari*."

I froze. I was shivering, shock and reaction, adrenaline curdling inside me. For months now those two names had haunted my every move. Mika Renar. Cal Amir. An Archmage and her apprentice who had tried to murder the world, irritated at me for spoiling their plans.

"Then who—"

With a snarl he rolled me, pushing me off to the side, and was up and running, reciting as he went. I felt the old familiar yellow drain of someone casting off of you, pulling your lifeblood out. My vision went blurry as I pushed myself up, ready to give chase, and then I stumbled to my knees as he completed his spell, and I could sense he was gone. There was an eerie quiet in the old church then, except for a low buzz of weeping somewhere.

At least he hadn't bled me to death. I assumed he'd just gotten clear of the church, just cast something fast to get over to the street.

I staggered back to the office, trying to pull myself together in case Carith Abdagnale had come to, ready to spit out some shrill spells. As I limped through the dusty corridor, the weeping got louder.

It didn't matter; Abdagnale was gone. Whether she'd fled or been taken, I didn't know. The office was a mess. The desk had been flipped over at some point. My shattered cage was a pile of metal shards, the other two cages intact. I shuffled over to Mel's and knelt with a wince as something caught in my back like a piano wire hooked in to my nerves. She was sitting with her knees up at her chest, her arms wrapped tightly around her legs. Staring at the floor of her cage.

She looked up at me, and her face froze the Words I'd been about to speak.

I turned my head. Sitting on the floor with his back to the overturned desk was the skinny black kid. He was a mess of dried stale blood and bruises. But he was alive and pretty healthy all things considered, one hand clamped over his own throat like he was keeping himself alive with direct pressure. Staring at us with a mean look, like he was trying to figure out the best way to kill us. Which I forgave. If I'd been abandoned after all that, I would probably be a little surly, too.

I looked back at Mel. Her eyes were wide, the dark makeup running down her face. We stared at each other for a few seconds as everything seemed to drain into my feet, bolting me to the floor.

I stood up again, back exploding, and turned around.

Mags was curled up on the floor of his cage. A shard of metal the size of my hand had clipped him in the throat. His hands were curled around the bars of the cage as if he'd tried to bend them, tried to break free. He was pale and inert, dirty and wild-looking.

He was dead.

I was on my knees. I didn't remember getting there. I stared at his hands.

I'd bled him. It hit me and then was obvious. His throat had been torn open by my brilliant, clever bit of Griefing, and I'd been too busy chasing down the Negotiator to realize I was casting off of Mags. I felt melted to the floor and became deadweight formed into something vaguely human. Then, with a lurch, my heart went into overdrive. I realized I'd been holding my breath, and emptied my lungs with a single forceful explosion of air. My brain activated: I ran through every trick I knew. Every Cantrip, every *mu*, I'd ever learned. Every bigger spell I'd ever heard, that Hiram had mentioned or written down in his notes. I reached out desperately for the trickle of gas leaking from the injured kid, a seeping head wound. Not enough. Not enough for anything *useful*.

Mags had been dead only a minute. This was fucking *magic*. There had to be something.

But I needed more gas.

I whirled, holding on to that spark of blood in the air, and barked my Word, gesturing numbly at the kid's chest. It smacked into him and he crashed backwards, the desk shattering into splinters beneath him.

"Vonnegan!" Billington shouted, her voice rusty.

And there was more gas in the air.

I barked the Word again and sent the kid spinning into the debris, grinding him down into it. He screamed once and went silent, and I did not give a shit. I tested the air. Enough gas. Enough for something useful. Something. *Something*.

"*Vonnegan!*"

"Shut up," I spat at the floor. "You're next."

For Mags, I would bleed the city. The world. I'd track down Mika Renar in person and help her do it, kill the world, save my friend.

Breathing hard, shivering, I ran through a spell Mags had cast on me, once, pumping energy into me, keeping me alive when I should have died. I recited it and recited it, pulling from the kid behind me. Not enough. Too thin.

I spun and launched myself over to my source, landing on top of him and tearing his shirt open with both hands. Sweating, I pulled my blade from my pocket and slashed downward at the jagged wound on his throat. Blood, black and hot, surged out of him, and as I spun around and threw myself back at the cage that held my friend, there was the dim thought, small and tinny in the background: *Murderer*.

I recited the spell. Nothing happened.

I'd been almost dead, but I'd still been alive—*it must matter*. I kept hold of the greasy flow of blood flowing from the kid and ran through everything again, every scrap of code I knew. It was all tricks. Tricks and death. Nothing *constructive*.

I sagged against the bars of his cage and shut my eyes. My heart thudded in my chest, pushing my eyes against their lids in rhythm. I would bleed for Mags. I'd open an artery and bleed out in a minute and a half if I could think of any fucking Words that would bring him back.

I didn't know any. All I had was the useless Revival spell. Everything else in my head was designed to cheat at cards or make someone like me, or other short cons. A few decent war Cantrips. Nothing *big*. I was the Asshole General of the Asshole Army, but I was still just a Trickster.

I stared at Mags's limp form. The way his hair was matted against his forehead. His comically big hands, slack and hanging. Tears dripped from my eyes. He hadn't deserved this. *In a fucking* cage. I'd had one job: Keep Mags calm, make him happier. One fucking job.

With a grunt, I seized the gas and turned, shouting my Word and smacking it into the kid again. Billington screamed. I tore at my jacket, fumbling out my blade. I needed more, every drop of it. Every drop in the kid, every drop in Mel Billington, every drop in me, every drop in every whore and customer in the whole fucking place. I'd drag people in from the streets.

I slashed at my arm with the blade. Deep. Mortal, my old Trickster sense told me, if I didn't do something about it. The old familiar burning felt good as the blood flowed, dark and rich, healthy after all this time of calm living.

Not enough. Not fast enough. I took the slick blade in my other hand, dragged it along the skin of my forearm, the pain icy cold.

I pushed my gushing arms through the bars and grabbed on to Mags. Closed my eyes. Started speaking the Words. The only spell I knew that had any chance. Because I was just a Trickster. I had nothing, no *gasam,* no Bleeders, no—

I spoke the spell again. Felt the old familiar yellow weariness sweep through me as the universe absorbed my energy and came back for more.

I spoke the spell again. Anger welled up in me, balancing out the nauseating wave of power being sucked out of me. The Thin Fuck in the nice white suit. The Negotiator. *Mika Renar did not contract for you.*

I spoke the spell again.

Someone was screaming behind me. More gas—Billington, I thought dimly, helping out. I was pulling from all three lines of gas, and pulling hard. I felt the energy drain from me, stared down at Mags through heavy, sweat-filled eyelids. Could feel the ground vibrating under me like a tiny, distant earthquake that was consuming cities miles away.

Everything was fading and shaky. Coming to me in bursts of data.

It had only been a minute. Just a minute. There was nothing, I told myself, nothing that couldn't be undone in one fucking *minute.*

I spoke the spell again. Felt Mags's body under my bloody hands get warmer. My vision swam, my head pounded. The universe sucking me dry. Bleeding me white. The cage trapping Mags started to shake and rattle. It lifted slightly off the ground, and Billington stopped screaming. Everything images sounds and heartbeat beating beat beating—

The ground was shaking under me, the slightest shivery vibration worming up through my feet and knees. Like an earthquake, sailing in to mark Mag's passing.

I spoke the spell again.

My vision swam, everything going wavy and indistinct. *Not yet,* I thought. *Too soon to be bleeding out.* There was a roaring in my ears, like a train rushing towards me from somewhere in the next room. At first I'd thought it was in my head, the rush of my own bleedout tricking my brain, but it wasn't. It was external, and it was loud, and the whole room seemed to go blurry and indistinct as the noise rose in volume.

Pushing through mud in my throat, I spoke the spell again.

Everything snapped back into clarity, and it was just Billington's scream in the air and I could feel

warm

exhaustion coursed through me like a liquid

almost fell over and did, he was that Mags—I stared down at him blearily—had he, did he—a twitch—the stupid fuck, had he *twitched*?

I spoke the spell again.

III.

GLAMOUR

31.

IT WAS EASIER TO STEAL a plane than it used to be. The world was broken. We had broken it.

We'd come loaded for bear. Six Bleeders and I'd been prepared to use them, but when we'd arrived at Teterboro there was no security to speak of. No one. The place abandoned, lit up and empty like a trap. Like someone had parked a couple of private jets and thousands of gallons of jet fuel and stepped back into the shadows to see what would happen, how many disasters could spring from this one epic moment of incompetence.

So we'd just walked up to the Grumman Albatross and climbed aboard. Neilsson, the drunk old bastard, had been a pilot lifetimes ago. At first he'd insisted on being sober for the flight, but seeing the old man trembling in the backseat of the limo gave me the shivers, so I'd gotten him a bottle of Mellow Corn and now he was his regular self, singing old Irish folk songs and telling me every five minutes that he'd been the one to tell me we needed to *do something* back on Mad Day. Neilsson had decided it was his fiery speech to me that had caused the Army of Assholes to form in the first place. Since no one else wanted the honor, we let it be.

As we'd climbed aboard, I'd asked myself whether Neilsson looked like a man trained on modern equipment, if I cared much about possibly dying over the ocean in a few hours.

The seats were the sort of soft leather that molded itself to you but were the color of shit. The air smelled stale and processed, like it was artificial, made in a lab and pumped in for the rich folks.

My Bleeders sat down a few rows behind me, noisy and excited. Kids, all of them. Kids in nearly identical black suits. None of them had been on a plane before. I turned and leaned out into the aisle to glare back at them, and they shut up, elbowing each other and looking down at the carpet.

I settled in and took out the bottle of Ballantine's I'd gotten. Two men in matching newsboy caps emerged from the cockpit, sweeping their heavy wool coats behind them as they straightened up and approached. One was young, maybe my age or a little younger. His partner was much older, stooped and white-haired, lined and wrinkled. They had the same face. Twins, save that one was forty years older. Two pairs of identical pale gray eyes scanned the cabin as they stopped next to me.

I waved and the younger one, Remy, nodded. Ducking into the galley, he emerged with a plastic cup. "The old man says buckle your seat belt, Mr. Vonnegan," he said, dropping the cup onto my fold-down table. Remy's black hair was shaggy, tufting out from under his ridiculous cap. I'd asked Mel where she'd found these two, and she'd just shrugged and told me not to worry, they were vetted. Mel was always fucking *vetting* people.

"He says about six hours, Mr. Vonnegan," Roman added. I'd asked the twins how they'd ended up this way. Remy had said they weren't twins. Roman had said something about a Ritual that had gone wrong and *Folded* them. I'd asked him what that meant, and he'd shrugged and said he didn't know. One minute he'd been home, the next he'd been *here,* and the *enustari* who'd fucked up had used that term and not bothered explaining.

The Twins creeped me out, but they were reliable.

I waved them off. Looking at those faces from opposite ends of time gave me a headache. And I was sick of being called *Mr. Vonnegan* by everyone. Even the old-timers like Neilsson had started on that bullshit, and it was wearying. Roman and Remy were the first of the New Recruits. The first of the *ustari* who had started looking at me differently after we dragged our asses back from the debacle in Abdagnale's church. Rumors had spread, fast—I was certain Melanie had started them all.

Recruitment had gone through the roof six months ago and continued to be strong. But I didn't want to think about that.

I grabbed the cup Remy had left and set it right side up. Pouring a generous three fingers, I went to hand it over to the big dumb bear next to me.

White-knuckled in his seat, Mags started shaking his head.

"Don't want it," he said through clenched teeth.

I shrugged, holding the cup in front of him. "I could cast something on you, calm you down."

He shook his head again.

I sighed. I could feel Mag's heart beat. Literally. It pulsed distantly next to my own, somehow. His heartbeat was so slow, it always alarmed me. My own pounded all the time, thundering in my chest, but Mags's just kept on, steady, deliberate. I stared at him. He had his miserable face on, reminding me of the time Hiram and I had tried to convince him to take cold medicine when he'd been sneezing huge green gobs of snot everywhere. It was the same face. It was Mags's face. I sat and stared at that face for a few seconds, squinting. Trying to see . . . something. Anything I hadn't noticed before. Anything that would prove he was really there.

Or that he wasn't.

"Suit yourself," I said, and placed the cup on my own table. I glanced out the window as we bit into the air and caught hold. Out in the distance, several huge fires were burning. I wondered if anyone was going to bother putting them out.

The world was broken. *We* had broken it.

IN THE DREAM, AS always, Claire Mannice was in a cage, in a circus attraction, snarling and banging up against the bars.

I WOKE UP AND looked out the window. I could feel us descending, the whiskey left in the bottle at a steep angle. I wondered, at that angle, whether it was insanely steep, if Neilsson knew what the fuck he was doing, or if I was going to end up in the drink. I imagined it: my last moment. A split second of alarm, maybe. Or silence. Would I feel the impact before anything else? A tremor up through my legs and into my back, then blackness, then not even blackness.

I reminded myself that I would have to cast before we hit and the water cut off my voice.

I thought of Claire. I thought of Claire often. I pictured her, defiant and half crazy, the way all girls under the age of thirty ought to be. Skinny, tall, long legs, short hair. That way of looking at you that made you think she was memorizing you, really seeing every hair on your face and every scar on your arms. Like she would be able to describe you to the sketch artist later and get a perfect picture of you for her trouble.

I shut my eyes for a moment. I didn't like thinking about Claire. It was actively dangerous to think about Claire. Claire, who was the key to the end of the world, or so I'd been told—and I had no reason not to believe it. I thought of a white apron on a pink skirt and the smell of bitter, overbrewed coffee. Then I shut it down, thinking about clouds, picturing them, white and fluffy and swirling, a time-lapse weather pattern.

The window was a square of total black, infinite, deep. I couldn't see anything, which clarified for me that I'd let an old drunk pilot a small jet, and as a result we were about to crash in the middle of the fucking ocean. And so went Lem Vonnegan, General of the Assholes.

But then, in the distance, the faint blue-gray shine of a coastline.

I looked over at Mags to say something reassuring. He sat bolt upright in the seat, eyes clenched shut. He was whimpering. My gaze lingered again. When you stared at something long enough, it became unreal. But his every movement, every scowl, and every whimper was spot-on, exactly as I recalled.

The air was like a damp sock stuffed into your mouth. From the plane, we stepped onto a private airstrip, just a strip of blacktop and a small office that was dark and locked up tight. We crowded into a pair of gleaming, brand-new SUVs, black and shiny and smelling like the shipping containers they'd recently occupied. I didn't know anything about the arrangements. Mel summoned us, and as I moved, things just fell into place. All the assholes in the black suits knew where to take me, knew how to get there, knew better than to talk to me. Everyone around me knowing more than I did.

Me and Mags took the front car, the rest pushed their way into the second. I didn't know any of their names. They'd come, months or weeks or days ago, and joined our little Army of Assholes, put on the uniform. Which was, apparently a cheap black suit. I didn't want to learn their names.

I rolled down the window in the back, then immediately rolled it back up. At speed, the heavy, hot air became a fist punching into the car's interior. Our destination had already been programmed in to the GPS by Melanie's invisible fingers, and we headed into the fucking jungle. I lit a cigarette. The branches of huge, damp trees slapped at the SUV and we barreled onward, the car bouncing along on the best suspension money could buy. Or that *idimustari* could steal.

Eventually, a pool of white light welled up on the horizon and we aimed for it. Then there was a paved driveway, six other black SUVs parked haphazardly with their lights on, three with their engines humming.

The gas in the air was stale and dying off, the remnants of some serious shit. The heat and wet slapped down on me as I poured myself out of the car and had that sense of murmured conversations stopping. A group of kids hung around. Muscle. Assholes, mostly, the runts Mel had put on walking perimeters, guys and girls who could barely form a fucking sentence in a *modern* language, much less the Words. They remained terrified of anyone with any actual ability. They'd heard stories about me—bullshit, mostly, but a grifter never pisses on a gift like that, so I let it ride. And they'd all heard *the* story about me. They all pissed their jammies and stared at their shoes as I walked towards the house, lighting a cigarette. Remy and Roman swaggering in front of me, my six personal Bleeders falling into line behind me. Strutting, I thought, because they were so fucking important that we'd chosen them to bleed out at the first sign of trouble.

When Mags passed, hands clenched and murder in his eyes—which I knew was anger at the sky for frightening him—the runts all took involuntary, instinctive steps backward. None of them were sure if they could cast faster than he could lunge, and half of them thought he was some sort of *dimma* or *gidim,* something I'd created using his dead body and some gas. He was already sweating through his jacket, and his long black hair was having some sort of weird chemical reaction with the water in the air.

The house was a modern catastrophe. Out in the middle of Nowhere, Colombia, a million miles from Bogotá or anyplace else. Drug lord country, militia country. Guys with no fucking teeth and automatic weapons ginned up from 3-D printers via templates downloaded from the Internet. It was white stucco and glass, glass everywhere. It sat on an ugly concrete slab but had a satellite hookup and three huge military-grade generators chugging away. Not to mention, I'd been told, a staff of fifteen professional security men and at least twenty Bleeders and a few *saganustari* set to defend their *enustari.*

I found what remained of most of these in the living room. It had been decorated in pure white: white rugs, white tile, white couch, white walls. There was so much dead blood all over the place that it had gone a nauseous pink. I stood running my eyes over the carnage. Saw several of our people in the black suits Mel issued them, torn to pieces. Someone had uttered something absolutely fucking terrible in this room, and it had gone through everyone like a buzz saw.

There was a hissing static noise in the air. The stereo, sizzling, smoke drifting upwards.

Walking deeper into the house, I tripped over a leg. Separated from its body, it was still encased in the shiny material of a truly awful suit and a perfectly preserved black shoe without a scuff or a mark on it. As I moved, the house grew quiet as more and more of Mel's team realized I was there. I hadn't gotten used to that.

I stopped. Didn't turn. "Everybody outside."

"Right," Roman said. I started forward again and he and Remy gathered up the others. I'd gotten used to this, to people doing things I told them to do. Mags turned and I had to grab him by the collar to remind him that he was not *everybody*.

In the bedroom, I met Rithy Kal, *enustari*.

We passed through what was left of a massive steel security door. It was bent and buckled, hanging from one final hinge. The bedroom beyond it was all white as well, but there was less blood. Less but still plenty. The lesson Mel kept teaching me was that if you had an *army*, it didn't matter how low-level the grunts were. A hundred *idimustari* who knew one spell each could do damage, and a single *enustari* could be whipped by a bunch of Tricksters if they all worked together. She stood off to the right just inside the door, wearing her blue pin-striped suit with an overcoat, even in the heat. Her long red hair was pulled back, her face a painting, layers of makeup coalesced into a reasonable facsimile of a perfect complexion. Mel might have been thirty or fifty and stood at rigid attention. She nodded at us once, then waved off someone behind me with a casual dismissal.

Seated in a thronelike padded white chair, a strip of black tape covering his mouth—and wrapped all the way around his head—was a plump, balding man, his brown skin shining with sweat. He'd let his limp black hair grow long, which gave him an astonishingly large forehead. He glanced at me with furtive intensity, then looked down at his bare lap, his hands having been taped to the arms of the chair.

My cigarette was being stubborn in the damp air. I placed it between my lips and knelt in front of the man.

"Rithy Kal," Mel said, sounding tired. Bored. "*Enustari*, one of the original conspirators. Supplied Renar and Amir with blood sacrifice in the building of the Renar Fabrication. Known to have purchased human beings through Slovenian slavers for the purpose of sacrifice. Known to—"

I held up my hand and she stopped talking. I didn't know how she decided the line between her purview and my authority. It was entirely up to her; I'd never asked her to pay attention to me. Some things she arranged on her own, without asking. Some things she waited for me. I couldn't read the system. It was a machine built by someone else.

I stared down at Kal. "I'm going to take the tape off," I said, cigarette bobbing up and down. "If you try to cast something, I will have my friend Pitr break every tooth in your mouth. Nod if you understand."

Even *ustari* had reason to worry about broken teeth. Kal's dancing eyes drifted to Mags, lingered for a stunned moment, traveling up from waist to chest, then jumped back to me. He nodded. I reached forward and tore the tape free.

"You are all *fucking dead,*" Rithy Kal hissed.

"And so are you!" I replied, throwing out my arms. "Guess you're not getting on the Immortal Bus with your friends." I shot my cuff and started rolling up my sleeve. "You ever been Charmed, Mr. Kal?"

Rithy Kal stared at my arm with a pop-eyed sneer. "You bleed for your own spells," he said softly. "Like a common thief."

"Jesus," Mel said. "We got *volunteers* for that, Chief."

I waved her away. Here was a true *enustari,* and there was a difference between him and me. I'd been losing sight of it. I thought of the black kid six months ago, thought of how I'd torn him up and crushed him under Words to squeeze him dry. I'd gotten used to bleeding people, but I was no Rithy Kal. It was time, I thought, to mark out the difference. To make it up, a little bit, with some sacrifice.

It was easy to steal things these days, and my switchblade was new. It had a glossy black shell that felt like skin as it warmed in my hand, with a set of dice showing snake eyes engraved on one side. Expensive, but the world was broken and everything was free.

I flicked it open and placed it against the skin of my forearm. Only a few of the scars there were recent. The rest had faded into pink, puckered memory, a skein of ancient roads I'd traveled down. The most recent ones were wide and thick, one on each arm, darker and wet-looking. The cold metal against my skin was familiar and comforting. I pushed and pulled, and the old searing pain released a thick flow of gas

into the air. I felt Mags and Billington react, subtle shifts in weight as
they sensed it and instinctively reached for it.

I spoke seven words. A mouthful for me. But I wanted the spell to
have some subtlety. Kal was *enustari;* he was a man who knew what a
Charm was. I had to be tricky, but there were more tricks than magical
ones: I'd used the word *Charm,* but I'd actually cast a Compulsion to
answer my questions. Misdirection. If he'd been paying attention, he'd
have heard the corresponding Words. But I still had my Trickster rat's
nose for people, and it was telling me that Rithy Kal had just survived
an assault, had his Bleeders and Security team slaughtered by a bunch
of schlubs one slice above Griefers, and had just seen the largest, angriest man in existence. So he might not be at his sharpest. Plus, Rithy Kal
hadn't had enough interaction with *idimustari* to know that we lied for
a living.

You worked grifts the same way; there was a method. Step one was
to start nonthreatening and establish a rapport. If you *could* establish a
rapport with a sweating man who was taped to a chair and pretty sure
you were going to kill him.

I glanced at Billington. *I* wasn't going to kill him. Mel had turned
out to be something of a hands-on fanatic on that point. The guilty
had to be punished, and execution had the extra benefit of taking resources away from Renar.

I looked back at Kal. "You know who I am?"

He nodded. Wary. "The Trickster."

I'd never been known as *the* anything before.

"Tell me where Mika Renar is."

There hadn't been any signs of Mika Renar or her pet in the two
years since Mad Day. Two years of hunting. We didn't even know for
sure whether Renar had survived, as old and frail as she was. Amir, I
was almost certain, had died—I'd seen him up close, in slow motion.
But Renar—she had an army of Bleeders and more money than some
small countries. Anything was possible. I didn't doubt that in the absence of her fucking *Biludha-tah-namus,* she would just organize an

endless Bleed, would find open veins to fuel some looped spell that would keep her alive one more second, then one more second, then one more.

Mel had found plenty of *conspirators*. Mel had *killed* plenty of conspirators. *Enustari* who had somehow helped Renar—helped her build her murder machine, helped her phrase the Rite of Death. Helped her in any way.

"I do not know," Kal said after a moment's hesitation as he struggled against my Compulsion. It was a subtle spell. It didn't make him want to answer me. It didn't make him want to tell the truth. It made him not want to *lie*. Kal would steel himself against being forced to say things. He wouldn't be ready for being forced to *not* say things.

It was like any grift: Keep them off-balance.

Of course, Kal was *enustari*. I had to accept the possibility that he might be fucking with *me*.

I didn't hesitate. You had to pepper them with questions, keep them from thinking. "Why is your house out here in the middle of fucking nowhere?"

He shrugged. "Before the—" He hesitated again. "Before, it was very difficult to acquire blood in the cities. This was . . . private."

I had never heard the word spoken with so much oily menace.

"Do you have an *urtuku*?"

The questions didn't matter. I was just training him to answer.

He shook his head. "I have learned this never goes well."

"Why is everything white?"

"So you can see the dirt."

"Who was your *gasam*?"

"You would not know her."

Not a lie. I let it pass. "How do you pronounce your name?"

"Ri-thee Kaal."

"Tell me where Mika Renar is."

"I don't *know*."

"Tell me where Cal Amir is."

"He is dead."

I hesitated for one second. Hearing it was somehow troubling. "Tell me what Renar is planning."

"I . . . don't wish to."

"Tell me what Renar is planning."

"No."

Not a lie. I pushed. "Tell me what Renar is planning."

"No!"

"Tell me *anything*." It was an old trap. Set up a pattern. Then abandon it, suddenly.

Kal answered before he could think. "The *kurre-nikas*."

The horrified look that immediately spread over his face told me I'd struck oil somehow. I paused, then let my cigarette drop to the floor. It was mostly ash anyway. *Kurre-nikas*. I'd never heard of anything like that, though a dirty translation would be *difference engine*. I rolled the phrase around in my head. Didn't like it.

"What is the *kurre-nikas*?"

He opened his mouth. The struggle was clear on his face, and then his expression clarified into anger. He'd caught on to my little trick. I stood up; the Compulsion was too weak to work against an active resistance. I began rolling my sleeve down over the clean, dry wound.

"We're going to kill you now, you know that?" I said.

He nodded. "Yes."

I looked down, then reached up and carefully put the tape back over his mouth. He watched the whole time, studying me.

"We found something," I heard Mel say behind me.

I put a fresh cigarette between my lips and let it dangle. Pushing my hands into my pockets as I looked at her over my shoulder. "Was it *inside* someone in the other room? Because *that* would explain a few things."

She grimaced and stepped forward, a thick bundle of papers in her hands. I took them and turned.

"So what is it?" I asked, walking past Kal to the immaculate bed, the largest one I'd ever seen. The bed was crisp and white, had a thick column at each corner, and was big enough to fit an entire normal-person bedroom on top of it. I dropped the stack of paper on it and spread it on the sheet with one hand, like a pack of cards.

"Plans," Mel said.

They were. Sheet after sheet of careful line drawings, equations in the margins, and runes. I didn't recognize the alphabet, but there were dozens—the written form of the Words didn't matter, and different *ustari* used different ones. I flipped through the pages more slowly. The drawings were layers, each page representing a level of an overall design. Lines, spidery and silvery, drawn by hand. Dozens of oversize pages, chalky blue, folded and scuffed, notes written haphazardly everywhere. None of it made any sense.

I paused, suddenly aware of a trembling in the room, the tiniest shiver under my feet, like a small earthquake. I realized the *s* in her saying *plans* had lingered, seemed to stretch out gritty and rubbery. I looked quickly over at Billington, but she was staring intently at Kal, deciding how she would execute him for his crimes. I looked at Kal, who appeared to be vibrating along with the room, his edges indistinct.

I looked at Mags. Mags looked back at me, his dark, flat face a mask of alarm. I watched to make sure he wasn't fading away.

A second, no longer, and then with a physical shock that left me swaying on my feet it was over. Everything was back to normal. I looked at Mags and held up my hand before he could say anything. It was clear from their body language that Billington and Kal hadn't noticed a thing.

I folded up the straight razor into its pearl handle and slipped it back into my pocket. Then I folded the sheaf of papers in half lengthwise and slipped it into my coat pocket. Getting up, I started for the door and felt rather than saw Mags fall into step behind me.

"That was fucking useful," Billington said, sounding bored. "You want to keep him around awhile, Chief? Try again?"

I shook my head. "No. He'll be on his toes," I said, "and I can't go body blows with an Archmage."

As we passed through into the white living room, stepping over the bodies with care, I felt the sharp flood of gas that was Rithy Kal's final gift to the universe. Billington liked the idea of that final humiliation: just wasting their blood, these *enustari*.

A second later, she was there behind me again. I took a deep breath as we stepped outside, all the Bleeders turning to look at us, quiet. The air in my lungs was damp and awful. "*Kurre-nikas.*" I rolled the words around in my mouth. A literal translation was something like *change maker*. "That mean anything to you?"

"No, Chief," Billington said. Which wasn't surprising. If I was uneducated, relatively speaking, then Melanie Billington was fucking illiterate.

I didn't even look at Mags.

The crowd of Bleeders parted in front of me, swirling behind as I walked. It took me a moment to realize there were soldiers crowding the driveway, sweating, unhappy men and women in ill-fitting dun yellow uniforms, caps on their heads, automatic rifles in their hands. A short older man with a thin mustache and a huge, overpowering nose stood in front of them all, relaxed. No rifle for him, just a leather holster on his hip and knee-high boots that gleamed with a fresh shine and provincial authority.

"Fuck," Mags spat. I paused to analyze him: his hair, his face, the way he'd spat the word. Was that Mags? Was that how he spoke, how he moved? Or had I been seeing an illusion for so long it seemed real?

Billington was in my ear. "We do not have time for this."

I turned my head slightly, keeping my eyes on the Little General. "Mel, you want to take on an army?" I shook my head. "I don't. I'm not *enustari*."

She grunted. "Look behind you, Chief. You sure?"

I turned a bit more. Three dozen men and women, sporting similar black suits in varying states of repair, cleanliness, and bloodsoakedness, were following us at a loose distance. My Army of Assholes.

My Bleeders. Each and every one of them convinced that I'd graduated to *enustari* six months ago, when I'd brought Mags back from the dead.

Except I hadn't. I couldn't have.

32.

IN MY DREAM, CLAIRE MANNICE stood on a porch with the pre-storm wind whipping her hair, holding a shotgun on me.

I STARTLED AWAKE WITH Mags's elbow in my ribs. The two of us were in the Little General's office, a plain room with pressed wood walls, a concrete floor, and four pieces of furniture: a metal desk that had seen better days, a wooden rolling chair, two stiff, uncomfortable guest chairs, and a filing cabinet. There were zero windows and one door. We'd been driven in the back of a truck for about an hour; I had no idea where we were.

Billington, typically, had suggested we shed a bit of gas and murder our way out. Me, I wondered about the coincidence of the Little General showing up in the middle of the jungle, and I decided to spend some time finding out. Time, I had. Two years and all we'd seen was death and tragedy, nary a hair on Renar's mummy head. We had gotten nowhere.

The troops had hovered, ready to leap into action, while Melanie debated my proposal. Finally, she'd nodded, made a waving gesture with her hand, and our people relaxed as one and let themselves be arrested and taken . . . somewhere.

It all felt surreal. A few hours ago I'd been in fucking *New Jersey,* for God's sake.

"Lem," Mags whispered. "I'm *starving.*"

I considered my pockets: some cash. Bandages. I shook my head.

He shifted his massive frame in the chair. "Fuck," he said. "It's *hot.*"

I'd been listening to Mags complain my whole life, it seemed, but I'd stopped being annoyed by it. I liked listening to Mags complain. I had caught some strain of Stockholm syndrome, I figured.

"Cast something," I said without looking at him, "and be not hungry."

Mags grunted in frustrated annoyance. I thought about the bodies back at Kal's, the black suits on the floor. Six or seven, I thought I'd counted. I didn't know anything about them—I'd lost track of all the *idimustari* who'd come to New York and taken service with Lem Vonnegan's Traveling Shadow Show. They were Billington's people, not mine.

Still, I saw myself stepping over them, careful not to get blood on my shoes.

The door opened, and the Little General entered with two slovenly soldiers. Up close, his army looked about as ragtag as mine. They were unshaved, smelled pretty ripe, and their boots were more tape than leather. The Little General was in better shape, but not by much.

He sat down behind his desk and smiled at us. He leaned back and laced his fingers over his immense belly. It was as if someone else's stomach had been grafted on to his skinny little body.

"Gentlemen," he said in a thick accent. "I have a difficulty."

We stared back at him. They'd taken my razor, and I didn't have my old collection of aching wounds to split open for a bit of gas. I'd gotten soft. There was nothing on the desk that was useful, nothing in sight at all. I could always bite my tongue for a little trickle. A little Charm. A Little General on my side. I wasn't worried.

"Señor Kal, he paid for protection, yes? I kept . . . elements away from him. Made him safe out in the middle of nowhere? I take my obligations very seriously."

I ran my hands over the sides of the chair. A ragged screw caught at my skin, a half-assed repair. I imagined pushing my palm against it and jerking my hand back and up. The ragged tear through my skin, the shock of warm pain, the gas in the air. Pure and unsullied. Just energy for the taking.

"So, you have invaded his privacy, and I am honor-bound to punish you." He leaned forward. "But, of course, Señor Kal, he is dead."

I knew a con when I smelled one. Colombia wasn't a country anymore; Bogotá was a ghost town, according to the news sites, half burned to the ground, claimed by dozens of gangs picking over the bones. Outside the cities were the remnants of the army and the police, formed up into militias. The bigger countries were holding it together. If you had dollars or euros or yuan, you could make things happen. I thought I could almost see the Little General's nose twitch.

I pinched the jagged piece of metal, jutting an eighth of an inch from the chair, between my thumb and forefinger. Waited for his pitch.

The Little General seemed nonplussed when we didn't respond, and glanced down at his hands. "You understand? There is . . . what is . . . there is *overhead*. There is the cleaning up of the house. The disposal of the . . . the *disposal*. There is the issue of the dead man. The fact that none of you are in Colombia legally."

I nodded, wondering what *affable* looked like and if I had the necessary facial muscles to project it. Wondered exactly who the Little General thought was going to give a shit about Colombia's border enforcement. I took a deep breath and slashed my hand against the nub of screw and tore my palm open. The pain was sudden, severe, and familiar. The gas filled the air like heavy syrup as I bled. I gave it three words. Felt the draining moment of exhaustion, but I was so flush and healthy these days, it didn't phase me in the least.

The Little General started to smile.

Your standard Charm was the tiny engine of the universe I was familiar with. Easy to cast, not very expensive in terms of blood, and infinitely pliable. A Word here, a Word not there, and the Charm became something completely different and wonderful. Assholes always hit the Charms hard, bleeding out a tub of gas and frying brains, but that was stupid. A light touch. Get in their heads and whisper.

I thought of the *Udug*. A fragment of rock that became a whispering voice in your head when you touched it. A shiver of combined fear and lust went through me.

Back at the house, there'd been too much chaos and too many guns. You started casting spells en masse it was hard to hide, hard to keep people from becoming alarmed. Hard for soldiers who looked like their training had involved identifying the boom end of a rifle and a hearty slap on the back to resist squeezing their triggers just because they didn't know what the fuck was going on. You saw it every day in the papers, what papers were left, or on the blogs, what blogs were left. Half the massacres that happened in the world, this world that we had broken, involved soldiers. I didn't want my people in the news, so I'd passed the word to stand fast until we had more advantageous circumstances. *Idimustari* worked better close up, one on one.

"You work for Rithy Kal?" I asked, keeping my voice neutral.

The Little General had recently fallen in love with me and his expression implied he was super curious as to what color underwear I had on.

"No, no," the Little General said, eyes bugging out. "Señor Kal is a *client*. Colonel Luis Suarez does not *work* for anyone." He frowned slightly, something poisoning my nice Charm. "Yes. But. No. Yes."

I resisted the urge to look at Mags. "What is it?"

The Little General's grin came and went like someone was sitting on a keyboard somewhere, hitting the ENTER key over and over. "*Del Traje Blanco,*" he muttered, and looked apologetic.

My Spanish . . . I had no Spanish aside from insults. But I knew enough. I thought of him. The Man in the White Suit.

I remembered his voice, nasal and flat. *Nonsense. I am the Negotiator.*

I struggled not to lean forward and slap the Little General. The poor sap had been Charmed so hard, his brain was half fried. "White suit?"

He nodded, happy again now that we were in agreement. "*Sí!* Yes. It is fair to say I work for him." His face darkened again. "Between you and me, *amigo*, I wish I did not. I will not be welcome in heaven, I will never see my poor mama again, this I know, but this . . . work . . . this is evil work."

I nodded. "Show me."

The Little General's smile returned, wide and exultant. He sat back and clapped his hands. "An excellent *idea,* señor! Come! I will show you everything."

The Charm. I told some of the young ones sometimes: If you could only manage to learn one fucking Cantrip, learn a fucking *Charm*.

"Is there anything to eat?" Mags wanted to know. He stood up, but the metal chair was too small for him and remained clamped on his ass. For a full twenty seconds the Little General and I stood there watching him spin around like a dog trying to chase its tail. When Mags finally got a hand on it and yanked himself free, he let it drop and stood there grinning shamefacedly.

As if nothing had happened, the Little General beckoned us, grinning. Outside his office, the two guards looked momentarily confused but managed an approximation of attention. Up close I could see that their rifles were rusty. I wondered how many hands had been blown off when they tried to fire them, as the men fell in behind us wordlessly.

The place had the feel of an abandoned school or hospital. Cinderblock walls, concrete floors. Echoes crowding us as we walked. Silence. No power, as far as I could tell, but the place had a stale residue of blood, an old shadow of magic. Someone had used it for some serious rituals. The Little General was all grins now that he had found a way to please us. Our tour guide into hell. He led us to a chained-shut set of double doors and told us pleasantly that Rithy Kal once owned this facility, and drug lords before him. That it had been given to the Little General as a base of operations.

He led us down the stairs.

The stairwells were little tubes of humidity. The stairs themselves were metal and groaned alarmingly as we stepped onto them. I could see bolts jiggling and working as we descended, flakes of rust raining down to announce us. Every flight brought us into a thick new layer of heat and wet, and a thick new layer of ancient, dried-up blood. I'd never been able to sense old blood like this. Usually, the gas burned off and was gone, clean. Of course I could always sense the fresh stuff in the air, even at a distance. But I'd never sensed the dry-rot, furry aura of dead gas.

A lot of people had died here, and not well.

Down and down. The heat, the wet, the death all getting stronger.

At the bottom level—the subbasement, I supposed—we stood in ankle-deep water, warm as piss, brown and smelling like sewage. I stood feeling the water soak my socks and the cuffs of my pants as the two guards worked another padlocked set of doors, and thought that I should have just stuck with the old thrift store suits I used to wear.

The doors squealed open, and we'd arrived: hell, population my Asshole Army.

The doors led to an underground holding area—a wide, low-ceilinged center aisle banked on either side by iron-barred cells that had been carved out of the soft, damp rock. It was completely silent save for the splashing of our feet. The heat and damp hit me in the face; I'd been über-sweating for the last ten minutes and hadn't noticed, my own level of humidity matching that of the air around me.

As Mags and I walked into the space, our people stared at us from the cells. Some of them hung off the bars, their faces pushed between them. Some leaned against the rear walls burning damp cigarettes that were trying hard to snuff out in the wet air. The Little General's guards, six of them, stood in the center with their rifles slung over their shoulders. They stared sightlessly, their bodies stiff, their breathing even and calm.

I let my eyes adjust to the gloom. Farther down, the other cells were crowded with people too. Locals. Dark-skinned men and women and children and babies. All dressed differently, all staring at us—or straining to. They were silent. They looked like they'd been there for a long time.

"All right," I said.

The cell doors nearest us groaned open. You couldn't hold a bunch of *idimustari* in fucking jail. They all swam out, kicking up the awful water and arranging themselves along the sides, shooting cuffs and pushing hair out of their faces, plucking cigarettes from behind their ears.

"Who are they?" I asked, gesturing at the locals.

The Little General shrugged. "They belong to *Del Traje Blanco*. Señor Kal, he holds them here."

"Chief."

I squinted through the gloom until I found Billington. She looked spotless, untouched by the heat and dirt. I had her pegged: She liked to look plain and unconcerned about her appearance, but I was almost certain she used a constant stream of *mu* to maintain her look.

I stepped away from Mags and the Little General and went over. She waited until I was right next to her, then turned to look down the rest of the aisle. I could just make out a large, heavy-looking door.

"It gets worse," she said, and started walking. I followed, pushing my hands into my pockets. Even after all this time I wasn't quite used to not feeling the burn of a dozen small wounds when I did that. The door resolved from the gloom, bloated, old, and wooden with rusted iron hinges, chained shut like everything else and green with moss or rot or both. As we got near, Billington raised an arm and snapped her fingers. A moment later, a tender shoot of gas trickled into the air. She spat two Words at the door and it sagged open, gentle, like a prom date.

Splashing forward and pulling it open, she gestured me through. I could still sense the tendril of gas burning into the universe's hungry maw, and with two Words of my own I had a neat yellow ball of light, a miniature sun, floating over my shoulder. I'd cribbed the basic spell and rubbed it down to its basics. Two Words.

I stepped through the doorway, and the light floated a few inches ahead. After one step, I stumbled over something. I looked up, and with a thought the ball expanded slightly, bringing more of the space into the light. I stared.

This next room was larger than the prison area. And it was *filled* with corpses.

33.

THEY WERE GUILTY.

The Little General, Charmed so hard I expected his ears to start bleeding. There were bits of food stuck in his yellowed teeth, which I knew because he never stopped smiling.

Del Traje Blanco *informed us of their guilt.*

I replayed his voice in my head as the car inched down Broadway. Neilsson, the old drunk, had gotten us home with just a small amount of cabin depressurization and queasy gravity shifts as he flew the jet like it was a fucking mobile home with wings. Mags had spent the entire flight with the lower half of his face thrust in a vomit bag, his eyes shooting rage everywhere, the expression somewhat ruined by his occasional whimper when we hit a pocket of turbulence.

The Little General, collecting bodies. Delivering them to Rithy Kal. The Negotiator. There was a missing step in there, something that would cause it all to make sense. I wasn't smart enough to see what it was.

Outside the car, crowds of people milled about. New York was truly never asleep anymore. Thousands of people lived on the streets, choking traffic, cooking and sleeping and just being awake constantly. The police had given up. They still cleared a street here and there when they needed to, but when you had a few hundred thousand people camped out, what could you do?

They were guilty, so we executed them.

The corpses had been stacked neatly. The smell was incredible, all that flesh rotting in the heat and the damp. Their hands were all tied behind their backs with rough twine. A strip of dirty white cloth had been tied around their eyes as a blindfold.

I smoked a stale cigarette someone had given me, and the back of the car filled up with smoke. I didn't want to crack a window. People were always sticking their fingers in, trying to push the window down, trying anything. Why not. Nothing was working, why not try whatever you could. See what happens.

We could have cast on the cars. I had Mags, Remy, and Roman, dusted off, their cuffs and shoes still smelling like shit, still damp. Mags was so irritated from the flight he probably would have killed anyone who came close enough, more or less by accident. We could have cast on the cars, but it was just too easy, casting and casting, bleeding and bleeding and not feeling any of it.

I'd been to and gone from Colombia in eighteen hours.

Our three cars averaged about six miles per hour through the meat of the city, but we never stopped. There was no cross traffic and no reason to stop for the lights, which were all blinking yellow anyway. So we actually made better time than we would have three years before. We pulled up outside Rue's, one car after the other, Wards on the curb keeping the sidewalk clear of other vehicles. A few vagrants shuffled along the sidewalk, but we didn't bother them and they didn't bother us, and none of them ever came into the bar. No one but us came in.

I sat in the car after we'd parked, thinking on it. A puzzle. Something was tickling me, trying to break through and become an epiphany. All this. Everything. I had Renar, everywhere for three terrifying weeks of my life two years ago, now missing since, like a ghost. But not dead, I thought. Too much to hope for that she was dead. In the meantime, no word of her, no word of anything. Just the slow unwinding of the world, spinning out under its own internal pressure. Mass suicides. Mass killings. Bombs. Poisonings. Mutinies.

Now we had a fucking tinpot general collecting blood for the Negotiator. *Del Traje Blanco.* And not voluntarily, I didn't think. There was a lot of daylight between an honorable bribe to protect Rithy Kal from the local authorities and actively rounding up your friends and neighbors to be bled white.

In the back room at Rue's, Billington was already working on a bottle of bourbon, leaning against one of the tables with her arms crossed under her tits. There'd been a discussion about moving the Asshole Army to a new location, because Rue's was known to be ours—we'd even pastured Kenny out of the picture with a payout and a Charmed kick in the ass. But I'd vetoed the idea. What difference did it make? If Renar or any of the death-crazy *enustari* wanted to find me, they'd find me. Mags had been gifted a candy bar, his nausea and terror forgotten as he did his level best to smear it all over himself without actually ingesting any of it.

A group of men and women in shitty black suits stood and sat across from him, watching him openly. But instead of wearing expressions of vague amusement and amazement, they looked like they were ready to scatter if he glanced up at them. Like he was something unexpected, supernatural.

"You'll read about it in the papers, on some newsfeed or other," Mel said without preamble. "*Colombian military slaughters innocent villagers wholesale for weirdo in red shoes.*"

I sat down and watched Mags eat, apparently via absorption. She was right—we'd gotten so used to the endless stream of horrors in what passed for the news these days that it had become numbing. But this shit . . . this was exactly the sort of thing you heard about and processed and ignored. *Five hundred corpses found in Colombian prison.* Huh, just five hundred? In Qinghai three weeks before, fifty-six people had been crushed to death by *elephants* from the southern provinces. Fucking elephants got you remembered. Just average everyday murder didn't even budge the needle.

"That whole place," Mags said thickly, sounding sticky, "reminded me of Fallon's workshop. Lem, remember when Fallon made himself into a giant? He told me he'd teach me that one, but he never did."

For a second I imagined Mags even larger.

Ev Fallon. An old man then, even older now. I recalled his sinewy, tough body, thin and scrappy, but somehow elegant. His huge, nimble hands. *Enustari,* easily. The only Fabricator I knew, and capable of building intricate, powerful magical Artifacts. Somehow the mechanical nature of the devices augmented or amplified the power, and spells could be bound to them permanently, sometimes without requiring repeated bleedings for repeated effects. Fallon had taken to teaching Mags the art of Fabrication, saying he had a touch for it. This was incredible, and so far I'd assumed Fallon was just being nice. Fallon didn't seem to notice that Mags *was* showing signs of improvement, ever since he'd . . . come back.

For the millionth time I thought about what had happened that day in Abdagnale's tiny universe. It certainly hadn't been *me* who brought him back. One second I'd been sinking into the cold, bled-white failure I was so familiar with, casting a useless spell on a dead body, and the next—the next, Mags was coughing and sputtering beneath me, kicking like a bucking horse, and I'd become a legend.Whatever had happened, it had changed him, and no one else seemed to notice. Fallon didn't. He still regarded Mag's lessons as charity, entertainment for the dim giant. But Mags had a better memory for the Words, more discipline when casting now. Which made me feel like an asshole because I'd spent the last ten, twelve years teaching my friend absolutely nothing. In fact, it could be argued that before the . . . incident, I'd somehow made him even *dumber* through his association with me, if that were technically possible.

I was not a good friend. I felt Mags's heartbeat, his respiration, *him,* like an invisible sun beating against me.

For his part, Fallon remained mysterious to me, but there was no harm in letting him teach Mags a few tricks. Fallon's lessons were widely spaced, the old man showing no urgency in scheduling them, but Mags was really *working* at it, and that was good for him, too, I guessed. Since I was not a good friend. At least he was trying to learn something. I remembered meeting Fallon for the first time, presenting him with the fact that he'd helped engineer the end of the fucking world, and then immediately having to fight for our lives. Which at the time hadn't been unusual, even though I hadn't been the fucking Leader of the Resistance back then or had a quote-unquote army. Yet since I'd acquired said army, since Mag's resurrection, no one had attacked me. There had been assassination attempts, wetwork-type attempts. But no invasions. No lightning bolts from the sky. No *dimma*.

Five hundred corpses in Colombia. On the Negotiator's order. Sucked dry, bled white, all of them marked, all of them under a simple *geas* even I could see, though there'd been no evidence of a spell cast from them. Nothing recent. Nothing. It was as if—

And the Negotiator had said he didn't work for Renar. None of it fit together. Except maybe one piece.

I looked at Mags, now busily licking his fat fingers for every tiny smear of chocolate he could locate. Fallon's workshop had been destroyed that night, but I remembered it. The Glamours in place to obfuscate its true purpose, both workshop . . . and Fabrication.

I stood up. "Tell Remy and Roman to get the cars."

Billington shot up instantly. No matter how many times I failed to be whatever it was Melanie Billington imagined I was, she never lost faith. And despite the fact that I hadn't seen so much as a sign from her, I knew the twins were already walking out to get the cars.

"Where're we going, Chief?"

"Just you and Pitr," I said. "We're visiting the Old Man."

THE DRIVE INTO HOBOKEN was creepy, as always. The tunnel was empty, unlit, and had two feet of water pooled at the deepest point, forcing us to slow to a crawl for a few minutes. One car passed us going the wrong way at about a hundred miles an hour. Billington, Mags, and I had our sleeves yanked up as it screamed past and splashed a tidal wave of dirty water over our car. No one had officially closed the tunnel. No one seemed to be keeping it open, either.

When we burst out on the other side, we passed the wall of toll-booths, empty and dark. There were a few other cars on the roads, but not many. Half the streetlights were out.

Fallon had set up a new workshop in a massive former warehouse down by the rail tracks. It was a big brick building with broken plate glass all around the perimeter, the interior of the first floor completely and utterly ransacked. The walls and floors had even been stolen, everything stripped down to studs and joists. We had to balance on the joists as we crept in, arms stretched out. Except Mags, who bounded forward at nearly a run, making the old wooden beams bounce under us like living things.

This time Fallon wasn't relying on complex Glamours to hide his workshop from the world. An abandoned building and a freight elevator that worked only if he wanted it to: elegant. As Mags arrived, the elevator kicked into life, rattling and coughing its way up from below.

The Old Man stood in the exact center of the carriage, wearing a pair of greasy yellow overalls that looked thick and hot enough to stop a bullet. A pair of blackened gloves hung out of one pocket. One of his too-long brown cigarettes dangled from one gray lip. Ev Fallon's face had only gotten more deeply lined, more shadowed in the last two years. There were dark circles under his eyes but those eyes were still bright and sharp.

"Mr. Mageshkumar," he said, thin brown cigarette bobbing, smoke spitting out into the cool air. "Mr. Vonnegan. Ms. Billington." His eyes landed on Remy and Roman standing silently behind us. "Assorted freaks. To what do I owe the pleasure?"

"Consultation," I said. "Regarding your area of expertise."

He nodded but didn't move. "I thought you were traveling," he said. "To bring justice to the world."

I didn't know if Fallon had had previous dealings with Rithy Kal. It was a touchy subject. Fallon was our only ally of substance, the only *enustari* we counted on our side. As much as he was on our side. Because he was also the man who'd designed Renar's murder machine.

The man who'd left us to die there. When he'd wandered into the dinner later, possibly filled with shame and remorse—though no guarantees there—he'd been fucking lucky to find us alive.

And, I reminded myself, for some reason hearing it in Hiram's booming actor voice, he'd waited until we'd *won*. Or at least: not lost.

"We did. What we came back with was *kurre-nikas*."

He studied me with a slight tightening of the eyes and reached up to pluck the cigarette from his mouth. He flicked it into the darkness and stepped aside, exhaling smoke. "Come, then."

We crowded into the elevator, and Fallon worked the doors and pressed the bottommost button. We lurched downward with just the screech of the old elevator around us.

"Mr. Mageshkumar," Fallon said without turning. "Say for me your Binding."

Mags choked and pushed his hands into his pockets, staring down at his surprisingly small feet. "Now?" he said shyly. "Wait—I made a spell. A *mu*. Make people bray like donkeys whenever they try to speak. I made it."

This was news, Mags making up a spell. Assuming it wasn't riddled with grammatical errors that would instead summon several dogs into the room, or mysteriously do nothing at all, it was almost amazing. The Mags I knew—the Mags I'd *known*, before he'd been brought back— had never been able to remember a spell for more than a few days, much less write one from scratch.

I studied the big bastard as the elevator rumbled down. Felt the strangeness again, like something had shifted in his face that was so subtle and minute, so tiny, that I couldn't place it. But my underbrain knew.

Fallon was not to be dissuaded. "That is well, Mr. Mageshkumar, but I did not ask if you had created a spell to make people bray like *donkeys*. At our last lesson, I asked you to memorize the Binding. Recite it now, please. Do not pause or start over even if you make your usual mistakes. Remember, a Binding is not your common spell. Mistakes do not warp its effects. Failure to complete will not release unfocused energy."

"Why is it different?" I asked. I'd taken it upon myself to be Mags's advocate. He didn't know what questions to ask.

"Because Fabrication is about simplification through repetition. Mass production of the *effect*. When you create a Fabrication, you are freeing yourself from the time and blood constraint of casting—but much of that must be invested *into* the Fabrication during its creation. That is what the Binding does—but come, this is not theory, Lemuel. Mr. Mageshkumar, say for me your Binding. When you can make your Binding *work,* then perhaps you are ready to know why it does so."

Ritual. It felt good. Hiram and Mags were dead, Claire was silent, the world was broken, but I had little rituals to cling to.

Hiram. Fallon's teaching style was like Hiram's, with the disdain, but without the profanity and sarcasm. It was comforting. I could close my eyes and imagine the slaps and insults, and it felt almost like old, fat, blackhearted Hiram was still with me.

Mags began to speak the Binding that Fallon had been laboriously trying to teach him for months now. The Binding was the final spell in the creation of any Fabrication. It imbued the machine or contraption or rock or whatever with the energy that made it work. That was the limit of my comprehension of the art, and I suspected that despite months of work, Mags's comprehension wasn't much better.

The Words were easy enough. Mags's problem was a brain that was at least three sizes too small. My problem was that my usual skills—my ability to cut the Words down, to reduce spells to their basics—worked against me. Because the first rule of Fabrication, of creating an Artifact, was that more Words meant more powerful. Always. More Words, bigger Artifacts—mass. More Words, more power—density. These were, so far, my only takeaways from Fallon's droning lectures.

When Mags finished, Fallon sighed, conveying infinite sadness and disappointment. He left it to Mags—and me—to figure out why he was disappointed. He always did.

The elevator ride, as usual, was disturbingly long. Hoboken was built on fucking sand. Though there wasn't a basement deeper than five feet in the whole town, the freight elevator just kept going. We rode out the last minute in silence, then the carriage settled loudly with a rusty scraping sound that made me dread the return trip. Fallon worked the doors again, and with a sweep of his long, thin arm beckoned us to enter his new workshop.

The place was a crowded machine shop. One big room, it wasn't cavernous like the last one, but it was big enough. A simple metal workbench stretched along the length of one wall, littered with scrap metal, hand tools, and other debris. There was a smell of solder in the air. Big machines with obscure uses were bolted into the concrete floor, and the place had a hot, greasy feel. There was a hum, too, barely there but somehow deep and inside me, resonating with my bones. I figured there was probably a hundred, two hundred thousand dollars' worth of equipment in the place: two hundred grand of the old money, when currency was worth something. But we *ustari*, we never paid for anything. Especially Archmages like Fallon.

"You know that name," I said, stepping through the thick air as Fallon crossed to the workbench and retrieved a pair of glasses that were so light and thin they were practically invisible. He slipped them on and turned, leaning back against the workbench and crossing his arms as his eyes landed on Pitr Mags, who was pulling on a long metal lever attached to something that looked like an overgrown coffee grinder and frowning in a way that signaled comedy or tragedy, coming soon.

Keeping his eyes on Mags, Fallon nodded slightly. "Yes."

"What does it mean?"

He looked at me for a long moment. "I do not know."

There was a sudden deep boom, and then Mags was scampering backwards from the machine, face red and alarmed. He slid to a halt and looked around at us, then pushed his hands deep into his pockets and hung his head.

I looked back at the old man. He was making a show of removing and cleaning his glasses. "You don't know?"

He sighed. "I know the term. I have heard it. But I cannot tell you what it is." He put his glasses back on. "The *kurre-nikas* involves some-one I used to know. A former acquaintance."

This was fucking fascinating. I'd begun to imagine that Fallon had emerged, fully formed, from the ground a few years ago, perhaps cre-ated by the power of my desperation. The idea that the man had a his-tory made me vibrate with excitement.

"Well," I said, "let's go have a chat with them."

Fallon hesitated, then nodded slowly, finally looking at me. "That will require some blood."

34.

AS HE SCRUBBED HIS ARMS up past the elbows with a yellow soap that smelled like gasoline and foamed ridiculously, making a sizzling noise, Fallon said, "You told Cal Amir about my Fab-rication," in a flat voice that was somehow threatening.

Ten feet behind us, Mags was practicing his Binding over and over. I didn't know what Billington was up to.

I shrugged, my own hands in my pockets. "At the time it was a tacti-cal decision." I remembered Cal Amir in the car. *There's a secret room in the basement. I will search for it.*

I looked at the sheaf of papers we'd taken from Kal's place, getting wet on the bench beside the sink. "How bad is it?"

He shrugged. "It is a mechanism for storing sacrificed energy, yes?"

I stared dumbly at the sketches. Looked up. "Like your old place."

"Yes, but on a much greater scale. This Fabricator has great skill. But this." He tapped a wet finger on the papers. "This component, if I am reading his notes correctly—they are in an unfamiliar cipher, so I may be misunderstanding, but I do not think so—allows the stored power to be broadcast. To be accessed long-distance."

I stared at his finger. The page under it was a folded-over blueprint, white markings and lines and numbers. I thought about the Little General telling us that the Man in the White Suit wanted executions; he and his men had been Charmed to the gills to keep doing it. "Could it be *stored* long-distance?"

Fallon didn't answer right away. When I looked up he was staring at me, his lined face blank, his body still. "Yes," he said curtly. He shook himself and turned away. "Yes."

Fallon snorted and went back to scrubbing. He was still wiry, and his hands with their inhumanly long fingers were still strong, the tendons on his forearm ropy with power. "That was foolish, Lemuel. Yes, my Fabrication would scale. Even to this degree. A battery, you called it. Fabrication is an art of scale. This can be in either the Binding, the Words, or the size of the Fabrication. Or all." He looked up into the mirror, his reflected eyes on me. "Yes, it could follow. Spur bloodshed and collect it all. Store it. It would require someone in the area, a point person. A trained mage who could direct the flow of energy. But in something based on my designs, it could be done."

A point person. I nodded. That would be Rithy Kal, contracted to direct the flow. One small piece in place.

I heard Mags unleash a series of soft *fuck*s under his breath. Ever since Fallon had taken on teaching him, Mags had treated the Fabricator with the same anxious deference he'd once reserved for Hiram. I could still picture the first time I'd braced Hiram in his apartment. I'd been young, impossibly young, and Hiram had seemed old, impossibly old, with his Santa beard and suspenders, his Earl Grey tea, and his fussy, crowded apartment. Mags had been sort of a servant or bodyguard, though as far as I could tell he'd made more messes than he'd cleaned up and had proved courageous only at unexpected moments.

I remembered him standing behind Hiram as the old man interviewed me. His hands had been clenched, and he'd just glared at me, his unibrow a hard line of anger. I remembered being afraid of Mags for the first and only time in my life.

"It's not *could* be done," I said. "It's *being* done. I didn't see it before, but I see it now. We haven't heard a peep from Renar and Amir. Nothing. *Nothing.* Meanwhile, the world is fucking tearing itself apart: Every day, thousands, tens of thousands, dead. We assumed it was ripples from Renar's *biludha,* but that's not it. It's a *grift,* Fallon. They're bleeding the world in slow motion, so we wouldn't be able to put it together. Bleeding it and storing it."

Fallon pushed the spigot closed with his elbow and stood with his arms up and dripping. "*Ya,* I said it *follows,* Mr. Vonnegan. You pointed them to my work, and they have extrapolated it, enlarged it. Made it global—an immense undertaking. But Mika's expiration date approaches, yes? She has no reason to be reasonable, to be careful. She is all in. Come."

He turned, arms held up by his chest, and I followed him past Mags, who glanced up nervously at us, then back down at his shoes.

"First let me state," the old man said as he walked, "that I am not the designer of this Artifact. It was inherited."

He led me to the back wall of the workshop, where a bank of storage cabinets had been arranged in a long, neat row. The upper cabinets had no doors, and each exposed shelf had several neatly arranged objects of varying size and shape. Fallon walked along the edge, peering into each one, until he made a clucking noise with his tongue and reached in, emerging with what looked like a tiny golden box, like a jewelry box. His personal collection of Fabrications, I supposed.

He turned and held it out to me. "*Gulla,*" he said.

Gulla. To destroy, to overwhelm. A good word for the Griefers— exciting things happened when you gassed up the air and shouted, *Gulla!* I reached out, but the old man pulled it back away from me.

"It is . . . invasive."

He turned it over, revealing that the underside of the little box was bristling with thin, delicate-looking needles.

"You will have to bleed for it," he continued. "And submit to its will."

I pulled my hand back. "What exactly does that *mean*?"

He shrugged, turning the box over in his hand. "You bleed for it, it will lead you to what you wish. This takes as long as it takes, limited by the physical limitations of your body and the speed with which it can travel." He looked back at me. "It will possess you. For some time, you will be . . . asleep, while the *gulla* accepts your sacrifice and does its work." The faintest smile flickered on his face. "I went through a period where all my Fabrications were boxes." He sobered suddenly, shaking his head once, curtly. "Our other choice would be to try to cast something to locate your Man in White—difficult, as he is certainly shielded from such spells—or locate him by more physical means, which may take a lot of time." He nodded at the small golden box. "This is, as they say, *under the radar*."

I stared at the golden box. I imagined the tiny bristle-like needles were moving, squirming. I remembered the slimy feel of the *Udug* in my hand, the whisper in my brain. I had no desire to relive that, and I wanted nothing more than to hear that silent voice again. My hands twitched.

"We don't have time," I said slowly. "This has been going on for *two fucking years*. Right under our noses. She's been bleeding the world and made it look like we were tearing ourselves apart." The world was broken. *We* had broken it. "Jesus Christ, it's a *con*. She's trying to fuel the *Biludha-tah-namus* again, just in slow motion this time."

Fallon squinted. "She cannot. The *Biludha-tah-namus* would require the Mannice girl. She is marked for the ritual but has not experienced the cadence. To complete it requires her, or her death."

I pictured Claire: shotgun in her hands, dry wind blowing her hair around. Skinny and fierce, telling me to go the fuck away and not look back. It was dangerous to even think about Claire, so I pushed her from my mind again.

"How does it work?"

Fallon shrugged and looked down contemplatively at the box. "Simply, from the perspective of the Client. You fix in your mind that which you seek. You take the *gulla* in your hand and bleed for it. You will awake sometime later where you need to be." He looked up at me. "We will follow you."

I swallowed. *Client.* It was, as I'd learned from overhearing Fallon's sessions with Mags, a term used by Fabricators to describe the people who used their creations.

"It is an old Fabrication," he continued softly, sounding lost in thought. "Predating electricity. I cannot tell you what you will experience, as no one who has used it has ever described it."

I nodded. "Evelyn, is that because they all died?"

He looked up sharply, fixing me in his piercing gray gaze for one terrible second, and I reminded myself that Fallon was *enustari* and capable of terrible, awful things. Then he threw his head back and burst into laughter.

"There are easier ways to kill, Mr. Vonnegan," he said, holding the *gulla* out to me, smiling. Ev Fallon smiling was attractive and disturbing. His face was and was not made for expressions of cheer. The smile made him look like a cheerful psychopath, the kind who made you laugh and then stabbed you with knitting needles. I didn't know much about Fallon and his motivations, but I reminded myself that he'd had years to fuck me over and hadn't.

I reached out and took the *gulla* from his hand. It was *dense.* It felt heavy in my hand, heavier than should have been possible. It was warm to the touch, and I was reminded of the slick *Udug.* Both objects had felt *alive* in my hand. I studied the Artifact and realized the tiny golden wires *were* moving, waving slightly as if in some private breeze of invisible particles.

I thought of Mika Renar. The dried-up old mummy in the wheelchair, her yellow eyes the only part of her still alive enough to move. I hesitated. Wherever she was, she would be protected. I'd blown her sky-high when I'd fucked up the *Biludha-tah-namus,* dropped a bomb on her fucking head, and she'd survived. If I showed up with Mags and

Billington and some harsh words as ammunition, I didn't think we'd get too far.

I thought of Claire. After so many months of refusing to think of her, of blocking her out of my mind, it felt strange and foreign to actively think of her. I pictured her not as she'd been the last time I'd seen her, but an idealized version: beautiful, dirty, mocking. This was all about her, in some way. She was the key. And if the Negotiator didn't work for Renar, than he worked for someone else who wanted to put hands on Claire.

And I couldn't allow that. *Time,* as Hiram might have said in his fussy, exasperated voice, *is of the essence.* And *Offense,* I thought, coining a Vonnegan original, *is always better than defense.*

I thought of the Man in the White Suit. The Negotiator. I felt a flush rise in my cheeks. I pictured his red shoes, his face, like a series of triangles stitched together, his pointy nose and pale, milky skin. Those dead, haunted eyes. Heard his imperious voice in my head. *Nonsense. I am the Negotiator.* Fixed an image in my mind of the skinny son of a bitch. Looked up at Fallon as he spoke.

"Mr. Vonnegan, we should discuss what—"

I turned the *gulla* over and pushed the needles down into my palm.

There was a second of sharp pain. I felt the wires under my skin, moving.

35. IN THE DREAM, AS ALWAYS, Claire Mannice was on fire. She stood with her back to me, leaning forward against the bar at Rue's, burning, the runes on her skin bright and perfectly clear for once, glowing blue and eldritch. No matter how I tried, I couldn't see her face.

/////

I WOKE UP TO a stinging pain, a weight on my chest, and the smell of mildew in the air. I opened my eyes to Fallon sitting on top of me, one huge hand cocked up by his face. He was peering intently down at me.

I realized I was holding my breath. Panic filled me. I opened my mouth but could not make my chest move. I lay there with my mouth open, goggle-eyed, Fallon over me like a terrible ancient bird about to spit something into my mouth.

With a grunt, Fallon swung his arm down and slapped me again.

My whole body went into a deep, painful spasm, every muscle tensing up into something rock-hard. My chest heaved, and a tiny pinprick of air trickled into my chest.

"Stupid," Fallon said with an air of disgust as he shifted his weight and climbed back to the floor. "You are very *stupid*. But alive. Which is a relief, as your giant Indian friend has informed me many times that he would break every bone in my body if you did not wake up."

I sat up, moving in jerky increments as if only certain muscles were getting oxygen, and those along a selected pattern. The pinprick slowly expanded into an airway, and I gulped in mildewy air hungrily, every muscle in my body burning. My head felt like someone had pushed something into the space between the skull and brain—too tight, the pulse of my blood sluggish and thickened. I turned my head and imagined I could hear every single sinew and tendon creak. Mags was standing right over me, breathing very loudly through his nose. He filled his shirt and jacket so thoroughly, it was safe to say he had reached *maximum* containment.

I tried to make my face into a smile for Mags. "Where," I said, my voice sounding like sandpaper on rocks. "Where—?"

"Stupid," Fallon repeated, stalking to a window and standing there staring at the drapes, hands in his pockets. He was wearing a beautiful cream-colored suit of an old style. It had wide shoulders and a gorgeous sheen and was the sort of suit I'd always wanted to wear but knew, on an unspoken, inarticulate level, I'd never be able to pull off.

"Seward," I heard Mel Billington say. "Seward, fucking-A-laska."

"It is a trap," Fallon said simply. "Perhaps someday we will discuss why you did not discuss your choices before invoking the *gulla*."

I looked down at my hand; the tiny golden box was gone. We were in a motel room. This came to me in chunks, like my brain was reconnecting. Done in browns and yellows—or maybe they'd been other colors a century ago, when the place was built—the room was dark and dusty, tired sunlight pushing anemically through the thick drapes to give us just enough light to see by. I was on the bed. It was fucking freezing. Mel was thrown into a broken-down chair, wrapped up in even more coats than usual, smoking a cigarette in the silver holder she favored.

Sitting on the orange rug were three of ours. Bloody messes. They'd stripped off their shirts and sat with fresh, puckered scars on both arms, a small stain spread out around them.

I looked at Mel. For a second I couldn't make my mouth work. "How—?"

"Three weeks," she said. She pointed the cigarette at me. "You've been a zombie for three weeks."

The stink in the room was overwhelming. It was rotten and damp, and it was in the air itself, attached to each molecule. I looked at Mags; he was smiling shyly.

"It's good to have you back," he said.

I swallowed something spiky and dry. Mags was my responsibility. Without me, people forgot to water and feed him. "What was it like, buddy?"

He looked down at his surprisingly small feet, dancer's feet. "You were, like, asleep. Your eyes were always closed. You got thinner and thinner and you were, like, gray. Like you were suffocating even though you were breathing. Sometimes you twitched. You just walked all the time. We had to tie you down, sometimes."

My feet, I realized, ached painfully.

"It is difficult to travel *by foot* in the modern world," Fallon groused. He gestured at the slumped forms of our Bleeders. "Ms. Billington had to employ much of her organizational skill to secure Bleeders so we could obscure ourselves. And we put much effort into getting you bundled into vehicles when we could, at which point you would thrash and kick—*possessed*." He paused, and then raised his voice just slightly, the result like a shout from anyone else. "By *foot*, Mr. Vonnegan!"

"The town," Mel added immediately, sounding almost cheerful, "is abandoned. As in, totally fucking empty. Which I am inclined to think isn't because of Mad Day or Mika Renar or what the fuck, but because Seward is a fucking hole no one should ever live in."

I felt like I'd been doing chin-ups for three weeks. Shuddering with some final spasm, I felt something mysterious unlock deep inside me, and my whole body relaxed into a steady, awful aching. I sucked in breath and moved my sand-dry tongue around in my mouth.

Fuckin' *magic*. It had been a long time since I'd felt that thrill. That thrill I'd felt thirty years before, watching that old gent levitate in a motel parking lot. That thrill of possibility. For a while now it had been survival, then nothing. Nothing for a long time.

I tried to move my legs, to swing them over the edge of the bed. This did not work, and I started to get a little alarmed. Fallon wasn't infallible, after all, and he seemed like he was in the mood to accidentally-on-purpose leave me paralyzed. As a lesson. We were not, I reminded myself, good people.

"Why the fuck Alaska?"

"You chose someone or something to find. The *gulla* has brought you to it." Fallon took a deep breath. "This place is damp with magic. Blood, everywhere, recently. I believe you have been *seen coming*, as the expression goes. Perhaps because we came here *by foot*."

The door opened. Mel leaped from her chair and all three of the kneeling Bleeders—white-faced and covered in a cold sheen of sweat— stiffened. But it was Remy and Roman, wearing identical pea coats and newsboy caps like father and son, or grandfather and grandson, doing grandfatherly things like dressing identically.

They glanced at me blankly for a second, then turned and took off their caps to Mel.

"Not a soul in town, Mum," Remy said, his voice serious and without humor. "We checked every place likely."

"Looks like they packed up nice and careful when movin' out," Roman added, twisting his cap in his hands.

"How long have we been here?" I asked.

Roman glanced at me, then back at Billington. She gave him a nod, studying her fingers, and he looked back at me.

"Two days."

I worked my jaw, which felt stiff and sore, like I'd been clenching my teeth for weeks. Which, I guessed, I had.

"*Lem*," Mags said suddenly, leaning down. "Are you *okay*?"

I nodded, reaching up and putting my hand on his neck, hot and tough, and pulled his face down into my shoulder. I'd brought Mags to meet the Negotiator, the man who'd killed him as far as I was concerned, and hadn't even told him. Stupid, as Fallon had said. I got a toe wiggling, stiff and painful. It was inspirational. "Let's take the tour."

No one moved until Billington nodded again. "Let's take the fucking tour, then," she said, and Roman and Remy snapped to and held the door open.

IT WAS OBVIOUS THAT Seward had been a hole before this, whatever this was. The sort of Alaskan town where I imagined people looked forward to seasonal affective disorder as a sort of vacation from their miserable lives.

It was cold. Felt like it had been so for decades straight, the sort of deep core cold that got into bones and made them fragile. The town was a long corridor along a road, open and exposed to the elements. One big restaurant, one small bar, a bunch of sad-looking houses. Everything gray. We went into the houses, the shops. Everything put up, but none of the doors locked. Clothes folded in drawers, dishes in the cabinets. It reminded me of a dozen stories on the news. Towns gone, abandoned, mass suicides and assorted mysteries.

Standing out in the middle of the main road, wind whipping at us, we felt like we were at the farthest point from anywhere in the world, the point where you had no choice but to turn back. I stood hunched over with the wind pushing at me, my army in miniature—three Bleeders, the Twins, Mags, Mel Billington, and Ev Fallon—standing around me, hands in pockets, faces grim.

I'd learned to have faith in magic. I'd learned that it always did exactly as it was told; the trick was in knowing what orders to give, what questions to ask. The *gulla* hadn't led me to this fucking ghost town as a joke. Someone was here. Or had been.

Shivering, I led them through every building, every room. The place had been sucked dry, I knew it. I sensed Fallon and Billington exchanging looks, trying to decide how much leeway to give me. How long to let me wander an empty town before they took charge and got us back on track. But I kept walking. I knew what I was going to find. As we moved through each antiseptic tableau, I had this idea that we were all repeating ourselves. Setting the same tragedies in motion over and over, stealing from the bloody massacres of the past. Cribbing blood from our predecessors in the same way we were repeating the same spells, no one making anything new.

Except this. This felt new. This draining of the earth in slow motion.

All of the buildings felt the same. Wood. Bad decor. Yellowing laminate. The smell of tobacco and used beer. Seward was not a place I would have chosen to live, but then, these days there was nowhere that made sense. Maybe Seward was as good as anywhere.

After about an hour, we turned a corner heading towards the water and found a suitcase sitting in the middle of the road, closed tight, its old vinyl battered and stained. A thin trail of luggage formed an almost straight line to the ocean, going off-road and curving around buildings, thickening as it went. Starting with that one suitcase, then a cluster of luggage a few feet later. Then a stream of rolling bags and trash bags filled with clothes, then an unbroken line of handbags, backpacks, and trunks, all just left on the ground.

People walking, growing tired, divesting themselves of their possessions.

The luggage thinned out as we got near the metallic shoreline, but we didn't need its direction anymore. We found everyone in the ice-cold gray water lapping at the town, erasing it a millimeter at a time.

All of them were fully dressed, all of them weighed down by different things: logs, stones, backpacks filled with power tools. They'd slashed their wrists, mostly, though some had opted for the throat. Self-inflicted, to judge by the angles and the variety of blades on the ground or in the water. They'd lined up on the edge of the freezing Pacific and opened their veins and tipped backwards into the water one by one. Not a drop of blood anywhere to be seen.

We stood for a moment or two, just studying their bloated gray bodies. I was shivering, hard. I heard someone approach and turned to find Fallon next to me, hands thrust in his coat pockets, breath steaming.

"Collected," he said. "The blood."

I nodded. "Everywhere."

I thought of Claire. Then unthought of her. The Ritual of Death had failed, but she was still marked for it in a way no one else could be. I didn't know why. My education was incomplete because I'd gotten my Master killed.

My shivering became epic. My whole body jerked and twitched. "What . . . do we do . . . about . . . this?" I managed to chatter through my clicking teeth.

My legs went out from under me, but Mags was there, catching me easily under the shoulders and then heaving me up, supporting me.

"You should be inside, Mr. Vonnegan," Fallon said, his hands strong and firm on my shoulders. "The *gulla* has brought you here. The thing you seek is here, somewhere. We cannot see it because *this is a trap.*"

I nodded. That made perfect sense. Or no sense at all. And Fallon was fading away anyway, turning into mist, and then I was passing out. It felt like I was falling into the water. A woman's bloated face, peeling away from her skull a few inches under the gray water, stared up at me, her teeth showing through her frayed cheek like an awful smile.

36.

IN THE DREAM, AS ALWAYS, Claire was wearing a bear costume, her leg a bloody mess, caught in a huge rusty trap bolted to the floor. Tiny flies swarmed the wound, laying eggs.

I WAS BACK IN the motel. I could tell from the rotten-egg appearance of the water-damaged popcorn ceiling. Remy, Roman, and our three Bleeders were sitting around and smoking cigarettes. Fallon, Mags, and Billington were playing cards. I didn't need to pay much attention to know that Melanie was winning. Mags's face was screwed up into the red mask of anger he wore when he was losing, and Fallon was up against true grift. You didn't win at cards with *idimustari*.

I lay still. Enjoying the silence, the space. I'd spent the last two years surrounded by people who were always looking at me like I was going to do something amazing at any moment, because I'd defeated Renar—if you could call near-total failure *defeating* somone. And ever since Billington had told everyone I'd brought Mags back to life—resurrected him—the Cult o' Lem had picked up its suffocating pace. Since she'd started building my myth, it was like I was always surrounded by people, but no one looked directly at me. So it was nice to be ignored. I felt my body ache for a while. But I felt warmer. And I wanted a cigarette, which was a good sign. I didn't know, with the whole town deserted, why we kept coming back to this shithole.

"Mr. Vonnegan," Fallon said. "A moment."

I took a deep breath and pushed myself up. Swung my legs over the edge of the bed. I felt like I'd been filled with molten copper. I stumped my way over to the table by the window where Fallon and Billington sat, their cards down. Fallon gestured at the window.

"We have visitors."

I looked up. Two men wearing heavy overcoats and ridiculous fur caps were standing in the parking lot of the motel. As I stared, a woman blinked into existence. One second empty space, the next a striking older woman in an expensive fur that looked at a distance like it might still have the claws attached to the sleeves.

I'd seen this trick once before. Except the time I'd seen it, the demonstration had involved a vagrant bled dry for the spell, but there was no sign that these people had bled anyone. As I thought of the memory, he appeared. Still wearing the same white suit, still icy blond and almost invisible, he was so pale. Still thin and still mocking. He wore the same red shoes, too. I had only fragments of his teleportation spell in my memory. I probably would be able to figure out the rest if I wanted to. I hadn't wanted to. Now I wished I had.

"Be ready for a fight," I said.

"Jesus, you *think*?" Billington spat.

I considered my Asshole Army in miniature.

Melanie Billington was useless. She wouldn't bleed. She considered herself too high up for that. She was shit with the Words. She knew some nifty *mu*, so in theory she could be of use. But she stuttered and warped Words in her mouth, spat out gibberish or spells that went awry. And not bleeding, she wouldn't get off anything useful.

Remy and Roman were scrappers. They'd never done anything amazing, but they were like me and the other Tricksters: roaches. They survived. It wasn't pretty, but I knew I could count on them to at least put up a fight.

Ev Fallon was *enustari*. He knew the Words and he knew how to use them. We were all scared shitless of Ev Fallon, and for good reason.

Pitr Mags had become a wild card. He still sneezed in the middle of reciting and caused minor explosions, but he'd been making progress with Fallon's lessons, and ever since he'd been dead for five minutes, he'd been sharper, darker, more focused.

The three Bleeders were halfway dead.

Fallon could do something with them, though. The rest of us would just kill them. He kept staring out the window and nodded, once. Crisp.

"Fallon doesn't bleed," I said, my voice rust and dust. "Everyone else fuels their own."

The Bleeders, reluctant, eyed the door for a few lingering seconds, until Roman glared back at them with an implied threat. I rolled up the sleeve of my right arm.

"That is Alfonse Alligherti," Fallon said quietly. "Alfonse, you are forever picking the wrong side of things! Be alert. He will use a Compulsion." He sighed almost sadly. "He always does."

Gas in the air. Multiple streams of it.

"If they didn't bring any Bleeders," Billington said slowly, "who will they cast from?"

Fallon sighed again. "Us."

I nodded. Before Renar, before everything, *enustari* never would have stooped to stealing gas from the likes of us. They'd have come with a dozen Bleeders, beefy men and women paid to fuel their spells. But back then they'd never have actually *fought* us, either—they would have ignored us. Now they weren't ignoring us; come to fight Tricksters, it made sense for them to use our tricks. Nothing worked the way it used to.

I didn't know many *enustari*. The ones I'd met were psychotic, murderous, and contemptuous of me and my kind. They were also usually too sure of themselves, surrounded by sycophants, the Charmed and Compelled. They were terrifying, but in all my dealings with them, they'd been arrogant and stupid, too. And these were no different. Bleeding out some poor son of a bitch so they could wink in like fucking demigods. Then assuming we would all just kneel down and present our throats so they could wink back to wherever they'd come from.

I had a spell. I sliced my arm. Before I could speak, Mags was reciting. I turned, gas leaking out of me, and there was the huge son of a bitch, eyes closed and brow furrowed in the traditional Mags-is-trying-to-think expression. He spoke sixteen Words, thirty-six syllables. It was awful. Sloppy and loose, stuffed with noises that made sense only to Mags. Halfway through, I knew how I could have cut it in half, sliced off the fat. I felt the drain as he cast from me, nausea and yellow exhaustion, old familiar friends. At the same moment, I felt *him* as he filled up with it, the awful strength passing through him, golden and shivery. I wavered a little on my feet as my vision went dark, went up to the line of unconsciousness then steadied.

I staggered to the window.

"Clever," Fallon said quietly as even more gas leaked into the air, thick, healthy streams of it, green with rot and horror. "Mr. Mageshkumar—clever. You have caught Perinine and Mugase by surprise. But Alligherti is Warded against such tricks as a matter of course."

Outside, the woman and one of the first men to arrive—short and round, jowly and yellow-skinned under his fur cap and thick coat—were frowning, hands at their throats in unknowing mimicry. As I watched, the woman opened her mouth and said something. Or tried to. What came out was the distinct bleating of a donkey: *Ee-ore, ee-ore.*

I smiled slightly, swaying on my feet. It once amused Pitr Mags for six days straight to cast a *mu* that threw his voice, startling people as we walked the streets. *Cast it one more time, Lem, just one more, c'mon, please.* Six days with a thumbtack in my pocket, making Mags giggle, and I'd been anemic and half-dead, but it had been worth it to keep him happy. It made sense that this kind of donkey ridiculousness would be the first spell Mags wrote all on his own. Even if it was the worst piece of writing I'd ever heard.

The third man and the Negotiator offered their colleagues brief ice-cold glances of almost total contempt. Fallon took in a deep breath and whispered. I felt him pulling the gas in the air, knew he was casting, but couldn't catch the Words he used. He spoke twenty-three syllables, but half of them were gibberish. Obfuscation. Slow—but secure. This was not waste but secrecy. I frowned in professional disapproval of such tactics.

The round man and white-haired woman, still braying as they tried to shake off Mags's spell, dropped to the ground in a simultaneous collapse. I wondered why Fallon hadn't gone after Alligherti, who seemed like the boss of this moment. There was a single fat second of silence between us, and then the old man spoke.

"In war, Mr. Vonnegan, it is always advisable to press your advantage—and never pass up low-hanging fruit." I was suddenly creeped out and terrified to be in the same room as Fallon. He was, after all, one of those *ustari* who stayed in the shadows, whispering out death.

Outside, Alligherti spoke, eyes closed. I strained to feel him pulling on our gas, sucking us dry to kill us, but there was nothing. He wasn't using our gas. He was casting from some other source, remote. Gas in the air but walled off from me, which meant there had to be something linking them to it, an Artifact. Everything was changing, and magic was starting to feel broken, too.

I thought of the designs we'd taken from Kal's place. I thought of Fallon's old workshop. A battery for magical energy, for blood, buried in some secret place and broadcasting. And the designs we'd taken had indicated the ability to broadcast that energy. How much gas had been stored? Two years now, the world had been breaking up. Two years of bloodbaths and massacres, two years of mass suicides and terrorist bombs, wars and assassinations. Two years of death on an epic, accelerated scale, stored somewhere.

"Jesus," I whispered, "he's got enough g—"

The room exploded. This happened in slow motion.

For a moment I didn't know what was happening; I stood there with my mouth open, the word *gas* like syrup in it, spilling out slowly. I watched seams open up between the window and the wall, like they were being pulled apart. Light slipping in. The floor tilted subtly, and we all rose off the ground a few centimeters as if gravity had gotten tired of holding us down. There was a low rumble of noise under it all, like an endless train going by six miles away, the sound of an explosion slowed down.

Slow. I had experience with slow. Hiram's lessons were still in my head, his theatrical voice, all boom and bombast, telling me about the Law of Perception, the Law of Volume. This was a second, a moment, and I was experiencing it in slow motion. I wondered why. Why blow us to hell but make it last?

Then I saw my answer.

The other Archmage, Alligherti, appeared in the room. Impeccable. He was swarthy, olive-skinned, but taut and healthy, not a scar on him. The idea of all that gas in a tank somewhere, always at your fingertips— fuck, I'd be casting *mu* to shave in the morning. I'd cast for *everything* if I didn't have to bleed, or bleed someone else. The *freedom* of it.

Shame bloated inside me. Freedom. I'd spent years thinking I was the best guy in the room because I wouldn't bleed anyone. I didn't touch anyone. I didn't do anything. And then I'd started bleeding people, and I remembered the first few months, feeling so powerful, so *free*.

It hadn't lasted. I'd gotten used to it. It didn't feel free anymore. It felt *normal*, and I twisted and itched against it. Freedom was a fucking moving target. I imagined myself pointing at one of our people and them tearing off a sleeve and opening a vein so I could cast anything and be just as strong afterwards.

Alligherti stood there surveying us, moving—from my perspective— normally. Or he was moving super-fast and we saw it as normal. Or something. He was a bear of a man, six feet, six three, wide in the shoulders, his hands wide and big with short fingers. A gold ring on every finger—plain bands, no gems, no etchings. His face was round and jowly, his lips delicate and pouty. Big bags under his eyes. The sort of face that always looked sad. The sort of guy who stood silent in the background, being ignored, then said one Word that killed everybody.

Our eyes met. His were old. Yellow and drippy, faded. He looked mid-forties and strong as a bull in his suit and coat. His eyes were ancient.

Alligherti leaned forward, put his arms around Roman, and then they both winked out of the room. Just gone.

I pondered this as all the old worn-out clamshell trim in the room began to split, jagged diagonal cracks appearing at the seams. A moment—one of my moments—went by, and Alligherti returned. He blinked back into existence as the low roar of the room exploding slowly built into intolerable noise around us. He laced one thick arm around Remy, and then they blinked away.

I knew all about time. At full speed, I figured, this was all happening in about two seconds. At full speed, I'd be standing there with my mouth open as the room burst into flame, superheated air expanding and swelling the room, smashing out the glass and tearing the walls from the studs. At full speed, I'd have time for about one Word.

You could and couldn't do a lot with one Word. The Griefers proved that. But you had to pick the right one. Not every Word could be used to Grief. Some were too vague, too dependent on context. They had to be action verbs. The sort of concepts the universe could not confuse. Otherwise you got a very tiny blowback on an unfinished spell, not enough to make any trouble.

The Word I chose was *dalra*.

Dal meant to fly. Adding the suffix made it more specific: to fly *out*.

I spoke it and began to drift. In real time, I was speeding through the air. In real time, the window did not slowly crack open as I put a shoulder to it, shards of glass like snowflakes around me as the cold air admitted me like a jelly behind a thin plastic sheet.

Without any other Words, I'd fly until I bled my people white. I twisted my head around as I drifted through the slow air in time to see Alligherti blink into space next to the Negotiator, holding Remy around the neck. As I approached, the Negotiator was shaking his head. They were hunting for someone. Someone the Negotiator had seen before, could identify. Someone the Negotiator was afraid to confront in person: me. Who else? Who else had beaten him bloody, made him run? I recalled the haunted look in his watery eyes. For all the flash, the Negotiator was half broken already.

I'd asked the *gulla* to find the Negotiator for me, to get the drop on him. And I'd fucked it up, like I'd fucked every other thing since the day I left home.

I felt for the thread of gas in the air, reached out one languorous hand as I swooped down. Took hold of the white jacket, and he rose up off the ground slowly, like a balloon, red shoes kicking the air. I marveled at the expression on his face as it shifted into shock and dismay. His sudden weight spun me around majestically, yanking at my arm in painful slow motion, ligaments popping like timpani drum fills. The air against my cheek and pulling at my hair was thick and warm despite the chill. Thinking in real time was disorienting: I thought of turning my head to see where I was headed, and my muscles responded in a lazy, frustrating swivel, dragging my gaze along the slightly blurred, blasted landscape of Seward: trees, snow, cars, exploding motel.

I moved like I was heavy, but I felt nothing: no weight, no drag, no inertia.

I remembered spinning Pitr Mags around like a parade float in Renar's murder hole. I remembered the feel of him, huge and alive, his hair long because I kept forgetting to make him cut it.

My head finally swiveled to face our trajectory, a copse of dead-looking trees jutting up from the ground like bones. I couldn't do the complex math needed to calculate how quickly we would get there. With the thin thread of our gas in hand, I whispered another Word: *silig*. Stop.

We stopped, but as happened with one-Word spells, not in the way I'd wanted. Instead of drifting to a slow-motion landing, everything rushed back to normal speed with a roar. With a visible stutter, time reasserted itself as the Negotiator and I smacked into a gnarled old tree and separated, each of us flying off at an angle. I hit the frosted, dead grass and skimmed along for a few feet, my leg twisted under my body, and finally rolled to a stop.

I pushed myself up onto one elbow, my leg sending red waves of agony directly into my brain, like I was having a stroke. My vision swam, but I felt for the gas and found more than there had been—me and White Suit feeding in to it, I guessed. I reminded myself that Alligherti had an endless supply of invisible gas stored somewhere. He could cast anything.

I pulled the gas from my people through me and spoke a Word. A Grief, but fuck it, I couldn't *think*.

The ground at Alligherti's feet exploded into a spray of snow and dirt, knocking him backwards. Roman dropped to the ground, limp. I muttered a cute little *mu* I'd picked up from Mags, perhaps the only thing the huge moron had ever taught me. I'd cut out some words. When he'd whispered it sixty or seventy times to keep me alive, once, he'd almost killed himself.

Six syllables, and I felt a flush of hot, rotten energy flow into me directly from my Bleeders. The pain went numb—still there, a throbbing that I could feel like audio through a wall, but blunted, rounded off.

I whispered it again and felt strong enough to stand up. I started walking towards Alligherti and whispered it again, another wave of awful, slimy energy filling me up, making my heart pound and my vision swim. I'd probably just killed someone; I didn't even know any of my Bleeders' names. I'd just bled some follower to death so I could stand up and fight. I was a fucking hero. I swallowed back something acid and thick, making it settle in my belly like a nest of spiders.

As I walked, Fallon appeared next to me. He stumbled slightly as he transitioned from the level floor of the motel to the rough ground outside.

"That was impressive," he said in his almost-accent.

"Do you know the names of the Bleeders?" I asked as we walked.

In my peripheral vision I saw him turn to look at me, then forward again. "It is best not to."

Roman wasn't dead. He was out cold but breathing. Alligherti was nowhere to be seen. Fallon knelt next to Roman and peered around like an owl.

"Where have you run, Alfonse?" he said quietly.

I stood there with the sickening energy pulsing through me, animating me. I looked around. The crumpled form of the Negotiator lay in the frosted grass where he'd landed. But the barrel-chested *enustari* who'd been plucking people from the room and presenting them to him for identification—he was gone.

I looked at Fallon. Thought, *He ran away from Fallon. From a man named* Evelyn. *Not from me—from Fallon.*

We needed to flush Alligherti out. I closed my eyes and pulled an old chestnut from my street days, plucking loose change from people's pockets with my own gas until I'd nearly passed out, Mags leading me around like a seeing-eye dog. Just four syllables, a rough outline of a spell, but enough to do the job. I felt the trickle of power flow through me, leaving me untouched. A second later, a piercing scream burst out of the air, its source a few feet away, where the blacktop of the motel parking lot met the frozen grass.

Fallon shifted and focused on the noise, then spoke rapidly, the same twisting, sliding verbiage, half of it sounds that could have been Words, were *almost* Words. I didn't waste time trying to catch it; I could steal from Fallon some other time. Mel Billington rolled up between us, bleeding from her scalp and panting.

"Light him up for us, Mel," I said, pushing myself into motion.

She nodded with assurance and began muttering something, but I knew it was a fifty-fifty shot whether she'd successfully cast anything.

Fallon finished speaking, and there was a burning man in front of us.

The burning *shape* of a man, because Alligherti was still invisible. It was the shape of a man outlined in flames, running full tilt towards the motel. I could hear him hissing out his own spell and was impressed. I tried to think of the things I'd be capable of doing while on fire, and the list was fucking *short*.

After a stunned second, I spat another Word.

Alligherti and I finished our spells simultaneously. The fire winked out, sputtering away into a few tendrils of icy white smoke. The ground at his feet exploded again; I had no pride—if something worked, *work it*. I wasn't some Archmage, no matter what Billington said. He was blown sideways but managed to keep his feet and kept running.

Billington finished her own spell a moment later and Alligherti flickered back into sight. The bastard was still on the move, his nice coat charred and smoking. Tough son of a bitch. I guess you didn't get invited into a cabal set to bleed the world dry by being fragile. Running, he suddenly spun and started reciting syllables in a ragged, strained voice that was almost a choked growl. But he would wear us down. He had access to a massive, invisible pool of blood. He would bury us. Long after our poor Bleeders had been killed, he would still be raining thunderbolts down on us.

As I was thinking this, Mags came roaring from the direction of the motel, head down and massive hands curled into fists, and Alligherti *did* begin raining thunderbolts down on us.

The Archmage hit his cadence when Pitr was three steps away. Sensing his opponent, the older man spun to face Mags, throwing out his hands and hissing five Words in a slithery accent. Mags was three, two, one step away and suddenly shot backwards, all four limbs splayed in the air, his face purple with receding rage as Alligherti began running again.

A second later, I felt Mags hit the ground.

For a moment, nothing else happened. Fallon was casting, muttering another twisty little spell. Billington was cutting and casting, using her own gas. I was casting my explosive *mu*, trying to time it so I could trip up Alligherti. Then a flash above us, and a bright blue-white bolt of energy cracked from the sky and slammed into the ground about two feet in front of Fallon, sending up a spray of dirt and rock like liquid, the air filling with greasy white smoke. The Old Man took one half-step back, keeping his balance without difficulty, never missing a beat. He finished his own spell just as another flash in the air signaled another bolt.

The second bolt hit Fallon. A direct hit, a slithering line of blue-white energy from the clouds above smacking right into him . . . and skittering away in a crackling, harmless scatter. The smell of ozone hit me, but Fallon hadn't been touched.

With the slightest smirk, he began walking towards Alligherti. The other *enustari* had begun a second spell, leaving the first to run its course. You could tie off spells to keep repeating, if you knew the tricks, the way to lead the grammar from one syllable to the next in a perfect, twisting loop. I knew one thing about Alligherti: He knew his way around the Words.

The gas that I could feel had gotten thin. At least one of our Bleeders was down. I tried to picture them, and couldn't. They were just faceless men in suits. And I'd never know a single additional fact about them. There had been a time when only the very worst and most powerful *enustari* had Bleeders. When someone like me wouldn't have been able to inspire anyone to bleed for them. But the world was broken now.

Fallon reached into his jacket pocket as a bolt of energy hit him square on target and sizzled away with another bitter breeze of ozone. He produced what looked like a small black box with a single white button on top. Small enough to fit in his palm. A Fabrication, I realized.

As I fell in behind the old man, Billington came limping alongside me, still bleeding, her own thin trickle of gas mixing into what was in the air. I thought: *The Asshole Army is shaping up nicely.* And then Fallon extended his arm, holding his little box out in front of him, vaguely in the direction of Alligherti.

"Good-bye, Alfonse," Fallon said in a conversational tone, and pressed the button.

For a few beats, nothing obvious happened. Fallon stopped walking; so did we. In the windy silence, I could hear Alligherti speaking the Words, distant. The sky began to flash again, a deep, almost subaudible rumble that heralded another bolt of energy. Just as I was wondering how far Fallon's protection spell could stretch, Alligherti stopped running and twisted his head around to stare at us, and then he froze in place instantaneously. His voice stopped.

"Shit," Billington snapped. "Down!"

We both dropped to our bellies. Up close, I stared at Fallon's shoes, fine brown leather without a hint of mud or snow or a single scuff. Alligherti's collapsing spell continued as a flash of light nearby, then swept over us in a rush of air and heat, painfully hot and dry for one brief second, then gone.

I looked up and squinted around Fallon's shoes. Alligherti was a few dozen feet away, frozen in place. His eyes were sliding around as if he'd been encased in a life-sized rubber suit of himself. As I watched, he began to tremble, as if a spot-specific earthquake had struck right under his feet. I could hear a crackling noise, like broken glass hitting a floor. Tiny lines inched their way along Alligherti's skin, fractures in what had become hard as stone.

His eyes kept moving, as fluid and alive as ever.

Then he began to crumble. For one terrible second the eyes, ancient and yellow, locked on me and I had a glimpse of the full force of his suffering. Then pieces of him fell away as he started to vibrate, first tiny chunks and then larger and larger pieces, each sifting into the wind as dust seconds after separating.

I looked away before it got to the eyes. Fucking *magic*.

Billington and I rolled up onto our asses and sat there behind Fallon. Mel squinted at the tiny Artifact in Fallon's hand. I looked at the back of Fallon's head, dread and awe battling within me. I hadn't known Alligherti. He'd been *enustari,* and that was usually good enough for me to say they deserved what they got.

But Fallon was *enustari,* too.

I scanned the horizon until Mags sat up, a surprising distance away, his face no longer purple with rage but wide-eyed with confusion.

Next to me, Billington whistled, low and appreciative. "*Biludha,*" she said, "in a box."

Fallon turned slightly and glanced down at his hand. "Just so," he said.

I shuddered.

37

THE ROOM SAGGED AND GROANED around us. Every structural piece of the place had been stretched beyond its engineered limits. Gaps had appeared around the door and window frames, letting the air in. The floor slanted sharply towards the bathroom, the carpet bulging in several spots where the subfloor had snapped. The wind howled in through the broken window, playing with the Negotiator's nearly white hair. The fresh air was helping with the smell of old blood, dead and useless.

I didn't know anything about the three *ustari* we'd just killed. Whether they were skilled, whether they were particularly evil people. I sat on the bed, legs spread, hands clasped between my knees. My pants were torn and had seen better days, and my hands were filthy.

We'd taped the Negotiator's arms to the desk chair with gray duct tape and put his back to the door. He'd come to a few minutes into the process and said nothing, just blinked around a bit, looking thoughtfully at Fallon as the old man stood at ease across the room, smoking one of his brown cigarettes.

I could hear Billington talking to Remy and Roman outside, voices low. Calming them down.

Mags stood next to me with those huge hands clenched into fists, barely restrained from beating the Negotiator until his hair fell out. I focused on the curious sensation of Mags's heartbeat: slow, ponderous. Too slow, I thought, for him to still be alive, as if the last year and a half had been a Glamour.

I'd been staring at the Negotiator. He'd been staring back. Suddenly, he took a deep breath and smiled. He had a young face, ruddy-cheeked and hairless. His lips were the same color as his shoes, bright red, like slashes of blood on a face that was all sharp lines, subtle shades of pink and salmon and white. His smile looked artificial to me, a definite put-on.

"You've made a mess," he said, chipper and fake.

I nodded. Something rusted and creaky inside of me spun into lurching motion. "We won't get the security deposit back, no. Speak one Word and I'll break your jaw."

He nodded. He looked as if he wanted very much to laugh at my joke but didn't have the spare energy. His eyes remained locked on mine. There was no hint of begging, no scent of desperation. I'd fought him back in New York. I'd managed to spark a little fear into his eyes that day. There was none now.

"You were here looking for me?" I asked.

His eyes tightened and he cocked his head slightly. "We have not come to an arrangement," he said, sounding apologetic. "What do I get if I tell you?"

I twisted my head around until I got a satisfying pop as a reward. I put my hands on my knees and pushed myself into a standing position. His gray eyes followed me up. I started taking my jacket off.

"It's been some long years," I said. "I used to not bleed people, did you know that? I used to be a fucking priest about it. I rode my own gas, period. Never touched anyone else. Almost bled myself out daily trying to stay alive, make ends meet."

The Negotiator continued to stare at me with his head cocked slightly. "I know." He jerked his head at the three dead men in the room, limp and bloodless, almost like wax figures. "You seem to have relieved yourself of that concern."

I didn't look at them. "They're not on me," I said.

He smiled. I'd left no scars on him from our last meeting. His face had healed and he was just as pretty as before. "Oh yes? Who are they *on*, then?"

I shrugged. "Mika Renar. Her little boy Cal Amir. It's on them." Every person I bled, every crime I committed, was theirs. Thinking that allowed me to sleep at night.

His smile bloomed into full, twitchy force. "Is that *so*?"

I worked the jacket off and made a show of folding it neatly, stains and tears and all. "And you, and yours, of course." I waited a beat. "Who sent you to find me?"

He shook his head, still smiling, still looking directly at me, as if no one else were in the room. "No, Mr. Vonnegan. We have not struck a deal. We must come to terms."

I shook my head, anger boiling deep inside. "There is no deal."

His smile turned comically sad, his mouth pulled down into a frown, his eyes still laughing. "Nonsense, Mr. Vonnegan. I am the Negotiator."

I was going to hit him. The knowledge was suddenly there. All my plans to play it cool, to play *enustari* and be mysterious and ominous, just melted away, and I was going to knock him down in the chair and beat him until the mocking look in his eyes died out. And this would have been mercy because it wouldn't be Mags doing the beating. Mags would crush him by accident and then hold his bloody hands out at me and whimper apologies.

Behind me, Fallon cleared his throat. "He has had a *geas* placed on him, Mr. Vonnegan," he said. "Powerful. Complex."

The Negotiator smiled again, nodding as he looked past me to Fallon. "Yes. My old *gasam*, bless her, was displeased with me. I have been punished." He looked back at me with those deep, tragic eyes. "Oh, how I have been *punished*, Mr. Vonnegan. Come, let us come to terms. You wish information. I must preserve my life. Let us strike a bargain. It is what I *do*."

I vibrated with the need to hit him, to tear at him. A black spot of weary hatred bloomed on those thoughts like mold, growing, spreading. Hadn't I killed enough fucking people today? I'd wasted half my life refusing to bleed the world. Now I couldn't wait to bleed one more person, for no real reason.

I twitched myself around to look at Fallon. "What kind of *geas*?" I asked, my voice surprising me by being ragged and rough, like I'd been crying for ten years. Or recently dead. Or dead for a long time.

"It is a cursory impression," Fallon said with a shrug. "But it appears he is compelled to speak the truth. Unadorned, without guile, without omission."

"Yes!" the Negotiator shouted, sounding exultant. "*Yes!* So simple. But that is not all! My old *gasam*, she is very *clever* when it comes to punishments." He laughed, sounding crazy. "I have been punished quite *thoroughly*."

I turned back to him. "Can I negotiate for *you*? For your life?"

His eyes widened slightly, then narrowed. He leaned towards me slightly. "State your terms."

My vision swam. The magical energy I'd bled out of the three dead men was fading, was now just a green scum of adrenaline floating on top of my thinned blood. "Or I could kill you." Bleed him out for another round of healing. If I took it all, I'd be right as rain when I was done. The thrill of desire that vibrated through me was visceral. My mouth watered.

The Negotiator shrugged. "You could. But then you would learn nothing from this. As you have already killed *everyone else*."

I could almost hear Billington saying, *You sure?*

"All right," I said. "Here are my terms. I want to know where Mika Renar *is*. I want to know why they've been bleeding the world a couple thousand people at a time, storing all that blood. If it's another go at the *tah-namus* or something else. I want to know what the *kurre-nikas* is."

The Negotiator nodded crisply. "Three questions. Very elegant, Mr. Vonnegan. You think well. As it happens, I can give you the opportunity to ask your questions. We will have to travel to accomplish this." He paused and studied me, cocking his head as if considering something. "Allow me to formalize our agreement," he said suddenly, that half-crazy smile touching his bloodred lips. "You wish to be transported to meet my employer. You wish to ask three questions as stated—the location of Mika Renar, the purpose of her activities these past few years, and the nature of the *kurre-nikas*. I guarantee answers to your questions. You stipulate to this wording of your terms?"

Something felt off, and I could feel a ripple of discomfort go through everyone in the room, but it sounded right enough. "Yes."

He nodded. "In return, you will be asked *one* question, and my term is to require you to answer it." He pursed his lips. "I will not reveal the question at this moment. I will tell you that you will not like it. It is why I was sent to fetch you all those many months ago. It is why I was sent to fetch you *today*."

I considered this man. This parasite. His suit was torn and stained but still had an essential crispness to it. He was ruddy with health, and he'd been riding along on the back of some major movers, serious *enustari*. He'd told me back in that church that he didn't work for Renar. Maybe he did. Maybe he didn't. There were other *enustari* at her level, but who said he was telling me the truth.

"If there is travel," Fallon said precisely, "we must have guarantees."

The Negotiator nodded. "Of course. I can guarantee your safety and return."

I turned and frowned at Fallon. "Are you fucking senile, finally?"

Fallon's smile was just a hint. "His *geas* is powerful. The *ustari* who crafted it spent time on it. Made it a complex flower of a spell. It has also made *him* powerful, by association." He shrugged. "He always speaks the truth, you see."

I stared for a moment, then shook my head. "What?"

"What the infamous Evelyn Fallon means, Mr. Vonnegan," our thin captive said cheerily, "is that when I have been engaged to speak on behalf of someone—to *negotiate*—the terms, I come to *become* the truth. The agreement is woven directly into reality. Into the future. If I say to you that you will not be harmed, you *will not be harmed*. If I say to you that you will be returned after your interview, you *will be returned*."

I kept looking at Fallon. "Jesus," I said.

"Only in the context of negotiation, of course. My old *gasam* hated me far too much to grant me such unfettered power. I can grant it only in the context of serving the interests of others, never my own. *Never* my own! And there are limits. There must be a true motivating factor for the negotiations—a need. Need is what drives my *geas*. I cannot negotiate simply to achieve my own aims." Reciting this, he sat up straighter. Looked like one of those prim, fluffy dogs at Westminster.

"Do we have an agreement, Mr. Vonnegan?"

I kept my eyes on Fallon. "Who in their right mind would give someone this kind of power and call it a *punishment*?"

Fallon smiled slightly. It was just a tick of the corners of his mouth, but it was a terrible expression. "You do not know much about punishment, Mr. Vonnegan. Being in the service of others, eternally, forced to negotiate all manner of things no matter your personal feelings—you do not find that terrible? I do."

I looked back at the Negotiator. The awful faked energy I'd siphoned from the three Bleeders was completely gone, and I was shivering again. I considered the power and skill required to create a *geas* of that complexity, duration, and power. I held up three fingers.

"Three questions—answered."

He nodded. "Agreed."

"Safe passage to and from."

"Agreed. And you will answer *one* question." He smiled, a twitchy thing that flickered on his face. "And guarantee safety in turn."

I turned to look at Fallon. He gave me a typically Fallon-like shrug. I looked at Mags. He was staring at the Negotiator intently, breathing loudly through his nose. I turned back to the skinny shit himself.

"Agreed."

38.

THE EXPERIENCE OF TELEPORTATION WAS that it was no experience at all.

The Negotiator cast it pretty plain, right out in the open, with no effort to obscure it or hide its format from me. Either he didn't know how or he had the usual disdain for *idimustari* and assumed I wouldn't be able to do anything with it. I paid attention, though. It wasn't about the specific Words, it was about the grammar and the structure. The way things led into other things. It was an impressive spell, and while I didn't manage to memorize it, I got ideas from it. And I had to admit it was both simpler and more clever than I would have imagined a teleportation spell to be.

He didn't bleed anyone. I recalled the time he'd appeared in Abdagnale's office, and he'd bled a man dry to get there. Something had changed in his circumstances. Hell, the whole universe had changed, because this was fucking *impossible*. At least so my incomplete education insisted.

He spoke his spell, and we were somewhere else. As he spoke, I cut my thumb open with a palmed blade, whispered a little insurance. An old survivor trick.

There was no sense of movement, no transition. No blurring, no wind, none of the bullshit a showy mage would have incorporated. He finished speaking and then we were all in a different room, just like that.

As we arrived, I finished my own *mu*. A tiny thing inspired by the deal I'd just made. A down-and-dirty Cantrip ideal for *idimustari*.

I wasn't sure if it would work in the context of the Negotiator's *geas,* which was a spell so convoluted and awful I had no idea where to even begin trying to suss it out. I couldn't see it without help, the way Fallon had; I still needed a witch light to trace runes or Wards or other marks. Even if I could have seen the *geas* plainly, I wasn't certain I'd be able to follow it. To make it reality simply by speaking it, even within the limitation of a third-party negotiation—who could create such a spell? Powerful fucking stuff. The sort of thing you bled a whole town to fuel, and according to the Negotiator, it had been done simply to *punish* him.

We are not good people. In recent months I'd realized we were worse than I'd ever imagined. I'd thought I knew awful. Then I'd met myself, bleeding volunteers dry without even knowing their names.

The space we found ourselves in was quiet. Muffled. Or maybe it was just the abrupt shift between a room that had been swollen outward and torn open, wind howling and freezing, and a sealed room. I fought the urge to stagger, my brain demanding there be motion and momentum even though there hadn't been. The floor was covered in several layers of thick oriental-style carpets, making it a little uneven. It was huge, a wide-open space that stretched away from me to a monolithic wall of plate glass looking out into darkness.

There was no furniture. The floor was littered with pillows and larger cushions and had different levels: three steps down into what was supposed to be a living area, after which rose three more steps to a dining area. I looked back towards the windows, like panes of obsidian, the darkness outside complete.

"The view o' Shanghai used to be *spectacular* at night, before the power shit the bed. All the skyscrapers. Fuckin' *spectacular.*"

I turned, somehow surprised that I could move. Walking from the kitchen was a young girl, twelve or thirteen, maybe. Not pretty, not ugly, just sort of there. Skinny with long dirty-blond hair cascading from her head in messy waves. A round and plump face, tan skin and dark eyebrows. Her voice was rough and sandpapery, kind of sexy. In one hand she held a cigarette pinched between her forefinger and middle finger and a tumbler of liquor almost too big for her hand. She was wearing a pair of loose jeans, a thin white T-shirt, and a bright yellow feather boa that was far too long for her.

We had arrived exactly as we'd been back at the World's Worst Motel: Fallon behind me, Mags a few feet off as if behind an invisible bed, the Negotiator tied to the chair. Billington and the Twins were nowhere to be seen. I glanced at the windows, the sort of blind plate glass that implied height, and I worried that they hadn't been merely left behind but had been teleported to a spot out there five hundred feet in the air.

"Mr. Harrows," said the Girl Who Was Clearly Not a Girl, "I see you have made your deal and brought me Mr. Vonnegan at last."

The Negotiator was still looking at me. He nodded without shifting his eyes. "Yes, ma'am." I'd known since our first meeting—somehow instinctively believing him—that this prim bastard in the white suit and red shoes wasn't working for Renar. And yet I was still surprised to find some other *enustari* here at the other end of the maze. Because, as far as I knew, Mika Renar was behind every atrocity in the world these days.

That there was another spider plotting and spinning out in the darkness was fucking *disturbing*.

The kid laughed and dropped into a large red pillow on the floor in front of me, managing somehow to not spill her drink or ash on herself. She reclined there, skinny body squirming to find a comfortable position, and put her eyes on me. "Oh, Richard. I assume I will not like the terms."

"Yes, ma'am."

"But I know you *must* serve my interests, as the party who engaged you. And as I know you *havta* be engaged by someone at all times or you'll *suffer*—your words, not mine!—I guess I'll just havta swallow it, huh?"

"Yes, ma'am." He paused to see if she was finished, then nodded. "Three questions answered, safe passage in return for one question from you, answered. All parties' safety guaranteed."

"Shit," the girl said, not looking the least bit put out. "Very well, Mr. Vonnegan, ask away."

It all felt wrong, which didn't make me a genius. I looked out the windows and realized I could see the faint, silvery outlines of buildings close by. Seeing the perfect pitch black of the night made no sense, because every light in the room was on, burning hot, pouring artificial light into the place. I turned and looked at Fallon. We stared at each other for a moment and then he cleared his throat and stepped forward.

"Mr. Vonnegan wonders," he said in his clipped almost-accent, "if any question he might now speak would be considered one of his *three*."

The Negotiator—Harrows—shook his head almost wearily. "The questions have been named already. They are the questions, no others."

"Evelyn Fallon," the girl sang out, sending a plume of smoke into the air. "You look awful."

"Elsa," Fallon said. "It has not been long enough."

"Evvy dislikes me, Mr. Vonnegan, though I do not understand why. We are old friends."

Fallon snorted. "We have never been *friends*, Elsa."

"*Comrades*, then, from past wars. Fallon's a deadly one, you know. A lot of blood on those old hands." She cackled, sounded like a preteen girl howling at some movie. "You're too young, Mr. Vonnegan. Our wars were long over by the time you learned your first *mu*."

I did not *feel* young. I did not say this. I was terrified of saying *anything*.

"I see you have . . . *refreshed* yourself," Fallon said, his voice dry and emotionless.

She smiled and ran her free hand from her throat to her belly, pulling up the thin T-shirt to expose an inch or two of flat, taut skin. "Oh, you *noticed*, you old charmer. Yes, being old and dried up, as you know, is no fun." She frowned. "I do hate being this young. So much you can't *do*. But *you* know, you have to start young. If you go in too late, they *resist*. I don't know why a few years makes such a difference, but it does," she concluded with a singsong lilt.

A green lump formed in the pit of my stomach. *There*, I thought. *There is the difference.* I was no *enustari*, no matter how many volunteers I bled. I studied the girl in front of me. Pictured her playing video games, watching movies. Saw her, in a brief flash, shivering in Hiram's apartment in tennis shoes covered with pink writing. Saw her strapped into a Fabrication under Mika Renar's house. Saw them all, sitting there in that yellow boa.

"What happens to her?" I asked before I remembered to be terrified.

Outside, in the distance, there was an explosion, bright enough to make me wince and close my eyes, loud enough to rattle the glass and make the floor dance underfoot. When I looked back, something was burning a mile away, a blob of shifting light in the frame of the windows.

The Girl Who Was Certainly Not a Girl looked at me for a long moment, one eyebrow raised. "I have her," she said slowly, "safe and sound. And someday, when I am done with this body, I will give it back. It is a kinder forever, in some ways, than what that old bitch Renar has planned, don't you think? One girl inconvenienced instead of a whole world dead? But Mika—Mika's too fancy for other bodies. She doesn't want to touch other people, much less inhabit their stinky, low-class bodies." She shrugged and looked back at Fallon. "So you see, Evvy, I am not as wicked as you imply."

Fallon grunted. "The Fabrication, then, Elsa?"

She smiled and stood up with an easy athleticism. "Why, yes, my ancient old friend. A Fabrication." She crossed to the kitchen area, where the counter held several small objects that looked like jewelry boxes made from bone or ivory. She picked one up and stood staring at it, her back to us. "She is very safe. I am merely *borrowing* her bones for a bit."

"Mika," Fallon said, sounding bored, like this was a conversation he'd had before, "does not like to work, Elsa. You know this. The constant changing of bodies, it wearies her. Easier—for her—to engage a final solution to her mortality problem."

All of them, crazy and terrified of death.

"Would you care for a demonstration?" she asked, striding over towards me with the box in a loopy, off-balance trot, then almost crashing into me. She pulled up, laughing, holding the box out towards me. "It's fucking *easy*. Wantta see? Maybe on your big dumb friend there? All you do is . . . touch 'em . . . on the forehead . . ." She reached the box up towards my face until I flinched away. "And *bang!* Transference." She smiled a dopey, thick smile, admiring the little box in the light. "A fuckin' *work of art*."

"Always talented, Elsa," Fallon said. "Always you could do amazing things. And yet always, your amazing things are *horrifying* things."

The girl-thing snorted. Turning and stumbling back the way she came, she replaced the box on the counter. I kept staring at it. A soul, someone in there. Trapped until this mercurial captor let them out. I imagined being twelve fucking years old and then boom, waking up and you were seventy. Or your body was. Was she aware, in there? Did she know that time was passing while some fucking Archmage used up her body? Would that be *better*?

Touch 'em on the forehead.

"You're one to talk. Better, Evvy, than hiding in that basement for thirty years, no? Better than pretending nothing was going on outside my walls, then making a pathetic ass of myself at the last minute, then spending the last two years following this *Trickster* about.

"Now," she said, draining her glass and dropping it onto the floor, "business. Mr. Vonnegan, you drive a hard bargain. Three questions. Let's get them over with."

She dropped back down on the pillow and crossed her skinny legs in front of her, biting one nail as she stared at me. A Fabricator in Fallon's class.

I licked my lips with a dry tongue. I realized that Mags and I hadn't moved at all. "Where," I said deliberately, "is Mika Renar?"

The Girl Who Was Not a Girl stared at me for a moment. Her expression was thoughtful, with a slight frown, the sort of look I'd seen a million times a second before a subtle Charm took hold and shifted everything in my favor. Then it shifted and became a half-puzzled, half-amused frown, like she assumed there was a trick but couldn't be sure. "Helsinki, last I heard." The smile bloomed into a lopsided, mean-spirited snarl. "I don't really know."

The Negotiator, months ago: *Mika Renar did not contract for you.*

Abdignale: *You are not the only person working to bring Renar to justice.*

I'd been conned. And stupid. I couldn't remember why I'd just assumed I could just ask where Renar was, except that Renar was *everywhere*, behind *everything*. I'd been conned.

I thought back to the Negotiator *formalizing* my terms, and then I wanted to kill him.

I wanted to kill *her*. Instinctively, I raised an arm in anger, and then I heard a choked grunt and felt Mags landing next to me. One of his hands began crushing my forearm as he took hold of it. I could feel him, his insides, burning with rage. He wanted to kill her, too.

This Girl Who Was Not a Girl had fucked us, and looked happy to be doing so.

We did nothing. I willed myself to move. To teach her a lesson about what years of pent-up frustration bought you. She was *right there*. But I couldn't move.

"Lem," Mags breathed, his voice hot and angry. And again, but now frightened and confused. "*Lem.*"

We couldn't do anything. Because we'd bargained in good faith, and our deal included *safety guaranteed*. I heard the voice of the Negotiator: *The things I say* become *the truth*. We had guaranteed everyone's safety. He had guaranteed me answers, but tricked me into asking the wrong fucking questions. Serving the interests of his employer.

I tried to move towards her. Anything. I tried clearing my mind of intention, imagining nothing, a field of static in my mind's eye. I was still bolted to the floor. I heard a slow, dry creaking noise and realized it was Pitr Mags's shoes as he strained against the *geas*.

"Your second question, Mr. Vonnegan? We are pressed for time. We havta get out of this craphole before the whole fuckin' *city* burns to the ground."

The Girl Who Was Not a Girl tilted her head slightly and lit a ciga-rette, smiling at me. She looked, for a moment, like any twelve-year-old girl at the fucking mall.

I turned to look at Fallon. "Who the fuck is she?"

"Mr. *Vonnegan!*" the girl sang out in a lilting, childish voice. "We do not have *time*—"

I kept my eyes on Fallon and just pointed at her. "Our fucking deal had no fucking time dimension, so shut the fuck up and I will stand here as long as I fucking *like*." I turned to look at her. "And *my* safety is fucking guaranteed, too."

She stared at me, still smiling. Then she glanced over at the Negoti-ator. Whatever he did in response, she sighed and looked back at me, nodding. "As you say."

I looked at Fallon. The old man pushed his hands into his pockets and looked down at the floor. "Elsa," he said slowly, "was my *urtuku* fifty-three years ago." His eyes lifted to meet mine. "She is . . . talented." His gray eyes moved to land on the girl's body. "She is . . . dangerous."

The girl burst into a fit of giggles. "Oh, *poor Evelyn!*" she hooted, twisting on the floor in orgiastic physical freedom, as if she could not believe how good it felt to be twelve. I wasn't old, but I was stiff, aching. I imagined, for a sick moment, sliding into a new body. No aching back. No old scars up and down the arms. "Poor, *poor* Evvy!" She pointed her cigarette at him. "You begged me to leave you alone, you wept and beat your breast because I had surpassed you, and I left

you alone *as a kindness*. And you buried yourself in that hole and tin-
kered. The only reason that cunt Renar hired you was because she
knew *I* wasn't dumb enough work with her. You built her something
grand, Evelyn, I'll give you that. It was *grand*. But it was the best
you'll ever do, and you *didn't even get dealt in*." She dissolved into
laughter again.

I felt our hearts pounding, Mags's and mine. I forced myself to look
at her. Wanted to shut her up. "What is the *kurre-nikas*?"

She didn't shut up. She *cackled*. She kicked her legs in the air and
dropped the cigarette on the carpet, where it smoldered and smoked.
She rolled around howling. Then she was up, so young and lithe it was
like an animal hunting in the wild. She vaulted over to Fallon and he
took two hurried steps backwards, his face screwing up into a mask of
fear. I'd seen Ev Fallon vaporize people just a few hours ago, and here
he was backing away from a tiny girl.

She stopped and stretched up on her tiptoes. "You *know*, Evvy, but
you do not tell him because you are a *coward*. You were a coward in '56
and a coward in '71 with that ridiculous fat friend of yours and a
coward in Belfast and a coward in Munich—and you are still a fucking
coward today. We are at *war*, and you went to ground. And now you
are not hiding anymore, but you are on the *wrong side*." She spun and
faced me but was still talking to the old man. "I gave you everything,
and you went to ground like a fucking *coward*. You are not the man I
thought you were."

He stared back at her, his face expressionless.

She spun to face me. "The *kurre-nikas*," she said with a little bow,
"as your *friend* here knows full well, is capable of some *serious* mis-
chief."

Fallon stared at the back of her head as if contemplating the well-
placed arc of a blade. "You are mad."

The little girl leaped on him—spun and sprang and wrapped herself
around the old man, forcing him to stagger backwards, twisting his
torso away from her shining eyes, her sharp white pebble teeth.

"Fucking *coward fucking coward fucking coward!*" she screeched. "All of you so fucking *afraid—all of you so fucking* afraid! *I did not build the fucking thing for her, Evvy! I am trying to save us, you god-damn coward!*"

With a snarl, Fallon took hold of her shoulders . . . and then froze. They wobbled there for a moment, each prevented from hurting the other. Each struggling against the force of the spell—a spell cast years ago, still suspended between the molecules of the universe.

Slowly, she climbed down. He released her almost reluctantly. Watched her back away from him with wary eyes.

"Mika has built it, Evvy. Mika has built it to try and right a wrong, or what she perceives as one. And I am merely trying to even up the playing field. Because where the fuck have *you* been during all of this?" She snorted and spat on the ground at Fallon's feet.

I stared at Fallon. Who was still a stranger after all this time. "You fucking *do* know what it is," I said. "You lied to me."

"For your protection, Mr. Vonnegan," he said, staring daggers at the Girl Who Was Not a Girl. "There was once a time when our order knew how dangerous knowledge was. It was portioned out when people were *ready.*" He turned his head to look at me. "*Kurre-nikas,*" he said slowly. He was slightly out of breath, his mysterious accent some-how suddenly thicker, making him sound like he was biting his words off one by one from some sheet. His yellowed eyes bore into me. "I apologize, Mr. Vonnegan, if I was reluctant to speak of it. I am old-fashioned. It is an ancient design. Predating the modern era. There was a time when knowing of it was a death sentence." He smiled thinly. "Luckily for us, the wars Elsa refers to destroyed much of that . . . civilization among us."

The girl spat on the floor and padded over to the bar. "Cunt," she hissed over her shoulder.

"If built correctly—precisely—the *kurre-nikas* does one simple, im-possible thing: It alters a single moment in the past."

I let that sink in. It got about an inch and then stalled. "What."

He shrugged. "Take a moment, a second, of your existence. You turn left and are attacked. So you go insane, you lose your humanity, you spend oceans of pain—"

The girl, pouring whiskey into a glass, giggled and muttered, "Cunt."

"—and suffering—"

"Cunt."

"—and blood—"

"*Cunt!*"

"—in order to create this Fabrication. The *kurre-nikas*. And you choose the moment when you went left, and you alter it so that you went right. And the universe, drawing on more oceans of blood and pain and suffering—"

"*Cunt, cunt, cunt,*" she chanted.

"—the universe, she *adjusts.*"

I stared at him blankly. "Adjusts. It's a wedge."

Fallon nodded. "Precisely. The sacrifice required to change reality wholesale is nearly as much as the *Biludha-tah-namus.* But to change one moment? Much easier. The moment changes. Every moment thereafter cascades in change as well. But at no blood cost. The universe *repairs* itself. You change one thing, the universe adjusts around it. Not always in predictable ways, of course; there is a lot of chance involved in the specifics. The universe chooses the *details.*" He pushed his huge hands back into his pockets. "So you see, Mr. Vonnegan: We do not speak of it unless we must. So that no one gets *ideas.*"

The girl cackled again. "Ideas! Evvy, when was the last idea *you* had that was not planted in your tiny brain as an *order*!" She spun, sloshing whiskey everywhere. The tumbler was as big as her fist and filled halfway. She was plastered. How fast did you burn through a body like that when you drank enough for everyone in the room?

"Mr. Fucking Vonnegan," Elsa slurred, swaying on her feet, her tan little face bright red. "You *moron.* One more question, you fucking asshole." She peeled her index finger from the glass and held it up, waving it slightly back and forth.

My mind was racing. Changing moments, changing reality. The possibilities were fucking endless, but in a way, it made sense for *one* possibility: I'd come along and fucked up Mika Renar's bid for immortality. But what if I hadn't? It wasn't like I'd been some fucking hero, casting *biludha* and kicking ass. There'd been so much *luck*, so much *dumb fucking luck*. If one moment had gone differently, I would have been dead. Or simply failed.

One moment.

Easier than trying to do it all over again. With me and my Army of Assholes watching, looking for it. Fucking misdirection. For a second, shame and a weird fevered excitement crashed through me. It was a great *con*. We'd spent the last two years looking for the *Biludha-tah-namus*. They weren't going to try that again. They were pouring their resources into the *kurre-nikas*. Tweak one moment, watch the future change around you. Reductive. Simple.

Dread filled me. It filled Mags, his heart rate lifting slightly as he got that terrified look that meant he had no fucking idea what was going on.

I knew my third question was a waste of time, and that once I'd asked it, I would be on the hook for *her* question, but I felt the pressure of the *geas* building behind me. I *had* to ask. I had another question suddenly. The Girl Who Was Not a Girl had no idea where Mika Renar was. They were on different teams—but what did that mean? What did she want, if not what Mika Renar wanted?

I'd been conned so fucking hard, I was amazed my ears weren't bleeding.

The *geas* pushed me along. "Why," I said thickly, "are you storing all the blood?"

The little girl laughed again, a shimmer of girlish giggles, and then tripped and fell on her face. The tumbler crashed to the floor and she popped back up, nose bleeding, a thick stream like chocolate syrup.

Gas in the air, strong, heavy, for the taking. Except I'd guaranteed her safety. I could feel the weight of the Negotiator's *geas* like a wet coat, tightening in admonishment.

"You mean why is *she* storing it, 'cause all we did was steal that trick. Why not? As dear Evvy has pointed out, there is no law anymore, no fucking secret society of mumblebeards keepin' the peace. We're not storing sacrifice to rape the world the way she is—we're playin' catch-up. Defense. Once we saw what that demented bat was up to, we figured out her battery idea and replicated it. Easy enough once you know the principle involved. I can see from your fuckin' stupid expression that *you* know the answer, too, you fuckin' moron. *She* needs it. For the *kurre-nikas*, of course!" Her voice had become a screech again. "Of *course*! And she did it right under your *fuckin' nose!*" She spat on the floor again. "That's the problem—we've been playin' catch-up. But we're gettin' there." She looked back at me. "And we're takin' out *insurance*."

The little girl's body was wracked with laughter. She knelt there with blood running down her chin, laughing, body shaking. After a few seconds she lurched forward, planted her hands flat on the carpet, and vomited a prodigious amount of clear liquid. She started laughing again, a thick string of saliva connecting her to the floor. She spoke between gasps.

"And . . . now . . . *my* . . . question!"

Next to me, Mags whimpered, like a kicked dog. Dread solidified inside me like a pebble I'd swallowed.

I'd been conned each and every way possible.

"Tell me," she said, her voice sludgy and thick, "where Claire Mannice is."

39.

I REMEMBERED HER IN THE stupid fucking uniform. Pink. A white apron. Her name tag read CAROL. She'd been wearing white tennis sneakers and had that tired look that got burned in after a while. I didn't even recognize her at first. She was just another too-skinny chick working the breakfast rush, trying to keep truckers from pinching her ass *too* much and exhausted from some other job or a kid or some other fucking thing.

When I realized who she was, I kept my eyes on her. I hadn't bled. I had four Bleeders roasting in the car out in the lot, sleepy and unhappy, but I hadn't let them bleed, either.

I didn't need to bleed to keep Claire from noticing me. She wasn't looking, for one, and I knew from bitter experience grifting my way through New York that half the time you didn't need to cast anything—people just didn't see what they didn't expect to see.

My own waitress was an older version of Claire. As if Claire had been cloned and terribly fast-forwarded thirty years and fifty pounds. She had a blurry tattoo on her forearm that I kept trying to steal a glance at, and she kept calling me *sugar* like it was a word she'd just invented and would grow famous for. I'd ordered pancakes and sausage and black coffee. It was all sitting in front of me on the greasy, sticky table in the booth by the bathrooms. The least popular booth in the whole place. But I had a good view.

I sat and watched and drank coffee. I wasn't hungry. I didn't bleed anymore, so I was never hungry. My body had reached a silent deal with the universe.

Claire never smiled. My waitress, Claire Mark Two, smiled constantly in a brain-aching way that had ruined my appetite. But Claire's face was set in the sort of determined expression that still scared me after all this time. The same expression as the girl who'd almost punched her way free of Gottschalk's place, the girl who'd killed two policemen in New York City. Her hair was tied back with a rubber band, and she had scratches up and down both legs.

On the television, the news was reporting that a pilot had flown an Airbus A340-600 into a mountain, killing 355 people. No one was paying any attention, because they were all discussing the shirt-factory floor manager who'd chained all the doors shut and set the place on fire, then sat outside and ate a brown-bag lunch of a PB and J and sixty-two sleeping pills, all washed down with a pint of bourbon. The debate evolved into the question of staying in town or packing up and trying to find higher ground. The world was broken. We had broken it. I wanted to lean over and explain to them that there was no such thing as higher ground. Not anymore.

My pancakes got cold. My waitress refilled my coffee every ten minutes, like clockwork. She'd been working the job so long, she didn't even have to think about it. I watched Claire get hassled by a bunch of sunburned assholes in plaid shirts who thought it was hilarious to call her *honey* and tell her that her sneakers were cute.

OUT IN THE PARKING lot, it was pitch-black and quiet. My Bleeders were all asleep in the car. I didn't give a shit. I hadn't asked them to come.

I stood in the shadows, leaning against a telephone pole, smoking. I still wasn't worried about being seen. Claire didn't want to see me, I knew that. But I'd spent enough time too tired to bleed; I knew a few tricks that didn't require any gas.

She came out of the diner with the second waitress and a short, round guy who was the manager or the owner or something. They said good night in those too-loud voices people used when they didn't give a rat's ass about each other but couldn't admit it. They spread out, heading for cars. There were four vehicles in the lot, and I already knew which one belonged to which person: The beat-to-shit hatchback on not one but *two* donuts belonged to the older waitress. I could picture the duct tape holding the engine together. The decade-old but well-maintained sedan was the manager's, bought after years of careful saving, and goddamn he was going to die in that car. The blue pickup was Claire's. It was old and rusted, but every pickup in the world had an old and rusted future and it didn't matter. Pickups were judged on a different track.

The fourth vehicle was a truck, too, and it was surrounded by the good ole boys who'd been fucking with Claire in the diner. Smoking cigarettes and laughing. I knew what the script was here. So did the other waitress and the manager, which was why they were trying like fucking hell to get into their cars as fast as possible and acting like they hadn't noticed the crew. So they could have plausible deniability later.

Leaving my cigarette burning between my lips, I fished in my pocket for my switchblade. Flicked it open and hiked my sleeve up. Dragged the blade in one sharp, quick motion. Not deep; I wouldn't need much gas for this.

As the manager and the other waitress drove off, Claire was just getting to her car. Like it had been planned that way. I expected the good ole boys to jump for her, but they didn't. They just started calling out to her from where they were.

"Good night!"

"Thanks for puttin' up with us!"

"Hope that tip keeps you warm tonight!"

I stood there with blood dripping off my fingers, uncertain. Maybe they weren't dangerous. Maybe they were just assholes. I'd have to recalibrate my Redneck Meter.

Claire didn't respond. She was struggling to open the truck's door. It looked like an old, familiar battle. After a few seconds, the rednecks took notice, and one of them, wearing a pair of brown heavy-duty pants and the classic white thermal shirt under a blue workshirt, peeled off from the group.

"Need a hand, there, honey?"

The other rednecks consulted in a series of whispers and chuckles and ambled to follow. I tensed up again. I glanced over at my Bleeders and they were all staring at me. Smelling the gas in the air. I shook my head and turned back. The rednecks had crowded around Claire.

I hesitated. Maybe I was being racist, in my way. Classist, something like that. Maybe these guys went home and read poetry; maybe they'd die to protect her. Maybe I was being an asshole from the northeast.

Claire decided for me.

I didn't see what sparked it. One second she was surrounded, the next there was a shout and the rednecks stumbled backwards. Claire had the first guy by the nose. Two fingers hooked into his nostrils with her arm wrapped around his neck, a small penknife in her other hand, pressing against his neck hard enough to draw a bead of blood.

I whispered a *mu*. Something short and sweet, simple. I felt the familiar push and pull of sour energy flowing from me, draining, and then . . . nothing happened.

I whispered it again. The same thing happened, but this time I could almost feel it flowing towards Claire. And disappearing, as if it had never been bled. I remembered how spells twisted around her, because of the runes. But they'd never just failed like this.

She was shouting, sounding calm, and the rednecks were backing off, hands up, looking honestly terrified and confused. When they were ten feet from her, she spun the first one away and landed a kick on his ass, sending him sprawling onto his hands and knees, sputtering.

Without another word, she turned back and—the key working easily this time—got into her truck. The rednecks waited until she'd started the motor and put the truck into gear before stepping forward to help their friend up.

I watched her drive off, chewing on it all. I felt the scabby, dry wound I'd opened up. I'd felt the energy flowing out, typical, familiar. It hadn't coalesced around the Words, for the first time in my life. It had flowed towards her . . . and disappeared.

Watching the rednecks help their fallen comrade to his truck, I slashed the wound open again, wincing slightly at the burning pain. Spoke another *mu*, similar, just as simple. Felt the old familiar drain, but this time it firmed up around the syllables and exploded outward, invisible and silent, and all four tires on the boys' truck blew out simultaneously, like shotgun blasts. They all jumped and hollered.

///////

WE SAT IN THE car in the darkness and watched the house. The so-called house. It was a faded wood structure that appeared to be standing more out of habit than good construction code. It was gray and splintery-looking, a one-floor bungalow with a porch that tilted to the left. The blue-rust pickup truck was parked in front. We were smoking in the darkness, and all I could see of any of them were the red coals of their cigarettes, three men whose names escaped me, although I'd been introduced to them many times. Three men who looked at me like I was fucking Jesus.

Billington was a shit mage, but she could fucking organize a cult like nobody's business.

Two hours, I sat there smoking one cigarette after another, watching her house. I got that heart-pounding, jittery feeling that meant too many cigarettes. I smoked more. At two hours fifteen minutes, a man stepped out and started in on his own cigarette, standing on the porch and staring out into the flat, featureless plains. Daryl Fucking Houy. Two years ago, Mags and I had Charmed him to love Claire because we needed his help, and either we were better at Charms than we'd suspected or we'd just happened to choose her soul mate as a chump. He looked pretty much the same. Slightly less stupid, even.

His middle name, as far as I was concerned, really was *Fucking*.

He finished his smoke and went back inside. The house was lit up blue and silver from an old TV.

I sat there and burned a few more cigarettes in the dark, thinking about it. Not about Daryl and Claire. Why not? Daryl had been Charmed into adoring her, but that had worn off long ago. Or maybe it hadn't; since I'd met her, magic had worked strangely around Claire, and maybe the spell was on eternal repeat. She was still marked for Renar's *biludha*, and though it had collapsed spectacularly, it was the most powerful spell ever attempted, so who knew what the blowback would be. And I'd just cast two spells that seemed to have been absorbed by her, like she was some sort of black hole for magical energy. Bending everything around her gravity.

I let two cigarettes burn to the filter in my hand. One more inhalation and I was going to turn and puke all over the Bleeder sitting next to me, ruining his black suit.

I wasn't getting out of the car.

I hadn't come to talk to Claire. I hadn't come to let her know how I'd found her. It hadn't been easy, and I was confident that no one else would be able to do it. Casting didn't help—she was still marked, and magic still went sideways around her, as I'd just learned. And now I knew: If you got close enough, magic plain didn't work when focused on her. Something had changed after the failed *biludha*. Something quantum and invisible had shifted. But I was *idimustari*. We Tricksters knew how to sniff out the dusty corners of the world. I hadn't come to talk to Claire. Just to see her. To satisfy myself that she was okay. That she was safe. Or as safe as she could be in a broken world. Which wasn't so much *safe* as *hidden*.

"Okay," I said. "Let's go."

The Bleeders didn't say a word or hesitate. They started the car and hit the gas like good little soldiers.

40.

I FELT THE WORDS RISING in my throat instantly. The Negotiator's *geas* reaching out its slender fingers and pulling words up from within me like meatball surgery, like someone gutting you on a battlefield and yanking out parts.

Mags took me by the shoulders, hands cracking my bones, and spun me to face him. "Lem! No!"

I stared at him and felt my mouth opening of its own volition. I reached up and clamped my hands over my mouth, staring into his eyes. He stared back in pop-eyed horror, shaking his head slightly.

"No, Lem, no," he whispered, his grip on my shoulders now actively painful.

I spun away from him. He tried to hold on to me, but comically, his hands slid away without purchase, and his arms windmilled as I staggered back. He stumbled as he tried to pursue me but was prevented. The *geas* wouldn't be denied.

"Speak, Mr. Vonnegan!" The Girl Who Was Not a Girl cackled. "You are *compelled*!"

I was. I could *feel* the words. They were like stones in my throat. I clamped my hands on my mouth harder but knew they would come loose. Soon enough. When the universe determined that they had to. The room spun as I staggered. I tripped and fell forward into Fallon, who straightened me up roughly and shook me vigorously.

"You *know where she is*?" he hissed. "You are a *fool,* Mr. Vonnegan!"

Claire. Claire was the most important girl in the world. As long as we'd kept her hidden and safe, Renar could do a great many terrible things, but her spell to bleed the world white so that she and her cohorts might live forever wasn't one of them.

Which didn't explain why Elsa wanted her, too. Assuming an insane bodysurfing alcoholic *enustari*-level Fabricator living in the middle of a dead city had things like *reasons*.

I twitched away from Fallon. He hung on to me for a moment and then pushed me away roughly. I stumbled backwards and spun back in time to see him slashing his arm with something small, a blade hidden entirely in his hand. I wanted to tell him it wouldn't work. Nothing would work. The power of the *geas* was filling me, crowding in to push the words out of me. It was immense. It was more power than I'd ever felt before in my life, even more than I'd felt at Renar's *biludha*. This was ancient, and it had an *intelligence,* as if it wasn't just blind energy shaped by Words spoken years ago, but a living, sentient thing.

My arms trembled as my hands were forced away from my face, centimeter by centimeter, by an unseen force. I clenched my teeth until my jaw hurt. Sweat dripping into my eyes.

"Men have bitten off their *tongues* in an effort to resist this *geas*," Elsa continued, her voice rough and ragged, like she was swallowing puke with every breath. "And yet found a way to answer! This is a far older power than your tricks. Or your mentor's *toys*. Wars were fought to destroy the dissemination of such things, Mr. Vonnegan, but you *cannot destroy* knowledge. It persists."

I heard the ligaments in my jaw creaking as I fought to keep my mouth clenched tight. I heard the girl giggling, a wet, warm sound worming into my ear.

I stiffened, arms flying out straight from my body. I convulsed, once, undulating from my knees up, and my mouth snapped open.

"Sh—"

Mags's tree-trunk arms slid around me and he pulled me close to him, his head on my shoulder. With a casual twitch of muscles, he hugged me. Hugged me so tight the breath hissed out of my lungs, a red pulse of light flashing across my vision. Mags routinely broke every coffee mug he encountered completely by accident, having been removed from his mother far too soon.

I could almost feel the *geas* pausing, waiting for a judgment as to whether this was violating my safety or preventing me from answering.

"No, Lem!" Mags whispered fiercely in my ear. "You can't!"

I was staring right at Elsa. Her chin and neck were covered in a slick of dark red, her shirt soaked in her own blood. She was kneeling on the floor, arms wrapped around her belly, staring back at me while she laughed. They were raw, physical guffaws like something being torn from inside her. I thought briefly that she must burn out these bodies before they turned twenty-five. Twenty. She must wake up one day and be the oldest twenty-year-old in the world.

"Mr. Mageshkumar," Fallon said, his voice like ashes, "you cannot stop him. We can do nothing. He has made a fool's deal, and he must now pay the consequences. *We* must pay the consequences."

The world was broken. I had broken it.

I felt Mags trembling around me, like I'd been buried underground just before an earthquake. He grunted in my ear. Mags would never hurt me, I was certain—not on *purpose*.

"*Lem.*"

For a second we were in sync. His heart beat, my heart beat twice. His heart was like a bass drum somewhere in the distance. Mine was a snare, beating double time. *Boom-tattattat-boom-tattattat*. I felt the blood pulsing through his veins, the sizzling chemical reactions as he breathed, as his kidneys filtered and his liver oozed and his intestines writhed and squeezed. We breathed in and breathed out as one.

Then his embrace loosened and he stepped back. I stared into Elsa's little-girl eyes, a striking dull green lit from within with something crazy, something terrible, something that was burning up her body at fifty times the normal rate.

She nodded, smiling blood. "Go on, kid. You ain't winnin' this."

I dropped to my knees and fell forward, catching myself on my palms. The rug was damp and scratchy. My whole body convulsed again, like I was vomiting the words, like I was going to puke up the address in brightly colored refrigerator magnets. Which, fuck all I knew, might be exactly how it worked. My education had been incomplete.

Slowly, my body calmed. I pushed myself back up, leaning back on my haunches, breathing hard. I could feel and hear Mags behind me, the smooth machine of his inner workings, the warm glow of him. I saw Fallon off to my left, head down on his chest, hands in his pockets, looking older than I'd ever seen him before.

I looked down at my hands. Mysteriously, my straight razor was clutched in my right hand, open, gleaming. I wondered if I could bleed. If I could speak the Words. Or if I could cut my own throat, solve the world's problems that way. I stared at the razor. Where had I gotten it? I couldn't remember.

The *kurre-nikas*. I wondered if they'd already used it. It was an obvious question. Why hadn't I asked it? Something like that would take calibration. Trial runs. Experimentation. I looked up at my big, dumb hetero life mate in silent appeal.

"Lem," Mags whispered.

But I knew it was useless. I would tell them. The realization calmed me. My body stopped trembling. My breathing and heart rate slowed. Everything went quiet and calm.

"It's okay, Magsie," I said.

It felt good to give in. I took a deep breath. Felt Mags take a deep breath.

And then I told them.

41.

I KNEW I WAS IN Nebraska, because there was nothing to see.

Again, teleportation was disorienting by its nonexperiential nature. There was no visual or audio cue; suddenly, you were somewhere else. I stumbled because the ground was uneven after the perfect floors of the Shanghai apartment. I was in a field. It was fucking freezing, and pitch-black, and the wind was so strong I thought if I held open my coat, I'd catch a breeze and take off. I immediately began shivering.

I spun around, peering into the gloom. I was alone. Fallon and Mags were nowhere to be seen. The Girl Who Was Not a Girl or Elsa or whatever had sent us to different spots. Safe passage didn't specify anything else, I supposed, and now the deal was done, so staying in the spot they'd sent me seemed unwise. I half expected a tiger to materialize out of thin air. Or a *dimma*.

Teleportation was an expensive spell for which I didn't have gas or the know-how, so I started walking. I'd taken three steps when I felt the faintest tremor, as if something had exploded far off in the distance. The world swam around me like I was about to pass out, but I felt fine. Everything blurred, then snapped back into place a second later.

I'd never had a chance to ask Hiram whether prolonged exposure to magic gave you brain tumors. Maybe that was what was wrong with *enustari*.

I resumed walking and sliced my thumb with my switchblade. Muttering three syllables, I closed my eyes and felt for a highway. Something with two lanes, at least. Felt a road beating softly against my left cheek and turned into the wind. I pulled my coat closed at the neck and started off in that direction.

The road was ice-cold and hadn't seen a car in hours. Maybe days. I stood shivering on the shoulder, my hand at my throat, and considered my options. I was somewhere. It *felt* the way I'd always imagined Nebraska to feel, though I couldn't be sure unless I found someone or put some gas into it. Fallon's old friend Elsa knew how to send someone to the fucking middle of nowhere, I had to give her that.

I chewed on the *kurre-nikas* and whether it had already been used.

Jesus. My brain snagged on that thought and wouldn't let go. The universe resetting around me, silent, my own fucking past being rewritten. And no one knowing, except Mika Renar. The spider in her web, rubbing the threads.

I stared into the inky dark and felt the wind pushing its fingers into every seam, every gap, between each and every hair to freeze my skin.

MY HEAD WAS SWIMMING and I felt hot.

The kids were all drunk. The kid driving, a girl named Lucy who the others called Loose, was probably the least drunk, but it was still kind of unnerving. I'd given them a hair too much Charm, three degrees west of innocent, and they were all looking at me with big drunk teenage eyes like I was their Prince Charming come to save them from working three years at Walmart and then having sixty kids. The car smelled like pot and bourbon, and the radio was playing a song I'd never heard, all rhythm, no guitars. The two in the backseat on either side of me kept touching me. Ten years before, I would have gone for it.

Ten years before, I reminded myself, these kids had been *seven*.

Lucy was tall and had black hair, not pretty at all, but skinny enough to finish high school pregnant. Her two blond friends and their unfortunate haircuts and too-tight tops were in the back with me. The redhead in the passenger seat had blue eyes, hadn't smiled once, and looked about ready to cry.

None of their phones worked. They didn't seem surprised. They said no one's phones worked, and they hadn't had Internet in weeks. I asked about landlines. They stared at me.

They started talking in a dreamy, drunken way about how fucked-up their town was. Half the place had moved away. The other half was made up of unemployed men who occasionally shot their wives and then themselves, and anyone else walking by. School had ended early this year. Two months ahead of schedule, they just called it a day. No one knew for sure if they were going to bother having school next autumn, and now, unexpectedly, the girls weren't sure they were happy about that.

They drove me to the interstate, and then the driver, Loose, seriously considered taking me the whole way. She idled in the middle of the empty road for a long time, the choppy engine on the Malibu like a giant clearing his throat. Her three friends sat there, befuddled and dreamy, and let her wait. I sat there with half an erection and a contact high, knowing what she was thinking. Why not go with me, wherever I was going?

I THOUGHT ABOUT NEW York, about Billington and the Army of Assholes she'd assembled.

The redhead was snoring slightly, her head resting on my shoulder as the bus bumped and turned. I'd gassed the driver into stopping in the middle of the fucking highway, cornfields rotting on either side of us, and then I'd gassed up five tickets. It didn't take much. The driver didn't have a uniform on. He was an older black guy with a friar's halo of white hair. Management, filling in. Odds were the official driver had stepped off the bus at a rest stop and just kept walking.

The Malibu, noble and last serviced in the previous decade, had died a slow, agonizing death. Everything got dim so slowly we didn't notice at first, and then we were driving in pitch darkness. The car was still running, but the lights and the dash had gone dark. For a minute or two we kept going, just driving into a wall of darkness, and then Loose cut the engine and let us coast to a stop, saved by the uncanny straightness of midwestern highways.

Red smelled like soap. Just simple soap, clean and dry. Lucy and the two blondes were sitting in the row behind us. The bus was deathly quiet. Twenty or twenty-five people, most of them young. None of them had any luggage. None of them had noticed we were taking a slight detour, the driver cheerfully gassed to be cooperative. Fifteen minutes in, I was the only one who had his overhead light on. I looked around and pulled my pack of cigarettes from my jacket pocket, shook one out, and placed it between my lips. I lit it with a cheap plastic lighter and wondered briefly if they were still making cheap plastic lighters somewhere, if the workers were still showing up, if there were still trucks carrying palettes of them around the country to filthy gas stations and head shops. I breathed in smoke, sent a plume into the air. Waited for anyone to complain. Two guys were sitting across the aisle from us. One was skinny with a shaved head and wore a button-down shirt and a sweater, his face thin and flushed. The other was younger, skinny with brown hair grown over the ears. This one couldn't sit still for one moment, constantly rearranging himself.

The older guy leaned over and jostled my knee. His scalp was pink and smooth. "Can I bum one?"

THE SHOCKS ON THE old Ford creaked alarmingly as we went a little too fast down the dirt road. Both windows down, it was colder *in* the cab than outside. The old man was dressed entirely in denim. Jeans, denim jacket, blue denim work shirt. He had white hair that shagged over his ears, and pink, permanently sunburned skin. He hadn't said three words since I'd gassed our way into his vehicle.

In the bed, the four girls and three guys were chattering. Smoking my cigarettes, freezing their asses off. I hadn't Charmed a single one after hitching my ride with Lucy. The three guys had told me their names, but I hadn't listened.

The old familiar burn of scars forming on my arm felt good. It had been too long. I used to go to bed every night with that burning sensation, collapsing into a pitch-black exhaustion, the pain and itch of a dozen short cons my only company. It felt good to get back into that dark, red place where everything throbbed and going to sleep was as easy as closing your eyes.

The driver reached forward and turned on the radio. It was an old beat-to-shit radio, perfect for an old beat-to-shit Ford. He scanned through static for a while. Not a single station. Then he gave up and pushed an ancient cassette in. George Strait began singing something depressing.

"You got a cigarette for me, son?" he said over the music. "I quit twenty-three years ago."

"YOU'RE A HARD PERSON to find."

She peered at me through the gloom, the oldest shotgun I'd ever seen in my life wedged into her tiny shoulder, an old triple shot. She was chewing gum. The shotgun had been sawed down to a ridiculous nub and would kill every living thing within twenty feet if it went off. She was wearing a black-and-blue Germs T-shirt, a pair of ratty jeans, and pink cowboy boots. Her black hair was short, but she'd contrived to have a lick of it hang in her face. Her nipples were hard, and I felt shitty for noticing.

For a few seconds Claire chewed her gum loudly. Then she slowly lowered the boomer. "Unfind me," she said.

The truck idled behind me, belching white exhaust into the cold air.

"I brought a few friends."

Her eyes flicked over my shoulder, then back to me. "They're fine where they are."

"It's time we talked, Claire."

She kept studying me, her face impassive. "How'd you find me?"

I sighed. "Every time I try to cast a spell on you or in your general direction, Claire, it bombs. Just falls flat, disappears." I grinned a little. "So a year ago I cast a few Seeking *mu* and got nothing until I figured it out. Figured out that when it's aimed directly at you, magic shits the fucking bed for some reason. So I did it the hard way, the *Trickster* way. I cast a spell to tell me where you *weren't*. Then narrowed it down." I shrugged. "It took a while."

Behind her, the front door to the saggy little house opened, and Daryl Fucking Houy emerged, a bottle of beer in his hand. He ambled to the top of the porch stairs and leaned against a post that was set on a bad angle. The wind blew his hair around—longer than I remembered. He'd let his beard grow a bit. It suited him.

"Holy heck," he said, smiling. "I remember you."

I nodded without taking my eyes off Claire. She was as pretty as I remembered. She'd gained a few pounds, and that suited her. "Daryl."

"Go on, Lem," Claire said tiredly. "We don't have anything to talk about."

"Except that I just told some *enustari* where you are."

For a second she just stared at me. Then she broke. It was something like hurt, something like betrayal. Like she'd thought we were friends. Her eyes got shiny and she looked away, swallowing something hard.

"Daryl," she said, her voice a little shaky. "Get the Run Bag."

I took a step forward, holding up one hand. "Wait!"

The shotgun came back up. "Jesus, Lem," she said, sounding angry now. "Wait for *what*?"

I smiled. "It's okay. I lied."

"AN OLD TRICK," I said, politely declining to ever take a second sip of the coffee Daryl Fucking Houy had just served me. "It's simple. If you believe something is true, if you really *believe* it, it fools everyone. It fools the universe."

I heard Hiram's booming voice. *Reality is perception.*

"Basically, I cast a little spell that ensured I believed a lie to be true for a while."

Buoyed by my own cleverness, the interior of the bungalow felt surprisingly charming. I sat at an old, weathered kitchen table, but the cabinetry and appliances were in great shape, and the whole place had a freshly painted glow to it. The kitchen had been done in a pale yellow that was cheerful, and through the kitchen doors I could see the living room, where my new friends were being entertained in fine style by Darryl Fucking Houy. It was done up in a baby blue that worked, somehow.

The domesticity of the scene made no sense. This was Claire Mannice. Murderer, survivor, marked.

"So you lied," she said, arms crossed in front of her chest, one hand with a cigarette clamped between two fingers, "and they believed you because they thought you *couldn't* lie."

I nodded. "The *enustari* always think too much of their spells. Sure, go after the main line and you'll get a bloody nose. You don't go after the main line. You get a wedge in the cracks."

She nodded. "Where'd you say I was?"

"North Korea."

"Seriously?"

I nodded. In the living room, a soft wave of low laughter went up. Daryl had served home-brewed beer and homemade deer sausage, proud as a new father. It sounded like it was going over well.

"We got lazy," Claire said suddenly, curling her hand so she could scowl down at her cigarette. "Haven't seen a soul out this way in months. Not a single car, not a single person. No mail, no cops. Months. Montana might as well be the moon, for all the traffic we've seen." She looked back at me. Her face was exactly as I recalled it, the exact lines and weight. "So we stopped being so careful. Otherwise you wouldn't have made it this close."

I shrugged. "I know a lot of tricks, Claire."

She gave me the slightest ghost of a smile. "All right, Vonnegan. I'm not saying I'm in, but what do you need me for? All this time I've been lying low so that dotty old bitch doesn't snatch me, and now you're here to bring me in from the cold."

I thought of my little spell being sucked into a black hole centered on Claire, the way her magic resistance had evolved, changed. "You're my secret weapon."

She looked back at her cigarette. "Tell me this is important. Tell me this isn't just some fucking grudge match."

Instead, I told her it wasn't over for her, even if she wished it were. I told her what they were doing. That she was the most important person in the world, and now two totally batshit insane *enustari* were after her. I told her that her empty town and its zero visitors were directly connected to stories on the news every day about endless tragedy and horror. I told her that Renar had been trying for years to find her, that she was still marked, that the world was cracking open like a rotten fruit from the pressure of being bled, bled, and bled again, all in preparation for Renar's next attempt at forever.

She frowned, snuffing out her cigarette in an old-school brass ashtray. "If they're going to change everything, why do they need me now?" She looked at me, genuinely curious. "If they change that moment and everything happens the way they want it to back in New York, why bother with me *now*? And the other one—the girl. Why does she need me in the first place?"

I thought for a moment. "I don't know," I said. I was used to her look of disappointment. All the recruits always looked at me that way the first time they realized I didn't know shit about shit. "Fallon told me it has to be you. If they try to cast the *tah-namus* again, it *has* to be you . . . but I don't know why." I shrugged. "Maybe it's just insurance— they'll fuck with reality if they have to, but if they can strap you in first, they'll go that route."

She nodded like this was always the most likely answer. Which it was. She reached for her pack of cigarettes. For a moment, the noise from the living room faded away, leaving us alone together in a dying world, smoking the last pack of cigarettes ever. Me and Claire at the end of the world felt right.

"All right, Chief," she said. "If I was going along with this, what would be the next step?"

This, at least, I'd thought about. "We're heading back to New York, first of all. That's where Fallon and Mags will be headed, and a few other folks you never met. We'll have a war council."

She looked at me sharply and stared for a few beats. "Pitr?"

I frowned. "Pitr Mags, sure. Why?"

Her expression didn't change. "Because he's been dead for two years, Lem."

42. **THE TOLLBOOTHS AT THE GEORGE** Washington Bridge were abandoned. All three of our cars sailed through, joining an anemic trickle of other vehicles heading in and out of New York. It was me and the old man, Claire and Daryl, and the eight people we'd picked up along the way. I hadn't asked any of the hangers-on to come along. They just had.

I sat in the cab with the old man and stared at the thick plume of black smoke rising out of Harlem and felt nothing. I looked down at the switchblade in my lap and wondered at it. Looked back at the plume of black smoke and thought about the *kurre-nikas*.

I remembered Mags standing next to me in that apartment in Shanghai. Remembered him tearing ass out of the motel in Seward. I couldn't sense him now, and I hadn't been able to since arriving in the middle of fucking nowhere courtesy of Elsa and friends. I didn't know what had happened to us when Mags had come back from death, but I'd felt him since then. His heartbeat, mainly, like a goddamn drum, but sometimes other things, like his temper or his breathing. At times it seemed like I could live inside his entire nervous system.

Now, nothing. He wasn't there. Had he been before? Had he really come back from the dead? Had he ever been there at all? Two fucking years, Claire'd said.

But he *had* been. And then . . . he hadn't. The *kurre-nikas*. It had to be. Why I retained this memory, I didn't know. But Renar had pulled the lever on her terrible difference engine and erased my friend from the universe. Claire told me Mags had bled out in the desanctified church and I'd bled some poor kid dead, tearing the place down, raging.

When had Renar first used the *kurre-nikas*? I wondered. Because Mags had been there, then he'd been dead, then somehow he'd come back—and I had no fucking faith I'd had fuck-all to do with that—and now he was dead again, the last few years a dream. Unless I'd fucking cracked and I'd been imagining Mags there, a Glamour, a ghost, and everyone staring at me in mixed pity and fear as I called the thin air a fucking moron.

Two years.

I'd asked Claire how she knew that, because in my memory I hadn't spoken a word to her since she'd melted away after the failed *biludha* in New York. And she'd told me I'd shown up in the parking lot at the diner one night, in bad shape, drunk and unhappy, and I'd told her. Who knew what the fuck else they'd changed. What if every other memory I had in my head was wrong? What if I was remembering things that never actually happened?

My head hurt. I folded up the knife and pushed it into my pocket.

I directed the old man to Broadway, and there was no traffic until we hit 158th Street. As if a switch had been thrown, there was suddenly nothing *but* traffic, a wall of idling cars blowing their horns. We sat there staring for a second. I was certain that if we walked about thirty blocks downtown, we'd find cars that had been sitting there so long they'd run out of gas.

"Well," the old man said, gesturing at the two cars idling behind us, "guess we walk."

I was picking through my memories for useful *mu*, something to clear the way. I thought about all the people in the cars behind us, following me around. They'd end up Bleeders, every one of them, unless Billington found a spark in one of them and someone else took the time to teach them a thing or two. I'd have nothing to do with their eventual fate, that much was for sure—it was all Billington.

"Cops," the old man said.

I glanced up and twisted around in the cracked seat of his truck. It was an unmarked car, a black sedan with a cherry in the dash.

"Fuck," I whispered. I hadn't seen a fucking cop in at least a year. As I stared, the passenger door opened and Ev Fallon climbed out. He appeared to have stopped for a new suit—cream-colored and spotless, with bold black piping, sharp and tailored. And a haircut.

Fucking *enustari* motherfuckers.

"Wait here," I said, opening the door.

"Nowhere to go," the old man said jovially enough.

"Mr. Vonnegan," Fallon said with a curt nod. "You look surprisingly alive."

"Safe passage," I said. I opened my mouth to say something else, something about Mags, but couldn't find the words. What could I say? Did Fallon remember the same way I did? Had anything I remembered actually happened? I felt like the ground was made of gelatin, unreliable, apt to shift under my feet without warning.

Before I could speak, Claire got out of Daryl's truck and stood eyeing us. Fallon turned at the sound of her door, hesitated, then turned back to me. "Hello, Ms. Mannice," he said loudly. "You have brought her. That is . . . incredible."

Behind me, blocks deeper into the endless traffic jam, the clear sound of gunfire split the air, followed by the muffled sound of screams.

I shrugged. "I played a trick," I said. The driver's-side door on the cop car opened and a tall black man half stood, one arm on the roof of the car. "Who's your friend?"

Fallon sighed, glanced down at his shoes, then gestured at the cop. "Detective Stanley James. He is . . . indebted to me. Stanley, this is my . . . colleague, Lem Vonnegan."

The stranger nodded once. He was the best-dressed cop I'd ever seen in my life. A few years ago, before you needed a box of twenties for bus fare, I would have said he had two, three thousand dollars on his back, including the big ruby tiepin and the gold watch, the big ring on his right hand. He was dark and tall and broad, and I had no doubt he'd won every fistfight he'd ever been in. His expression wasn't exactly friendly, wasn't exactly mean. It was open.

Behind me, the gunfire spat again. It seemed just as far away, but the screams were closer. Like a distant tide heading towards us.

"C'mon," the cop said, his voice a deep, satisfying drawl I'd never heard. "I'll make a hole for you."

I studied him a moment longer, then looked back at Fallon and shrugged. "Rue's, then."

"Is that safe, Mr. Vonnegan?"

"We've been there for years, Ev," I said, feeling tired. "It hasn't exactly been a secret." I was losing track of who might have been searching for me—Renar, Elsa, all the insane *enustari* trying to live forever in different ways. One by eating the world, one by switching bodies every few years. *Del Traje Blanco*, twin girls hiding under my bed—despite Billington's efforts to shield me, I'd been found plenty of times. And after Shanghai, I knew I'd been conned. Everyone always knew my next move. So why start being *clever* now?

"That would be my *point*. And you have some extra . . . cargo whose absence perhaps protected you in the past."

That might have been true. Everyone really wanted Claire. If they took down Rue's they might never find her. Renar, Elsa, all of them might have taken a wait-and-see approach, see if she washed up on the curb one day. "And we have a fucking *army* waiting for us there." I paused. "A *useless* army, sure, but an army nonetheless." I turned and walked back towards the truck. "Rue's!"

As I got back in the truck, James's sedan swung out around me. Going about ten miles an hour, it bumped a few pedestrians roughly out of the way just as a wave of people streamed uptown, running in panic, screams trailing behind them. James spiked his siren and drove up onto the sidewalk, crawling along as the pedestrians made a sullen corridor for him. We steered behind him, and the wave of humanity streamed past us in one direction as we crawled in the other, following the spinning cherry top.

After a block or so, I tasted a thread of gas in the air, and then the sidewalk opened up as people began scrambling out of our way instinctively. James goosed the sedan and we followed suit. The people were still running, screaming past us, but now they were a blur, and I closed my eyes and let the old man steer. Then the George Strait tape was back on and the screams were drowned out.

I WALKED INTO RUE'S in silence, a hundred eyes on me.

They were all there, in their ratty black suits, lined up behind the bar, in front of the bar, on the other side of the room. I don't know, if I'd let Mags die—if I'd accidentally killed my friend back at the church—why they were all still here. If I hadn't had my little god moment, why would they all treat me like I had? I walked in leading everyone and they all just watched me, like always. Mags's absence didn't feel real. He'd been alive a day ago, not two years. He'd been there and I'd felt his heart beating. But if he were alive, he'd be walking with me. He'd be looming over my shoulder and scowling at everyone, daring them to keep looking at me.

His absence surrounded me, and I felt the nothing that had been his heartbeat just the day before. I began to tremble. There had been that one terrible moment in the church when I'd not only thought I'd lost Pitr but when I knew I'd *bled him to death*. In the heat of battle, I'd grabbed on to that thick full-throated line of gas in the air that had been *him,* had been Pitr, and bled him white to save myself.

The world had shimmered, I remembered that. I'd been speaking the spell, the useless piece-of-shit *mu* that was all I'd been able to think of. Just speaking it and peaking it and pouring blood and Words into the universe's hungry maw, and I'd known it was doomed, it was useless.

And Mags had come back. And Billington had told everyone what she'd seen. That I'd brought him back. Done the impossible, considering my skill, the spell itself, the blood on hand.

Except I hadn't.

Halfway to the back door that led to what once was the banquet room, my legs began to shake and my knees went out from under me. Arms shot out and righted me, lifting me to my feet, settling me, patting me on the back. I managed two more steps and stumbled again, catching myself on someone, and another four sets of hands pushed in and held me until I took a deep breath, closed my eyes, and nodded.

I hadn't.

They followed me into the back room. All of them. The Bleeders whose names I'd never learned, who'd been crawling in from around the world for two years expecting miracles and getting nothing but a cheap black suit and abuse. I'd still defeated Renar. Still stopped the first attempt at the *tah-namus*. That much remained real. Fallon, his pet cop James. Claire and Daryl, dusty and tired. The eight newbies we'd picked up along the way like a fucking magnet picking up debris, as if the universe had been remade just for me and they could sense it. Suckers who would get their own black suits as soon as Billington made her way back to New York.

Assuming Billington, in this new reality created by the *kurre-nikas*, was still alive.

Pitr was dead.

Hands helped me up onto a chair. I stood there while the room settled, and then looked up at them all, my vision blurry and damp. Someone handed a lit cigarette up to me. After a moment someone took it and placed it between my lips.

I heard Billington in Colombia: *You sure?* If that had still happened.

My eyes roamed the room and settled on Ev Fallon's ancient eyes, wrinkled and puffy from his own brand of exhaustion. All of us except him in black, in the back room of a bar. A wake. For Pitr. For the fucking world, splitting apart outside as it was bled by Renar, the death throes not pretty.

The world was broken. I had broken it.

"We," I said in a voice that wasn't more than a croak, "have been conned."

All of it a grift. Two years, I'd been fucked with. They'd played my own game and *beaten me*. Two years they'd been dangling something in one hand, and I'd been staring at it like a simp, while the other hand picked our pockets. I'd gone tearing ass to Alaska, the smartest man in the room, and they'd fucked me *again*. Three questions for one. And I hadn't wanted any of the answers.

The room shifted its weight. Everyone breathed.

"What do you do when you've been conned?" I asked quietly. I was still trembling, the cigarette dancing in my mouth. Pitr was dead and I'd let it happen twice. And brought him back once.

You sure?

I took a deep drag on the cigarette and plucked it from my mouth, flicked it off into the air. Thought of Pitr, who'd been taken away from me—because he *had* been there. He *had* come back. And been taken away again. Leaving me nothing left to lose.

"You go to war."

43.

"A SUMMONING," FALLON SAID, MAKING the word sound like it tasted bad, "is very dangerous. With someone of his level."

"Ev, I'd say the time for worrying about safety is passed." Pitr was dead. "They've already used the fucking *kurre-nikas* once, maybe twice. Who knows? They've been bleeding the world for years, poking away at this. You think it matters if we play it *safe*? Do we just sit on our dicks and wait for them to use it again?"

He held up his hands in a placating gesture. "A Summoning is not a typical spell, Mr. Vonnegan. It violates many things. The will of the summoned. The physical laws of the universe. Violate one, yes, it can be done easily. Violate *both* and you have the potential for a viol*ent* outcome." He glanced around the room, his dry, careful eyes landing on Claire and Daryl before flitting back to me. Everyone else had crowded back out into the bar area. "What do you accomplish if you attempt to Summon him and he resists, and you . . . do not survive the attempt?"

Truth be told, I hadn't realized death was a possible consequence of a failed spell like this. Summoning someone—even someone as powerful and strange as the Negotiator—seemed straightforward enough.

"They resist, Mr. Vonnegan," he continued, as if reading my mind. "They feel you pulling at them, and they resist. A normal person, not part of our *guild*, has little to resist with. This Negotiator, Mr. Harrows, he is skilled. His resistance would be more intense."

He sighed. For a moment we all just existed in silence.

"Hey."

I jumped a little and turned to look at Claire.

"So, I'm fucking *here*," she said. "*Why* am I fucking here?"

Fallon beat me to it, so I let him talk.

"You are here, Ms. Mannice, because everyone wishes to kill you. Mika Renar for her interrupted Rite—you are the only person who may be bled as the cornerstone of the Ritual. Mika worked diligently to create you, Ms. Mannice. She wishes to use you as she intended."

It was one way of saying Mika Renar had played geneticist with her own apprentice and created dozens of daughters, all marked for the Ritual, who would give their mother eternal life. I saw no profit in reminding Claire of that.

"Elsa—whom you have not had the pleasure of meeting—wishes to kill you outside Renar's Ritual, thereby rendering it moot. For, without you there can *be* no Ritual, I assume, as I do not caucus with Elsa anymore. I must extrapolate."

Fallon in his nifty cream suit. Like he was on vacation. "You are irreplaceable," he said softly. "You are the most unique person in the world, Ms. Mannice."

She stared at him, a half-smile on her face. "No, I'm not."

Fallon closed his eyes. "When the *kurre-nikas* is used, it essentially creates an alternate universe. In one universe, the previous moment. In the new, the adjustment. We do this constantly simply by making decisions. This is why the Fabrication is possible without bleeding the world dry each time—the mechanics already exist.

"In each of these universes, a version of you exists. It is possible, although unlikely, that in every other possible universe, you have died. You no longer exist there. You have reached what we call *Terminus*." He opened his tired, sharp eyes. "You are truly unique. As a Terminus, there remains only one of you. Only one." He opened his eyes and glanced at me. "There is much we fought to keep secret."

No one said anything. Or moved. After a few seconds Fallon clucked his tongue in a way I recognized from my lessons with Hiram, when the old man thought I was being particularly stupid.

"I fire a gun at your head," he said, making a gun-shape with his nimble, age-spotted hand. "In one universe, you are killed. In another, you live. In the latter, I fire the gun again—the process repeats. On and on, branching, branching. This is a simplification, you understand, for your *benefit*. Over a long enough time—or if assisted by magical meddling, say in the construction of a large *biludha* of which you are the cornerstone—there is only one version of you left, the version that lives each time. The last version.

"Ms. Mannice, if you die here, in *this* universe, you cease to exist anywhere. You remain marked because Renar's *biludha* cannot be cast without you. She has been trumped by a force more fundamental and powerful than magic."

I thought of Pitr, thought of him in another dimension or some shit, exactly the same, hanging out with someone just like me but *not* me. My head was spinning. "How do you know she's a fucking *Terminus*?"

"The runes. They should have disappeared when the *tah-namus* collapsed, but they remained. The *biludha* is trapped with you."

She blew out a breath and leaned back. "Ah, fuck all of you," she said tiredly, scrubbing her face. "Just tell me what it fucking *means*."

"It means they can't use anyone else as the keystone of the Ritual. It's all suspended in you," I said, pulling off my jacket and draping it over a chair. "*That's* why the whole fucking world didn't end when we stopped the ritual. It didn't really collapse; it's been suspended *in* you ever since. Because there's no place else for it to go. And it means this."

I slashed a quick line of blood down my arm and spoke four Words. Felt the energy move from me, draining me. And nothing happened.

Fallon sat forward. "Remarkable."

"This is new. *Before* Mad Day, magic curved around you, warped because of the power of the Rite. Now you're like a fucking black hole," I said. "Everything cast within a few feet of you just dies on the vine. The gas is sucked into you and gone." I smiled, thinking of Pitr, alive somewhere. "You're a secret weapon, Claire. You fuck up magic in ways I don't even pretend to understand, and we've barely scratched the surface. Who knows what happens if someone casts a really big spell on you."

"Well, bully for fucking me," she said, scowling and crossing her arms under her breasts.

I looked at Fallon and wondered whether I'd be up for stopping her if she tried to leave. I knew she felt some sense of debt to me because I'd saved her. I knew she had some affection for me—more for Pitr but some for me, too. I also knew she was the Survivor Type, and it all came down to what she saw as her currently running best shot. I couldn't Charm her, and I couldn't Compel her. For the first time in my life, I was dependent entirely on someone's goodwill.

I felt sick. But hell, it was good to have her smell in the room again. "So," I said, tearing my eyes from her. "A Summoning?"

Fallon sighed and closed his eyes again. "I regret . . . There was an Artifact, once in my possession, that would be of use here. It required some amount of sacrifice, but it made such a Summoning much easier."

I rolled my sleeve down to the wrist. "What happened to it?"

Fallon opened one eye. "Your old *gasam*, Bosch, stole it. As he stole *everything*."

I paused, staring down at the buttons on my sleeve. "Describe it."

He waved his wand in the air. "It was decades ago—"

"Describe it!"

He closed his eye again. "A small ivory box. A symbol of a scarab on it inlaid in gold. No obvious way to open it."

"I know where it is."

The eye opened. I looked at Claire. "You up for some breaking and entering?"

"THIS IS CREEPY."

I sighed, staring at the building from across the street. "Tell me one moment you've spent in my company that *wasn't* creepy."

She didn't respond, and we went back to staring at Hiram's old building. We were in the alley where she'd killed two cops not so long ago.

"How do you know it's still in there?" she asked.

"It's Warded. Pitr . . . Pitr and me, we made the whole place invisible."

I walked through the time line in my head. We'd done the Warding *before* we'd gone to Abdagnale's place. *Before* Pitr had died. So it had really happened, still.

I was pretty sure.

She chewed that for a moment. It was dark and quiet and the only streetlight was half a block away. The rest of the building blazed with light. Hiram's blown-out windows were dark and forgotten. The alley smelled like garbage and rain.

"Why?"

I thought of Hiram. I hadn't seen much of him in those later years. I'd ignored him, resented him, made no effort to stay in touch with him—and yet at the end, when I was desperate, I'd had no compunction about begging him for help in spite of it all. Now he was gone, and I still wasn't used to that.

That made me think of Pitr. My Pitr wouldn't even have a stinking, rotting apartment as a headstone. No one but me would remember him, and soon enough I'd be gone, too.

"I didn't want anyone else living there," I said honestly. "And I didn't want to have to go through all the shit Hiram stole, burned out or not. So we just *hid* it. Come on."

Claire followed me across the alley to the bottom of the fire escape, where we'd barely escaped Cal Amir two years prior. I started climbing.

"What about everyone else who lives here? They just don't think about it?"

She was right behind me. I hadn't heard her jump onto the ladder or start climbing. I tried to control my heavy, out-of-shape breathing but couldn't manage it. "Pretty much," I agreed. "They just don't think about it."

The windows to Hiram's kitchen were empty, and so the world had invaded his pristine space. What I remembered as a clean white room with appliances that were rarely touched, aside from the burner where he brewed his tea, had become a nesting place for birds, unaffected by my Wards. I felt those Wards as we crossed the plane from outside to in. They weren't heavy artillery, just some simple tricks to inspire people not to notice this place.

As Claire pushed one leg through the window, I felt the Wards vanish. Just be absorbed by her, a walking magical black hole. I felt exposed, because for the first time in years anyone could see Hiram's apartment, would notice it, think of it, wonder about the smell.

The whole apartment was a damp, rotting mess. The floors were covered in mold and felt soft and spongy under my feet. Doors had sagged off the cabinets, and the whole place smelled like shit. As we climbed in, a riot of disturbed birds flew up in a panic, causing two seconds of sheer crazy as they fluttered around, escaping the way we'd come.

"Fuck," Claire said, "you couldn't come up with any goddamn magic to keep the place *clean*?"

The areas not directly exposed to the elements were preserved under a layer of white dust. The walls were scorched from Hiram's battle with Amir, the debris from the explosion all that was left of the furniture. We crunched through to the tiny closet he'd used as his office. As we moved, all the Wards and Glamours we'd laid on the apartment vanished one by one, but that shit had worked: No one had been here in all the time we'd left it. I could remember Pitr and me working the place over, both of us eager to leave, to get out of Hiram's mausoleum. For a second I wasn't sure I could trust the memory. I remembered things that had not actually happened. How could I be certain of any memory if I didn't know what moments the *kurre-nikas* had altered? What else I didn't know about because my memories came from a different version of the world?

In the tiny office, even the invisible keys that protected the safe melted away as she entered, exposing everything. I glanced at Claire and considered this new idea that she was the last of herself. Which wasn't much different mathematically than the day before, when I'd thought, like most people did, that all of us were the one and only— and thus the last—of ourselves. This following right on the new idea that we all had various versions of ourselves, that when Renar had tweaked reality with her *kurre-nikas* she'd created a new me, leaving the old me behind. Terminus. There were no other Claires, and despite having no fucking idea what that meant, it made me sad.

"You know why I'm doing this, right?" Claire said suddenly, leaning in close to watch my hands, her smell cigarettes and something vanilla. "I'm doing it 'cause I pay my debts."

I nodded, not looking at her. I was very still.

"I want to be clear, because I get the feeling that for you we're some sort of love story."

I nodded again. I loved Claire's nearly sociopathic directness. I did. But I wanted to cast something that would shut her up. Except it was increasingly clear that I'd never manage to cast another spell on Claire Mannice ever again. I reached down and pulled Hiram's old floor safe open. She knelt down next to me, our sides touching. "Oooh, pretty!"

She reached into the safe and pulled out a gold bracelet inlaid with green and red gems. I had no idea if it was paste or real, an Artifact or just something that had caught Hiram's eye. Claire slipped it on her wrist with all the bravado of someone who'd been stealing since birth. I started picking through the rest of the safe's contents. I'd left everything. Even the money, wads of cash in rubber bands. Cash was cash, there was nothing magical or sentimental about it, but taking anything from Hiram's panic hole had felt like stealing.

For a second, I thought of the *Udug*, heard its slithery voice in my ear. Wanted to hear it again so badly my balls ached.

Then I spotted the little white box. I knew everything Hiram had ever stolen. I'd lived in the house for years, and even after our estrangement, I knew on my infrequent visits exactly what was new, what had been acquired recently. The white box had been on Hiram's desk that first day when I'd shown up and asked the fat old man to be my *gasam*, to teach me. That first day with Pitr standing behind him, staring at me so fucking *angry* . . .

If that had still really happened.

At some point the white box had migrated, first to the shelves in the office and then, finally, into the safe. I realized with a start that I hadn't been aware Fallon and Hiram had known each other well enough, or long enough, for Hiram to steal things from the Fabricator.

After a moment's hesitation, I reached into the safe and took hold of the box. It felt normal. No current running through it, no Wards on the lid. I wondered if just being near Claire had killed it, short-circuited it. It was heavier than I would have expected. But it didn't crawl against my skin the way the *Udug* had. I studied it for a moment and then slipped it into my pocket. I let my eyes roam over the remaining trinkets in Hiram's safe, wondering what else might be of value.

"How come him?" Claire suddenly asked. "If Fallon can use this to snatch anyone, why not *her*? Snatch her, hit her over the head, be done with it."

I didn't blame her. If someone was trying to murder me ritualistically—and even change reality so that they already *had* murdered me ritualistically—I might be voting for their murder, too. "First of all, she's *enustari,* Claire. Even if she doesn't expect it, she'd be fucking hell to beat in a battle. Always go for someone you know you can *beat*. And second, Renar can't *negotiate.*"

"Why does that fucking matter?"

I let that hang. I didn't want to answer.

"Excuse me."

We both turned. An older woman was standing in the room behind us, dark skin, bright red and very fake hair. She was wearing a black cloth coat a little too long for her and carrying a tiny, shivering dog in her arms. She was wearing a pair of cheap red slippers, the kind you bought in a drugstore and got change for five bucks.

The expression on her face was best described as *alarmed*. "What," she said, eyes everywhere, "have you *done*?"

44. **DETECTIVE JAMES WAS STANDING AT** the bar, drinking a shot of bourbon with a Coke chaser. There were three empty shot glasses in front of him. One of the Bleeders was playing bartender, instructed by Fallon to treat him as a guest.

"Mr. Lem Vonnegan," the cop said in a pleasing baritone without turning around. "I ever tell you me and Jim Holloway were old friends?" His face cheerful in the mirror opposite him. "I guess not, as I've been here just four hours or so, waiting on your friend. You maybe remember the man? Picked you up a few years ago."

Alarm flashed through me. Holloway. Marichal. Two cops in over their heads and totally unaware of that right up until Claire killed them both. In self-defense, sure, but I had a feeling Detective Stanley James would give two small shits about the distinction.

"Sure, I remember," I said. "It was right before . . . before everything went to hell."

Mad Day. A stupid name, but it was the one the cable talking heads had started using, with their slick graphics and grainy footage, so it had stuck. Death toll in one day: six hundred fifty-nine thousand people. A few hundred thousand a week for months afterwards. Cities—hell, *countries*—had disappeared under that weight. I remembered Pitr Mags crashing into the precinct to save me, a cannonball. Indestructible.

James turned around, nodding. He was smiling, but there wasn't anything very friendly about it, and I didn't like cops in the first place. Definitely not cops like this one, who dressed beyond their pay grade and acted like their shield meant they could do whatever the fuck they wanted. The sort of cop, I was pretty certain, who carried a set of brass knuckles in his pocket just in case some citizen complained.

"Sure!" he said. "See, Jim got killed shortly after he sweated you. For obvious reasons, the case never got a real workout, you know? But he was a friend, and I've been trying to work it in my spare time, right? Shit, police work is all for show these days anyway, ain't it?" He shook his head in a world-weary way. "You know, two days ago an old man— must have been ninety years old, truth—got out his old rifle from when he was in the service and shot everyone in his building. Went door-to-door, knocked, and blew whoever opened up straight to hell. Then cleared the apartment. Then went on to the next one." He shook his head. "You know what? He must've made one *hell* of a noise, you know? All that knocking and shooting. Thing is, *no one* ran. No one called *us*. And no one thought, *Shit, no way I'm answering when he* knocks. He killed everyone. Does that make any fucking sense? Any sense at all?"

It did. Because the world was broken. *I* had broken it.

I opened my mouth to say something, then thought that it actually did make sense if everyone in the fucking building was Charmed. A man in a white suit in the jungle, collecting blood for his boss. Why not a man in a white suit in Manhattan doing the same? The idea dovetailed perfectly with everything else and made me feel smart.

When I didn't answer, he shrugged. "So your name is like the last name in his notes. You walked out of the precinct after a little scuffle, right? Jim didn't make too many notes on that. Just said you came in, got a little sweating, and then you left. Bam! Few days later, Jim's dead." He sighed, a big theatrical production. "Shit, police just a gang now. You got a gang"—he waved one huge hand around the room—"I got a gang. No difference anymore."

He downed his shot and made a show of looking around. "Seems like you moved up some, huh? Own this place now?"

A few years ago this would have been intimidating. A few years ago I would have shit my pants and prayed for an intervention. Instead of answering, I pointed at him. "Give me your gun."

He frowned. "Excuse me, now?"

"Your gun," I said slowly. "We need it."

He smiled. It was an impressive smile, big white teeth and bright red gums. "How bad?"

In my pocket, I had the switchblade positioned against the inner seam, ready to slice my thigh if I pushed the button. A simple *mu* sitting on the back of my tongue, ready to turn him into a newly erected statue of Detective Stanley James if necessary.

"You're standing here," I said slowly, "waiting to be dismissed by Ev Fallon, right? Because he owns you."

James didn't flinch, but the smile had become a mask, lifeless. Humorless.

"I don't know what he's got on you. Magic, money, shame, whatever, it doesn't fucking matter, Detective. He's got something. Else you wouldn't be standing here like some fucking valet, would you? So, I can go and get Mr. Fallon and ask him to ask you for your gun. Or we can cut the shit and you can just give it to me."

He stared at me with bloody eyes. A second later, he shook his head, forcing a laugh, and pulled open his coat. Reaching in, he produced a stainless-steel semiautomatic pistol with a black grip. He spun it around and gave it to me handle-first.

"Never liked those Glocks they tried to push on us. This is a good all-American gun. You know anything about guns?"

I shook my head, feeling the weight. It wasn't heavy at all. "Never needed one."

James winked. "That's right. Jim Holloway was fucking *strangled*, wasn't he? From behind, his own goddamn handcuffs." He turned back to the bar. "You tell your man Evelyn that we are dangerously close to me considering my debt *paid*, okay?"

I took the gun back to the banquet room, feeling the eyes of the Bleeders on me. They were all standing around, smoking cigarettes, chatting. Doing nothing because Billington wasn't around to organize them. I shut the door behind me and found that Fallon had taken off his jacket and cleared the furniture to the edges of the room, except for a single chair. He glanced from the gun to me, then to Claire, who stood behind the second bar with Daryl. The small white box sat on the chair.

Suddenly, from beyond the door, shouts and commotion. Noise resolved into cheers, then applause, and a familiar female voice booming out instructions. The cheers warped into the sound of industry, and then the banquet room door banged open and Mel Billington strutted into the room, trailed by Remy and Roman.

"Jesus fucking *Christ*," she shouted. "Don't fucking fall all over yourselves looking for us. I mean, it's not like we were fucking *abandoned* in the wilderness or something."

I tried hard not to smile. "You were left at a *motel*," I pointed out.

She grinned, looking dirty and rumpled, like they'd been Charming their way south and east without pausing for rest. "That place was deadly. We left to sleep under the stars in order to *survive*."

I grinned back. *Idimustari*—we were like roaches. We could not be killed by normal means.

"We will need blood," Fallon said, gesturing at the chair by way of explanation.

Billington winked at me. "Good to see you, too, old man." She cocked her head. "Maybe I need a bit more before I tell the kids to open the floodgates, huh?"

"No," Fallon said. "It must be Mr. Vonnegan's sacrifice."

She hesitated and looked back at me. I swallowed a sudden ball of anxiety that made no sense. I'd bled before. I was fresh. "Go have a drink. Keep an eye on the cop out there."

She blew out an explosive breath. "You got it, Chief. Need-to-know and all that. I get it."

I looked at Remy and Roman, who stood, hats literally in hands, looking dirty and stiff. "You, too. Out. Get a drink."

They looked at me impassively until Billington gestured at them. Then they nodded, waited for her to pass, and followed her out.

"She is a good general," Fallon said, sounding almost jaunty. "It is important to have someone who organizes. Who keeps everyone in line."

I nodded, staring down at the white box. "So how will this work?"

Fallon followed my gaze. "*Gespu*," he began. "There were once dozens of these. Fabricators before my time—known then as Thaumaturges—created them frequently, as a Rite of Passage. These and other Artifacts and Fabrications. Simple bindings, really, with powerful effects. There was once a concentration on simple things that had great effect. Much of this knowledge has been lost." He looked up at me and blinked. "It is simple. You open the *gespu*, speak the name of the person you wish to summon, and bleed. He will be Summoned." The

404 ///   JEFF SOMERS

old man paused to purse his lips. "The amount of sacrifice required will be determined by how much he resists."

I nodded. "So he might *resist* me to death?"

A crisp nod. "Certainly."

"And I can't take volunteers?"

"The *gespu* requires a connection between you and the subject. Ideally, you will picture him as you bleed."

The fucking universe was fucking *greedy*.

Fallon smiled tiredly. "Artifacts and Fabrications make things easier, in a way," he said gently. "But there is always a price, and it must be paid somehow. You can put in the work, or you can put in the blood. It is an old saying."

"Fine," I said, and crossed to the chair, taking off my jacket. "Daryl? Claire?"

Without Pitr, my Trust Circle had gotten small. I had an army milling about in the bar and in the general area, but they weren't really mine. Every time I gave an order, they all looked at Billington for confirmation.

They glanced at each other, a lovers' glance, and I swallowed a pang of anger at seeing it. Not because I was jealous. Just because it wasn't fair. She stepped around the bar and walked over to me.

"He'll be in the chair?" I asked Fallon over my shoulder.

"Yes."

I looked at Claire. "Step out of the room," I said.

She squinted at me. "If you fucking think—"

"Spells go sideways around you," I said. "That's why you're *here*. To be a secret weapon. We cast this and you're standing here, we'll get a goddamn purple gorilla in this chair instead of him. Or nothing."

She looked from me to Fallon, over my shoulder, and then back again. "Fucking fine," she finally said, turned, and walked to the door. She didn't open it, though. She leaned against it, crossing her arms. I sighed and looked at Daryl, standing behind the chair like he'd seen this movie before and was afraid of it.

"When he shows up," I said, "you make sure he doesn't make a *sound*."

Daryl nodded. It wasn't convincing.

Fallon was next to me, his own tiny penknife in hand. He leaned down and opened the small white box, then took hold of my arm. He was brusque, businesslike. A man who had bled plenty of people. With a single deft movement, he opened a vein and my blood began pouring out of me, down my forearm, through my hand, and into the white cube. It should have filled the tiny box in seconds, but it didn't.

"Think of him, Mr. Vonnegan," Fallon said. "Picture him. Call to him."

The moment my blood splashed down on the box, I felt it reach up into me, like invisible spiders climbing rapidly up my body. I was connected to it in a way I'd never felt, and I could feel . . . something waiting patiently for me to interact, to feed it. Patience. I could feel its patience as a physical thing, like a wall, softly throbbing, unhurried.

It waited. It would wait, I was certain, until I bled to death.

I pictured the Negotiator. Realized I knew his name and struggled, for a moment, to turn back in my mind to the apartment in Shanghai, to the Girl Who Was Not a Girl slurring it at him.

Harrows, I thought. *Richard Harrows.*

The invisible, patient thing throbbed and pulled at me, jerking the gas from me in a greedy lunge that made me stagger slightly. And then I felt him. Like he was on the other side of a wall, a heat signature. And I knew two things: To pull him through, I would have to move quickly, before he realized what was happening; and I would have to pull him *through* the wall before I bled to death.

I concentrated, and the *gespu* grabbed hold. And the Negotiator started kicking.

I could feel the Artifact working; smoky, insubstantial tendrils twisted and hooked into something soft and yielding—him. His resistance grew frenzied, pushing back until I closed my eyes and began to tremble with the effort of keeping my mind focused on him. It was like someone trying to distract you, to break your concentration, except instead of just losing my train of thought, I was being squeezed for blood. I felt it pouring out of me like someone had attached a straw to my arm and started sucking.

When he started to come through that wall, it began to *hurt*.

Someone had taken hold of the nub end of a nerve that looped in a single line around my entire body and started pulling at it. When I pulled at the presence that was the Negotiator, the nerve got pulled in the other direction, a burning line of agony that started in my belly and snaked around to every limb, every toe, every finger. I felt myself drop to my knees, holding my arm up over the *gespu* with increasing effort. I heard Claire shouting something that I imagined was encouraging.

And then, without warning, all the resistance and pain ceased and I rocketed back onto my ass, a warm spray of my own blood landing on my face. I was suddenly conscious of being soaked in sweat and shivering like an old drunk. It wasn't the most I'd ever bled, but it had been a long time, and I was out of practice.

I looked up and my eyes met his. The pale, skinny shit was right there, breathing hard, eyes popping in shock. We stared at each other for exactly one heartbeat. Then he opened his mouth. Claire skipped forward with the animal grace I remembered, a superpower, and hit him over the head with a sap that had appeared in her hand. He twisted off the chair and crumpled to the floor.

I looked at her. I looked at Daryl, who just stood there, arms out in shock.

Claire shrugged. "Well, your spell was finished," she said, "and he didn't make a sound."

45.

"ONE PIECE OF GREEN GLASS, six hundred and fifteen dollars in what appears to be pre–World War Two currency, one small jade figurine." Claire nudged the Negotiator's body with her foot. "Glad we weren't trying to rob him or I'd be fucking *pissed*."

Fallon and I knelt on the floor next to the bound and gagged man and examined the slim pickings of his pockets. Fallon reached down and picked up the piece of glass. It was a jagged and nasty hunk and had some dried blood on it. I guessed it came from the thick bottom of a beer bottle.

"Crude, but I suppose it gets the job done." Fallon looked past it at me. "You should move quickly. Elsa will be searching for him. And she will find him soon enough."

I nodded. "We'll ask Billington to get a bleed going and obscure him a little."

Claire reached down and snatched the figurine from the floor, let out a yelp of surprise and dropped it. It rolled towards me; it was square and resembled some sort of ancient god, eyes angry, mouth open. I picked up the milky-green thing and a jolt of buzzing energy instantly coursed up my arm. I recognized the gas right away, but it was more than I'd ever felt in my life. An ocean of roiling, *living* energy, like someone had recently bled a stadium full of people five seconds ago.

"Jesus," I whispered.

Fallon reached out for it. I instinctively pulled my hand away. No *enustari* should ever have this much gas in their hands. He left his hand outstretched for a moment, then smiled slightly and glanced down at his shoes.

"A Token, I believe. A connection to all that sacrifice they've been storing." He sighed. "That is *wonderful* work. Elsa has a touch." He frowned. "It is likely a copy of the existing piece. Although I am unaware of any other Fabricator capable of this."

I nodded. So simple. I could feel it, seemingly endless power vibrating inside the tiny statue, ready and willing to be drawn out and used. I closed my fist around it and spent two heartbeats exulting in it, just imagining what could be done with that kind of gas on demand, always in your pocket.

I thought of Pitr. All that gas—it felt infinite—and yet it wasn't enough to bring someone back, to reach back two years and erase a death. If it had been, Renar would have reached back and reworked everything already.

I looked at Claire and Daryl, who always seemed to be hulking behind her, simultaneously protective and completely confused. I pushed the Token into my pocket. I could feel it humming against my thigh.

"Help me tie him to the chair," I said.

THE NEGOTIATOR CAME TO while we were covering the knots of his binding with duct tape so he couldn't pick at them even if he managed to get his fingers free. He jerked awake, tried to speak through the ball and gag, rocked his bindings a bit, then instantly calmed, his eyes going around the room before finally settling on me. Fallon leaned against the bar to his left. Claire and Daryl were still behind him. The room was silent except for the low hum of drinkers' voices leaking under the door. I felt hot and sweaty.

I turned and dragged one of the other chairs over, pushed it close to him. Pulling James's gun from my pocket, I sat down so that our knees were touching, and held it flat against my thigh. I could smell myself. It wasn't pretty. His eyes darted to the gun and then back to me.

I smiled. "You can't speak yourself out of a bullet, eh?"

He just stared.

"I'm going to let you speak. If you try to cast, it will go very badly for you. Do you understand?"

He nodded once. He looked confident. He knew what was coming, or thought he did.

I glanced up at Claire, and she shrugged and reached savagely around, took hold of the gag, and yanked it free with one brutal pull.

The Negotiator howled. "*That* is quite unnecessary, Mr. Vonnegan!"

I nodded. We were all friends here. "Tell me, Mr. Harrows, can you negotiate on your own behalf?"

His eyes went to the gun again and lingered a bit longer. "Yes."

I leaned forward. "Can you negotiate under *duress*?" He didn't answer. I nodded. "Sure you can. Because this was a punishment, right? This was designed to ruin you. So sure, you can negotiate under *all sorts* of conditions, can't you?"

The Negotiator and I stared at each other. I reminded myself that in this world, in this *version* that Mika Renar had created, he had killed Pitr. Or caused me to kill Pitr. Either way, I let that thought bloat and push against my brain.

"If I refuse to engage in . . . *negotiations?*"

"I don't think you can," I said. "Because where's the suffering if you can *refuse?*"

He snorted, a crooked smile forming on his face. "Do you believe this is the first time I have been used thus? Mr. Vonnegan, this has been my existence for many years. I have been reduced to a tool. And I am used roughly."

I was an old hand at bullshit. For years, Pitr and I had made our meager living on bullshit. I was a fucking expert, and I could see, behind the jolly calm, that the Negotiator was agitated. Upset. Worried. I tipped my hand down and fired a shell into the floor. Everyone but me jumped. The noise outside the door went quiet.

"Boo-hoo, Mr. Harrows." I glanced up. "Daryl, check the door and tell anyone who inquires that everything's fine. And pass a message to Billington to get a bleed going and hide this place as best she can."

Daryl nodded and turned to go. I could hear him whispering my instructions to himself. He'd been with me a few hours and was already one of us. I heard Billington with her perpetual question: *You sure?* I wasn't winning, but in small ways, in ways that felt important, everything was coming up Lem, like an invisible hand was guiding things or my own invisible gravity had increased. I didn't know what kind of weird aura the universe had me wrapped up in, but it was fucking useful, that was for sure.

The Negotiator had closed his eyes. "Very well," he said. "Let us *negotiate.*"

He spoke the word as if it tasted like poison.

I nodded. I took a deep breath and kept my eyes on his angular, flushed face. "I want Pitr Mageshkumar."

I HAD SAT IN the cold, disturbingly clean kitchen and eyed the cup of tea steaming in front of me with dread. It was probably just tea, but there was something about the fruity, rotten smell wafting from it that made me imagine exotic, poisonous roots and berries. There was steady, disturbing breathing filling the air. It was right across from me, blowing the warm scent of sour cream and onion potato chips into my face. I was afraid to look up, because the largest man in the world might hit me again.

He was also the angriest man in the world.

I reached out and took hold of the teacup. It was excessively fragile, decorated with whimsical drawings of kittens with umbrellas. The edge of the cup was gilded, and it gleamed as I brought the hot liquid up to my nose for a sniff. The old bastard had added cream and sugar without asking if I wanted either.

My stomach rumbled.

I looked up. The Huge Indian Man was staring at me, his eyebrows knitted into one angry bar. He sat two feet across from me with his shovel-like hands clasped tightly in front of him, breathing with his mouth open like a panting lion.

I set the tea down. The possibility that it was deadly seemed suddenly very real. I picked up the spoon from the saucer and shook the cold pool of tea from it onto the table. I heard the Big Man grunt in disapproval. Holding the spoon up, I flashed out my other hand in a theatrical gesture, drawing his eye.

"Want to see a trick?"

By the time he'd reoriented on me, I'd bent the spoon between my thumb and forefinger, just at the neck. The dumbest trick in the world. But I suspected I had the dumbest audience in the world, too. He nodded curtly, hands now curled into fists, like he was thinking that if my trick sucked, he would hit me.

"I'm going to bend this spoon with just my mind," I said.

He frowned. "No blood?"

I frowned back. "No, no blood. Just my mind."

He nodded back, serious. "All right."

Holding the spoon so it was at a straight-on angle to him, I began waggling it back and forth, holding my free hand over it in various mystical shapes. "Bend," I commanded. "Bend!" As I waggled, I increased the angle so that from his point of view the spoon did appear to bend slowly. All it was really doing was inching towards him, revealing the bend that was already there. I'd won two beers and one punch for this one. I wasn't very good at it. But I'd never met a man more easily distracted than this hulk.

His face froze, his eyes wide and his mouth open. He stopped breathing. He lunged forward and grabbed the spoon from my hand, almost breaking a finger.

"Holy shit!" he said, rubbing his thumb along the spoon. "You didn't even *speak*!"

I smiled and opened my mouth to say something. He surged up out of his chair with a whoop and spun, taking hold of one of the cabinet drawers behind him and pulling it out so hard that it popped right off the tracks and crashed to the floor, making me jump. He dived down and popped back up, spun, and dumped about two dozen spoons of various sizes and purposes onto the table.

"Show me how!"

I looked from the spoons to his wide, excited face, without a shred of threat. I picked up my cup of tea and gestured at his chair. "Sit down, I'll show you."

"FEKETE KUTYA," **FALLON MUTTERED.** Out of the corner of my eye, I saw him throw his hands up and turn away.

The Negotiator blinked and began shaking his head slightly, his brow furrowing. This represented the most lines I'd seen in his face since I'd met him. It felt like a minor victory.

"What?"

"The things you say *become the truth*," I quoted. "Those are my terms."

He licked his lips. "This is . . . This is not possible. You have to be—"

I fired another shell into the floor. "Say the word *reasonable* and the negotiation is over."

He was breathing in short little gasps. For me, Pitr had been dead four days. To everyone else, he'd been gone for two years. But I knew what was possible. Mika Renar had ginned up an ocean of blood and built herself a Fabrication that changed moments. I'd felt that change, I realized. More than once. Standing in the middle of nowhere Nebraska, feeling smug for a little trick I'd managed, I'd *felt* it. And when I'd come out on the other side, Pitr Mageshkumar had been dead for two years.

"This, I cannot grant this," he said, craning his neck forward.

I shook my head. "I think you can." I was betting on it. "I think the Archmage who punished you with this *geas* doesn't know how to do anything lightly. I think she hammered this into place with every bit of skill she had. And I think if you *negotiate* in good faith, you can make any-fucking-thing happen, because *the things you say become the truth*." Hiram had taught me: Reality is *perception*. "And I think your *geas* allows you to negotiate for your own life because it was designed as a punishment."

He flew into a constrained frenzy then, rocking in the chair and straining against his bonds. He stopped suddenly and was still, his nearly white hair disheveled, sticking up in every direction. "Punishment! You know nothing of punishment. Of suffering. I reject your terms!"

I nodded. "Then I'll kill you."

"You won't."

I brought the gun up to his head. Claire let out a yelp. The Negotiator flinched away, sucking in a breath and then breathing rapidly, shallowly, straining his head back from it. It was always the way: People got used to having the gas at their fingertips, got used to people bleeding for them. They didn't react well to threats.

"Please!"

I resisted the ridiculous urge to cock the hammer. "Pitr Mageshku-mar," I said. "You know him."

He closed his eyes as I nudged the gun into his temple. "I . . . do know him, yes, I know him! But you do not understand, there is a *price* to be—" He stopped suddenly. Shook his head. "You do not understand. I have existing arrangements. With my former *gasam*. She is not so foolish as to allow me to work directly against her. I have already made my deals with her, precluding me from ever working directly against her interests."

"*Directly,*" I said, "is full of wiggle room. Be creative." I jabbed him with the gun. "My terms are fucking *clear*, Mr. Harrows."

"I have a counteroffer!"

I froze. I could feel the power of his *geas* pushing against me, demanding. This was apparently an acceptable action in the negotiation, and I was aware of being powerless to deny him.

"I will tell you everything I know. Every conversation. Every detail I can recall. I will willingly tell you *everything* to use as you will. In return for my guaranteed safety and release."

He opened his eyes and looked at me. I saw desperation and hope. Clearly, he thought he'd played a trump; he might even have believed that everything else was just a ploy to get him to break.

I nodded. "I reject your terms." I pushed the gun into his head again. "Mageshkumar."

The floor under my feet began to tremble.

"Holy fucked," Claire muttered.

Fallon was in my ear, leaning down, smelling like tobacco and coffee. "Lemuel, I urge you to *think*—"

"Mr. Harrows?"

"Please," he said in a soft, low voice. "There is a *price*. And I must pay it. *Please.*"

I nodded. "I will release you. And guarantee your safety. In exchange for Pitr Mageshkumar. Alive."

A low, agonizing tearing noise became audible. The Negotiator was sweating. Rivulets of sweat rolled down his pale face, the sharp angles.

The *kurre-nikas* was an immense Fabrication, running on an ocean of gas. The Negotiator's *geas* was an old and powerful spell applied by an *enustari*. I had set something in motion, and I didn't know if it was powerful enough, or how the gears of both machines would grind against one another.

We were going to find out.

"Mr. Vonnegan," he whimpered, slumping, "*please.*" He looked away, lips moving with nervous energy. "I would remove myself. I would end it all. A blade across the neck, a waste, I would waste my lifeblood. I *would*. But I am *prevented.*" He closed his eyes. "I am *prevented*. Even by someone else's hand, I cannot."

I just waited. The *geas* had rules, and every Trickster knew where there were rules there were tricks. I just let him work it out for himself: If he couldn't allow himself to die, he was out of options.

The hum had gotten loud enough to make it difficult to hear anything else. The floor was dancing under us like we were on a ship going down.

"*Please!*"

I paused for breath. "I will count to three! One—"

"*Very well! I accept your terms!*"

Something exploded. Everything went black.

46.

IN THE DREAM, AS ALWAYS, Claire had been set on fire. As she burned, she shrank.

"SHE IS *COMING*."

I opened my eyes and couldn't see anything. I could smell sawdust and shit, something like a skunk's terror in the air. I could feel the splintery old floorboards under my hands, dry and pitted. My chest convulsed and I lay coughing, hands curling into claws as the coughing went on and on endlessly, painfully, each wave making my whole body tense up, every muscle cramping simultaneously.

Each time I convulsed, there was a flash of dull red in my vision, and I thought, *Not blind, at least.*

"*Please*—she is *coming*."

A strange noise swallowed the air. It sounded like rain but wasn't.

The convulsions stopped, but I just lay there, breathing. I felt like I was vibrating softly, every bone under my flesh jittering.

"Please . . ."

The voice died off and was replaced with a grunting, pain-soaked noise, a wet noise, like gurgling. As I pushed myself up onto my hands, the gurgling stopped, replaced by the Words, familiar. I sensed immediately what he was casting, but he stumbled on the third syllable and it collapsed, a warm breeze of dull power pushing past me.

The skittering, dry-rain noise was still there. Louder? It was hard to tell. It sounded like the universe was being eaten by something. It sounded the way I always imagined time-lapse video of maggots might.

After what sounded like a deep breath, the Negotiator whispered, "*Please*." Then he started casting again. Now that I knew to look for it, I could sense the line of gas in the air—more than a trickle, but not by much. A bitten cheek or lip. The *enustari* were turning into Tricksters, one by one. You got desperate enough, you lost your fancy ways.

Meanwhile, pounding at the door. The Army of Assholes. More gas in the air, big streams of it as my Bleeders got into the act, and a second later the door blew in, a hollow drumlike noise. I tried to speak, but my throat was tight and knotted.

The Negotiator fucked up again, mangling his fourth Word, and the spell collapsed again. Feet on the floorboards, shouts, and then hands on me, pulling me up.

"Please," I heard the Negotiator say. "Please, she is coming. Please, I am willing to be accommodating. Please! We can come to an arrangement."

I was held up between two people, my legs numb and useless. I struggled to speak. "Shut him up," I croaked. "Shut him the fuck up."

"Chief," Billington shouted. "Chief! You okay?"

"Fucking immortal," I spat, swaying between my invisible supports. A chair scraped behind me and I was dropped into it. "I'm a fucking roach—you *can't* kill me!"

The dry rain had gotten louder. "Can you hear that shit?"

"Watch him!"

"Fuck!"

He was on me, the Negotiator, damp and warm and clinging to my shirt with his hands. "Mr. Vonnegan! Mr. Vonnegan! Please! We can help each other—but we must be *quick*!"

Someone was trying to pull him off, but he held fast. I thought I could just make out his outline right in front of me, a squirming shadow of terror.

"Mr. Vonnegan! We must come to an arrangement for safe passage! For both of us! We can *help* each other, but we must be *quick! Please! SHE IS COMING!*"

"Who?" I croaked, waving off whoever was tugging at him.

"*Renar,*" he wept, fingers curling into the fabric of my shirt. "My old *gasam*. She is *coming*!"

A spike of fear drove through me. She was an ancient, mummified old woman in a wheelchair, but I remembered those malevolent, dry yellow eyes and the way they'd stabbed at me during the *Biludha-tah-namus,* and I wanted to piss myself. Something about watching someone try to bleed the whole fucking world took the starch out of a person.

The dry rain was maddening. It was like a distant wave of water. You knew it was out there, could tell it was coming to swamp you, to flood you out, but you had no idea how far, how long, how deep. It got louder and louder a tick at a time, impossible to catch in the act.

"Mr. Vonnegan! *We must make a deal!*"

I stared around, blind. I could make out shapes. Shapes were everywhere. My Bleeders, standing around leaking gas, their dicks in their hands. My heart pounded crazily in my chest, but I was aware of something else. Steady, slow, like a truck in low gear making its lazy way up a steep incline. In between my crazy pre-stroke heartbeat, someone else's.

I surged up and swayed, nearly falling down. "Mags!"

It had been a long time since magic had amazed me. A long time since I'd thought of it as a way to do the impossible, the amazing, instead of just a way to make fifty dollars, a way to hide from the police, a way to make people do what I needed them to do, or just something to be terrified of. I remembered the first time I'd seen the old man, floating inches off the ground in that grungy parking lot. My bleeding hands, the first time I'd cast a spell by myself. Since then, there hadn't been much amazement.

Now I was amazed.

"Mags!"

And he was there, his hands on me with crushing force.

"I'm here, Lem," he said in his concerned voice, two shades south of fury, ready to destroy anything that had hurt me, anything that had made me even momentarily unhappy. Though I'd done nothing but contemplate leaving him behind, nothing but ruin his life and condemn him to a lifetime of starving and grifting and then one day led him into a fucking apartment that hadn't been touched in fifty years and destroyed us both.

I reached up and put my hands on his face. "You okay, buddy?" I let out a crazy laugh. "You all right?"

Jesus fucking Christ, was I crying?

"Hey!"

Claire's voice, deep into pissed-off territory, barely cutting through the hissing noise. "Hey! Did you hear the part about the psycho witch coming and *what the fuck is that noise?* Let's fucking focus here, okay?"

I shifted one hand to Mags's shoulder and blinked rapidly. Everything was in twilight, but I could make out lines and shades. When I had some vacation time, I'd do some at-home studying and figure out what had happened to me, what price the universe had extracted from me for fucking with it.

"She is *coming for me!*" the Negotiator shouted, grabbing me again. Mags hesitated, then reached over and plucked the writhing man up by his collar, holding him an inch or two off the floor. If I concentrated, I could make out his face. I squinted, then wished I hadn't. If I'd been sitting around wondering what complete despair looked like, this would have been a good answer.

The room was filled with voices and the intense sizzling noise that was like the fucking sound of insanity creeping up on us. I spun away from him.

"Everybody *shut UP!*" I shouted.

The voices died off. The dry rain got louder, as if in response.

I spun back and leaned in towards the Negotiator. I could see details now. His chin and neck were covered in blood. It looked black and slick on his face. His careful hair was a tousled mess, and his suit, for the first time, looked like it didn't fit him right.

"All right," I said. "Talk."

He nodded and raised his hands up between us. Strands of rope and tape still clung to them, and I made a note to ask if he'd really snapped his bonds through sheer terror.

"We," he said in a slow, shaking voice, as if he was containing his fear with extreme effort. He reached forward slightly as if to touch my face, then pulled back. "We must make a *deal,* Mr. Vonnegan, granting each other safe passage in return for understandings, concessions— anything. But we must do so *quickly.*"

"A deal," I said. "We make a deal giving each other safe fucking passage, and she can't hurt us." It was cons on cons on cons. Fucking cons all the way down.

"Yes!" he shouted, reaching out for me again so suddenly I staggered backwards. He took his hands back and held them up in a placating gesture. "Yes—yes, if the language is *precise,* if the arrangement is *carefully constructed.* But luckily I have experience with such contracts!" He smiled, and I was willing to go blind again. The black blood, the white teeth, the deep dark holes that were his eyes. He was triumphant. "We have been *punished,* Mr. Vonnegan!" he shouted. "But we have *learned!*"

The dry rain was almost too loud to shout over. "What about my people? What about their *safe passage?*"

He began to shake his head, his eyes going wide. "I—I cannot construct—there must be believable gain on both sides! What can they offer me, all of them? *I cannot make this work for so many! Please! She is* coming!"

I stared at him. He'd been Renar's *gasam* after Amir. When I'd met him at Abdagnale's, he'd already become the Negotiator. Whatever had happened between him and Renar, it had happened *quick.* He'd been a tool ever since. Kidnapped, no doubt, on a regular basis. Negotiating for his life over and over—I hadn't been the first fucking genius to come up with that idea. He'd ping-ponged from one horror to another, and then he'd hooked up with Elsa. Revenge. I supposed they couldn't come up with a way to make a deal to ruin Renar—or maybe they had, in a way. He'd thought he was free for a bit.

And now here he was. I assumed Renar would not be in a mood to consider his debt paid.

"Mags," I shouted. "Me and Mags. Safety fucking guaranteed or however you want to phrase it. Fallon!" I yelled. I needed someone who knew all this shit. "Fallon!"

"Why the *fuck* are you calling his name?" Claire demanded, leaning in close to shout directly into my ear. "When was the last time you saw that old man?"

I hesitated. I started to say *He was just here* and then wondered if he really had been. Mags hadn't been here. Now he was.

"Mr. *Vonnegan!*" the Negotiator shouted, his voice distant, buried under the sound of hail hitting a tin roof, fed directly into an overcharged amplifier. "I will phrase as needed. I accept your terms! You must hear and accept—"

I had brought Pitr back to life. I had brought Pitr back to life by abusing this man, and I wondered what else I might accomplish. "Jesus *fuck* me," I hissed. "Your *terms,* Mr. Harrows!"

Again I heard Billington say, *You sure?*

"I offer you information! I offer to answer any question you ask! I offer your safety guaranteed! Your *terms,* Mr. Vonnegan!"

"I offer to fucking *have this conversation!*"

He looked ready to weep. "My *safety,* Mr. Vonnegan!"

"Jesus—I offer your safety guaranteed, okay?"

Relief swept over his face, damp with perspiration. "I accept your terms!"

My vision clicked back into focus, bright and clear. I focused on movement just over Mags's shoulder, a narrow casement window that was open. I felt something go loose and wonky inside me.

It was an insect the size of a baby. Except so much worse.

47

"WE SHOULD DISCUSS A SUBJECT very foreign to both you and our oversize friend, Mr. Vonnegan. Intelligence. In the sense of a Summoned inhuman presence."

I tried to listen to Hiram over the growling of my stomach. Part of our arrangement as *gasam* and *urtuku* was that Hiram would feed me and let me sleep in his kitchen at night. So far there had been an endless supply of weak pale tea and no food. I'd been feeding Mageshkumar and myself from regular raids on the coffee cart and the lunch cart that traded off on the corner a few blocks away. I waited until the end of their shift, and when they were hooking their cart up to the car—a dilapidated old wood-paneled station wagon for the coffee guy, a surprisingly sleek new SUV for the lunch guy—I just walked by on the street side, reached in, and took whatever I could.

Mags was demonstrating a worrying tendency to be able to eat anything I gave him in one swallow and then declare he was still starving. I had the growing sense that Hiram had bequeathed Mags to me.

The really curious thing was that there was no food in the house. Tea, yes. Milk and sugar cubes. And nothing else. Hiram Bosch was a round man with a full, red face behind that white beard. He was so round that he wore a belt *and* suspenders. But there wasn't a bite to eat in the place and I had *looked*.

Being Hiram's apprentice was exhausting. Lessons came whenever Hiram was in the mood, without structure or planning. Sometimes he woke me up in the middle of the night when he made himself a cup of tea, and he would talk for an hour about shit I could not for the life of me apply in any practical way to the burning issues of *Jesus, I'm hungry* or *How do I cast fucking magic spells*. I'd decided to give it another week, and then I was going to find someone else. Hiram had told me the oath of *urtuku* bound me to him, but Hiram said a lot of shit.

"It will not surprise you to learn that there are alternate worlds, or universes. It will not surprise you that these alternate worlds can be very similar or dissimilar to our own. Some of the intelligences encountered are novel. And therefore useful. They can be imprisoned. They can be contacted, forced, and imprisoned into an Artifact or Fabrication and their energies and properties utilized in a focused, aware manner."

Artifact. Fabrication. I'd heard the old man use the words, but he hadn't bothered to explain them. I'd tried requesting those definitions, but that had only prompted an hour of roaring rage from him, redfaced as he lectured me on the proper behavior of *urtuku*: silent, servile, grateful. I'd weathered that storm easy; I'd been on my own long enough to be unimpressed by anger, especially when it came from round old men wearing both suspenders and a belt. But Mageshkumar, the biggest motherfucker I'd ever seen, had once been reduced to tears by the man. It had taken me fifteen minutes to coax Mags out of the bathroom where he'd fled, and he'd spent the rest of the day watching

Hiram with wide, fearful eyes. I'd decided not to piss off Hiram Bosch with Mageshkumar in the room ever again.

"There are many forms of intelligence you can master, imprison, and use. Today we will discuss one particular type: *gidim*. What is the meaning of this word, *gidim*?"

A pang of anxiety settled in my stomach. Hiram was insane. He had provided me with no reference materials and yet seemed to assume I could somehow actually learn this fucking vocabulary he kept referring to.

He waited a moment, then sighed. I tensed up. I'd been with Hiram for just two weeks, but I already knew this could go one of two ways: punishment or a lecture. He wasn't an imposing man physically—or he *was,* but not in a threatening way—but he knew hundreds of what he called *Cantrips,* tiny spells he hissed out so fast you couldn't hope to stop him, most of them designed to make you hurt a little or a lot.

"Literally, it means *sickness demon,* but it is commonly and poetically translated as *coming darkness.* The *gidim* are formed from sacrifices. They take on the physical form of that which is sacrificed to summon them. This makes them unusual in that they will form an organic body to live in, a physical, corporeal body. Most other intelligences you may Summon must be confined in artificial constructions designed at least partially for the purpose—your Artifacts, or your more modern Fabrications. The *gidim* create bodies from those sacrificed to Summon them. Some of our order view this as evidence that they are a more elegant or efficient manner of creation." He sighed, rubbing his belly. "Those who think so are fools. You need only see a *gidim* once to understand."

He looked up at me. Whether it was the expression of slight doubt and boredom on my face or the fact that I'd once again inexplicably failed to study the materials he had never supplied, I knew immediately that the old man was about to make me bleed.

"Come! A demonstration. A pint, no more." His eyes burned with a malevolent cheer, then shifted to the hulking form of Mageshkumar. "Pitr, perhaps you would like to be elsewhere. This may upset you."

I knew this was more concern for his property than for anything else. The big baby could do some damage when he got freaked out.

But Mageshkumar shook his head, frowning, his face becoming fierce and bloody. "I'm here to learn, too. Just like him."

He stabbed one gigantic finger at me. Mageshkumar had been camped out at Hiram's for months now, begging to be taken on as an apprentice. Hiram had refused. The big idiot thought we were in competition for the post, despite the fact that I'd been bonded to Hiram in a disturbing ceremony involving far more of my own blood than I would have liked.

Hiram sighed. "Very well. Mr. Vonnegan, prepare yourself."

He shuffled off into the dim, mysterious interior of his apartment. I hadn't been allowed anywhere aside from the bathroom and the kitchen. With a sigh, I rolled up my sleeve and studied the eight or nine healing scars already present, a sharp contrast to the milky white skin everywhere else. Somehow, despite my father, I'd never had a serious injury. No broken bones. No stitches. I was all original equipment—or I had been until I'd apprenticed myself to Hiram Bosch.

I wasn't used to cutting myself yet. It hurt like a motherfucker every time, and the sensation of my lifeblood running out of me still freaked me out. And I was tired all the time. Every second of every day, I could close my eyes and just fall asleep.

I pulled the simple razor blade I'd been using from my shirt pocket. It was clean and sharp. A thrill of horror went through me.

Hiram bustled back into the kitchen carrying a birdcage, in which a bright blue bird bounced and chirped, and a small wooden bowl. In the bowl wriggled a collection of slimy-looking earthworms.

"You may be tempted to think the *gidim* we produce here today is gruesome because of these chosen forms we will sacrifice," he said. My eyes flickered to the tiny blue bird, and a stab of panic hit me. "But I assure you: *Gidim* always assume the worst possible form based on the sacrifices. They are *malevolent*. Do not mistake this. Now: a pint, please."

I hesitated. "Do we . . . Do we have to kill the bird?"

He sighed. "Mr. Vonnegan," he said without looking up, busying himself with a long, curved blade he extracted from a velvet sheath, "this is old magic. Our roots, as it were. Violent and barbaric. You must *know* this, or you will fail. Magic is not power. It is not freedom. It is not faith or luck. Magic is *violence*. When you are comfortable with violence, when you are willing to inflict it on yourself and others, then you will be ready to master it." He nodded and opened the cage, thrusting a plump hand inside. "*Gidim* are the true face of magic, Mr. Vonnegan. Better you see it now than later."

Mageshkumar shifted in his chair and made what I would have sworn was a whimpering noise. I turned to stare at him. The big guy looked like he had already murdered several people. Now he was staring at the bird like he was going to burst into tears.

"Mr. Vonnegan?"

I looked back at my arm and held the blade over it. *Not too deep,* Hiram had taught me. *Deep enough, only.* Important not to sever any arteries, not to kill yourself by accident. Although the wounds healed right away. I hadn't gotten used to that yet, either.

I pushed the blade down and pulled it across my arm. For a second nothing seemed to happen. There was no blood, no pain. Then they both came. A searing line of pain and a thick gush of blood, spilling out of me onto the table.

Hiram began speaking and strangled the bird.

48.

"KIDS," I SAID IN A conversational tone, inaudible to everyone, "what we got here is an everyone-for-themselves sort of situation."

The wings were like thin diamonds, fluttering. The body was humanoid, two legs, a trunk, two arms. Cherubic hands. Covered in the coarse black hair of a fly. The head was triangular, sporting two shiny yellow eyes that glittered in the light, covering most of the skull. A long, thin tubelike proboscis extended a foot or two from the front of its head. There was no mouth.

The Negotiator was shouting at me, but I couldn't hear him. I was staring at the humanoid body and those tiny, perfect little hands—*baby's* hands, my brain kept telling me, reminding me cheerfully how, exactly, a *gidim* was created—bristling with a fly's coarse fur, opening and closing into tiny fists. *Gidim* took the form of the things sacrificed to create them. The tiny hands were the worst thing I'd ever seen in my life.

The proboscis was the second worst.

The *gidim's* tiny, perfect little feet suddenly curled over the edge of the windowsill and it launched itself into the air, streaking three or four feet into the loose crowd gathered in the room. One of my Bleeders, a chubby black guy whose suit had been tailored for a much larger man, spun at the last second, and I had a glimpse of his face as he registered complete and utter shock for the last full second of his life. Then the *gidim* landed on him and, with one savage jerk of its neck, sank the needlelike proboscis directly into his skull.

The *gidim's* body convulsed, as if it was pumping something into the Bleeder. The big man jittered and shook like a fish on the line, and then it whirled away, leaping to the nearest body, a middle-aged woman with long hair that was just a mass of split ends. For his part, the bug guy continued to jitter and shake, and then his head began to swell, to distort in agonizing jerks, like something was pounding at his skull from the inside.

A moment before I realized what was happening, two tiny, perfect hands, glistening, reached out of his distended mouth and began to force his jaw apart from the inside.

The Bleeder crashed to the floor. Something crashed against the door. The sound of the *gidim's* wings was now beyond loud; we had reached the point where the world had gone deaf, the collected noise of their buzzing wings pushing everyone's ears into the red zone. I tried, briefly, to imagine how many were outside, how many filled the neighborhood—or New York entirely, the fucking *world*—and then spun to grab hold of Pitr Mags's jacket and pull him close.

He was shouting. Everyone was shouting. Holding on to him, I turned and put my other hand on Claire, yanking her close. I thought of everyone else. I thought of Daryl, and Melanie, and all the stupid fucks whose names I'd never bothered to learn, the kids who had hitchhiked and bled and tramped here over the last few years, and then I pushed them out of my thoughts. They'd come to bleed for me. And I wouldn't be able to save them now, if there'd ever been a slim possibility that I might. I had to try to save who I could.

Claire shoved me away violently, spinning and searching for Daryl, who'd gotten lost in the panic and noise. For a split second I swallowed down anger and jealousy—I couldn't believe that even in the face of death she didn't want me. After all this time. After all we'd been through. I was fucking smarter than that dumb hick. I had fucking *followers*. And if I'd put her in a position to not only get killed but to be the last version of herself, her whole fucking existence burned out of the cosmos because of me, well, I fucking hadn't *meant* to.

Four *gidim* now spat around the room, three still shining from their recent birth throes. I didn't look down to see what was left of their incubators. I lunged for Claire, but she slipped between two bodies and was gone. Before I could think of what to do, someone took hold of me in a sweating panic and lifted me off the floor. I felt Mags's heart skip a beat, and then it was Mags lifting me off the floor and we were on the move. Mags tossed people aside like he was running for the goal. I could feel him shouting, the deep vibration of air through his lungs. I planted my feet and hauled against him, and he whirled, face lit up by dark red blood, eyes flashing. He continued to shout at me.

There was gas in the air, but it . . . tasted wrong, as if contact with the *gidim* had poisoned it. I tore my jacket off and fished my straight razor from my pocket. Stared down at the switchblade that came out instead. Pressed the button and slashed my arm, a little deeper and longer than necessary, blood spilling down my arm. I ran down the pieces, the tiny *mu* I would stitch together into a larger spell, and began reciting.

I felt the breeze of wings against my neck and dead-dropped to the floor. Kept spitting out Words, one *mu* after another, four syllables, two, three. Felt the universe reaching and sucking me dry, the giddy power of my life passing through me like I was a mere conduit—which we all were, I supposed, just borrowing our molecules and eventually giving them all back again. It was weird to not hear my voice as I cast—I felt disoriented, like I might be mispronouncing things without realizing it. When I finished, I looked up in time to see one of the *gidim* explode into wet pink gibs, splattering the people around it. There was a flare of gas in the air, awful and thin, but there. The *gidim* could be bled.

Shaking with the sudden weariness of sloppy spells, I pushed myself up and scanned the room. All the *gidim* had been turned into messy spots on the floor—six of them, alongside six corpses—but the casement window was still open, and as I looked, I saw two of those tiny, perfect little hands reaching in.

I took a deep breath. Clear the room, seal the room, turn the volume down. Then think about what to do.

Do? There is nothing to be done except die.

The voice was dry and silent, inside my head. My ears were full of the fluttering wings. I recognized it immediately, the dry, mocking tone, the dull headache that pulsed with each consonant. Renar. I thought for a moment, looking to come up with a devastating comeback.

Fuck you, I managed.

The room froze. Everyone, everything. Me. The two *gidim* slipping in through the window. The crowd of people caught midscrum, struggling against each other, still locked in panic, still freaked out. Blades were in the air, caught in the act of slashing down. I saw Claire and Daryl, hand in hand, frozen in the act of spinning towards the door. Pitr right at my elbow, snarling at something, a hand on his shoulder, his jacket whipped open as if he'd been in the act of whirling around.

The door to the room opened, and there was a faint tremor in the floorboards, like the beginnings of a distant earthquake. Alarm shot through me; I had felt this before. When the details of the room seemed to become slippery, like the things I was looking at might not actually be the things I was looking at, I fought back an urge to turn and run, blind. Just run. But I was trapped, sucked into the invisible amber of Mika Renar's spell.

Did you believe yourself to be special? she breathed into my mind. *Did you imagine you had been chosen? Chosen to defeat* me?

She stepped into the room. Her Glamour. Floating that centimeter off the ground, the second time she'd been in this back room. My blood vessels constricted, and a buzzing lust seeped into my head as I smelled her, the imaginary smell of her, magic, warm cherries and an autumn breeze. She was wearing the same dress, bright red, her skin pale like ice cream, her face perfection. Again I wondered how accurate it was. If Mika Renar had been this beautiful in real life eighty years ago, I didn't understand how she hadn't conquered the planet and killed everyone, showing Oppenheimer and the rest of the Manhattan Project geeks how it was done.

The tremor under my feet grew more pronounced. The room seemed to be shaking, or it was just my vision.

You have been fooled. You have been distracted. I am here to claim my revenge.

She glided towards me. As she encountered obstacles, she passed through them, dissolving like a hologram and then re-forming. She was crisp and sharp even as the rest of the room was getting dim, indistinct. She grew larger as she approached, and a faint sound of tinkling bells followed her. She had been shaping and layering this Glamour for decades. She'd had the time and the blood, and she'd been tweaking it for *decades,* and now it wasn't just a Glamour. It was *her* more her than her own shriveled body was.

Behind her, trailing a few feet, the wheelchair, and the brittle body, motionless except for the faint movement of her gray lips as she whispered the Words. The head tilted to one side. Always together, the Glamour and its creator.

I am here to witness my triumph.

Everything seemed to stretch except her. The room, the people, they went indistinct, as if they'd never really been there, like they were the half-remembered shadows of something I'd imagined.

It took some effort, but we have discovered the correct combinations. The kurre-nikas. *You must experiment. The moment must be personal, personally experienced. You alter one, but the time line does not arrange as you desired. You try again. Eventually, you discover the settings, the order of events. You* have given us enough time to perform our research and experiments.

With a noise almost like a sigh, soft and nearly subaudible, most of the people in the room just faded away. Renar grew even brighter, more distinct and sharp. She seemed to fill my vision entirely, stretching and shifting until she was all I could see.

Reality changes. And again you persist.

Her words in my head started to hurt. Each word stabbed into me.

This is something you will regret.

I finally unhinged my own mind enough to think back, *I already do, lady.*

She blinked out of existence. So did just about everyone else. Everything snapped back into normal motion, and I staggered backward, found nothing to stop me, and slipped and fell on my ass. A cloud of dust went up around me, as if something had exploded.

Darkness. Around me, coughs and exclamations. Not the loud, busy noise of two dozen men and women but the echoed noise of three people. A bit of gas in the air, and then a glowing white ball of light bloomed in the center of the room. Pitr Mags loomed ahead of me, spinning in place and muttering *Fuck?* like a question over and over.

The Negotiator. On his hands and knees. Breathing hard, staring down at the floor.

Pitr Mags spied me and launched himself at me. As I got onto my elbows, he took hold of one arm and pulled me up so forcefully, a bolt of red pain shot up my arm.

"Lem!" he shouted as my feet left the floor and then landed again.

I held up a hand and turned to look around. Everyone was gone. The Asshole Army, all of them gone. The room looked weathered. Cobwebs had sprung up in the corners like fields of mold. The window was missing, torn out of the wall, and a diminishing spray of rot and water damage spread from the opening. Parts of the walls were charred. I looked up. Half the ceiling was missing, the innards of the second floor yawning above us.

I looked back down. The room was full of skeletons.

They were dressed, the clothes still in good shape. The skeletons were yellowed and greasy-looking, like bones recently sucked clean by hungry mouths. They weren't my people. There were twelve, maybe fifteen of them, dressed by turns in suits and jeans, dresses and sweatpants. Jewelry still on their hands. Glasses perched on the bones of their face.

The room had a dry, funeral smell to it.

"She has succeeded," the Negotiator whispered. "She has used the *kurre-nikas* and adjusted the world."

I jerked free from Mags's grip and ran. I burst into the old main room of the bar. Kicking up immense clouds of gray-white dust, I stumbled and spun as I ran, staring at the collection of skeletons arranged around the place like someone had dressed and posed them, two dozen, looking like they'd been sitting around having a few drinks before being flash-flayed. Glasses and plates and silverware still sat on the tables.

I stumbled through the front door and out into the evening. It was raining. It was almost perfectly dark. I couldn't see anything. Cursing, I fumbled for my straight razor, flicked it open with a jerk of my wrist, and bled for three Words and a second ball of white light, the first *mu* anyone gets taught.

It was a dead city.

I made it out into the middle of the street, between two cars that had crashed into each other. Each was filled with more of the eerie, posed skeletons. The rain poured into the open windows, inches deep on the cars' floors. I looked up the street and there was an endless line of old, rusting cars, each filled with its own voting population of dead people. Of *skeletons,* every one slimy and relatively recent and picked clean by the hungry universe. The rain sizzled around me. There was no other noise behind it. Nothing.

Two years ago, I thought. She'd done it two years ago. Killed Claire, run her Ritual. Murdered the world entire. She'd gone back and changed one moment and ensured that nothing else I remembered doing had ever happened.

And I understood.

The world was broken.

I had broken it.

IV.
FABRICATOR

49.

THERE WAS BOOZE IN THE bottles. Two years wasn't so long, and anything with a decent cork had stayed pretty fresh. Mags and I sat in the back room, each with a bottle, trying to get as drunk as possible. The Negotiator stood apart with his arms wrapped around his thin frame, his hair in his face, his suit stained and torn. I avoided looking at him, but I knew he was there. We were bound together. We had given each other safe passage to this new future. We had saved each other's lives.

Claire, I reminded myself, was dead in this world. At first I felt like her just winking out of existence wasn't anything like the dreams I'd been having of her—on fire, burning—and then I remembered that she had died burning. Suffering. Screaming. Strapped in to Renar's Fabrication, because I hadn't saved her.

For a moment, I was filled with lead, everything too heavy to move, even my lungs. Everything had been for nothing. Everything. I could have done nothing for the past few years and it wouldn't have made any difference. I wanted to start drinking and simply not stop, just wait until I died, because I should have, a long time ago. It would have made things a lot easier, and it would have saved everyone a lot of fucking trouble. Maybe even improved things. And the world would have ended anyway, but at least I wouldn't have known a fucking thing about it.

I closed my eyes tightly, fighting to maintain control, and imagined Claire as I'd last seen her, running with Daryl, hair whipping around, her hand in his. Desperate, as always, to survive. Something she'd been good at until she met Mika Renar. And me. So far, I thought, I'd killed every woman I'd known in my adult life with the exception of my mother. Who had saved me the trouble herself.

And now it was too late to sit and study *that* thought.

I opened my eyes again and took a deep breath. Because it was habit, another in a long series of deep breaths, none of which had mattered in any way. None of us looked at the remnants of the people. In this world, Renar had successfully cast the *Biludha-tah-namus*, and in a few moments of what I could only imagine as complete and utter terror, almost every single living thing in the world had been killed, their blood absorbed and regurgitated as immortality for Renar's cadre of conspirators. I hoped it had been sudden enough. I doubted it had. That wasn't Renar's style.

I saw her again, huge, encompassing, mocking me. She'd assumed I'd die along with everyone else, but the Negotiator's *geas* had stepped in and saved me. We had, after all, made a deal.

Mags was stealing glances at both of us, trying to match the mood but not entirely sure what the mood *was*. Mags had at least learned to keep his mouth shut when he wasn't sure what the mood was.

The Negotiator was rocking himself slightly. I had a feeling he'd thought himself miserable *before* this.

The silence was intimidating. I didn't want to make any noise. The sun had risen, the light turning a greenish gray and then sweetening until we were in full-blown morning, the rain gone and the air fresh. And there was no noise. No birds. No shouts. No car horns or flybys or phones ringing. The remnants of Rue's Morgue were cold and damp, stuffed with the skeletal remains of people I'd once known—I thought back two years to the gang who had hung out here. Neutral territory. We came in to announce our big scores, to plot, to plan.

I stood up. Half a bottle of Old Grand-Dad and I felt nothing. Mags looked up, tracking me with his eyes, but I didn't walk towards him. I pushed my free hand into my pocket—and gasped as a spike of buzzing electricity shot up into my chest. The Token I'd taken from the Negotiator. Somehow, in this new time line, I'd still managed to steal it. Fallon had said that the universe adjusted when the *kurre-nikas* was used. It had found letting me keep the Token was easier than routing around that event.

I walked over to Harrows. Stood in front of him, studying him. I tried to remember seeing him for the first time, how powerful and mysterious he'd seemed. Now he was just another broken servant. He'd tried to wriggle out from under her, set up his tent with someone else, and it hadn't gone well for him.

"What did you do, anyway?"

He oriented on me as if coming back from a very long trip. "What?"

"To earn a punishment from Renar. What did you do?"

He smiled and looked over my shoulder. His eyes were shining with something I was terrified would turn into tears. "I refused to . . . perform a sacrifice."

"You wouldn't bleed someone?" For the first time in a while, I pictured the girl I'd refused to cut: shivering, her sneakers with all the marker, her snotty nose. Hiram telling me she would be compensated. I'd thought of her so often. She'd been part of my life every day. And I couldn't remember the last time I'd thought of her, that unnamed girl I'd refused to bleed. "That's it?"

He grimaced. "Not just *someone*, Mr. Vonnegan." He looked past me, staring into nothing. "Not just . . . Mika needed servants, you see. She had forgotten she would be marooned in this future with no one. But she did not wish to use up blood. She was afraid to reduce the amount of blood in the world too greatly, lest her Ritual fail. So she got creative. And she instructed me to create the first few. She said they were so *small*, their contribution would be so *small* . . ." He swallowed and looked back at me. "And I refused."

A shot of horror lanced through my chest. "The *gidim*," I said, my voice low.

He nodded, and I saw in his face something bottomless. "I have seen much and been punished for it, Mr. Vonnegan. Oh, how I have been *punished*." Then he looked over my shoulder again. "Your Mr. Fallon is here."

I froze. Fallon. I didn't know how it was possible that I remembered who knew how many alternate time lines simultaneously. Fallon had been with me in this room and then he hadn't. Having him back didn't fill me up with hope and cheer.

I turned myself around slowly. He looked good. He looked fantastic. Under an immense fur coat, he was still wearing the cream-colored suit I'd last seen him in. He wore black leather gloves and looked young, well preserved, like the last few years of living in a dead world had been good to him.

I wondered if it was my absence from his life these last few years that had been a tonic for him. For one second I felt the gulf of time between us—Ev Fallon hadn't been in this room with me just hours ago, hadn't accompanied me to Alaska, to Shanghai. He'd been somewhere else, being someone else. And I found I could tell. I could see it in his face.

"Mr. Vonnegan," he said crisply. "Mr. Mageshkumar." He looked past me. "Mr. Harrows. We have never met."

"Have we not?"

I heard Billington's voice, a ghost of a memory: *You sure?*

Fallon shook his head. "No, we have not." He returned his gaze to me. "Mr. Vonnegan, I am surprised to find you here. But having found you, I am glad. I would have spared you if it were in my power to do so. I am glad you were spared in the event."

I felt the old, familiar buzzing sense of trouble coming. A fight. A challenge.

So I stepped forward and held up the bottle. "Can I buy you a drink?"

He glanced around the room and nodded. Mags was staring up at him like he was seeing a ghost.

Up close, Fallon looked even better. Clean. Groomed. He pulled his gloves off and accepted the bottle from me. Sniffed it with an arched eyebrow and took a sip. Nothing adventurous or enthusiastic. Just polite.

I waited him out. I wanted to hear what he'd been up to. What he remembered. He hadn't been there at the end, and I didn't know what that meant, how that affected his . . . his what? Time line? Existence? Jesus, my head was pounding. I'd spent my life giving a clinic on how to fuck up in slow motion. I had slow-motion-fuckup whiplash.

"You should not stay here," he said, looking around. "It is depressing."

I nodded, cocking my head. "Why are you here, Ev?"

I felt a pinprick of gas in the air, and my skin crawled. Mags, I figured. Giving voice to the weird anxiety I felt. Fallon hesitated, glancing upward, sensing it as well. He seemed amused. I thought of the Token in my pocket. Wondered if he remembered me taking it, if he imagined I still had it. My glancing touch had told me that whatever else had happened in this new future, the reservoir of blood still existed, and my Token still connected to it. I wondered if I would survive were I to try and cast from it.

"I am to give you a message."

An awful prickling made its way up my spine. I heard dimly, in a memory of something that hadn't actually happened, the Little General saying, *Del Traje Blanco informed us of their guilt.* The Man in the White Suit.

"From who?"

He shrugged, looking away suddenly, as if finding one of the skeletons unexpectedly fascinating. "From Mika, Lemuel."

Mika. I pushed my hand into my pocket and touched the Token. Instantly, my arm went numb, the buzzing power bridged through that tiny humanoid slamming into it. Nothing else happened. Fallon showed no sign of sensing it. Feeling it, I questioned whether I had the skill to control it, to bring through just what I needed. I wished Hiram were alive to explain things to me. In the most painful, awful way possible, but still.

I stared at Fallon's suit. A light cream, almost white. Certainly it would be considered white against a dark canopy of jungle. "You," I said, my voice thick with failure and anger. "It was you in Colombia. You overseeing the . . . harvesting."

He nodded. "Yes."

"How long—?"

"Almost immediately after her first failure," he said simply. "I was not part of the original group. I was shocked when you came to me, revealed her plans to me. I'll admit I felt foolish. For being deceived . . . and for being left out. So, when we parted company, I went to make amends."

I remembered Fallon on Mad Day, saying, *I have not been particularly smart or heroic today. I thought perhaps I could at least still be useful?* And I'd thought he was talking to *me*.

"And here you are," I croaked.

"And here I am. As are you!"

"Immortal."

He nodded gravely. "And free from the burdens of staying that way. Although I don't share Mika's rather *epic* distaste for such work, I will admit the freedom is exhilarating. But not for you." He smiled slightly. "I *am* glad to see you, Lemuel. As I said, I would have spared you, had it been in my power. It was not, yet you have been spared. And I am glad for that."

Cons, all the way down.

There was a roar, and a flood of gas in the air, hot and vibrant. You never knew how much Pitr understood. Sometimes he was like a child, or perhaps a really smart bear, blinking in confusion and perpetually assuming you were making fun of him in some subtle way. Other times he was a fucking genius. I spun and he was standing there, five feet away, his hands on fire. It was Hiram's old fireball spell, and I spent a second marveling that he'd memorized it all those years ago, having heard it once, and in a reality that had no longer ever existed.

"Mr. Mageshkumar," Fallon said with a heavy sigh, "you will hurt yourself."

He whispered five quick syllables, two of which, I was pretty sure, were hokum. Pitr continued to stand there. His hands continued to be on fire. A tendril of flame caught on to his jacket sleeve and licked it.

My arm buzzed with the energy of thousands, tens of thousands, stolen and trapped.

"Mika does not know you, Lemuel," Fallon said, eyes on Pitr, "in this reality. The universe has been reset, and in this time line your paths never crossed. She will not remember you, and she will not molest you. She did not spend enough time with you, as I had—yes, I recall our time that never was. That universe exists, separate from us. Split off. But Mika is unconnected to it." He looked back at me. Pitr's arm was completely on fire. "And she will not *hear* of you. For that, you can thank me. Most of her comrades, or fellow *conspirators,* as you would know them, have not been so lucky."

My arm buzzed, but I couldn't think of a single spell. I'd thought I was doing something. Billington, with all her hunting and her Drum Trials. We'd just wasted our time, misdirected.

"Live out your life," Fallon said. "You are no longer our concern." He glanced at Pitr. "Better put him out before he burns to death."

He turned to go. He would be Fallon, forever. He would be eternal, with an ocean of stored blood hidden away somewhere. Plenty to cast from.

"You'll end up destroying each other," I said, the words bubbling up from somewhere deep and bitter inside me. I'd saved myself. I'd saved Pitr. I'd let everyone else die. Hiram was dead. Claire and Daryl. Mel. *Everyone.* "You know that. Whatever peace you have now between you, it's going to go to hell."

He didn't stop walking. "Of course."

My hand was clasped around the Token so tightly it hurt. Something fast. Dirty and painful. Something that would incapacitate him, shut him up. Then what? I couldn't go up against all of those *enustari.* Even with the Token, it was me and Pitr, who, even if we assumed he had a few other useful spells finally memorized, was unreliable at best. And the Negotiator. Who was a strong mage, I knew, but not *enustari. Saganustari,* probably. The sort who ended up a servant, who sold his life for knowledge and then got screwed.

The three of us up against Renar, Fallon, who knew who else. Useless. And even if we did manage to—what, I didn't know. Could they *be* killed? They were immortal, but maybe only from fate. Maybe if someone slit their throats the old-fashioned way, it would work. And if it did, then what?

I thought of Claire. In this reality, she *had* died at Renar's mansion. In this reality, she *had* been burned up, the final link in the chain reaction. The Skinny Fuck had grabbed her up, dragged her there, and fed her into the machine. I could picture it perfectly—I'd *been* there, in that old, destroyed reality. I thought of a hundred other people I'd failed, fucked over, misled, conned. They would all be just as dead.

I watched Fallon leave.

Both of Pitr's arms were on fire. Still clutching the Token, I whispered two Words. With a sudden breeze confined to the inch of airspace surrounding him, the flames guttered out and he animated, bringing his smoking fists up, growling. Then he froze again, his face collapsing into panic and confusion.

I turned to the Negotiator. "We have an arrangement," I said.

He oriented on me slowly, as if his thoughts had been distant and muddled. He blinked. "Yes. Of course."

I nodded. "You owe me information. Tell me something useful."

50.

WE COULD HEAR OUR FOOTSTEPS echoing off the cars, the canyon walls of skyscrapers. Skeletons in the cars, skeletons littering the street. A huge number of skeletons, all still dressed, lying one on top of the other. A crowd in the street, thousands upon thousands, killed instantly and simultaneously. We had to pick our way carefully, trying not to trip over them or crush their delicate skulls under our shoes.

I paused to squint up through the dazzling sunshine up at the building, endlessly tall, slender. It looked perfect, like two years of neglect and weather hadn't yet had any lasting effect. As if there might still be a chance to forestall its eventual destruction. If we could bring everyone back. If we could undo what had been done.

"You sure she's here?"

The Negotiator answered immediately. "I'm certain. If Elsa's alive, she's here. She's been here for sixty years."

I looked around Shanghai, dead, all the Chinese on the neon signs dark and forgotten. "In that reality," I said sourly.

He didn't say anything. I started picking my way across the street again.

"Mr. Vonnegan."

I glanced over at Harrows. Still tall and thin and icy, but his suit had been repaired with a roll of duct tape, and he had grown a scum of beard. It was the first time, aside from the moments when I'd been literally beating him with my fists, he didn't appear to be perfectly coiffed. He jerked his head back across the street. I followed his chin and there was Pitr, huge, hair down past his ears, staring in horror at the yellowed skeletons littering the street. He kept shifting his weight from one foot to another.

"Jesus fucking Christ," I said. The world had fucking ended and I was standing in a field of fucking *skeletons* and it was *still* comedy. "One step at a time, Magsie. Take it slow."

He nodded, his eyes glued to the bones, and took one slow, careful step forward. There was an audible crunching sound, and he froze, arms out for balance, like some huge bird.

"Ah, shit," I muttered. "They're already fucking *dead,* Magsie!"

He nodded, staring down in horror. "I know, Lem. I just wouldn't want someone walking on me after I was dead. You know?"

I sighed. "Climb the cars, Pitr," I said. "Stepping-stones."

He looked around at the cars that sat in the middle of the street and nodded, then kept nodding. He judged the distance to the nearest one, a black BMW with four long-dead occupants, gritty with dust, all four tires flat. He leaped for it, coat fluttering out behind him, and landed on the back bumper with a perfect stick landing, arms slapping down on the roof and grabbing hold of the bike rack perched up there.

As Pitr leaped from car to car, landing each time with a thunderous crash that was batted back and forth by the concrete and glass, the Negotiator ambled over, hands in his pockets, and stood next to me. We watched Pitr make his painful way across the street.

"This is pointless, of course," the Negotiator said, sounding cheerful. For a second I thought he wanted a response, but then he went on, talking to himself. "But what can you do? You remain. You must continue in motion. You have to do *something*. So why not this? Something to do. Doomed. But if you admit that, you might as well just lie down, wait to be found by *her*."

"You're a fucking pleasure to be with," I said, watching as Pitr stood on the roof of a rusting SUV, dismayed. There was about six or seven feet between him and the relatively clear sidewalk. He couldn't make any jump that didn't result in crunching bones. "Climb down, pick your spots," I called out. "Come on—you want to be out here when the sun goes down?"

That got him. He looked up sharply, the horror of that thought seeping in. Total darkness, surrounded by the skeletal remains of the whole fucking world, and every time he twitched in his sleep—and Pitr did nothing *but* twitch when he was asleep, pawing at the air and muttering—he would crush someone beneath him.

"I should have died a long time ago," the Negotiator said, and I realized he was responding to me. "In a more just world, I would have."

"You could have died back there."

He shook his head. "Not that way. Not her. Never *her*. I have dreamed of my own death. Imagined it. I would like it to be quick, and painless, and perhaps peaceful, looking out on something beautiful. A moment of quiet, just in case you carry with you your last thoughts. But she would never allow that. Never *her*."

I pictured her, huge and all-encompassing, beautiful, terrible. I thought I understood.

Pitr was putting serious, sweat-inducing effort into every step. It was like watching a bear play a game of Twister. I was seized with a fierce affection for him. I had squandered an advantage to bring him back. And yet I knew I would always make that same decision, every time. The universe could be reset over and over again, and I would always use every bit of my strength and every trick up my sleeve to bring him back. Because I couldn't stand to think of Pitr in a dark place, in the ground, alone.

When he made the final leap for the sidewalk and landed on a clear patch of concrete, he turned to beam at me, triumphant, a perfect organism.

In the lobby, there wasn't a single corpse. It was stuffy and smelled like rot and mold. The humidity was intense, and I figured somewhere there was a persistent water leak. Something that had been going on for years.

"What floor?" I asked.

"The top."

Of course. We walked over to the stairs and pulled the heavy metal door open. The dark was nearly perfect, the steps disappearing into gloom just a few feet in. The smell was worse.

"Lem—"

I held up a hand to Pitr. "Give me some gas, Magsie."

I hadn't reminded the Negotiator about the Token I'd taken from him. I didn't know if he remembered it, and if I couldn't articulate why I thought it mattered, instinct told me to hold on to every advantage I had. He knew I hadn't just teleported us to Shanghai by pricking my finger, but that didn't mean I was just going to make it obvious for him.

Looking up at the ceiling of the lobby, I thought I could piece together something to put us on the top floor, but the specifics made me nervous. I'd never cast anything like that without being able to see where I was going. The Words were easy enough, but the details, I'd never been good with the details. I'd come to realize how much I didn't know, and that was worse than anything, the sudden feeling of having nothing beneath your feet.

I felt Pitr's blood in the air, strong and tempting. We'd both cut ourselves so often it was easy.

I closed my eyes and felt my way through it. The Rule of Perception: Reality was what you believed to be true. I could let the Negotiator handle it, but I hadn't allowed him to cast and wasn't ready to take that chance. I reminded myself that I'd cast a teleportation spell just a few hours ago. But that had been different. The spatial dynamics of steering us to the airport off the East China Sea hadn't been so fucking complicated with all that open space. I'd been flush with success for a moment, then froze up: The thought of teleporting through the dense city scared the shit out of me. We'd all end up embedded in concrete, impaled on streetlights. As with everything in fucking magic, the huge and amazing was easier than the small and simple. It had always been that way.

Closer in, I felt more confidence. Wishing for a flask of something to settle my nerves, I pushed my hand into my pocket and touched the Token, gas from another reality coursing up my arm and making me giddy. I strung together six syllables, half-Words molded together, forming new ones. I felt my gravity shift, and when I opened my eyes we were back in the apartment. The floor-to-ceiling windows looked out on the skyline of Shanghai, now lit up by the blood-orange sun and gleaming back at us, and if you squinted, it was like nothing had happened. It was a beautiful sight.

The apartment was trashed. It stank worse than anything else in the building. It stank like garbage and body odor and stale blood, used gas. And something worse, something primitive and rotten. The furniture had been broken up and the floors gouged and shattered, like a battle had been fought.

We found her in the bedroom. She was different.

Instead of the fresh twelve-year-old body I'd met her in, she was in her late teens. A pale, red-haired girl in a dirty, shapeless dress. A dirty, shapeless girl. She lay on the floor in a crumpled heap, breathing in a ragged, phlegmy rhythm. There were bottles of pills everywhere, empties, fulls, some marked with neat printed prescription labels, others mysterious and naked. There were bottles and glasses and plastic bowls everywhere. Some of the bowls appeared to be filled with her shit and piss.

She was covered in the old familiar scars, most of them relatively new. *Enustari*, I thought, *with no one to bleed.*

"She passed out yesterday," someone said, a voice so simultaneously familiar and foreign that I froze and stared at a spot directly across from me, where a half-closed door led to the bathroom. "I have not tried to revive her too hard."

Pitr made a strangled noise.

I turned slowly, heart pounding. She was seated in a plush chair that had once been part of a stately seating area by the windows. She looked older than I remembered, but her long red hair was still woven into a complex braid. She was wearing the remnants of a very nice man's suit, charcoal gray with wide white pin stripes hugging her figure.

"Mr. Vonnegan," Melanie Billington said without any trace of a smile. "I assume this is all your fucking fault."

51.

I STARED AT MY OLD lieutenant as she stood up and glided over to us. She moved exactly the way I remembered, surprisingly graceful for a woman without any grace. When she came near, she stared at me in a disconcerting way. She strode warmly up to Pitr, who leaned in and wrapped his immense arms around her, lifting her off the floor and then dropping her with a whoop.

"Yes!" Billington said breathlessly, taking one calculated step back. "It is good to see you as well, Pitr."

I stepped around in front of her and leaned down slightly to stare. "You remember?" I said. Then felt stupid for having spoken.

"Remember? What, the fucking universe being folded up and *replaced*?" She huffed, grinning. "*Yes*. And found myself in fucking *Alabama,* which I had fucking left *twenty years prior,* as far as I can remember, yeah?" She shivered. "I don't know what *this* version of me did, but she fucked *that* part up."

I had no idea how far back the adjustment had been. Renar had used the *kurre-nikas* to change one moment, but which moment? How far back? How much of what I remembered—now muddied by who knew how many layered realities we'd cycled through—was still accurate? How much was basically my imagination now? Fallon had said that Renar *didn't* remember. But we did. Maybe because we wanted to. Because we needed to. Maybe that was part of the deal we'd negotiated.

I realized I didn't know what, in this new reality, I'd been up to for the last two years. I didn't know why we *remembered* lives that hadn't, technically, happened. Maybe once you became aware of the shift, you could hold on to yourself. I thought of Claire, the way magic bent around her, deflected. It had made spells unpredictable back before the *Biludha-tah-namus.* Then, after she'd come right to the edge of being absorbed into that spell, we'd pulled her card and she'd become this black hole of magical energy. In those last seconds of the reality I remembered, she'd been right there, bending and absorbing and

And now she was dead. A *Terminus,* Fallon had said. She was as dead as dead got. I swallowed something thick and yellow that was suddenly in my throat. Again, I thought I should have tried to actually learn something. Years and years, I thought, wasted.

Billington was chewing her lip, studying me. "So I spent about a year wandering, trying to figure out what the fuck to do, and I saw exactly zero other living things. Zero. And then *she* showed up one fucking day in the middle of the street and told me she'd been scouring what was left of the fucking world for anyone with the ability to cast, and she'd found me. Told me to come with her, and fuck all if I had any better ideas. She was the only other soul I'd seen." Billington looked down at the prone figure, thick white drool pooling on the carpet. "She knew what was comin', she said. Started work on a plan, but she's . . . fucked-up."

Hope swelled up inside me at the words *a plan*. Elsa was *enustari*. She'd told Ev Fallon to go fuck himself and he'd seemed afraid of her. If Elsa had a plan, maybe the arrival of a few more arms to bleed would make the difference. I thought it was fucking perfect fate for me to end my days as a Bleeder.

Then I thought of Claire again, and the black smoke of despair settled over me again.

"But fuck, she is unreliable," Billington said, in the tone of someone giving a performance review at a job. "Amoral. Insane? Yeah, I think so. But skilled, sure enough. And I think she was the only mage of rank who opposed Renar at the end." She shrugged. "I am here to help, as I can. And to keep her alive, as I can."

I stared down at the girl. She breathed heavily, as if an invisible weight had settled on her. She was sweating, and her skin had a familiar green, rubbery look. Based on all the Tricksters I'd known in my time—the whole circus—I had an eye for it. I gave her a year, maybe two.

"I met her," I said, looking down at her. "In a different body."

"She told me that was an unfortunate habit of hers."

I looked up. "An *unfortunate habit*? The original owner of this fucking body is *where*, exactly?"

"Fuck, what does it *matter*, as we can now only cast what we can fund ourselves. Transference is an *expensive* spell." She glanced in the direction of the Negotiator and then back at me. "Why is *he* here?"

I looked over at Harrows. He had gotten thinner, I thought, if that was possible. Skeletal. His suit had yellowed, the clumsy repairs somehow worse than the tears and scuffs. His red shoes had faded to an awful, uneven pink. He still stood with the unexpected elegance of the tall, one hand thrust into his trouser pocket, a look of blank misery on his angular, almost alabaster face.

"He's—he was—working with her."

There was a beat. Melanie said nothing. The Negotiator sighed. "Another reality. I don't know what I am, *here*. Now."

Melanie didn't seem convinced. I remembered her as the *idimustari* who had spent years hunting down mages much more powerful than she was and punishing them.

"So what do we do?" I asked. I was eager, I realized, to just let Melanie run the show. I'd spent two years fucking up being The One. I didn't want it anymore. "What's the fucking plan? What's she been *doing* here?"

She nodded, eyes dancing around the room. "Come with me."

THE TRIP DOWN TO the parking garage took twenty minutes, skipping down the stairs following Melanie's flickering, electric-blue light, a ball of it crackling silently above her shoulder. Was she better with the Words than I remembered? It had seemed like the spell was tighter than her usual. Better planned. More effective. Mags had gotten better, too, studying with Fallon. As if their repeated reinventions had somehow improved them both.

The stairwells were hot and damp, and I was sweating pretty freely by the time we were halfway down. We could have cast something, of course, but Melanie pointed out that we were on our own for gas and couldn't be wasting any of it on anything unnecessary, and I was still reluctant to reveal the Token in my pocket. How this reality had conspired to let me retain possession of it, I didn't know. But I suspected the Negotiator's continued presence had something to do with it.

On the landing between the twentieth and nineteenth floors, there was a single human skeleton and the skeleton of a medium-sized dog. A blanket had been spread on the floor, and a collection of pathetic possessions, including a metal food bowl for the animal. The person had been sitting on the landing with their back to the wall, the dog in their lap, when Renar had cast the *Biludha-tah-namus* and made a select few immortal.

I looked away as we all gave the bodies a wide berth. An overwhelming black depression settled on my shoulders and pushed.

We went down past the first floor, deep into the bowels of the building where it only got hotter and darker, and then Billington struggled with the rusted metal door for a moment, humming out curses and breathing loudly. When she finally got the door pried open, there was a moment of relief as cooler air flooded into the space. As we moved into the parking level underground, Billington cleared her throat and spoke two more Words, goosing it with a bit of extra gas squeezed out of the wound on her palm, and the flickering blue orb of light expanded and floated upwards, giving us a view of the whole space.

It was a parking garage, all right, but the cars had been moved somewhere—or else the owners had decided to take their cars out for a ride right before the *tah-namus*. In place of the cars, someone had built something.

It was a mass of PVC piping, dirty white and clamped together to form big, thick bundles, then clamped on to the ceiling and running down the columns. When the pipes reached the floor, black cables emerged, zip-tied together and snaking along the concrete floor in two directions: back towards us, where they came together in one monumental gathering of cables that swelled to about six feet high and then narrowed down bit by bit into a single rubbery cable that terminated inside a featureless black box attached to the headrest of what looked like an old dentist's chair, complete with straps on the armrests. The cables then snaked away from us, spreading out to the sides of the garage like a spiderweb and then turning in and diving down into the huge, deep crater in the floor that looked like the result of a bomb detonation.

There was no sound. No movement.

"What is it?" Pitr asked in a small, shy voice.

"This," Melanie said in a small, scared voice, "is the *kurre-nikas*."

52.

"SHE BUILT IT," MELANIE SAID, rolling up her sleeves. We'd walked back up one step at a time and had arrived in the apartment sweating and red-faced. "She's the best Fabricator I have ever known. Admittedly, she is one of *two* Fabricators I have known. But of those two, she's the best. The bowl, Pitr, please."

She built it. I remembered my one meeting with Elsa, back in a different time line. *I am merely trying to even up the playing field,* she'd said. And why not? If you knew how to build a Fabrication that could alter one moment, why not fight fire with fire? Why not try to play the same dirty trick? Except she'd run out of time. Out of time in a lot of different ways, I thought, thinking about the pill bottles and the way she'd been drinking when I'd met her. The body she was in looked to be mid-twenties. That was a lot of wear and tear with someone like Elsa burning you on both ends.

"Pitr, bring that bowl," she commanded.

Pitr was Johnny-on-the-spot with a metal bowl, still beaming to have met an old friend and found her alive. Melanie had rolled Elsa over onto her back, and now she lowered herself into a kneeling position. "Petey, a bit of blood, okay?"

I tensed, but Pitr didn't glance at me or hesitate. The feeling of doom pressed down harder. He was used to it. To being bled. I had done that. I'd trained my best friend like that.

"She began working on it as soon as she understood what Renar was working on. She stopped sleeping, she said, trying to finish on time." Melanie paused, letting her hands fall on her thighs as she rocked back on her ankles briefly. "She was not, perhaps, careful in how she acquired resources for the project."

I thought: *Translation, she bled everyone she could knock unconscious, probably to death.* I'd never seen a more complex Fabrication. Every cable, Melanie had explained, had been meticulously inscribed with runes in specific order, then wrapped and tied together, then snaked through the space in a precise pattern that involved the sort of math I'd fallen asleep listening to in school. Even the murder machine that Ev Fallon had built for Renar looked small in comparison.

"But the *tah-namus* was enacted too soon. She was caught off guard. She has tried to continue work, but she is . . . not in the best of health." For a moment, we all stared down at the fleshy, red-haired girl. A rash, deep red and angry-looking, had spread from her neck down into the shadowed recesses of her housedress.

"We know what it is, Melanie," I said. I glanced at Pitr, who was staring at Elsa and humming to himself. "*I* know what it is. As far as I know, I've been . . . adjusted . . . at least twice by it."

She laughed. "Fuuuuuck you, Mr. Fancy-pants Vonnegan. You haven't been here for months being lectured by a drunken teenager about this shit. You don't know *half* what I know about that contraption. The *kurre-nikas* needs a focus. A person. It is not required, per se, but if you have a target focus, it is much easier to guide, to control the specific way the adjustments are made. Elsa had a focus in mind when she began work. But that person is lost to us now."

Claire. It was obvious it had been Claire. That was why she'd been searching for her in the other version of reality I still remembered. Maybe. It might have been to kill her, as Fallon had suggested; Elsa was feral. I thought about how the Elsa I'd known, in her brand-new tanned and toned little girl's body, had wanted Claire so badly. Had contracted with the Negotiator to get her.

Melanie, I recalled, hadn't been there for that, so I gave her the thirty-second version.

She looked around at Pitr and the Negotiator. Lingered on the latter, cocking her head. "All right, Creepshow, what's your story?"

I knew her well enough to know she was probing for his involvement with the *tah-namus*. She wanted to know which side he'd been on.

"I worked with Elsa in another life," Harrows said softly. "I was once *urtuku* to Mika Renar. I was the Negotiator, under *geas* as punishment." He looked over at me, orienting slowly as if seeing me from a very far distance. "My *geas* has been removed."

I blinked. "What?" For a moment, this was shocking. Then I put it up against the whole of reality being rewritten, and I wasn't surprised at all.

"Broken, more likely," he said. "When Renar used the *kurre-nikas* in our original world." He sounded dreamy. "I do not know what my own life was in *this* reality. But I am not under *geas*."

Melanie raised an eyebrow and nodded with sarcastic enthusiasm. "Very well. You are not who you once were. Which of us is?" She looked at Pitr and smiled. "Aside from you, Petey! You are the rock on which we anchor."

Pitr smiled the slightly terrified smile he offered when totally confused.

"All right, let's get this shit going. Pete, you ready?"

"I'm ready," Pitr said in a tiny voice, holding his blade over his forearm, crisscrossed with the familiar skein of scars.

Melanie nodded, and the big man cut him himself with experienced precision. "Mr. Vonnegan, would you support her, please," she said.

I hesitated, but after over a decade and two fucking reality resets, I wasn't giving up now. I bent down and slipped my arms under Elsa's shoulders. She was red-hot, damp with sweat, and breathing shallowly. Getting my back into it, I lifted her into a semblance of a sitting position, and Melanie, once again showing more skill than I remembered her having, began to recite.

It was an unfamiliar spell. Elsa convulsed in my arms, stiffened, and with a guttural moaning noise opened her mouth and vomited. It was thick and yellow and there was much more of it than seemed possible. It filled the bowl to overflowing, and then she proceeded to spasm, jerking her body and coughing up sprays mixed with a little blood. Melanie averted her face but made no move to avoid the mess. Pitr danced backwards, squawking.

The Negotiator, I noticed, had left the room.

When she'd stopped spewing, Melanie turned her head back, leaned forward, and slapped Elsa across the face hard enough to nearly unbalance me as I tried to hold on to her. The *enustari* screamed, then hung limp in my arms, breathing heavily. "Touch me again," Elsa said between gasps, "you cunt, and I will fuckin' gut you like a pig."

From the main living area: a gunshot. And the bubbling sizzle of gas in the air, fresh and vital.

HOW HE'D GOTTEN THE gun from me, I wasn't sure. I didn't remember a moment. I hadn't put the gun down anywhere or noticed any casting. But he'd gotten it, and he'd walked over to the big floor-to-ceiling windows, and he'd put a bullet in his head. I recalled our negotiations over Pitr. *Prevented,* he'd said. Prevented by the terms of his *geas* to kill himself or allow himself to be killed. That had been the overriding factor in his decision to come to terms with me—he might have wanted to die, but he couldn't allow it. I'd had a gun to his head, and in the end he'd made his deal.

And now he was free of his *geas,* and as soon as he'd realized that, he'd blown his brains out. *I would like it to be quick, and painless, and perhaps peaceful, looking out on something beautiful,* he'd said. I looked out through the massive windows onto a bloodred Shanghai cloaked in the setting sun and congratulated him.

Melanie, Pitr, and I stood around his body, the last few ounces of blood seeping into the carpet. The splatter had painted the windows, the sizzling gas in the air already fading, dying away, wasted.

Melanie sighed. "That's one less Bleeder," she said in a flat voice. I was reminded forcefully why I'd never liked her.

"Who the fuck is this, then?"

The voice was like gravel being pushed through a sieve, deep and roasted, like lava bubbling. Upright, Elsa looked worse: Her face was swollen, her eyes a deep, unhealthy red and yellow.

No one said anything. After a moment, she staggered over to the couch, making Pitr scramble in terror when she drew close to him along the way. She dropped onto the filthy cushions and draped one arm over her eyes.

"Fucking *Christ* I feel like hell. Anyone got any booze? Anything? Shit, I'd drink fucking *schnapps* if you had it."

Again, no one said anything. I stared through the Negotiator's blood at the dead city beyond, thinking about all the skeletons in suits and track clothes and under sheets and in bathtubs all over the city, right across the street, everywhere. I didn't feel them. I felt the hundred or two hundred who had been following me around, convinced that I was special, that I'd been chosen instead of *lucky*, and that for just a short time. I felt Claire. But everyone else? I'd just figured out that none of it mattered. We came back. If we didn't come back, there were other versions of us.

Except Claire, if Fallon had been telling the truth. And why wouldn't he?

"Does it work?" I asked the air, watching the city, perfectly still, motionless. Not even any birds.

"It ain't Bound, so no, it don't fucking *work*," Elsa snarled. "Did you fucking *see* that monstrosity? I built half that fucking thing *myself*, with just my *own blood*." She cleared her throat noisily and spat. "But it ain't *Bound*, so it's just a bunch of shit in the fucking basement."

I pushed my hand into my pocket until my fingertips brushed the Token, shocks of energy rattling up my arm and making my teeth click and clack against each other. "If you had the blood, you could finish it? Make it work?"

She barked a laugh. "Fucking tooth just came out. Yah, sure, if I had a goddamn *city* of blood, I could get the binding done and that monster running once, maybe twice. But then you gotta calibrate it. Figure it out. Takes a few stabs to get the feel of it. Or so my understandin' is." She coughed. "Ah, fucking hell, just when I thought I couldn't puke *any more*."

I stared out at the dead city. I was tired. The last few years, from my subjective point of view, had been an endless mindfuck. I thought I'd been scrambling, going after Renar. All I'd been doing was falling for cons. Cons all the way down.

Movement caught my eye.

It was a tiny dot moving through the sky. I stared at it dumbly at first, my mind blank. I focused in on it as it grew larger, banking in the air to head straight towards us. Alarm fought against the thick blanket of exhaustion draped over me. Some people had survived the *tah-namus*, I told myself. Maybe a few birds had. Why not?

I stared at the dot as it approached. Not a bird.

Melanie was saying something in her razor-burned voice, sizzling and raspy. I kept expecting the dot to bank again as it zoomed towards us, to avoid the building, but it kept coming. A second before it hit the glass, I took a step back.

The sound was like someone punching a side of meat. The glass starred and the whole bank of windows shook and shimmied. The *gidim* ruptured, spilling entrails out onto the glass and then slowly sliding down, its tiny, perfect baby hands clutching spasmodically as it slid from view. There was a pinprick of gas in the air, there and gone, like a spark.

Everyone had stopped.

"Get ready," I said.

"For what?" Melanie asked in a hoarse whisper.

I closed my eyes. The sky had filled with tiny black dots. "A fight."

53.

"WHY WOULD THEY COME *NOW*?" Melanie said to herself, pacing. "They left us unmolested. Renar has been smug and *quiet*, the bitch. She's been happy to watch us age and die. Why *now*?" She looked at me almost reluctantly. I thought of Fallon, and it seemed suddenly obvious: He'd lied. Of *course* they were coming to take care of the details. He'd been running some sort of game when he'd braced us in the tomb that had been Rue's. Just because I couldn't see what the game had been didn't make it untrue.

I'd come full circle. I remembered, if that was the right word, Melanie asking me *You sure?* Now I wasn't. Whatever I might have been evolving into in that old reality, I wasn't anymore. It was just me and Mags and Mel, like old times.

Like old times, except with an ocean of gas at my fingertips.

I told myself I should give the Token to Elsa. She had more experience, knew more. She'd made Ev Fallon flinch, and survived the *tahnamus* when no one else at her rank had—unless they'd been hooked in with Renar. She knew more about weaponized *mu* than I did. But I didn't want to. I didn't know her. I wasn't sure I knew anyone anymore.

"Shit," Elsa said right next to me, making me jump. Silent as a fucking cat. She smelled liked sour milk. "I don't want to die fucking *sober*."

Another *gidim* slammed into the glass a few feet over from the first, exploding just as dramatically. Though the glass didn't star or shatter, the whole wall of glass shook again. A moment later, two more slammed into the building, and there was a dry, grinding sound of cracking glass.

"Bullshit," Melanie huffed. She had a small blade in hand, one sleeve rolled up in preparation to go down fighting. "Such *bullshit*."

A cluster of *gidim* slapped into the building, with a flying wall of them right behind. I pushed my hand into my pocket and took hold of the Token, the roar of power surging up my arm, becoming real, becoming something I could touch. It was as immense as I recalled, the stored-up gas of hundreds of thousands, of millions, systematically murdered for years. How it was still active, I didn't know. I remembered Fallon's little lesson on the *kurre-nikas* and alternate universes. Somewhere, two or three realities back, that universe still existed. With me? With Mags? I didn't know. But that ocean of fucking gas was *there,* and the Token was *here,* and it was able to pull that blood across whatever void there was between. It made my head hurt to think about it.

It didn't matter. I had the lifeblood of millions, torn from their bodies with ruthless efficiency, and I wasn't responsible. I'd table the discussion about whether using it made me culpable. I'd argue that later. Right now, I had it, I hadn't killed anyone for it, and I was going to *use* it.

I ran through the spells I knew. They were still mostly tricks, but you could beef anything up if you were good with the Words. The one thing everyone, even Hiram, had ever agreed on was that I was good with the Words. I'd just never had the blood to do anything dramatic.

Until now.

There was a spell we'd used a few times when we ran a grift called the Fake Friend: You Charmed some poor guy just enough to make him think highly of you, like you were his just-discovered soul mate. Then your partner ran a simple con on him. Something easy, low-risk and low-profit. Then you stepped in like a good friend and pointed out the con, and you were their hero. And they very much wanted to given their new best friend and current hero a reward. A reward you were happy to suggest, of course. Then the problem was getting your new friend to walk away—the Charmed had a habit of following you around, making it hard to count your money and find another mark. So you cast a spell to make your belly impervious to a blade, and you started a fight with your partner. They pretended to stab you. The mark ran, and then *we* ran. It was a terrible grift. Too complicated. Too many moving parts. But the blade spell was useful, and I dredged it up from memory now.

Within that spell, I swapped two Words and added a modifier, and—treating the Token like an open wound on a giant—I sped through the Words, felt the power surge through me, as much as I needed. The glass in the windows shimmered briefly, and when the wave of *gidim* slammed into it, they all burst like melons, an explosion of gore that made the three of us flinch away, arms raised in silent defense. The windows would hold, one-way. Not a single crack more, not even another groaning noise of brittle surrender.

In my peripheral vision, I saw Melanie glance at me. "What have you been up to, Mr. Vonnegan?"

"Failing," I said. "In slow motion."

To my surprise, she exploded into laughter—big, round, rich, and sincere.

I spun and looked around. Renar's pattern included the predictable appearance of her Glamour, sent in like a fucking bomb to unnerve, arouse, and mock. I knew when it appeared, she would be nearby. I didn't know if she knew about the Token. Fallon, who had seen me take the Token in an earlier iteration of our existence, hadn't remembered, or at least had said nothing. She might not. If she didn't I had an advantage.

I sensed the thin, reedy lines of gas fed into the air by Melanie, Pitr, and Elsa, who swayed on her feet next to me, barely maintaining consciousness as the blood dripped down her arm. They didn't have any Tokens, and they couldn't touch the ocean of gas in my pocket. They would have to fend for themselves.

Outside, more and more *gidim* crashed into the building, until the windows were smeared from top to bottom with their guts, each impact crashing through the space like a snare drum. The din was deafening.

"It was good to finally see you again, Vonnegan!" Melanie shouted over it. "I wish the circumstances were better!"

I spun again, then lunged and grabbed hold of Elsa. She yelped and twisted in my grip, but she wasn't very strong. She was red-hot, like she was burning on the inside like a coal fire underground. "Can you make it work?"

She kept staring at the windows. "No blood, you dim cunt. Need at least a healthy male for the Binding. *Then* an army to run the goddamn thing." Slowly, her yellow eyes drifted in my direction. "You got an army, *idimustari*?" She burst into an off-balance laugh.

I shook her. Hard. "If you *had the fucking blood,* could you make it work?"

She reached up and put a hot, dry hand on my cheek. "Sure, darling. You wanna bleed out for it? I'll make it feel *so good.*"

I spun away and heard her laughing behind me as I raced back towards Melanie, trying to put my eyes everywhere, waiting for the Glamour. Renar wouldn't resist coming in person. She never could.

I vaulted onto the ruined couch and heard the laugh turn . . . strangled. I spun and stumbled backwards off the cushions. Elsa had gone still, her face frozen in a jaundiced smile, mouth open, eyes wide, head tilted. Then she . . . settled. Her face slackened, going blank, then firmed up, going rigid. She walked off towards the kitchen.

I turned. Melanie was still staring out the windows, hands pushed into her trouser pockets. As I watched, she slowly pulled her hands free, her tiny blade in one hand. In the reflection of the glass, her face had settled into the same rigid, half-dreamy expression as Elsa's, and panic flooded into my veins. Charm. They were being Charmed. I was about to have an *enustari*-caliber Fabricator and poor old Melanie Billington, much improved since our last meeting, come at me with everything they had.

I looked at Pitr, and the panic hit my heart and sent it into overdrive.

His face had the frozen, deranged look Elsa's had just sported. His hands were held up halfway to his face, locked into fists.

Taking hold of the Token, I jumped over the couch and ran for him. "Pitr!" I shouted, the roar of gas flooding into me. I crashed into him and he stumbled back. I bounced and landed on my ass, teeth clicking. Scrambling to my feet, I thought furiously and then stopped. He was being Charmed. The easiest thing to do was Charm right back.

Charms were easy. I'd cast a million, easing our way over pissed-off security guards, suspicious landlords, cops, waitresses—everyone in old New York, back when people were still alive. I had one that was just two Words. It wasn't anything. It was brute force, just an unfocused feeling of goodwill, but I had enough gas at my disposal for once in my life to make it into a fucking sledgehammer that would turn anyone's brain to fucking jelly. I spat it out, pulling on the Token for all I was worth. The sensation of power flowing through me was brief but glorious and disgusting. All those lives, all those *people,* pushed through me like golden sewage.

Mags twitched, his whole massive body convulsing, and his legs went out from under him. I felt a presence behind me and whirled, my hand coming off the Token as I whipped my arms up in shock and surprise; Elsa had crept up right behind me, one of her tiny jeweled boxes in one hand.

With a cackle, she lunged at me, swinging the box at my head.

"Whoa!" I dived under her and slipped again. Backwards, on my hands and feet, I scrambled away as she lunged for me once more, the sour-milk smell crowding in on me each time. Outside, the wet impacts of the *gidim* were coming fast.

I thought of the Token in my pocket. She kept coming with a new, manic energy, her face locked in a crazy smile, eyes wide, teeth bared. Every time she swung the jeweled box at me, she grunted a little, like this was some sort of spectator sport.

I rolled, managing to get under one of her lunges and scramble to my feet. At the windows, Melanie had formed a ball of flame in between her hands. Everybody had decided fireballs were in this year.

The grin on Melanie's face was demented. It was, I realized, the same expression on Mika Renar's face—her real face, stiffened and drained by existence. The drifting mouth, the never-blinking eyes, the twisted and arrested cheeks and lips. *She* was inside them, pulling the strings, yanking the levers.

Pushing my hand in my pocket, I dropped back to the floor. The carpet was filthy and smelled literally like shit. Some last-second instinct made me roll again, and the jeweled box in the clawed hand stabbed into the carpet I'd just vacated. I kept rolling and got to my feet again but kept moving with no particular direction—just movement, constant movement.

I thought of the gun. Where the fuck had the Negotiator dropped it?

"Lem!"

A wave of relief gave me a second of respite. I looked, and there was Mags, good old Mags, sitting up and rubbing his head, an expression of bafflement on his face.

"Mags!" I shouted, and then there was a flash in the corner of my vision. A fireball the size of Melanie herself, sizzling through the air at me. I started to run, then gripped the Token even harder, pulling more gas through than I'd felt since the *tah-namus,* and I spat a single two-syllable word at it.

"*Gulla!*"

The wave of energy passing through me was incredible. It felt inexhaustible, eternal. The fireball winked out of existence, sputtering into a faint wisp of white smoke along with a ragged chunk of the couch and half a light fixture hanging from the ceiling. Holy shit, *Griefing.* Griefing with this much gas was like a fucking nuclear weapon. The subtlety and detail that made even the work of Tricksters more powerful than any one Word didn't matter *at all* when you had this kind of volume behind it.

Something hit me from behind, knocking me to the floor. On instinct, I tore my hand free from my pocket, trying to bring it up to break my fall, and it was trapped painfully under our weight. I managed to block the tiny, delicate-looking jeweled box in her hand with my other arm for one second, which was all I needed. I took hold of her wrist and twisted, and the tiny box dropped to the floor. With a murderous roar, Pitr knocked her from me. I rolled over in time to see him pick her up and lift her, wriggling, over his head.

"Pitr—Ah, *shit!*"

Melanie, face still frozen in that terrifying Renar expression, had turned to orient on Mags and Elsa, a fresh ball of flame singing her jacket. I could see her lips moving in the bright, flickering light of the fire, the gash on her arm weeping blood that never hit the floor, and the fireball exploded from her hands as I got my hand back on the Token.

Mags spun and, with a yell, threw Elsa into the air. She collided with the fireball and was engulfed, the flame losing shape and spreading over her like a jelly as she crashed straight down to the floor, where she thrashed, shrieking.

Pitr stared, wide-eyed. He looked at me in panicked tears. "I'm sorry! Lem, I'm sorry!"

For one heartbeat, doom crashed through me. Elsa, crazy, possessed—whatever—had been the key to everything. Without her, this was just futile survival.

But futile survival was what Tricksters did best. Futile survival felt like *home*.

Snatching up Elsa's jeweled box, I clawed my way back to my knees and pushed my hand back into my pocket. Melanie already had another fireball growing between her hands. As the gas flowed right back into me from the Token, I thrust out my other hand, box and all, in a fit of burned-in grifter theatrics, and I Griefed again, shouting, "*Sutaka!*"

She sailed backwards as if hit in the belly by a bowling ball, the fireball exploding upwards at an angle and bursting like a shell, the ceiling catching fire and burning enthusiastically.

Elsa was still shrieking. The apartment had become fire and screams.

Up on shaking legs, I recalled the Charm spell I'd used on Mags, and pulled from the Token as I spat it at Melanie's prone form.

"Lem!"

I spun back. "It's *okay*, Magsie!" I took a deep shuddering breath. "It doesn't fucking matter anyway." I stared down at Elsa as she burned, quiet and still, the whole place filled with the greasy smell of burning skin. "The Fabrication can't be bound without her," I said between gasps, black rage seeping into my veins. I closed my eyes, listening to the crackle of flames and the thud of *gidim* as they slapped into the building. "We're *done*."

I had the gas. I would go out and I would go up against Mika Renar and I would use every spell and every trick I knew, and she would tear me to pieces and that would be the end of that. I didn't have the education. I remembered Fallon casting in Alaska—fast and obfuscated, tricky wormy spells, *devastating*. I'd tricked Renar in another life. I wasn't sure I had enough tricks left.

Outside, a howling noise like a high wind had begun, spinning up in pitch every few seconds. I stared at the tiny box in my hand. It felt warm and heavy, like I could literally feel the people, the person, trapped inside. Could I free them? Did it fucking matter?

"I can speak the Binding."

For a moment I just kept staring at the box. The apartment was hot, the air almost too hot and thick to breathe. Renar didn't even have to come in. She just had to wait for us to cook.

Then I looked up at my friend. "What?"

Mags stepped forward until we were on either side of the smoldering remains of Elsa, wisps of inky black smoke wafting up. "I can speak the Binding, Lem. I can do it. Fallon, he taught me."

A thrill went through me. "This isn't Baby's First Fabrication, Pitr. This isn't—"

"It doesn't matter, Lem. Fallon told me. The Rule of the Words. The bigger the Fabrication, the more Words." He leaned forward, his long hair falling into his eyes. "I can *do* it, Lem!"

I stared at him. And then I burst into laughter.

Melanie's voice, behind us, breathless and hoarse. "*Evelyn Fallon!* You can't fucking trust *Evelyn* fucking *Fallon!*"

I ignored her. It fit. It *fucking* fit. This was the way the world ends. It ends with Pitr Mags trying to remember how to speak a spell.

"Lem," he said as the flames from the ceiling began licking down the wall behind him, "I can *do* it. I just . . . I can't do it myself . . . I need . . ."

I sobered, and another wave of pure affection for the big idiot flooded me, carrying away everything else, all the doubt and anger. It was me and Pitr, like always, and no matter what else happened, it was enough. It was plenty.

I pulled the Token from my pocket, the roar of awful, beautiful gas buzzing up my arm, and held it out to him. "All the gas you need, buddy," I said. He took it, slowly, eyes widening as he made contact. He held it out from his face, staring in pure wonder. I put my hands on his shoulders, looking up at that uncomplicated face, the closest thing to an absolute good I'd ever met in the whole damn world. "I'll keep her busy, Pitr," I said over the roar of flames. "I'll give you as much time as I can."

He swallowed, staring at the tiny green statue, and nodded.

The wind outside became a sudden, earsplitting roar, and then I felt invisible fingers take hold of me. My eyes locked with Pitr's, and when I was pulled through the air, he lunged for me, his fingers brushing mine as I sailed backwards, smashing through the starred glass of the windows, into the air fifty stories up.

54.

FOR A MOMENT IT WAS peaceful. There was no gravity, no friction. The glass dissolved around me, slicing me in a million places, but there was no pain at first. Shock and adrenaline masked everything, made it okay. It felt good to be out of the heat of the burning apartment, the cool air taking me in as I spread out, unfolding my legs and arms and feeling the wind take me, like a sail.

And then the *gidim* came.

There were thousands of them. I didn't know how that was possible. Renar had killed practically everyone in the world to fuel her *biludha*. I had seen Renar's *gidim* reproducing—this many of them should not have been possible. But then, what the fuck did I know.

In the instant I realized I was being suspended in the air against the wishes of gravity, the *gidim* all noticed me. The fluttering of their glassy wings stopped as one, and for a single fraction of a second it was silent, almost peaceful. I found the thin, ragged lines of my own blood in the air, vibrant but in short supply, my wounds not nearly mortal enough for this. It didn't matter; I could open up an artery and bleed out in five minutes and it wouldn't be enough, not nearly enough, to take on Mika Renar. Even the Big Spells I did know weren't particularly weaponized.

I could slow down time, as I'd done once before, but fueling it on the blood I could spare would kill me, and not even create a bubble of Slow Time large enough to make a difference.

I could teleport. Maybe twice before I had bled myself white, depending on range.

Tricks, I thought. It would have to be tricks.

And I remembered the rats, ten, twelve years ago. The goddamn rats.

"HOW MANY OF THEM do you think there are?"

I sighed, feeling woozy. I hadn't eaten in two days. We'd left Hiram's with thirteen dollars in our pocket. Or *I'd* left Hiram's with thirteen dollars in my pocket, and Mags had followed me out the door without asking permission or saying a word. I'd spent thirteen dollars on hamburgers since then, all of them going to him. He ate them in one bite and then looked sad. Having Mags as a friend was like having a huge dog that just stared at you whenever you weren't actively feeding it.

The alley was behind a row of restaurants and sported a line of rusting, filth-caked garbage Dumpsters, each one a thriving condominium for the biggest rats I'd ever seen.

"I dunno, Magsie. Hundreds."

"How many do we need?"

I shrugged. "All of them."

Hiram's tutelage had been harsh and grinding and had centered more on how much I could steal on his behalf than anything else. It was almost an equation; for every package of fucking socks we stole for Hiram, for every jeweled paperweight we Charmed out of a shop on Forty-Seventh Street, he would go ahead and teach me something. Mags had started off pretending to pay attention, but he got bored so easy, so now he watched TV while Hiram slapped me in the face every time I fucked up a Word or let a spell collapse with a rush of wind and heat.

But somehow, one thing I'd definitely learned was that there was a link, mysterious and unexplored, between the intelligence and genetic complexity of a creature and the power its blood gave to a spell. A human being was the top of the pyramid. A single pint of human blood could fuel some pretty amazing spells. A dog's blood was weaker; you needed more of it to get the same Volume. A spider barely registered.

So I did the math: One pint of human blood was what, twenty or thirty rats? I watched them wiggling around, looking for their dinner in the rotting recesses of the Dumpsters. They were *fucking monstrous,* so maybe we would get away with fifteen, eighteen. But what was the point of going through this and coming up short? They were *rats.* I was doing the city a fucking service.

Mags didn't see it that way. He hadn't minded the idea of bleeding the girl. Or anyone. He wasn't bloodthirsty, but he didn't cry about it. It had taken me a long time to get him to understand that if he was going to follow me around like a goddamn puppy, he couldn't do things like that. He couldn't bleed me, not some street trash Hiram paid twenty bucks to, no one. Mags finally got it, his face ashen, his eyes wide, because he thought I was mad at him. I wasn't. I was just *mad.*

But animals, even the fucking rats, Mags shed tears for. Fat, hot tears of mourning for the rats and possums and raccoons of the world, of which there were more in New York City than you might imagine. I'd suggested we give it a try because I'd been casting off my own gas for a week and was tired and fuzzy around the edges. I couldn't keep it up much longer.

"We can't kill all those rats," Mags said, his voice shocked and horrified. He cleared his throat and put on a manly tone. "I mean, you kill one, the rest are gonna run."

I shook my head. Hiram wasn't a great teacher, but he got into a bottle now and then, and when he did he liked to lecture as long as I kept my mouth shut. One of his favorite topics was the *enustari,* the really fucking evil people of the world. Powerful, bloodthirsty, the people who had a way with the Words and no compunction about bleeding out a football team or a stadium or half a fucking country to do what they wanted. He liked to tell stories about Fujan, who engineered the deaths of over a hundred thousand soldiers two thousand years ago in order to cast a *biludha*. He always sounded half impressed, half admiring, and half disgusted by the idea.

Hiram had no scruples when it came to individuals, though he was careful not to kill anyone. He took what his small spells needed and no more, and felt good about himself. Proud.

"What the *enustari* do," I told Mags, who didn't remember anything for long, "is they set up a chain reaction."

He nodded, very serious. "A chain reaction."

"Like dominoes. You kill one sacrifice and the spell you cast kills two more, and so on, and so you kill them all in one moment, and then you use *that* gas to cast the big spell."

He nodded, pursing his lips wisely. "Right. Okay. How?"

I didn't know, but I knew the Words. Spells were just putting the Words together and pushing some gas through them as you spoke. You start with the Word for *death,* not the static Word, *ug,* but the dynamic word, the fucking infinitive, *to die, namus*. You started there, and you figured out the rest.

With no gas in the air, I went through it, building it syllable by syllable. I cribbed some of it from spells I'd heard Hiram recite, dropping the bullshit he insisted on adding for "color." I cut myself, wincing and sucking in my breath at the burning, sizzling pain I didn't think I'd ever get used to, and spoke fifteen Words, eighteen syllables. And the rats began to die.

THE GIDIM CAME AT me. I knew I would have to time it. I forgot that I was suspended in midair. I forgot that nothing mattered anymore anyway. I forgot about Claire, dead and erased, about everything. I had the faintest sliver of my own blood feeding out into the air from a million scratches and cuts. I spoke seven Words, eight syllables. And the *gidim* began to die.

I kept reciting.

The feeling of exhausting energy being pulled from me, draining me, while the *gidim* combined into a decent amount of gas in the air, was confusing; the Words were like cement in my mouth. I slowed down and sped up as the *gidim* burst, dissolving into greasy pink clouds that were immediately consumed by my spell, and I hit my cadence just as the last of the bloated things were destroyed. And I was somewhere else.

I hadn't had a lot of time to choose a destination for the Teleport spell; I'd cut it down to something halfway elegant, which had allowed me to time it exactly. I ended up three or four feet over the roof of the building I'd chosen, and I fell, arms and legs in the air, head bouncing off the spongy black surface. I lay there a second, staring up at the almost transparent sky that still had demons exploding all over it. Then I dug into my pocket and pulled out the switchblade, sliced about halfway down my forearm, blood welling up nice and thick and healthy.

When I tried to move, I found myself pinned by the familiar old invisible fist. My whole body frozen. Except I could breathe, and move my eyes, and swallow, and move my tongue. I lay there bugging my eyes and probing my mouth, my hand frozen on the blade, the blade stuck in my skin, burning.

I closed my eyes and felt Pitr's heartbeat, dim and far but steady. When I opened my eyes, there was just the wind and the sky and my old friend the invisible fist.

And then Mika Renar floated up over the edge of the roof. The Glamour, absurdly decked out in a long black coat that billowed realistically in the wind as she floated up and over, her usual red dress underneath and everything *perfect*.

She floated near, settling in slow motion into a believable pose of kneeling over me, like someone had taken the time to motion-capture her every move. The scent of cherries, thick and too sweet, made my stomach churn even as goose bumps raised up all over my skin, even as my mouth watered. The illusory face leaned down close, the eyes flicking around me. Mika was able to see and hear through the Glam-

our, and even inches away I was amazed at the artistry. This was someone who was good with the Words. I was just a scratcher. A Trickster.
A Trickster who was out of tricks.

"Who," she said with the barest hint of doubt in her voice, "are
you?"

I took a deep breath and thought about Words with the right conso-
nants and vowels. If I could have moved my lips, I would have smiled. I
drew on the heavy cloud of gas I was bleeding into the air and, without
moving my lips, managed to hiss out those two Griefer-friendly syllables: *gulla*.

To destroy, to overwhelm.

Not enough gas behind it to do much, but it tore the Glamour to
shreds. Her beautiful face puffed up and her expression changed in
minute increments from blank curiosity to surprise and shock to
anger, feral and terrible. Her whole body swelled like a hundred *gidim*
had taken root inside her all at once, and then she burst into fragments
that were caught in some solar wind, scattered everywhere, flickering
and extinguishing like multicolored sparks.

The invisible fist vanished.

I sat up. It hadn't accomplished much, but it had *felt* good, which
was true of most tricks. You got away with pennies, loose change, but
you'd fooled people and proved you were smarter than they were. I
didn't know where she was getting the gas in this dead world, but she'd
been made a fool, and that felt good.

I tore the blade free from my arm; the wound had sealed around it
and the fresh cut hurt like hell. I knew Renar would regroup quickly
and come roaring back, so I needed to stay one step ahead of her.
Blood flowing down my arm, heart pounding in my chest, I thought,
Two can play this game. Glamours were a dime a dozen. I put it together in seconds, snatches of old *mu* fit together like a puzzle: a piece
of an old duplication spell, a few syllables to mimic and mirror the
wind on my hair, my clothes, two Words to link it to me. I spoke it and
felt the drain, heavier than before because the Glamour was going to

be half decent and thus was expensive. And then there was a decent version of me standing right there. I didn't pause to think about how bad it looked, how thin and gaunt, how gray the hair was getting. I didn't study the way the hair moved realistically in the wind. It was a nice job, but I instantly regretted the blood it cost. I'd gotten lazy, with the Asshole Army following me around, waiting for more miracles. I'd gotten used to casting off other people.

As I stumbled for the green door and the slim cover offered by the stub of the stairwell, feeling giddy with blood loss I'd almost forgotten how to operate under, the Glamour stayed behind, dumb. I scrambled behind the wall and leaned against it, panting, cold sweat all over me, and watched as her Glamour reappeared, just winking into existence right where it had been. With a wince I hated myself for, I slashed my arm again, hoping I would be able to get to the streets without killing myself.

A sixth sense made me spin. Melanie Billington grabbed me by the shoulders.

"Shut the fuck up," she hissed, "and follow me."

55.

WE HIT THE GROUND LIKE feathers, settling down to our weight by increments. I could feel the cartilage in my joints compressing by degrees as the world took us back. I glanced up at the building, hundreds of feet up, and then looked at Billington. The whole front of her suit had been singed, the buttons melted and the fabric charred.

"Come on," she said. "I know where the bitch is."

She strode off, and I hesitated. What were we going to do? Cast, sure. Bleed, and cast, and that would burn up a few minutes of her time and then we'd be anemic and half dead and exhausted and the old mummy would whisper at us and that would be that. Then I trotted off after Melanie. What else was there? I couldn't help Pitr with the Binding. Neither could Melanie. And there was *literally* no one else. All we could do was be a distraction as long as we could manage, give Pitr every chance we could to get it right. No matter how unlikely that seemed.

Billington led me down the street, our heels making thunderous, echoing noise in the empty air, then pressed herself against the polished stone of a skyscraper and waved me to do the same. I leaned over and peered around the corner. Renar was alone, slumped in the familiar pose in her wheelchair. It was suddenly incredible, this ancient woman, so feeble and so completely abandoned, sitting alone after destroying the world so that she might live forever . . . as an ancient old crone in a metal contraption.

I reminded myself she was the most dangerous *enustari* in history, and could not quite believe it. Then thought, what did she have to fear? Whoever she had brought with her into this empty world, whoever had helped her to cast the *tah-namus* and become immortal—she had turned on them. She had betrayed them. How could she not? She was Mika Renar.

"We can't let her speak," Billington whispered.

We did nothing. I knew our window was closing; my Glamour wouldn't fool *hers* for long. I pushed myself back against the wall and closed my eyes. You could do a lot with two relatively healthy people a pint or so down between them. You could do plenty. But it had to be right. It had to work the first time.

I pushed my hands into my pockets and found the tiny jeweled box I'd taken from Elsa.

I didn't have a name for it. It was warm and heavy in my hand, and when she'd tried to use it on me there had been no spell, no Words at all. A Fabrication, built and bound. A tap to the forehead. Fucking *magic*.

Reaching across myself, I gently tugged Melanie until she turned to me. Her face was deeply lined. I'd never noticed before, or maybe she'd aged in this weird time line I'd never experienced. She said she'd woken up in Alabama. I'd never asked her where she was from, what she'd been through, and hadn't wondered. And she hadn't asked me.

"Keep her distracted," I said. Her eyes flicked to the box, then back to me. She nodded and started to turn away, but I caught her. "*Distracted,*" I repeated.

She smiled. "We're fucking Tricksters, Chief," she whispered. "That's all we do."

She lifted her blade with one hand and her thick, heavy braid with the other, revealing a bloody mess behind her ear. "Head wounds," she said simply. I nodded.

As the gas filled the air, she began to whisper the Words. Again, I was struck by how much more skilled she was than she had been. When she hit the cadence, twenty or thirty of her blinked into existence. It was clever—each one moved in a way that was a half inch towards wonky, making them all seem like individual versions, acting independently.

"Wish me luck," she said, then let out a whoop at the top of her lungs and ran around the corner. A second later, her army of Glamours followed, whooping in concert.

I cut myself. I spoke ten Words, fifteen syllables. Fucking with the physical universe was hard as hell, but fooling people's perceptions was easy. That had always been the rule. I turned the corner and started walking, slow.

Melanie was making a real effort. Her two dozen Glamours were racing around Renar, who looked already dead, frail and motionless in her wheelchair. I glanced up and over my shoulder, and there was Renar's Glamour—her eyes and ears, I realized, the only way she could see or hear—terrible in its beauty, floating down to the street, the beautiful face locked in a frown, the black coat fluttering in realistic detail. She looked like she couldn't quite believe what she was seeing. I didn't blame her. Who came at Mika fucking Renar like this?

I kept walking. Slow and steady. I could feel Pitr's heart out of sync with mine, five beats of mine to one of his. I clung to it. I felt like that connection was the only thing real; everything else was bullshit.

I stared at Renar, the dozens of Billingtons racing between us. I avoided them as best I could; illusions were easy to ruin with a quick physics lesson, and Renar hadn't lived to be forever and a day (and counting up to eternity) by being *unobservant*. I kept walking. I side-stepped the Melanies. When Renar's Glamour passed over me, there was no shadow, and I was momentarily pleased to note one fucking mistake in that spell. One fucking mistake.

Then her Glamour was right in front of me. I drafted it as it glided forward, slightly faster than I was walking. Tricks on tricks on tricks. We were a few feet away from the mummy in the chair. Tension built inside me, and I couldn't believe I was this close to Mika Renar.

The Glamour suddenly reached out one hand and pointed. The mummy's white lips moved. One of the Melanies exploded into bone and blood, and a hard consonant sound, the beginnings of a scream, cut off. The other Melanies disappeared, just gone, in an instant. I froze. I was two feet away. The Glamour, Renar's eyes and ears, was turned away from me.

I held my breath. The Glamour surveyed the remains of Melanie Billington calmly. The quiet was once again complete. I'd gotten one more person killed, inching towards my perfect record of killing *everyone I came in contact with*.

I felt Pitr's heart beating. I thought of Claire. And I launched myself forward.

I passed through the Glamour, like flying through dry clouds, red and black and pink. The mummy's slitted eyes leaped to me at the last second. The rest of her tiny, puppet body remained perfectly still. I thought I could feel those eyes physically. It was like jumping on top of a sharp spike in the ground, belly-first. I stretched out my arm just as the Glamour began to shout something, as the mummy's mouth began to twitch.

I felt something slide around my neck, like a snake, cold and dry.

The jeweled box, seemingly tiny and fragile, slammed into Renar's forehead like a rock. A jolt of fire lanced up my arm, agony for one split second and then complete, buzzing numbness as the box leaped from my hand and hit the ground, thudding there like a much larger, much heavier object. I fell to my knees in front of it, my left hand going to my throat, where they found a thin silver wire, like a garrote, wrapped around my neck. It tingled at the touch.

I looked up. Renar's Glamour was gone.

The mummy held the same position, but the eyes had gone flat and staring, and there was no sign of her slight, labored breathing. I looked from her to the box.

The silver wire around my neck tightened. My right arm still hung at my side, and I couldn't move it, so I worked the fingers of my left hand under and tugged at it. There was a jerk on the wire and I flipped over, searing pain burning into the skin of my neck as someone gave it an enthusiastic yank.

I rolled onto my belly and lay there, panting. I looked up, following the length of the nearly invisible, thin silver wire to where Ev Fallon stood, looking dapper in a well-tailored white suit.

"Hurry up, now," he said with a kindly grin. "It is time."

56.

"A VERY OLD ARTIFACT," FALLON said conversationally as he led me on what was essentially a leash through the bone-strewed streets of Shanghai. "Perhaps two thousand years old. Amazing that such things have been preserved. I discovered it in a storage unit in Miami, Florida, seventy-odd years ago. Just coiled in an unmarked wooden box. Artifacts are always like this, mischievous. Always falling through cracks and becoming lost, always seeking to be found by those who do not know how to control them. The intelligences imprisoned within them are . . . resentful."

The pain was constant, a sensation of burning. My right arm was still numb and useless, and I'd found that I could only answer questions; I could not say anything else. If I tried to resist being led through the streets like a dog, the pain doubled, and tripled, and then made my vision turn red and my brain threaten to explode. So I was following the old man in silence.

"That is the main difference between an Artifact, as we call them, and a Fabrication. Fabrications are more complex, of course, but the main difference is this intelligence. This awareness. Artifacts of the old school involved Summonings, intelligences. Fabrications usually do not. They simply manipulate energy in mechanical ways."

I wondered if this was a lesson he had taught Pitr.

Fallon turned, transferring the end of the leash to his right hand and producing the jeweled box from his right pocket and holding it up. "This, not so old. In fact, I created this."

I stared at him.

He nodded. "Yes! Elsa liked to take credit for things. Elsa is not nearly so old as I am, and not nearly as talented, despite what others— quoting Elsa herself—may have told you. I am the Fabricator, Mr. Vonnegan. When you encounter a beautiful Fabrication, a Fabrication that works and is clever, you have found some of my work." He laughed. "I am, I believe, the oldest man in history. And now, thanks to dear Mika, I will always be. Elsa was talented, yes. She had the ability to see something, once, and then replicate it, perfectly. Extraordinary, in her way . . ." Trailing off, he studied me for a moment as he walked backwards and I followed, limping slightly, and then he sighed and turned away. "You have questions. Ask them."

I didn't know what to say. I could still feel Pitr somewhere, and I hoped he wasn't panicked or scared or just failing. I didn't know where Fallon was taking me, or what he planned to do to me.

"It was you all along," I said at last. "Wasn't it? Behind everything."

He laughed. Fallon had laughed so infrequently in my experience that it sounded bizarre and disconcerting. "No! No, Mr. Vonnegan, that is the fun of it. I remember our previous existences, as you do. I was not aware of Mika's plans when I originally designed her custom work. And I did not know what it was intended for. I have lived for centuries using the *barna* like this one. I have been here a long time, Mr. Vonnegan. I was content to work and study and use only the occasional body to perpetuate myself. I am of the old school. You do not leave marks. You stay hidden, you do not discuss certain lore. You control the situation." He sighed. "I was content. I worked, and when my body became too old to function, or when it become ill, I borrowed another. But only then. Not as Elsa did, reckless, ruthless. Cruel. In this way I did intend to live forever, Mr. Vonnegan, and for that you may judge me. But Mika's plan was her own."

He walked a few steps in silence.

"But your visit shocked me. Because I had never considered the possibility of another *enustari* ending *me*. Almost as an afterthought. As if I did not matter—me, who had lived so *long*. So when you had thrown your wrench into the plan, I approached Mika, and made terms, and worked with her to solve the problem you had created. I held no harsh feelings towards you, Mr. Vonnegan. I would have been happy for you to survive. However, Mika was no fool, and when she accepted me into her camp, I was forced to agree to terms."

I nodded to myself. Tried speaking again and found I could. "The Negotiator."

There was no gas in the air, so I pulled the tired old trick of biting my tongue. The tongue bleeds. It's filled with vessels, and it *bleeds*. Iron and salt filled my mouth and the gas hit the air, and I didn't waste a second: I pulled on it hard and tried whispering my new favorite word: *gulla*. My throat locked, and I choked. I tried again and made a gagging noise, the silver leash seeming to tighten around my neck.

"Mr. Harrows, yes," Fallon said without acknowledging my attempt to cast. "I pledged not to harm Mika directly. This became problematic when we found ourselves both on the other side of the *tah-namus*, yes? Like we were an old married couple. Marriage always ends in divorce, you know. Among our kind, divorce can be quite final. And Mika thought she was clever: *She* was not bound by the same restriction to respect the existence of her colleagues. One by one, she isolated them and destroyed them. They all had their *pride* and attempted to take her on, directly, without tricks, without guile. And they were *destroyed*. And then only I remained."

I nodded. It was funny, I thought, how it all became clear when someone was explaining it to you. "You let me live so I could kill her for you." I had a slight lisp from my bitten tongue.

"Oh, Mr. Vonnegan, I let you live so you could *try*." He laughed and spun around again. "And look at you! You have succeeded! It was a dirty trick, especially against an *enustari* of such history and reputation. But certainly I do not blame you."

I swallowed. I was sweating. "What happens to me?"

He turned again. "And Mr. Mageshkumar? Do not worry, Mr. Vonnegan, you will not die. You will *bleed*, for I find myself in need of blood. The reserves I have so carefully maintained will last some time. But not forever. It is good to have some living stock to work with, so you will join the others I have acquired, rather painstakingly." His free hand went up in a classic rhetoric gesture. "I will observe the ancient traditions of *ustari* and *siskur*."

Siskur. I'd heard the Word. I wasn't sure where. I'd never heard anyone else use it, but then I didn't spend a lot of time hanging around with Archmages. If I had to guess—and I did—I would guess it meant *Bleeder*.

The silver leash squirmed on my neck like a living thing.

"And right now?" I asked. It was a big world. A big empty world. I tried to comprehend the three of us being the last people in the world. It was impossible. The *Biludha-tah-namus* wouldn't have killed everyone. Someone had survived, maybe even hundreds, thousands of people. A tiny amount, but still—someone.

Fallon stopped suddenly. I stopped too, curiously. Forced by the leash. For a second I thought I was still moving, my brain sending the signals to my legs, but they wouldn't obey.

He turned slowly, almost posing, like he was in a photo shoot for a fashion magazine. *Old Coots Who Dress Better* or something.

He looked at me with a sort of wry half-smile. "Where *is* Mr. Mageshkumar?"

We stared at each other. My mind was blank. For the first time in as long as I could remember, I had nothing smart to say.

He wrapped the silver leash around his hand two, three times, then slowly tugged it closer to him. The leash tightened around my neck, making my eyes bulge and my face turn hot red. I tried to stagger towards him but couldn't.

"Mr. Vonnegan, *where* is Mr. Mageshkumar? *Exactly?*"

I remembered Pitr grabbing me by the shoulders in another time line, telling me I couldn't tell them where Claire was. I clamped my teeth together and hoped I had some tricks left.

Fallon sighed, conveying the irritated affection of a man whose patience was tried by fools. "I can, if need be, Compel you, Mr. Vonnegan."

I nodded. "You're . . . going to . . . have to," I ground out, my voice thick and ragged as the silver leash squeezed.

My mind raced over ideas. I could gas up a little, and either Fallon couldn't sense it in the air like a squirming cloud of energy anymore or he didn't care, because the other side of it was, I couldn't cast. The Words got stuck in my throat. And soon Fallon was going to cut himself—or *me*—and cast a Charm or a Compulsion, or he was going to pull another fucking gadget from his pockets that he would insert into my ear and it would wriggle in and turn me into a fucking zombie slave and that would be that.

"He's in the apartment," I managed to squeeze out, my own pulse pounding in my head. "I told him to hide. In . . . the . . . closet."

The silver leash tightened until I couldn't breathe as Fallon studied me with that half-smile.

"No, he is not," he finally said, sighing heavily. He began walking back towards me. "Now I will have to bleed you, and Compel you, and then I will be forced to punish both you and Mr. Mageshkumar. Which is unfortunate. I *like* Mr. Mageshkumar. He is rather like a trained dog, yes? I recall our teaching sessions. Very pleasant. He is a man who has no deceit in him, which is refreshing. And he was so conscientious about his lessons! I recall when we were studying the Binding Ritual, he almost had it! And almost, I suspect, is—"

He stopped, and as my consciousness began to recede in strangled waves, red pulses in my eyes, he stared at me again.

He chuckled. "Oh, Mr. Vonnegan, don't tell me—"

Dying twice and coming back, I thought grimly, *seemed to improve a man, and Pitr was better with the Words than he had been.*

Except, Fallon didn't *know* that.

Beneath us, there was a deep, shaking rumble. It went on and on, second after second, mutating rapidly into a high-pitched grinding noise that kept getting higher- and higher-pitched until it seemed to fade away. But I had a feeling it was still there, fluttering my heart valves and lungs, just too high up on the register for me to hear.

My vision had pinned down to a hazy tunnel. I couldn't breathe. Fallon just stood there, suddenly blackly austere, chewing his lip and watching me suffocate.

"*Fekete kutya,*" he said, grimacing. Then he pushed his free hand into his coat pocket and a second later, without transition, we were in the parking garage under Elsa's building.

I stared around, smiling. A warm bloom of pride, maybe, spread through my chest.

Pitr Mageshkumar, I thought, *today you are a man.*

I wanted to jump and shout for him. I wanted to let the stupid bastard give me one of his patented bone-crushing hugs. It wasn't *right,* that Pitr would pull something like this off and not be able to give me that aw-shucks grin while dancing on his tiny feet like an embarrassed schoolboy.

The *kurre-nikas* had come to life. I dropped to my knees and put my left hand uselessly up to the silver wire, tugging feebly at it. Through the pinhole, I could see a faint blue glow suffusing all the cables, similar to the faerie light I'd summoned to reveal runes and other hidden things. Runes covered the walls, flickering in and out of solidity as if they existed in more than one plane, as if they were slipping back and forth, first in one time line, then another, or maybe all time lines at once.

The work was immense. The runes were precise and tiny and covered the walls and floor and all of the cable and other components, written by hand in a steady, unwavering line. I'd never seen so much written work, all of it Bound, infused into the mechanics of the Fabrication. It must have taken months. It must have taken months and endless bleeding, endless.

Pitr Mags was nowhere to be seen.

57

"ACH," FALLON SPAT, A RAW sound of disgust brought up from his chest. "This, this is a waste of time." He scanned the area. "Mr. Mageshkumar!" he shouted. "I commend you on your first successful Binding! I must admit I am surprised. But not unpleasantly so!"

Jesus fucking Christ, I thought dimly. This was different from Renar's brand of evil. This was a guy who'd been devouring souls in order to survive for so long he didn't think twice about it. He didn't have any bad feelings towards us. He was just fucking *irritated* that we were complicating his merry day of genocide and revenge followed by a calming evening of tea, Fabrication, and the bleeding of acquaintances.

"Reveal yourself, Mr. Mageshkumar. I know you are not as foolhardy as your friend here. Who is well, as you can see!" Fallon glanced back at me, and his face registered exasperation as he realized he had just contradicted himself. He muttered something, closing his eyes. A second later, the silver wire loosened, and blood rushed back to my brain as I sucked in a chestful of damp, cold air. Immediately, I began coughing.

Fallon waited, turning slowly as his old gray eyes scanned the gloom. Then he sighed and looked down at his shiny shoes, the black leather like mirrors. "*Stupid* man," he said to no one. Then he turned and looked back at me. "Mr. Vonnegan, I am afraid your new career will begin a bit earlier than expected. Attend to me, please."

The silver leash tugged at me gently. Still fighting for each breath, I staggered to my feet and started towards him. I wasn't sure if I was volunteering or if I was being compelled by the Artifact. It didn't matter much. This would be, if something creative didn't occur to me first, the rest of my miserable existence: the leash, Fallon's smooth politeness, the occasional choking hazard.

"Kneel," Fallon said absentmindedly. I recognized the tone of the in-charge, the *enustari* who couldn't fathom *not* being obeyed. Fallon had always had an air of command about him, an air of aristocracy. It was just that he'd never had a fucking leash around my neck before. Even when he'd been playing me for a fool, working around the world to bleed the crowds for Renar's *kurre-nikas* while pretending to be my reluctant Wise Man, available for counsel and advice and the occasional murder of his fellow Archmages, he'd always had the expectation that he would be obeyed, listened to, worried over.

I peered up at him through eyes that felt red and burst. "How old are you, then?"

Fallon was affixing the other end of the leash to his wrist to free up both hands. He snorted. "I am six hundred and thirty-three years old. I was born a sixth daughter to a poor man and was set out in the woods to die of exposure. Or so I have been told. And here I am, six and a half centuries later." The knot finished, he reached into his coat and extracted a straight razor. It had a pearl handle and looked strangely familiar.

"Mika," he said with a shake of his head. "You see how I could never take her seriously? Her power lay in her cruelty. Mika was willing to do *anything*. People feared her because of it. But her ideas . . . the *tah-namus*! So *unnecessary*. And all to avoid slumming, as she saw it. The wrong type of body. The wrong *class*. Silly woman." He sighed. "I could not openly oppose her. She had gathered too many powerful, stupid *ustari* around her banner. And she was dangerous in battle, when she was prepared."

The world was dead, and Fallon didn't seem to care one way or another.

He took hold of my greasy, unkempt hair and pulled my head back to expose my neck, then laid the cold steel of the blade against it.

"Mr. Mageshkumar!" he shouted. "The spell I will cast will bleed Mr. Vonnegan deeply. I cannot swear he will survive. If you would save him, I would reveal myself!"

The tortured grammar, I thought, would just confuse Pitr. I was as good as dead while he puzzled out.

"If you had the whole immortal thing solved," I asked, my throat burning, "why let Renar do it?"

Fallon sighed, looking around the dark for any sign of Pitr. "I will admit, Mr. Vonnegan, that after so many years, this did start to seem *easier*. Especially since someone else had done most of the work. But as I said, stopping Mika and her confederates would not have been easy, and carried with it the risk of defeat. I examined the odds, and I made my choice." He nodded, once, firmly. "Mr. Mageshkumar! Last opportunity!"

Silence greeted us. *Good for you, Pitr,* I thought. I'd been worried he was going to try something ridiculous and Mags-like by trying to attack the man who was, after all, the most powerful *enustari* in the world now.

Fallon sighed. "Very well, then." He looked down at me, his face almost kindly. "Mr. Vonnegan, it has been a pleasure."

I smirked. "Fuck you."

He nodded. "Do not move; do not speak." And though I didn't feel anything, I knew, with the silver leash around my neck, that I would not be able to.

The blade was sharp and well cared for, and cut me with a gentle nudge from Fallon. He didn't slit my throat entirely, just precisely opened the carotid artery so that a warm cascade of my blood swarmed out in gentle waves. The shock burned through me, and my nervous system went into instinctive overdrive. But I couldn't move. I just knelt there, bleeding. I could already feel a tingling drain in the center of my body, that shivery, exhausted feeling I'd once known so well. The feeling of bleeding to death in slow motion. Except this wouldn't be over the course of weeks or months but minutes.

I knew bleeds. I gave myself two minutes before I lost consciousness. Maybe two more before I was dead. Maybe one more. I was already in pretty sad shape.

Unexpected, horrifyingly, tears welled up. I watched them drop to the concrete floor, where they beaded like the floor had been treated with something, rolling this way and that and mixing with the blood that had begun to drip from me. Nothing had gone according to plan, as usual, but I'd always assumed that when my time came, Pitr would be there. I guessed he *was* somewhere nearby, but I felt all alone.

I closed my eyes and concentrated and could feel his heartbeat. I'd never had a chance to figure out why I was able to feel him like this. We were linked. Had been since the first time the *kurre-nikas* had brought him back. Twice that bastard had come back from the dead.

My thoughts were getting slow and heavy. I kept losing track. Breathing was suddenly a lot of fucking trouble.

I slumped on the dirty concrete, bleeding out. I thought that if he could at least keep himself hidden, if he could be *smart* for one time in his life, Mags would slip away. Fallon was *enustari* and might be able to track him down. But Fallon didn't want to use the gas. He had a finite supply in this dead world he'd helped create, and he might decide Pitr was too stupid to worry over and just let him go.

Fallon made a *tsk*-ing noise with his mouth. "Mr. Mageshkumar!"

Another two heartbeats, echoed with Pitr's somewhere nearby. I knew I would have fallen over by now if the leash had allowed it.

"Very well," Fallon said. "Let us see where you are hiding, then." He closed his eyes and began to recite.

Fallon finished and the spell drew energy from me, and I was so fucking cold all of a sudden, shivering. Shivering so hard my teeth rattled in my head. I opened my eyes slowly, each one heavy as a boulder, their natural state closed. And there was Pitr, standing right next to Fallon. He looked terrified. In one hand he held the Token, clutching it like I had, white-knuckled and shaking. He could have reached out and hit Fallon with it.

In his other hand, he held the gun I'd taken from Detective Stanley in another life, still smeared with the Negotiator's blood, dead and tasteless.

Fallon remained standing with his eyes shut. When he opened them, he jerked back and barked a single Word—my new favorite Word, I thought dreamily—just as Pitr squeezed the trigger.

And for the third time that I knew of, Pitr Mags died.

I CAME TO LIKE I was buried in snow, light trickling down in photons so big and fat I felt like I could reach up and grab them like globes. For some time I didn't know if I was awake or alive. I just was. I marveled at the light and the cold and the awful, searing dry pain in my neck and just lay there and marveled and lay there and marveled and there was no time.

The pain in my neck grew worse and worse. It was a rusty, jagged pain, and every time I sipped some air, my breathing shallow and rapid, it swelled up and hurt like hell. And that led to a thought: Fallon had cast off my wound. He'd used the gas I'd been pouring into the air to reveal Pitr's Glamour, and my wound had scarred up.

The one gift the universe gave back to the Bleeder: It healed the cuts.

The concrete I was lying on was ice-cold and stained black with my blood. Fallon had let me just bleed, wasting it. I assumed he'd intended to take me to the edge of death and then pull me back so he could nurse me back to health to be bled again. Instantly that seemed pretty obvious what he had planned to do. Bleed Pitr and me repeatedly, storing the gas in his fancy Fabrication, so that one day when we finally died he'd have gotten his money's worth.

I couldn't stop shivering. I reached up and pulled the silver leash from my neck. It squirmed and hummed against my skin, then seemed to rush away when I dropped it.

A few feet away from me, two upright sets of shoes. Fallon's were the super-shiny dress shoes, black leather, sturdy black laces, soles like new, without a scratch. Pitr's were tennis shoes. Duct tape wrapped around them, holding the crumbling rubber soles on. They were muddy and torn. I should have paid more attention to his feet. I should have gotten him new shoes. I could have gotten him a new pair of shoes at any time.

Shaking, I rubbed my dry tongue against my scratchy teeth and began to drag myself towards him. My right arm was still numb and useless, so I had to rely on my left to do all the work, and it seemed to resent this.

My fingernails peeled up. I didn't have enough blood left to bleed. I weighed a thousand pounds, and progress was slow. My breathing came in short, rapid bursts of hot, dry air. It was all carbon dioxide, in and out. When I was close enough, I grabbed on to Pitr's feet and used his weight as an anchor, pulling myself towards him, on top of him, until I lay panting on top of him.

I CAME TO LIKE I'd been dipped in glue. My eyes didn't want to open. My nose was clogged with dried blood, and my mouth had hung open so I could breathe and was so dry my tongue was literally glued to the top of my mouth. I gagged and twitched. It took me a moment to realize I was trying to cough.

When it had passed, I looked down at Pitr.

His eyes were open, and I hated that. Still shaking, I dragged my left hand up and slapped with ragged, bloody fingers at his eyes until I'd managed to drag his lids down. They fluttered back up, making him look half asleep. I decided that was better.

The world was broken. I had broken it.

I rolled off him and found the Token, thrown from him and bounced off the wall, lying in a cold, jelly-like puddle of blood mixed from Fallon and Pitr. As my hand closed around it, the roar of gas filled me. I closed my eyes and remembered the spell I'd tried once to bring him back.

Pulling as hard as I could, I spoke the spell. Felt the power pass through me, making me shiver even harder. Croaking, I spoke the spell again, but my lips and tongue betrayed me, scratchy and dry, and I flubbed the fifth Word. A tiny explosion of the universe's displeasure tore around the garage. I closed my eyes and barked an incoherent scream.

Then I struggled for a deep breath, my chest feeling tight and compressed, like something heavy was on it, or like a lung had collapsed, and spoke the spell again.

I watched Pitr's feet, all I could see. I spoke the spell again, and in the middle of it, I dissolved into a paroxysm of coughs, and this time the explosion was more violent, lifting me and the corpses briefly from the floor and smacking us down.

I spoke the spell again. Felt the rush of power directed at Pitr's body. But there was no twitch, there was no sign of anything.

I spoke the spell again. I watched his feet for any kind of movement, but there was none.

I started to speak the spell—

I CAME TO IN slow motion, the roar of gas still coursing through me, a chorus of demons screaming from somewhere distant inside of me. I thought I would cry, but I was dry as a desert, and Pitr had died twice before, and recently.

I fell asleep.

58

I DIDN'T KNOW WHAT DAY it was supposed to be, so I'd just randomly started assigning names to the days. I'd started with Monday. Then I'd decided the next day should be called Muddle. I went along that way for a while, then lost track. I'd started over at zero and counted up. I'd lost track a few more times, but I was pretty sure it was somewhere between three hundred and three hundred twenty-five.

I'd taken to walking around everywhere with a scratchy brown blanket wrapped around me like a cloak. I'd found it in Elsa's apartment and liked it because it didn't match. Everything else was new and expensive—or had been three years before, when the world had ended—and soulless and designed. The brown blanket was old and dirty, a blanket from the time before blankets were meant to be comfortable. From a time when a blanket would be listed as a prized possession, something you'd fight and cut and scream to hang on to, not something you gave to Goodwill and bought new. Plus, it had ancient old bloodstains on it. It was perfect. It had meant something to that daffy old bitch, and now it meant something to me.

My arm never came all the way back. I started to get feeling a day or so after the end, and could move it, but I'd lost some of the fine motor control, somehow, and dropped things all the time.

I'd buried Pitr on the roof. *Buried* was the wrong word. I'd built, with the help of the Token, a mausoleum out of stone, fused to the structure and open to the elements on the top. Because Pitr had always liked the sun and the rain, and he'd hated being inside small spaces.

I'd ransacked Elsa's apartment in slow motion. I tried not to use the Token for everything, reminding myself that I had no way of knowing how much there was, how deep that vein went. You had to imagine I could cast anything I wanted for decades and not exhaust it, but if I had a brilliant idea and found I had wasted too much gas to get it done, I wouldn't get another shot.

I had the Token. I had the *kurre-nikas*. I had everything I needed. Except the fucking *knowledge*.

I'd searched every corner of the apartment. Elsa had been *someone,* she'd been *enustari,* she'd built the fucking *kurre-nikas* in a parking garage. Assuming the fucking thing actually worked and had been built according to the fucking directions in Norwegian or whatever, because what the fuck did I know? I had no fucking education. There had to be something. A cache of Artifacts. A journal with her meticulous notes about building something huge like the *kurre-nikas.* Something. Anything.

There was nothing but the *barna,* the jeweled boxes, each, I assumed, containing the insane imprisoned soul of someone Elsa had stolen a body from. And pill bottles, and liquor bottles, and cigarettes. A whole closet filled with cartons of cigarettes, all brands, all varieties. She had created the *kurre-nikas,* the most complex Fabrication I'd ever seen, from scratch.

Three times a day I ate a can of SPAM and a can of green beans because if I didn't I would die. Every day I drank a bottle of bourbon or sometimes two because if I didn't I would die. Every day I spent an hour or four staring out the cracked, starred windows, covered in the dried, flaking guts of *gidim,* and thought of nothing.

At night, when I invariably couldn't sleep, listening to the immense emptiness of the world outside the windows, I walked down to the garage level, passing the skeletons I'd named Bob and Boy, and sat in the soft glow of the Fabrication, willing it to tell me how to use it. I'd left Fallon where he was. It no longer smelled.

I wrote spells. I used a phonetic alphabet I'd invented as shorthand. No one but me would be able to understand any of it. I only tested them sometimes, bleeding myself, and the endless scars on my body that had faded during my time as General of the Asshole Army began reassembling, resurfacing, red and angry. I would lose myself in the work, drinking steadily and piecing them together, then scratching out the bullshit and shading them down to a tighter group of sounds. I tried to think big, to come up with huge ideas and make spells for them. I'd spent a few days attempting to come up with something like the *kurre-nikas,* something that would adjust the whole fucking pattern, but I got lost in the weeds. Where did you even start?

I started talking to myself. Talking to Pitr, really, but I reminded myself that Pitr was gone and I was the only one left. I wandered back and forth in my blanket, having entire conversations with myself. I worked out complex grammars and nested reaction loops. I invented new approaches to old problems. From memory, I recorded every line of the *Biludha-tah-namus* that I could remember from my time in the murder machine at Renar's mansion, trying to puzzle out the mechanics of that Ritual. I figured since the *tah-namus* played with the very bones of reality, making the impossible possible, I might learn something I could apply to understanding the *kurre-nikas.* Somewhere deep inside both things was a fundamental concept, a technique, a trick that Fallon and Elsa and Renar had learned. Something I'd never heard of, because I'd had the equivalent of a third-grade education in magic.

I let my beard grow. It was a mistake, but every day I took pleasure in not correcting it.

Fallon had been carrying a collection of Fabrications and Artifacts in his pockets. I didn't recognize any of them or have any idea what they did. I organized them on the kitchen counter and thought that eventually I'd make a try at them, see what they did. But seeing as I was one of a handful—maybe—of people left in the world, or maybe the only person left, who knew, I didn't feel a strong need for weaponized Fabrications. And I doubted Fallon had a Reset the Universe button mixed in there.

Sometimes I went out and wandered. I took the stairs. I saw no need to waste blood, my own or the phantom sufferings of a million people in some other dimension. And I needed the exercise. So I walked down, saying hello to Bob and Boy, and wandered the streets. The skeletons didn't bother me anymore. And it didn't matter if I got lost. I had the Token for emergencies, and there were a million places to sleep.

I found interesting things. Signs that the *tah-namus* had taken long enough for some people to see what was happening. People banded together in unusual places: public buildings, temples. Skeletons clasping each other, holding on to each other. Not many examples. I assumed it had been fast but not instantaneous. Some people had seen their neighbors burning up in an eldritch flame, being sucked dry in nanoseconds by a force they had never been taught existed, and they'd clawed their way to each other and huddled.

Several miles away, on an elevated road crammed with cars that were, in turn, crammed with skeletons, a single man in an expensive suit lay on the pavement, his bony fingers still curled around the handle of a black suitcase filled with yuan.

Here and there, suicides. People fast enough to get a belt around their neck, or a gun out of a cabinet. People who had beaten Renar, too fast for her ritual. I wondered if they had attained a better fate. If they were more at peace. If it mattered, how you died.

The people didn't bother me too much. I'd bled enough now, and seen enough people die on my account or for my mistakes. The pets, though, the animals. They bothered me. Pitr rubbing off on me. The cats and the dogs. I could imagine how confused the people had been, how terrified. I couldn't imagine the animals, how it had seemed to them. When I came across a pet, I got all choked up and wondered if I'd finally just completely lost it, when billions of skeletons didn't bother me but the dead dogs and cats did.

On what was either day three hundred fifty or three hundred seventy-something, I stood with my blanket clutched around my neck, looking out and counting the windows, when movement, tiny and distant, caught my eye. I stared down at the figure walking along the street for a while, unable to process it. A person. A person, walking the streets of Shanghai. Another person, alive.

Or at least it looked like a person. It appeared to have two heads.

There was no time to race down the stairs. By the time I made it they might have taken a turn, disappeared into the city. Lost. I didn't

even pause to bleed. I ran to the bedroom and retrieved the gun. I had
no idea how many bullets remained or if I was supposed to have kept
up some sort of maintenance during all this time. I stuffed the gun into
my pocket and raced back to the main part of the apartment, grabbing
the Token from its place on the countertop. I whispered the Teleportation spell that was my only gift of enduring value from the Negotiator,
and a moment later I stumbled and staggered on the street, having, as
usual, appeared about three or four inches above the ground.

The figure was a few blocks away, walking with confident strides, a
staff or walking stick in one hand, a large pack strapped to their back.
Still holding the Token, the rush of eager, awful energy pushing against
my thoughts, I began to walk towards them, waving my arms.

It was a man, average height, older. A man with a monkey on his
shoulder, a small humanoid with big eyes and tiny hands who peered
at me with a disturbing intelligence that felt somehow malevolent. As
the man drew closer, I slowed down, recognition dawning. He wore a
heavy military-style coat, but underneath were trousers, a white dress
shirt, and red suspenders. When we were close enough to make out
each other's faces, I stopped suddenly. He took the last few feet with
imperious, impatient strides.

"Mr. Vonnegan," Hiram Bosch said through a bushy yellowing
beard, his voice a gravelly, rusty instrument as he looked me up and
down. "You look . . . precisely as bad as I would have imagined."

59.

"IT IS *ASAG*, A SUMMONING," Hiram said, lighting a cigar and
sending a cloud of smoke into the air. "The animal. A demon,
of course. Bound to me, paid for in blood." He closed his eyes. "It offers
advice. It has been my sole companion for years now."

The monkey sat on its haunches on the couch behind him, its hands
folded on top of its belly. It appeared to be sleeping.

"How did you know to come here?"

Hiram shook his head, eyes still closed. We were seated on the floor of Elsa's apartment. "I knew her. Towards the end, Elsa attempted to rally us against Renar. She sent word to every *ustari* of any rank she could track down and put out the alarm. This has been done many times. We have banded together against one of our own for the good of all of us. We were too late, of course. Too many had been tricked over to Renar's side—promised eternal life—and we simply did not have the power, the skill, so we failed every attempt to stop her." He sighed and opened his eyes. "I spent much time here, in those last days, as we worked." He offered a muted smile. "Even I, the great Hiram Bosch, was valued. Very few of any skill made the attempt."

We sat in silence for some time. "Pitr's dead," I said finally.

He nodded. "I assumed as much, Mr. Vonnegan. Although I was extremely amazed to arrive here and learn *you* were alive. When you convinced me to sever our bond—what was it, eight? Nine years ago?—I thought I would find you were dead soon enough. Yet, here you are. Of all people."

I looked closely at him, but there was no malice. None of the old Hiram venom, the insults and red-faced attacks. After a moment I smiled. "Of all fucking people," I agreed. "It's good to see you, Hiram."

"Mr. Vonnegan! Of course it is. Under the circumstances it is good to see *anybody,* yes?"

We both laughed. It was ridiculous. The pent-up release of months of solitude for both of us. We laughed harder and longer than the tiny joke deserved, throwing our bodies around the dusty living room, hooting and bellowing, tears streaming down our faces.

"*You!*" I gasped. "And *me,* at the *end of the world!*"

Hiram, thinner but still with that round red face, put up his hands in mock surrender, unable to speak.

I looked up, gasping. The monkey had opened its eyes and was staring at me, its tiny hands still folded on its belly. The hands reminded me of the *gidim,* and the eyes were . . . deep.

We sat in silence for a bit, catching our breath. "If you were here with Elsa, where did you go?"

Hiram sighed. "Elsa is dead?"

I nodded.

"Did she die as badly as I imagine?"

Remembering Pitr and the fireball, I shook my head. "Worse."

He raised a snowy eyebrow but didn't say anything for a moment. "I went . . . on a quest." He rubbed his eyes with both hands, like a kid, and behind him the monkey did the same. "Towards the end, we knew we had failed. The *Biludha-tah-namus* was being cast, every *ustari* in the world could feel it. Most melted away to die as they saw fit. Elsa had a Fabrication to preserve a few people, and I was among them. We survived the *tah-namus,* and in the dawn of a dead world she sent me to try to locate and retrieve an Artifact. An Artifact she suspected had wriggled free from its master, as Artifacts often do." He sighed. "She was half mad, of course. Watching her newest body wither under her assault, with no hope to replace it." He sighed. I was reminded that Hiram was the sort who would feel sympathy for someone like Elsa, and not spend a single thought on the long list of poor assholes she'd preyed on like some sort of vampire.

He looked at me. "And you? How in the world did you wind up here? Certainly you would not have been on Elsa's contact list."

There was a brief stab of the old anger. *Certainly.* But it didn't matter. I had been an asshole. I'd been an asshole for so long I'd gotten used to it. When I'd had an army and something worth doing, I'd still been an asshole and here we were.

I told Hiram the story as best I could. While I went down each path, each time line that folded back on itself, he grew silent and attentive. Behind him, the monkey again mimicked him. Mouth open—mouth open. Eyes wide—eyes wide. Frown—frown. With a jolt, I realized the monkey's face somewhat resembled Hiram's, if his beard had been shaved. And I thought, *So much for sleep tonight.* And then I thought,

Of course Hiram creates a companion for the apocalypse that looks and acts just like him.

He chewed one lip. "Was she coherent when you arrived? Had she been working on anything? Did she tell you anything?"

I nodded. "I'll show you."

I didn't tell Hiram about the Token or teleport us. Something made me want to keep secrets. Part of it, I thought, was because I didn't know him. Not *this* version of him. In this time line, Hiram and I had never crossed paths again. We had merely drifted, and he had apparently thought me dead long before the *tah-namus*. Part of it was the fact that the Hiram I *had* known would have simply demanded the Token, insisting he had the superior knowledge and experience.

So we walked down the stairs. The monkey rode on Hiram's shoulder, holding on to his collar with one brown hand for balance. As we passed Bob and Boy, I had to resist the urge to wave and greet them as I normally did. It was strange to suddenly have to remember how to behave.

"Did you see anyone else when you were out there?" I asked.

Hiram didn't answer right away. "Once I thought I had," he finally answered. He sounded out of breath even though we were going down. "I followed shadows for some days. To this moment, I am unsure if there really was someone or not. It has been a long, long time. A long time."

His hand was pushed into his pocket, as if touching something.

"It was terrible at the end," he said. "So many in the world did not know what was coming for them. Business, as they say, went on as usual. And yet *we* knew. And we knew we would fail. And then afterwards . . . so few of us. So many things I would *not* have done. Would *never* have done."

He was talking to himself, I realized.

"Evelyn Fallon," he said slowly, sounding amazed. "I had been told he was long dead, after the war to remove Quyen Vinh in the 1960s. Had attained for himself a high command and used it to perform experiments, driving his battalions into the desert and killing them by the thousands. To his superiors, with a bit of Charm, he justified the executions and throat-slitting and torturous bleeding as fighting fire with fire. And the people at home wondered how the war became so brutal, so horrifying." He shook his head and looked up at me. "I was told the war's notoriety was what sent him underground, but that he'd been killed in Munich in the 1970s by his fellow *enustari* because he was considered uncontrollable. Obsessed with the storing of blood for future use and taking excessive chances to test his theories." He took a deep breath. "It is . . . curiously exciting and unnerving to hear that name here, now."

I reflected on my lost educational chances with Hiram. I wondered if he might teach me again, if we failed to find a way back.

We had reached the bottom landing, and I opened the squealing metal door that led to the parking garage. "This is what Elsa worked on after you left," I said as he passed me, stepping through. I thought about telling him that Pitr had spoken the Binding, because it seemed right that Hiram should know that. But I didn't say anything.

"Jesus *Christ*," Hiram breathed. "What *is* this?"

I had to force back the urge to crow a bit, knowing more than my old *gasam*. "The *kurre-nikas*," I said as dramatically as I could.

"My God, the *kurre-nikas*," Hiram whispered, stepping slowly into the space, looking around. The monkey did the same. "She was a genius."

I thought of Ev Fallon's opinion of Elsa. Every mage I'd ever met was crazy and self-important, including me. Who knew who was smart or skilled or what. But Hiram's awe seemed genuine. He turned to look at me, smiling, the monkey's tiny face smiling behind him.

"My God, Mr. Vonnegan! We can *make adjustments*! We can go back. Change the past. We can wipe the last few years away!"

I stared at the monkey. "If we knew how to use it, Hiram. You got any ideas?"

He shook his head, pushing his hands into his pockets. "No, Mr. Vonnegan," he said, staring at the Fabrication. "But this does."

Without turning around, he pulled a silver chain from his pocket and held it up for my inspection. It was long. Dangling from the bottom, shining with a skinlike gleam, was a small irregular hunk of green stone.

The *Udug*.

60.

I WANTED TO TOUCH IT, and I wanted to burn it into ash.

I could still feel the voice of the *Udug*, toneless, pitiless, constantly in motion, telling me amazing things. I knew it would be able to offer us perfect, exact instructions on how to operate the *kurrenikas*. I had no doubt in my mind about that. It would also offer a lot of information we didn't need to know. Or that I didn't *want* to know.

My hands twitched every time I thought of that toneless voice. I'd never imagined I'd see it again, and that had made it bearable.

I watched Hiram as he stood there, hand clasped around the chip of green stone. He'd been holding it much longer than I'd ever dared, twenty minutes or more. His lips, delicate and pink as always, almost girlish, moved slightly as he took in the instructions. I kept picturing the sudden move: snatching the chain, yanking the Artifact free from his grasp. Could I cast something to slow him down simultaneously? Why not. He was old, and he wasn't expecting it. Unless the *Udug* told him to expect it.

I wanted that voice in my head again.

I never wanted to hear that voice again.

Pacing, I wanted a cigarette, but I was afraid to leave Hiram alone. Somehow it seemed to make sense that my presence was a necessary control. As if it mattered.

Suddenly, Hiram produced his fussy little blade, a tiny thing you would normally use to open wine bottles, though sharpened to a razor's edge, and cut himself on the forearm. The gas wasn't much. I stopped pacing and watched him, excited. Maybe this was it. Maybe this was the beginning, the first step towards making that Fabrication lurch into motion and change the universe again, one final time if we were lucky.

The Words were . . . I realized I couldn't follow them because Hiram was . . . He was . . . The apartment began spinning, his words getting louder and slower and more elastic, like someone had taken hold of one end of the sentence and pulled, and then it all went black.

IN THE DREAM, AS always, Pitr and Claire were waltzing. As they spun, I caught glimpses of each from the front and back. From the front they looked normal. From the back they had been torn to pieces, bloody hunks of flesh hanging, bone and muscles exposed and moving, blood oozing everywhere and forming a slime trail on the floor.

"IT INSISTS."

Choking. I surged up, swinging my arms at the attacker, but there was no one there. I felt the hands on my throat, the aching pain of my windpipe being compressed. My eyes bugged and my dry tongue swelled, but there was no one there.

I turned my head, making meaningless glottal noises as I tried to suck air into myself. Hiram sat next to me, hand still pushed into his pocket. He was shirtless, and stared at me with a tortured, horrified look. He still clutched the *Udug* in his hand, the knuckles white, the arm trembling. His eyes seemed to tremble, too, as if the involuntary muscle movement couldn't be controlled. Our eyes locked.

"It *insists*."

It, I knew, was the *Udug*. I remembered the Skinny Fuck who had come for Claire. I remembered casting on his dead body so I could experience his existence, because we needed information. I remembered him almost like it was me, his years of touching that thing, its slimy, almost living surface, squirming under his fingers, the voice in his head, helping. I had a flash of Hiram on the road alone with his fucking monkey, terrified, afraid, *alone*. And then that voice, whispering to him. At first a few minutes a day, then hours. Then *all the time*.

Red dots appeared in my vision. Why in hell strangulation had become everyone's favorite way of killing me, I didn't know. Something to try and remember in the next time line, something to ponder. For the moment, I fell back to the floor and dug under the scratchy brown blanket until my hand clasped the handle of the gun, warm from my body heat, just like the *Udug*, squirming against my skin with its own sort of intelligence, bloodthirsty and mechanical. Hiram leaped on me, pinning my arms, his unblinking eyes foreign and alien. This wasn't the man I'd known and disliked intensely. This wasn't the reluctant but fundamentally good man who'd tried to help Claire and Pitr and me, who'd given his life so we might escape. This was a man who'd seen the end of the world, seen what men and women of power could do, and spent the last few years alone with a demon whispering in his ear. The *Udug* had broken him. As my chest began to burn again, the fucking unfortunately *familiar* sensation of being strangled to death, I was almost reluctant to shoot him in the face.

"It insists, Mr. Vonnegan!" he hissed, breathing hard as I bucked and struggled beneath him. "I don't wish to do this! But it must be done! You must trust me!"

The monkey was screeching in the background.

"Please, Mr. Vonnegan! Don't be so *selfish*. Great things will come of this. *Great things*. You cannot be allowed to use the *kurre-nikas*. You will not know what to adjust, how to set things right. You do not . . . have . . . the *knowledge*." He shook his head, shooting his white eyebrows up, his bloodshot eyes fixed on my face as I struggled. "You have never understood what it is we do! You have never done the *work*, Mr. Vonnegan! You have sought the easy answers. You only ever wanted to *get by*, to scam your living, and as soon as you had been taught the *basics*, you wished to break free, to betray the sacred trust of *gasam* and *urtuku*." He bared his teeth, sweat pouring from his face and dripping onto mine. "You will interfere. It insists on this point. This *must* be done!"

With my vision flashing red, I bucked with all my might and managed to roll out from under his weight. I got onto my hands and knees as my head swam, my chest heaving against an invisible plug in my throat, and leaped on top of him. There was less of him than I remembered. He was thin. Crazy thin, the sort of thin you got when you started spending your evenings listening to a demon whispering in your head instead of foraging for food.

I got my hands around his throat and squeezed for all I was worth. My right hand was still weak, and it was an imperfect job, but it shut him up and made his eyes pop out. He thrashed under me, and then the fucking monkey jumped on my back and began tearing at my hair and scalp, screeching, and blood ran into my eyes, the gas light and sweet in the air.

For one second, I thought: *What if he's right?*

What had I ever done to convince myself that I was the one to save everything? I'd done nothing but make things worse. I'd fumbled every chance and killed everyone. More than once, in some cases. For a moment, I eased my hands and stared down at him, my old teacher. What if the *Udug* was telling him the fucking truth?

I started to get light-headed and thought: *Fuck it.*

Staring down at the familiar face, I knew I didn't want to kill him. My mind was getting foggy, a red pulse overlaying my vision with every heartbeat, but then Hiram's thrashing slowed. He opened his mouth and his tongue lolled out, pale and liverish, and the light in his eyes changed. It was like watching someone swim to the surface. His eyes tightened, as if in sudden pain, and then closed as he went limp under me.

The plug dissolved in my throat and I collapsed onto Hiram's unconscious form, heaving and gasping. The monkey gave me one last tiny swipe with its claws and scampered back to the couch. When I eventually turned over, exhausted, it was sitting quietly, hands folded over its belly again, staring at me with those deep eyes.

I used the blood leaking from my million monkey-inflicted wounds to wrap Hiram up in Binding Cantrip and weld him to the floor, then a Muting to take his voice away. Still shaking, every breath painful, I pushed my hands into his pockets until a glancing touch

secret panel in ceiling

brought the dry, affectless voice from the *Udug* into my brain. I cried out and threw myself backwards, goose bumps springing up all over my body. I wanted to hold it again so fucking badly, and my stomach turned at the thought.

I turned my head. The monkey was a few inches away. It regarded me calmly, flaring its black nostrils.

Slowly, I crawled back to Hiram and put my hand in his pocket more carefully, finding the metal chain he'd attached to the *Udug*. I drew it out. All the light in the dim room seemed to leap for it, leaving everything else in shadow. I'd stopped breathing and had to force myself to resume.

"Not tonight," I whispered to myself. "Tomorrow. In the daylight."

The monkey made a little sighing grunt. I turned. It had closed its eyes and settled in to sleep, hands still folded over its belly.

I DIDN'T SLEEP. I sat and stared at the *Udug* until the sun rose. Hiram's eyes tracked me from the bedroom to the kitchen, where I ate my breakfast straight from some cans and lit a cigarette. The monkey leaped up on the counter and stared at me intently until I spooned some canned meat out for it. It took handfuls and nibbled, making tiny grunts of satisfaction.

"Hiram, it appears I have stolen your *asag*."

Hiram did nothing, unable to move or speak. I felt bad for a second, then winced as my chest caught on something sharp, and I didn't feel bad anymore. I took the Token, the gun, and the *Udug* and walked down to the lobby and out onto the street. As I stepped outside, the monkey streaked out and danced around my feet, making cute cooing noises.

The sun felt good. I sat down in the street and smoked three more cigarettes. Then I went back in, down to the parking level, stood near the huge, ugly chair, pulled the *Udug* from my pocket, and dangled it in front of me. I thought back over my past experience with it, in another time line. You could control it, I thought. At least in the short term. My weak right arm trembled as I held it up, making it dance in the low light.

Some warm-up exercises, I thought. *Get into the swing of it.*

I closed my eyes and thought, *are we the last people alive in the world,* kept thinking it on repeat, over and over, and closed my left hand around the *Udug*.

Without transition, the slithering voice was in my head.

trees, the trees there are five hundred five hundred left look for the red trees

I let go. I was breathing hard and bathed in sweat. Five fucking hundred people left.

I thought, concentrating, *should I kill the monkey*

I clutched the *Udug*.

you or the monkey one of you will kill the other Artifact most powerful Artifact in history buried in desert coordinates

I let go. I looked at the monkey. I would have sworn it knew what I was thinking.

I took a deep breath. I cleared my mind. *How the fuck do I use the kurre-nikas?*

I clutched the *Udug*.

she is her thread is she is gone truly gone it must be personal must be personal remember every detail must be remember remember choose wisely what could be different to change everything what could be different sit and concentrate sit and listen listen here are the Words

Holding the *Udug* tightly, I sat in the old dentist's chair. And listened.

61.

I WAS OUT OF BREATH by the third floor, head spinning and heart thudding weakly in my chest. For a moment I clung to the banister, gasping as everything receded and I almost lost my footing. Then Mags had me, the seams of my jacket groaning as he took hold of it and set me on my feet, steadying me with his other hand on my chest, almost squeezing me to death.

"I got you, Lem," he said. "Take a moment."

I took a moment.

I stood there taking in great gasps of air, waiting for the dots to clear out of my vision. The old familiar pain in my throat returned, a strange burning on my neck as if someone had tied a rope around it and given it a good tug, and a sharp pain that caught at my lungs as I breathed. It didn't always happen, but it happened often enough to make me worry. Too bad *idimustari* didn't have group health care.

I raised my right hand and flexed it, fighting through another bout of the strange numbness I'd been experiencing. It came and went. Sometimes I was totally normal, and then all of a sudden I'd get weak and numb and my hand would feel like it belonged to someone else. I was fucking falling apart.

On top of that, I was bled white. Our luck kept getting worse and worse, and we were five minutes from living on the street. We'd started the day with seventeen dollars and a bit more gas in our veins, and through a spectacular series of complete bullshit decisions, I'd managed to back us into a final play that had almost zero chance of working out. And if I bled for three more spells, I was going to pass out.

The building smelled like tobacco and cabbage. I wasn't sure how I managed to identify those two smells, but it was absolutely accurate.

I lowered myself into a sitting position on the stairs by inches, shaky. Mags dropped down like a bomb next to me, making me jump an inch. He blew an explosive sigh through his lips and began twiddling his thumbs.

"Don't worry, Lem," he said cheerfully. "Things're gonna be great now. This is gonna be a Win."

I wanted to tell him to shut up. I wanted to tell him that he was getting dumber, somehow, as impossible as that was. I wanted to tell him that he'd made a huge mistake following me out of Hiram's apartment all those years ago. It had been slow, and easy to ignore, but looking back it was obvious: Mags had been near the bottom of the world when we'd met. And all I'd managed to do was drag him down closer to it.

"Right, Lem?" he said, nudging me hard enough to bruise.

"Right!" I said, a little too loud. My heart felt thready, thin and too fast.

"Treasure," he said. "That's what it is. Gold and shit."

I stared down at my bandaged hands. Two fingers without bandages. I'd gotten tired of cutting my forearms, scarring the same skin over and over again, some of the scars hard and raised, making me feel like a mutant.

Footsteps above us, and I felt Mags stiffen in terror, going silent. We just sat and waited, and eventually, the Oldest Man in the World appeared, huffing his way down the hall from the opposite end; the landings just opened out into the hallways, and you had to walk past a bunch of apartment doors to get from one flight to the next. The green carpet was ancient, sending up little clouds of dust as the old man walked. He was wearing what appeared to be a smoking jacket, black socks, and sock garters with no pants.

He stepped nimbly past us down the stairs. We kept our heads down. I didn't have it in me to cast a Charm. I'd fall asleep on the stairs.

A few seconds after the old man had disappeared around the next landing, Mags snorted. "Nielsson, that cocksucker. Did you know he used to be a pilot?"

I was in no mood to joke about the old man, who had sat there laughing with his green teeth and bottomless liver while we piled on the gassed-up dollar bills and made him stupid. It had taken forever, and I was about to vomit and pass out because of it.

"Now he's all alone," Mags said, getting dreamy and sad. "That's why he's always at Rue's, you know? Because he's got nowhere else to be. I remember when I was living with Hiram and it was scary and he yelled at me all the time but I was happy because I had somewhere to be, you know?"

He settled himself more firmly. Patient. Happy to wait. He began humming to himself.

I turned my head. Here was Pitr Mags, the perfect organism. You could feed him garbage and he would grow strong. You could treat him terribly and he would love you. You could frighten him to death and he would wade into fire to defend you. You could drag him onto the streets and make him live in poverty and he would refer to you as home. Pitr Mags, the perfect organism.

I reached up and tousled his hair, then patted him on the neck. For a strange moment I imagined I could feel his nervous system, his heart beating, his lungs filling and deflating. I took a deep breath and felt almost human again.

"All right," I said, hauling myself up. "Hurry up now. It's time."

The door looked like a normal, everyday kind of door. I stared at it with a stone roughly the size and shape of a bowling ball in my stomach. The handle seemed to pulse with evil energy. I had this feeling that if I grasped it, I would be shocked or stabbed or burned.

Mags was almost dancing, he was so excited. "This it?" he asked. "Huh, Lem? Is this the right door?"

In Mags's head, we were already sitting down to a steak dinner and renting a suite at some Times Square hotel. We were rich. Mags couldn't count very high, so his idea of *rich* was kind of a funny one, but whatever the word meant, Mags assumed we were moments away. As if gold coins would spill out into the hallway once we managed to open the fucking door, maybe with a leprechaun surfing down the wave, giggling and farting clovers. It was the right door. And it wouldn't take more than a drop or two of gas to pop. But I stood there staring at it. My arm had gone numb again, and in the back of my mind, a whisper—or a memory.

She is gone.

I stood there, hands at my sides, and listened to it. A strange voice, flat, with no emotion.

She is gone.

"Lem? C'mon, Lem, before someone *comes*."

Mags was dancing again. Now, though, it was out of fear and anxiety.

I looked at my numb hand, holding it up in front of my face. Three fingers and the thumb sported flesh-colored bandages, damp from recent wounds. The cuts always healed, but sometimes lightly, and they tore open again. My whole body had sizzled in slight, tiny pain for years. I rarely noticed anymore.

She is gone.

I blinked. I turned and looked at Mags. He had discovered a piece of hard candy somewhere in his pockets and was unwrapping it, his face a wide-open mask of pleasure. He was my best and only friend. I looked back at the door and thought about what, if anything, we might find behind it. Then I looked at Mags again and laughed; he'd put the candy in his mouth, and his big, broad face had screwed up into a cartoonish mask of distaste, which was a risk when you ate random candy of unknown vintage found in pockets.

I felt like the biggest asshole on the planet, because Mags deserved to be dressed in jammies and put in a warm, dry bed and told a story every night, not terrified and exhausted.

I thought, *Start tonight.* I had no money, and one more good bleed would make me pass out. And I thought, *Start tonight anyway.* Because I thought of Mags happy, laughing, delighted, and relaxed, and it made *me* happy.

I reached out and touched his shoulder. He frowned a little. "Lem?"

I looked back at the door. In between the unsteady, ragged beat of my heart, I felt the thunderous, slow march of Mag's pulse somehow. It felt natural and familiar, and sleeping under an overpass one more night didn't seem like such a bad idea.

ACKNOWLEDGMENTS

EVERY NOVEL HAS A team of people behind it. First of all, and most important, there is the author, the person who actually wrote it, that is to say, me. I'd like to start off my thanking myself for all those poor decisions in life that have conspired in complex and unknowable ways to bring me to this junction in my life.

Behind every author is a person who whispers encouragement and dire threats in his ear as he writes, and for me that person is and has been my lively wife, Danette, to whom I owe everything and who knew I would sell this book, this book you are now holding in your hands, before I had even actually written it, such are the powers my wife possesses.

Let's see how many commas I can squeeze in here, want to? Commas are fun, and underappreciated, much like writers.

Every author, the guy who actually writes the book, that is, me, has somcone in a windowless room somewhere collecting the pennies that cascade in from our crime syndicates and book sales, and also who buys the author drinks, and that person is my redoubtable literary agent, Janet Reid.

Every author, that is, the guy who actually writes the books, which is to say, me again, every author needs hooligans who tempt him from serious work and encourage him to consume adult beverages in lieu of pious labor, and my hooligans, aside from my aforementioned literary agent, who on many occasions incapacitated me with drink when I should have been home tapping words into a hard disk, aside from her the hooligans in question were fellow authors Sean Ferrell and Dan Krokos, who so often suggested I spend my time drinking curated whiskeys while viewing Internet Celebrity Gossip sites, supposedly in an ironic manner, although I suspect the irony was a pose as I really do enjoy celebrity gossip.

Above and beyond all of these, of course, Olympian and leviathan-like, stands the man who actually signs the contract that sends those pennies cascading to be collected in unused mason jars by my afore-mentioned literary agent on behalf of me, the author, the guy who ac-tually writes the book, and that person is, of course, my editor, Adam Wilson, whose suggestions and ideas for the book were disturbingly intelligent and interesting, and I thank him for it while simultaneously becoming enraged that anyone might contribute something to my story I did not myself think of, and whenever I express these feelings of rage to my aforementioned literary agent, she pours out two glasses of good Scotch and at first I think she's going to have a belt with me but then I slowly realize these are medicinally intended for me. And she's right, I feel lots better.

GLOSSARY OF MAGICAL TERMS

ARTIFACT: nonmechanical magical object, often but not always inhabited by an intelligence that guides it

ASAG: demon companion

BARNA: an Artifact

BILUDHA: Rite, Ritual, a major spell

BILUDHA TAH NAMUS: The Rite of Death

DALRA: literally, to fly out

DIMMA: golem, an animated sculpture or object, guided by an intelligence

ENUSTARI: Archmage

FABRICATION: mechanical magical object, trapping a demonic intelligence or reproducing a complex spell with no, or only a very small, sacrifice

GASAM: teacher, Master

GEAS: curse, obligation

GESPU: an Artifact

GIDIM: demon, Summoned by a dual sacrifice from which it takes form

GLAMOUR: illusion

GULLA: a Fabrication, literally, to overwhelm, destroy

IDIMUSTARI: little magician, Trickster

KURRE: literally, change, alter

MU: Cantrip, minor spell

NAMUS: to die, death

NIKAS: literally, result

SAGANUSTARI: high magician

SILIG: literally, to stop

SISKUR: a Bleeder

SUTAKA: literally, to push at

UDUG: demon, a specific Artifact

URTUKU: apprentice

USTARI: mage, magician

ABOUT THE AUTHOR

JEFF SOMERS was born in Jersey City, New Jersey, but as a student of history, you already knew that. Credited with being the first author to discover a penchant for drinking booze and laying about, he frequently forgets what day it is and where, precisely, his pants might be at any given moment. As a young child his family was hopeful he might grow up to make a difference in the world, but as he made his way through his schooling they slowly lowered their expectations. When he announced a desire to write fiction they collectively threw up their hands and stopped paying attention. He oftens claims to have invented the dance known as the Dougie.

In 1995 Jeff began publishing his own magazine, *The Inner Swine* (www.innerswine.com). His first novel, *Lifers*, was published in 2001; the Avery Cates series, beginning with *The Electric Church*, was published by Orbit Books from 2007–2011; and in 2013 republished *Chum* with Tyrus Books. He's also had stories published in many magazines, most of which regret the connection. His story "Ringing the Changes" was chosen for "Best American Mystery Stories 2006" and his story "sift, almost invisible, through" appeared in *Crimes by Moonlight* edited by Charlaine Harris in 2010.

He currently lives in Hoboken, New Jersey, with his lovely wife, Danette, and their plump, imperious cats Pierre, Oliver, Spartacus, Otto, Coco, and Homer Spit. Jeff insists the cats would be delicious.

In between all this and writing, too, Jeff plays guitar, chess, and staves off despair with whiskey.